ABSENT IN THE SPRING

• A N D   O T H E R   N O V E L S •

Also by Agatha Christie writing as Mary Westmacott

A Daughter's a Daughter
The Burden
Unfinished Portrait

A MARY WESTMACOTT OMNIBUS

ABSENT IN THE SPRING

· A N D   O T H E R   N O V E L S ·

Absent in the Spring

Giant's Bread

The Rose and the Yew Tree

AGATHA CHRISTIE

writing as MARY WESTMACOTT

ST. MARTIN'S MINOTAUR

NEW YORK

www.minotaurbooks.com

Library of Congress Cataloging-in-Publication Data

Westmacott, Mary, 1890–1976.
    Absent in the spring and other novels / Mary Westmacott, also known as Agatha Christie.—1st ed.
        p. cm.—(Mary Westmacott omnibus; no. 1)
    ISBN 0-312-27322-3
    1. Middle-class women—Fiction. 2. Young women—Fiction. 3. Composers—Fiction. 4. England—Fiction. I. Title. II. Series.

PR6005.H66 A6 2001
823'914—dc21   2001019169

First St. Martin's Minotaur Edition: September 2001

10   9   8   7   6   5   4   3   2   1

CONTENTS

· ABSENT IN THE SPRING ·

From you I have been absent in the Spring...

Chapter One

Joan Scudamore screwed up her eyes as she peered across the dimness of the Rest House dining room. She was slightly short-sighted.

"Surely that's—no it isn't—I believe it *is*. Blanche Haggard."

Extraordinary—right out in the wilds—to come across an old schoolfriend whom she hadn't seen for—oh quite fifteen years.

At first, Joan was delighted by the discovery. She was by nature a sociable woman, always pleased to run across friends and acquaintances.

She thought to herself, But, poor dear, how dreadfully she's changed. She looks years older. Literally *years*. After all, she can't be more than—what, forty-eight?

It was a natural sequence after that to glance at her own appearance in the mirror that happened, most conveniently, to hang just beside the table. What she saw there put her in an even better humor.

Really, thought Joan Scudamore, I've worn very well.

She saw a slender middle-aged woman with a singularly unlined face, brown hair hardly touched with gray, pleasant blue eyes and a cheerful smiling mouth. The woman was dressed in a neat cool traveling coat and skirt and carried a rather large bag containing the necessities of travel.

Joan Scudamore was traveling back from Baghdad to London by the overland route. She had come up by the train from Baghdad last night. She was to sleep in the Railway Rest House tonight and go on by car tomorrow morning.

It was the sudden illness of her younger daughter that had brought her posthaste out from England, her realization of William (her son-in-law's) impracticability, and of the chaos that would arise in a household without efficient control.

Well, that was all right now. She had taken charge, made arrangements. The baby, William, Barbara convalescent, everything had been planned and set in good running order. Thank goodness, thought Joan, I've always had a head on my shoulders.

William and Barbara had been full of gratitude. They'd pressed her to stay on, not to rush back, but she had smilingly, albeit with a stifled sigh, refused. For there was Rodney to consider—poor old Rodney stuck in Crayminster, up to his ears in work and with no one in the house to look after his comfort except servants.

"And after all," said Joan, "what are servants?"

Barbara said:

"*Your* servants, mother, are always perfection. You see to that!"

She had laughed, but she had been pleased all the same. Because when all was said and done one did like appreciation. She had sometimes wondered if her family took a little too much for granted the smooth running of the house and her own care and devotion.

Not really that she had any criticism to make. Tony, Averil and Barbara were delightful children and she and Rodney had every reason to be proud of their upbringing and of their success in life.

Tony was growing oranges out in Rhodesia, Averil, after giving her parents some momentary anxiety, had settled down as the wife of a wealthy and charming stockbroker. Barbara's husband had a good job in the Public Works department in Iraq.

They were all nice-looking healthy children with pleasant manners. Joan felt that she and Rodney were indeed fortunate—and privately she was of the opinion that some of the credit was to be ascribed to them as parents. After all, they had brought the children up very carefully, taking infinite pains over the choice of nurses and governesses, and later of schools and always putting the welfare and well-being of the children first.

Joan felt a little gentle glow as she turned away from her image in the glass. She thought, Well, it's nice to feel one's been a success at one's job. I never wanted a career, or anything of that kind. I was quite content to be a wife and mother. I married the man I loved, and he's been a success at his job—and perhaps that's owing to me a bit too. One can do so much by influence. Dear Rodney!

And her heart warmed to the thought that soon, very soon, she would be seeing Rodney again. She'd never been away from him for very long before. What a happy peaceful life they had had together.

Well, perhaps *peaceful* was rather overstating it. Family life was never quite peaceful. Holidays, infectious illnesses, broken pipes in winter. Life really was a series of petty dramas. And Rodney had always worked very hard, harder perhaps than was good for his health. He'd been badly run-down that time six years ago. He hadn't, Joan thought with compunction, worn quite as well as she had. He stooped rather, and there was a lot of white in his hair. He had a tired look, too, about the eyes.

Still, after all, that was life. And now, with the children married, and the firm doing so well, and the new partner bringing fresh money in, Rodney could take things more easily. He and she would have time to enjoy themselves. They must entertain more—have a week or two in London every now and then. Rodney, perhaps, might take up golf. Yes, really she couldn't think why she hadn't persuaded him to take up golf before. So healthy, especially when he had to do so much office work.

Having settled that point in her mind, Mrs. Scudamore looked across the dining room once more at the woman whom she believed to be her former schoolfriend.

Blanche Haggard. How she had adored Blanche Haggard when they were at St. Anne's together! Everyone was crazy about Blanche. She had been so daring, so amusing, and yes, so absolutely *lovely*. Funny to think of that now, looking at that thin, restless, untidy elderly woman. What extraordinary clothes! And she looked—really she looked—at least sixty. . . .

Of course, thought Joan, she's had a very unfortunate life.

A momentary impatience rose in her. The whole thing seemed such a wanton waste. There was Blanche, twenty-one, with the world at her feet—looks, position, everything—and she had had to throw in her lot with that quite unspeakable man. A vet—yes, actually a *vet*. A vet with a wife, too, which made it worse. Her people had behaved with commendable firmness, taking her round the world on one of those pleasure cruises. And Blanche had actually got off the boat somewhere, Algiers, or Naples, and come home and joined her vet. And naturally he had lost his practice, and started drinking, and his wife hadn't wished to divorce him. Presently they'd left Crayminster and after that Joan hadn't heard anything of Blanche for years, not until she'd run across her one day in London at Harrods where they had met in the shoe department, and after a little discreet conversation (discreet on Joan's part, Blanche had never set any store by discretion) she had discovered that Blanche was now married to a man called Holliday who was in an insurance office, but Blanche thought he was going to resign soon because he wanted to write a book about Warren Hastings and he wanted to give all his time to it, not just write scraps when he came back from the office.

Joan had murmured that in that case she supposed he had private means? And Blanche had replied cheerfully that he hadn't got a cent! Joan had said that perhaps to give up his job would be rather unwise, unless he was sure the book would be a success. Was it commissioned? Oh dear me, no, said Blanche cheerfully, and as a matter of fact she didn't really think the book would be a success, because though Tom was very keen on it, he really didn't write very well. Whereupon Joan had said with some warmth that Blanche must put her foot down, to which Blanche had responded with a stare and a "But he wants to write, the poor pet. He wants it more than anything." Sometimes, Joan said, one had to be wise for two. Blanche had laughed and remarked that she herself had never even been wise enough for one!

Thinking that over, Joan felt that it was only too unfortunately true. A year later she saw Blanche in a restaurant with a peculiar flashy-looking woman and two flamboyantly artistic men. After that the only reminder she had had of Blanche's existence was five years later when Blanche wrote and asked for a loan of fifty pounds. Her little boy, she said, needed an operation. Joan had sent her twenty-five and a kind letter asking for details. The response was a postcard with scrawled on it: *Good for you, Joan. I knew you wouldn't let me down*—which was gratifying in a way, but hardly satisfactory. After that, silence. And now here, in a Near Eastern Railway Rest House, with kerosene lamps flaring and spluttering amidst a smell of rancid mutton fat and paraffin and Flit, was the friend of so many years ago, incredibly aged and coarsened and the worse for wear.

Blanche finished her dinner first and was on her way out when she caught sight of the other. She stopped dead.

"Holy Moses, it's Joan!"

A moment or two later she had pulled up her chair to the table and the two were chatting together.

Presently Blanche said:

"Well, *you've* worn well, my dear. You look about thirty. Where have you been all these years? In cold storage?"

"Hardly that. I've been in Crayminster."

"Born, bred, married and buried in Crayminster," said Blanche.

Joan said with a laugh:

"Is that so bad a fate?"

Blanche shook her head.

"No," she said seriously. "I'd say it was a pretty good one. What's happened to your children? You had some children, didn't you?"

"Yes, three. A boy and two girls. The boy is in Rhodesia. The girls are married. One lives in London. I've just been visiting the other one out in Baghdad. Her name is Wray—Barbara Wray."

Blanche nodded.

"I've seen her. Nice kid. Married rather too young, didn't she?"

"I don't think so," said Joan stiffly. "We all like William very much, and they are happy together."

"Yes, they seem to be settling down all right now. The baby has probably been a settling influence. Having a child does sort of steady a girl down. Not," added Blanche thoughtfully, "that it ever steadied me. I was very fond of those two kids of mine—Len and Mary. And yet when Johnnie Pelham came along, I went off with him and left them behind without a second thought."

Joan looked at her with disapprobation.

"Really, Blanche," she said warmly. "How could you?"

"Rotten of me, wasn't it?" said Blanche. "Of course I knew they'd be all right with Tom. He always adored them. He married a really nice domestic girl. Suited him far better than I ever did. She saw that he had

decent meals and mended his underclothes and all that. Dear Tom, he
was always a pet. He used to send me a card at Christmas and Easter
for years afterwards which was nice of him, don't you think?"

Joan did not answer. She was too full of conflicting thoughts. The
predominant one was wonder that this—*this*—could be Blanche Haggard—that well-bred, high-spirited girl who had been the star pupil at
St. Anne's. This really slatternly woman with apparently no shame in
revealing the more sordid details of her life, and in such common language too! Why, Blanche Haggard had won the prize for English at St.
Anne's!

Blanche reverted to a former topic.

"Fancy little Barbara Wray being your daughter, Joan. That just
shows how people get things wrong. Everyone had got it into their heads
that she was so unhappy at home that she'd married the first man who
asked her in order to escape."

"How ridiculous. Where do these stories come from?"

"I can't imagine. Because I'm pretty sure of one thing, Joan and that
is that you've always been an admirable mother. I can't imagine you
being cross or unkind."

"That's nice of you, Blanche. I think I may say that we've always
given our children a very happy home and done everything possible for
their happiness. I think it's so important, you know, that one should be
friends with one's children."

"Very nice—if one ever can."

"Oh, I think you can. It's just a question of remembering your own
youth and putting yourself in their place." Joan's charming, serious face
was bent a little nearer to that of her former friend. "Rodney and I have
always tried to do that."

"Rodney? Let me see, you married a solicitor, didn't you? Of
course—I went to their firm at the time when Harry was trying to get a
divorce from that awful wife of his. I believe it was your husband we
saw—Rodney Scudamore. He was extraordinarily nice and kind, most
understanding. And you've stayed put with him all these years. No fresh
deals?"

Joan said rather stiffly:

"Neither of us have wanted a fresh deal. Rodney and I have been perfectly contented with one another."

"Of course you always were as cold as a fish, Joan. But I should have said that husband of yours had quite a roving eye!"

"Really, Blanche!"

Joan flushed angrily. A roving eye, indeed. Rodney!

And suddenly, discordantly, a thought slipped and flashed sideways across the panorama of Joan's mind, much as she had noticed a snake flash and slip across the dust-colored track in front of the car only yesterday—a mere streak of writhing green, gone almost before you saw it.

The streak consisted of three words, leaping out of space and back into oblivion.

The Randolph girl. . . .

Gone again before she had time to note them consciously.

Blanche was cheerfully contrite.

"Sorry, Joan. Let's come into the other room and have coffee. I always did have a vulgar mind, you know."

"Oh no," the protest came quickly to Joan's lips, genuine and slightly shocked.

Blanche looked amused.

"Oh, yes, don't you remember? Remember the time I slipped out to meet the baker's boy?"

Joan winced. She had forgotten that incident. At the time it had seemed daring and—yes—actually romantic. Really a vulgar and unpleasant episode.

Blanche settling herself in a wicker chair and calling to the boy to bring coffee, laughed to herself.

"Horrid precocious little piece I must have been. Oh well, that's always been my undoing. I've always been far too fond of men. And always rotters! Extraordinary, isn't it? First Harry—and *he* was a bad lot all right—though frightfully good looking. And then Tom who never amounted to much, though I was fond of him in a way. Johnnie Pelham—that was a good time while it lasted. Gerald wasn't much good, either . . ."

At this point the boy brought the coffee, thus interrupting what Joan could not but feel was a singularly unsavory catalogue.

Blanche caught sight of her expression.

"Sorry, Joan, I've shocked you. Always a bit straitlaced, weren't you?"

"Oh I hope I'm always ready to take a broad-minded view."

Joan achieved a kindly smile.

She added rather awkwardly:

"I only mean I'm—I'm so *sorry*."

"For me?" Blanche seemed amused by the idea. "Nice of you, darling, but don't waste sympathy. I've had lots of fun."

Joan could not resist a swift sideways glance. Really, had Blanche any idea of the deplorable appearance she presented? Her carelessly dyed hennaed hair, her somewhat dirty, flamboyant clothes, her haggard, lined face, an old woman—an old raddled woman—an old disreputable gypsy of a woman!

Blanche, her face suddenly growing grave, said soberly:

"Yes, you're quite right, Joan. You've made a success of your life. And I—well, I've made a mess of mine. I've gone down in the world and you've gone—no, you've stayed where you were—a St. Anne's girl who's married suitably and always been a credit to the old school!"

Trying to steer the conversation towards the only ground that she and Blanche had in common now, Joan said:

"Those were good days, weren't they?"

"So so." Blanche was careless in her praise. "I got bored sometimes. It was all so smug and consciously healthy. I wanted to get out and see the world. "Well," her mouth gave a humorous twist, "I've seen it. I'll say I've seen it!"

For the first time Joan approached the subject of Blanche's presence in the Rest House.

"Are you going back to England? Are you leaving on the convoy tomorrow morning?"

Her heart sank just a little as she put the question. Really, she did not want Blanche as a traveling companion. A chance meeting was all very well, but she had grave doubts of being able to sustain the pose of friendship all the way across Europe. Reminiscences of the old days would soon wear thin.

Blanche grinned at her.

"No, I'm going the other way. To Baghdad. To join my husband."

"Your husband?"

Joan really felt quite surprised that Blanche should have anything so respectable as a husband.

"Yes, he's an engineer—on the railway. Donovan his name is."

"Donovan?" Joan shook her head. "I don't think I came across him at all."

Blanche laughed.

"You wouldn't, darling. Rather out of your class. He drinks like a fish anyway. But he's got a heart like a child. And it may surprise you, but he thinks the world of me."

"So he ought," said Joan loyally and politely.

"Good old Joan. Always play the game, don't you? You must be thankful I'm not going the other way. It would break even your Christian spirit to have five days of my company. You needn't trouble to deny it. I know what I've become. Coarse in mind and body—that's what you were thinking. Well, there are worse things."

Joan privately doubted very much whether there were. It seemed to her that Blanche's decadence was a tragedy of the first water.

Blanche went on:

"Hope you have a good journey, but I rather doubt it. Looks to me as though the rains are starting. If so, you may be stuck for days, miles from anywhere."

"I hope not. It will upset all my train reservations."

"Oh well, desert travel is seldom according to schedule. So long as you get across the wadis all right, the rest will be easy. And of course the drivers take plenty of food and water along. Still it gets a bit boring to be stuck somewhere with nothing to do but think."

Joan smiled.

"It might be rather a pleasant change. You know, one never has time as a rule to relax at all. I've often wished I could have just one week with really nothing to do."

"I should have thought you could have had that whenever you liked?"

"Oh no, my dear. I'm a very busy woman in my small way. I'm the Secretary of the Country Gardens Association— And I'm on the Committee of our local Hospital. And there's the Institute—and the Guides. And I take quite an active part in politics. What with all that and running the house and then Rodney and I go out a good deal and have people in to see us. It's so good for a lawyer to have plenty of social background I always think. And then I'm very fond of my garden and like to do quite a good deal in it myself. Do you know, Blanche, that there's hardly a moment, except perhaps a quarter of an hour before dinner, when I can really sit down and rest? And to keep up with one's reading is quite a task."

"You seem to stand up to it all pretty well," murmured Blanche, her eyes on the other's unlined face.

"Well, to wear out is better than to rust out! And I must admit I've always had marvelous health. I really *am* thankful for that. But all the same it would be wonderful to feel that one had a whole day or even two days with nothing to do but think."

"I wonder," said Blanche, "what you'd think about?"

Joan laughed. It was a pleasant, tinkling, little sound.

"There are always plenty of things to think about, aren't there?" she said.

Blanche grinned.

"One can always think of one's sins!"

"Yes, indeed." Joan assented politely though without amusement.

Blanche eyed her keenly.

"Only that wouldn't give *you* occupation long!"

She frowned and went on abruptly:

"You'd have to go on from them to think of your good deeds. And all the blessings of your life! Hm—I don't know. Might be rather dull. I wonder," she paused, "if you'd nothing to think about but yourself for days and days I wonder what you'd find out about yourself—"

Joan looked skeptical and faintly amused.

"Would one find out anything one didn't know before?"

Blanche said slowly:

"I think one might . . ." She gave a sudden shiver. "I shouldn't like to try it."

"Of course," said Joan, "some people have an urge towards the contemplative life. I've never been able to understand that myself. The mystic point of view is very difficult to appreciate. I'm afraid I haven't got that kind of religious temperament. It always seems to me to be rather extreme, if you know what I mean."

"It's certainly simpler," said Blanche, "to make use of the shortest prayer that is known." And in answer to Joan's enquiring glance she said abruptly, " 'God be merciful to me, a sinner.' That covers pretty well everything."

Joan felt slightly embarrassed.

"Yes," she said. "Yes, it certainly does."

Blanche burst out laughing.

"The trouble with you, Joan, is that you're *not* a sinner. That cuts you off from prayer! Now I'm well-equipped. It seems to me sometimes that I've never ceased doing the things that I ought not to have done."

Joan was silent because she didn't know quite what to say.

Blanche resumed again in a lighter tone:

"Oh well, that's the way of the world. You quit when you ought to stick, and you take on a thing that you'd better leave alone; one minute life's so lovely you can hardly believe it's true—and immediately after that you're going through a hell of misery and suffering! When things are going well you think they'll last for ever—and they never do—and when you're down under you think you'll never come up and breathe again. That's what life is, isn't it?"

It was so entirely alien to any conception Joan had of life or to life as she had known it that she was unable to make what she felt would be an adequate response.

With a brusque movement Blanche rose to her feet.

"You're half asleep, Joan. So am I. And we've got an early start. It's been nice seeing you."

The two women stood a minute, their hands clasped. Blanche said quickly and awkwardly, with a sudden rough tenderness in her voice:

"Don't worry about your Barbara. She'll be all right—I'm sure of it.

Bill Wray is a good sort, you know—and there's the kid and everything. It was just that she was very young and the kind of life out here—well, it goes to a girl's head sometimes."

Joan was conscious of nothing but complete bewilderment.

She said sharply:

"I don't know what you mean."

Blanche merely looked at her admiringly.

"That's the good old school tie spirit! Never admit anything. You really haven't changed a bit, Joan. By the way I owe you twenty-five pounds. Never thought of it until this minute."

"Oh, don't bother about that."

"No fear." Blanche laughed. "I suppose I meant to pay it back, but after all if one ever does lend money to people one knows quite well one will never see one's money again. So I haven't worried much. You were a good sport, Joan—that money was a godsend."

"One of the children had to have an operation, didn't he?"

"So they thought. But it turned out not to be necessary after all. So we spent the money on a bender and got a rolltop desk for Tom as well. He'd had his eye on it for a long time."

Moved by a sudden memory, Joan asked:

"Did he ever write his book on Warren Hastings?"

Blanche beamed at her.

"Fancy your remembering that! Yes, indeed, a hundred and twenty thousand words."

"Was it published?"

"Of course not! After that Tom started on a life of Benjamin Franklin. That was even worse. Funny taste, wasn't it? I mean such dull people. If I wrote a life, it would be of someone like Cleopatra, some sexy piece—or Casanova, say, something spicy. Still, we can't all have the same ideas. Tom got a job again in an office—not so good as the other. I'm always glad, though, that he had his fun. It's awfully important, don't you think, for people to do what they really want to do?"

"It rather depends," said Joan, "on circumstances. One has to take so many things into consideration."

"Haven't you done what you wanted to do?"

"I?" Joan was taken aback.

"Yes, *you*," said Blanche. "You wanted to marry Rodney Scudamore didn't you? And you wanted children? And a comfortable home." She laughed and added, "And to live happily ever afterwards, world without end, Amen."

Joan laughed too, relieved at the lighter tone the conversation had taken.

"Don't be ridiculous. I've been very lucky, I know."

And then, afraid that that last remark had been tactless when confronted by the ruin and bad luck that had been Blanche's lot in life, she added hurriedly:

"I really *must* go up now. Good night—and it's been marvelous seeing you again."

She squeezed Blanche's hand warmly (Would Blanche expect her to kiss her? Surely not.) and ran lightly up the stairs to her bedroom.

"Poor Blanche," thought Joan as she undressed, neatly laying and folding her clothes, putting out a fresh pair of stockings for the morning. "Poor Blanche. It's really too tragic."

She slipped into her pyjamas and started to brush her hair.

"Poor Blanche. Looking so awful and so coarse."

She was ready for bed now, but paused irresolutely before getting in.

One didn't, of course, say one's prayers every night. In fact it was quite a long time since Joan had said a prayer of any kind. And she didn't even go to church very often.

But one did, of course, *believe*.

And she had a sudden odd desire to kneel down now by the side of this rather uncomfortable-looking bed (such nasty cotton sheets, thank goodness she had got her own soft pillow with her) and well—say them properly—like a child.

The thought made her feel rather shy and uncomfortable.

She got quickly into bed and pulled up the covers. She picked up the book that she had laid on the little table by the bed head, *The Memoirs of Lady Catherine Dysart*—really most entertainingly written—a very witty account of mid-Victorian times.

She read a line or two but found she could not concentrate.

"I'm too tired," she thought.

She laid down the book and switched off the light.

Again the thought of prayer came to her. What was it that Blanche had said so outrageously—"that cuts you off from prayer." Really, what did she mean?

Joan formed a prayer quickly in her mind—a prayer of isolated words strung together.

God—thank thee—poor Blanche—thank thee that *I* am not like that—great mercies—all my blessings—and especially not like poor Blanche—poor Blanche—really dreadful. Her own fault of course—dreadful—quite a shock—thank God—I am different—poor Blanche. . . .

Joan fell asleep.

Chapter Two

It was raining when Joan Scudamore left the Rest House the following morning, a fine gentle rain that seemed somehow incongruous in this part of the world.

She found that she was the only passenger going west—a sufficiently uncommon occurrence, it appeared, although there was not much traffic this time of year. There had been a large convoy on the preceding Friday.

A battered-looking touring car was waiting with a European driver and a native relief driver. The Manager of the Rest House was on the steps in the gray dawn of the morning to hand Joan in, yell at the Arabs until they adjusted the baggage to his satisfaction, and to wish Mademoiselle, as he called all his lady guests, a safe and comfortable journey. He bowed magnificently and handed her a small cardboard container in which was her lunch.

The driver yelled out cheerily:

"Bye bye, Satan, see you tomorrow night or next week—and it looks more like next week."

The car started off. It wound through the streets of the oriental city with its grotesque and unexpected blocks of occidental architecture. The horn blared, donkeys swerved aside, children ran. They drove out through the western gate and onto a broad unequally paved road that looked important enough to run to the world's end.

Actually it petered out abruptly after two kilometers and an irregular track took its place.

In good weather it was, Joan knew, about seven hours run to Tell Abu Hamid which was the present terminus of the Turkish railway. The train from Stamboul arrived there this morning and would go back again at eight-thirty this evening. There was a small Rest House at Tell Abu Hamid for the convenience of travelers, where they were served with what meals they might need. They should meet the convoy coming east about halfway along the track.

The going was now very uneven. The car leapt and jumped and Joan was thrown up and down in her seat.

The driver called back that he hoped she was all right. It was a bumpy bit of track but he wanted to hurry as much as possible in case he had difficulty crossing the two wadis they had to negotiate.

From time to time he looked anxiously up at the sky.

The rain began to fall faster and the car began to do a series of skids, zigzagging to and fro and making Joan feel slightly sick.

They reached the first wadi about eleven. There was water in it, but they got across and after a slight peril of sticking on the hill up the other side drew out of it successfully.

About two kilometers farther on they ran into soft ground and stuck there.

Joan slipped on her mackintosh coat and got out, opening her box of lunch and eating as she walked up and down and watched the two men working, digging with spades, flinging jacks at each other, putting boards they had brought with them under the wheels. They swore and toiled and the wheels spun angrily in the air. It seemed to Joan an impossible task, but the driver assured her that it wasn't a bad place at all. Finally, with unnerving suddenness the wheels bit and roared, and the car quivered forward onto drier ground.

A little further on they encountered two cars coming in the opposite direction. All three stopped and the drivers held a consultation, giving each other recommendations and advice.

In the other cars were a woman and a baby, a young French officer, an elderly Armenian and two commercial-looking Englishmen.

Presently they went on. They stuck twice more and again the long, laborious business of jacking up and digging out had to be undertaken.

The second wadi was more difficult of negotiation than the first one. It was dusk when they came to it and the water was rushing through it.

Joan asked anxiously:

"Will the train wait?"

"They usually give an hour's grace. They can make up that on the run, but they won't delay beyond nine-thirty. However the track gets better from now on. Different kind of ground—more open desert."

They had a bad time clearing the wadi—the further bank was sheer slippery mud. It was dark when the car at last reached dry ground. From then on, the going was better but when they got to Tell Abu Hamid it was a quarter past ten and the train to Stamboul had gone.

Joan was so completely done up that she hardly noticed her surroundings.

She stumbled into the Rest House dining room with its trestle tables, refused food but asked for tea and then went straight to the dimlit bleak room with its three iron beds and taking out bare necessaries, she tumbled into bed and slept like a log.

She awoke the next morning her usual cool competent self. She sat up in bed and looked at her watch. It was half past nine. She got up, dressed and came out into the dining room. An Indian with an artistic turban wrapped round his head appeared and she ordered breakfast. Then she strolled to the door and looked out.

With a slight humorous grimace she acknowledged to herself that she had indeed arrived at the middle of nowhere.

This time, she reflected, it looked like taking about double the time.

On her journey out she had flown from Cairo to Baghdad. This route was new to her. It was actually seven days from Baghdad to London—three days in the train from London to Stamboul, two days on to Aleppo, another night to the end of the railway at Tell Abu Hamid, then a day's motoring, a night in a Rest House and another motor drive to Kirkuk and on by train to Baghdad.

There was no sign of rain this morning. The sky was blue and cloudless, and all around was even-colored golden brown sandy dust. From the Rest House itself a tangle of barbed wire enclosed a refuse dump of tins and a space where some skinny chickens ran about squawking loudly. Clouds of flies had settled on such tins as had recently contained nourishment. Something that looked like a bundle of dirty rags suddenly got up and proved to be an Arab boy.

A little distance away, across another tangle of barbed wire was a squat building that was evidently the station with something that Joan took to be either an Artesian well or a big water tank beside it. On the far horizon to the north was the faint outline of a range of hills.

Apart from that, nothing. No landmarks, no buildings, no vegetation, no humankind.

A station, a railway track, some hens, what seemed to be a disproportionate amount of barbed wire—and that was all.

Really, Joan thought, it was very amusing. Such an odd place to be held up.

The Indian servant came out and said that the Memsahib's breakfast was ready.

Joan turned and went in. The characteristic atmosphere of a Rest House, gloom, mutton fat, paraffin and Flit greeted her with a sense of rather distasteful familiarity.

There was coffee and milk (tinned milk), a whole dish of fried eggs, some hard little rounds of toast, a dish of jam, and some rather doubtful-looking stewed prunes.

Joan ate with a good appetite. And presently the Indian reappeared and asked what time the Memsahib would like lunch.

Joan said not for a long time—and it was agreed that half past one would be a satisfactory hour.

The trains, as she knew, went three days a week, on Monday, Wednesday and Friday. It was Tuesday morning, so she would not be able to leave until tomorrow night. She spoke to the man asking if that was correct.

"That right, Memsahib. Miss train last night. Very unfortunate. Track very bad, rain very heavy in night. That means no cars can go to and fro from here to Mosul for some days."

"But the trains will be all right?"

Joan was not interested in the Mosul track.

"Oh yes, train come all right tomorrow morning. Go back tomorrow night."

Joan nodded. She asked about the car which had brought her.

"Go off this morning early. Driver hope get through. But I think not. I think him stick one, two days on way there."

Again without much interest Joan thought it highly probable.

The man went on giving information.

"That station, Memsahib, over there."

Joan said that she had thought, somehow, that it might be the station.

"Turkish station. Station in Turkey. Railway Turkish. Other side of wire, see. That wire frontier."

Joan looked respectfully at the frontier and thought what very odd things frontiers were.

The Indian said happily:

"Lunch one-thirty exactly," and went back into the Rest House. A minute or two later she heard him screaming in a high angry voice from somewhere at the back of it. Two other voices chimed in. A spate of high, excited Arabic filled the air.

Joan wondered why it was always Indians who seemed to be in charge of Rest Houses like this one. Perhaps they had had experience of European ways. Oh well, it didn't much matter.

What should she do with herself this morning? She might go on with the amusing *Reminiscences of Lady Catherine Dysart*. Or she might write some letters. She could post them when the train got to Aleppo. She had a writing pad and some envelopes with her. She hesitated on the threshold of the Rest House. It was so dark inside and it smelt so. Perhaps she would go for a walk.

She fetched her thick double-felt hat—not that the sun was really dangerous at this time of year, still it was better to be careful. She put on her dark glasses and slipped the writing pad and her fountain pen into her bag.

Then she set out, past the refuse dump and the tins, in the opposite direction to the railway station, since there might, possibly, be international complications if she tried to cross the frontier.

She thought to herself, How curious it is walking like this . . . there's nowhere to walk *to*.

It was a novel and rather interesting idea. Walking on the downs, on moorland, on a beach, down a road—there was always some objective in view. Over that hill, to that clump of trees, to that patch of heather, down this lane to the farm, along the high road to the next town, by the side of the waves to the next cove.

But here it was *from*—not *to*. Away from the Rest House—that was all. Right hand, left hand, straight ahead—just bare dun-colored horizon.

She strolled along not too briskly. The air was pleasant. It was hot, but not too hot. A thermometer, she thought, would have registered seventy. And there was a faint, a very faint breeze.

She walked for about ten minutes before turning her head.

The Rest House and its sordid accompaniments had receded in a very accommodating manner. From here it looked quite pleasant. Beyond it, the station looked like a little cairn of stones.

Joan smiled and strolled on. Really the air was delicious! There was a purity in it, a freshness. No staleness here, no taint of humanity or civilization. Sun and sky and sandy earth, that was all. Something a little intoxicating in its quality. Joan took deep breaths into her lungs. She was enjoying herself. Really this was quite an adventure! A most welcome break in the monotony of existence. She was quite glad she had missed the train. Twenty-four hours of absolute quiet and peace would be good for her. It was not as though there were any absolute urgency in her return. She could wire to Rodney from Stamboul explaining the delay.

Dear old Rodney! She wondered what he was doing now? Not, really, that there was anything to wonder about, because she knew. He would be sitting in his office at Alderman, Scudamore and Witney's—quite a nice room on the first floor looking out over the Market Square. He had moved into it when old Mr. Witney died. He liked that room—she remembered how she had come in one day to see him and had found him standing by the window staring out at the market (it was market day) and at a herd of cattle that was being driven in. "Nice lot of short-horns, those," he had said. (Or perhaps it wasn't shorthorns—Joan wasn't very good at farming terms—but something like that, anyway.) And she had said, "About the new boiler for the central heating, I think Galbraith's estimate is far too high. Shall I see what Chamberlain would charge?"

She remembered the slow way Rodney had turned, taking off his glasses and rubbing his eyes and looking at her in an absent far-away

manner as though he didn't really see her, and the way he had said
"boiler?" as though it was some difficult and remote subject he had never
heard of, and then saying—really rather stupidly, "I believe Hoddesdon's
selling that young bull of his. Wants the money, I suppose."

She thought it was very nice of Rodney to be so interested in old
Hoddesdon at Lower Mead farm. Poor old man, everyone knew he was
going down the hill. But she did wish Rodney would be a little quicker
at listening to what was said to him. Because, after all, people expected
a lawyer to be sharp and alert, and if Rodney was to look at clients in
that vague way it might create quite a bad impression.

So she had said with quick affectionate impatience:

"Don't *wool-gather*, Rodney. It's the *boiler* I'm talking about for the
central heating." And Rodney had said certainly have a second estimate
but that costs were bound to be higher and they must just make up their
minds to it. And then he had glanced at the papers piled up on his desk
and she had said that she mustn't keep him—it looked as though he had
a lot of work to do.

Rodney smiled and said that as a matter of fact he had got a lot of
work piled up—and he'd been wasting time already watching the market. "That's why I like this room," he said. "I look forward to Fridays.
Listen to 'em now."

And he had held up his hand, and she had listened and heard a good
deal of mooing and lowing—really a very confused and rather ugly noise
of cattle and sheep—but Rodney, funnily enough, seemed to like it. He
stood there, his head a little on one side, smiling. . . .

Oh well, it would not be market day today. Rodney would be at his
desk with no distractions. And her fears about clients thinking Rodney
vague had been quite unfounded. He was by far the most popular member of the firm. Everyone liked him which was half the battle in a country
solicitor's practice.

And but for me, thought Joan proudly, he'd have turned the whole
thing down!

Her thoughts went to that day when Rodney had told her about his
uncle's offer.

It was an old-fashioned flourishing family business and it had always
been understood that Rodney should go into it after he had passed his

law exams. But Uncle Harry's offer of a partnership and on such excellent terms was an unexpectedly happy occurrence.

Joan had expressed her own delight and surprise and had congratulated Rodney warmly before she noticed that Rodney didn't seem to be sharing in her sentiments. He had actually uttered the incredible words, "If I accept—"

She had exclaimed, dismayed, "But Rodney!"

Clearly she remembered the white set face he had turned to her. She hadn't realized before what a nervous person Rodney was. His hands picking up blades of turf were trembling. There was a curious pleading look in his dark eyes. He said:

"I hate office life. I hate it."

Joan was quick to sympathize.

"Oh I know, darling. It's been awfully stuffy and hard work and just sheer grind—not even interesting. But a partnership is different—I mean you'll have an interest in the whole thing."

"In contracts, leases, messuages, covenants, whereas, insomuch as heretofore—"

Some absurd legal rigmarole he had trotted out, his mouth laughing, his eyes sad and pleading—pleading so hard with her. And she loved Rodney so much!

"But it's always been understood that you'd go into the firm."

"Oh I know, I know. But how was I to guess I'd hate it so?"

"But—I mean—what else—what do you want to do?"

And he had said, very quickly and eagerly, the words pouring out in a rush:

"I want to farm. There's Little Mead coming into the market. It's in a bad state—Horley's neglected it—but that's why one could get it cheap—and it's good land, mark you . . ."

And he had hurried on, outlining plans, talking in such technical terms that she had felt quite bewildered for she herself knew nothing of wheat or barley or the rotation of crops, or of pedigreed stocks or dairy herds.

She could only say in a dismayed voice:

"Little Mead—but that's right out under Asheldown—*miles* from anywhere."

"It's good land, Joan—and a good position . . ."

He was off again. She'd had no idea that Rodney could be so enthusiastic, could talk so much and with such eagerness.

She said doubtfully, "But darling, would you ever make a living out of it?"

"A living? Oh yes—a bare living anyway."

"That's what I mean. People always say there's no money in farming."

"Oh, there isn't. Not unless you're damned lucky—or unless you've got a lot of capital."

"Well, you see—I mean, it isn't *practical*."

"Oh, but it is, Joan. I've got a little money of my own, remember, and with the farm paying its way and making a bit over we'd be all right. And think of the wonderful life we'd have! It's grand, living on a farm!"

"I don't believe you know anything about it."

"Oh yes, I do. Didn't you know my mother's father was a big farmer in Devonshire? We spent our holidays there as children. I've never enjoyed myself so much."

It's true what they say, she had thought, men are just like children. . . .

She said gently, "I daresay—but life isn't holidays. We've got the future to think of, Rodney. There's Tony."

For Tony had been a baby of eleven months then.

She added, "And there may be—others."

He looked a quick question at her, and she smiled and nodded.

"But don't you see, Joan, that makes it all the better? It's a good place for children, a farm. It's a healthy place. They have fresh eggs and milk, and run wild and learn how to look after animals."

"Oh but, Rodney, there are lots of other things to consider. There's their schooling. They must go to good schools. And that's expensive. And boots and clothes and teeth and doctors. And making nice friends for them. You can't just do what *you* want to do. You've got to consider children if you bring them into the world. After all, you've got a duty to them."

Rodney said obstinately, but there was a question in his voice this time, "They'd be happy . . ."

"It's not practical, Rodney, really it isn't. Why, if you go into the firm you may be making as much as two thousand pounds a year some day."

"Easily, I should think. Uncle Harry makes more than that."

"There! You see! You can't turn a thing like that down. It would be madness!"

She had spoken very decidedly, very positively. She had got, she saw, to be firm about this. She must be wise for the two of them. If Rodney was blind to what was best for him, she must assume the responsibility. It was so dear and silly and ridiculous this farming idea. He was like a little boy. She felt strong and confident and maternal.

"Don't think I don't understand and sympathize, Rodney," she said. "I do. But it's just one of those things that isn't real."

He had interrupted to say that farming was real enough.

"Yes, but it's just not in the picture. *Our* picture. Here you've got a wonderful family business with a first-class opening in it for you—and a really quite amazingly generous proposition from your uncle—"

"Oh, I know. It's far better than I ever expected."

"And you can't—you simply *can't* turn it down! You'd regret it all your life if you did. You'd feel horribly guilty."

He muttered, "That bloody office!"

"Oh, Rodney, you don't really hate it as much as you think you do."

"Yes, I do. I've been in it five years remember. I ought to know what I feel."

"You'll get used to it. And it will be different now. Quite different. Being a partner, I mean. And you'll end by getting quite interested in the work—and in the people you come across. You'll see, Rodney— you'll end by being perfectly happy."

He had looked at her then—a long sad look. There had been love in it, and despair and something else, something that had been, perhaps, a last faint flicker of hope. . . .

"How do you know," he had asked, "that I shall be happy?"

And she had answered briskly and gaily, "I'm quite sure you will. You'll see."

And she had nodded brightly and with authority.

He had sighed and said abruptly: "All right then. Have it your own way."

Yes, Joan thought, that was really a very narrow shave. How lucky for Rodney that she had held firm and not allowed him to throw away his career for a mere passing craze! Men, she thought, would make sad messes of their lives if it weren't for women. Women had stability, a sense of reality. . . .

Yes, it was lucky for Rodney he'd had her.

She glanced down at her wristwatch. Half past ten. No point in walking too far—especially (she smiled) as there was nowhere to walk to.

She looked over her shoulder. Extraordinary, the Rest House was nearly out of sight. It had settled down into the landscape so that you hardly saw it. She thought, I must be careful not to walk too far. I might get lost.

A ridiculous idea—no—perhaps not so ridiculous after all. Those hills in the distance, you could hardly see them now—they were indistinguishable from cloud. The station didn't exist.

Joan looked round her with appreciation. Nothing. No one.

She dropped gracefully to the ground. Opening her bag she took out her writing pad and her fountain pen. She'd write a few letters. It would be amusing to pass on her sensations.

Who should she write to? Lionel West? Janet Annesmore? Dorothea? On the whole, perhaps, Janet.

She unscrewed the cap of her fountain pen. In her easy flowing handwriting she began to write:

Dearest Janet:

You'll never guess where I'm writing this letter! In the middle of the desert. I'm marooned here between trains—they only go three times a week. There's a Rest House with an Indian in charge of it, and a lot of hens and some peculiar-looking Arabs and me. There's no one to talk to and nothing to do. I can't tell you how I am enjoying it.

The desert air is wonderful—so incredibly fresh. And the stillness, you'd have to feel it to understand. It's as though for the first time for years I could hear myself think! One leads such a dreadfully busy life, always rushing from one thing to the other. It can't be helped, I suppose, but one ought really to make time for intervals of thought and recuperation.

I've only been here half a day but I feel miles better already. No people. I never realized how much I wanted to get away from people. It's soothing to the nerves to know that all round you for hundreds of miles there's nothing but sand and sun. . . .

Joan's pen flowed on, evenly, over the paper.

Chapter Three

Joan stopped writing and glanced at her watch.

A quarter past twelve.

She had written three letters and her pen had now run out of ink. She noted, too, that she had nearly finished her writing pad. Rather annoying, that. There were several more people she could have written to.

Although, she mused, there was a certain sameness in writing after a while.... The sun and the sand and how lovely it was to have time to rest and think! All quite true—but one got tired of trying to phrase the same facts slightly differently each time....

She yawned. The sun had really made her feel quite sleepy. After lunch she would lie on her bed and have a sleep.

She got up and strolled slowly back toward the Rest House.

She wondered what Blanche was doing now? She must have reached Baghdad—she had joined her husband. The husband sounded rather a dreadful kind of man. Poor Blanche—dreadful to come down in the world like that. If it hadn't been for that very good-looking young vet, Harry Marston—if Blanche had met some nice man like Rodney. Blanche herself had said how charming Rodney was.

Yes, and Blanche had said something else. What was it? Something about Rodney's having a roving eye. Such a common expression—and quite untrue! *Quite* untrue! Rodney had never—never once—

The same thought as before, but not so snakelike in its rapidity, passed across the surface of Joan's mind.

The Randolph girl. . . .

Really, thought Joan indignantly, walking suddenly just a little faster as though to outpace some unwelcome thought, I can't imagine why I keep thinking of the Randolph girl. It's not as though Rodney. . . .

I mean, there's nothing in it. . . .

Nothing at all. . . .

It was simply that Myrna Randolph was that kind of a girl. A big dark luscious-looking girl. A girl who, if she took a fancy to a man, didn't seem to have any reticence about advertising the fact.

To speak plainly, she'd made a dead set at Rodney. Kept saying how wonderful he was. Always wanted him for a partner at tennis. Had even got a habit of sitting at parties devouring him with her eyes.

Naturally Rodney had been a little flattered. Any man would have been. In fact, it would have been quite ridiculous if Rodney hadn't been flattered and pleased by the attentions of a girl years younger than he was and one of the best-looking girls in the town.

Joan thought to herself, If I hadn't been clever and tactful about the whole thing. . . .

She reviewed her conduct with a gentle glow of self-approbation. She had handled the situation very well—very well indeed. The light touch.

"Your girlfriend's waiting for you, Rodney. Don't keep her waiting. . . . Myrna Randolph of course . . . Oh, yes, she is, darling . . . Really she makes herself quite ridiculous sometimes."

Rodney had grumbled.

"I don't want to play tennis with the girl. Put her in that other set."

"Now don't be ungracious, Rodney. You must play with her."

That was the right way to handle things—lightly—playfully. Showing quite well that she knew that there couldn't be anything serious in it. . . .

It must have been rather nice for Rodney—for all that he growled and pretended to be annoyed. Myrna Randolph was the kind of girl that practically every man found attractive. She was capricious and treated her admirers with deep contempt, saying rude things to them and then beckoning them back to her with a sideways glance of the eyes.

Really, thought Joan (with a heat that was unusual in her) a most detestable girl. Doing everything she could to break up my married life.

No, she didn't blame Rodney. She blamed the girl. Men were so easily flattered. And Rodney had been married then about—what—ten years? Eleven? Ten years was what writers called a dangerous period in married life. A time when one or the other party had a tendency to run off the rails. A time to get through warily until you settled down beyond it into comfortable set ways.

As she and Rodney had . . .

No, she didn't blame Rodney—not even for that kiss she had surprised.

Under the mistletoe indeed!

That was what the girl had had the impudence to say when she came into the study.

"We're christening the mistletoe, Mrs. Scudamore. Hope you don't mind."

Well, Joan thought, I kept my head and didn't show anything.

"Now, hands off my husband, Myrna! Go and find some young man of your own."

And she had laughingly chivvied Myrna out of the room. Taking it all as a joke.

And then Rodney had said, "Sorry, Joan. But she's an attractive wench—and it's Christmas time."

He had stood there smiling at her, apologizing, but not looking really sheepish or upset. It showed that the thing hadn't really gone far.

And it shouldn't go any further! She had made up her mind to that. She had taken every care to keep Rodney out of Myrna Randolph's way. And the following Easter Myrna had got engaged to the Arlington boy.

So really the whole incident amounted to exactly nothing at all. Perhaps there had been just a little fun in it for Rodney. Poor old Rodney—he really deserved a little fun. He worked so hard.

Ten years—yes, it was a dangerous time. Even she herself, she remembered, had felt a certain restlessness. . . .

That rather wild-looking young man, that artist—what was his name now? Really she couldn't remember. Hadn't she been a little taken with him herself?

She admitted to herself with a smile that she really had been—yes—

just a little silly about him. He had been so earnest—had stared at her with such disarming intensity. Then he had asked if she would sit for him.

An excuse, of course. He had done one or two charcoal sketches and then torn them up. He couldn't "get" her on canvas, he had said.

Joan remembered her own subtly flattered, pleased, feelings. Poor boy, she had thought, I'm afraid he really *is* getting rather fond of me. . . .

Yes, that had been a pleasant month. . . .

Though the end of it had been rather disconcerting. Not at all according to plan. In fact, it just showed that Michael Callaway (Callaway, that was his name, of course!) was a thoroughly unsatisfactory sort of person.

They had gone for a walk together, she remembered, in Haling Woods, along the path where the Medaway comes twisting down from the summit of Asheldown. He had asked her to come in a rather gruff shy voice.

She had envisaged their probable conversation. He would tell her, perhaps, that he loved her, and she would be very sweet and gentle and understanding and a little—just a little—regretful. She thought of several charming things she might say, things that Michael might like to remember afterwards.

But it hadn't turned out like that.

It hadn't turned out like that at all!

Instead, Michael Callaway had, without warning, seized her and kissed her with a violence and a brutality that had momentarily deprived her of breath, and letting go of her had observed in a loud and self-congratulatory voice:

"My God, I wanted that!" and had proceeded to fill a pipe with complete unconcern and apparently deaf to her angry reproaches.

He had merely said, stretching his arms and yawning, "I feel a lot better now."

It was exactly, thought Joan, remembering the scene, what a man might say after downing a glass of beer on a thirsty day.

They had walked home in silence after that—in silence on Joan's part, that is. Michael Callaway seemed, from the extraordinary noises he made, to be attempting to sing. It was on the outskirts of the wood, just before they emerged onto the Crayminster Market Wopling high road, that he had paused and surveyed her dispassionately, and then remarked in a contemplative tone:

"You know, you're the sort of woman who ought to be raped. It might do you good."

And, whilst she had stood, speechless with anger and astonishment, he had added cheerfully:

"I'd rather like to rape you myself—and see if you looked the least bit different afterwards."

Then he had stepped out onto the high road, and giving up trying to sing had whistled cheerfully.

Naturally she had never spoken to him again and he had left Crayminster a few days later.

A strange, puzzling and rather disturbing incident. Not an incident that Joan had cared to remember. In fact, she rather wondered that she had remembered it now. . . .

Horrid, the whole thing had been, quite horrid.

She would put it out of her mind at once. After all, one didn't want to remember unpleasant things when one was having a sun and sand rest cure. There was so much to think of that was pleasant and stimulating.

Perhaps lunch would be ready. She glanced at her watch, but saw that it was only a quarter to one.

When she got back to the Rest House, she went to her room and hunted in her suitcase to see if she had any more writing paper with her. No, she hadn't. Oh, well, it didn't matter really. She was tired of writing letters. There wasn't much to say. You couldn't go on writing the same thing. What books had she got? Lady Catherine, of course. And a detective story that William had given her last thing. Kind of him, but she didn't really care for detective stories. And *The Power House* by Buchan. Surely that was a very old book. She had read it years ago.

Oh, well, she would be able to buy some more books at the station at Aleppo.

Lunch consisted of an omelette (rather tough and overcooked), curried eggs, and a dish of salmon (tinned) and baked beans and tinned peaches.

It was rather a heavy meal. After it Joan went and lay down on her bed. She slept for three quarters of an hour, then woke up and read Lady Catherine Dysart until teatime.

She had tea (tinned milk) and biscuits and went for a stroll and came back and finished Lady Catherine Dysart. Then she had dinner: omelette, curried salmon and rice, a dish of eggs and baked beans and tinned apricots. After that she started the detective story and finished it by the time she was ready for bed.

The Indian said cheerfully:

"Good night, Memsahib. Train come in seven-thirty tomorrow morning but not go out till evening, half past eight."

Joan nodded.

There would be another day to put in. She'd got *The Power House* still. A pity it was so short. Then an idea struck her.

"There will be travelers coming in on the train? Oh, but they go straight off to Mosul, I suppose?"

The man shook his head.

"Not tomorrow, I think. No cars arrive today. I think track to Mosul very bad. Everything stick for many days."

Joan brightened. There would be travelers off the train in the Rest House tomorrow. That would be rather nice—there was sure to be someone to whom it would be possible to talk.

She went to bed feeling more cheerful than she had ten minutes ago. She thought, There's something about the atmosphere of this place—I think it's that dreadful smell of rancid fat! It quite depresses one.

She awoke the next morning at eight o'clock and got up and dressed. She came out into the dining room. One place only was laid at the table. She called, and the Indian came in.

He was looking excited.

"Train not come, Memsahib."

"Not come? You mean it's late?"

"Not come at all. Very heavy rain down line—other side Nissibin. Line all wash away—no train get through for three four five six days perhaps."

Joan looked at him in dismay.

"But then—what do I do?"

"You stay here, Memsahib. Plenty food, plenty beer, plenty tea. Very nice. You wait till train come."

Oh dear, thought Joan, these Orientals. Time means nothing to them. She said, "Couldn't I get a car?"

He seemed amused.

"Motor car? Where would you get motor car? Track to Mosul very bad, everything stuck other side of wadi."

"Can't you telephone down the line?"

"Telephone where? Turkish line. Turks very difficult people—not do anything. They just run train."

Joan thought, rallying with what she hoped was amusement, This really *is* being cut off from civilization! No telephones or telegraphs, no cars.

The Indian said comfortingly:

"Very nice weather, plenty food, all very comfortable."

Well, Joan thought, it's certainly nice weather. That's lucky. Awful if I had to sit inside this place all day.

As though reading her thoughts, the man said:

"Weather good here, very seldom rain. Rain nearer Mosul, rain down the line."

Joan sat down at the laid place at the table and waited for her breakfast to be brought. She had got over her momentary dismay. No good making a fuss—she had much too much sense for that. These things couldn't be helped. But it was rather an annoying waste of time.

She thought with a half smile, It looks as though what I said to Blanche was a wish that has come true. I said I should be glad of an interval to rest my nerves. Well, I've got it! Nothing whatever to do here. Not even anything to read. Really it ought to do me a lot of good. Rest cure in the desert.

The thought of Blanche brought some slightly unpleasant association—something that, quite definitely, she didn't want to remember. In fact, why think of Blanche at all?

She went out after breakfast. As before, she walked a reasonable distance from the Rest House and then sat down on the ground. For some time she sat quite still, her eyes half closed.

Wonderful, she thought, to feel this peace and quiet oozing into her. She could simply *feel* the good it was doing her. The healing air, the lovely warm sun—the peace of it all.

She remained so for a little longer. Then she glanced at her watch. It was ten minutes past ten.

She thought, The morning is passing quite quickly. . . .

Supposing she were to write a line to Barbara? Really it was extraordinary that she hadn't thought of writing to Barbara yesterday instead of those silly letters to friends in England.

She got out the pad and her pen.

"Darling Barbara," she wrote. "I'm not having a very lucky journey. Missed Monday night's train and now I'm held up here for days apparently. It's very peaceful and lovely sunshine so I'm quite happy."

She paused. What to say next. Something about the baby—or William? What on earth could Blanche have meant—*"don't worry about Barbara."* Of course! That was why Joan hadn't wanted to think about Blanche. Blanche had been so peculiar in the things she had said about Barbara.

As though she, Barbara's mother, wouldn't know anything there was to know about her own child.

"I'm sure she'll be all right now." Did that mean that things *hadn't* been all right?

But in what way? Blanche had hinted that Barbara was too young to have married.

Joan stirred uneasily. At the time, she remembered, Rodney had said something of the kind. He had said, quite suddenly, and in an unusually peremptory way:

"I'm not happy about this marriage, Joan."

"Oh, Rodney, but *why?* He's so nice and they seem so well suited."

"He's a nice enough young fellow—but she doesn't love him, Joan."

She'd been astonished—absolutely astonished.

"Rodney—really—how *ridiculous!* Of *course* she's in love with him! Why on earth would she want to marry him otherwise?"

He had answered—rather obscurely: "That's what I'm afraid of."

"But, darling—*really*—aren't you being a little ridiculous?"

He had said, paying no attention to her purposely light tone, "If she doesn't love him, she mustn't marry him. She's too young for that—and she's got too much temperament."

"Well, really, Rodney, what do *you* know about temperament?"

She couldn't help being amused.

But Rodney didn't even smile. He said, "Girls do marry sometimes— just to get away from home."

At that she had laughed outright.

"Not homes like Barbara's! Why, no girl ever had a happier home life."

"Do you really think that's true, Joan?"

"Why, of course. Everything's always been perfect for the children here."

He said slowly, "They don't seem to bring their friends to the house much."

"Why, darling, I'm always giving parties and asking young people! I make a point of it. It's Barbara herself who's always saying she doesn't want parties and not to ask people."

Rodney had shaken his head in a puzzled unsatisfied way.

And later, that evening, she had come into the room just as Barbara was crying out impatiently:

"It's no good, Daddy, I've got to get away. I can't stand it any longer—and don't tell me to go and take a job somewhere, because I should hate that."

"What's all this?" Joan said.

After a pause, a very slight pause, Barbara had explained, a mutinous flush on her cheek.

"Just Daddy thinking he knows best! He wants me to be engaged for years. I've told him I can't stand that and I want to marry William and go away to Baghdad. I think it will be wonderful out there."

"Oh dear," said Joan anxiously. "I wish it wasn't so far away. I'd like to have you under my eye as it were."

"Oh, *Mother!*"

"I know, darling, but you don't realize how young you are, how inexperienced. I should be able to help you so much if you were living somewhere not too far away."

Barbara had smiled and had said, "Well, it looks as though I should have to paddle my own canoe without the benefit of your experience and wisdom."

And as Rodney was going slowly out of the room, she had rushed after him and had suddenly flung her arms round his neck hugging him and saying, "Darling Dads. Darling, darling, darling . . ."

Really, thought Joan, the child is becoming quite demonstrative. But it showed, at any rate, how entirely wrong Rodney was in his ideas. Barbara was just reveling in the thought of going out East with her William—and very nice it was to see two young things in love and so full of plans for the future.

Extraordinary that an idea should have got about Baghdad that Barbara had been unhappy at home. But it was a place that seemed absolutely full of gossip and rumors, so much so that one hardly liked to mention anyone.

Major Reid, for instance.

She herself had never met Major Reid, but he had been mentioned quite often in Barbara's letters home. Major Reid had been to dinner. They were going shooting with Major Reid. Barbara was going for the summer months up to Arkandous. She and another young married woman had shared a bungalow and Major Reid had been up there at the same time. They had had a lot of tennis. Later, Barbara and he had won the mixed doubles at the Club.

So it had really been quite natural for Joan to ask brightly about Major Reid—she had heard so much about him, she said, that she was really longing to see him.

It was quite ludicrous the embarrassment her question had caused. Barbara had turned quite white, and William had gone red, and after a minute or two he had grunted out in a very odd voice:

"We don't see anything of him now."

His manner had been so forbidding that she really hadn't liked to say anything more. But afterwards when Barbara had gone to bed Joan reopened the subject, saying smilingly, that she seemed to have put her foot in it. She'd had an idea that Major Reid was quite an intimate friend.

William got up and tapped his pipe against the fireplace.

"Oh, I dunno," he said vaguely. "We did a bit of shooting together and all that. But we haven't seen anything of him for a long time now."

It wasn't, Joan thought, very well done. She had smiled to herself, men were so transparent. She was a little amused at William's old-fashioned reticence. He probably thought of her as a very prim strait-laced woman—a regular mother-in-law.

"I see," she said. "Some scandal."

"What do you mean?" William had turned on her quite angrily.

"My dear boy!" Joan smiled at him. "It's quite obvious from your manner. I suppose you found out something about him and had to drop him. Oh, I shan't ask questions. These things are very painful, I know."

William said slowly, "Yes—yes, you're right. They *are* painful."

"One takes people so much at their own valuation," said Joan. "And then, when one finds out that one has been mistaken in them, it's all so awkward and unpleasant."

"He's cleared out of this country, that's one good thing," said William. "Gone to East Africa."

And suddenly Joan remembered some scraps of conversation overheard one day at the Alwyah Club. Something about Nobby Reid going to Uganda.

A woman had said, "Poor Nobby, it's really not his fault that every little idiot in the place runs after him."

And another, older, woman had laughted spitefully and said, "He takes a lot of trouble with them. Dewy innocents—that's what Nobby likes. The unsophisticated bride. And I must say he has a wonderful technique! He can be terribly attractive. The girl always thinks he's passionately in love with her That's usually the moment when he's just thinking of passing on to the next one."

"Well," said the first woman. "*We* shall all miss him. He's so amusing."

The other laughed.

"There's a husband or two who won't be sorry to see him go! As a matter of fact very few men like him."

"He's certainly made this place too hot to hold him."

Then the second woman had said, "Hush," and lowered her voice and Joan hadn't heard anymore. She had hardly noticed the conversation at the time, but it came back to her now, and she felt curious.

If William didn't want to talk about it, perhaps Barbara might be less reticent.

But instead of that Barbara had said quite clearly and rather disagreeably:

"I don't want to talk about him, Mother, do you mind?"

Barbara, Joan reflected, never did want to talk about anything. She had been quite incredibly reticent and touchy about her illness, and its cause. Some form of poisoning had started it all, and naturally Joan had taken it to be food poisoning of some kind. Ptomaine poisoning was very common in hot climates, so she believed. But both William and Barbara had been most unwilling to go into details—and even the doctor to whom she had naturally applied for information as Barbara's mother, had been taciturn and uncommunicative. His principal care was to stress the point that young Mrs. Wray must not be questioned or encouraged to dwell on her illness.

"All she needs now is care and building up. Whys and wherefores are very unprofitable subjects of discussion and talking about all that will do the patient no good. That's just a hint I'm giving you, Mrs. Scudamore."

An unpleasant dour kind of man, Joan had found him, and not at all impressed, as he easily might have been, by the devotion of a mother in rushing out from England posthaste.

Oh well, Barbara had been grateful, at all events. At least Joan supposed so . . . She had certainly thanked her mother very prettily. William, too, had said how good of her it was.

She had said how she wished she could have stayed on, and William had said Yes, he wished so too. And she had said now they mustn't press her—because it was really too tempting and she'd love to have a winter in Baghdad—but after all there was Barbara's father to consider, and it wouldn't be fair on him.

And Barbara, in a faint little voice had said, "Darling Dads," and after a moment or two had said, "Look here, Mother, why don't you stay?"

"You must think of your father, darling."

Barbara said in that rather curious dry voice she used sometimes that she *was* thinking of him, but Joan said, no, she couldn't leave poor dear Rodney to servants.

There was a moment, a few days before her departure, when she had almost changed her mind. She might, at any rate, stay another month. But William had pointed out so eloquently the uncertainties of desert travel if she left it too late in the season that she had been quite alarmed and had decided that it was best to stick to her original plan. After that William and Barbara had been so nice to her that she almost changed her mind again—but not quite.

Though really, however late in the season she had left it, nothing could be much worse than this.

Joan looked at her watch again. Five minutes to eleven. One seemed to be able to think a great deal in quite a short space of time.

She rather wished she'd brought *The Power House* out here with her, though perhaps as it was the only thing she had to read it was wise to keep it back—something in reserve.

Two hours to put in before lunchtime. She had said she would have lunch at one o'clock today. Perhaps she had better walk on a little, only it seemed rather silly just walking aimlessly with nowhere particular to walk to. And the sun was quite hot.

Oh well, how often she had wished she could have just a little time to herself, to think things out. Now, if ever, was her opportunity. What things were there that she had wanted to think out so urgently?

Joan searched her mind—but they seemed mostly to have been matters of local importance—remembering where she had put this, that or the other, deciding how to arrange the servants' summer holidays, planning the redecorating of the old schoolroom.

All these things seemed now rather remote and unimportant. November was rather far in advance to plan the servants' holidays, and besides, she had to know when Whitsuntide was and that needed next year's almanac. She could, however, decide about the schoolroom. The walls a light shade of beige and oatmeal covers with some nice bright cushions? Yes, that would do very well.

Ten minutes past eleven. Redecorating and doing up the schoolroom hadn't taken long!

Joan thought vaguely, If I'd only known, I could have brought along some interesting book on modern science and discoveries, something that would explain things like the quantum theory.

And then she wondered what had put the quantum theory into her head and thought to herself, Of course—the covers—and Mrs. Sherston.

For she remembered that she had once been discussing the vexed questions of chintzes or cretonnes for drawing room covers with Mrs. Sherston, the Bank Manager's wife—and right in the middle of it Mrs. Sherston had said in her abrupt way, "I do wish I was clever enough to understand the quantum theory. It's such a fascinating idea, isn't it, energy all done up in little parcels."

Joan had stared at her, for she really couldn't see what scientific theories had to do with chintzes, and Mrs. Sherston had got rather red and said, "Stupid of me, but you know the way things come into your head quite suddenly—and it *is* an exciting idea, isn't it?"

Joan hadn't thought the idea particularly exciting and the conversation had ended there. But she remembered quite well Mrs. Sherston's own cretonne—or rather handprinted linen covers. A design of leaves in browns and grays and reds. She had said, "These are very unusual, were they very expensive?" And Mrs. Sherston had said yes, they were. And she had added that she had got them because she loved woods and trees and the dream of her life was to go somewhere like Burma or Malay where things grew really *fast! Really* fast, she had added, in an anxious tone, and making a rather clumsy gesture with her hands to express impatience.

Those linens, reflected Joan now, must have cost at least eighteen and six a yard, a fantastic price for those days. One ought, by realizing what Captain Sherston gave his wife for housekeeping and furnishing, to have had at least an inkling of what was to come out later.

She herself had never really liked the man. She remembered sitting in his office at the bank, discussing the reinvestment of some shares, Sherston opposite her, behind his desk—a great big breezy man exuding *bonhomie*. A rather exaggeratedly social manner . . . "I'm a man of the world, dear lady," he seemed to be saying, "don't think of me as just a money machine—I'm a tennis player, a golfer, a dancer, a bridge player. The real me is the chap you meet at a party, not the official who says 'no further overdraft.' "

A great overblown windbag, thought Joan indignantly. Crooked, always crooked. Even then he must have started on his falsification of the books, or whatever the swindle was. And yet nearly everyone had liked him, had said what a good sort old Sherston was, not at all the usual type of Bank Manager.

Well, that was true enough. The usual type of Bank Manager doesn't embezzle bank funds.

Well, Leslie Sherston had, at any rate, got her handprinted linen covers out of it all. Not that anyone had ever suggested that an extravagant wife had led to Sherston's dishonesty. You only had to look at Leslie Sherston to see that money meant nothing particular to her. Always wearing shabby green tweeds and grubbing around in her garden or tramping through the countryside. She never bothered much about the children's clothes, either. And once, much later, Joan remembered an afternoon when Leslie Sherston had given her tea, fetching a big loaf and a roll of butter and some homemade jam and kitchen cups and teapot—everything bundled anyhow on a tray and brought in. An untidy, cheerful, careless sort of woman, with a one-sided slouch when she walked and a face that seemed all on one side too, but that one-sided smile of hers was rather nice, and people liked her on the whole.

Ah, well, poor Mrs. Sherston. She'd had a sad life, a very sad life.

Joan moved restlessly. Why had she let that phrase, a sad life, come into her mind? It reminded her of Blanche Haggard (though that was quite a different kind of sad life!) and thinking of Blanche brought her back again to Barbara and the circumstances surrounding Barbara's illness. Was there nothing one could think of that did not lead in some painful and undesired direction?

She looked at her watch once more. At any rate, handprinted linens and poor Mrs. Sherston had taken up nearly half an hour. What could she think about now? Something pleasant, with no disturbing sidelines.

Rodney was probably the safest subject to think about. Dear Rodney. Joan's mind dwelt pleasurably on the thought of her husband, visualizing him as she had last seen him on the platform at Victoria, saying goodbye to her just before the train pulled out.

Yes, dear Rodney. Standing there looking up at her, the sun shining full on his face and revealing so mercilessly the network of little lines at the corners of his eyes—such tired eyes. Yes, tired eyes, eyes full of a deep sadness. (Not, she thought, that Rodney *is* sad. It's just a trick of construction. Some animals have sad eyes.) Usually, too, he was wearing his glasses and then you didn't notice the sadness of his eyes. But he certainly looked a very tired man. No wonder, when he worked so hard. He practically never took a day off. (I shall change all that when I get back, thought Joan. He must have more leisure. I ought to have thought of it before.)

Yes, seen there in the bright light, he looked as old or older than his years. She had looked down on him and he up at her and they had exchanged the usual idiotic last words.

"I don't think you have to go through any customs at Calais."

"No, I believe one goes straight through to the Simplon express."

"Brindisi carriage, remember. I hope the Mediterranean behaves."

"I wish I could stop off a day or two in Cairo."

"Why don't you?"

"Darling, I must hurry to Barbara. It's only a weekly air service."

"Of course. I forgot."

A whistle blew. He smiled up at her.

"Take care of yourself, little Joan."

"Goodbye, don't miss me too much."

The train started with a jerk. Joan drew her head in. Rodney waved, then turned away. On an impulse she leaned out again. He was already striding up the platform.

She felt a sudden thrill at seeing that well-known back. How young he looked suddenly, his head thrown back, his shoulders squared. It gave her quite a shock . . .

She had an impression of a young carefree man striding up the platform.

It reminded her of the day she had first met Rodney Scudamore.

She had been introduced to him at a tennis party and they had gone straight onto the court.

He had said: "Shall I play at the net?"

And it was then that she had looked after him as he strode up to take his place at the net and thought what a very attractive back he had . . . the easy confident way he walked, the set of his head and neck . . .

Suddenly she had been nervous. She had served two lots of double faults running and had felt all hot and bothered.

And then Rodney had turned his head and smiled at her encouragingly—that kind friendly smile of his. And she had thought what a very attractive young man . . . and she had proceeded straight away to fall in love with him.

Looking out from the train, watching Rodney's retreating back until the sight of it was blotted out by the people on the platform, she relived that summer's day so many years ago.

It was as though the years had fallen away from Rodney, leaving him once more an eager confident young man.

As though the years had fallen away . . .

Suddenly, in the desert, with the sun pouring down on her, Joan gave a quick uncontrollable shiver.

She thought, No, no—I don't want to go on—I don't want to think about this. . . .

Rodney, striding up the platform, his head thrown back, the tired sag of his shoulders all gone. A man who had been relieved of an intolerable burden. . . .

Really, what was the matter with her? She was imagining things, inventing them. Her eyes had played a trick on her.

Why hadn't he waited to see the train pull out?

Well, why should he? He was in a hurry to get through what business he had to do in London. Some people didn't like to see trains go out of stations bearing away someone they loved.

Really it was impossible that anyone could remember so clearly as she did exactly how Rodney's back had looked!

She was imagining—

Stop, that didn't make it any better. If you imagined a thing like that, it meant that such an idea was already in your head.

And it couldn't be true—the inference that she had drawn simply could not be true.

She was saying to herself (wasn't she?) that Rodney was glad she was going away . . .

And that simply couldn't be true!

Chapter Four

Joan arrived back at the Rest House definitely overheated. Unconciously she had increased her pace so as to get away from that last unwelcome thought.

The Indian looked at her curiously and said:

"Memsahib walk very fast. Why walk fast? Plenty time here."

Oh God, thought Joan, plenty time indeed!

The Indian and the Rest House and the chickens and the tins and the barbed wire were all definitely getting on her nerves.

She went on into her bedroom and found *The Power House.*

At any rate, she thought, it's cool in here and dark.

She opened *The Power House* and began to read.

By lunchtime she had read half of it.

There was omelette for lunch and baked beans round it, and after it there was a dish of hot salmon with rice, and tinned apricots.

Joan did not eat very much.

Afterwards she went to her bedroom and lay down.

If she had a touch of the sun from walking too fast in the heat, a sleep would do her good.

She closed her eyes but sleep did not come.

She felt particularly wide awake and intelligent.

She got up and took three aspirins and lay down again.

Every time she shut her eyes she saw Rodney's back going away from her up the platform. It was insupportable!

She pulled aside the curtain to let in some light and got *The Power House*. A few pages before the end she dropped asleep.

She dreamt that she was going to play in a tournament with Rodney. They had difficulty in finding the balls but at last they got to the court. When she started to serve she found that she was playing against Rodney and the Randolph girl. She served nothing but double faults. She thought, "Rodney will help me," but when she looked for him she could not find him. Everyone had left and it was getting dark. "I'm all alone," thought Joan. "I'm all alone."

She woke up with a start.

"I'm all alone," she said aloud.

The influence of the dream was still upon her. It seemed to her that the words she had just said were terribly frightening.

She said again, "I'm all alone."

The Indian put his head in.

"Memsahib call?"

"Yes," she said. "Get me some tea."

"Memsahib want tea? Only three o'clock."

"Never mind, I want tea."

She heard him going away and calling out, "Chaichai!"

She got up from the bed and went over to the fly-spotted mirror. It was reassuring to see her own normal pleasant-looking face.

"I wonder," said Joan addressing her reflection, "whether you can be going to be ill? You're behaving very oddly."

Perhaps she *had* got a touch of the sun?

When the tea came she was feeling quite normal again. In fact the whole business was really very funny. She, Joan Scudamore, indulging in *nerves!* But of course it wasn't nerves, it was a touch of the sun. She wouldn't go out again until the sun was well down.

She ate some biscuits and drank two cups of tea Then she finished *The Power House*. As she closed the book, she was assailed by a definite qualm.

She thought, "Now I've got nothing to read."

Nothing to read, no writing materials, no sewing with her. Nothing at all to do, but wait for a problematical train that mightn't come for days.

When the Indian came in to clear tea away she said to him:

"What do you do here?"

He seemed surprised by the question.

"I look after travelers, Memsahib."

"I know." She controlled her impatience. "But that doesn't take you all your time?"

"I give them breakfast, lunch, tea."

"No, no, I don't mean that. You have helpers?"

"Arab boy—very stupid, very lazy, very dirty—I see to everything myself, not trust boy. He bring bath water—throw away bath water—he help cook."

"There are three of you, then, you, the cook, the boy? You must have a lot of time when you aren't working. Do you read?"

"Read? Read what?"

"Books."

"I not read."

"Then what do you do when you're not working?"

"I wait till time do more work."

It's no good, thought Joan. You can't talk to them. They don't know what you mean. This man, he's here always, month after month. Sometimes, I suppose, he gets a holiday, and goes to a town and gets drunk and sees friends. But for weeks on end he's here. Of course he's got the cook and the boy. . . . The boy lies in the sun and sleeps when he isn't working. Life's as simple as that for him. They're no good to me, not any of them. All the English this man knows is eating and drinking and "Nice weather."

The Indian went out. Joan strolled restlessly about the room.

"I mustn't be foolish. I must make some kind of plan. Arrange a course of—of thinking for myself. I really must *not* allow myself to get—well—rattled."

The truth was, she reflected, that she had always led such a full and occupied life. So much interest in it. It was a civilized life. And if you had all that balance and proportion in your life, it certainly left you rather at a loss when you were faced with the barren uselessness of doing nothing at all. The more useful and cultured a woman you were, the more difficult it made it.

There were some people, of course, even at home, who often sat about for hours doing nothing. Presumably they would take to this kind of life quite happily.

Even Mrs. Sherston, though as a rule she was active and energetic enough for two, had occasionally sat about doing nothing. Usually when she was out for walks. She would walk with terrific energy and then drop down suddenly on a log of wood, or a patch of heather and just sit there staring into space.

Like that day when she, Joan, had thought it was the Randolph girl. . . .

She blushed slightly as she remembered her own actions.

It had, really, been rather like spying. The sort of thing that made her just a little ashamed. Because she wasn't, really, that kind of woman.

Still, with a girl like Myrna Randolph. . . .

A girl who didn't seem to have any moral sense. . . .

Joan tried to remember how it had all come about.

She had been taking some flowers to old Mrs. Garnett and had just come out of the cottage door when she had heard Rodney's voice in the road outside the hedge. His voice and a woman's voice answering him.

She had said goodbye to Mrs. Garnet quickly and come out into the road. She was just able to catch sight of Rodney and, she felt sure, the Randolph girl, swinging round the corner of the track that led up to Asheldown.

No, she wasn't very proud of what she had done then. But she had felt, at the time, that she had to know. It wasn't exactly Rodney's fault— everyone knew what Myrna Randolph was.

Joan had taken the path that went up through Haling Wood and had come out that way onto the bare shoulder of Asheldown and at once she had caught sight of them—two figures sitting there motionless staring down over the pale shining countryside below.

The relief when she had seen that it wasn't Myrna Randolph at all, but Mrs. Sherston! They weren't even sitting close together. There were four feet at least between them. Really a quite ridiculous distance— hardly friendly! But then Leslie Sherston wasn't really a very friendly person—not, that is, a demonstrative one. And she certainly could not be regarded as a siren—the mere idea would have been ludicrous. No, she had been out on one of her tramps and Rodney had overtaken her and with his usual friendly courtesy, had accompanied her.

Now, having climbed up Asheldown Ridge, they were resting for a while and enjoying the view before going back again.

Astonishing, really, the way that neither of them moved nor spoke. Not, she thought, very companionable. Oh well, presumably they both had their own thoughts. They felt, perhaps, that they knew each other well enough not to have to bother to talk or to make conversation.

For by that time, the Scudamores had got to know Leslie Sherston very much better. The bombshell of Sherston's defalcations had burst upon a dismayed Crayminster and Sherston himself was by now serving his prison sentence. Rodney was the solicitor who had acted for him at the trial and who also acted for Leslie. He had been very sorry for Leslie, left with two small children and no money. Everybody had been prepared to be sorry for poor Mrs. Sherston and if they had not gone on being quite so sorry that was entirely Leslie Sherston's own fault. Her resolute cheerfulness had rather shocked some people.

"She must, I think," Joan had said to Rodney, "be rather insensitive."

He had replied brusquely that Leslie Sherston had more courage than anyone he had ever come across.

Joan had said, "Oh, yes, *courage*. But courage isn't everything!"

"Isn't it?" Rodney had said. He'd said it rather queerly. Then he'd gone off to the office.

Courage was a virtue one would certainly not deny to Leslie Sherston. Faced with the problem of supporting herself and two children, and with no particular qualifications for the task she had managed it.

She'd gone to work at a market gardener's until she was thoroughly conversant with the trade, accepting in the meantime a small allowance from an aunt, and living with the children in rooms. Thus, when Sherston had come out of prison, he'd found her established in a different part of the world altogether, growing fruit and vegetables for the market. He'd driven the truck in and out from the nearby town, and the children had helped and they'd managed somehow to make not too bad a thing of it. There was no doubt that Mrs. Sherston had worked like a

Trojan and it was particularly meritorious because she must, at that time, have begun to suffer a good deal of pain from the illness that eventually killed her.

Oh well, thought Joan, presumably she loved the man. Sherston had certainly been considered a good-looking man and a favorite with women. He looked rather different when he came out of prison. She, Joan, had only seen him once, but she was shocked by the change in him. Shifty eyed, deflated, still boastful, still attempting to bluff and bluster. A wreck of a man. Still, his wife had loved him and stuck by him and for that Joan respected Leslie Sherston.

She had, on the other hand, considered that Leslie had been absolutely wrong about the children.

That same aunt who had come to the rescue financially when Sherston was convicted had made a further offer when he was due to come out of prison.

She would, she said, adopt the younger boy, and an uncle, persuaded by her, would pay the school fees of the elder boy and she herself would take them both for the holidays. They could take the uncle's name by deed poll and she and the uncle would make themselves financially responsible for their future.

Leslie Sherston had turned this offer down unconditionally and in that Joan thought she had been selfish. She was refusing for her children a much better life than she could give them and one free from any taint of disgrace.

However much she loved her boys, she ought, Joan thought, and Rodney agreed with her, to think of their lives before her own.

But Leslie had been quite unyielding and Rodney had washed his hands of the whole matter. He supposed, he had said with a sigh, that Mrs. Sherston knew her own business best. Certainly, Joan thought, she was an obstinate creature.

Walking restlessly up and down the Rest House floor, Joan remembered Leslie Sherston as she had looked that day sitting on Asheldown Ridge.

Sitting hunched forward, her elbows on her knees, her chin supported on her hands. Sitting curiously still. Looking out across the farmland and the plough to where slopes of oaks and beeches in Little Havering wood were turning golden red.

She and Rodney sitting there—so quiet—so motionless—staring in front of them.

Quite why she did not speak to them, or join them, Joan hardly knew.

Perhaps it was the guilty consciousness of her suspicions of Myrna Randolph?

Anyhow she had not spoken to them. Instead she had gone quietly back into the shelter of the trees and had taken her way home. It was an incident that she had never liked very much to think about—and she had certainly never mentioned it to Rodney. He might think she had ideas in her head, ideas about him and Myrna Randolph.

Rodney walking up the platform at Victoria. . . .

Oh goodness, surely she wasn't going to begin *that* all over again?

What on earth had put that extraordinary notion into her head? That Rodney (who was and always had been devoted to her) was enjoying the prospect of her absence?

As though you could tell anything by the way a man walked!

She would simply put the whole ridiculous fancy out of her mind.

She wouldn't think any more about Rodney, not if it made her imagine such curious and unpleasant things.

Up to now, she'd never been a fanciful woman.

It *must* be the sun.

Chapter Five

The afternoon and evening passed with interminable slowness. Joan didn't like to go out in the sun again until it was quite low in the sky. So she sat in the Rest House.

After about half an hour she felt it unendurable to sit still in a chair. She went into the bedroom and began to unpack her cases and repack them. Her things, so she told herself, were not properly folded. She might as well make a good job of it.

She finished the job neatly and expeditiously. It was five o'clock. She might safely go out now surely. It was so depressing in the Rest House. If only she had something to read. . . .

Or even, thought Joan desperately, a wire puzzle!

Outside she looked with distaste at the tins and the hens and the barbed wire. What a horrible place this was. Utterly horrible.

She walked, for a change, in a direction parallel with the railway line and the Turkish frontier. It gave her a feeling of agreeable novelty. But after a quarter of an hour the effect was the same. The railway line, running a quarter of a mile to her right, gave her no feeling of companionship.

Nothing but silence—silence and sunlight.

It occurred to Joan that she might recite poetry. She had always been supposed as a girl to recite and read poetry very well. Interesting to see what she could remember after all these years. There was a time when she had known quite a lot of poetry by heart.

The quality of mercy is not strained,
It droppeth as the gentle rain from heaven

What came next? Stupid. She simply couldn't remember.

Fear no more the heat of the sun

(That began comfortingly anyway! Now how did it go on?)

Nor the furious winter's rages
Thou thy worldly task has done
Home art gone and ta'en thy wages
Golden lads and girls all must
As chimney sweepers come to dust.

No, not very cheerful on the whole. Could she remember any of the sonnets? She used to know them. The *marriage of true minds* and that one that Rodney had asked her about.

Funny the way he had said suddenly one evening:

"*And thy eternal summer shall not fade*—that's from Shakespeare, isn't it?"

"Yes, from the sonnets."

And he had said:

"*Let me not unto the marriage of true minds admit impediment?* That one?"

"No, the one that begins, *Shall I compare thee to a summer's day.*"

And then she had quoted the whole sonnet to him, really rather beautifully, with a lot of expression and all the proper emphasis.

At the end, instead of expressing approbation, he had only repeated thoughtfully:

"*Rough winds do shake the darling buds of May* . . . but it's October now, isn't it?"

It was such an extraordinary thing to say that she had stared at him. Then he had said:

"Do you know the other one? The one about the marriage of true minds?"

"Yes." She paused a minute and then began:

"Let me not to the marriage of true minds
Admit impediments. Love is not love
Which alters where it alteration finds,
Or bends with the remover to remove:
O, no, it is an ever-fixed mark
That looks on tempests and is never shaken,
It is the star to every wandering bark
Whose worth's unknown, although his height be taken.
Love's not Time's fool, though rosy lips and cheeks
Within his bending sickle's compass come;
Love alters not with his brief hours and weeks,
But bears it out even to the edge of doom.
If this be error, and upon me prov'd
I never writ, nor no man ever lov'd."

She finished, giving the last lines full emphasis and dramatic fervor.

"Don't you think I recite Shakespeare rather well? I was always supposed to at school. They said I read poetry with a lot of expression."

But Rodney had only answered absently, "It doesn't really need expression. Just the words will do."

She had sighed and murmured, "Shakespeare *is* wonderful, isn't he?"

And Rodney had answered, "What's really so wonderful is that he was just a poor devil like the rest of us."

"Rodney, what an extraordinary thing to say."

He had smiled at her, then, as though waking up. "Is it?"

Getting up, he had strolled out of the room murmuring as he went:

"Rough winds do shake the darling buds of May
And summer's lease hath all too short a date."

Why on earth, she wondered, had he said, "But it's October now"? What could he have been thinking about?

She remembered that October, a particularly fine and mild one.

Curious, now she came to think of it, the evening that Rodney had asked her about the Sonnets had been the actual evening of the day when she had seen him sitting with Mrs. Sherston on Asheldown. Perhaps Mrs. Sherston had been quoting Shakespeare, but it wasn't very likely. Leslie Sherston was not, she thought, at all an intellectual woman.

It had been a wonderful October that year.

She remembered quite plainly, a few days later, Rodney asking her in a bewildered tone:

"Ought this thing to be out this time of year?"

He was pointing to a rhododendron. One of the early flowering ones that normally bloom in March or the end of February. It had a rich blood red blossom and the buds were bursting all over it.

"No," she had told him. "Spring is the time, but sometimes they do come out in Autumn if it's unusually mild and warm."

He had touched one of the buds gently with his fingers and had murmured under his breath:

"The darling buds of May."

March, she told him, not May.

"It's like blood," he said, "heart's blood."

How unlike Rodney, she thought, to be so interested in flowers.

But after that he had always liked that particular rhododendron.

She remembered how, many years later, he had worn a great bud of it in his buttonhole.

Much too heavy, of course, and it had fallen out as she knew it would.

They'd been in the churchyard, of all extraordinary places, at the time.

She'd seen him there as she came back past the church and had joined him and said, "Whatever are you doing here, Rodney?"

He had laughed and said, "Considering my latter end, and what I'll have put on my tombstone. Not granite chips, I think, they're so genteel. And certainly not a stout marble angel."

They had looked down then at a very new marble slab which bore Leslie Sherston's name.

Following her glance Rodney had spelled out slowly:

"Leslie Adeline Sherston, dearly beloved wife of Charles Edward Sherston, who entered into rest on May 11th, 1930. And God shall wipe away their tears."

Then, after a moment's pause, he had said:

"Seems damned silly to think of Leslie Sherston under a cold slab of

marble like that, and only a congenital idiot like Sherston would ever
have chosen that text. I don't believe Leslie ever cried in her life."

Joan had said, feeling just a little shocked and rather as though she
was playing a slightly blasphemous game:

"What would you choose?"

"For her? I don't know. Isn't there something in the Psalms? *In thy
presence is the fullness of joy.* Something like that."

"I really meant for yourself."

"Oh, for me?" He thought for a minute or two—smiled to himself.
"The Lord is my shepherd. He leadeth me in green pastures. That will do
very well for me."

"It sounds rather a dull idea of Heaven, I've always thought."

"What's your idea of Heaven, Joan?"

"Well—not all the golden gates and that stuff, of course. I like to
think of it as a *state.* Where everyone is busy helping, in some wonderful
way, to make this world, perhaps, more beautiful and happier. Service—
that's my idea of Heaven."

"What a dreadful little prig you are, Joan." He had laughed in his
teasing way to rob the words of their sting. Then he had said, "No, a
green valley—that's good enough for me—and the sheep following the
shepherd home in the cool of the evening—"

He paused a minute and then said, "It's an absurd fancy of mine,
Joan, but I play with the idea sometimes that, as I'm on my way to the
office and go along the High Street, I turn to take the alley into the Bell
Walk and instead of the alley I've turned into a hidden valley, with green
pasture and soft wooded hills on either side. It's been there all the time,
existing secretly in the heart of the town. You turn from the busy High
Street into it and you feel quite bewildered and say perhaps, 'Where am
I?' And then they'd tell you, you know, very gently, that you were
dead. . . ."

"Rodney!" She was really startled, dismayed. "You—you're ill. You
can't be well."

It had been her first inkling of the state he was in—the precursor of
that nervous breakdown that was shortly to send him for some two
months to the sanatorium in Cornwall where he seemed content to lie

silently listening to the gulls and staring out over the pale, treeless hills to the sea.

But she hadn't realized until that day in the churchyard that he really had been overworking. It was as they turned to go home, she with an arm through his, urging him forward, that she saw the heavy rhododendron bud drop from his coat and fall on Leslie's grave.

"Oh, look," she said, "your rhododendron," and she stooped to pick it up. But he had said quickly:

"Let it lie. Leave it there for Leslie Sherston. After all—she was our friend."

And Joan had said quickly, what a nice idea, and that she would bring a big bunch of those yellow chrysanthemums herself tomorrow.

She had been, she remembered, a little frightened by the queer smile he gave her.

Yes, definitely she had felt that there was something wrong with Rodney that evening. She didn't, of course, realize that he was on the edge of a complete breakdown, but she did know that he was, somehow, different. . . .

She had plied him with anxious questions all the way home but he hadn't said much. Only repeated again and again:

"I'm tired, Joan . . . I'm very tired."

And once, incomprehensibly, "We can't *all* be brave. . . ."

It was only about a week later that he had, one morning, said dreamily, "I shan't get up today."

And he had lain there in bed, not speaking or looking at anyone, just lain there, smiling quietly.

And then there had been doctors and nurses and finally the arrangements for him to go for a long rest cure to Trevelyan. No letters or telegrams and no visitors. They wouldn't even let Joan come and see him. Not his own wife.

It had been a sad, perplexing, bewildering time. And the children had been very difficult too. Not helpful. Behaving as though it was all her, Joan's, fault.

"Letting him slave and slave and slave at that office. You know perfectly well, Mother, Father's worked far too hard for years."

"I know, my dears. But what could I do about it?"

"You ought to have yanked him out of it years ago. Don't you *know* he hates it? Don't you know *anything* about Father?"

"That's quite enough, Tony. Of course I know all about your father— far more than you do."

"Well, sometimes I don't think so. Sometimes I don't think you know anything about *anybody*."

"Tony—really!"

"Dry up, Tony—" That was Averil. "What's the good?"

Averil was always like that. Dry, unemotional, affecting a cynicism and a detached outlook beyond her years. Averil, Joan sometimes thought despairingly, had really no heart at all. She disliked caresses and was always completely unaffected by appeals to her better self.

"Darling Daddy—" it was a wail from Barbara, younger than the other two, more uncontrolled in her emotions. "It's all your fault, Mother. You've been cruel to him—*cruel*—always."

"Barbara!" Joan quite lost patience. "What do you think you're talking about? If there is one person who comes first in this house, it's your father. How do you think you could all have been educated and clothed and fed if your father hadn't worked for you? He's sacrificed himself for *you*—that's what parents have to do—and they do it without making any fuss about it."

"Let me take this opportunity of thanking you, Mother," said Averil, "for all the sacrifices *you* have made for us."

Joan looked at her daughter doubtfully. She suspected Averil's sincerity. But surely the child couldn't be so impertinent. . . .

Tony distracted her attention. He was asking gravely:

"It's true, isn't it, that Father once wanted to be a farmer?"

"A farmer? No, of course he didn't. Oh well, I believe years ago— just a kind of boyish fancy. But the family have always been lawyers. It's a family firm, and really quite famous in this part of England. You ought to be very proud of it, and glad that you're going into it."

"But I'm not going into it, Mother. I want to go to East Africa and farm."

"Nonsense, Tony. Don't let's have this silly nonsense all over again. Of course you're going into the firm! You're the only son."

"I'm not going to be a lawyer, Mother. Father knows and he's prom-ised me."

She stared at him, taken aback, shaken by his cool certainty.

Then she sank into a chair, tears came to her eyes. So unkind, all of them, browbeating her like this.

"I don't know what's come over you all—talking to me like this. If your father were here—I think you are all behaving very unkindly!"

Tony had muttered something and, turning, had slouched out of the room.

Averil, in her dry voice, said, "Tony's quite set on being a farmer, Mother. He wants to go to an Agricultural College. It seems quite batty to me. I'd much rather be a lawyer if I was a man. I think the law is jolly interesting."

"I never thought," sobbed Joan, "that my children could be so unkind to me."

Averil had sighed deeply. Barbara, still sobbing hysterically in a corner of the room, had called out:

"I know Daddy will die. I know he will—and then we'll be all alone in the world. I can't bear it. Oh, I can't bear it!"

Averil sighed again, looking with distaste from her frenziedly sobbing sister to her gently sobbing mother.

"Well," she said, "if there isn't anything I can do—"

And with that she had quietly and composedly left the room. Which was exactly like Averil.

Altogether a most distressing and painful scene, and one that Joan hadn't thought of for years.

Easily understandable, of course. The sudden shock of their father's ill-ness, and the mystery of the words "nervous breakdown." Children always felt better if they could feel a thing was someone's fault. They had made a kind of scapegoat of their mother because she was nearest to hand. Both Tony and Barbara had apologized afterwards. Averil did not seem to think that there was anything for which she needed to apologize, and perhaps, from her own point of view, she was justified. It wasn't the poor child's fault that she really seemed to have been born without any heart.

It had been a difficult, unhappy time altogether while Rodney was away. The children had sulked and been bad tempered. As far as possible they had kept out of her way and that had made her feel curiously lonely. It was, she supposed, the effect of her own sadness and preoccupation. They all loved her dearly, as she knew. Then, too, they were all at difficult ages—Barbara at school still, Averil a gawky and suspicious eighteen. Tony spent most of his time on a neighboring farm. Annoying that he should have got this silly idea about farming into his head, and very weak of Rodney to have encouraged him. Oh, dear, Joan had thought, it seems too hard that *I* should always have to do all the unpleasant things. When there are such nice girls at Miss Harley's, I really cannot think why Barbara has to make friends with such undesirable specimens. I shall have to make it quite plain to her that she can only bring girls here that I approve of. And then I suppose there will be another row and tears and sulks. Averil, of course, is no help to me, and I do hate that funny sneering way she has of talking. It sounds so badly to outside people.

Yes, thought Joan, bringing up children was a thankless and difficult business.

One didn't really get enough appreciation for it. The tact one had to use, and the good humor. Knowing exactly when to be firm and when to give way. Nobody really knows, thought Joan, what I had to go through that time when Rodney was ill.

Then she winced slightly—for the thought brought up a memory of a remark uttered caustically by Dr. McQueen to the effect, that during every conversation, sooner or later somebody says, "Nobody knows what I went through at that time!" Everybody had laughed and said that it was quite true.

Well, thought Joan, wriggling her toes uneasily in her shoes because of the sand that had got in, it's perfectly true. Nobody does know what I went through at that time, not even Rodney.

For when Rodney had come back, in the general relief, everything had swung back to normal, and the children had been their own cheerful, amiable selves again. Harmony had been restored. Which showed, Joan thought, that the whole thing had really been due to anxiety. Anxiety had made her lose her own poise. Anxiety had made the children nervous and bad tempered. A very upsetting time altogether and why she had got to select those particular incidents to think about now—when what she wanted was happy memories and not depressing ones—she really couldn't imagine.

It had all started—what had it started from? Of course—trying to remember poetry. Though really could anything be more ridiculous, thought Joan, than to walk about in a desert spouting poetry! Not that it mattered since there wasn't anybody to see or hear.

There wasn't anybody—no, she adjured herself, no, you must not give way to panic. This is all silliness, sheer nerves. . . .

She turned quickly and began to walk back towards the Rest House.

She found that she was forcing herself not to break into a run.

There was nothing to be afraid of in being alone—nothing at all. Perhaps she was one of those people who suffered from—now, what was the word? Not claustrophobia, that was the terror of confined spaces—the thing that was the opposite of that. It began with an A. The fear of open spaces.

The whole thing could be explained scientifically.

But explaining it scientifically, though reassuring, didn't at the moment actually help.

Easy to say to yourself that the whole thing was perfectly logical and reasonable, but not so easy to control the curious odds and ends of thoughts that popped in and out of your head for all the world like lizards popping out of holes.

Myrna Randolph, she thought, like a snake—these other things like lizards.

Open spaces—and all her life she'd lived in a box. Yes, a box with toy children and toy servants and a toy husband.

No, Joan, what are you saying—how can you be so silly? Your children are real enough.

The children were real, and so were Cook and Agnes, and so was Rodney. Then perhaps, thought Joan, *I'm* not real. Perhaps I'm just a toy wife and mother.

Oh dear, this was dreadful. Quite incoherent she was getting. Perhaps if she said some more poetry. She must be able to remember *something*.

And aloud, with disproportionate fervor, she exclaimed:

"From you have I been absent in the Spring."

She couldn't remember how it went on. She didn't seem to want to. That line was enough in itself. It explained everything, didn't it? Rodney, she thought, Rodney . . . *From you have I been absent in the Spring.* Only she thought, it's not Spring, it's November. . . .

And with a sudden sense of shock—"But that's what *he* said—that evening . . ."

There was a connection there, a clue, a clue to something that was waiting for her, hiding behind the silence. Something from which, she now realized, she wanted to escape.

But how could you escape with lizards popping out of holes all round?

So many things one mustn't let oneself think of. Barbara and Baghdad and Blanche (all Bs, how very curious). And Rodney on the platform at Victoria. And Averil and Tony and Barbara all being so unkind to her.

Really—Joan was exasperated with herself—why didn't she think of the *pleasant* things? So many delightful memories. So many—so very many. . . .

Her wedding dress, such a lovely oyster-shell satin . . . Averil in her bassinette, all trimmed with muslin and pink ribbons, such a lovely fair baby and so well behaved. Averil had always been a polite, well-mannered child. "You bring them up so beautifully, Mrs. Scudamore." Yes, a satisfactory child, Averil—in public, at any rate. In private life given to interminable argument, and with a disconcerting way of looking at you, as though she wondered what you were really like. Not at all the sort of way a child ought to look at its mother. Not, in any sense of the word, a loving child. Tony, too, had always done her credit in public though he was incurably inattentive and vague over things. Barbara was the only difficult child in the family, given to tantrums and storms of tears.

Still, on the whole, they were three very charming, nice-mannered, well-brought-up children.

A pity children had to grow up and start being difficult.

But she wouldn't think of all that. Concentrate on them in their childhood. Averil at dancing class in her pretty pink silk frock. Barbara in that nice little knitted dress from Liberty's. Tony in those cheery patterned rompers that Nannie made so cleverly—

Somehow, thought Joan, surely she could think of something else except the clothes the children wore! Some charming, affectionate things that they had said to her? Some delightful moments of intimacy?

Considering the sacrifices one made, and the way one did everything for one's children—

Another lizard popping its head out of a hole. Averil enquiring politely, and with that air of reasonableness that Joan had learned to dread:

"What do you *really* do for us, Mother? You don't *bathe* us, do you?"

"No—"

"And you don't give us our dinners, or brush our hair. Nannie does all that. And she puts us to bed and gets us up. And you don't make our clothes—Nannie does that, too. And she takes us for walks—"

"Yes, dear. I employ Nannie to look after you. That is to say I pay her her wages."

"I thought Father paid her her wages. Doesn't Father pay for all the things we have?"

"In a way, dear, but it's all the same thing."

"But *you* don't have to go to the office every morning, only Father. Why don't you have to go to the office?"

"Because I look after the house."

"But don't Kate and Cook and—"

"That will do, Averil."

There was one thing to be said for Averil, she always subsided when told. She was never rebellious nor defiant. And yet her submission was often more uncomfortable than rebellion would have been.

Rodney had laughed once and said that with Averil, the verdict was always Non Proven.

"I don't think you ought to laugh, Rodney. I don't think a child of Averil's age ought to be so—so critical."

"You think she's too young to determine the nature of evidence?"

"Oh, don't be so legal."

He said, with his teasing smile, "Who made me into a lawyer?"

"No, but seriously, I think it's disrespectful."

"I call Averil unusually polite for a child. There's none of the usual devastating frankness children can employ—not like Babs."

It was true, Joan admitted. Barbara, in one of her states, would shout

out, "You're ugly—you're horrible—I hate you. I wish I was dead. You'd be sorry if I was dead."

Joan said quickly. "With Babs it's just temper. And she's always sorry afterwards."

"Yes, poor little devil. And she doesn't mean what she says. But Averil has got quite a flair for detecting humbug."

Joan flushed angrily, "Humbug! I don't know what you mean."

"Oh, come now, Joan. The stuff we feed them up with. Our assumption of omniscience. The necessity we are under of pretending to do what is best, to know what is best, for those helpless little creatures who are so absolutely in our power."

"You talk as though they were slaves, not children."

"Aren't they slaves? They eat the food we give them and wear the clothes we put on them, and say more or less what we tell them to say. It's the price they pay for protection. But every day they live they are growing nearer to freedom."

"Freedom," Joan said scornfully. "Is there any such thing?"

Rodney said slowly and heavily, "No, I don't think there is. How right you are, Joan . . ."

And he had gone slowly out of the room, his shoulders sagging a little. And she had thought with a sudden pang, I know what Rodney will look like when he is old . . .

Rodney on Victoria platform—the light showing up the lines in his tired face—telling her to take care of herself.

And then, a minute later . . .

Why must she eternally come back to that? It wasn't true! Rodney was missing her a great deal! It was miserable for him in the house alone with the servants! And he probably never thought of asking people in for dinner—or only somebody stupid like Hargrave Taylor—such a dull man, she never could think why Rodney liked him. Or that tiresome Major Mills who never talked of anything but pasture and cattle breeding . . .

Of course Rodney was missing her!

Chapter Six

She arrived back at the Rest House and the Indian came out and asked: "Memsahib have nice walk?"

Yes, Joan said, she had had a very nice walk.

"Dinner ready soon. Very nice dinner, Memsahib."

Joan said she was glad of that, but the remark was clearly a ritual one, for dinner was exactly the same as usual, with peaches instead of apricots. It might be a nice dinner, but its disadvantage was that it was always the same dinner.

It was far too early to go to bed when dinner was over and once again Joan wished fervently that she had brought either a large supply of literature or some sewing with her. She even attempted to reread the more entertaining passages of *Lady Catherine Dysart's Memoirs* but the attempt was a failure.

If there were *anything* to do, Joan thought, anything at *all!* A pack of cards, even. She could have played patience. Or a game—backgammon, chess, draughts—she could have played against herself! *Any* game—halma, snakes and ladders. . . .

Really a very curious fancy she had had out there. Lizards popping their heads out of holes. Thoughts popping up out of your mind . . . frightening thoughts, disturbing thoughts . . . thoughts that one didn't want to have.

But if so, why have them? After all one could control one's thoughts—or couldn't one? Was it possible that in some circumstances one's thoughts controlled oneself . . . popping up out of holes like lizards—or flashing across one's mind like a green snake.

Coming from *somewhere*. . . .

Very odd that feeling of panic she had had.

It must be agoraphobia. (Of course that was the word—agoraphobia. It showed that one could always remember things if one only thought hard enough). Yes, that was it. The terror of open spaces. Curious that she had never known before that she suffered from it. But of course she had never before had any experience of open spaces. She had always lived in the midst of houses and gardens with plenty to do and plenty of people. Plenty of people, that was the thing. If only there was someone here to talk to.

Even Blanche. . . .

Funny to think how she had been appalled by the possibility that Blanche might be making the journey home with her.

Why, it would have made all the difference in the world to have had Blanche here. They could have talked over the old days at St. Anne's. How very long ago that seemed. What was it Blanche had said? "You've gone up in the world and I've gone down." No, she had qualified it afterwards—she had said, "You've stayed where you were—a St. Anne's girl who's been a credit to the school."

Was there really so little difference in her since those days? Nice to think so. Well, nice in a way, but in another way not so nice. It seemed rather—rather stagnant somehow.

What was it Miss Gilbey had said on the occasion of the leave-taking talk? Miss Gilbey's leave-taking talks to her girls were famous, a recognized institution of St. Anne's.

Joan's mind swept back over the years and the figure of her old Headmistress loomed immediately into her field of vision with startling clarity. The large aggressive nose, the pince-nez, the mercilessly sharp eyes with their compelling gaze, the terrific majesty of her progress through the school, slightly preceded by her bust—a restrained disciplined bust that had about it only majesty and no suggestion of softness.

A terrific figure, Miss Gilbey, justly feared and admired and who could produce just as frightening an effect on parents as on pupils. No denying it, Miss Gilbey *was* St. Anne's!

Joan saw herself entering that sacred room, with its flowers, its Medici prints, its implications of culture, scholarship and social graces.

Miss Gilbey, turning majestic from her desk—

"Come in, Joan. Sit down, dear child."

Joan had sat down as indicated in the cretonne-covered armchair. Miss Gilbey had removed her pince-nez, had produced suddenly an unreal and distinctly terrifying smile.

"You are leaving us, Joan, to go from the circumscribed world of school into the larger world which is life. I should like to have a little talk with you before you go in the hope that some words of mine may be a guide to you in the days that are to come."

"Yes, Miss Gilbey."

"Here, in these happy surroundings, with young companions of your own age, you have been shielded from the perplexities and difficulties which no one can entirely avoid in this life."

"Yes, Miss Gilbey."

"You have, I know, been happy here."

"Yes, Miss Gilbey."

"And you have done well here. I am pleased with the progress you have made. You have been one of our most satisfactory pupils."

Slight confusion—"Oh—er—I'm glad, Miss Gilbey."

"But life opens out before you now with fresh problems, fresh responsibilities—"

The talk flowed on. At the proper intervals Joan murmured:

"Yes, Miss Gilbey."

She felt slightly hypnotized.

It was one of Miss Gilbey's assets in her career to possess a voice that was, according to Blanche Haggard, orchestral in its compass. Starting with the mellowness of a cello, administering praise in the accents of a flute, deepening to warning in the tones of a bassoon. Then to those girls of marked intellectual prowess the exhortation to a career was proclaimed in terms of brass—to those of more domestic caliber the duties of wifehood and motherhood were mentioned in the muted notes of the violin.

Not until the end of the discourse did Miss Gilbey, as it were, speak pizzicato.

"And now, just a special word. No *lazy thinking*, Joan, my dear! Don't just accept things at their face value—because it's the easiest way, and because it may save you pain! Life is meant to be lived, not glossed over. And don't be too pleased with yourself!"

"Yes—no, Miss Gilbey."

"Because, just *entre nous*, that *is* a little your failing, isn't it, Joan? Think of others, my dear, and not too much of yourself. And be prepared to accept responsibility."

And then on to the grand orchestral climax:

"Life, Joan, must be a continual progress—a rising on the stepping stones of our dead selves to higher things. Pain and suffering will come. They come to all. Even Our Lord was not immune from the sufferings of our mortal life. As he knew the agony of Gethsemane, so you will know it—and if you do not know that, Joan, then it will mean that your path has veered far from the true way. Remember this when the hour of doubt and travail comes. And remember, my dear, that I am glad to hear from my old girls at any time—and always ready to help them with advice if they should ask for it. God bless you, dear."

And thereupon the final benediction of Miss Gilbey's parting kiss, a kiss that was less a human contact than a glorified accolade.

Joan, slightly dazed, was dismissed.

She returned to her dormitory to find Blanche Haggard, wearing Mary Grant's pince-nez, and with a pillow stuffed down the front of her gym tunic, giving an orchestral recital to an enraptured audience:

"You are going," boomed Blanche, "from this happy world of school into the larger more perilous world of life. Life opens out before you with its problems, its responsibilities . . ."

Joan joined the audience. The applause grew as Blanche worked up to her climax.

"To you, Blanche Haggard, I say but one word. Discipline. Discipline your emotions, practice self-control. Your very warmth of heart may prove perilous. Only by strict discipline can you attain the heights. You have great gifts, my dear. Use them well. You have a lot of faults, Blanche—a lot of faults. But they are the faults of a generous nature and they can be corrected.

"Life—" Blanche's voice rose to a shrill falsetto, "is a continual progress. Rise on the stepping stones of our dead selves—(see Wordsworth). Remember the old school and remember that Aunt Gilbey gives advice and help at any time if a stamped addressed envelope is enclosed!"

Blanche paused, but to her surprise neither laughter nor applause greeted the pause. Everyone looked as though turned into marble and all heads were turned to the open doorway where Miss Gilbey stood majestically, pince-nez in hand.

There was an agonized silence. Then Miss Gilbey said:

"If you are thinking of taking up a stage career, Blanche, I believe there are several excellent schools of dramatic art where they would teach you proper voice control and elocution. You seem to have some talents in that direction. Kindly return that pillow to its proper place at once."

And with that she moved swiftly away.

"Whew," said Blanche. "The old tartar! Pretty sporting of her—but she does know how to make you feel small."

Yes, thought Joan, Miss Gilbey had been a great personality. She had finally retired from St. Anne's just a term after Averil had been sent there. The new Headmistress had lacked her dynamic personality, and the school had started to go down in consequence.

Blanche had been right, Miss Gilbey had been a tartar. But she had known how to make herself felt. And she had certainly, Joan reflected, been quite right about Blanche. Discipline—that was what Blanche had needed in her life. Generous instincts—yes, possibly. But self-control had been notably lacking. Still, Blanche *was* generous. That money, for instance, the money that Joan had sent her—Blanche hadn't spent it on herself. It had bought a rolltop desk for Tom Holliday. A rolltop desk was the last thing in the world that Blanche would have wanted. A warm-hearted kindly creature, Blanche. And yet she had left her children, gone off callously and deserted the two little creatures she herself had brought into the world.

It just showed that there were people who had simply no maternal instinct whatsoever. One's children, thought Joan, should always come first. She and Rodney had always agreed on that. Rodney was really very unselfish—if it was put to him, that is, in the right way. She had pointed out to him, for instance, that that nice sunny dressing room of his really ought to be the children's day nursery and he had agreed quite willingly to move into the little room overlooking the stable yard. Children should have all the sun and light there was.

She and Rodney had really been very conscientious parents. And the children had really been very satisfactory, especially when they were quite small—such attractive handsome children. Much better brought up than the Sherston boys, for instance. Mrs. Sherston never seemed to mind what those children looked like. And she herself seemed to join them in the most curious activities, crawling along the ground as a Red Indian—uttering wild whoops and yells—and once when they were attempting a reproduction of a circus, giving a most lifelike imitation of a sea lion!

The fact was, Joan decided, that Leslie Sherston herself had never properly grown up.

Still, she'd had a very sad life, poor woman.

Joan thought of the time when she had so unexpectedly run across Captain Sherston in Somerset.

She had been staying with friends in that part of the world and had had no idea the Sherstons were living there. She had come face to face with Captain Sherston as he emerged (so typical) from the local pub.

She had not seen him since his release and it was really quite a shock to see the difference from the old days of the jaunty, confident Bank Manager.

That curiously deflated look that big aggressive men got when they had failed in the world. The sagging shoulders, the loose waistcoat, the flabby cheeks, the quick shifty look of the eyes.

To think that anyone could ever have trusted this man.

He was taken aback by meeting her, but he rallied well, and greeted her with what was a painful travesty of his old manner:

"Well, well, well, Mrs. Scudamore! The world is indeed a small place. And what brings you to Skipton Haynes?"

Standing there, squaring his shoulders, endeavoring to put into his voice the old heartiness and self-assurance. It was a pitiful performance and Joan had, in spite of herself, felt quite sorry for him.

How dreadful to come down in the world like that! To feel that at any moment you might come across someone from the old life, someone who might refuse even to recognize you.

Not that she had any intention herself of behaving that way. Naturally she was quite prepared to be kind.

Sherston was saying, "You must come back and see my wife. You must have tea with us. Yes, yes, dear lady, I insist!"

And the parody of his old manner was so painful that Joan, albeit rather unwillingly, allowed herself to be piloted along the street, Sherston continuing to talk in his new uneasy way.

He'd like her to see their little place—at least not so little. Quite a good acreage. Hard work, of course, growing for the market. Anemones and apples were their best line.

Still talking he unlatched a somewhat dilapidated gate that needed painting and they walked up a weedy drive. Then they saw Leslie, her back bent over the anemone beds.

"Look who's here," Sherston called and Leslie had pushed her hair back from her face and had come over and said this *was* a surprise!

Joan had noticed at once how much older Leslie looked and how ill. There were lines carved by fatigue and pain on her face. But otherwise she was exactly the same as usual, cheerful and untidy and terrifically energetic.

As they were standing there talking, the boys arrived home from school, charging up the drive with loud howls and rushing at Leslie, butting at her with their heads, shouting out Mum, Mum, Mum, and Leslie after enduring the onslaught for some minutes suddenly said in a very peremptory voice, "Quiet! Visitors."

And the boys had suddenly transformed themselves into two polite angels who shook hands with Mrs. Scudamore, and spoke in soft hushed voices.

Joan was reminded a little of a cousin of hers who trained sporting dogs. On the word of command the dogs would sit, dropping to their haunches, or on another word dash wildly for the horizon. Leslie's children, she thought, seemed trained much on the same plan.

They went into the house and Leslie went to get tea with the boys helping her and presently it came in on a tray, with the loaf and the butter and the homemade jam, and the thick kitchen cups and Leslie and the boys laughing.

But the most curious thing that happened was the change in Sherston.

That uneasy shifty painful manner of his vanished. He became suddenly
the master of the house and the host—and a very good host. Even his
social manner was in abeyance. He looked suddenly happy, pleased with
himself and with his family. It was as though, within these four walls,
the outer world and its judgment ceased to exist for him. The boys
clamored for him to help them with some carpentry they were doing,
Leslie adjured him not to forget that he had promised to see to the hoe
for her and ought they to bunch the anemones tomorrow or could they
do it Thursday morning?

Joan thought to herself that she had never liked him better. She understood, she felt, for the first time Leslie's devotion to him. Besides, he
must have been a very good-looking man once.

But a moment or two later she got rather a shock.

Peter was crying eagerly, "Tell us the funny story about the warder
and the plum pudding!"

And then, urgently, as his father looked blank:

"*You* know, when you were in prison, what the warder said, and the
other warder?"

Sherston hesitated and looked slightly shamefaced. Leslie's voice said
calmly:

"Go on, Charles. It's a very funny story. Mrs. Scudamore would like
to hear it."

So he had told it, and it was quite funny—if not so funny as the boys
seemed to think. They rolled about squirming and gasping with laughter.
Joan laughed politely, but she was definitely startled and a little shocked,
and later, when Leslie had taken her upstairs she murmured delicately:

"I'd no idea—they *knew!*"

Leslie—really, Joan thought, Leslie Sherston must be most insensitive—looked rather amused.

"They'd be bound to know someday," she said. "Wouldn't they? So
they might just as well know now. It's simpler."

It was simpler, Joan agreed, but was it wise? The delicate idealism of
a child's mind, to shatter its trust and faith—she broke off.

Leslie said she didn't think her children were very delicate and idealistic. It would be worse for them, she thought, to know there was
something—and not be told what it was.

She waved her hands in that clumsy, inarticulate way she had and said, "Making mysteries—all that—*much* worse. When they asked me why Daddy had gone away I thought I might just as well be natural about it, so I told them that he'd stolen money from the Bank and gone to prison. After all, they know what stealing is. Peter used to steal jam and get sent to bed for it. If grown-up people do things that are wrong they get sent to prison. It's quite simple."

"All the same, for a child to look *down* on its father instead of *up* to him—"

"Oh they don't look down on him." Leslie again seemed amused. "They're actually quite sorry for him—and they love to hear all about the prison life."

"I'm sure that's *not* a good thing," said Joan decidedly.

"Oh don't you think so?" Leslie meditated. "Perhaps not. But it's been good for Charles. He came back simply cringing—like a dog. I couldn't bear it. So I thought the only thing to do was to be quite natural about it. After all, you can't pretend three years of your life have never existed. It's better, I think, to treat it as just one of those things."

And that, thought, Joan, was Leslie Sherston, casual, slack, and with no conception of any finer shades of feeling! Always taking the way of least resistance.

Still, give her her due, she had been a loyal wife.

Joan had said kindly, "You know, Leslie, I really think you have been quite splendid, the way you have stuck to your husband and worked so hard to keep things going while he was—er—away. Rodney and I often say so."

What a funny one-sided smile the woman had. Joan hadn't noticed it until this minute. Perhaps her praise had embarrassed Leslie. It was certainly in rather a stiff voice that Leslie asked:

"How is—Rodney?"

"Very busy, the poor lamb. I'm always telling him he ought to take a day off now and again."

Leslie said, "That's not so easy. I suppose in his job—like mine—it's pretty well full-time. There aren't many possible days off."

"No. I daresay that's true, and of course Rodney is very conscientious."

"A full-time job," Leslie said. She went slowly towards the window and stood there staring out.

Something about the outline of her figure struck Joan—Leslie usually wore things pretty shapeless, but surely—

"Oh Leslie," Joan exclaimed impulsively. "Surely you aren't—"

Leslie turned and meeting the other woman's eyes slowly nodded her head.

"Yes," she said. "In August."

"Oh my dear." Joan felt genuinely distressed.

And suddenly, surprisingly, Leslie broke into passionate speech. She was no longer casual and slack. She was like a condemned prisoner who puts up a defense.

"It's made all the difference to Charles. All the difference! Do you see? I can't tell you how he feels about it. It's a kind of symbol—that he's not an outcast—that everything's the same as it always was. He's even tried to stop drinking since he's known."

So impassioned was Leslie's voice that Joan hardly realized until afterwards the implication of the last sentence.

She said, "Of course you know your own business best, but I should have thought it was unwise—at the moment."

"Financially, you mean?" Leslie laughed. "Oh we'll weather the storm. We grow pretty well all we eat anyway."

"And, you know, you don't look very strong."

"Strong? I'm terribly strong. Too strong. Whatever kills me won't kill me easily, I'm afraid."

And she had given a little shiver—as though—even then—she had had some strange prevision of disease and racking pain. . . .

And when they had gone downstairs again, and Sherston had said he would walk with Mrs. Scudamore to the corner and show her the short-cut across the fields, and, turning her head as they went down the drive, she saw Leslie and the boys all tangled up and rolling over and over on the ground with shrieks of wild mirth. Leslie, rolling about with her young, quite like an animal, thought Joan with slight disgust, and then bent her head attentively to listen to what Captain Sherston was saying.

He was saying in rather incoherent terms that there never was, never had been, never would be, any woman like his wife.

"You've no idea, Mrs. Scudamore, what she's been to me. No idea. Nobody could. I'm not worthy of her. I know that . . ."

Joan observed with alarm that the easy tears were standing in his eyes. He was a man who could quickly become maudlin.

"Always the same—always cheerful—seems to think that everything that happens is interesting and amusing. And never a word of reproach. Never a word. But I'll make it up to her—I swear I'll make it up to her."

It occurred to Joan that Captain Sherston could best show his appreciation by not visiting the Anchor and Bell too frequently. She very nearly said so.

She got away from him at last, saying, Of course, of course, and what he said was so true, and it had been so nice to see them both. She went away across the fields and looking back as she crossed the stile, she saw Captain Sherston at a standstill outside the Anchor and Bell, looking at his watch to decide how long it was to opening time.

The whole thing, she said to Rodney, when she got back, was very sad.

And Rodney, seemingly purposefully dense, had said, "I thought you said that they all seemed very happy together?"

"Well, yes, in a way."

Rodney said that it seemed to him as though Leslie Sherston was making quite a success of a bad business.

"She's certainly being very plucky about it all. And just think—she's actually going to have another child."

Rodney had got up on that and walked slowly across to the window. He had stood there looking out—very much, now she came to think of it, as Leslie had stood. He said, after a minute or two, "When?"

"August," she said, "I think it's extremely foolish of her."

"Do you?"

"My dear, just consider. They're living hand to mouth as it is. A young baby will be an added complication."

He said slowly, "Leslie's shoulders are broad."

"Well, she'll crack up if she tries to take on too much. She looks ill now."

"She looked ill when she left here."

"She looks years older, too. It's all very well to say that this will make all the difference to Charles Sherston."

"Is that what she said?"

"Yes. She said it *had* made all the difference."

Rodney said thoughtfully, "That's probably true. Sherston is one of those extraordinary people who live entirely on the esteem in which other people hold them. When the judge passed sentence on him he collapsed just like a pricked balloon. It was quite pitiful and at the same time quite disgusting. I should say the only hope for Sherston is to get back, somehow or other, his self-respect. It will be a full-time job."

"Still I really do think that another child—"

Rodney interrupted her. He turned from the window and the white anger of his face startled her.

"She's his wife, isn't she? She'd only got two courses open to her— to cut loose entirely and take the kids—or to go back and damn well *be* a wife to him. That's what she's done—and Leslie doesn't do things by halves."

And Joan had asked if there was anything to get excited about? and Rodney replied, "Certainly not," but he was sick and tired of a prudent careful world that counted the cost of everything before doing it and never took a risk! Joan said she hoped he didn't talk like that to his clients, and Rodney grinned and said, No fear, he always advised them to settle out of court!

Chapter Seven

It was, perhaps, natural that Joan should dream that night of Miss Gilbey. Miss Gilbey in a solar topee, walking beside her in the desert and saying in an authoritative voice, "You should have paid more attention to lizards, Joan. Your natural history is weak." To which, of course, she had replied, "Yes, Miss Gilbey."

And Miss Gilbey had said, "Now don't pretend you don't know what I mean, Joan. You know perfectly well. Discipline, my dear."

Joan woke up and for a moment or two thought herself back at St. Anne's. It was true the Rest House was not unlike a school dormitory. The bareness, the iron beds, the rather hygienic-looking walls.

Oh, dear, thought Joan, another day to get through.

What was it Miss Gilbey had said in her dream? "Discipline."

Well, there was something in that. It had really been very foolish of her the day before to get into that queer state all about nothing! She must discipline her thoughts, arrange her mind systematically—investigate once and for all this agoraphobia idea.

Certainly she felt quite all right now, here in the Rest House. Perhaps it would be wiser not to go out at all?

But her heart sank at the prospect. All day in the gloom, with the smell of mutton fat and paraffin and Flit—all day with nothing to read—nothing to do.

What did prisoners do in their cells? Well, of course they had exercise

and they sewed mailbags or something like that. Otherwise she supposed, they would go mad.

But there was solitary confinement . . . that did send people mad.

Solitary confinement—day after day—week after week.

Why, she felt as though she had been here for *weeks!* And it was—
how long—two days?

Two days! Incredible. What was that line of Omar Khayyam's? "Myself with Yesterday's Ten Thousand Years." Something like that. Why
couldn't she remember anything properly?

No, no, not again. Trying to remember and recite poetry hadn't been
a success—not at all a success. The truth is there was something very
upsetting about poetry. It had a poignancy—a way of striking through
to the spirit. . . .

What was she talking about? Surely the more spiritual one's thoughts
were the better. And she had always been a rather spiritual type of
person . . .

"You always were as cold as fish . . ."

Why should Blanche's voice come cutting through to her thoughts?
A very vulgar and uncalled for remark—really, just like Blanche! Well,
she supposed that that was what it must seem like to someone like
Blanche, someone who allowed themselves to be torn to pieces by their
passions. You couldn't really blame Blanche for being coarse—she was
simply made that way. It hadn't been noticeable as a girl because she
had been so lovely and so well bred, but the coarseness must always
have been there underneath.

Cold as a fish indeed! Nothing of the kind.

It would have been a good deal better for Blanche if *she* had been a
little more fishlike in temperament herself!

She seemed to have led the most deplorable life.

Really *quite* deplorable.

What had she said? "One can always think of one's sins!"

Poor Blanche! But she had admitted that that wouldn't give Joan
occupation long. She did realize, then, the difference between herself
and Joan. She had pretended to think that Joan would soon get tired of
counting her blessings. (True, perhaps, that one did tend to take one's

blessings for granted!) What was it she had said after that? Something rather curious. . . .

Oh yes. She had wondered what, if you had nothing to do but think about yourself for days and days, you might find out about yourself. . . .

In a way, rather an interesting idea.

In fact, quite an interesting idea.

Only Blanche had said that she, herself, wouldn't like to try it. . . .

She had sounded—almost—*afraid*.

I wonder, thought Joan, if one *would* make any discoveries about oneself.

Of course I'm not *used* to thinking of myself. . . .

I've never been a self-centered sort of woman.

. . . I wonder, thought Joan, how I appear to other people?

. . . I don't mean in general—I mean in particular.

She tried to remember any instances of things people had said to her. . . .

Barbara, for instance:

"Oh, *your* servants, Mother, are always perfection. *You* see to that."

Quite a tribute, in a way, showing that her children did consider her a good manager and housewife. And it was true, she did run her house well and efficiently. And her servants liked her—at least, they did what she told them. They weren't, perhaps, very sympathetic if she had a headache, or wasn't feeling well, but then she hadn't encouraged them on those lines. And what was it that that very excellent cook had said when she had given her notice, something about not being able to go on forever without any appreciation—something quite ridiculous.

"Always being told when a thing's wrong, Ma'am, and never a word of praise when it's right—well, it takes the heart out of you."

She had answered coldly, "Surely you realize, Cook, that if nothing is said it is because everything is all right and perfectly satisfactory."

"That may be, Ma'am, but it's disheartening. After all, I'm a human being—and I did take a lot of trouble over that Spanish Ragout you asked for, though it was a lot of trouble and I'm not one that cares for made-up dishes myself."

"It was quite excellent, Cook."

"Yes, Ma'am. I thought it must have been as you finished it all in the dining room, but nothing was said."

Joan said impatiently, "Don't you think you are being rather silly? After all, you are engaged to do the cooking at a very good salary—"

"Oh, the wages are quite satisfactory, Ma'am."

"—and therefore the understanding is that you are a sufficiently good cook. If anything is *not* satisfactory, I mention it."

"You do indeed, Ma'am."

"And apparently you resent the fact?"

"It's not that, Ma'am, but I think we'd best say no more about it and I'll leave at the end of my month."

Servants, thought Joan, were very unsatisfactory. So full of feelings and resentments. They all adored Rodney, of course, simply because he was a man. Nothing was ever too much trouble to do for the Master. And Rodney would sometimes come out with the most unexpected knowledge concerning them.

"Don't pitch into Edna," he would say surprisingly. "Her young man's taken up with another girl and it's thrown her right out of gear. That's why she's dropping things and handing the vegetables twice and forgetting everything."

"How on earth do you know, Rodney?"

"She told me this morning."

"Very extraordinary that she should talk to *you* about it."

"Well, I asked her what was wrong, as a matter of fact. I noticed her eyes were red as though she had been crying."

Rodney, thought Joan, was an unusually kind person.

She had said to him once, "I should think that with your experience as a lawyer, you would get tired of human tangles."

And he had answered, thoughtfully, "Yes, one might think so. But it doesn't work that way. I suppose a country family solicitor sees more of the seamy side of human relationships than almost anybody else, except a doctor. But it only seems to deepen one's pity for the whole human race—so vulnerable, so prone to fear and suspicion and greed—and sometimes so unexpectedly unselfish and brave. That is, perhaps, the only compensation there is—the widening of one's sympathies."

It had been on the tip of her tongue to say, "Compensation? What do you mean?" But for some reason she hadn't said it. Better not, she thought. No, better to say nothing.

But she had been disturbed sometimes by the practical expression of Rodney's easily awakened sympathies.

The question, for instance, of old Hoddesdon's mortgage.

She had learned about that, not from Rodney, but from the garrulous wife of Hoddesdon's nephew, and she had come home seriously perturbed.

Was it true that Rodney had advanced the money out of his private capital?

Rodney had looked vexed. He had flushed and answered heatedly: "Who's been talking?"

She told him and then said, "Why couldn't he borrow the money in the ordinary way?"

"Security isn't good enough from the strictly business point of view. It's difficult to raise mortgages on farmland just now."

"Then why on earth are *you* lending it?"

"Oh, I shall be all right. Hoddesdon's a good farmer really. It's lack of capital and two bad seasons that have let him down."

"The fact remains that he's in a bad way and has to raise money. I really can't feel that this is good business, Rodney."

And quite suddenly and unexpectedly, Rodney had lost his temper.

Did she understand the first thing, he had asked her, about the plight that farmers all over the country were in? Did she realize the difficulties, the obstacles, the shortsighted policy of the Government? He had stood there pouring out a welter of information concerning the whole agricultural position of England, passing from that to a warm, indignant description of old Hoddesdon's particular difficulties.

"It might happen to anyone. No matter how intelligent and hardworking he was. It might have happened to me if I'd been in his position. It's lack of capital to begin with and bad luck following on. And anyway, if you don't mind my saying so, it isn't your business, Joan. I don't interfere with your management of the house and the children. That's your department. This is mine."

She had been hurt—quite bitterly hurt. To take such a tone was most unlike Rodney. It was really the nearest they had come to having a quarrel.

And all over that tiresome old Hoddesdon. Rodney was besotted about the stupid old man. On Sunday afternoons he would go out there and spend the afternoon walking round with Hoddesdon and come back full of information about the state of the crops and cattle diseases and other totally uninteresting subjects of conversation.

He even used to victimize their guests with the same kind of talk.

Why, Joan remembered how at a garden party she had noticed Rodney and Mrs. Sherston sitting together on one of the garden seats, with Rodney talking, talking, talking. So much so that she had wondered what on earth he had been talking about and had gone up to them. Because really he seemed so excited, and Leslie Sherston was listening with such apparently tense interest.

And apparently all he was talking about were dairy herds and the necessity of keeping up the level of pedigree stock in this country.

Hardly a subject that could be of any interest to Leslie Sherston, who had no particular knowledge of or interest in such matters. Yet she had been listening with apparently deep attention, her eyes on Rodney's eager, animated face.

Joan had said lightly, "Really, Rodney, you mustn't bore poor Mrs. Sherston with such dull things." (For that had been when the Sherstons first came to Crayminster and before they knew them very well.)

The light had died out of Rodney's face and he had said apologetically to Leslie:

"I'm sorry."

And Leslie Sherston had said quickly and abruptly, in the way she always spoke:

"You're wrong, Mrs. Scudamore. I found what Mr. Scudamore was saying very interesting."

And there had been a gleam in her eye which had made Joan say to herself, "Really, I believe that woman has got quite a temper . . ."

And the next thing that had happened was that Myrna Randolph had come up, just a little out of breath, and had exclaimed:

"Rodney darling, you must come and play in this set with *me*. We're waiting for you."

And with that charming imperious manner that only a really good-looking girl can get away with, she had stretched out both hands, pulled Rodney to his feet and smiling up into his face, had simply swept him away to the tennis court. Whether Rodney had wanted to or not!

She had walked beside him, her arm familiarly slipped through his, turning her head, gazing up into his face.

And Joan had thought angrily to herself, It's all very well, but men don't like girls who throw themselves at their heads like that.

And then had wondered, with a sudden queer cold feeling, whether perhaps men *did* like it after all!

She had looked up to find Leslie Sherston watching her. Leslie no longer looked as though she had a temper. She looked, instead, as though she was rather sorry for her, Joan. Which was impertinence if nothing else.

Joan stirred restlessly in her narrow bed. How on earth had she got back to Myrna Randolph? Oh, of course, wondering what effect she herself had on other people. Myrna, she supposed, had disliked her. Well, Myrna was welcome to do so. The kind of girl who would break up anybody's married life if she got the chance!

Well, well, no need getting hot and bothered about that now.

She must get up and have breakfast. Perhaps they could poach an egg for her as a change? She was so tired of leathery omelettes.

The Indian, however, seemed impervious to the suggestion of a poached egg.

"Cook egg in water? You mean boil."

No, Joan said, she didn't mean boil. A boiled egg in the Rest House, as she knew by experience, was always hard-boiled. She tried to explain the science of the poached egg. The Indian shook his head.

"Put egg in water—egg all go away. I give Memsahib nice fried egg."

So Joan had two nice fried eggs, well frizzled outside and with hard firm, pale yolks. On the whole, she thought, she preferred the omelette.

Breakfast was over all too soon. She inquired for news of the train, but there was no news.

So there she was fairly and squarely up against it. Another long day ahead of her.

But today, at any rate, she would plan her time out intelligently. The trouble was that up to now she had just tried to pass the time.

She had been a person waiting at a railway station for a train, and naturally that engendered in one a nervy, jumpy frame of mind.

Supposing she were to consider this as a period of rest and—yes, *discipline*. Something in the nature of a Retreat. That is what Roman Catholics called it. They went for Retreats and came back spiritually refreshed.

There is no reason, thought Joan, why I should not be spiritually refreshed too.

Her life had been, perhaps, too slack lately. Too pleasant, too easy-going.

A wraithlike Miss Gilbey seemed to be standing at her side and saying, in the well-remembered bassoon-like accents, "Discipline!"

Only actually that was what she had said to Blanche Haggard. To Joan she had said (really rather unkindly), *"Don't be too pleased with yourself, Joan."*

It was unkind. For Joan never had been in the least bit pleased with herself—not in that fatuous sort of way. *"Think of others, my dear, and not too much of yourself."* Well, that is what she had done—always thought of others. She hardly ever thought of herself—or put herself first. She had always been unselfish—thinking of the children—of Rodney.

Averil!

Why did she have suddenly to think of Averil?

Why see so clearly her elder daughter's face—with its polite slightly scornful smile.

Averil, there was no doubt of it, had never appreciated her mother properly.

The things she said sometimes, quite sarcastic things, were really most irritating. Not exactly rude, but—

Well, but what?

That look of quiet amusement, those raised eyebrows. The way Averil would stroll gently out of a room.

Averil was devoted to her, of course, all her children were devoted to her—

Were they?

Were her children devoted to her—did they really care for her at all?

Joan half rose out of her chair, then sank back.

Where did these ideas come from? What made her think them? Such frightening, unpleasant ideas. Put them out of her head—try not to think of them. . . .

Miss Gilbey's voice—*pizzicato*—

"No lazy thinking, Joan. Don't accept things at their face value, because that's the easiest way, and because it may save you pain. . . ."

Was that why she wanted to force these ideas back? To save herself pain?

Because they certainly were painful ideas. . . .

Averil. . . .

Was Averil devoted to her? Was Averil—come now, Joan, face it—was Averil even *fond* of her?

Well, the truth was that Averil was rather a peculiar kind of girl—cool, unemotional.

No, not perhaps unemotional. Actually Averil had been the only one of the three children to give them real trouble.

Cool, well-behaved, quiet Averil. The shock it had given them!

The shock it had given *her!*

She had opened the letter without the least suspicion of its contents. Addressed in a scrawled, illiterate hand, she had taken it to be from one of her many charitable pensioners.

She had read the words almost uncomprehendingly.

> This is to let you know as how your eldest daughter is carry-
> ing on with the Dr. up at the Saniturum. Kissing in the woods
> something shameful it is and ought to be stopped.

Joan stared at the dirty sheet of paper with a definite feeling of nausea. What an abominable—what a disgusting—thing—

She had heard of anonymous letters. She had never received one before. Really, it made one feel quite sick.

Your eldest daughter—Averil? Averil of all people in the world? *Carry-*

ing on (disgusting phrase) *with the Dr. up at the Saniturum.* Dr. Cargill?
That eminent distinguished specialist who had made such a success of
his tubercular treatment, a man at least twenty years older than Averil,
a man with a charming invalid wife.

What rubbish! What disgusting rubbish.

And at that moment, Averil herself had walked into the room and
had asked, but with only mild curiosity, for Averil was never really curious, "Is anything the matter, Mother?"

Joan, the hand that held the letter shaking, had hardly been able to
reply.

"I don't think I had better even show it to you, Averil. It's—it's too
disgusting."

Her voice had trembled. Averil, raising those cool, delicate eyebrows
of hers in surprise, said, "Something in a letter?"

"Yes."

"About me?"

"You'd better not even see it, dear."

But Averil, walking across the room, had quietly taken the letter out
of her hand.

Had stood there a minute reading it, then had handed it back, and
had said in a reflective, detached voice, "Yes, not very nice."

"Nice? It's disgusting—quite disgusting. People should be punished
by law for telling such lies."

Averil said quietly, "It's a foul letter, but it's not a lie."

The room had turned a somersault and revolved round and round.
Joan had gasped out:

"What do you mean—what can you mean?"

"You needn't make such a fuss, Mother. I'm sorry this has come to
you this way, but I suppose you would have been bound to know sooner
or later."

"You mean it's *true?* That *you* and—and Dr. Cargill—"

"Yes." Averil had just nodded her head.

"But it's wicked—it's disgraceful. A man of that age, a married man—
and a young girl like you—"

Averil said impatiently, "You needn't make a kind of village melodrama out of it. It's not in the least like that. It's all happened very

gradually. Rupert's wife is an invalid—has been for years. We've—well, we've simply come to care for each other. That's all."

"That's all, indeed!" Joan had plenty to say, and said it. Averil merely shrugged her shoulders and let the storm play round her. In the end, when Joan had exhausted herself, Averil remarked:

"I can quite appreciate your point of view, Mother. I daresay I should feel the same in your place—though I don't think I should have said some of the things you've chosen to say. But you can't alter facts. Rupert and I care for each other. And although I'm sorry, I really don't see what you can do about it."

"Do about it? I shall speak to your father—at once."

"Poor Father. Must you really worry him about it?"

"I'm sure he'll know just what to do."

"He really can't do anything at all. And it will simply worry him dreadfully."

That had been the beginning of a really shattering time.

Averil, at the heart of the storm, had remained cool and apparently unperturbed.

But also completely obdurate.

Joan had repeated to Rodney again and again, "I can't help feeling it's all a *pose* on her part. It's not as though Averil were given to really strong feeling of any kind."

But Rodney had shaken his head.

"You don't understand Averil. With Averil it is less her senses than her mind and heart. When she loves, she loves so deeply that I doubt if she will ever quite get over it."

"Oh, Rodney, I really do think that is nonsense! After all, I know Averil better than you do. I'm her mother."

"That doesn't mean that you really know the least thing about her. Averil has always understated things from choice—no, perhaps from necessity. Feeling a thing deeply she belittles it purposely in words."

"That sounds very farfetched to me."

Rodney said slowly, "Well, you can take it from me that it isn't. It's true."

"I can't help thinking that you are exaggerating what is simply a silly schoolgirl flirtation. She's been flattered and likes to imagine—"

Rodney had interrupted her.

"Joan, my dear—it's no good trying to reassure yourself by saying things that you yourself don't believe. Averil's passion for Cargill is serious."

"Then it's disgraceful of *him*—absolutely disgraceful . . ."

"Yes, that's what the world will say all right. But put yourself in the poor devil's place. A wife who's a permanent invalid and all the passion and beauty of Averil's young, generous heart offered to you on a platter. All the eagerness and freshness of her mind."

"Twenty years older than she is!"

"I know, I know. If he were only ten years younger the temptation wouldn't be so great."

"He must be a horrid man—perfectly horrid."

Rodney sighed.

"He's not. He's a fine and very humane man—a man with an intense enthusiastic love for his profession—a man who has done outstanding work. Incidentally, a man who has always been unvaryingly kind and gentle to an ailing wife."

"Now you are trying to make him out a kind of saint."

"Far from it. And most saints, Joan, have had their passions. They were seldom bloodless men and women. No, Cargill's human enough. Human enough to fall in love and to suffer. Human enough, probably, to wreck his own life—and to nullify his lifework. It all depends."

"Depends on what?"

Rodney said slowly, "It depends on our daughter. On how strong she is—and how clear-sighted."

Joan said energetically, "We must get her away from here. How about sending her on a cruise? To the northern capitals—or the Greek Islands? Something like that."

Rodney smiled.

"Aren't you thinking of the treatment applied to your old school friend, Blanche Haggard? It didn't work very well in her case, remember."

"Do you mean that Averil would come rushing back from some foreign port?"

"I rather doubt whether Averil would even start."

"Nonsense. We would insist."

"Joan dear, do try and envisage realities. You cannot apply force to an adult young woman. We can neither lock Averil in her bedroom nor force her to leave Crayminster—and actually I don't want to do either. Those things are only palliatives. Averil can only be influenced by factors that she respects."

"And those are?"

"Reality. Truth."

"Why don't you go to him—to Rupert Cargill. Threaten him with the scandal."

Again Rodney sighed.

"I'm afraid, terribly afraid, Joan, of precipitating matters."

"What do you mean?"

"That Cargill will throw up everything and that they will go away together."

"Wouldn't that be the end of his career?"

"Undoubtedly. I don't suppose it would come under the heading of unprofessional conduct, but it would completely alienate public opinion in his special circumstances."

"Then surely, if he realizes that—"

Rodney said impatiently, "He's not quite sane at the moment. Don't you understand anything at all about love, Joan?"

Which was a ridiculous question to ask! She said bitterly:

"Not *that* kind of love, I'm thankful to say . . ."

And then Rodney had taken her quite by surprise. He had smiled at her, had said, "Poor little Joan" very gently, had kissed her and had gone quietly away.

It was nice of him, she thought, to realize how unhappy she was over the whole miserable business.

Yes, it had indeed been an anxious time. Averil silent, not speaking to anybody—sometimes not even replying when her mother spoke to her.

I did my best, thought Joan. But what are you to do with a girl who won't even listen?

Pale, wearily polite, Averil would say:

"Really, Mother, must we go on like this? Talking and talking and talking? I do make allowances for your point of view, but won't you just accept the plain truth, that nothing you can say or do will make the least difference?"

So it had gone on, until that afternoon in September when Averil, her face a little paler than usual, had said to them both:

"I think I'd better tell you. Rupert and I don't feel we can go on like this any longer. We are going away together. I hope his wife will divorce him. But if she won't it makes no difference."

Joan had started on an energetic protest, but Rodney had stopped her.

"Leave this to me, Joan, if you don't mind. Averil, I must talk to you. Come into my study."

Averil had said with a very faint smile, "Quite like a headmaster, aren't you, Father."

Joan burst out, "I'm Averil's mother. I insist—"

"Please, Joan. I want to talk to Averil alone. Would you mind leaving us?"

There had been so much quiet decision in his tone that she had half turned to leave the room. It was Averil's low, clear voice that stopped her.

"Don't go away, Mother. I don't want you to go away. Anything Father says to me I'd rather he said in front of you."

Well at least that showed, thought Joan, that being a mother had some importance.

What a very odd way Averil and her father had of looking at each other, a wary, measuring, unfriendly way, like two antagonists on the stage.

Then Rodney smiled slightly and said, "I see. *Afraid!*"

Averil's answer came cool and slightly surprised, "I don't know what you mean, Father."

Rodney said, with sudden irrelevance, "A pity you weren't a boy, Averil. There are times when you are quite uncannily like your Great Uncle Henry. He had a wonderful eye for the best way to conceal the weakness in his own case, or to expose the weakness of his opponent's case."

Averil said quickly, "There isn't any weakness in my case."

Rodney said deliberately, "I shall prove to you that there is."

Joan exclaimed sharply, "of course you are not going to do anything so wicked or so foolish, Averil. Your father and I will not allow it."

And at that Averil had smiled just a little and had looked not at her mother, but at her father, offering as it were her mother's remark to him.

Rodney said, "Please, Joan, leave this to me."

"I think," said Averil, "that Mother is perfectly entitled to say just what she thinks."

"Thank you, Averil," said Joan. "I am certainly going to do so. My dear child, you must see that what you propose is quite out of the question. You are young and romantic and you see everything in quite a false light. What you do on an impulse now you will bitterly regret later. And think of the sorrow you will cause your father and me. Have you thought of that? I'm sure you don't want to cause us pain—we have always loved you so dearly."

Averil listened quite patiently, but she did not reply. She had never taken her eyes from her father's face.

When Joan finished, Averil was still looking at Rodney and there was still a faint, slightly mocking smile on her lips.

"Well, Father," she said. "Have you anything to add?"

"Not to add," said Rodney. "But I have something of my own to say."

Averil looked at him inquiringly.

"Averil," said Rodney, "do you understand exactly what a marriage is?"

Averil's eyes opened slightly. She paused and then said, "Are you telling me that it is a sacrament?"

"No," said Rodney. "I may consider it as a sacrament, or I may not. What I am telling *you* is that marriage is a *contract*."

"Oh," said Averil.

She seemed a little, just a little, taken aback.

"Marriage," said Rodney, "is a contract entered into by two people, both of adult years, in the full possession of their faculties, and with a full knowledge of what they are undertaking. It is a specification of partnership, and each partner binds himself and herself specifically to honor the terms of that contract—that is, to stand by each other in certain eventualities—in sickness and in health, for richer for poorer, for better for worse.

"Because those words are uttered in a church, and with the approval and benediction of a priest, they are none the less a contract, just as any agreement entered into between two people in good faith is a contract. Because some of the obligations undertaken are not enforcible in a court of law, they are none the less binding on the persons who have assumed them. I think you will agree that, equitably, that is so."

There was a pause and then Averil said, "That may have been true once. But marriage is looked upon differently nowadays and a great many people are not married in church and do not use the words of the church service."

"That may be so. But eighteen years ago Rupert Cargill did bind himself by using those words in a church, and I challenge you to say that he did not, at that time, utter those words in good faith and meaning to carry them out."

Averil shrugged her shoulders.

Rodney said, "Will you admit that, although not legally enforcible, Rupert Cargill did enter into such a contract with the woman who is his wife? He envisaged, at the time, the possibilities of poverty and of sickness, and directly specified them as not affecting the permanence of the bond."

Averil had gone very white. She said, "I don't know where you think you are getting by all this."

"I want an admission from you that marriage is, apart from all sentimental feeling and thinking, an ordinary business contract. Do you admit that, or don't you?"

"I'll admit it."

"And Rupert Cargill proposes to break that contract with your connivance?"

"Yes."

"With no regard for the due rights and privileges of the other party to the contract?"

"She will be all right. It's not as though she were so terribly fond of Rupert. All she thinks of is her own health and—"

Rodney interrupted her sharply, "I don't want sentiment from you, Averil. I want an admission of *fact*."

"I'm not sentimental."

"You are. You have no knowledge at all of Mrs. Cargill's thoughts and feelings. You are imagining them to suit yourself. All I want from you is the admission that she has *rights*."

Averil flung her head back.

"Very well. She has rights."

"Then you are now quite clear exactly what it is you are doing?"

"Have you finished, Father?"

"No, I have one more thing to say. You realize, don't you, that Cargill is doing very valuable and important work, that his methods in treating tuberculosis have met with such striking success that he is a very prominent figure in the medical world, and that, unfortunately, a man's private affairs can affect his public career. That means that Cargill's work, his usefulness to humanity, will be seriously affected, if not destroyed, by what you are both proposing to do."

Averil said, "Are you trying to persuade me that it's my duty to give Rupert up so that he can continue to benefit humanity?"

There was a faint sneer in her voice.

"No," said Rodney. "I'm thinking of the poor devil himself. . . ."

There was sudden vehement feeling in his voice.

"You can take it from me, Averil, that a man who's not doing the work he wants to do—the work he was made to do—is only half a man. I tell you as surely as I'm standing here, that if you take Rupert Cargill away from his work and make it impossible for him to go on with that work, the day will come when you will have to stand by and see the man you love unhappy, unfulfilled—old before his time—tired and disheartened—only living with half his life. And if you think your love, or any woman's love, can make up to him for that, then I tell you plainly that you're a damned sentimental little fool."

He stopped. He leaned back in his chair. He passed his hand through his hair.

Averil said, "You say all this to me. But how do I know—" She broke off and began again, "How do I know—"

"That it's true? I can only say that it's what I believe to be true and that *it is what I know of my own knowledge.* I'm speaking to you, Averil, as a man—as well as a father."

"Yes," said Averil. "I see. . . ."

Rodney said, and his voice was tired now and sounded muffled:

"It's up to you, Averil, to examine what I have told you, and to accept or reject it. I believe you have courage and clear-sightedness."

Averil went slowly towards the door. She stopped with her hand on the handle and looked back.

Joan was startled by the sudden bitter vindictiveness of her voice when she spoke.

"Don't imagine," she said, "that I shall ever be grateful to you, Father. I think—I think I hate you."

And she went out and closed the door behind her.

Joan made a motion to go after her, but Rodney stopped her with a gesture.

"Leave her alone," he said. "Leave her alone. Don't you understand? We've won. . . ."

Chapter Eight

A nd that, Joan reflected, had been the end of that.

Averil had gone about, very silent, answering in monosyllables when she was spoken to, never spoke if she could help it. She had got thinner and paler.

A month later she had expressed a wish to go to London and train in a secretarial school.

Rodney had assented at once. Averil had left them with no pretense of distress over the parting.

When she had come home on a visit three months later, she had been quite normal in manner and had seemed, from her account, to be having quite a gay life in London.

Joan was relieved and expressed her relief to Rodney.

"The whole thing has blown over completely. I never thought for a moment it was really serious—just one of those silly fancies girls get."

Rodney looked at her, smiled, and said, "Poor little Joan."

That phrase of his always annoyed her.

"Well, you must admit it *was* worrying at the time."

"Yes," he said, "it was certainly worrying. But it wasn't your worry, was it, Joan?"

"What do you mean? Anything that affects the children upsets me far more than it upsets them."

"Does it?" Rodney said. "I wonder. . . ."

It was true, Joan thought, that there was now a certain coldness between Averil and her father. They had always been such friends. Now there seemed little except formal politeness between them. On the other hand, Averil had been quite charming, in her cool, non-committal way, to her mother.

I expect, thought Joan, that she appreciates me better now that she doesn't live at home.

She herself certainly welcomed Averil's visits. Averil's cool good sense seemed to ease things in the household.

Barbara was now grown up and was proving difficult.

Joan was increasingly distressed by her younger daughter's choice of friends. She seemed to have no kind of discrimination. There were plenty of nice girls in Crayminster, but Barbara, out of sheer perversity, it seemed, would have none of them.

"They're so hideously *dull*, Mother."

"Nonsense, Barbara. I'm sure both Mary and Alison are charming girls, full of fun."

"They're perfectly awful. They wear *snoods*."

Joan had stared, bewildered.

"Really, Barbara—what do you mean? What can it matter?"

"It does. It's a kind of symbol."

"I think you're talking nonsense, darling. There's Pamela Grayling— her mother used to be a great friend of mine. Why not go about with her a bit more?"

"Oh, Mother, she's hopelessly dreary, not amusing a bit."

"Well, I think they're all very nice girls."

"Yes, nice and deadly. And what does it matter what *you* think?"

"That's very rude, Barbara."

"Well, what I mean is, you don't have to go about with them. So it's what *I* think matters. I like Betty Earle and Primrose Deane but you always stick your nose in the air when I bring them to tea."

"Well, frankly, darling, they are rather dreadful—Betty's father runs those awful charabanc tours and simply hasn't got an *h*."

"He's got lots of money, though."

"Money isn't everything, Barbara."

"The whole point is, Mother, can I choose my own friends, or can't I?"

"Of course you can, Barbara, but you must let yourself be guided by me. You are very young still."

"That means I can't. It's pretty sickening the way I can't do a single thing I want to do! This place is an absolute prison house."

And it was just then that Rodney had come in and had said, "What's a prison house?"

Barbara cried out, "Home is!"

And instead of taking the matter seriously Rodney had simply laughed and had said teasingly, "Poor little Barbara—treated like a black slave."

"Well, I am."

"Quite right, too. I approve of slavery for daughters."

And Barbara had hugged him and said breathlessly, "Darling Dads, you are so—so—ridiculous. I never can be annoyed with you for long."

Joan had begun indignantly, "I should hope not—"

But Rodney was laughing, and when Barbara had gone out of the room, he had said, "Don't take things too seriously, Joan. Young fillies have to kick up their heels a bit."

"But these awful friends of hers—"

"A momentary phase of liking the flamboyant. It will pass. Don't worry, Joan."

Very easy, Joan had thought indignantly, to say "Don't worry." What would happen to them all if she didn't worry? Rodney was far too easy-going, and he couldn't possibly understand a mother's feelings.

Yet trying as Barbara's choice of girl friends had been, it was as nothing to the anxiety occasioned by the men she seemed to like.

George Harmon and that very objectionable young Wilmore—not only a member of the rival solicitor's firm (a firm that undertook the more dubious legal business of the town) but a young man who drank too much, talked too loudly, and was too fond of the race track. It was with young Wilmore that Barbara had disappeared from the Town Hall on the night of the Christmas Charity Dance, and had reappeared five dances later, sending a guilty but defiant glance towards where her mother was sitting.

They had been sitting out, it seemed, on the roof—a thing that only fast girls did, so Joan told Barbara, and it had distressed her very much.

"Don't be so Edwardian, Mother. It's absurd."

"I'm not at all Edwardian. And let me tell you, Barbara, a lot of the old ideas about chaperonage are coming back into favor. Girls don't go about with young men as they did ten years ago."

"Really, Mother, anyone would think I was going off weekending with Tom Wilmore."

"Don't talk like that, Barbara, I won't have it. And I hear you were seen in the Dog and Duck with George Harmon."

"Oh, we were just doing a pub crawl."

"Well, you're far too young to do anything of the kind. I don't like the way girls drink spirits nowadays."

"I was only having beer. Actually we were playing darts."

"Well, I don't like it, Barbara. And what's more I won't have it. I don't like George Harmon or Tom Wilmore and I won't have them in the house anymore, do you understand?"

"O.K., Mother, it's your house."

"Anyway I don't see what you like in them."

Barbara shrugged her shoulders. "Oh, I don't know. They're exciting."

"Well, I won't have them asked to the house, do you hear?"

After that Joan had been annoyed when Rodney brought young Harmon home to Sunday supper one night. It was, she felt, so weak of Rodney. She herself put on her most glacial manner, and the young man seemed suitably abashed, in spite of the friendly way Rodney talked to him, and the pains he took to put him at his ease. George Harmon alternately talked too loud, or mumbled, boasted and then became apologetic.

Later that night, Joan took Rodney to task with some sharpness.

"Surely you must realize I'd told Barbara I wouldn't have him here?"

"I knew, Joan, but that's a mistake. Barbara has very little judgment. She takes people at their own valuation. She doesn't know the shoddy from the real. Seeing people against an alien background, she doesn't know where she is. That's why she needs to see people against her own background. She's been thinking of young Harmon as a dangerous and dashing figure, not just a foolish and boastful young man who drinks too much and has never done a proper day's work in his life."

"*I* could have told her that!"

Rodney smiled.

"Oh, Joan, dear, nothing that you and I say is going to impress the younger generation."

The truth of that was made plain to Joan when Averil came down on one of her brief visits.

This time it was Tom Wilmore who was being entertained. Against Averil's cool critical distaste, Tom did not show to advantage.

Afterwards Joan caught a snatch of conversation between the sisters. "You don't like him, Averil?"

And Averil, hunching disdainful shoulders had replied crisply, "I think he's dreadful. Your taste in men, Barbara, is really too awful."

Thereafter, Wilmore had disappeared from the scene, and the fickle Barbara had murmured one day, "Tom Wilmore? Oh, but he's dreadful." With complete and wide-eyed conviction.

Joan set herself to have tennis parties and ask people to the house, but Barbara refused stoutly to cooperate.

"Don't fuss so, Mother. You're always wanting to ask people. I hate having people, and you always will ask such terrible duds."

Offended, Joan said sharply that she washed her hands of Barbara's amusement. "I'm sure I don't know *what* you want!"

"I just want to be let alone."

Barbara was really a most difficult child, Joan said sharply to Rodney. Rodney agreed, a little frown between his eyes.

"If she would only just say what she wants," Joan continued.

"She doesn't know herself. She's very young Joan."

"That's just why she needs to have things decided for her."

"No, my dear—she's got to find her own feet. Just let her be—let her bring her friends here if she wants to, but don't *organize* things. That's what seems to antagonize the young."

So like a man, Joan thought with some exasperation. All for leaving things alone and being vague. Poor, dear, Rodney, he always had been rather vague, now she came to think of it. It was she who had to be the practical one! And yet everyone said that he was such a shrewd lawyer.

Joan remembered an evening when Rodney had read from the local paper an announcement of George Harmon's marriage to Primrose Deane and had added with a teasing smile:

"An old flame of yours, eh, Babs?"

Barbara had laughed with considerable amusement.

"I know. I was awfully keen on him. He really is pretty dreadful, isn't he? I mean, he really *is*."

"I always thought him a most unprepossessing young man. I couldn't imagine what you saw in him."

"No more can I now." Barbara at eighteen spoke detachedly of the follies of seventeen. "But really, you know, Dads, I did think I was in love with him. I thought mother would try to part us, and then I was going to run away with him, and if you or mother stopped us, then I made up my mind I should put my head in the gas oven and kill myself."

"Quite the Juliet touch!"

With a shade of disapproval, Barbara said, "I meant it, Daddy. After all, if you can't bear a thing, you just *have* to kill yourself."

And Joan, unable to bear keeping silent any longer, broke in sharply:

"Don't say such wicked things, Barbara. You don't know what you're talking about!"

"I forgot you were there, Mother. Of course, *you* wouldn't ever do a thing like that. *You'd* always be calm and sensible, whatever happened."

"I should hope so indeed."

Joan kept her temper with a little difficulty. She said to Rodney when Barbara had left the room:

"You shouldn't encourage the child in such nonsense."

"Oh, she might as well talk it out of her system."

"Of course, she'd never really do any of these dreadful things she talks about."

Rodney was silent and Joan looked at him in surprise.

"Surely you don't think—"

"No, no, not really. Not when she's older, when she's got her balance. But Barbara is very unstable emotionally, Joan, we might as well face it."

"It's all so ridiculous!"

"Yes, to us—who have a sense of proportion. But not to her. She's always in deadly earnest. She can't see beyond the mood of the moment. She has no detachment and no humor. Sexually, she is precocious—"

"Really, Rodney! You make things sound like—like one of those horrid cases in the police court."

"Horrid cases in the police court concern living human beings, remember."

"Yes, but nicely brought-up girls like Barbara don't—"

"Don't what, Joan?"

"Must we talk like this?"

Rodney sighed.

"No. No, of course not. But I wish, yes, I really do wish that Barbara could meet some decent young fellow and fall properly in love with him."

And after that it had really seemed like an answer to prayer, when young William Wray had come home from Iraq to stay with his aunt, Lady Herriot.

Joan had seen him first one day about a week after his arrival. He had been ushered into the drawing room one afternoon when Barbara was out. Joan had looked up surprised from her writing table and had seen a tall sturdily built young man with a jutting-out chin, a very pink face, and a pair of steady blue eyes.

Blushing still pinker, Bill Wray had mumbled to his collar that he was Lady Herriot's nephew and that he had called—er—to return Miss Scudamore's racket which she had—er—left behind the other day.

Joan pulled her wits together and greeted him graciously.

Barbara was so careless, she said. Left her things all over the place. Barbara was out at the moment, but probably she would be back before long. Mr. Wray must stay and have some tea.

Mr. Wray was quite willing, it seemed, so Joan rang the bell for tea, and inquired after Mr. Wray's aunt.

Lady Herriot's health occupied about five minutes, and then conversation began to halt a little. Mr. Wray was not very helpful. He remained very pink in the face and sat very bolt upright and had a vague look of suffering some internal agony. Luckily tea came and made a diversion.

Joan was still prattling kindly, but with a slight sense of effort when Rodney, much to her relief, returned a little earlier than usual from the office. Rodney was very helpful. He talked of Iraq, drew the boy out with some simple questions, and presently some of Bill Wray's agonized stiffness began to relax. Soon he was talking almost easily. Presently Rodney took him off to his study. It was nearly seven o'clock when Bill, still it seemed reluctantly, took his departure.

"Nice lad," said Rodney.

"Yes, quite. Rather shy."

"Decidedly." Rodney seemed amused. "But I don't think he's usually quite so diffident."

"What a frightfully long time he stayed!"

"Over two hours."

"You must be terribly tired, Rodney."

"Oh, no, I enjoyed it. He's got a very good headpiece, that boy, and rather an unusual outlook on things. The philosophic bent of mind. He's got character as well as brains. Yes, I liked him."

"He must have liked you—to stay talking as long as he did."

Rodney's look of amusement returned.

"Oh, he wasn't staying to talk to me. He was hoping for Barbara's return. Come, Joan, don't you know love when you see it? The poor fellow was stiff with embarrassment. That's why he was as red as a beet-root. It must have taken a great effort for him to nerve himself to come here—and when he did, no glimpse of his lady. Yes, one of those cases of love at first sight."

Presently when Barbara came hurrying into the house, just in time for dinner, Joan said:

"One of your young men has been here, Barbara, Lady Herriot's nephew. He brought back your racket."

"Oh, Bill Wray? So he did find it? It seemed to have disappeared completely the other evening."

"He was here some time," said Joan.

"Pity I missed him. I went to the pictures with the Crabbes. A frightfully stupid film. Did you get awfully bored with Bill?"

"No," said Rodney. "I liked him. We talked Near Eastern politics. You'd have been bored, I expect."

"I like to hear about queer parts of the world. I'd love to travel. I get so fed up always staying in Crayminster. At any rate, Bill is different."

"You can always train for a job," suggested Rodney.

"Oh, a job!" Barbara wrinkled up her nose. "You know, Dads, I'm an idle devil. I don't like work."

"No more do most people, I suspect," said Rodney.

Barbara rushed at him and hugged him.

"You work much too hard. I've always thought so. It's a shame!"

Then, releasing her hold, she said, "I'll give Bill a ring. He said something about going to the point to point over at Marsden . . ."

Rodney stood looking after her as she walked away towards the telephone at the back of the hall. It was an odd look, questioning, uncertain.

He had liked Bill Wray, yes, undoubtedly he had liked Bill from the first. Why, then, had he looked so worried, so harassed, when Barbara had burst in and announced that she and Bill were engaged and they meant to be married at once so that she could go back to Baghdad with him?

Bill was young, well connected, with money of his own, and good prospects. Why then, did Rodney demur, and suggest a longer engagement? Why did he go about, frowning, looking uncertain and perplexed?

And then, just before the marriage, that sudden outburst, that insistence that Barbara was too young?

Oh well, Barbara had soon settled that objection, and six months after she had married her Bill and departed for Baghdad, Averil in her turn had announced her engagement to a stockbroker, a man called Edward Harrison-Wilmott.

He was a quiet, pleasant man of about thirty-four and extremely well-off.

So really, Joan thought, everything seemed to be turning out splendidly. Rodney was rather quiet about Averil's engagement, but when she pressed him he said, "Yes, yes, it's the best thing. He's a nice fellow."

After Averil's marriage, Joan and Rodney were alone in the house.

Tony, after training at an Agricultural College and then failing to pass his exams, and altogether causing them a good deal of anxiety, had finally gone out to South Africa where a client of Rodney's had a big orange farm in Rhodesia.

Tony wrote them enthusiastic letters, though not very lengthy ones. Then he had written and announced his engagement to a girl from Durban. Joan was rather upset at the idea of her son marrying a girl they had never even seen. She had no money, either—and really, as she said to Rodney, what did they know about her? Nothing at all.

Rodney said that it was Tony's funeral, and that they must hope for the best. She looked a nice girl, he thought, from the photographs Tony had sent, and she seemed willing to begin with Tony in a small way up in Rhodesia.

"And I suppose they'll spend their entire lives out there and hardly ever come home. Tony ought to have been forced to go into the firm—I said so at the time!"

Rodney had smiled and said that he wasn't very good at forcing people to do things.

"No, but really, Rodney, you ought to have *insisted*. He would soon have settled down. People do."

Yes, Rodney said, that was true. But it was, he thought, too great a risk.

Risk? Joan said she didn't understand. What did he mean by risk?

Rodney said he meant the risk that the boy mightn't be happy.

Joan said she sometimes lost patience with all this talk of happiness. Nobody seemed to think of anything else. Happiness wasn't the only thing in life. There were other things much more important.

Such as, Rodney had asked?

Well, Joan said—after a moment's hesitation—duty, for instance.

Rodney said that surely it could never be a duty to become a solicitor.

Slightly annoyed, Joan replied that he knew perfectly what she meant. It was Tony's duty to please his father and not disappoint him.

"Tony hasn't disappointed me."

But surely, Joan exclaimed, Rodney didn't like his only son being far away half across the world, living where they could never see the boy.

"No," said Rodney with a sigh. "I must admit that I miss Tony very much. He was such a sunny, cheerful creature to have about the house. Yes, I miss him. . . ."

"That's what I say. You should have been firm!"

"After all, Joan, it's Tony's life. Not ours. Ours is over and done with, for better or worse—the active part of it, I mean."

"Yes—well—I suppose that's so in a way."

She thought a minute and then she said, "Well, it's been a very nice life. And still is, of course."

"I'm glad of that."

He was smiling at her. Rodney had a nice smile, a teasing smile. Sometimes he looked as though he was smiling at something that you yourself didn't see.

"The truth is," said Joan, "that you and I are really very well suited to each other."

"Yes, we haven't had many quarrels."

"And then we've been lucky with our children. It would have been terrible if they'd turned out badly or been unhappy or something like that."

"Funny Joan," Rodney had said.

"Well but, Rodney, it really *would* have been very upsetting."

"I don't think anything would upset you for long, Joan."

"Well," she considered the point. "Of course I have got a very equable temperament. I think it's one's duty, you know, not to give way to things."

"An admirable and convenient sentiment!"

"It's nice, isn't it," said Joan smiling, "to feel one's made a success of things?"

"Yes." Rodney had sighed. "Yes, it must be very nice."

Joan laughed and putting her hand on his arm, gave it a little shake.

"Don't be modest, Rodney. No solicitor has got a bigger practice round here than you have. It's far bigger than in Uncle Henry's time."

"Yes, the firm is doing well."

"And there's more capital coming in with the new partner. Do you mind having a new partner?"

Rodney shook his head.

"Oh no, we need young blood. Both Alderman and I are getting on."

Yes, she thought, it was true. There was a lot of gray in Rodney's dark hair.

Joan roused herself, and glanced at her watch.

The morning was passing quite quickly, and there had been no recurrence of those distressing chaotic thoughts which seemed to force themselves into her mind so inopportunely.

Well, that showed, didn't it, that "discipline" was the watchword needed. To arrange one's thoughts in an orderly manner, recalling only those memories that were pleasant and satisfactory. That is what she had done this morning—and see how quickly the morning had passed. In about an hour and a half it would be lunchtime. Perhaps she had better go out for a short stroll, keeping quite near the Rest House. That would just make a little change before coming in to eat another of those hot, heavy meals.

She went into the bedroom, put on her double-felt hat and went out.

The Arab boy was kneeling on the ground, his face turned towards Mecca, and was bending forward and straightening himself, uttering words in a high nasal chant.

The Indian, coming up unseen, said instructively just behind Joan's shoulder, "Him make midday prayer."

Joan nodded. The information, she felt, was unnecessary. She could see perfectly well what the boy was doing.

"Him say Allah very compassionate, Allah very merciful."

"I know," said Joan and moved away, strolling gently towards the barbed-wire conglomeration that marked the railway station.

She remembered having seen six or seven Arabs trying to move a dilapidated Ford that had stuck in the sand, all pulling and tugging in opposite directions, and how her son-in-law, William, had explained to her that in addition to these well meant but abortive efforts, they were saying hopefully, "Allah is very merciful."

Allah, she thought, had need to be, since it was certain that nothing but a miracle would extract the car if they all continued to tug in opposite directions!

The curious thing was that they all seemed quite happy about it and enjoying themselves. Inshallah, they would say, if God wills, and would thereupon bend no intelligent endeavor on the satisfaction of their desires. It was not a way of living that commended itself to Joan. One should take thought and make plans for the morrow. Though perhaps if one lived in the middle of nowhere like Tell Abu Hamid it might not be so necessary.

If one were here for long, reflected Joan, one would forget even what day of the week it was . . .

And she thought, Let me see, today is Thursday . . . yes, Thursday, I got here on Monday night.

She had arrived now at the tangle of barbed wire and she saw, a little way beyond it, a man in some kind of uniform with a rifle. He was leaning up against a large case and she supposed he was guarding the station or the frontier.

He seemed to be asleep and Joan thought she had better not go any further in case he might wake up and shoot her. It was the sort of thing, she felt, that would not be at all impossible at Tell Abu Hamid.

She retraced her steps, making a slight detour so as to encircle the Rest House. In that way she would eke out the time and run no risk of that strange feeling of agoraphobia (if it had been agoraphobia).

Certainly, she thought with approval, the morning had gone very successfully. She had gone over in her mind the things for which she had to be thankful. Averil's marriage to dear Edward, such a solid, dependable sort of man—and so well-off, too Averil's house in London was quite delightful—so handy for Harrod's. And Barbara's marriage. And Tony's—though that really wasn't quite so satisfactory—in fact they knew nothing about it—and Tony himself was not as entirely satisfactory as a son should be. Tony should have remained in Crayminster and gone into Alderman, Scudamore and Witney's. He should have married a nice English girl, fond of outdoor life, and followed in his father's footsteps.

Poor Rodney, with his dark hair streaked with gray, and no son to succeed him at the office.

The truth was that Rodney had been much too weak with Tony. He should have put his foot down. Firmness, that was the thing. Why, thought Joan, where would Rodney be, I should like to know, if I hadn't put *my* foot down? She felt a warm little glow of self-approval. Crippled with debts, probably, and trying to raise a mortgage like Farmer Hoddesdon. She wondered if Rodney really quite appreciated what she had done for him. . . .

Joan stared ahead of her at the swimming line of the horizon. A queer watery effect. Of course, she thought, mirage!

Yes, that was it, mirage . . . just like pools of water in the sand. Not at all what one thought of as mirage—she had always imagined trees and cities—something much more concrete.

But even this unspectacular watery effect was queer—it made one feel—what *was* reality?

Mirage, she thought, mirage. The word seemed important.

What had she been thinking of? Oh, of course, Tony, and how exceedingly selfish and thoughtless he had been.

It had always been extremely difficult to get at Tony. He was so vague, so apparently acquiescent, and yet in his quiet, amiable, smiling way, he did exactly as he liked. Tony had never been quite so devoted to her as she felt a son ought to be to his mother. In fact he really seemed to care for his father most.

She remembered how Tony, as a small boy of seven, in the middle of the night, had entered the dressing room where Rodney was sleeping, and had announced quietly and unromantically:

"I think, Father, I must have eaten a toadstool instead of a mushroom, because I have a very bad pain and I think I am going to die. So I have come here to die with you."

Actually, it had been nothing to do with toadstools or mushrooms. It had been acute appendicitis and the boy had been operated on within twenty-four hours. But it still seemed to Joan queer that the child should have gone to Rodney and not to her. Far more natural for Tony to have come to his mother.

Yes, Tony had been trying in many ways. Lazy at school. Slack over games. And though he was a very good-looking boy and the kind of boy she was proud to take about with her, he never seemed to want to be taken about, and had an irritating habit of melting into the landscape just when she was looking for him.

"Protective coloring," Averil had called it, Joan remembered. "Tony is much cleverer at protective coloring than we are," she had said.

Joan had not quite understood her meaning, but she had felt vaguely a little hurt by it. . . .

Joan looked at her watch. No need to get too hot walking. Back to the Rest House now. It had been an excellent morning—no incidents of any kind—no unpleasant thoughts, no sensations of agoraphobia—

Really, some inner voice in her exclaimed, you are talking just like a hospital nurse. What do you think you are, Joan Scudamore? an invalid? a mental case? And why do you feel so proud of yourself and yet so tired? Is there anything extraordinary in having passed a pleasant, normal morning?

She went quickly into the Rest House, and was delighted to see that there were tinned pears for lunch as a change.

After lunch she went and lay down on her bed.

If she could sleep until teatime. . . .

But she did not feel even inclined to sleep. Her brain felt bright and wakeful. She lay there with closed eyes, but her body felt alert and tense, as though it were waiting for something . . . as though it were watchful, ready to defend itself against some lurking danger. All her muscles were taut.

I must relax, Joan thought, I must relax.

But she couldn't relax. Her body was stiff and braced. Her heart was beating a little faster than was normal. Her mind was alert and suspicious.

The whole thing reminded her of something. She searched and at last the right comparison came to her—a dentist's waiting room.

The feeling of something definitely unpleasant just ahead of you, the determination to reassure yourself, to put off thinking of it, and the knowledge that each minute was bringing the ordeal nearer . . .

But what ordeal—what was she expecting?

What was going to happen?

The lizards, she thought, have all gone back into their holes . . . that's because there's a storm coming . . . the quiet—before a storm . . . waiting . . . waiting. . . .

Good Heavens, she was getting quite incoherent again.

Miss Gilbey . . . discipline . . . a Spiritual Retreat . . .

A Retreat! She must meditate. There was something about repeating Om . . . Theosophy? Or Buddhism. . . .

No, no, stick to her own religion. Meditate on God. On the love of God. *God* . . . Our Father, which art in Heaven . . .

Her own father—his squarely trimmed Naval brown beard, his deep piercing blue eyes, his liking for everything to be trim and shipshape in the house. A kindly martinet, that was her father, a typical retired Admiral. And her mother, tall, thin, vague, untidy, with a careless sweetness that made people, even when she most exasperated them, find all kinds of excuses for her.

Her mother going out to parties with odd gloves and a crooked skirt and a hat pinned askew to a bun of iron gray hair, and happily and serenely unconscious of anything amiss about her appearance. And the anger of the Admiral—always directed on his daughters, never on his wife.

"Why can't you girls look after your mother? What do you mean by letting her go out like that! I will *not* have such slackness!" he would roar. And the three girls would say submissively:

"No, Father." And afterwards, to each other, "It's all very well, but really Mother is impossible!"

Joan had been very fond of her mother, of course, but her fondness had not blinded her to the fact that her mother was really a very tiresome woman—her complete lack of method and consistency hardly atoned for by her gay irresponsibility and warmhearted impulsiveness.

It had come as quite a shock to Joan, clearing up her mother's papers after her mother's death, to come across a letter from her father, written on the twentieth anniversary of their marriage.

> I grieve deeply that I cannot be with you today, dear heart.
> I would like to tell you in this letter all that your love has
> meant to me all these years and how you are more dear to
> me today than you have ever been before. Your love has been
> the crowning blessing of my life and I thank God for it and
> for you. . . .

Somehow she had never realized that her father felt quite like that about her mother. . . .

Joan thought, Rodney and I will have been married twenty-five years this December. Our silver wedding. How nice, she thought, if he were to write such a letter to me. . . .

She concocted a letter in her mind.

Dearest Joan—I feel I must write down all I owe to you—
and what you have meant to me—You have no idea, I am
sure, how your love has been the crowning blessing. . . .

Somehow, Joan thought, breaking off this imaginative exercise, it
didn't seem very real. Impossible to imagine Rodney writing such a
letter . . . much as he loved her . . . much as he loved her. . . .

Why repeat that so defiantly? Why feel such a queer, cold little
shiver? What had she been thinking about before that?

Of course! Joan came to herself with a shock. She was supposed to
be engaged in spiritual meditation. Instead of that she had been thinking
of mundane matters—of her father and mother, dead these many years.

Dead, leaving her alone.

Alone in the desert. Alone in this very unpleasant prison-like room.
With nothing to think about but herself.

She sprang up. No use lying here when one couldn't go to sleep.

She hated these high rooms with their small gauze-covered windows.
They hemmed you in. They made you feel small, insect-like. She wanted
a big airy drawing room, with nice cheerful cretonnes and a crackling
fire in the grate and people—lots of people—people you could go and
see and people who would come and see you. . . .

Oh, the train *must* come soon—it had got to come soon. Or a car—or
something. . . .

"I can't stay here," said Joan aloud. "I can't stay here!"

(Talking to yourself, she thought, that's a very bad sign.)

She had some tea and then she went out. She didn't feel she could
sit still and think.

She would go out and walk, and she wouldn't think.

Thinking, that was what upset you. Look at these people who lived
in this place—the Indian, the Arab boy, the cook. She felt quite sure
they never thought.

Sometimes I sits and thinks, and sometimes I just sits. . . .

Who had said that? What an admirable way of life!

She wouldn't think, she would just walk. Not too far away from the
Rest House just in case—well, just in case. . . .

Describe a large circle. Round and round. Like an animal. Humiliating. Yes, humiliating but there it was. She had got to be very, very careful of herself. Otherwise—

Otherwise what? She didn't know. She hadn't any idea.

She mustn't think of Rodney, she mustn't think of Averil, she mustn't think of Tony, she mustn't think of Barbara. She mustn't think of Blanche Haggard. She mustn't think of scarlet rhododendron buds. (Particularly she mustn't think of scarlet rhododendron buds!) She mustn't think of poetry. . . .

She mustn't think of Joan Scudamore. But that's myself! No, it isn't. Yes, it is. . . .

If you had nothing but yourself to think about what would you find out about yourself?

"I don't want to know," said Joan aloud.

The sound of her voice astonished her. What was it that she didn't want to know?

A battle, she thought, I'm fighting a losing battle.

But against whom? Against what?

Never mind, she thought. I don't want to know—

Hang on to that. It was a good phrase.

Odd the feeling that there was someone walking with her. Someone she knew quite well. If she turned her head . . . well, she had turned her head but there was no one. No one at all.

Yet the feeling that there was someone persisted. It frightened her. Rodney, Averil, Tony, Barbara, none of them would help her, none of them could help her, none of them wanted to help her. None of them cared.

She would go back to the Rest House and get away from whoever it was who was spying on her.

The Indian was standing outside the wire door. Joan was swaying a little as she walked. The way he stared annoyed her.

"What is it?" she said. "What's the matter?"

"Memsahib not look well. Perhaps Memsahib have fever?"

That was it. Of course, that was it. She had fever! How stupid not to have thought of that before.

She hurried in. She must take her temperature, look for her quinine. She had got some quinine with her somewhere.

She got out her thermometer and put it under her tongue.

Fever—of course it was fever! The incoherence—the nameless dreads—the apprehension—the fast beating of her heart.

Purely physical, the whole thing.

She took out the thermometer and looked at it.

98.2. If anything she was a shade below normal.

She got through the evening somehow. She was by now really alarmed about herself. It wasn't sun—it wasn't fever—it must be nerves.

"Just nerves," people said. She had said so herself about other people. Well, she hadn't known. She knew now. Just nerves, indeed! Nerves were hell! What she needed was a doctor, a nice, sympathetic doctor, and a nursing home and a kindly, efficient nurse who would never leave the room. "Mrs. Scudamore must never be left alone." What she had got was a whitewashed prison in the middle of a desert, a semi-intelligent Indian, a completely imbecile Arab boy, and a cook who would presently send in a meal of rice and tinned salmon and baked beans and hard-boiled eggs.

All wrong, thought Joan, completely the wrong treatment for my sort of case. . . .

After dinner she went to her room and looked at her aspirin bottle. There were six tablets left. Recklessly she took them all. It was leaving her nothing for tomorrow, but she felt she must try something. Never again, she thought, will I go traveling without some proper sleeping stuff with me.

She undressed and lay down apprehensively.

Strangely enough she fell asleep almost immediately.

That night she dreamed that she was in a big prison building with winding corridors. She was trying to get out but she couldn't find the way, and yet, all the time, she knew quite well that she *did know it.* . . .

You've only got to remember, she kept saying to herself earnestly, you've only got to remember.

In the morning she woke up feeling quite peaceful, though tired.

"You've only got to remember," she said to herself.

She got up and dressed and had breakfast.

She felt quite all right, just a little apprehensive, that was all.

I suppose it will all start again soon, she thought to herself. Oh well, there's nothing I can do about it.

She sat inertly in a chair. Presently she would go out, but not just yet.

She wouldn't try to think about anything in particular—and she wouldn't try not to think. Both were much too tiring. She would just let herself drift.

The outer office of Alderman, Scudamore and Witney—the deed boxes labeled in white. Estate of Sir Jasper Ffoulkes, deceased. Colonel Etchingham Williams. Just like stage properties.

Peter Sherston's face looking up bright and eager from his desk. How very like his mother he was—no, not quite—he had Charles Sherston's eyes. That quick, shifty, sideways look. I wouldn't trust him too far if I were Rodney, she had thought.

Funny that she should have thought that!

After Leslie Sherston's death, Sherston had gone completely to pieces. He had drunk himself to death in record time. The children had been salvaged by relations. The third child, a little girl, had died six months after its birth.

John, the eldest boy, had gone into Woods and Forests. He was somewhere out in Burma now. Joan remembered Leslie and her handprinted linen covers. If John was like his mother, and had her desire to see things that grew fast, he must be very happy now. She had heard that he was doing very well.

Peter Sherston had come to Rodney and had expressed his desire to be taken into the office.

"My mother told me she was sure you would help me, Sir."

An attractive, forthright boy, smiling, eager, always anxious to please—the more attractive, Joan had always thought, of the two.

Rodney had been glad to take the boy. It had made up to him a little, perhaps, for the fact that his own son had preferred to go overseas and had cut himself off from his family.

In time, perhaps, Rodney might have come to look upon Peter almost as a son. He was often at the house and was always charming to Joan. Easy, attractive manners—not quite so unctous as his father's had been.

And then one day Rodney had come home looking worried and ill.

In response to her questions he had replied impatiently that it was noth-ing, nothing at all. But about a week later he mentioned that Peter was leaving—had decided to go to an aircraft factory.

"Oh, Rodney, and you've been so good to him. And we both liked him so much!"

"Yes—an attractive lad."

"What was the trouble? Was he lazy?"

"Oh no, he's a good head for figures and all that sort of thing."

"Like his father?"

"Yes, like his father. But all these lads are attracted to the new dis-coveries—flying—that kind of thing."

But Joan was not listening. Her own words had suggested to her a certain train of thought. Peter Sherston had left very suddenly.

"Rodney—there wasn't anything *wrong*, was there?"

"Wrong? What do you mean?"

"I mean—well, like his father. His mouth is like Leslie's—but he's got that funny shifty look in the eyes that his father always had. Oh, Rodney, it's true, isn't it? He *did* do something?"

Rodney said slowly, "There was just a little trouble."

"Over the accounts? He took money?"

"I'd rather not talk about it, Joan. It was nothing important."

"Crooked like his father! Isn't heredity queer?"

"Very queer. It seems to work the wrong way."

"You mean he might just as well have taken after Leslie? Still, she wasn't a particularly efficient person, was she?"

Rodney said in a dry voice, "I'm of the opinion that she was very efficient. She stuck to her job and did it well."

"Poor thing."

Rodney said irritably, "I wish you wouldn't always pity her. It annoys me."

"But, Rodney, how unkind of you. She really had an awfully sad life."

"I never think of her that way."

"And then her death—"

"I'd rather you didn't talk about that."

He turned away.

Everybody, thought Joan, was afraid of cancer. They flinched away from the word. They called it, if possible, something else—a malignant

growth—a serious operation—an incurable complaint—something internal. Even Rodney didn't like the mention of it. Because, after all, one
never knew—one in every twelve, wasn't it, died of it? And it often
seemed to attack the healthiest people. People who had never had anything else the matter with them.

Joan remembered the day that she had heard the news from Mrs.
Lambert in the Market Square.

"My dear, have you heard? Poor Mrs. Sherston!"

"What about her?"

"Dead!" With gusto. And then the lowered voice. "Internal, I believe . . . Impossible to operate . . . She suffered terrible pain, I hear. But
very plucky. Kept on working until only a couple of weeks before the
end—when they really *had* to keep her under morphia. My nephew's
wife saw her only six weeks ago. She looked terribly ill and was as thin
as a rail, but she was just the same, laughing and joking. I suppose people
just can't believe they can never get well. Oh well, she had a sad life,
poor woman. I daresay it's a merciful release. . . ."

Joan had hurried home to tell Rodney, and Rodney had said quietly,
Yes, he knew. He was the executor of her will, he said, and so they had
communicated with him at once.

Leslie Sherston had not had very much to leave. What there was was
to be divided between her children. The clause that did excite Crayminster was the direction that her body should be brought to Crayminster for burial. "Because," so ran the will, "I was very happy there."

So Leslie Adeline Sherston was laid to rest in the churchyard of St.
Mary's, Crayminster.

An odd request, some people thought, considering that it was in Crayminster that her husband had been convicted of fraudulent appropria-
tion of bank funds. But other people said that it was quite natural. She
had had a happy time there before all the trouble, and it was only natural
that she should look back on it as a kind of lost Garden of Eden.

Poor Leslie—a tragic family altogether, for young Peter, after training
as a test pilot, had crashed and been killed.

Rodney had been terribly cut up about it. In a queer way he seemed
to blame himself for Peter's death.

"But really, Rodney, I don't see how you make that out. It was noth-ing to do with you."

"Leslie sent him to me—she told him that I would give him a job and look after him."

"Well, so you did. You took him into the office."

"I know."

"And he went wrong, and you didn't prosecute him or anything—you made up the deficit yourself, didn't you?"

"Yes, yes—it isn't that. Don't you see, that's *why* Leslie sent him to me, because she realized that he was weak, that he had Sherston's un-trustworthiness. John was all right. She trusted me to look after Peter, to guard the weak spot. He was a queer mixture. He had Charles Sher-ston's crookedness and Leslie's courage. Armadales wrote me that he was the best pilot they'd had—absolutely fearless and a wizard—that's how they phrased it—with planes. The boy volunteered, you know, to try out a new secret device on a plane. It was known to be dangerous. That's how he was killed."

"Well, I call that very creditable, very creditable indeed."

Rodney gave a short dry laugh.

"Oh yes, Joan. But would you say that so complacently if it was your own son who had been killed like that? Would you be satisfied for Tony to have a creditable death?"

Joan stared.

"But Peter wasn't our son. It's entirely different."

"I'm thinking of Leslie . . . of what she would have felt. . . ."

Sitting in the Rest House, Joan shifted a little in her chair.

Why had the Sherstons been so constantly in her thoughts ever since she had been here? She had other friends, friends who meant much more to her than any of the Sherstons had ever done.

She had never liked Leslie so very much, only felt sorry for her. Poor Leslie under her marble slab.

Joan shivered. I'm cold, she thought. I'm cold. Somebody is walking over my grave.

But it was Leslie Sherston's grave she was thinking about.

It's cold in here, she thought, cold and gloomy. I'll go out in the sunlight. I don't want to stay here any longer.

The churchyard—and Leslie Sherston's grave. And the scarlet, heavy rhododendron bud that fell from Rodney's coat.

Rough winds do shake the darling buds of May....

Chapter Nine

Joan came out into the sunlight at almost a run.

She started walking quickly, hardly glancing at the dump of tins and the hens.

That was better. Warm sunlight.

Warm—not cold any longer.

She had got away from it all. . . .

But what did she mean by "got away from it all"?

The wraith of Miss Gilbey seemed suddenly to be close beside her, saying in impressive tones:

"Discipline your thoughts, Joan. Be more precise in your terms. Make up your mind exactly what it is from which you are running away."

But she didn't know. She hadn't the least idea.

Some fear, some menacing and pursuing dread.

Something that had been always there—waiting—and all she could do was to dodge and twist and turn. . . .

Really, Joan Scudamore, she said to herself, you are behaving in a very peculiar manner. . . .

But saying so didn't help matters. There must be something badly wrong with her. It couldn't exactly be agoraphobia—(had she got that name right, or not? It worried her not to be sure) because this time she was anxious to escape from those cold confining walls—to get out from them into space and sunlight. She felt better now that she was outside.

Go out! Go out into the sunshine! Get away from these thoughts.

She'd been here long enough. In this high-ceilinged room that was like a mausoleum.

Leslie Sherston's grave, and Rodney . . .

Leslie . . . Rodney . . .

Get out . . .

The sunshine . . .

So cold—in this room . . .

Cold, and alone. . . .

She increased her pace. Get away from that dreadful mausoleum of a Rest House. So grim, so hemmed in. . . .

The sort of place where you could easily imagine ghosts.

What a stupid idea—it was practically a brand new building, only put up two years ago.

There couldn't be ghosts in a new building, everybody knew that.

No, if there were ghosts in the Rest House, then she, Joan Scudamore, must have brought them with her.

Now that was a *very* unpleasant thought. . . .

She quickened her pace.

At any rate, she thought determinedly, there's nobody with me now. I'm quite alone. There's not even anybody I could meet.

Like—who was it—Speke and Livingstone? Meeting in the wilds of Africa.

Dr. Livingstone, I presume.

Nothing like that here. Only one person she could meet here and that was Joan Scudamore.

What a comic idea! *"Meet Joan Scudamore." "Pleased to meet you, Mrs. Scudamore."*

Really—quite an interesting idea. . . .

Meet yourself. . . .

Meet yourself. . . .

Oh, God, she was frightened. . . .

She was horribly frightened. . . .

Her steps quickened into a run. She ran forward, stumbling a little. Her thoughts stumbled just like her feet did.

. . . I'm frightened. . . .

. . . Oh, God, I'm so frightened. . . .

... If only there was someone here. Someone to be with me. . . .

Blanche, she thought. I wish Blanche were here.

Yes, Blanche was just the person she wanted.

Nobody near and dear to her. None of her friends.

Just Blanche. . . .

Blanche, with her easy warmhearted kindness. Blanche was kind. You couldn't surprise Blanche or shock her.

And anyway, Blanche thought she was nice. Blanche thought she had made a success of life. Blanche was fond of her.

Nobody else was. . . .

That was it—that was the thought that had been with her all along— that was what the real Joan Scudamore knew—had always known. . . .

Lizards popping out of holes. . . .

Truth. . . .

Little bits of truth, popping out like lizards, saying "Here am I. You know me. You know me quite well. Don't pretend you don't."

And she did know them—that was the awful part of it.

She could recognize each one of them.

Grinning at her, laughing at her.

All the little bits and pieces of truth. They'd been showing themselves to her ever since she'd arrived here. All she needed to do was to piece them together.

The whole story of her life—the real story of Joan Scudamore. . . .

It was here waiting for her. . . .

She had never needed to think about it before. It had been quite easy to fill her life with unimportant trivialities that left her no time for self-knowledge.

What was it Blanche had said?

"If you'd nothing to think about but yourself for days on end I wonder what you'd find out about yourself?"

And how superior, how smug, how stupid had been her answer:

"Would one find out anything one didn't know before?"

Sometimes, Mother, I don't think you know anything about anybody. . . .

That had been Tony.

How right Tony had been.

She hadn't known anything about her children, anything about Rodney. She had loved them but she hadn't known.

She should have known.

If you loved people you should know about them.

You didn't know because it was so much easier to believe the pleasant easy things that you would like to be true, and not distress yourself with the things that really were true.

Like Averil—Averil and the pain that Averil had suffered.

She hadn't wanted to recognize that Averil had suffered. . . .

Averil who had always despised her. . . .

Averil who had seen through her at a very early age. . . .

Averil who had been broken and hurt by life and who, even now perhaps, was still a maimed creature.

But a creature with courage. . . .

That was what she, Joan, had lacked. Courage.

"Courage isn't everything," she had said.

And Rodney had said, *"Isn't it? . . ."*

Rodney had been right. . . .

Tony, Averil, Rodney—all of them her accusers.

And Barbara?

What had been wrong with Barbara? Why had the doctor been so reticent? What was it they had all been hiding from her?

What had the child done—that passionate undisciplined child, who had married the first man who asked her so as to get away from home.

Yes, it was quite true—that was exactly what Barbara had done. She'd been unhappy at home. And she'd been unhappy because Joan hadn't taken the least trouble to make home happy for her.

She'd had no love for Barbara, no kind of understanding. Cheerfully and selfishly she had determined what was good for Barbara without the least regard for Barbara's tastes or wishes. She had had no welcome for Barbara's friends, had gently discouraged them. No wonder the idea of Baghdad had seemed to Barbara like a vista of escape.

She had married Bill Wray hastily and impulsively, and without (so Rodney said) loving him. And then what had happened?

A love affair? An unhappy love affair? That Major Reid, probably. Yes, that would explain the embarrassment when Joan had mentioned his name. Just the kind of man, she thought, to fascinate a silly child who wasn't yet properly grown up.

And then, in desperation, in one of those violent paroxysms of despair to which she had been prone from early childhood, those catacylysms when she lost all sense of proportion, she had tried—yes, that must be it—to take her own life.

And she had been very, very ill—dangerously ill.

Had Rodney known, Joan wondered? He had certainly tried to dissuade her from rushing out to Baghdad.

No, surely Rodney couldn't have known. He would have told her. Well, no, perhaps he wouldn't have told her. He certainly had done his best to stop her going.

But she had been absolutely determined. She had felt, she said, that she simply couldn't endure not to go out to the poor child.

Surely *that* had been a creditable impulse.

Only—wasn't even that a part, only, of the truth?

Hadn't she been attracted by the idea of the journey—the novelty— seeing a new part of the world? Hadn't she enjoyed the idea of playing the part of the devoted mother? Hadn't she seen herself as a charming impulsive woman being welcomed by her ill daughter and her distracted son-in-law? How good of you, they would say, to come rushing out like that.

Really, of course, they hadn't been at all pleased to see her! They had been, quite frankly, dismayed. They had warned the doctor, guarded their tongues, done everything imaginable to prevent her from learning the truth. They didn't want her to know because they didn't trust her. Barbara hadn't trusted her. Keep it from Mother—that had probably been her one idea.

How relieved they had been when she had announced that she must go back. They had hidden it quite well, making polite protestations, suggesting that she might stay on for a while. But when she had, just for a moment actually thought of doing so, how quick William had been to discourage her.

In fact, the only possible good that she had done by her hurried rush Eastwards was the somewhat curious one of drawing Barbara and William together in their united effort to get rid of her and keep their secret.

Odd if, after all, some positive good might come from her visit. Often, Joan, remembered, Barbara, still weak, had looked appealingly at William, and William, responding, had hurried into speech, had explained some doubtful point, had fended off one of Joan's tactless questions.

And Barbara had looked at him gratefully—affectionately.

They had stood there on the platform, seeing her off. And Joan remembered how William had held Barbara's hand, and Barbara had leaned a little towards him.

"Courage, darling," that was what he had been meaning. "It's nearly over—she's going. . . ."

And after the train had gone, they would go back to their bungalow at Alwyah and play with Mopsy—for they both loved Mopsy, that adorable baby who was such a ridiculous caricature of William—and Barbara would say, "Thank goodness she's gone and we've got the house to ourselves."

Poor William, who loved Barbara so much and who must have been so unhappy, and yet who had never faltered in his love and tenderness.

"Don't worry about her!" Blanche had said. "She'll be all right. There's the kid and everything."

Kind Blanche, reassuring an anxiety that simply hadn't existed.

All she, Joan, had had in her mind was a superior disdainful pity for her old friend.

I thank thee, Lord, that I am not as this woman.

Yes, she had even dared to pray. . . .

And now, at this moment, she would have given anything to have had Blanche with her!

Blanche, with her kindly easy charity—her complete lack of condemnation of any living creature.

She had prayed that night at the Railway Rest House wrapped in that spurious mantle of superiority.

Could she pray now, when it seemed to her that she had no longer a rag to cover her?

Joan stumbled forward and fell on her knees.

. . . *God*, she prayed, *help me.* . . .

. . . *I'm going mad, God.* . . .

. . . *Don't let me go mad.* . . .

. . . Don't let me go on thinking. . . .

Silence. . . .

Silence and sunlight. . . .

And the pounding of her own heart. . . .

God, she thought, *has forsaken me. . . .*

. . . God won't help me. . . .

. . . I am alone—quite alone. . . .

That terrible silence . . . that awful loneliness. . . .

Little Joan Scudamore . . . silly futile pretentious little Joan Scudamore. . . .

All alone in the desert.

Christ, she thought, *was alone in the desert.*

For forty days and forty nights. . . .

. . . No, no, nobody could do that—nobody could bear it. . . .

The silence, the sun, the loneliness . . .

Fear came upon her again—the fear of the vast empty spaces where man is alone except for God. . . .

She stumbled to her feet.

She must get back to the Rest House—back to the Rest House.

The Indian—the Arab boy—the hens—the empty tins . . .

Humanity.

She stared round her wildly. There was no sign of the Rest House—no sign of the tiny cairn that was the station—no sign, even, of distant hills.

She must have come farther than ever before, so far that all around her there was no discernible landmark.

She didn't, horror upon horror, even know in which direction the Rest House lay. . . .

The hills—surely those distant hills couldn't disappear—but all around on the horizon were low clouds . . . Hills? Clouds? One couldn't tell.

She was lost, completely lost. . . .

No, if she went north—that was right—north.

The sun. . . .

The sun was directly overhead . . . there was no way of telling her direction from the sun. . . .

She was lost—lost—she would never find the way back. . . .

Suddenly, frenziedly she began to run.

First in one direction, then, in sudden panic back the other way. She ran to and fro, wildly, desperately.

And she began to cry out—shouting, calling. . . .

Help. . . .

Help. . . .

(They'll never hear me, she thought . . . I'm too far away . . .)

The desert caught up her voice, reduced it to a small bleating cry. Like a sheep, she thought, like a sheep. . . .

He findeth his sheep. . . .

The Lord is my Shepherd. . . .

Rodney—green pastures and the valley in the High Street . . .

Rodney, she called, *help me, help me. . . .*

But Rodney was going away up the platform, his shoulders squared, his head thrown back . . . enjoying the thought of a few weeks' freedom . . . feeling, for the moment, young again. . . .

He couldn't hear her.

Averil—Averil—wouldn't Averil help her?

I'm your mother, Averil, I've always done everything for you. . . .

No, Averil would go quietly out of the room, saying perhaps:

"There isn't really anything I can do . . ."

Tony—Tony would help her.

No, Tony couldn't help her. He was in South Africa.

A long way away. . . .

Barbara—Barbara was too ill . . . Barbara had got food poisoning.

Leslie, she thought. Leslie would help me if she could. But Leslie is dead. She suffered and she died. . . .

It was no good—there was no one. . . .

She began to run again—despairingly, without idea or direction—just running. . . .

The sweat was running down her face, down her neck, down her whole body. . . .

She thought, This is the end. . . .

Christ, she thought . . . *Christ. . . .*

Christ would come to her in the desert. . . .

Christ would show her the way to the green valley.

... Would lead her with the sheep. ...

... The lost sheep. ...

... The sinner that repented. ...

... Through the valley of the shadow. ...

... (No shadow—only sun ...)

... Lead kindly light. (But the sun wasn't kindly ...)

The green valley—the green valley—she must find the green valley. ...

Opening out of the High Street, there in the middle of Crayminster. Opening out of the desert. ...

Forty days and forty nights.

Only three days gone—so Christ would still be there.

Christ, she prayed, *help me.* ...

Christ. ...

What was that?

Over there—far to the right—that tiny blur upon the horizon!

It was the Rest House ... she wasn't lost ... she was saved ...

Saved. ...

Her knees gave way—she crumpled down in a heap. ...

Chapter Ten

Joan regained consciousness slowly. . . .
 She felt very sick and ill. . . .

And weak, weak as a child.

But she was saved. The Rest House was there. Presently, when she felt a little better, she could get up and walk to it.

In the meantime she would just stay still and think things out. Think them out properly—not pretending anymore.

God, after all, had not forsaken her. . . .

She had no longer that terrible consciousness of being alone. . . .

But I must think, she said to herself. *I must think.* I must get things straight. That is why I'm here—to get things straight. . . .

She had got to know, once and for all, just what kind of a woman Joan Scudamore was. . . .

That was why she had had to come here, to the desert. This clear terrible light would show her what she was. Would show her the truth of all the things she hadn't wanted to look at—the things that, really *she had known all along.*

There had been one clue yesterday. Perhaps she had better start with that. For it had been then, hadn't it, that that first sense of blind panic had swept over her?

She had been reciting poetry—that was how it had begun.

From you have I been absent in the Spring.

That was the line—and it had made her think of Rodney and she had
said, "But it's November now. . . ."

Just as Rodney had said that evening, "But it's October. . . ."

The evening of the day that he had sat on Asheldown with Leslie
Sherston—the two of them sitting there in silence—with four feet of
space between them. And she had thought, hadn't she, that it wasn't
very friendly?

But she knew now—and of course she must really have known then—
why they sat so far apart.

It was because, wasn't it, they didn't dare to be nearer. . . .

Rodney—and Leslie Sherston. . . .

Not Myrna Randolph—never Myrna Randolph. She had deliberately
encouraged the Myrna Randolph myth in her own mind because she
knew there was nothing in it. She had put up Myrna Randolph as a
smoke screen so as to hide what was really there.

And partly—be honest now, Joan—partly because it was easier for
her to accept Myrna Randolph than Leslie Sherston.

It would hurt her pride less to admit that Rodney had been attracted by
Myrna Randolph who was beautiful and the kind of siren who could be supposed to attract any man not gifted with superhuman powers of resistance.

But Leslie Sherston—Leslie who was not even beautiful—who was
not young—who was not even well turned out. Leslie with her tired face
and her funny one-sided smile. To admit that Rodney could love Leslie—
could love her with such passion that he dared not trust himself nearer
than four feet—that was what she hated to acknowledge.

That desperate longing, that aching unsatisfied desire—that force of
passion that she herself had never known. . . .

It had been there between them that day on Asheldown—and she
had felt it—it was because she had felt it that she had hurried away so
quickly and so shamefacedly, not admitting to herself for a moment the
thing that she really knew. . . .

Rodney and Leslie—sitting there silent—not even looking at each
other—because they dared not.

Leslie, loving Rodney so desperately, that she wanted to be laid when
dead in the town where he lived. . . .

Rodney looking down at the marble slab and saying, "It seems damned silly to think of Leslie Sherston under a cold slab of marble like that." And the rhododendron bud falling, a scarlet splash.

"Heart's blood," he had said. "Heart's blood."

And then, afterwards, how he had said, "I'm tired, Joan. I'm tired." And later, so strangely, "We can't all be brave. . . ."

He had been thinking of Leslie when he said that. Of Leslie and her courage.

"Courage isn't everything . . ."

"Isn't it?"

And Rodney's nervous breakdown—Leslie's death had been the cause of that.

Lying there peacefully in Cornwall, listening to the gulls, without interest in life, smiling quietly. . . .

Tony's scornful boyish voice:

"Don't you know *anything* about Father?"

She hadn't. She hadn't known a thing! Because, quite determinedly, she hadn't wanted to know.

Leslie looking out of the window, explaining why she was going to have Sherston's child.

Rodney, saying as he too looked out of the window, "Leslie doesn't do things by halves. . . ."

What had they seen, these two, as they stood there? Did Leslie see the apple trees and the anemones in her garden? Did Rodney see the tennis court and the goldfish pond? Or did both of them see the pale smiling countryside and the blur of woods on the further hill that you saw from the summit of Asheldown. . . .

Poor Rodney, poor tired Rodney. . . .

Rodney with his kind teasing smile, Rodney saying Poor Little Joan . . . always kind, always affectionate, never failing her. . . .

Well, she'd been a good wife to him, hadn't she?

She'd always put his interests first. . . .

Wait—had she?

Rodney, his eyes pleading with her . . . sad eyes. Always sad eyes.

Rodney saying, "How was I to know I'd hate the office so?" looking at her gravely, asking, "How do you know that I'll be happy?"

Rodney pleading for the life he wanted, the life of a farmer.

Rodney standing at the window of his office watching the cattle on market day.

Rodney talking to Leslie Sherston about dairy herds.

Rodney saying to Averil, "If a man doesn't do the work he wants to do, he's only half a man."

That was what she, Joan, had done to Rodney. . . .

Anxiously, feverishly, she tried to defend herself against the judgment of her new knowledge.

She had meant it for the best! One had to be practical! There were the children to think of. She hadn't done it from selfish motives.

But the clamor of protestation died down.

Hadn't she been selfish?

Hadn't it been that *she* didn't want to live on a farm herself? She'd wanted her children to have the best things—but what *was* the best? Hadn't Rodney as much right to decide what his children should have as she had?

Hadn't he really the prior right? Wasn't it for a father to choose the life his children should live—the mother to care for their well-being and to follow out, loyally, the father's idea of life?

Life on a farm, Rodney had said, was a good life for children—

Tony would certainly have enjoyed it.

Rodney had seen to it that Tony should not be balked of the kind of life that he wanted.

"I'm not very good," Rodney had said, "at forcing people to do things."

But she, Joan, hadn't scrupled to force Rodney. . . .

With a sudden, agonizing pang, Joan thought, But I *love* Rodney. I *love* Rodney. It wasn't that I didn't love him. . . .

And that, she saw, with a sudden revealing vision, was just what made it so unforgivable.

She loved Rodney and yet she had done this thing to him.

If she had hated him it could be excused.

If she had been indifferent to him, it wouldn't have mattered so much.

But she had loved him, and yet, loving him, she had taken from his his birthright—the right to choose his manner and way of life.

And because of that, because she had used, unscrupulously, her woman's weapons, the child in the cradle, the child that her body was bearing within it—she had taken something from him that he had never recovered. She had taken from him a portion of his manhood.

Because, in his gentleness, he had not fought with her and conquered her, he was so much the less, for all his days on the earth, a man. . . .

She thought, Rodney . . . Rodney. . . .

She thought, And I can't give it back to him . . . I can't make it up to him . . . I can't do *anything.* . . .

But I love him—I do love him. . . .

And I love Averil and Tony and Barbara. . . .

I always loved them. . . .

(But not enough—that was the answer—not enough—)

She thought, Rodney—Rodney, is there *nothing* I can do? Nothing I can say?

From you have I been absent in the Spring.

Yes, she thought, for a long time . . . ever since the Spring . . . the Spring when we first loved each other. . . .

I've stayed where I was—Blanche was right—I'm the girl who left St. Anne's. Easy living, lazy thinking, pleased with myself, afraid of anything that might be painful. . . .

No *courage.* . . .

What can I do, she thought. What can I do?

And she thought, I can go to him. I can say, "I'm sorry. Forgive me . . ."

Yes, I can say that . . . I can say, "Forgive me. I didn't know. I simply didn't know. . . ."

Joan got up. Her legs felt weak and rather silly.

She walked slowly and painfully—like an old woman.

Walking—walking—one foot—then the other—

Rodney, she thought, Rodney. . . .

How ill she felt—how weak . . .

It was a long way—a very long way.

The Indian came running out from the Rest House to meet her, his face wreathed in smiles. He waved, gesticulated:

"Good news, Memsahib, good news!"

She stared at him.

"You see? Train come! Train at station. You leave by train tonight."

The train? The train to take her to Rodney.

("Forgive me, Rodney . . . forgive me. . . .")

She heard herself laughing—wildly—unnaturally—the Indian stared and she pulled herself together.

"The train has come," she said, "just at the right time. . . ."

Chapter Eleven

It was like a dream, Joan thought. Yes, it was like a dream. Walking through the convolutions of barbed wire—the Arab boy carrying her suitcases and chattering shrilly in Turkish to a big fat suspicious-looking man who was the Turkish station master.

And there, waiting for her, the familiar sleeping car with the Wagon Lits man in his chocolate uniform leaning out of a window.

Alep-Stamboul on the side of the coach.

The link that bound this resting place in the desert to civilization!

The polite greeting in French, her compartment thrown open, the bed already made with its sheets and its pillow.

Civilization again. . . .

Outwardly Joan was once more the quiet efficient traveler, the same Mrs. Scudamore that had left Baghdad less than a week ago. Only Joan herself knew of that astonishing, that almost frightening change that lay behind the facade.

The train, as she had said, had come just at the right moment. Just when those last barriers which she herself had so carefully erected had been swept away in a rising tide of fear and loneliness.

She had had—as others had had in days gone by—a Vision. A vision of *herself*. And although she might seem now the commonplace English traveler, intent on the minor details of travel, her heart and mind were held in that abasement of self-reproach that had come to her out there in the silence and the sunlight.

She had answered almost mechanically the Indian's comments and questions.

"Why not Memsahib come back for lunch? Lunch all ready. Very nice lunch. It nearly five o'clock now. Too late lunch. Have tea?"

Yes, she said, she would have tea.

"But where Memsahib go? I look out, not see Memsahib anywhere. Not know which way Memsahib gone."

She had walked rather far, she said. Farther than usual.

"That not safe. Not safe at all. Memsahib get lost. Not know which way to go. Perhaps walk wrong way."

Yes, she said, she had lost her way for a time, but luckily she had walked in the right direction. She would have tea now, and then rest. What time did the train go?

"Train go eight-thirty. Sometimes wait for convoy to come in. But no convoy come today. Wadi very bad—lot of water—rush through like that. Whoosh!"

Joan nodded.

"Memsahib look very tired. Memsahib, got fever, perhaps?"

No, Joan said, she hadn't got fever—now.

"Memsahib look different."

Well, she thought, Memsahib *was* different. Perhaps the difference showed in her face. She went to her room and stared into the fly-stained mirror.

Was there any difference? She looked, definitely, older. There were circles under her eyes. Her face was streaked with yellow dust and sweat.

She washed her face, ran a comb through her hair, applied powder and lipstick and looked again.

Yes, there was definitely a difference. Something had gone from the face that stared so earnestly back at her. Something—could it be smugness?

What a horribly smug creature she had been. She felt still the keen disgust that had come to her out there—the self-loathing—the new humility of spirit.

Rodney, she thought, Rodney. . . .

Just his name, repeated softly in her thoughts. . . .

She held to it as a symbol of her purpose. To tell him everything, not to spare herself. That, she felt, was all that mattered. They would make together, so far as was possible at this late date, a new life. She would say, "I'm a fool and a failure. Teach me, out of your wisdom, out of your gentleness, the way to live."

That, and forgiveness. For Rodney had a lot to forgive. And the wonderful thing about Rodney, she realized now, was that he had never hated her. No wonder that Rodney was loved so much—that his children adored him (even Averil, she thought, behind her antagonism, has never stopped loving him) that the servants would do anything to please him, that he had friends everywhere. Rodney, she thought, has never been unkind to anyone in his life. . . .

She sighed. She was very tired, and her body ached all over.

She drank her tea and then lay down on her bed until it was time to have dinner and start for the train.

She felt no restlessness now—no fear—no longing for occupation or distraction. There were no more lizards to pop out of holes and frighten her.

She had met herself and recognized herself. . . .

Now she only wanted to rest, to lie with an empty peaceful mind and with always, at the back of that mind, the dim picture of Rodney's kind dark face. . . .

And now she was in the train, had listened to the Conductor's voluble account of the accident on the line, had handed over to him her passport and her tickets and had received his assurance that he would wire to Stamboul for fresh reservations on the Simplon Orient Express. She also entrusted him with a wire to be sent from Alep to Rodney. *Journey delayed all well love Joan.*

Rodney would receive it before her original schedule had expired.

So that was all arranged and she had nothing more to do or to think about. She could relax like a tired child.

Five days' peace and quiet whilst the Taurus and Orient Express rushed westwards bringing her each day nearer to Rodney and forgiveness.

• • •

They arrived at Alep early the following morning. Until then Joan had been the only passenger, since communications with Iraq were interrupted, but now the train was filled to overflowing. There had been delays, cancelations, confusions in the booking of sleepers. There was a lot of hoarse excited talking, protests, arguments, disputes—all taking place in different languages.

Joan was traveling first class and on the Taurus Express the first-class sleepers were the old double ones.

The door slid back and a tall woman in black came in. Behind her the Conductor was reaching down through the window where porters were handing him up cases.

The compartment seemed full of cases—expensive cases stamped with coronets.

The tall woman talked to the attendant in French. She directed him where to put things. At last he withdrew. The woman turned and smiled at Joan, an experienced cosmopolitan smile.

"You are English," she said.

She spoke with hardly a trace of accent. She had a long, pale, exquisitely mobile face and rather strange light gray eyes. She was, Joan thought, about forty-five.

"I apologize for this early morning intrusion. It is an iniquitously uncivilized hour for a train to leave, and I disturb your repose. Also these carriages are very old-fashioned—on the new ones the compartments are single. But still—" she smiled—and it was a very sweet and almost childlike smile—"we shall not get too badly on each other's nerves. It is but two days to Stamboul, and I am not too difficult to live with. And if I smoke too much you will tell me. But now I leave you to sleep I go to the restaurant car that they put on at this moment," she swayed slightly as a bump indicated the truth of her words, "and wait there to have breakfast. Again I say how sorry I am you have been disturbed."

"Oh, that's quite all right," Joan said. "One expects these things when traveling."

"I see you are sympathetic—good—we shall get on together famously."

She went out and as she drew the door to behind her, Joan heard her being greeted by her friends on the platform with cries of "Sasha—Sasha" and a voluble burst of conversation in some language that Joan's ear did not recognize.

Joan herself was by now thoroughly awake. She felt rested after her night's sleep. She always slept well in a train. She got up and proceeded to dress. The train drew out of Alep when she had nearly finished her toilet. When she was ready, she went out into the corridor, but first she took a quick look at the labels on her new companion's suitcases.

Princess Hohenbach Salm.

In the restaurant car she found her new acquaintance eating breakfast and conversing with great animation to a small stout Frenchman.

The Princess waved a greeting to her and indicated the seat at her side.

"But you are energetic," she exclaimed. "If it was me, I should still lie and sleep. Now, Monsieur Baudier, go on with what you are telling me. It is most interesting."

The Princess talked in French to M. Baudier, in English to Joan, in fluent Turkish to the waiter, and occasionally across the aisle in equally fluent Italian to a rather melancholy-looking officer.

Presently the stout Frenchman finished his breakfast and withdrew, bowing politely.

"What a good linguist you are," said Joan.

The long pale face smiled—a melancholy smile this time.

"Yes—why not? I am Russian, you see. And I was married to a German, and I have lived much in Italy. I speak eight, nine languages—some well, some not so well. It is a pleasure, do you not think, to converse? All human beings are interesting, and one lives such a short time on this earth! One should exchange ideas—experiences. There is not enough love on the earth, that is what I say. Sasha, my friends say to me, there are people it is impossible to love—Turks, Armenians—Levantines. But I say no. I love them all. *Garçon, l'addition.*"

Joan blinked slightly for the last sentence had been practically joined to the one before it.

The restaurant car attendant came hurrying up respectfully and it was borne in upon Joan that her traveling companion was a person of considerable importance.

All that morning and afternoon they wound across the plains and then climbed slowly up into the Taurus.

Sasha sat in her corner and read and smoked and occasionally made unexpected and sometimes embarrassing remarks. Joan found herself being fascinated by this strange woman who came from a different world and whose mental processes were so totally different from anything she herself had previously come across.

The mingling of the impersonal and the intimate, had an odd compelling charm for Joan.

Sasha said to her suddenly:

"You do not read—no? And you do nothing with your hands. You do not knit. That is not like most Englishwomen. And yet you look most English—yes, you look exactly English."

Joan smiled.

"I've actually nothing to read. I was held up at Tell Abu Hamid owing to the breakdown on the line, so I got through all the literature I had with me."

"But you do not mind? You did not feel it necessary to get something at Alep. No, you are content just to sit and look out through the window at the mountains, and yet you do not see them—you look at something that *you yourself see*, is it not so? You experience in your mind some great emotion, or you have passed through one. You have a sorrow? Or a great happiness?"

Joan hesitated, with a slight frown.

Sasha burst out laughing.

"Ah but that is so English. You think it impertinent if I ask the questions that we Russians feel are so natural. It is curious that. If I were to ask you where you had been, to what hotels, and what scenery you had seen, and if you have children and what do they do, and have you traveled much, and do you know a good hairdresser in London—all that you would answer with pleasure. But if I ask something that comes into my mind—have you a sorrow, is your husband faithful—do you sleep much with men—what has been your most beautiful experience in life— are you conscious of the love of God? All those things would make you draw back—affronted—and yet they are much more interesting than the others, nicht wahr?"

"I suppose," said Joan slowly, "that we are very reserved as a nation."

"Yes, yes. One cannot even say to an Englishwoman who has recently been married, are you going to have a baby? That is, one cannot say so, across the table at luncheon. No, one has to take her aside, to *whisper* it. And yet if the baby is there, in its cradle, you can say, 'How is your baby?' "

"Well—it is rather intimate, isn't it?"

"No, I do not see it. I met the other day a friend I have not seen for many years, a Hungarian. Mitzi, I say to her, you are married—yes, several years now, you have not a baby, why not? She answers me she cannot think why not! For five years, she says she and her husband have tried hard—but oh! how hard they have tried! What, she asks, can she do about it? And, since we are at a luncheon party, everyone there makes a suggestion. Yes, and some of them very practical. Who knows, something may come of it."

Joan looked stolidly unconvinced.

Yet she felt suddenly welling up in her a strong impulse to open her own heart to this friendly peculiar foreign creature. She wanted, badly, to share with someone the experience that she had been through. She needed, as it were, to assure herself of its reality. . . .

She said slowly, "It is true—I have been through rather an upsetting experience."

"Ach, yes? What was it? A man?"

"No. No, certainly not."

"I am glad. It is so often a man—and really in the end it becomes a little boring."

"I was all alone—at the Rest House at Tell Abu Hamid—a horrible place—all flies and tins and rolls of barbed wire, and very gloomy and dark inside."

"That is necessary because of the heat in summer, but I know what you mean."

"I had no one to talk to—and I soon finished my books—and I got—I got into a very peculiar state."

"Yes, yes, that might well be so. It is interesting what you tell me. Go on."

"I began to find out things—about myself. Things that I had never known before. Or rather things that I *had* known, but had never been willing to recognize. I can't quite explain to you—"

"Oh but you can. It is quite easy. I shall understand."

Sasha's interest was so natural, so unassumed, that Joan found herself talking with an astonishing lack of self-consciousness. Since to Sasha to talk of one's feelings, and one's intimate relationships was perfectly natural, it began to seem natural to Joan also.

She began to talk with less hesitation, describing her uneasiness, her fears, and her final panic.

"I daresay it will seem absurd to you—but I felt that I was completely lost—alone—that God himself had forsaken me—"

"Yes, one has felt that—I have felt it myself. It is very dark, very terrible. . . ."

"It was not dark—it was light—blinding light—there was no shelter—no cover—no shadow."

"We mean the same thing, though. For you it was light that was terrible, because you had hidden so long under cover and in deep shade. But for me it was darkness, not seeing my way, being lost in the night. But the agony is the same—it is the knowledge of one's own nothingness and of being cut off from the love of God."

Joan said slowly, "And then—*it happened*—like a miracle. I saw everything. Myself—and what I had been. All my silly pretenses and shams fell away. It was like—it was like being born again. . . ."

She looked anxiously at the other woman. Sasha bent her head.

"And I knew what I had to do. I had to go home and start again. Build up a new life . . . from the beginning. . . ."

There was a silence. Sasha was looking at Joan thoughtfully and something in her expression puzzled Joan. She said, with a slight flush:

"Oh I daresay it sounds very melodramatic and far-fetched—"

Sasha interrupted her.

"No, no, you do not understand me. Your experience was real—it has happened to many—to St. Paul—to others of the Saints of God—and to ordinary mortals and sinners. It is conversion. It is vision. It is the soul knowing its own bitterness. Yes, it is real all that—it is as real as eating your dinner or brushing your teeth. But I wonder—all the same, I wonder. . . ."

"I feel I've been so unkind—done harm to—to someone I love—"

"Yes, yes, you have remorse."

"And I can hardly wait to get there—to get home, I mean. There is so much I want to say—to tell him."

"To tell whom? Your husband?"

"Yes. He has been so kind—so patient always. But he has not been happy. I have not made him happy."

"And you think you will be better able to make him happy now?"

"We can at least have an explanation. He can know how sorry I am. He can help me to—oh what shall I say?" The words of the Communion service flashed through her mind. "To lead a new life from now on."

Sasha said gravely, "That is what the Saints of God were able to do."

Joan stared.

"But I—I am not a saint."

"No. That is what I meant." Sasha paused, then said with a slight change of tone, "Forgive me that I should have said that. And perhaps it is not true."

Joan looked slightly bewildered.

Sasha lit another cigarette and began to smoke violently, staring out of the window.

"I don't know," said Joan uncertainly, "why I should tell you all this—"

"But naturally because you wish to tell someone—you wish to speak of it—it is in your mind and you want to talk of it, that is natural enough."

"I'm usually very reserved."

Sasha looked amused.

"And so proud of it like all English people. Oh, you are a very curious race—but very curious. So shamefaced, so embarrassed by your virtues, so ready to admit, to boast of your deficiencies."

"I think you are exaggerating slightly," said Joan stiffly.

She felt suddenly very British, very far away from the exotic pale-faced woman in the opposite corner of the carriage, the woman to whom, a minute or two previously, she had confided a most intimate personal experience.

Joan said in a conventional voice, "Are you going through on the Simplon Orient?"

"No, I stay a night in Stamboul and then I go to Vienna." She added carelessly, "It is possible that I shall die there, but perhaps not."

"Do you mean—" Joan hesitated, bewildered, "that you've had a premonition?"

"Ah no," Sasha burst out laughing. "No, it is not like that! It is an operation I am going to have there. A very serious operation. Not very often is it that it succeeds. But they are good surgeons in Vienna. This one to whom I am going—he is very clever—a Jew. I have always said it would be stupid to annihilate all the Jews in Europe. They are clever doctors and surgeons, yes, and they are clever artistically too."

"Oh dear," said Joan. "I am so sorry."

"Because I may be going to die? But what does it matter? One has to die sometime. And I may not die. I have the idea, if I live, that I will enter a convent I know of—a very strict order. One never speaks—it is perpetual meditation and prayer."

Joan's imagination failed to conceive of a Sasha perpetually silent and meditating.

Sasha went on gravely, "There will be much prayer needed soon—when the war comes."

"War?" Joan stared.

Sasha nodded her head.

"But yes, certainly war is coming. Next year, or the year after."

"Really," said Joan. "I think you are mistaken."

"No, no. I have friends who are very well informed and they have told me so. It is all decided.

"But war where—against whom?"

"War everywhere. Every nation will be drawn in. My friends think that Germany will win quite soon, but I—I do not agree. Unless they can win very very quickly indeed. You see, I know many English and Americans and I know what they are like."

"Surely," said Joan, "nobody really wants war."

She spoke incredulously.

"For what else does the Hitler Youth movement exist?"

Joan said earnestly, "But I have friends who have been in Germany a good deal, and they think that there is a lot to be said for the Nazi movement."

"Oh la la," cried Sasha. "See if they say that in three years' time."

Then she leaned forward as the train drew slowly to a standstill.

"See, we have come to the Cilician Gates. It is beautiful, is it not? Let us get out."

They got out of the train and stood looking down through the great gap in the mountain chain to the blue hazy plains beneath. . . .

It was close on sunset and the air was exquisitely cool and still.

Joan thought: How beautiful. . . .

She wished Rodney was here to see it with her.

Chapter Twelve

Victoria. . . .

Joan felt her heart beating with sudden excitement.

It was good to be home.

She felt, just for a moment, as though she had never been away. England, her own country. Nice English porters. . . . A not so nice, but very English, foggy day!

Not romantic, not beautiful, just dear old Victoria station just the same as ever, looking just the same, smelling just the same!

Oh, thought Joan, I'm *glad* to be back.

Such a long weary journey, across Turkey and Bulgaria and Yugoslavia and Italy and France. Customs officers, and passport examinations. All the different uniforms, all the different languages. She was tired— yes, definitely tired—of foreigners. Even that extraordinary Russian woman who had traveled with her from Alep to Stamboul had got rather tiresome in the end. She had been interesting—indeed quite exciting— to begin with, simply because she was so different. But by the time they had been running down beside the Sea of Marmora to Haidar Pacha, Joan had been definitely looking forward to their parting. For one thing it was embarrassing to remember how freely, she, Joan, had talked about her own private affairs to a complete stranger. And for another—well, it was difficult to put it into words—but something about her had made Joan feel definitely *provincial*. Not a very pleasant feeling. It had been no good to say to herself that she hoped she, Joan, was as good as anybody! She didn't really think so. She felt uneasily conscious that Sasha, for all her friendliness, was an aristocrat whilst she herself was middle class, the unimportant wife of a country solicitor. Very stupid, of course, to feel like that. . . .

But anyway all that was over now. She was home again, back on her native soil.

There was no one to meet her for she had sent no further wire to Rodney to tell him when she was arriving.

She had had a strong feeling that she wanted to meet Rodney in their own house. She wanted to be able to start straightaway on her confession without pause or delay. It would be easier so, she thought.

You couldn't very well ask a surprised husband for forgiveness on the platform at Victoria!

Certainly not on the arrival platform, with its hurrying mob of people, and the customs sheds at the end.

No, she would spend the night quietly at the Grosvenor and go down to Crayminster tomorrow.

Should she, she wondered, try and see Averil first? She could ring Averil up from the Hotel.

Yes, she decided. She might do that.

She had only hand luggage with her and as it had already been examined at Dover, she was able to go with her porter straight to the hotel.

She had a bath and dressed and then rang up Averil. Fortunately Averil was at home.

"Mother? I'd no idea you were back."

"I arrived this afternoon."

"Is Father up in London?"

"No. I didn't tell him when I was arriving. He might have come up to meet me—and that would be a pity if he's busy—tiring for him."

She thought that she heard a faint note of surprise in Averil's voice as she said:

"Yes—I think you were right. He's been very busy lately."

"Have you seen much of him?"

"No. He was up in London for the day about three weeks ago and we had lunch together. What about this evening, Mother? Would you like to come out and have dinner somewhere?"

"I'd rather you came here, darling, if you don't mind. I'm a little tired with traveling."

"I expect you must be. All right, I'll come round."

"Won't Edward come with you?"

"He's got a business dinner tonight."

Joan put down the receiver. Her heart was beating a little faster than usual. She thought, Averil—my Averil. . . .

How cool and liquid Averil's voice was . . . calm, detached, impersonal.

Half an hour later they telephoned up that Mrs. Harrison-Wilmott was there and Joan went down.

Mother and daughter greeted each other with English reserve. Averil looked well, Joan thought. She was not quite so thin. Joan felt a faint thrill of pride as she went with her daughter into the dining room. Averil was really very lovely, so delicate and distinguished looking.

They sat down at a table and Joan got a momentary shock as she met her daughter's eyes.

They were so cool and uninterested. . . .

Averil, like Victoria Station, had not changed.

It's I who have changed, thought Joan, but Averil doesn't know that.

Averil asked about Barbara and about Baghdad. Joan recounted various incidents of her journey home. Somehow or other, their talk was rather difficult. It did not seem to flow. Averil's inquiries after Barbara were almost perfunctory. It really seemed as though she had an inkling that more pertinent questions might be indiscreet. But Averil couldn't know anything of the truth. It was just her usual delicate, incurious attitude.

"The truth," Joan thought suddenly, *"how do I know it is the truth?"* Mightn't it, just possibly, be all imagination on her part? After all, there was no concrete evidence. . . .

She rejected the idea, but the mere passing of it through her head had given her a shock. Supposing she was one of those people who imagined things. . . .

Averil was saying in her cool voice, "Edward has got it into his head that there's bound to be war with Germany one day."

Joan roused herself.

"That's what a woman on the train said. She seemed quite certain about it. She was rather an important person, and she really seemed to know what she was talking about. I can't believe it. Hitler would never *dare* to go to war."

Averil said thoughtfully, "Oh I don't know. . . ."

"Nobody *wants* war, darling."

"Well, people sometimes get what they don't want."

Joan said decidedly, "I think all this talk of it is very dangerous. It puts ideas into people's heads."

Averil smiled.

They continued to talk in rather a desultory fashion. After dinner, Joan yawned, and Averil said she wouldn't stay and keep her up—she must be tired.

Joan said, Yes, she was rather tired.

On the following day Joan did a little shopping in the morning and caught the 2:30 train to Crayminster. That would get her there just after four o'clock. She would be waiting for Rodney when he came home at teatime from the office . . .

She looked out of the carriage window with appreciation. Nothing much in the way of scenery to see this time of year—bare trees, a faint misty rain falling—but how natural, how homelike. Baghdad with its crowded bazaars, its brilliant blue-domed and golden mosques, was far away—unreal—it might never have happened. That long fantastic journey, the plains of Anatolia, the snows and mountain scenery of the Taurus, the high bare plains—the long descent through mountain gorges to the Bosphorus, Stamboul with its minarets, the funny ox wagons of the Balkans—Italy with the blue Adriatic Sea glistening as they left Trieste—Switzerland and the Alps in the darkening light—a panorama of different sights and scenes—and all ending in this—this journey home through the quiet winter countryside. . . .

I might never have been away, thought Joan. *I might never have been away. . . .*

She felt confused, unable to coordinate her thoughts clearly. Seeing Averil last night had upset her—Averil's cool eyes looking at her, calm, incurious. *Averil*, she thought, *hadn't seen any difference in her*. Well, after all, why should Averil see a difference?

It wasn't her physical appearance that had changed.

She said very softly to herself, *"Rodney. . . ."*

The glow came back—the sorrow—the yearning for love and for-giveness. . . .

She thought, It's all true . . . I *am* beginning a new life. . . .

She took a taxi up from the station. Agnes opened the door and displayed a flattering surprise and pleasure.

The Master, Agnes said, *would* be pleased.

Joan went up to her bedroom, took off her hat, and came down again. The room looked a little bare, but that was because it had no flowers in it.

I must cut some laurel tomorrow, she thought, and get some carnations from the shop at the corner.

She walked about the room feeling nervous and excited.

Should she tell Rodney what she had guessed about Barbara? Supposing that, after all—

Of course it wasn't true! She had *imagined* the whole thing. Imagined it all because of what that stupid woman Blanche Haggard—no, Blanche Donovan—had said. Really, Blanche had looked too terrible—so old and coarse.

Joan put her hand to her head. She felt as though, within her brain, was a kaleidoscope. She had had a kaleidoscope as a child and loved it, had held her breath as all the colored pieces whirled and revolved, before settling down into a pattern. . . .

What *had* been the matter with her?

That horrible Rest House place and that very odd experience she had had in the desert. . . . She had imagined all sorts of unpleasant things—that her children didn't like her—that Rodney had loved Leslie Sherston (of course he hadn't—what an idea! Poor Leslie). And she had even been regretful because she had persuaded Rodney out of that extraordinary fancy of his to take up farming. Really, she had been very sensible and far seeing. . . .

Oh dear, why was she so confused? All those things she had been thinking and believing—such unpleasant things. . . .

Were they actually true? Or weren't they? *She didn't want them to be true.*

She'd got to decide—she'd got to decide. . . .

What had she got to decide?

The sun—thought Joan—the sun was very hot. The sun does give you hallucinations. . . .

Running in the desert . . . falling on her hands and knees . . . praying. . . .

Was *that* real?

Or was *this*?

Madness—absolute madness the things she had been believing. How comfortable, how pleasant to come home to England and feel you had never been away. That everything was just the same as you had always thought it was. . . .

And of *course* everything was just the same.

A kaleidoscope whirling . . . whirling. . . .

Settling presently into one pattern or the other.

Rodney, forgive me—I didn't know. . . .

Rodney, here I am. I've come home!

Which pattern? *Which?* She'd got to choose.

She heard the sound of the front door opening—a sound she knew so well—so very well. . . .

Rodney was coming.

Which pattern? Which pattern? *Quick!*

The door opened. Rodney came in. He stopped, surprised.

Joan came quickly forward. She didn't look at once at his face. *Give him a moment,* she thought, *give him a moment. . . .*

Then she said gaily, *"Here I am, Rodney . . . I've come home. . . ."*

Epilogue

Rodney Scudamore sat in the small low-backed chair while his wife poured out tea, and clanked the teaspoons, and chattered brightly about how nice it was to be home again and how delightful it was to find everything exactly the same and that Rodney wouldn't believe how wonderful it was to be back in England again, and back in Crayminster, and back in her own home!

On the windowpane a big bluebottle, deceived by the unusual warmth of the early November day, buzzed importantly up and down the glass.

Buzz, buzz, buzz, went the bluebottle.

Tinkle, tinkle, tinkle went Joan Scudamore's voice.

Rodney sat smiling and nodding his head.

Noises, he thought, noises. . . .

Meaning everything to some people, and nothing at all to others.

He had been mistaken, he decided, in thinking that there was something wrong with Joan when she first arrived. There was nothing wrong with Joan. She was just the same as usual. Everything was just the same as usual.

Presently Joan went upstairs to see to her unpacking, and Rodney went across the hall to his study where he had brought some work home from the office.

But first he unlocked the small top right-hand drawer of his desk and took out Barbara's letter. It had come by Air Mail and had been sent off a few days before Joan's departure from Baghdad.

It was a long closely written written and he knew it now almost by heart. Nevertheless, he read it through again, dwelling a little on the last page.

—So now I have told you everything, darling Dads. I daresay you guessed most of it already. You needn't worry about me. I do realize just what a criminal wicked little fool I have been. Remember, Mother knows *nothing*. It wasn't too easy keeping it all from her, but Dr. McQueen played up like a trump and William was wonderful. I really don't know what I should have done without him—he was always there, ready to fend Mother off, if things got difficult. I felt pretty desperate when she wired she was coming out. I know you must have tried to stop her, darling, and that she just wouldn't be stopped—and *I* suppose it was really rather sweet of her in a way—only of course she *had* to rearrange our whole lives for us and it was simply maddening, and I felt too weak to struggle much! I'm only just beginning to feel that Mopsy is my own again! She *is* sweet. I wish you could see her. Did you like us when we were babies, or only later? Darling Dads, I'm so glad I had you for a father. Don't worry about me. I'm all right now.

Your loving Babs

Rodney hesitated a moment, holding the letter. He would have liked to have kept it. It meant a great deal to him—that written declaration of his daughter's faith and trust in him.

But in the exercise of his profession he had seen, only too often, the dangers of kept letters. If he were to die suddenly Joan would go through his papers and come across it, and it would cause her needless pain. No need for her to be hurt and dismayed. Let her remain happy and secure in the bright confident world that she had made for herself.

He went across the room and dropped Barbara's letter into the fire. Yes, he thought, she would be all right now. They would all be all right. It was for Barbara he had feared most—with her unbalanced deeply emotional temperament. Well, the crisis had come and she had escaped, not unscathed, but alive. And already she was realizing that Mopsy and Bill were truly her world. A good fellow, Bill Wray. Rodney hoped that he hadn't suffered too much.

Yes, Barbara would be all right. And Tony was all right in his orange groves in Rhodesia—a long way away, but all right—and that young wife of his sounded the right kind of girl. Nothing had ever hurt Tony much—perhaps it never would. He had that sunny type of mind.

And Averil was all right too. As always, when he thought of Averil, it was pride he felt, not pity. Averil with her dry legal mind, and her passion for understatement. Averil, with her cool sarcastic tongue. So rock-like, so staunch, so strangely unlike the name they had given her.

He had fought Averil, fought her and vanquished her with the only weapons her disdainful mind would recognize, weapons that he himself had found it distasteful to use. Cold reasons, logical reasons, pitiless reasons—she had accepted those.

But had she forgiven him? He thought not. But it didn't matter. If he had destroyed her love for him, he had retained and enhanced her respect—and in the end, he thought, to a mind like hers and to her flawless rectitude, it is respect that counts.

On the eve of her wedding day, speaking to his best-loved child across the great gulf that now separated them, he had said:

"I hope you will be happy."

And she had answered quietly, "I shall try to be happy."

That was Averil—no heroics—no dwelling on the past—no self-pity. A disciplined acceptance of life—and the ability to live it without help from others.

He thought, They're out of my hands now, the three of them

Rodney pushed back the papers on his desk and came over to sit in the chair on the right of the fireplace. He took with him the Massingham lease and sighing slightly started to read it over.

"The Landlord lets and the tenant take all that farm-house buildings lands and hereditaments situate at. . . ." He read on and turned the page, "not to take more than two white straw crops of corn from any part of the arable lands without a summer fallow (a crop of turnips and rape sown on land well cleaned and manured and eaten on such land with sheep to be considered equivalent to a fallow) and. . . ."

His hand relaxed and his eyes wandered to the empty chair opposite.

That was where Leslie had sat when he argued with her about the children and the undesirability of their coming in contact with Sherston. She ought, he had said, to consider the children.

She *had* considered them, she said—and after all, he *was* their father.

A father who had been in prison, he said—an ex-jailbird—public opinion—ostracism—cutting them off from their normal social existence—penalizing them unfairly. She ought, he said, to think of all that. Children, he said, should not have their youth clouded. They should start fair.

And she had said, "That's just it. He *is* their father. It isn't so much that *they* belong to *him* as that *he* belongs to *them*. I can wish, of course, that they'd had a different kind of father—but it isn't so."

And she had said, "What kind of a start in life would it be—to begin by running away from what's there?"

Well, he saw her idea, of course. But it didn't agree with his ideas. He'd always wanted to give his children the best of things—indeed, that was what he and Joan had done. The best schools, the sunniest rooms in the house—they'd practiced small economies themselves to make that possible.

But in their case there had never been any moral problem. There had been no disgrace, no dark shadow, no failure, despair and anguish, no question of that kind when it would have been necessary to say, "Shall we shield them? Or let them share?"

And it was Leslie's idea, he saw, that they should share. She, although she loved them, would not shrink from placing a portion of her burden on those small untrained backs. Not selfishly, not to ease her own load, but because she did not want to deny them even the smallest, most unendurable part of reality.

Well, he thought that she was wrong. But he admitted, as he had always admitted, her courage. It went beyond courage for herself. She had courage for those she loved.

He remembered Joan saying that Autumn day as he went to the office: "Courage? Oh, yes, but courage isn't everything."

And he had said, "Isn't it?"

Leslie sitting there in his chair, with her left eyebrow going slightly up and her right eyebrow down and with the little twist at the right-hand corner of her mouth and her head against the faded blue cushion that made her hair look—somehow—green.

He remembered his voice, slightly surprised, saying:

"Your hair's not brown. It's *green*."

It was the only personal thing he'd ever said to her. He'd never thought, very much, what she looked like. Tired, he knew, and ill—and yet, withal, *strong*—yes, physically strong. He had thought once, incongruously, She could sling a sack of potatoes over her shoulder just like a man.

Not a very romantic thought and there wasn't, really, anything very romantic that he could remember about her. The right shoulder higher than the left, the left eyebrow growing up and the right down, the little twist at the corner of her mouth when she smiled, the brown hair that looked green against a faded blue cushion.

Not much, he thought, for love to feed on. And what was love? In Heaven's name, what *was* love? The peace and content that he'd felt to see her sitting there, in his chair, her head green against the blue cushion. The way she had said suddenly, "You know, I've been thinking about Copernicus—"

Copernicus? Why in Heaven's name, Copernicus? A monk with an idea—with a vision of a differently shaped world—and who was cunning and adroit enough to compromise with the powers of the world and to write his faith in such a form as would pass muster.

Why should Leslie, with her husband in prison, and her living to earn and her children to worry about, sit there running a hand through her hair and say, "I've been thinking about Copernicus."

Yet because of that, for always, at the mention of Copernicus his own heart would miss a beat, and up there, on the wall, he had hung an old engraving of the monk, to say to him, *"Leslie."*

He thought, I should at least have told her that I loved her. I might have said so—once.

But had there been any need? That day on Asheldown—sitting there in the October sunlight. He and she together—together and apart. The agony and the desperate longing. Four feet of space between them—four feet because there couldn't safely be less. She had understood that.

She must have understood that. He thought confusedly, That space between us—like an electric field—charged with longing.

They had not looked at each other. He had looked down over the
ploughland and the farm, with the distant faint sound of the tractor and
the pale purple of the upturned earth. And Leslie had looked beyond
the farmland to the woods.

Like two people gazing at a Promised Land to which they could not
enter in. He thought, I should have told her that I loved her then.

But neither of them had said anything—except just that once when
Leslie had murmured, *"And thy eternal summer shall not fade."*

Just that. One hackneyed line of quotation. And he didn't even know
what she had meant by it.

Or perhaps he did. Yes, perhaps he did.

The chair cushion had faded. And Leslie's face. He couldn't remember her face clearly, only that queer twist of the mouth.

And yet for the last six weeks she had sat there every day and talked
to him. Just fantasy, of course. He had invented a pseudo Leslie, and
put her there in the chair, and put words into her mouth. He had made
her say what he wanted her to say, and she had been obedient, but her
mouth had curved upwards at the side as though she had laughed at
what he was doing to her.

It had been, he thought, a very happy six weeks. He'd been able to
see Watkins and Mills and there had been that jolly evening with Hargrave Taylor—just a few friends and not too many of them. That pleasant
tramp across the hills on Sunday. The servants had given him very good
meals and he'd eaten them as slowly as he liked, with a book propped
up against the soda water syphon. Some work to finish sometimes after
dinner, and then a pipe and finally, just in case he might feel lonely,
false Leslie arranged in her chair to keep him company.

False Leslie, yes, but hadn't there been, somewhere, not very far away,
real Leslie?

And thy eternal summer shall not fade.

He looked down again at the lease.

> "... and shall in all respects cultivate the said farm in due
> and regular course of good husbandry."

He thought wonderingly, I'm really quite a good lawyer.

And then, without wonder (and without much interest), *"I'm successful."*

Farming, he thought, was a difficult heartbreaking business.

"My God, though," he thought, "I'm tired."

He hadn't felt so tired for a long time.

The door opened and Joan came in.

"Oh, Rodney—you can't read that without the light on."

She rustled across behind him and turned the light on. He smiled and thanked her.

"You're so stupid, darling, to sit here ruining your eyes when all you've got to do is just to turn a switch."

She added affectionately as she sat down, "I don't know what you'd do without me."

"Get into all sort of bad habits."

His smile was teasing, kindly.

"Do you remember," Joan went on, "when you suddenly got an idea you wanted to turn down Uncle Henry's offer and take up farming instead?"

"Yes, I remember."

"Aren't you glad now I wouldn't let you?"

He looked at her, admiring her eager competence, the youthful poise of her neck, her smooth pretty unlined face. Cheerful, confident, affectionate. He thought, Joan's been a very good wife to me.

He said quietly, "Yes, I'm glad."

Joan said, "We all get impractical ideas sometimes."

"Even you?"

He said it teasingly, but was surprised to see her frown. An expression passed over her face like a ripple across smooth water.

"One gets nervy sometimes—morbid."

He was still more surprised. He could not imagine Joan nervy or morbid. Changing the subject he said:

"You know I quite envy you your journey out East."

"Yes, it was interesting. But I shouldn't like to have to live in a place like Baghdad."

Rodney said thoughtfully, "I'd like to know what the desert is like. It must be rather wonderful—emptiness and a clear strong light. It's the idea of the light that fascinates me. To see clearly—"

Joan interrupted him. She said vehemently, "It's hateful—hateful—just arid nothingness!"

She looked round the room with a sharp nervous glance. Rather, he thought, like an animal that wants to escape.

Her brow cleared. She said, "That cushion's dreadfully old and faded. I must get a new one for that chair."

He made a sharp instinctive gesture, then checked himself.

After all, why not? A cushion was faded. Leslie Adeline Sherston was in the churchyard under a marble slab. The firm of Alderman, Scudamore and Witney was forging ahead. Farmer Hoddesdon was trying to raise another mortgage.

Joan was walking round the room, testing a ledge for dust, replacing a book in the bookshelf, moving the ornaments on the mantelpiece. It was true that in the last six weeks the room had acquired an untidy shabby appearance.

Rodney murmured to himself softly, "The holidays are over."

"What?" she whirled round on him. "What did you say?"

He blinked at her disarmingly. "Did I say anything?"

"I thought you said 'the holidays are over.' You must have dropped off and been dreaming—about the children going back to school."

"Yes," said Rodney, "I must have been dreaming."

She stood looking at him doubtfully. Then she straightened a picture on the wall.

"What's this? It's new, isn't it?"

"Yes. I picked it up at Hartley's sale."

"Oh," Joan eyed it doubtfully. "Copernicus? Is it valuable?"

"I've no idea," said Rodney. He repeated thoughtfully, "I've no idea at all. . . ."

What was valuable, what was not? Was there such a thing as remembrance?

"You know, I've been thinking about Copernicus. . . ."

Leslie, with her shifty jailbird of a husband—drunkenness, poverty, illness, death.

"Poor Mrs. Sherston, such a sad life."

But, he thought, Leslie wasn't sad. She walked through disillusion-ment and poverty and illness like a man walks through bogs and over plough and across rivers, cheerfully and impatiently, to get to wherever it is he is going. . . .

He looked thoughtfully at his wife out of tired but kindly eyes.

So bright and efficient and busy, so pleased and successful. He thought, She doesn't look a day over twenty-eight.

And suddenly a vast upwelling rush of pity swept over him.

He said with intense feeling, "Poor little Joan."

She stared at him. She said, "Why poor? And I'm not little."

He said in his old teasing voice, *"Here am I, little jumping Joan. If nobody's with me I'm all alone."*

She came to him with a sudden rush, almost breathlessly, she said: "I'm not alone. I'm not alone. I've got *you*."

"Yes," said Rodney. "You've got me."

But he knew as he said it that it wasn't true. He thought:

You are alone and you always will be. But, please God, you'll never know it.

· GIANT'S BREAD ·

Prologue

It was the opening night of London's new National Opera House and consequently an occasion. Royalty was there. The Press were there. The fashionable were there in large quantities. Even the musical, by hook and by crook, had managed to be there—mostly very high up in the final tier of seats under the roof.

The musical composition given was *The Giant*, a new work by a hitherto unknown composer, Boris Groen. In the interval after the first part of the performance a listener might have collected the following scraps of conversation:

"Quite divine, darling." "They say it's simply the—the—*the* latest!! Everything out of tune on purpose . . . and you have to read Einstein in order to understand it. . . ." "Yes, dear, I shall tell everyone it's too marvelous. But, privately, it does make one's head ache!"

"Why can't they open a British opera house with a decent British composer? All this Russian tomfoolery!" Thus a peppery colonel.

"Quite so," drawled his companion. "But, you see, there are no British composers. Sad, but there it is!"

"Nonsense—don't tell me, sir. They just won't give them a chance—that's what it is. Who is this fellow Levinne? A dirty foreign Jew. That's all he is!"

A man nearby, leaning against the wall half concealed by a curtain, permitted himself to smile—for he was Sebastian Levinne, sole owner of the National Opera House, familiarly known by the title of the World's Greatest Showman.

He was a big man, rather too well covered with flesh. His face was yellow and impassive, his eyes beady and black, two enormous ears stood out from his head and were the joy of caricaturists.

The surge of talk eddied past him.

"Decadent . . . morbid . . . neurotic . . . childish . . ."

Those were critics.

"Devastating . . . too divine . . . marvelous, my dear . . ."

Those were women.

"The thing's nothing but a glorified revue." "Amazing effects in the second part, I believe. Machinery, you know. This first part, 'Stone,' is only a kind of introduction. They say old Levinne has simply gone all out over this. Never been anything like it." "Music's pretty weird, isn't it?" "Bolshy idea, I believe. Noise orchestras, don't they call them?"

Those were young men, more intelligent than the women, less prejudiced than the critics.

"It won't catch on. A stunt, thath all. Yet, I don't know—there's a feeling for this cubist thtuff." "Levinne's shrewd." "Dropths money deliberately thometimes—but getth it back." "Cost . . . ?" The voices dropped, hushed themselves mysteriously as sums of money were mentioned.

Those were members of his own race. Sebastian Levinne smiled.

A bell rang—slowly the crowd drifted and eddied back to their seats.

There was a wait, filled with chattering and laughter—then the lights wavered and sank. The conductor mounted to his place. In front of him was an orchestra just six times as large as any Covent Garden orchestra and quite unlike an ordinary orchestra. There were strange instruments in it of shining metal like misshapen monsters, and in one corner an unaccustomed glitter of crystal. The conductor's baton was stretched out, then fell, and immediately there was a low rhythmic beating as of hammers on anvils. Every now and then a beat was missed—lost—and then came floating back taking its place out of turn, jostling the others.

The curtain rose. . . .

At the back of a box on the second tier Sebastian Levinne stood and watched.

This was no opera, as commonly understood. It told no story, featured no individuals. Rather was it on the scale of a gigantic Russian ballet. It contained spectacular effects, strange and weird effects of lighting—effects that were Levinne's own inventions. His revues had for long been proclaimed as the last word in sheer spectacular sensation. Into this, more artist than producer, he had put the whole force of his imagination and experience.

The prologue had represented Stone—Man's infancy.

This—the body of the work—was a supreme pageant of machinery—fantastic, almost awful. Power houses, dynamos, factory chimneys, cranes, all merging and flowing. And men—armies of men—with cubist robot faces—defiling in patterns.

The music swelled and eddied—a deep sonorous clamor came from the new strangely shaped metal instruments. A queer high sweet note sounded above it all, like the ringing of innumerable glasses.

There was an Episode of Skyscrapers—New York seen upside down as from a circling airplane in the early dawn of morning. And the strange inharmonious rhythm beat ever more insistently, with increasing menacing monotony. It drew on through other episodes to its climax: a giant-seeming steel erection—thousands of steel-faced men welded together into a Giant Collective Man.

The Epilogue followed immediately. There was no interval, the lights did not go up.

Only one side of the orchestra spoke. What was called in the new modern phrase "the Glass."

Clarion ringing notes.

The curtain dissolved into mist ... the mist parted ... the sudden glare made one wish to shield one's eyes.

Ice—nothing but ice ... great bergs and glaciers ... shining.

And on the top immense pinnacle a little figure—facing away from the audience toward the insufferable glare that represented the rising of the sun ...

The ridiculous puny figure of a man.

The glare increased—to the whiteness of magnesium. Hands went instinctively to eyes with a cry of pain.

The glass rang out—high and sweet—then crashed—and broke—literally broke—into tinkling fragments.

The curtain dropped and the lights rose.

Sebastian Levinne with an impassive face received various congratulations and side hits.

"Well, you've done it this time, Levinne. No half measures, eh?"

"A damned fine show, old man. Blessed if I know what it's all about, though."

"The Giant, eh? That's true, we live in an age of machinery all right."

"Oh! Mr. Levinne, it's simply too frightening for words! I shall dream of that horrid steel Giant."

"Machinery as the Giant that devours, eh? Not far wrong, Levinne. We want to get back to Nature. Who's Groen? A Russian?"

"Yes, who's Groen? He's a genius, whoever he is. The Bolshevists can boast they've produced one composer at last."

"Too bad, Levinne, you've gone Bolshy. Collective Man. Collective Music, too."

"Well, Levinne, good luck to you. Can't say I like this damned caterwauling they call music nowadays, but it's a good show."

Almost last came a little old man, slightly bent, with one shoulder higher than the other. He said with a very distinct utterance:

"Like to give me a drink, Sebastian?"

Levinne nodded. This little old man was Carl Bowerman, the most distinguished of English musical critics. They went together to Levinne's own sanctum.

In Levinne's room they settled down in two armchairs. Levinne provided his guest with a whisky and soda. Then he looked across at him inquiringly. He was anxious for this man's verdict.

"Well?"

Bowerman did not reply for a minute or two. At last he said slowly:

"I am an old man. There are things in which I take pleasure; there are other things—such as the music of today—which do not give me pleasure. But all the same I know genius when I meet it. There are a hundred charlatans—a hundred breakers down of tradition who think that by doing so they have accomplished something wonderful. And there is the hundred and first—a creator, a man who steps boldly into the future."

He paused, then went on:

"Yes, I know genius when I meet it. I may not like it—but I recognize it. Groen, whoever he is, has genius. . . . *The music of tomorrow* . . ."

Again he paused, and again Levinne did not interrupt, but waited.

"I don't know whether your venture will succeed or fail. I think succeed—but that will be mainly because of your personality. You have the art of forcing the public to accept what you want them to accept. You have a talent for success. You've made a mystery about Groen—part of your press campaign, I suppose."

He looked at Sebastian keenly.

"I don't want to interfere with your press campaign, but tell me one thing—Groen's an Englishman, isn't he?"

"Yes. How did you know, Bowerman?"

"Nationality in music is unmistakable. He has studied in the Russian revolutionary school, yes—but—well, as I said nationality is unmistakable. There have been pioneers before him—people who have tried tentatively the things he has accomplished. We've had our English school— Holst, Vaughan Williams, Arnold Bax. All over the world musicians have been drawing nearer to the new ideal—the Absolute in Music. This man is the direct successor of that boy who was killed in the war. What was his name? Deyre—Vernon Deyre. He had promise." He sighed. "I wonder, Levinne, how much we lost through the war."

"It's difficult to say, sir."

"It doesn't bear thinking of. No, it doesn't bear thinking of." He rose. "I mustn't keep you. You've a lot to do, I know." A faint smile showed on his face. "*The Giant!* You and Groen have your little joke all to yourselves, I fancy. Everyone takes it for granted the Giant is the Moloch of Machinery. They don't see that the real Giant is that pygmy figure—man. The individualist who endures through Stone and Iron and who, though civilization crumble and die, fights his way through yet another Glacial Age to rise in a new civilization of which we do not dream."

His smile broadened.

"As I grow older I am more and more convinced that there is nothing so pathetic, so ridiculous, so absurd, and so absolutely wonderful as Man."

He paused by the doorway, his hand on the knob.

"One wonders," he said, "what has gone to the making of a thing like the Giant? What produces it? What feeds it? Heredity shapes the instrument—environment polishes and rounds it off—sex wakens it. . . . But there's more than that. There's its food.

> *"Fee, fie, fo, fum,*
> *I smell the blood of mortal Man.*
> *Be he alive or be he dead,*
> *I'll grind his bones to make my bread."*

A cruel giant, genius, Levinne! A monster feeding on flesh and blood. I know nothing about Groen, yet I'd swear that he's fed his Giant with his own flesh and blood and perhaps the flesh and blood of others too. . . . Their bones ground to make the Giant's bread. . . .

"I'm an old man, Levinne. I have my fancies. We've seen the end tonight—I'd like to know the beginning."

"Heredity—environment—sex," said Levinne slowly.

"Yes. Just that. Not that I have any hopes of your telling me."

"You think I—know?"

"I'm sure you know."

There was a silence.

"Yes," said Levinne at last, "I do know. I would tell you the whole story if I could . . . but I cannot. There are reasons."

He repeated slowly: "There are reasons."

"A pity. It would have been interesting."

"I wonder . . ."

BOOK ONE

ABBOTS PUISSANTS

Chapter One

There were only three people of real importance in Vernon's world: Nurse, God, and Mr. Green.

There were, of course, the nursemaids. Winnie, the present one, and behind her Jane and Annie and Sarah and Gladys. Those were all the ones that Vernon could remember, but there were lots more. Nursery maids never stayed long because they couldn't get on with Nurse. They hardly counted in Vernon's world.

There was also a kind of twin deity called Mummy-Daddy mentioned by Vernon in his prayers and also connected with going down to dessert. They were shadowy figures, rather beautiful and wonderful—especially Mummy—but they again did not belong to the real world—Vernon's world.

The things in Vernon's world were very real indeed. There was the drugget on the nursery floor, for instance. It was of green and white stripes and rather scrubbly to bare knees, and in one corner of it was a hole which Vernon used surreptitiously to make bigger by working his fingers round in it. There were the nursery walls where mauve irises twined themselves interminably upward round a pattern that was sometimes diamonds and sometimes, if you looked at it long enough, crosses. That seemed very interesting to Vernon and rather magical.

There was a rocking horse against one wall, but Vernon seldom rode on it. There was a basketwork engine and some basketwork trucks

which he played with a good deal. There was a low cupboard full of
more or less dilapidated toys. On an upper shelf were the more delec-
table contents that you played with on a wet day or when Nurse was in
an unusually good temper. The Paint Box was there and the Real Camel
Hair Brushes and a heap of illustrated papers for Cutting Out. In fact,
all the things that Nurse said were "that messy she couldn't abear them
about." In other words, the best things.

And in the center of this realistic nursery universe, dominating everything, was Nurse herself. Person No. I of Vernon's Trinity. Very big and
broad, very starched and crackling. Omniscient and omnipotent. You
couldn't get the better of Nurse. She knew better than little boys. She
frequently said so. Her whole lifetime had been spent looking after little
boys (and incidentally little girls, too, but Vernon was not interested in
them) and one and all they had grown up to be a Credit to her. She
said so and Vernon believed her. He had no doubt that he also would
grow up to be a Credit to her, though sometimes it didn't seem likely.
There was something awe-inspiring about Nurse, but at the same time
infinitely comfortable. She knew the answer to everything. For instance,
Vernon propounded the riddle about the diamonds and the crosses on
the wallpaper.

"Ah! well," said Nurse, "there's two ways of looking at everything.
You must have heard that."

And as Vernon had heard her say much the same to Winnie one day,
he was soothed and satisfied. On the occasion in question Nurse had
gone on to say that there were always two sides to a question and in
future Vernon always visualized a question as something like a letter A
with crosses creeping up one side of it and diamonds going down the
other.

After Nurse, there was God. God was also very real to Vernon, mainly
because he bulked so largely in Nurse's conversation. Nurse knew most
things that you did, but God knew *everything*, and God was, if anything,
more particular than Nurse. You couldn't see God, which, Vernon always felt, gave him rather an unfair advantage over you, because he could
see you. Even in the dark he could see you. Sometimes, when Vernon
was in bed at night, the thought of God looking down at him through
the darkness used to give him a creepy feeling down the spine.

But on the whole, God was an intangible person compared with Nurse. You could conveniently forget about him most of the time. That was, until Nurse lugged him deliberately into the conversation.

Once Vernon essayed revolt.

"Nurse, do you know what I shall do when I'm dead?"

Nurse, who was knitting stockings, said: "One, two, three, four—there now, I've dropped a stitch. No, Master Vernon, I'm sure I don't."

"I shall go to Heaven—I shall go to Heaven—and I shall go right up to God—right up to him I shall go, and I shall say: 'You're an 'orrible man and I 'ate you!' "

Silence. It was done. He had said it. Unbelievable, unparalleled audacity! What would happen? What awful punishment terrestrial or celestial would descend upon him? He waited—breathless.

Nurse had picked up the stitch. She looked at Vernon over the top of her spectacles. She was serene—unruffled.

"It's not likely," she remarked, "that the Almighty will take any notice of what a naughty little boy says. Winnie, give me those scissors, if you please."

Vernon retired crestfallen. It was no good. You couldn't down Nurse. He might have known.

2

And then there was Mr. Green. Mr. Green was like God in that you couldn't see him, but to Vernon he was very real. He knew, for instance, exactly what Mr. Green looked like—of middle height, rather stout, a faint resemblance to the village grocer who sang an uncertain baritone in the village choir, bright red cheeks and muttonchop whiskers. His eyes were blue, a very bright blue. The great thing about Mr. Green was that he played—he loved playing. Whatever game Vernon thought of, that was just the game that Mr. Green loved to play. There were other points about him. He had, for instance, a hundred children. And three others. The hundred, in Vernon's mind, were kept intact, a joyous mob that raced down the yew alleys behind Vernon and Mr. Green. But the three others were different. They were called by the three most beautiful names that Vernon knew: Poodle, Squirrel and Tree.

Vernon was, perhaps, a lonely little boy, but he never knew it. Because, you see, he had Mr. Green and Poodle, Squirrel, and Tree to play with.

3

For a long time Vernon was undecided as to where Mr. Green's home was. It came to him quite suddenly that of course Mr. Green lived in the Forest. The Forest had always been fascinating to Vernon. One side of the Park bordered on it. There were high green palings and Vernon used to creep along them hoping for a crack that would let him see through. There were whisperings and sighings and rustlings all along, as though the trees were speaking to each other. Halfway down there was a door, but alas, it was always locked, so that Vernon could never see what it was really like inside the Forest.

Nurse, of course, would never take him there. She was like all nurses and preferred a good steady walk along the road, and no messing your feet up with them nasty damp leaves. So Vernon was never allowed to go in the Forest. It made him think of it all the more. Some day he would take tea there with Mr. Green. Poodle and Squirrel and Tree were to have new suits for the occasion.

4

The nursery palled on Vernon. It was too small. He knew all there was to know about it. The garden was different. It was really a very exciting garden. There were so many different bits of it. The long walks between the clipped yew hedges with their ornamental birds, the water garden with the fat goldfish, the walled fruit garden, the wild garden with its almond trees in springtime and the copse of silver birch trees with bluebells growing underneath, and best of all the railed-off bit where the ruins of the old Abbey were. That was the place where Vernon would have liked to be left to his own devices—to climb and explore. But he never was. The rest of the garden he did much as he liked in. Winnie was always sent out with him, but since by a remarkable coincidence they always seemed to encounter the second gardener, he could play his own games unhindered by too much kind attention on Winnie's part.

5

Gradually Vernon's world widened. The twin star, Mummy-Daddy, separated, became two distinct people. Daddy remained nebulous, but Mummy became quite a personage. She often paid visits to the nursery to "play with my darling little boy." Vernon bore her visits with grave politeness, though it usually meant giving up the game that he himself was engaged upon and accepting one which was not, in his opinion, nearly so good. Lady visitors would sometimes come with her, and then she would squeeze Vernon tightly (which he hated) and cry.

"It's so wonderful to be a mother! I never get used to it! To have a darling baby boy of one's very own!"

Very red, Vernon would extricate himself from her embrace. Because he wasn't a baby boy at all. He was three years old.

Looking across the room one day, just after a scene like the above, he saw his father standing by the nursery door with sardonic eyes, watching him. Their eyes met. Something seemed to pass between them: comprehension—a sense of kinship.

His mother's friends were talking.

"Such a pity, Myra, that he doesn't take after you. Your hair would be too lovely on a child."

But Vernon had a sudden feeling of pride. He was like his father.

6

Vernon always remembered the day that the American lady came to lunch. To begin with, because of Nurse's explanations about America which, as he realized later, she confused with Australia.

He went down to dessert in an awe-stricken state. If this lady had been at home in her own country she would be walking about upside down with her head hanging down. Quite enough, this, to make him stare. And then, too, she used odd words for the simplest things.

"Isn't he too cute? See here, honey, I've gotten a box of candy for you. Won't you come and fetch it?"

Vernon came gingerly; accepted the present. The lady clearly didn't know what she was talking about. It wasn't candy, but good Edinburgh Rock.

There were two gentlemen there also, one the husband of the American lady. This one said:

"Do you know half a crown, my boy, when you see it?"

And it presently turned out that the half crown was to be for his very own keep. Altogether it was a wonderful day.

Vernon had never thought very much about his home. He knew that it was bigger than the Vicarage where he sometimes went to tea, but he seldom played with any other children or went to their homes. So it came to him with a shock of wonder that day. The visitors were taken all over the house, and the American lady's voice rose ceaselessly.

"My, if that isn't too wonderful! Did you ever see such a thing? Five hundred years, you say? Frank, listen to that. Henry the Eighth—if it isn't just like listening to English history. And the Abbey older still, you say?"

They went everywhere, through the long picture gallery where faces strangely like Vernon's, with dark eyes set close together and narrow heads, looked out from the painted canvas arrogantly or with cold tolerance. There were meek women there in ruffs or with pearls twisted in their hair—the Deyre women had done best to be meek, married to wild lords who knew neither fear nor pity—who looked appraisingly at Myra Deyre, the last of their number, as she walked beneath them. From the picture gallery they went to the square hall, and from there to the Priest's Chamber.

Vernon had been removed by Nurse long since. They found him again in the garden feeding the goldfish. Vernon's father had gone into the house to get the keys of the Abbey ruins. The visitors were alone.

"My Frank," said the American lady, "isn't it *too* wonderful? All these years. Handed down from father to son. Romantic, that's what I call it, just too romantic for anything. All these years. Just fancy! How is it done?"

It was then that the other gentleman spoke. He was not much of a

talker, so far Vernon had not heard him speak at all. But he now un-
closed his lips and uttered one word—a word so enchanting, so mysterious, so delightful that Vernon never forgot it.

"Brumagem," said the other gentleman.

And before Vernon could ask him (as he meant to do) what that
marvelous word meant, another diversion occurred.

His mother came out of the house. There was a sunset behind her—a
scene painter's sunset of crude gold and red. Against that background
Vernon saw his mother—saw her for the first time—a magnificent
woman with white skin and red-gold hair—a being like the pictures in
his fairy book; saw her suddenly as something wonderful, wonderful and
beautiful.

He was never to forget that strange moment. She was his mother and
she was beautiful and he loved her. Something hurt him inside, like a
pain—only it wasn't a pain. And there was a queer booming noise inside
his head—a thundering noise that ended up high and sweet like a bird's
note. Altogether a very wonderful moment.

And mixed up with it was that magic word *Brumagem*.

Chapter Two

Winnie the nursemaid was going away. It all happened very suddenly. The other servants whispered together. Winnie cried. She
cried and cried. Nurse gave her what she called a Talking To and after
that Winnie cried more than ever. There was something terrible about
Nurse; she seemed larger than usual and she crackled more. Winnie,
Vernon knew, was going away because of Father. He accepted that fact
without any particular interest or curiosity. Nursemaids did sometimes
go away because of Father.

His mother was shut in her room. She too was crying. Vernon could
hear her through the door. She did not send for him and it did not occur
to him to go to her. Indeed he was vaguely relieved. He hated the noise
of crying, the gulping sound, the long-drawn sniffs, and it always hap-

pened so close to your ears. People who were crying always hugged you. Vernon hated those kinds of noises close to his ears. There was nothing in the world he hated more than the wrong sort of noise. It made you feel all curled up like a leaf in your middle. That was the jolly part about Mr. Green. He never made the wrong kind of noise.

Winnie was packing her boxes. Nurse was in with her—a less awful Nurse now—almost a human Nurse.

"Now you let this be a warning to you, my girl," said Nurse. "No carryings-on in your next place."

Winnie sniffed something about no real harm.

"And no more there wouldn't be, I should hope, with Me in charge," said Nurse. "A lot comes, I dare say, of having red hair. Red-haired girls are always flighty, so my dear mother used to say. I'm not saying you're a bad girl. But what you've done is Unbecoming. Unbecoming—I can't say more than that."

And, as Vernon had often noticed after using this particular phrase, she proceeded to say a good deal more. But he did not listen, for he was pondering on the word "unbecoming." Becoming, he knew, was a thing you said about a hat. Where did a hat come in?

"What's unbecoming, Nurse?" he asked later in the day.

Nurse with her mouth full of pins, for she was cutting out a linen suit for Vernon, replied:

"Unsuitable."

"What's unsuitable?"

"Little boys going on asking foolish questions," said Nurse with the deftness of a long professional career behind her.

2

That afternoon Vernon's father came into the nursery. There was a queer furtive look about him—unhappy and defiant. He winced slightly before Vernon's round interested gaze.

"Hullo, Vernon."

"Hullo, Father."

"I'm going to London. Good-bye, old chap."

"Are you going to London because you kissed Winnie?" inquired Vernon with interest.

His father uttered the kind of word that Vernon knew he was not suppose to hear—much less ever repeat. It was, he knew, a word that gentlemen used but little boys didn't. So great a fascination did that fact lend it that Vernon was in the habit of sending himself to sleep by repeating it over to himself in company with another forbidden word. The other word was Corsets.

"Who the devil told you that?"

"Nobody told me," said Vernon, after reflecting a minute.

"Then how did you know?"

"Didn't you, then?" inquired Vernon.

His father crossed the room without answering.

"Winnie kisses me sometimes," remarked Vernon. "But I don't like it much. I have to kiss her, too. The gardener kisses her a lot. He seems to like it. I think kissing's silly. Should I like kissing Winnie better if I was grown up, Father?"

"Yes," his father said deliberately, "I think you would. Sons, you know, sometimes grow up very like their fathers."

"I'd like to be like you," said Vernon. "You're a jolly good rider. Sam said so. He said there wasn't your equal in the county and that a better judge of horse flesh never lived." Vernon brought out the latter words rapidly. "I'd rather be like you than Mummy. Mummy gives a horse a sore back. Sam said so."

There was a further pause.

"Mummy's gotaheadacheanlyingdown," proceeded Vernon.

"I know."

"Have you said good-bye to her?"

"No."

"Are you going to? Because you'll have to be quick. That's the dog-cart coming round now."

"I expect I shan't have time."

Vernon nodded wisely.

"I dare say that would be a good plan. I don't like having to kiss people when they're crying. I don't like Mummy kissing me much anyway. She squeezes too hard and she talks in your ear. I think I'd almost rather kiss Winnie. Which would you, Father?"

He was disconcerted by his father's abrupt withdrawal from the room. Nurse had come in a moment before. She stood respectfully aside to let the Master pass, and Vernon had a vague idea that she had managed to make his father uncomfortable.

Katie, the under-housemaid, came in to lay tea. Vernon built bricks in the corner. The old peaceful nursery atmosphere closed round him again.

3

There was a sudden interruption. His mother stood in the doorway. Her eyes were swollen with crying. She dabbed them with a handkerchief. She stood there theatrically miserable.

"He's gone," she cried. "Without a word to me. Without a word. Oh! my little son. My little son."

She swept across the floor and gathered Vernon in her arms. The tower, at least one story higher than any he had ever built before, crashed into ruins. His mother's voice, loud and distraught, burrowed into his ear.

"My child—my little son—swear that you'll never forsake me. Swear it—swear it."

Nurse came across to them.

"There, ma'am, there, ma'am, don't take on so. You'd better get back to bed. Edith shall bring you a nice cup of hot tea."

Her tone was authoritative—severe.

His mother still sobbed and clasped him closer. Vernon's whole body began to stiffen in resistance. He could bear it a little while longer—a very little while longer—and he'd do anything Mummy wanted if only she'd let go of him.

"You must make up to me, Vernon—make up to me for the suffering your father has caused me. Oh! my God, what shall I do?"

Somewhere, in the back of his mind, Vernon was aware of Katie, silent, ecstatic, enjoying the scene.

"Come along, ma'am," said Nurse. "You'll only upset the child."

The authority in her voice was so marked this time that Vernon's mother succumbed to it. Leaning weakly on Nurse's arm, she allowed herself to be led from the room.

Nurse returned a few minutes later very red in the face.

"My," said Katie, "didn't she take on? Regular hysterics—that's what they call it! Well, this has been a to-do! You don't think she'll do a mischief to herself, do you? Those nasty ponds in the garden. The Master is a one—not that he hasn't a lot to put up with from Her. All them scenes and tantrums——"

"That'll do, my girl," said Nurse. "You can get back to your work, and under-servants discussing a matter of this kind with their betters is a thing that I've never known take place in a gentleman's house. Your mother ought to have trained you better."

With a toss of her head, Katie withdrew. Nurse moved round the nursery table, shifting cups and plates with unwonted sharpness. Her lips moved, muttering to herself.

"Putting ideas into the child's head. I've no patience with it. . . ."

Chapter Three

A new nursemaid came, a thin white girl with protruding eyes. Her name was Isabel, but she was called Susan as being More Suitable. This puzzled Vernon very much. He asked Nurse for an explanation.

"There are names that are suitable to the gentry, Master Vernon, and names that are suitable for servants. That's all there is to it."

"Then why is her real name Isabel?"

"There are people who when they christen their children set themselves up to ape their betters."

The word "ape" had a distracting influence on Vernon. Apes were monkeys. Did people christen their children at the Zoo?

"I thought people were christened in church."

"So they are, Master Vernon."

Very puzzling. Why was everything so puzzling? Why were things more puzzling than they used to be? Why did one person tell you one thing and another person something quite different?

"Nurse, how do babies come?"

"You've asked me that before, Master Vernon. The little angels bring them in the night through the window."

"That Am-am-am—"

"Don't stammer, Master Vernon."

"Amenkun lady who came—she said I was found under a gooseberry bush."

"That's the way they do with American babies," said Nurse serenely.

Vernon heaved a sigh of relief. Of course! He felt a throb of gratitude to Nurse. She always knew. She made the unsteady swaying universe stand still again. And she never laughed. His mother did. He had heard her say to other ladies: "He asks me the quaintest questions. Just listen to this. . . . Aren't children funny and adorable."

But Vernon couldn't see that he was funny or adorable at all. He just wanted to know. You'd got to *know*. That was part of growing up. When you were grown up you knew everything and had gold sovereigns in your purse.

2

The world went on widening.

There were, for instance, uncles and aunts.

Uncle Sydney was Mummy's brother. He was short and stout and had rather a red face. He had a habit of humming tunes and of rattling the money in his trouser pockets. He was fond of making jokes, but Vernon did not always think his jokes very funny.

"Supposing," Uncle Sydney would say, "I were to put on your hat. Hey? What should I look like, do you think?"

Curious, the questions grown-up people asked! Curious—and also difficult, because if there was one thing that Nurse was always impressing upon Vernon, it was that little boys must never make personal remarks.

"Come now," said Uncle Sydney perseveringly. "What should I look like? There—" he snatched up the linen affair in question and balanced it on top of his head—"what do I look like, eh?"

Well, if one must answer, one must. Vernon said politely and a little wearily:

"I think you look rather silly."

"That boy of yours has no sense of humor, Myra," said Uncle Sydney to his mother. "No sense of humor at all. A pity."

Aunt Nina, Father's sister, was quite different.

She smelt nice, like the garden on a summer's day, and she had a soft voice that Vernon liked. She had other virtues—she didn't kiss you when you didn't want to be kissed, and she didn't insist on making jokes. But she didn't come very often to Abbots Puissants.

She must be, Vernon thought, very brave, because it was she who first made him realize that one could master the Beast.

The Beast lived in the big drawing room. It had four legs and a shiny brown body. And it had a long row of what Vernon had thought, when he was very small, to be teeth. Great yellow shining teeth. From his earliest memory Vernon had been fascinated and terrified by the Beast. For if you irritated the Beast it made strange noises, an angry growling or a shrill angry wail—and somehow those noises hurt you more than anything in the world could. They hurt you right down in your inside. They made you shiver and feel sick, and they made your eyes sting and burn, and yet by some strange enchantment you couldn't go away.

When Vernon had stories read to him about dragons he always thought of them as like the Beast. And some of the best games with Mr. Green were where they killed the Beast—Vernon plunging a sword into his brown shining body whilst the hundred children whooped and sang behind.

Now that he was a big boy he knew better, of course. He knew that the Beast's name was Grand Piano, and that when you deliberately attacked its teeth, that was called "playingtherpiano"! and that ladies did it after dinner to gentlemen. But in his inmost heart he was still afraid and dreamed sometimes of the Beast pursuing him up the nursery stairs—and he would wake up screaming.

In his dreams the Beast lived in the Forest, and was wild and savage, and the noises it made were too terrible to be borne.

Mummy sometimes did "playingtherpiano," and that Vernon could just bear with difficulty. The Beast, he felt, would not really be waked up by what she was doing to it. But the day Aunt Nina played was different.

Vernon had been conducting one of his imaginary games in a corner. He and Squirrel and Poodle were having a picnic and eating lobsters and chocolate eclairs.

His Aunt Nina had not even noticed that he was in the room. She had sat down on the music stool and was playing idly.

Fascinated, Vernon crept nearer and nearer. Nina looked up at last to see him staring at her, the tears running down his face and great sobs shaking his small body. She stopped.

"What's the matter, Vernon?"

"I 'ate it," sobbed Vernon. "I 'ate it. I 'ate it. It hurts me *here*." His hands clasped his stomach.

Myra came into the room at that minute. She laughed.

"Isn't it odd? That child simply hates music. So very queer."

"Why doesn't he go away if he hates it?" said Nina.

"I can't," sobbed Vernon.

"Isn't it ridiculous?" said Myra.

"I think it's rather interesting."

"Most children are always wanting to strum on the piano. I tried to show Vernon chopsticks the other day, but he wasn't a bit amused."

Nina remained staring at her small nephew thoughtfully.

"I can hardly believe a child of mine can be unmusical," said Myra in an aggrieved voice. "I played quite difficult pieces when I was eight years old."

"Oh! well," said Nina vaguely. "There are different ways of being musical."

Which, Myra thought, was so like the silly sort of thing the Deyre family would say. Either one was musical and played pieces, or one was not. Vernon clearly was not.

3

Nurse's mother was ill. Strange unparalleled nursery catastrophe. Nurse, very red-faced and grim, was packing with the assistance of Susan Isabel. Vernon, troubled, sympathetic, but above all interested, stood nearby, and out of his interest asked questions.

"Is your mother very old, Nurse? Is she a hundred?"

"Of course not, Master Vernon! A hundred indeed!"

"Do you think she is going to die?" continued Vernon, longing to be kind and understand.

Cook's mother had been ill and died. Nurse did not answer. Instead she said sharply:

"The boot bags out of the bottom drawer, Susan. Step lively now, my girl."

"Nurse, will your mother—"

"I haven't time to be answering questions, Master Vernon."

Vernon sat down on the corner of a chintz-covered ottoman and gave himself up to reflection. Nurse had said that her mother wasn't a hundred, but she must, for all that, be very old. Nurse herself he had always regarded as terribly old. To think that there was a being of superior age and wisdom to Nurse was positively staggering. In a strange way it reduced Nurse herself to the proportions of a mere human being. She was no longer a figure secondary only to God himself.

The universe shifted—values were readjusted. Nurse, God, and Mr. Green—all three receded, becoming vaguer and more blurred. Mummy, his father, even Aunt Nina—they seemed to matter more. Especially Mummy. Mummy was like the princesses with long beautiful golden hair. He would like to fight a dragon for Mummy—a brown shiny dragon like the Beast.

What was the word—the magic word? Brumagem—that was it—Brumagem. An enchanting word! The Princess Brumagem! A word to be repeated over to himself softly and secretly at night at the same time as Damn and Corsets.

But never, never, never must Mummy hear it, because he knew only too well that she would laugh—she always laughed, the kind of laugh that made you shrivel up inside and want to wriggle. And she would say things—she always said things, just the kind of things you hated. "Aren't children too *funny?*"

And Vernon knew that he wasn't funny. He didn't like funny things— Uncle Sydney had said so. If only Mummy wouldn't . . .

Sitting on the slippery chintz he frowned perplexedly. He had a sud-

den imperfect glimpse of two Mummies. One, the princess, the beautiful
Mummy that he dreamed about, who was mixed up for him with sunsets
and magic and killing dragons—and the other, the one who laughed and
who said, "Aren't children too *funny?*" Only, of course, they were the
same. . . .

He fidgeted and sighed. Nurse, flushed from the effort of snapping
to her trunk, turned to him kindly.

"What's the matter, Master Vernon?"

"Nothing," said Vernon.

You must always say, "Nothing." You could never tell. Because, if
you did, no one ever knew what you meant. . . .

4

Under the reign of Susan Isabel the nursery was quite different. You
could be, and quite frequently were, naughty. Susan told you not to do
things and you did them just the same! Susan would say: "I'll tell your
mother." But she never did.

Susan had at first enjoyed the position and authority she had in
Nurse's absence. Indeed, but for Vernon, she would have continued to
enjoy it. She used to exchange confidences with Katie, the under-
housemaid.

"Don't know what's come over him, I'm sure. He's like a little demon
sometimes. And him so good and well behaved with Mrs. Pascal."

To which Kate replied:

"Ah! she's a oner, she is! Takes you up sharp, doesn't she?"

And then they would whisper and giggle.

"Who's Mrs. Pascal?" Vernon asked one day.

"Well, I never, Master Vernon! Don't you know your own nurse's
name?"

So Nurse was Mrs. Pascal. Another shock. She had always been just
Nurse. It was rather as though you had been told that God's name was
Mr. Robinson.

Mrs. Pascal! Nurse! The more you thought of it, the more extraordinary it seemed. Mrs. Pascal—just like Mummy was Mrs. Deyre and

Father was Mr. Deyre. Strangely enough, Vernon never cogitated on the possibility of a Mr. Pascal. (Not that there was any such person. The Mrs. was a tacit recognition of Nurse's position and authority.) Nurse stood alone in the same magnificence as Mr. Green, who in spite of the hundred children (and Poodle, Squirrel, and Tree) was never thought of by Vernon as having a Mrs. Green attached to him!

Vernon's inquiring mind wandered in another direction.

"Susan, do you like being called Susan? Wouldn't you like being called Isabel better?"

Susan (or Isabel) gave her customary giggle.

"It doesn't matter what I like, Master Vernon."

"Why not?"

"People have got to do what they're told in this world."

Vernon was silent. He had thought the same until a few days ago. But he was beginning to perceive that it was not true. You needn't do as you were told. It all depended on who told you.

It was not a question of punishment. He was continually being sat on chairs, stood in the corner, and deprived of sweets by Susan. Nurse, on the other hand, had only to look at him severely through her spectacles with a certain expression on her face, and anything but immediate capitulation was out of the question.

Susan had no authority in her nature, and Vernon knew it. He had discovered the thrill of successful disobedience. Also, he liked tormenting Susan. The more worried and flustered and unhappy Susan got, the more Vernon liked it. He was, as was proper to his years, still in the Stone Age. He savoured the full pleasure of cruelty.

Susan formed the habit of letting Vernon go out to play in the garden alone. Being an unattractive girl, she had not Winnie's reasons for liking the garden. And besides, what harm could possibly come to him?

"You won't go near the ponds, will you, Master Vernon?"

"No," said Vernon, instantly forming the intention to do so.

"You'll play with your hoop like a good boy?"

"Yes."

The nursery was left in peace. Susan heaved a sigh of relief. She took from a drawer a paper-covered book entitled *The Duke and the Dairymaid*.

Beating his hoop, Vernon made the tour of the walled fruit garden. Escaping from his control, the hoop leaped upon a small patch of earth which was at the moment receiving the meticulous attentions of Hopkins, the head gardener. Hopkins firmly and authoritatively ordered Vernon from the spot, and Vernon went. He respected Hopkins.

Abandoning the hoop, Vernon climbed a tree or two. That is to say, he reached a height of perhaps six feet from the ground, employing all due precautions. Tiring of this perilous sport, he sat astride a branch and cogitated as to what to do next.

On the whole, he thought the ponds. Susan having forbidden them, they had a distinct fascination. Yes, he would go to the ponds. He rose, and as he did so another idea came into his head, suggested by an unusual sight.

The door into the Forest was open!

5

Such a thing had never happened before in Vernon's experience. Again and again he had secretly tried that door. Always it was locked.

He crept up to it cautiously. The Forest! It stood a few steps away outside the door. You could plunge straightway into its cool green depths. Vernon's heart beat faster.

He had always wanted to go into the Forest. Here was his chance. Once Nurse came back, any such thing would be out of the question.

And still he hesitated. It was not any feeling of disobedience that held him back. Strictly speaking, he had never been forbidden to go into the Forest. His childish cunning was all ready with that excuse.

No, it was something else. Fear of the unknown—of those dark leafy depths. Ancestral memories held him back.

He wanted to go—but he didn't want to go. There might be Things there—Things like the Beast. Things that came up behind you—that chased you screaming. . . .

He moved uneasily from one foot to the other.

But Things didn't chase you in the daytime. And Mr. Green lived in the Forest. Not that Mr. Green was as real as he used to be. Still, it would be rather jolly to explore and find a place where you would pretend Mr. Green did live. Poodle, Squirrel, and Tree would each have a house of his own—small leafy houses.

"Come on, Poodle," said Vernon to an invisible companion. "Have you got your bow and arrow? That's right. We'll meet Squirrel inside."

He stepped out jauntily. Beside him, plain to Vernon's inner eye, went Poodle dressed like the picture of Robinson Crusoe in his picture book.

It was wonderful in the Forest—dim and dark and green. Birds sang and flew from branch to branch. Vernon continued to talk to his friend—a luxury he did not dare to permit himself often, since someone might overhear and say, "Isn't he too *funny?* He's pretending he's got another little boy with him." You had to be so very careful at home.

"We'll get to the Castle by lunchtime, Poodle. There are going to be roasted leopards. Oh! Hullo, here's Squirrel. How are you, Squirrel? Where's Tree?

"I tell you what. I think it's rather tiring walking. I think we'll ride."

Steeds were tethered to an adjacent tree. Vernon's was milk white, Poodle's was coal black—the color of Squirrel's he couldn't quite decide.

They galloped forward through the trees. There were deadly dangerous places, morasses. Snakes hissed at them and lions charged them. But the faithful steeds did all their riders required of them.

How silly it was playing in the garden—or playing anywhere but *here!* He'd forgotten what it was like, playing with Mr. Green and Poodle, Squirrel, and Tree. How could you help forgetting things when people were always reminding you that you were a funny little boy playing make-believe?

On strutted Vernon, now capering, now marching with solemn dignity. He was great, he was wonderful! What he needed, though he did not know it himself, was a tom-tom to beat whilst he sang his own praises.

The Forest! He had always known it would be like this, and it was! In front of him suddenly appeared a crumbling moss-covered wall. The wall of the Castle! Could anything be more perfect? He began to climb it.

The ascent was easy enough really, though fraught with the most agreeable and thrilling possibilities of danger. Whether this was Mr.

Green's Castle, or whether it was inhabited by an Ogre who ate human flesh, Vernon had not yet made up his mind. Either was an entrancing proposition. On the whole, he inclined to the latter, being at the moment in a warlike frame of mind. With a flushed face he reached the summit of the wall and looked over the other side.

And here there enters into the story, for one brief paragraph, Mrs. Somers West, who was fond of romantic solitude (for short periods) and had bought Woods Cottage as being "delightfully remote from anywhere and really, if you know what I mean, in the very heart of the Forest— at one with Nature!" And since Mrs. Somers West, as well as being artistic, was musical, she had pulled down a wall, making two rooms into one, and had thus provided herself with sufficient space to house a grand piano.

And at the identical moment that Vernon reached the top of the wall, several perspiring and staggering men were slowly propelling the aforesaid grand piano toward the window, since it wouldn't go in by the door. The garden of Woods Cottage was a mere tangle of undergrowth—wild Nature, as Mrs. Somers West called it. So that all Vernon saw was the Beast! The Beast, alive and purposeful, slowly crawling toward him, malign and vengeful. . . .

For a moment he stayed rooted to the spot. Then, with a wild cry, he fled. Fled along the top of the narrow crumbling wall. The Beast was behind him, pursuing him. . . . It was coming, he knew it. He ran—ran faster than ever. His foot caught in a tangle of ivy. He crashed downward—falling—falling . . .

Chapter Four

Vernon woke, after a long time, to find himself in bed. It was, of course, the natural place to be when you woke up, but what wasn't natural was to have a great hump sticking up in front of you in the bed. It was whilst he was staring at this that someone spoke to him. That someone was Dr. Coles, whom Vernon knew quite well.

"Well, well," said Dr. Coles, "and how are we feeling?"

Vernon didn't know how Dr. Coles was feeling. He himself was feeling rather sick and said so.

"I dare say, I dare say," said Dr. Coles.

"And I think I hurt somewhere," said Vernon. "I think I hurt very much."

"I dare say, I dare say," said Dr. Coles again—not very helpfully, Vernon thought.

"Perhaps I'd feel better if I got up," said Vernon. "Can I get up?"

"Not just now, I'm afraid," said the doctor. "You see, you've had a fall."

"Yes," said Vernon. "The Beast came after me."

"Eh? What's that? The Beast? What Beast?"

"Nothing," said Vernon.

"A dog, I expect," said the doctor. "Jumped at the wall and barked. You mustn't be afraid of dogs, my boy."

"I'm not," said Vernon.

"And what were you doing so far from home, eh? No business to be where you were."

"Nobody told me not to," said Vernon.

"Hum, hum, I wonder. Well, I'm afraid you've got to take your punishment. Do you know, you've broken your leg, my boy?"

"Have I?" Vernon was gratified—enchanted. He had broken his leg. He felt very important.

"Yes, you'll have to lie here for a bit, and then it will mean crutches for a while. Do you know what crutches are?"

Yes, Vernon knew. Mr. Jobber, the blacksmith's father, had crutches. And he was to have crutches! How wonderful.

"Can I try them now?"

Dr. Coles laughed.

"So you like the idea? No. I'm afraid you'll have to wait a bit. And you must try and be a brave boy, you know. And then you'll get well quicker."

"Thank you," said Vernon politely. "I don't think I do feel very well. Can you take this funny thing out of my bed? I think it would be more comfortable then."

But it seemed that the funny thing was called a cradle, and that it couldn't be taken away. And it seemed, too, that Vernon would not be able to move about in bed because his leg was all tied up to a long piece of wood. And suddenly it didn't seem a very nice thing to have a broken leg after all.

Vernon's underlip trembled a little. He was not going to cry—no, he was a big boy and big boys didn't cry. Nurse said so. And then he knew that he wanted Nurse—wanted her badly. He wanted her reassuring presence, her omniscience, her creaking rustling majesty.

"She'll be coming back soon," said Dr. Coles. "Yes, soon. In the meantime, this nurse is going to look after you—Nurse Frances."

Nurse Frances moved into Vernon's range of vision and Vernon studied her in silence. She too was starched and crackling; that was all to the good. But she wasn't big like Nurse. She was thinner than Mummy— as thin as Aunt Nina. He wasn't sure . . .

And then he met her eyes—steady eyes, more green than gray, and he felt, as most people felt, that with Nurse Frances things would be "all right."

She smiled at him—but not in the way that visitors smiled. It was a grave smile, friendly but reserved.

"I'm sorry you feel sick," she said. "Would you like some orange juice?"

Vernon considered the matter and said he thought he would. Dr. Coles went out of the room and Nurse Frances brought him the orange juice in a most curious-looking cup with a long spout. And it appeared that Vernon was to drink from the spout.

It made him laugh, but laughing hurt him, and so he stopped. Nurse Frances suggested he should go to sleep again, but he said he didn't want to go to sleep.

"Then I shouldn't go to sleep," said Nurse Frances. "I wonder if you can count how many irises there are on that wall? You start on the right side, and I'll start on the left side. You can count, can't you?"

Vernon said proudly that he could count up to a hundred.

"That is a lot," said Nurse Frances. "There aren't nearly as many irises as a hundred. I guess there are seventy-five. Now what do you guess?"

Vernon guessed that there were fifty. There couldn't, he felt sure, possibly be more than that. He began to count, but somehow, without knowing it, his eyelids closed and he slept. . . .

2

Noise . . . noise and pain. He woke with a start. He felt hot, very hot, and there was a pain all down one side. And the noise was coming nearer. It was the noise that one always connected with Mummy. . . .

She came into the room like a whirlwind, a kind of cloak affair she wore swinging out behind her. She was like a bird—a great big bird— and like a bird, she swooped down upon him.

"Vernon—my darling—Mummy's own darling! What have they done to you? How awful! How terrible! My child!"

She was crying. Vernon began to cry too. He was suddenly frightened. Myra was moaning and weeping.

"My little child. All I have in the world. God, don't take him from me. Don't take him from me! If he dies I shall die too!"

"Mrs. Deyre—"

"Vernon—Vernon—my baby—"

"Mrs. Deyre—please!"

There was crisp command in the voice rather than appeal.

"Please don't touch him. You will hurt him."

"Hurt him? I? His mother?"

"You don't seem to realize, Mrs. Deyre, that his leg is broken, I must ask you, please, to leave the room."

"You're hiding something from me. Tell me—tell me—will the leg have to be amputated?"

A wail came from Vernon. He had not the least idea what "amputated" meant, but it sounded painful—and more than painful, terrifying. His wail broke into a scream.

"He's dying!" cried Myra. "He's dying—and they won't tell me. But he shall die in my arms."

"Mrs. Deyre—"

Somehow Nurse Frances had got between his mother and the bed.

She was holding his mother by the shoulder. Her voice had the tone that Nurse's had had when speaking to Katie, the under-housemaid.

"Mrs. Deyre, listen to me. You must control yourself. You *must!*" Then she looked up. Vernon's father was standing in the doorway. "Mr. Deyre, please take your wife away. I cannot have my patient excited and upset."

His father nodded—a quiet understanding nod. He just looked at Vernon once and said: "Bad luck, old chap. I broke an arm once."

The world became suddenly less terrifying. Other people broke legs and arms. His father had hold of his mother's shoulder, he was leading her toward the door, speaking to her in a low voice. She was protesting, arguing, her voice high and shrill with emotion.

"How can you understand? You've never cared for the child like I have. It takes a mother. How can I leave my child to be looked after by a stranger? He needs his mother. . . . You don't understand. I *love* him. There's nothing like a mother's care—everyone says so."

"Vernon darling"—she broke from her husband's clasp, came back toward the bed—"you want me, don't you? You want Mummy?"

"I want Nurse," sobbed Vernon. "I want Nurse."

He meant his own Nurse, not Nurse Frances.

"Oh!" said Myra. She stood there quivering.

"Come, my dear," said Vernon's father gently. "Come away."

She leaned against him, and together they passed from the room. Faint words floated back into the room.

"My own child, to turn from me to a stranger."

Nurse Frances smoothed the sheet and suggested a drink of water.

"Nurse is coming back very soon," she said. "We'll write to her to-day, shall we? You shall tell me what to say."

A queer new feeling surged over Vernon—a sort of odd gratitude. Somebody had actually understood. . . .

3

When Vernon, later, was to look back upon his childhood, this one period was to stand out quite clearly from the rest. "The time I broke my leg" marked a distinct era.

He was to appreciate, too, various small incidents that were accepted by him at the time as a matter of course. For instance, a rather stormy interview that took place between Dr. Coles and his mother. Naturally this did not take place in Vernon's sick room, but Myra's raised voice penetrated closed doors. Vernon heard indignant exclamations of "I don't know what you mean by upsetting him. . . . I consider I ought to nurse my own child. . . . Naturally I was distressed—I'm not one of these people who simply have no heart—no heart at all. Look at Walter— never turned a hair!"

There were many skirmishes too, not to say pitched battles, fought between Myra and Nurse Frances. In these cases Nurse Frances always won, but at a certain cost. Myra Deyre was wildly and furiously jealous of what she called "the paid nurse." She was forced to submit to Dr. Coles's dictums, but she did so with a bad grace and with an overt rudeness that Nurse Frances never seemed to notice.

In after years Vernon remembered nothing of the pain and tedium that there must have been. He remembered only happy days of playing and talking as he had never played and talked before. For in Nurse Frances he found a grown-up who didn't think things "funny" or "quaint." Somebody who listened sensibly and who made serious and sensible suggestions. To Nurse Frances he was able to speak of Poodle, Squirrel, and Tree, and of Mr. Green and the hundred children. And instead of saying "What a *funny* game!" Nurse Frances merely inquired whether the hundred children were girls or boys—an aspect of the matter which Vernon had never thought of before. But he and Nurse Frances decided that there were fifty of each, which seemed a very fair arrangement.

If sometimes, off his guard, he played his make-believe games aloud, Nurse Frances never seemed to notice or to think it unusual. She had the same calm comfortableness of old Nurse about her, but she had something that mattered far more to Vernon: the gift of answering questions—and he knew, instinctively, that the answers were always true. Sometimes she would say, "I don't know that myself," or, "You must ask someone else. I'm not clever enough to tell you that." There was no pretense of omniscience about her.

Sometimes, after tea, she would tell Vernon stories. The stories were never the same two days running—one day they would be about naughty little boys and girls, and the next day they would be about enchanted princesses. Vernon liked the latter kind best. There was one in particular that he loved, about a princess in a tower with golden hair and a vagabond prince in a ragged green hat. The story ended up in a forest, and it was possibly for that reason that Vernon liked it so much.

Sometimes there would be an extra listener. Myra used to come in and be with Vernon during the early afternoon when Nurse Frances had her time off, but Vernon's father used sometimes to come in after tea when the stories were going on. Little by little it became a habit. Walter Deyre would sit in the shadows just behind Nurse Frances's chair, and from there he would watch, not his child, but the storyteller. One day Vernon saw his father's hand steal out and close gently over Nurse Frances's wrist.

And then something happened which surprised him very much. Nurse Frances got up from her chair.

"I'm afraid we must turn you out for this evening, Mr. Deyre," she said quietly. "Vernon and I have things to do."

This astonished Vernon very much, because he couldn't think what those things were. He was still more puzzled when his father got up also and said in a low voice:

"I beg your pardon."

Nurse Frances bent her head a little, but remained standing. Her eyes met Walter Deyre's steadily. He said quietly:

"Will you believe that I am really sorry, and let me come tomorrow?"

After that, in some way that Vernon could not have defined, his father's manner was different. He no longer sat so near Nurse Frances. He talked more to Vernon and occasionally they all three played a game—usually Old Maid, for which Vernon had a wild passion. They were happy evenings enjoyed by all three.

One day, when Nurse Frances was out of the room, Walter Deyre said abruptly:

"Do you like that nurse of yours, Vernon?"

"Nurse Frances? I like her lots. Don't you, Father?"

"Yes," said Walter Deyre, "I do."

There was a sadness in his voice which Vernon felt.

"Is anything the matter, Father?"

"Nothing that can be put right. The horse that gets left at the post never has much chance of making good—and the fact that it's the horse's own fault doesn't make matters any better. But that's double Dutch to you, old man. Anyway, enjoy your Nurse Frances while you've got her. There aren't many of her sort knocking about."

And then Nurse Frances came back and they played Animal Grab.

But Walter Deyre's words had set Vernon's mind to work. He tackled Nurse Frances next morning.

"Aren't you going to be here always?"

"No. Only till you get well—or nearly well."

"Won't you stay always? I'd like you to."

"But, you see, that's not my work. My work is to look after people who are ill."

"Do you like doing that?"

"Yes, very much."

"Why?"

"Well, you see, everyone has some particular kind of work that they like doing and that suits them."

"Mummy hasn't."

"Oh, yes, she has. Her work is to look after this big house and see that everything goes right, and to take care of you and your father."

"Father was a soldier once. He told me that if ever there was a war he'd go and be a soldier again."

"Are you very fond of your father, Vernon?"

"I love Mummy best, of course. Mummy says little boys always love their mothers best. I like *being* with Father, of course, but that's different. I expect it's because he's a man. What shall I be when I grow up, do you think? I want to be a sailor."

"Perhaps you'll write books."

"What about?"

Nurse Frances smiled a little.

"Perhaps about Mr. Green, and Poodle and Squirrel and Tree."

"But everyone would say that that was silly."

"Little boys wouldn't think so. And besides, when you grow up you will have different people in your head—like Mr. Green and the children, only grown-up people. And then you could write about them."

Vernon thought for a long time, then he shook his head.

"I think I'll be a soldier like Father. Most of the Deyres have been soldiers, Mummy says. Of course you have to be very brave to be a soldier, but I think I would be brave enough."

Nurse Frances was silent a moment. She was thinking of what Walter Deyre had said of his small son:

"He's a plucky little chap—absolutely fearless. Doesn't know what fear is! You should see him on his pony."

Yes, Vernon was fearless enough in one sense. He had the power of endurance, too. He had borne the pain and discomfort of his broken leg unusually well for so young a child.

But there was another kind of fear. She said slowly after a minute or two:

"Tell me again how you fell off the wall that day."

She knew all about the Beast, and had been careful to display no ridicule. She listened now to Vernon, and as he finished she said gently:

"But you've known for quite a long time, haven't you, that it isn't a real Beast? That it's only a thing made of wood and wires."

"I do *know*," said Vernon. "But I don't dream it like that. And when I saw it in the garden coming at me—"

"You ran away—which was rather a pity, wasn't it? It would have been much better to have stayed and *looked*. Then you'd have seen the men, and would have known just what it was. It's always a good thing to *look*. Then you can run away afterward if you still want to—but you usually don't. And Vernon, I'll tell you something else."

"Yes?"

"Things are never so frightening in front of you as they are behind you. Remember that. Anything seems frightening when it's behind your back and you can't see it. That's why it's always better to turn and face things—and then very often you find they are nothing at all."

Vernon said thoughtfully: "If I'd turned round I wouldn't have broken my leg, would I?"

"No."

Vernon sighed.

"I don't mind having broken my leg very much. It has been very nice having you to play with."

He thought Nurse Frances murmured "Poor child" under her breath, but that, of course, was absurd. She said smiling:

"I've enjoyed it too. Some of my ill people don't like to play."

"You really do like playing, don't you?" said Vernon. "So does Mr. Green."

He added rather stiffly, for he felt shy:

"Please don't go away very soon, will you?"

4

But as it happened, Nurse Frances went away much sooner than she might have done. It all happened very suddenly, as things in Vernon's experience always did.

It started very simply—something that Myra offered to do for Vernon and that he said he would rather have done by Nurse Frances.

He was on crutches now for a short and painful time every day, enjoying the novelty of it very much. He soon got tired, however, and was ready to go back to bed. Today his mother had suggested his doing so, saying she would help him. But Vernon had been helped by her before. Those big white hands of hers were strangely clumsy. They hurt where they meant to help. He shrank from her well-meant efforts. He said he would wait for Nurse Frances, who never hurt.

The words came out with the tactless honesty of children, and in a minute Myra Deyre was at white heat.

Nurse Frances came in two or three minutes later to be received with a flood of reproach.

Turning the boy against his own mother—cruel—wicked. They were all alike—everyone was against her. She had nothing in the world but Vernon and now he was being turned against her too.

So it went on—a ceaseless stream. Nurse Frances bore it patiently enough, without surprise or rancor. Mrs. Deyre, she knew, was that kind of woman. Scenes were a relief to her. And hard words, Nurse Frances reflected with grim humor, can only harm if the utterer is dear to you. She was sorry for Myra Deyre for she realized how much real unhappiness and misery lay behind these hysterical outbursts.

It was an unfortunate moment for Walter Deyre to choose to enter the nursery. For a moment or two he stood surprised, then he flushed angrily.

"Really, Myra, I'm ashamed of you. You don't know what you're saying."

She turned on him furiously.

"I know what I'm saying well enough. And I know what you've been doing. Slinking in here every day—I've seen you. Always making love to some woman or other. Nurse-maids, hospital nurses—it's all one to you."

"Myra—be quiet!"

He was really angry now. Myra Deyre felt a throb of fear. But she hurled her last piece of invective.

"You're all alike, you hospital nurses. Flirting with other women's husbands. You ought to be ashamed of yourself. Before the innocent child too—putting all sorts of things into his head. But you'll go out of my house. Yes, you'll go right out—and I shall tell Dr. Coles what I think of you."

"Would you mind continuing this edifying scene elsewhere?" Her husband's voice was as she hated it most—cold and sneering. "Hardly judicious in front of your innocent child, is it? I apologize, Nurse, for what my wife has been saying. Come, Myra."

She went—beginning to cry—weakly frightened at what she had done. As usual, she had said more than she meant.

"You're cruel," she sobbed. "Cruel. You'd like me to be dead. You hate me."

She followed him out of the room. Nurse Frances put Vernon to bed. He wanted to ask questions but she talked of a dog, a big St. Bernard that she had had when she was a little girl, and he was so much interested that he forgot everything else.

Much later that evening Vernon's father came to the nursery. He looked white and ill. Nurse Frances rose and came to where he stood in the doorway.

"I don't know what to say. How can I apologize—the things my wife said—"

Nurse Frances replied in a quiet matter-of-fact voice:

"Oh! it's quite all right. I understand. I think, though, that I had better go as soon as it can be arranged. My being here makes Mrs. Deyre unhappy, and then she works herself up."

"If she knew how wide of the mark her wild accusations are. That she should insult *you*—"

Nurse Frances laughed—not, perhaps, very convincingly.

"I always think it's absurd when people complain about being insulted," she said cheerfully. "Such a pompous word, isn't it? Please don't worry or think I mind. You know, Mr. Deyre, your wife is—"

"Yes?"

Her voice changed. It was grave and sad.

"A very unhappy and lonely woman."

"Do you think that is entirely my fault?"

There was a pause. She lifted her eyes—those steady green eyes.

"Yes," she said, "I do."

He drew a long breath.

"No one else but you would have said that to me. You—I suppose it's courage in you that I admire so much—your absolutely fearless honesty. I'm sorry for Vernon that he should lose you before he need."

She said gravely: "Don't blame yourself for things you needn't. This has not been your fault."

"Nurse Frances." It was Vernon, eagerly from bed. "I don't want you to go away. Don't go away, please—not tonight."

"Of course not," said Nurse Frances. "We've got to talk to Dr. Coles about it."

Nurse Frances left three days later. Vernon wept bitterly. He had lost the first real friend he had ever had.

Chapter Five

The years from five to nine remained somewhat dim in Vernon's memory. Things changed—but so gradually as not to matter. Nurse did not return to her reign over the nursery. Her mother had had a stroke and was quite helpless and she was obliged to remain and look after her.

Instead, a Miss Robbins was installed as nursery governess. A creature so extraordinarily colorless that Vernon could never afterward even recall what she looked like. He must have become somewhat out of hand under her regime for he was sent to school just after his eighth birthday. On his first holidays he found his cousin Josephine installed.

On her few visits to Abbots Puissants, Nina had never brought her small daughter with her. Indeed her visits had become rarer and rarer. Vernon, knowing things without thinking about them, as children do, was perfectly well aware of two facts. One, that his father did not like Uncle Sydney but was always exceedingly polite to him. Two, that his mother did not like Aunt Nina and did not mind showing it. Sometimes, when Nina was sitting talking to Walter in the garden, Myra would join them, and in the momentary pause that nearly always followed she would say:

"I suppose I'd better go away again. I see I'm in the way. No, thank you, Walter [this in answer to a protest, gently murmured], I can see plainly enough when I'm not wanted."

She would move away, biting her lip, nervously clasping and unclasping her hands, tears in her brown eyes. And, very quietly, Walter Deyre would raise his eyebrows.

One day Nina broke out: "She's impossible! I can't speak to you for ten minutes without an absurd scene. Walter, why did you do it? Why *did* you do it?"

Vernon remembered how his father had looked round, gazing up at the house, then letting his eyes sweep far afield to where the ruins of the old Abbey just showed.

"I cared for the place," he said slowly. "In the blood, I suppose. I didn't want to let it go."

There had been a brief silence and then Nina had laughed—a queer short laugh.

"We're not a very satisfactory family," she said. "We've made a pretty good mess of things, you and I."

There was another pause and then his father had said: "Is it as bad as that?"

Nina had drawn in her breath with a sharp hiss. She nodded.

"Pretty well. I don't think, Walter, that I can go on much longer. Fred hates the sight of me. Oh! we behave very prettily in public—no one would guess—but my God, when we're alone!"

"Yes, but my dear girl . . ."

And then, for a while, Vernon heard no more. Their voices were lowered, his father seemed to be arguing with his aunt. Finally his voice rose again.

"You can't take a mad step like that. It's not even as though you cared for Anstey. You don't."

"I suppose not—but he's crazy about me."

His father said something that sounded like Social Ostriches. Nina laughed again.

"That? We'd neither of us care."

"Anstey would in the end."

"Fred would divorce me—only too glad of the chance. Then we could marry."

"Even then—"

"Walter on the social conventions! It has its humorous side!"

"Women and men are very different," said Vernon's father dryly.

"Oh! I know—I know. But anything's better than this everlasting misery. Of course, at the bottom of it all is that I still care for Fred—I always did. And he never cared for me."

"There's the kid," said Walter Deyre. "You can't go off and leave her?"

"Can't I? I'm not much of a mother, you know. As a matter of fact, I'd take her with me. Fred wouldn't care. He hates her as much as he hates me."

There was another pause, a long one this time. Then Nina said slowly:

"What a ghastly tangle human beings can get themselves into. And in your case and mine, Walter, it's all our own fault. We're a nice family! We bring bad luck to ourselves and to anyone we have anything to do with."

Walter Deyre got up. He filled a pipe abstractedly, then moved slowly away. For the first time Nina noticed Vernon.

"Hullo, child," she said. "I didn't see you were there. How much did you understand of all that, I wonder?"

"I don't know," said Vernon vaguely, shifting from foot to foot.

Nina opened a chain bag, took out a tortoise-shell case, and extracted a cigarette which she proceeded to light. Vernon watched her, fascinated. He had never seen a woman smoke.

"What's the matter?" said Nina.

"Mummy says," said Vernon, "that no nice woman would ever smoke. She said so to Miss Robbins."

"Oh! well," said Nina. She puffed out a cloud of smoke. "I expect she was quite right. I'm not a nice woman, you see, Vernon."

Vernon looked at her, vaguely distressed.

"I think you're very pretty," he said rather shyly.

"That's not the same thing." Nina's smile widened. "Come here, Vernon."

He came obediently. Nina put her hands on his shoulders and looked him over quizzically. He submitted patiently. He never minded being touched by Aunt Nina. Her hands were light—not clutching like his mother's.

"Yes," said Nina, "you're a Deyre—very much so. Rough luck on Myra, but there it is."

"What does that mean?" said Vernon.

"It means that you're like your father's family and not like your mother's—worse luck for you."

"Why worse luck for me?"

"Because the Deyres, Vernon, are neither happy nor successful. And they can't make good."

What funny things Aunt Nina said! She said them half laughingly, so perhaps she didn't mean them. And yet, somehow, there was something in them that, though he didn't understand, made him afraid.

"Would it be better," he said suddenly, "to be like Uncle Sydney?"

"Much better. Much much better."

Vernon considered.

"But then," he said slowly, "if I was like Uncle Sydney—"

He stopped, trying to get his thoughts into words.

"Yes, well?"

"If I was Uncle Sydney I should have to live at Larch Hurst—and not here."

Larch Hurst was a stoutly built red brick villa near Birmingham where Vernon had once been taken to stay with Uncle Sydney and Aunt Carrie. It had three acres of superb pleasure grounds, a rose garden, a pergola, a goldfish tank, and two excellently fitted bathrooms.

"And wouldn't you like that?" asked Nina, still watching him.

"No!" said Vernon. A great sigh broke from him, heaving his small chest. "I want to live *here*—always, always, always!"

2

Soon after this something queer happened about Aunt Nina. His mother began to speak of her and his father managed to hush her down with a sideways glance at himself. He carried away only a couple of phrases: "It's that poor child I'm so sorry for. You've only got to look at Nina to see she's a Bad Lot and always will be."

The poor child, Vernon knew, was his cousin Josephine, whom he had never seen, but to whom he sent presents at Christmas and duly received others in return. He wondered why Josephine was "poor" and why his mother was sorry for her, and also why Aunt Nina was a Bad Lot—whatever that meant. He asked Miss Robbins, who got very pink and told him he mustn't talk about "things like that." Things like that? Vernon wondered.

However, he didn't think much more about it till four months later, when the matter was mentioned once more. This time no one noticed Vernon's presence—feelings were running too high for that. His mother and father were in the middle of a vehement discussion. His mother, as usual, was vociferous, excited. His father was very quiet.

"Disgraceful!" Myra was saying. "Within three months of running away with one man to go off with another. It shows her up in her true light. I always knew what she was like. Men, men, men, nothing but men!"

"You're welcome to any opinion you choose, Myra. That's not the point. I knew perfectly how it would strike you."

"And anyone else too, I should think! I can't understand you, Walter. You call yourself an old family and all that—"

"We are an old family," he put in quietly.

"I should have thought you'd have minded a bit about the honor of your name. She's disgraced it—and if you were a real man you'd cast her off utterly as she deserves."

"Traditional scene from the melodrama, in fact."

"You always sneer and laugh! Morals mean nothing to you—absolutely nothing."

"At the minute, as I've been trying to make you understand, it's not a question of morals. It's a question of my sister being destitute. I must go out to Monte Carlo and see what can be done. I should have thought anyone in their senses would see that."

"Thank you. You're not very polite, are you? And whose fault is it she's destitute, I should like to know? She had a good husband—"

"No—not that."

"At any rate, he married her."

It was his father who flushed this time. He said, in a very low voice:

"I can't understand you, Myra. You're a good woman—a kind honorable upright woman—and yet you can demean yourself to make a nasty mean taunt like that."

"That's right! Abuse me! I'm used to it! You don't mind what you say to me."

"That's not true. I try to be as courteous as I can."

"Yes. And that's partly why I hate you—you never do say right out.

Always polite and sneering—your tongue in your cheek. All this keeping up appearances—why should one, I should like to know? Why should I care if everyone in the house knows what I feel?"

"I've no doubt they do—thanks to the carrying power of your voice."

"There you are—sneering again. At any rate I've enjoyed telling you what I think of your precious sister. Running away with one man, going off with a second—and why can't the second man keep her, I should like to know? Or is he tired of her already?"

"I've already told you, but you didn't listen. He's threatened with galloping consumption—has had to throw up his job. He's no private means."

"Ah! Nina brought her pigs to a bad market that time."

"There's one thing about Nina—she's never been actuated by motives of gain. She's a fool, a damned fool, or she wouldn't have got herself into this mess. But it's always her affections that run away with her common sense. It's the deuce of a tangle. She won't touch a penny from Fred. Anstey wants to make her an allowance—she won't hear of it. And, mind you, I agree with her. There are things one can't do. But I've certainly got to go and see to things. I'm sorry if it annoys you, but there it is."

"You never do anything I want! You hate me! You do this on purpose to make me miserable. But there's one thing. You don't bring this precious sister of yours under this roof while I'm here. I'm not accustomed to meeting that kind of woman. You understand?"

"You make your meaning almost offensively clear."

"If you bring her here, I go back to Birmingham."

There was a faint flicker in Walter Deyre's eyes, and suddenly Vernon realized something that his mother did not. He had understood very little of the actual words of the conversation though he had grasped the essentials. Aunt Nina was ill or unhappy somewhere and Mummy was angry about it. She had said that if Aunt Nina came to Abbots Puissants she would go back to Uncle Sydney at Birmingham. She had meant that as a threat—but Vernon knew that his father would be very pleased if she did go back to Birmingham. He knew it quite certainly and uncomprehendingly. It was like some of Miss Robbins's punishments, like not speaking for half an hour. She thought you minded that as much as not having jam for tea, and fortunately she had never discovered that you didn't really mind it at all—in fact rather enjoyed it.

Walter Deyre walked up and down the room. Vernon watched him, puzzled. That his father was fighting out a battle in his own mind, he knew. But he couldn't understand what it was all about.

"Well?" said Myra.

She was rather beautiful just at that moment—a great big woman, magnificently proportioned, her head thrown back and the sunlight streaming in on her golden-red hair. A fit mate for some Viking seafarer.

"I made you the mistress of this house, Myra," said Walter Deyre. "If you object to my sister coming to it, naturally she will not come."

He moved toward the door. There he paused and looked back at her. "If Llewellyn dies—which seems almost certain—Nina must try to get some kind of a job. Then there will be the child to think of. Do your objections apply to her?"

"Do you think I want a girl in my home who will turn out like her mother?"

His father said quietly: "Yes or No would have been quite sufficient answer."

He went out. Myra stood staring after him. Tears stood in her eyes and began to fall. Vernon did not like tears. He edged toward the door—but not in time.

"Darling, come to me."

He had to come. He was enfolded—hugged. Fragments of phrases reiterated in his ears:

"You'll make up to me—you, my own boy. You shan't be like them—horrid, sneering. You won't fail me—you'll never fail me—will you? Swear it—my boy, my own boy!"

He knew it all so well. He said what was wanted of him—Yes and No in the right places. How he hated the whole business! It always happened so close to your ears.

That evening after tea Myra was in quite another mood. She was writing a letter at her writing table and looked up gaily as Vernon entered.

"I'm writing to Daddy. Perhaps, very soon, your Aunt Nina and your cousin Josephine will come to stay. Won't that be lovely?"

But they didn't come. Myra said to herself that really Walter was incomprehensible. Just because she'd said a few things she really didn't mean. . . .

Vernon was not very surprised, somehow. He hadn't thought they would come.

Aunt Nina had said she wasn't a nice woman—but she was very pretty.

Chapter Six

If Vernon had been capable of summing up the events of the next few years, he could best have done it in one word—scenes! Everlasting and ever-recurring scenes.

And he began to notice a curious phenomenon. After each scene his mother looked larger and his father looked smaller. Emotional storms of reproach and invective exhilarated Myra mentally and physically. She emerged from them refreshed, soothed—full of good will toward all the world.

With Walter Deyre it was the opposite. He withdrew into himself, every sensitive fiber in his nature shrinking from the onslaught. The faint polite sarcasm that was his weapon of defense never failed to goad his wife to the utmost fury. His quiet weary self-control exasperated her as nothing else could have done.

Not that she was lacking for very real grounds of complaint. Walter Deyre spent less and less time at Abbots Puissants. When he did return his eyes had baggy pouches under them and his hand shook. He took little notice of Vernon, and yet the child was always conscious of an underlying sympathy. It was tacitly understood that Walter should not "interfere" with the child. A mother was the person who should have the say. Apart from supervising the boy's riding, Walter stood aside. Not to do so would have roused fresh matter for discussion and reproach. He was ready to admit that Myra had all the virtues and was a most careful and attentive mother.

And yet he sometimes had the feeling that he could give the boy something that she could not. The trouble was that they were both shy of each other. To neither of them was it easy to express his feelings—a thing Myra would have found incomprehensible. They remained gravely polite to each other.

But when a scene was in progress Vernon was full of silent sympathy. He knew exactly how his father was feeling—knew how that loud angry voice hurt the ears and the head. He knew, of course, that Mummy must be right—Mummy was always right, that was an article of belief not to be questioned—but all the same, he was unconsciously on his father's side.

Things went from bad to worse—came to a crisis. Mummy remained locked in her room for two days—servants whispered delightedly in corners—and Uncle Sydney arrived on the scene to see what he could do.

Uncle Sydney undoubtedly had a soothing influence over Myra. He walked up and down the room, jingling his money as of old, and looking stouter and more rubicund than ever.

Myra poured out her woes.

"Yes, yes, I know," said Uncle Sydney, jingling hard. "I know, my dear girl. I'm not saying you haven't had a lot to put up with. You have. Nobody knows that better than I do. But there's give and take, you know. Give and take. That's married life in a nutshell—give and take."

There was a fresh outburst from Myra.

"I'm not sticking up for Deyre," said Uncle Sydney. "Not at all. I'm just looking at the whole thing as a man of the world. Women lead sheltered lives and they don't look at these things as men do—quite right that they shouldn't. You're a good woman, Myra, and it's always hard for a good woman to understand these things. Carrie's just the same."

"What has Carrie got to put up with, I should like to know?" cried Myra. "*You* don't go off racketing round with disgusting women. *You* don't make love to the servants."

"N-no," said her brother. "No, of course not. It's the principle of the thing I'm talking about. And mind you, Carrie and I don't see eye to eye over everything. We have our tiffs—why, sometimes we don't speak to each other for two days on end. But bless you, we make it up again,

and things go on better than before. A good row clears the air—that's
what I say. But there must be give and take. And no nagging afterward.
The best man in the world won't stand nagging."

"I never nag," said Myra tearfully, and believed it. "How can you say
such a thing?"

"Now don't get the wind up, old girl. I'm not saying you do. I'm just
laying down general principles. And remember, Deyre's not our sort.
He's kittle cattle—the touchy sensitive kind. A mere trifle sets them off."

"Don't I know it?" said Myra bitterly. "He's impossible. Why did I
ever marry him?"

"Well, you know, Sis, you can't have it both ways. It was a good
match. I'm bound to admit it was a good match. Here you are, living in
a swell place, knowing all the county, as good as anybody short of royalty. My word, if poor old Dad had lived, how proud he'd have been!
And what I'm getting at is this—everything's got its seamy side. You
can't have the halfpence without one or two of the kicks as well. They're
decadent, these old families, that's what they are—decadent, and you've
just got to face the fact. You've just got to sum up the situation in a
businesslike way—advantages, so and so; disadvantages, ditto. It's the
only way. Take my word for it, it's the only way."

"I didn't marry him for the sake of 'advantages,' as you call it," said
Myra. "I hate this place. I always have. It's because of Abbots Puissants
he married me—not for myself."

"Nonsense, Sis, you were a jolly pretty girl—and still are," he added
gallantly.

"Walter married me for the sake of Abbots Puissants," said Myra
obstinately. "I tell you I know it."

"Well, well," said her brother. "Let's leave the past alone."

"You wouldn't be so calm and cold-blooded about it if you were
me," said Myra bitterly. "Not if you had to live with him. I do everything
I can think of to please him—and he only sneers and treats me like this."

"You nag him," said Sydney. "Oh! yes, you do. You can't help it."

"If only he'd answer back! If he'd say something—instead of just
sitting there."

"Yes, but that's the kind of fellow he is. You can't alter people in
this world to suit your fancy. I can't say I care for the chap myself—too

la-di-da for me. Why, if you put him in to run a concern it would be bankrupt in a fortnight! But I'm bound to say he's always been very polite and decent to me. Quite the gentleman. When I've run across him in London he's taken me to lunch at that swell club of his, and if I didn't feel too comfortable there that wasn't his fault. He's got his good points."

"You're so like a man," said Myra. "Carrie would understand! He's been unfaithful to me, I tell you. Unfaithful!"

"Well, well," said Uncle Sydney, with a great deal of jingling and his eyes on the ceiling. "Men will be men."

"But Syd, you never—"

"Of course not," said Uncle Sydney hastily. "Of course not—of course not. I'm speaking generally, Myra—generally, you understand."

"It's all finished," said Myra. "No woman could stand more than I've stood. And now it's the end. I never want to see him again."

"Ah!" said Uncle Sydney. He drew a chair to the table and sat down with the air of one prepared to talk business. "Then let's get down to brass tacks. You've made up your mind? What is it you do want to do?"

"I tell you I never want to see Walter again!"

"Yes, yes," said Uncle Sydney patiently. "We're taking that for granted. Now what do you want? A divorce?"

"Oh!" Myra was taken aback. "I hadn't thought . . ."

"Well, we must get the thing put on a businesslike footing. I doubt if you'd get a divorce. You've got to prove cruelty, you know, as well, and I doubt if you could do that."

"If you knew the suffering he's caused me—"

"I daresay. I'm not denying it. But you want something more than that to satisfy the law. And there's no desertion. If you wrote to him to come back he'd come, I suppose?"

"Haven't I just told you I never want to see him again?"

"Yes, yes, yes. You women do harp on a thing so. We're looking at the thing from a business point of view now. I don't think a divorce will wash."

"I don't want a divorce."

"Well, what do you want, a separation?"

"So that he could go and live with that abandoned creature in London? Live with her altogether? And what would happen to me, I should like to know?"

"Plenty nice houses near me and Carrie. You'd have the boy with you most of the time, I expect."

"And let Walter bring disgusting women into this very house, perhaps? No, indeed, I don't intend to play into his hands like that!"

"Well, dash it all Myra, what do you want?"

Myra began to cry again.

"I'm so miserable, Syd, I'm so miserable. If only Walter were different!"

"Well, he isn't—and he never will be. You must just make up your mind to it, Myra. You've married a fellow who's a bit of a Don Juan—and you've got to try and take a broad-minded view of it. You're fond of the chap. Kiss and make friends—that's what I say. We're none of us perfect. Give and take—that's the thing to remember—give and take."

His sister continued to weep quietly.

"Marriage is a ticklish business," went on Uncle Sydney in a ruminative voice. "Women are too good for us, not a doubt of it."

"I suppose," said Myra in a tearful voice, "one ought to forgive and forgive—again and again."

"That's the spirit," said Uncle Sydney. "Women are angels and men aren't, and women have got to make allowances. Always have had to and always will."

Myra's sobs grew less. She was seeing herself now in the role of the forgiving angel.

"It isn't as if I didn't do everything I could," she sobbed. "I run the house and I'm sure nobody could be a more devoted mother."

"Of course you are," said Uncle Sydney. "And that's a fine youngster of yours. I wish Carrie and I had a boy. Four girls—it's a bit thick. Still, as I always say to her: 'Better luck next time, old girl.' We both feel sure it's going to be a boy this time."

Myra was diverted.

"I didn't know. When is it?"

"June."

"How is Carrie?"

"Suffering a bit with her legs—swelled, you know. But she manages to get about a fair amount. Why, hullo, here's that young shaver. How long have you been here, my boy?"

"Oh! a long time," said Vernon. "I was here when you came in."

"You're so quiet," complained his uncle. "Not like your cousins. I'm sure the racket they make is almost too much to bear sometimes. What's that you've got there?"

"It's an engine," said Vernon.

"No, it isn't," said Uncle Sydney. "It's a milk cart!"

Vernon was silent.

"Hey," said Uncle Sydney. "Isn't it a milk cart?"

"No," said Vernon. "It's an engine."

"Not a bit of it. It's a milk cart. That's funny, isn't it? You say it's an engine and I say it's a milk cart. I wonder which of us is right?"

Since Vernon knew that he was, it seemed hardly necessary to reply.

"He's a solemn child," said Uncle Sydney, turning to his sister. "Never sees a joke. You know, my boy, you'll have to get used to being teased at school."

"Shall I?" said Vernon, who couldn't see what that had to do with it.

"A boy who can take teasing with a laugh, that's the sort of boy who gets on in the world," said Uncle Sydney, and jingled his money again, stimulated by a natural association of ideas.

Vernon stared at him thoughtfully.

"What are you thinking about?"

"Nothing," said Vernon.

"Take your engine on the terrace, dear," said Myra.

Vernon obeyed.

"Now I wonder how much that little chap took in of what we were talking about?" said Sydney to his sister.

"Oh! he wouldn't understand. He's too little."

"H'm," said Sydney. "I don't know. Some children take in a lot—my Ethel does. But then she's a very wide-awake child."

"I don't think Vernon ever notices anything," said Myra. "It's rather a blessing in some ways."

2

"Mummy," said Vernon later, "what's going to happen in June?"

"In June, darling?"

"Yes—what you and Uncle Sydney were talking about."

"Oh! that—" Myra was momentarily discomposed. "Well, you see—it's a great secret."

"Yes?" said Vernon eagerly.

"Uncle Sydney and Aunt Carrie hope that in June they will have a dear little baby boy. A boy cousin for you."

"Oh!" said Vernon, disappointed. "Is that all?"

After a minute or two he said:

"Why are Aunt Carrie's legs swelled?"

"Oh! well—you see—she has been rather overtired lately."

Myra dreaded more questions. She tried to remember what she and Sydney had actually said.

"Mummy?"

"Yes, dear."

"Do Uncle Sydney and Aunt Carrie want to have a baby boy?"

"Yes, of course."

"Then why do they wait till June? Why don't they have it now?"

"Because, Vernon, God knows best. And God wants them to have it in June."

"That's a long time to wait," said Vernon. "If I were God I'd send people things at once, as soon as they wanted them."

"You mustn't be blasphemous, dear," said Myra gently.

Vernon was silent. But he was puzzled. What was blasphemous? He rather thought that it was the same word Cook had used speaking of her brother. She had said he was a most—something—man and hardly ever touched a drop! She had spoken as though such an attitude was highly commendable. But evidently Mummy didn't seem to think the same about it.

Vernon added an extra prayer that evening to his usual petition of "God bless Mummy and Daddy and makemeagooboy armen."

"Dear God," he prayed. "Will you send me a puppy in June!—or July would do if you are very busy."

"Now why in June?" said Miss Robbins. "You *are* a funny little boy. I should have thought you would have wanted the puppy now."

"That would be blamafous," said Vernon, and eyed her reproachfully.

3

Suddenly the word became very exciting. There was a war—in South Africa—and Father was going to it!

Everyone was excited and upset. For the first time, Vernon heard of some people called the Boers. They were the people that Father was going to fight.

His father came home for a few days. He looked younger and more alive and a great deal more cheerful. He and Mummy were quite nice to each other and there weren't any scenes or quarrels.

Once or twice, Vernon thought, his father squirmed uneasily at some of the things his mother said. Once he said irritably:

"For God's sake, Myra, don't keep talking of brave heroes laying down their lives for their country. I can't stand that sort of cant."

But his mother had not got angry. She only said:

"I know you don't like me saying it. But it's *true*."

On the last evening before he left, Vernon's father called to his small son to go for a walk with him. They strolled all round the place, silently at first, and then Vernon was emboldened to ask questions.

"Are you glad you're going to the war, Father?"

"Very glad."

"Is it fun?"

"Not what you'd call fun, I expect. But it is in a way. It's excitement, and then, too, it takes you away from things—right away."

"I suppose," said Vernon thoughtfully, "there aren't any ladies at the war?"

Walter Deyre looked sharply at his son, a slight smile hovering on his lips. Uncanny, the way the boy sometimes hit the nail on the head quite unconsciously.

"That makes for peace, certainly," he said gravely.

"Will you kill a good many people, do you think?" inquired Vernon interestedly.

His father replied that it was impossible to tell accurately beforehand.

"I hope you will," said Vernon, anxious that his father should shine. "I hope you'll kill a hundred."

"Thank you, old man."

"I suppose—" began Vernon, and then stopped.

"Yes?" said Walter Deyre encouragingly.

"I suppose—sometimes—people do get killed in war."

Walter Deyre understood the ambiguous phrase.

"Sometimes," he said.

"You don't think you will, do you?"

"I might. It's all in the day's work, you know."

Vernon considered the phrase thoughtfully. The feeling that underlay it came dimly to him.

"Would you mind if you were, Father?"

"It might be the best thing," said Walter Deyre, more to himself than to the child.

"I hope you won't," said Vernon.

"Thank you."

His father smiled a little. Vernon's wish had sounded so politely conventional. But he did not make the mistake Myra would have done, of thinking the child unfeeling.

They had reached the ruins of the Abbey. The sun was just setting. Father and son looked round and Walter Deyre drew in his breath with a little intake of pain. Perhaps he might never stand here again.

"I've made a mess of things," he thought to himself.

"Vernon?"

"Yes, Father?"

"If I am killed Abbots Puissants will belong to you. You know that, don't you?"

"Yes, Father."

Silence again. So much that he would have liked to say—but he wasn't used to saying things. These were the things that one didn't put into words. Odd, how strangely at home he felt with that small person, his son. Perhaps it had been a mistake not to have got to know the boy better. They might have had some good times together. He was shy of the boy—and the boy was shy of him. And yet, somehow, they were curiously in harmony. They both of them disliked saying things.

"I'm fond of the old place," said Walter Deyre. "I expect you will be too."

"Yes, Father."

"Queer to think of the old monks—catching their fish—fat fellows. That's how I always think of them—comfortable chaps."

They lingered a few minutes longer.

"Well," said Walter Deyre, "we must be getting home. It's late."

They turned. Walter Deyre squared his shoulders. There was a leave-taking to be got through—an emotional one, if he knew Myra—and he rather dreaded it. Well, it would soon be over. Good-byes were painful things—better if one made no fuss about them, but then of course Myra would never see it that way.

Poor Myra! She'd had a rotten deal on the whole. A fine-looking creature, but he'd married her really for the sake of Abbots Puissants—and she had married him for love. That was the root of the whole trouble.

"Look after your mother, Vernon," he said suddenly. "She's been very good to you, you know."

He rather hoped, in a way, that he wouldn't come back. It would be best so. Vernon had his mother.

And yet, at that thought, he had a queer traitorous feeling. As though he were deserting the boy. . . . .

4

"Walter," cried Myra, "you haven't said good-bye to Vernon."

Walter looked across at his son, standing there wide-eyed.

"Good-bye, old chap. Have a good time."

"Good-bye, Father."

That was all. Myra was scandalized. Had he no love for the boy? He hadn't even kissed him. How queer they were—the Deyres. So casual. Strange, the way they had nodded to each other across the width of the room. So alike. . . .

"But Vernon," said Myra to herself, "shall not grow up like his father."

On the walls around her Deyres looked down and smiled sardonically.

Chapter Seven

Two months after his father sailed for South Africa Vernon went to school. It had been Walter Deyre's wish and arrangement, and Myra, at the moment, was disposed to regard any wish of his as law. He was her soldier and her hero, and everything else was forgotten. She was thoroughly happy at this time. Knitting socks for the soldiers, urging on energetic campaigns of "white feather," sympathizing and talking with other women whose husbands had also gone to fight the wicked ungrateful Boers.

She felt exquisite pangs parting with Vernon. Her darling—her baby—to go so far away from her. What sacrifices mothers had to make! But it had been his father's wish.

Poor darling, he was sure to be most terribly homesick! She couldn't bear to think of it.

But Vernon was not homesick. He had no real passionate attachment to his mother. All his life he was to be fondest of her when away from her. His escape from her emotional atmosphere was felt by him as a relief.

He had a good temperament for school life. He had an aptitude for games, a quiet manner, and an unusual amount of physical courage. After the dull monotony of life under the reign of Miss Robbins, school was a delightful novelty. Like all the Deyres, he had the knack of getting on with people. He made friends easily.

But the reticence of the child who so often answered "Nothing" clung to him. Except with one or two people, that reticence was to go through life with him. His school friends were people with whom he shared "doing things." His thoughts he was to keep to himself and share with only one person. That person came into his life very soon.

On his very first holidays he found Josephine.

2

Vernon was welcomed by his mother with an outburst of demonstrative affection. Already rather self-conscious about such things, he bore it manfully. Myra's first raptures over, she said:

"There's a lovely surprise for you, darling. Who do you think is here? Your cousin Josephine, Aunt Nina's little girl. She has come to live with us. Now, isn't that nice?"

Vernon wasn't quite sure. It needed thinking over. To gain time, he said:

"Why has she come to live with us?"

"Because her mother has died. It's terribly sad for her and we must be very, very kind to her to make up."

"Is Aunt Nina dead?"

He was sorry Aunt Nina was dead. Pretty Aunt Nina with her curling cigarette smoke.

"Yes. You can't remember her, of course, darling."

He didn't say that he remembered her perfectly. Why should one say things?

"She's in the schoolroom, darling. Go and find her and make friends."

Vernon went slowly. He didn't know whether he was pleased or not. A girl! He was at the age to despise girls. Rather a nuisance having a girl about. On the other hand, it would be jolly having *someone*. It depended what the kid was like. One would have to be decent to her if she'd just lost her mother.

He opened the schoolroom door and went in. Josephine was sitting on the windowsill swinging her legs. She stared at him, and Vernon's attitude of kindly condescension fell from him.

She was a squarely built child of about his own age. She had dead black hair cut very straight across her forehead. Her jaw stuck out a little in a determined way. She had a very white skin and enormous eyelashes. Although she was two months younger than Vernon, she had the sophistication of twice his years—a kind of mixture of weariness and defiance.

"Hullo," she said.

"Hullo," said Vernon, rather feebly.

They went on looking at each other, suspiciously, as is the manner of children and dogs.

"I suppose you're my cousin Josephine," said Vernon.

"Yes, but you'd better call me Joe. Everyone does."

"All right—Joe."

There was a pause. To bridge it, Vernon whistled.

"Rather jolly, coming home," he observed at last.

"It's an awfully jolly place," said Joe.

"Oh! do you like it?" said Vernon, warming to her.

"I like it awfully. Better than any of the places I've lived."

"Have you lived in a lot of places?"

"Oh! yes. At Coombes first—when we were with Father. And then at Monte Carlo with Colonel Anstey. And then at Toulon with Arthur—and then a lot of Swiss places because of Arthur's lungs. And then I went to a convent for a bit after Arthur died. Mother couldn't be bothered with me just then. I didn't like it much—the nuns were so silly. They made me have a bath in my chemise. And then, after Mother died, Aunt Myra came and fetched me here."

"I'm awfully sorry—about your mother, I mean," said Vernon awkwardly.

"Yes," said Joe. "It's rotten in a way—though much the best thing for her."

"Oh!" said Vernon, rather taken aback.

"Don't tell Aunt Myra," said Joe. "Because I think she's rather easily shocked by things—rather like the nuns. You have to be careful what you say to her. Mother didn't care for me an awful lot, you know. She was frightfully kind and all that—but she was always soppy about some man or other. I heard some people say so in the hotel, and it was quite true. She couldn't help it, of course. But it's a very bad plan. I shan't have anything to do with men when I grow up."

"Oh!" said Vernon. He was still feeling very young and awkward beside this amazing person.

"I liked Colonel Anstey best," said Joe reminiscently. "But of course Mother only ran away with him to get away from Father. We stayed at much better hotels with Colonel Anstey. Arthur was very poor. If I ever do get soppy about a man when I grow up, I shall take care that he's rich. It makes things so much easier."

"Wasn't your father nice?"

"Oh! Father was a devil—Mother said so. He hated us both."

"But why?"

Joe wrinkled her straight black brows in perplexity.

"I don't quite know. I think—I think it was something to do with *me* coming. I think he had to marry Mother because she was going to have me—something like that—and it made him angry."

They looked at each other, solemn and perplexed.

"Uncle Walter's in South Africa, isn't he?" went on Joe.

"Yes. I've had three letters from him at school. Awfully jolly letters."

"Uncle Walter's a dear. I loved him. He came out to Monte Carlo, you know."

Some memory stirred in Vernon. Of course, he remembered now. His father had wanted Joe to come to Abbots Puissants then.

"He arranged for me to go to the convent," said Joe. "Reverend Mother thought he was lovely—a true type of high-born English gentleman—such a funny way of putting it."

They both laughed a little.

"Let's go out in the garden. Shall we?" said Vernon.

"Yes, let's. I say, I know where there are four different nests—but the birds have all flown away."

They went out together, amicably discussing birds' eggs.

3

To Myra, Joe was a perplexing child. She had nice manners, answered promptly and politely when spoken to, and submitted to caresses without returning them. She was very independent and gave the maid told to attend to her little or nothing to do. She could mend her own clothes and keep herself neat and tidy without any outside urging. She was, in fact, the sophisticated hotel child whom Myra had never happened to come across. The depths of her knowledge would have horrified and shocked her aunt.

But Joe was shrewd and quick-witted, well used to summing up the people with whom she came in contact. She refrained carefully from "shocking Aunt Myra." She had for her something closely akin to a kindly contempt.

"Your mother," she said to Vernon, "is very good—but she's a little stupid too, isn't she?"

"She's very beautiful," said Vernon hotly.

"Yes, she is," agreed Joe. "All but her hands. Her hair's lovely. I wish I had red-gold hair."

"It comes right down below her waist," said Vernon.

He found Joe a wonderful companion, quite unlike his previous conception of "girls." She hated dolls, never cried, was as strong if not stronger than he was, and was always ready and willing for any dangerous sport. Together they climbed trees, rode bicycles, fell and cut and bumped themselves, and ended up by taking a wasp's nest together, with a success due more to luck than skill.

To Joe, Vernon could talk and did. She opened up to him a strange new world, a world where people ran away with other people's husbands and wives, a world of dancing and gambling and cynicism. She had loved her mother with a fierce protective tenderness that almost reversed the roles.

"She was too soft," said Joe. "I'm not going to be soft. People are mean to you if you are. Men are beasts anyway, but if you're a beast to them first, they're all right. All men are beasts."

"That's a silly thing to say, and I don't think it's true."

"That's because you're going to be a man yourself."

"No, it isn't. And anyway I'm not a beast."

"No, but I daresay you will be when you're grown up."

"But, look here, Joe, you'll have to marry someone someday, and you won't think your husband a beast."

"Why should I marry anyone?"

"Well—girls do. You don't want to be an old maid like Miss Crabtree."

Joe wavered. Miss Crabtree was an elderly spinster who was very active in the village and who was very fond of "the dear children."

"I shouldn't be the kind of old maid Miss Crabtree is," she said weakly. "I should—oh! I should do things. Play the violin, or write books, or paint some marvelous pictures."

"I hope you won't play the violin," said Vernon.

"That's really what I should like to do best. Why do you hate music so, Vernon?"

"I don't know. I just do. It makes me feel all horrible inside."

"How queer! It gives me a nice feeling. What are you going to do when you grow up?"

"Oh! I don't know. I'd like to marry someone very beautiful and live at Abbots Puissants and have lots of horses and dogs."

"How dull!" said Joe. "I don't think that would be exciting a bit."

"I don't know that I want things to be very exciting," said Vernon.

"I do," said Joe. "I want things to be exciting the whole time without ever stopping."

4

Joe and Vernon had few other children to play with. The Vicar, whose children Vernon had played with when he was younger, had gone to another living, and his successor was unmarried. Most of the children of families in the same position as the Deyres lived too far away for more than a very occasional visit.

The only exception was Nell Vereker. Her father, Captain Vereker, was agent to Lord Coomberleigh. He was a tall stooping man, with very pale blue eyes and a hesitating manner. He had good connections but was inefficient generally. His wife made up in efficiency for what he lacked. She was a tall commanding woman, still handsome. Her hair was very golden and her eyes were very blue. She had pushed her husband into the position he held, and in the same way she pushed herself into the best houses of the neighbourhood. She had birth but, like her husband, no money. Yet she was determined to make a success of life.

Both Vernon and Joe were bored to death by Nell Vereker. She was a thin pale child with fair straggly hair. Her eyelids and the tip of her nose were faintly tinged with pink. She was no good at anything. She couldn't run and she couldn't climb. She was always dressed in starched white muslin and her favorite games were dolls' tea parties.

Myra was very fond of Nell. "Such a thorough little lady," she used to say. Vernon and Joe were kindly and polite when Mrs. Vereker brought Nell to tea. They tried to think of games she would like, and they used to give whoops of delight when at last she departed, sitting up very straight beside her mother in the hired carriage.

It was in Vernon's second holidays, just after the famous episode of the wasp's nest, that the first rumors came about Deerfields.

Deerfields was the property adjoining Abbots Puissants. It belonged to old Sir Charles Alington. Some friends of Mrs. Deyre's came to lunch and the subject came up for discussion.

"It's quite true. I had it from an absolutely authentic source. It's been sold to these people. . . . Yes—*Jews!* Oh! of course—enormously wealthy. . . . Yes, a fancy price. I believe. Levinne, the name is. . . . No, Russian Jews, so I heard. . . . Oh! of course *quite* impossible. Too bad of Sir Charles, I say. . . . Yes, of course there's the Yorkshire property as well, and I hear he's lost a lot of money lately. . . . No, no one will call. Naturally."

Joe and Vernon were pleasurably excited. All titbits about Deerfields were carefully stored up. At last the strangers arrived and moved in. There was more talk of the same kind.

"Oh! absolutely impossible, Mrs. Deyre. . . . Just as we thought. . . . One wonders what they think they are doing. . . . What do they expect? . . . I dare say they'll sell the place and move away. . . . Yes, there is a family. A boy. About your Vernon's age, I believe."

"I wonder what Jews are like," said Vernon to Joe. "Why does everyone dislike them? We thought one boy at school was a Jew, but he eats bacon for breakfast, so he can't be."

The Levinnes proved to be a very Christian brand of Jew. They appeared in church on Sunday, having taken a whole pew. The interest of the congregation was breathless. First came Mr. Levinne—very round and stout, tightly frock-coated—an enormous nose and a shining face. Then Mrs.—an amazing sight. Colossal sleeves! Hour-glass figure! Chains of diamonds! An immense hat decorated with feathers and black tightly curling ringlets underneath it! With them was a boy rather taller than Vernon with a long yellow face and protruding ears.

A carriage and pair was waiting for them when service was over. They got into it and drove away.

"Well!" said Miss Crabtree.

Little groups formed, talking busily.

5

"I think it's rotten," said Joe.

She and Vernon were in the garden together.

"What's rotten?"

"Those people."

"Do you mean the Levinnes?"

"Yes. Why should everyone be so horrid about them?"

"Well," said Vernon, trying to be strictly impartial, "they did look queer, you know."

"Well, I think people are beasts."

Vernon was silent. Joe, a rebel by force of circumstances, was always putting a new point of view before him.

"That boy," continued Joe. "I dare say he's awfully jolly, even though his ears do stick out."

"I wonder," said Vernon. "It would be jolly to have someone else. Kate says they're making a swimming pool at Deerfields."

"They must be frightfully, frightfully rich," said Joe.

Riches meant little to Vernon. He had never thought about them.

The Levinnes were the great topic of conversation for some time. The improvements they were making at Deerfields! The workmen they had had down from London!

Mrs. Vereker brought Nell to tea one day. As soon as she was in the garden with the children she imparted news of fascinating importance.

"They've got a motor car."

"A motor car?"

Motor cars were almost unheard of then. One had never been seen in the Forest. Storms of envy shook Vernon. A motor car!

"A motor car *and* a swimming pool," he murmured.

It was too much.

"It's not a swimming pool," said Nell. "It's a sunk garden."

"Kate says it's a swimming pool."

"Our gardener says it's a sunk garden."

"What is a sunk garden?"

"I don't know," confessed Nell. "But it is one."

"I don't believe it," said Joe. "Who'd want a silly sort of thing like that when they could have a swimming pool?"

"Well, that's what our gardener says."

"I know," said Joe. A wicked look came into her eyes. "Let's go and see."

"What?"

"Let's go and see for ourselves."

"Oh! but we couldn't," said Nell.

"Why not? We can creep up through the woods."

"Jolly good idea," said Vernon. "Let's."

"I don't want to," said Nell. "Mother wouldn't like it, I know."

"Oh! don't be a spoilsport, Nell. Come on."

"Mother wouldn't like it," repeated Nell.

"All right. Wait here, then. We won't be long."

Tears gathered slowly in Nell's eyes. She hated being left. She stood there sullenly, twisting her frock between her fingers.

"We won't be long," Vernon repeated.

He and Joe ran off. Nell felt she couldn't bear it.

"Vernon!"

"Yes?"

"Wait for me. I'm coming too."

She felt heroic as she made the announcement. Joe and Vernon did not seem particularly impressed by it. They waited with obvious impatience for her to come up with them.

"Now then," said Vernon, "I'm leader. Everyone to do as I say."

They climbed over the Park palings and reached the shelter of the trees. Speaking in whispers under their breath, they flitted through the undergrowth, drawing nearer and nearer toward the house. Now it rose before them, some way ahead to the right.

"We'll have to get farther still and keep a bit more uphill."

They followed him obediently. And then suddenly a voice broke on their ears, speaking from a little behind them to the left.

"You're trethpassing," it said.

They turned—startled. The yellow-faced boy with the large ears stood there. He had his hands in his pockets, and was surveying them superciliously.

"You're trethpassing," he said again.

There was something in his manner that awoke immediately antagonism. Instead of saying, as he had meant to say, "I'm sorry," Vernon said, "Oh!"

He and the other boy looked at each other—the cool measuring glance of two adversaries in a duel.

"We come from next door," said Joe.

"Do you?" said the boy. "Well, you'd better go back there. My father and mother don't want you in here."

He managed to be unbearably offensive as he said this. Vernon, unpleasantly conscious of being in the wrong, flushed angrily.

"You might manage to speak politely," he said.

"Why should I?" said the boy.

He turned as a footstep sounded coming through the undergrowth.

"Is that you, Sam?" he said. "Just turn these trethpassing kids off the place, will you?"

The keeper, who had stepped out beside him, grinned and touched his forehead. The boy strolled away, as though he had lost all interest. The keeper turned to the children and put on a ferocious scowl.

"Out of it, you young varmints! I'll turn the dogs loose on you unless you're out of here in double-quick time."

"We're not afraid of dogs," said Vernon haughtily as he turned to depart.

"Ho, you're not, h'aren't you? Well, then, I've got a rhinoceros here and I'm a-going to loose that this minute."

He stalked off. Nell gave a terrified pull at Vernon's arm.

"He's gone to get it," she cried. "Oh! hurry—hurry!"

Her alarm was contagious. So much had been retailed about the Levinnes that the keeper's threat seemed a perfectly likely one to the children. With one accord they ran for home. They plunged in a beeline, pushing their way through the undergrowth. Vernon and Joe led. A piteous cry arose from Nell.

"Vernon—Vernon! Oh! do wait. I've got stuck."

What a nuisance Nell was! She couldn't run or do anything. He turned back, gave her frock a vigorous pull to free it from the brambles with which it was entangled (a good deal to the frock's detriment), and hauled her to her feet.

"Come on, do."

"I'm so out of breath. I can't run anymore. Oh! Vernon, I'm so frightened."

"Come *on*."

Hand in hand, he pulled her along. They reached the Park palings, scrambled over. . . .

6

"We-ell," said Joe, fanning herself with a very dirty linen hat. "That *was* an adventure."

"My frock's all torn," said Nell. "What shall I do?"

"I hate that boy," said Vernon. "He's a beast."

"He's a beastly beast," agreed Joe. "We'll declare war on him. Shall we?"

"Rather!"

"What shall I do about my frock?"

"It's very awkward their having a rhinoceros," said Joe thoughtfully. "Do you think Tom Boy would go for it if we trained him to?"

"I shouldn't like Tom Boy to be hurt," said Vernon.

Tom Boy was the stable dog, a great favorite of his. His mother had always vetoed a dog in the house, so Tom Boy was the nearest Vernon had got to having a dog of his own.

"I don't know what Mother will say about my frock."

"Oh, bother your frock, Nell! It's not the sort of frock for playing in the garden, anyway."

"I'll tell your mother it's my fault," said Vernon impatiently. "Don't be so like a girl."

"I am a girl," said Nell.

"Well, so is Joe a girl. But she doesn't go on like you do. She's as good as a boy any day."

Nell looked ready to cry, but at that minute they were called from the house.

"I'm sorry, Mrs. Vereker," said Vernon. "I'm afraid I've torn Nell's frock."

There were reproaches from Myra, civil disclaimers from Mrs. Vereker. When Nell and her mother had gone Myra said:

"You must not be so rough, Vernon darling. When a little girl friend comes to tea you must take great care of her."

"Why have we got to have her to tea? We don't like her. She spoils everything."

"Vernon! Nell is such a dear little girl."

"She isn't, Mother. She's awful."

"Vernon!"

"Well, she is. I don't like her mother either."

"I don't like Mrs. Vereker much," said Myra. "I always think she's a very hard woman. But I can't think why you children don't like Nell. Mrs. Vereker tells me she's absolutely devoted to you, Vernon."

"Well, I don't want her to be."

He escaped with Joe.

"War," he said. "That's what it is—war! I dare say that Levinne boy is really a Boer in disguise. We must plan out our campaign. Why should he come and live next door to us and spoil everything?"

The kind of guerilla warfare that followed occupied Vernon and Joe in a most pleasurable fashion. They invented all kinds of methods of harassing the enemy. Concealed in trees, they pelted him with chestnuts. They stalked him with peashooters. They outlined a hand in red paint and crept secretly up to the house one night after dark and left it on the doorstep with the word "Revenge" printed at the bottom of the sheet of paper.

Sometimes their enemy retaliated in kind. He, too, had a peashooter, and it was he who laid in wait for them one day with a garden hose.

Hostilities had been going on for nearly ten days when Vernon came upon Joe sitting on a tree stump looking unusually despondent.

"Hullo! What's up? I thought you were going to stalk the enemy with those squashy tomatoes Cook gave us."

"I was. I mean I did."

"What's the matter, Joe?"

"I was up a tree and he came right by underneath. I could have got him beautifully."

"Do you mean to say you didn't?"

"No."

"Why ever not?"

Joe's face became very red and she began to speak very fast.

"I couldn't. You see, he didn't know I was there, and he looked— oh! Vernon, he looked so awfully *lonely*—as though he were simply hating things. You know, it must be pretty beastly having no one to do things with."

"Yes, but—"

Vernon paused to adjust his ideas.

"Don't you remember how we said it was all rotten?" went on Joe. "People being so beastly about the Levinnes, and now we're being as beastly as anyone."

"Yes, but he was beastly to *us!*"

"Perhaps he didn't mean to be."

"That's nonsense."

"No, it isn't. Look at the way dogs bite you if they're afraid or suspicious. I expect he just expected us to be beastly to him, and wanted to start first. Let's be friends."

"You can't be in the middle of a war."

"Yes, you can. We'll make a white flag, and then you march with it and demand a parley, and see if you can't agree upon honorable terms of peace."

"Well," said Vernon, "I don't mind if we do. It would be a change, anyway. What shall we use for a flag of truce—my handkerchief or your pinafore?"

Marching with the flag of truce was rather exciting. It was not long before they encountered the enemy. He stared in complete surprise.

"What's up?" he said.

"We want a parley," said Vernon.

"Well, I'm agreeable," said the other boy, after a moment's pause.

"What we want to say is this," said Joe. "If you'll agree, we'd like to be friends."

They looked from one to the other.

"Why do you want to be friends?" he asked suspiciously.

"It seems a bit silly," said Vernon, "living next door and not being friends, doesn't it?"

"Which of you thought of that first?"

"I did," said Joe.

She felt those small jet-black eyes boring into her. What a queer boy he was. His ears seemed to stick out more than ever.

"All right," said the boy, "I'd like to."

There was a minute's embarrassed pause.

"What's your name?" said Joe.

"Sebastian."

There was just the faintest lisp, so little as hardly to be noticed.

"What a funny name. Mine's Joe and this is Vernon. He's at school. Do you go to school?"

"Yes. I'm going to Eton later."

"So am I," said Vernon.

Again a faint tide of hostility rose between them. Then it ebbed away—never to return.

"Come and see our swimming pool," said Sebastian. "It's rather jolly."

Chapter Eight

The friendship with Sebastian Levinne prospered and throve apace. Half the zest of it lay in the secrecy that had to be adopted. Vernon's mother would have been horrified if she had guessed at anything of the kind. The Levinnes would certainly not have been horrified—but their gratification might have led to equally dire results.

Schooltime passed on leaden wings for poor Joe, cooped up with a
daily governess who arrived every morning and who subtly disapproved
of her outspoken and rebellious pupil. Joe lived only for the holidays.
As soon as they came she and Vernon would set off to a secret meeting place where there was a convenient gap in a hedge. They had invented a code of whistles and many unnecessary signals. Sometimes
Sebastian would be there before time—lying on the bracken, his yellow
face and jutting ears looking strangely at variance with his knicker-
bocker suit.

They played games, but they also talked—how they talked! Sebastian
told them stories of Russia. They learned of the persecution of Jews—
of pogroms! Sebastian himself had never been in Russia, but he had
lived for years amongst other Russian Jews and his own father had nar-
rowly escaped with his life in a pogrom. Sometimes he would say sen-
tences in Russian to please Vernon and Joe. It was all entrancing.

"Everybody hates us down here," said Sebastian. "But it doesn't matter. They won't be able to do without us because my father is so rich.
You can buy everything with money."

He had a certain queer arrogance about him.

"You can't buy everything," objected Vernon. "Old Nicoll's son has
come home from the war without a leg. Money couldn't make his leg
grow again."

"No," admitted Sebastian. "I didn't mean things like that. But money
would get you a very good wooden leg and the best kind of crutches."

"I had crutches once," said Vernon. "It was rather fun. And I had
an awfully nice nurse to look after me."

"You see, you couldn't have had that if you hadn't been rich."

Was he rich? He supposed he was. He'd never thought about it.

"I wish I was rich," said Joe.

"You can marry me when you grow up," said Sebastian, "and then
you will be."

"It wouldn't be nice for Joe if nobody came to see her," objected
Vernon.

"I wouldn't mind that a bit," said Joe. "I wouldn't care what Aunt
Myra or anybody said. I'd marry Sebastian if I wanted to."

"People will come and see her then," said Sebastian. "You don't realize. Jews are frightfully powerful. My father says people can't do without them. That's why Sir Charles Alington had to sell us Deerfields."

A sudden chill came over Vernon. He felt without putting the thought into words that he was talking to a member of an enemy race. But he felt no antagonism toward Sebastian. That was over long ago. He and Sebastian were friends—somehow he was sure they always would be.

"Money," said Sebastian, "isn't just buying things. It's ever so much more than that. And it isn't only having power over people. It's—it's—being able to get together lots of beauty."

He made a queer un-English gesture with his hands.

"What do you mean," said Vernon, "by 'get together'?"

Sebastian didn't know what he meant. The words had just come.

"Anyway," said Vernon, "things aren't beauty."

"Yes, they are. Deerfields is beautiful—but not nearly so beautiful as Abbots Puissants."

"When Abbots Puissants belongs to me," said Vernon, "you can come and stay there as much as ever you like. We're always going to be friends, aren't we? No matter what anyone says?"

"We're always going to be friends," said Sebastian.

2

Little by little the Levinnes made headway. The church needed a new organ—Mr. Levinne presented it with one. Deerfields was thrown open on the occasion of the choir boys' outing and strawberries and cream provided. A large donation was given to the Primrose League. Turn where you would, you came up against the opulence and the kindness of the Levinnes.

People began to say: "Of course they're impossible—but Mrs. Levinne is wonderfully *kind*."

And they said other things.

"Oh! of course—*Jews!* But perhaps it is absurd of one to be prejudiced. Some very good people have been Jews."

It was rumored that the Vicar had said: "Including Jesus Christ," in answer. But nobody really believed that. The Vicar was unmarried, which was very unusual, and had odd ideas about Holy Communion, and sometimes preached very incomprehensible sermons, but nobody believed that he would have said anything really sacrilegious.

It was the Vicar who introduced Mrs. Levinne to the Sewing Circle which met twice a week to provide comforts for our brave soldiers in South Africa. And meeting her twice a week there certainly made it awkward.

In the end, Lady Coomberleigh, softened by the immense donation to the Primrose League, took the plunge and called. And where Lady Coomberleigh led, everybody followed.

Not that the Levinnes were ever admitted to intimacy. But they were officially accepted, and people were heard saying:

"She's a very *kind* woman—even if she does wear impossible clothes for the country."

But that, too, followed. Mrs. Levinne was adaptable like all her race. A very short time elapsed before she appeared in even tweedier tweeds than her neighbors.

Joe and Vernon were solemnly bidden to tea with Sebastian Levinne.

"We must go this once, I suppose," said Myra sighing. "But we need never get really intimate. What a queer-looking boy he is. You won't be rude to him, will you, Vernon darling?"

The children solemnly made the official acquaintance of Sebastian. It amused them very much.

But the sharp-witted Joe fancied that Mrs. Levinne knew more about their friendship than Aunt Myra did. Mrs. Levinne wasn't a fool. She was like Sebastian.

3

Walter Deyre was killed a few weeks before the war ended. His end was a gallant one. He was shot when going back to rescue a wounded comrade under heavy fire. He was awarded a posthumous V.C. and the letter his colonel wrote to Myra was treasured by her as her dearest possession.

Never [wrote the Colonel] have I known anyone so fearless of danger. His men adored him and would have followed him anywhere. He has risked his life again and again in the gallantest way. You can indeed be proud of him.

Myra read that letter again and again. She read it to all her friends. It wiped away the faint sting that her husband had left no last word or letter for her.

"But, being a Deyre, he wouldn't," she said to herself.

Yet Walter Deyre had left a letter "in case I should be killed." But it was not to Myra and she never knew of it. She was grief-stricken, but happy. Her husband was hers in death as he had never been in life, and with her easy power of making things as she wished them to be, she began to weave a convincing romance of her wonderfully happy married life.

It is difficult to say how Vernon was affected by his father's death. He felt no actual grief—was rendered even more stolid by his mother's obvious wish for him to display emotion. He was proud of his father—so proud that it almost hurt—yet he understood what Joe had meant when she said that it was better for her mother to be dead. He remembered very clearly that last evening walk with his father—the things he had said—the feeling there had been between them.

His father, he knew hadn't really wanted to come back. He was sorry for his father—he always had been. He didn't know why.

It was not grief he felt for his father—it was more a kind of heart-gripping loneliness. Father was dead—Aunt Nina was dead. There was Mother, of course, but that was different.

He couldn't satisfy his mother—he never had been able to. She was always hugging him, crying over him, telling him they must be all in all to each other now. And he couldn't, he just couldn't, say the things she wanted him to say. He couldn't even put his arms round her neck and hug her back.

He longed for the holidays to be over. His mother, with her red eyes and her widow's weeds of the heaviest crape—somehow she overpowered things.

Mr. Flemming, the lawyer from London, came down to stay, and Uncle Sydney came from Birmingham. He stayed two days. At the end of them Vernon was summoned to the library.

The two men were sitting at the long table. Myra was sitting in a low chair by the fire, her handkerchief to her eyes.

"Well, my boy," said Uncle Sydney, "we've got something to talk to you about. How would you like to come and live near your Aunt Carrie and me at Birmingham?"

"Thank you," said Vernon, "but I'd rather live here."

"A bit gloomy, don't you think?" said his uncle. "Now I've got my eye on a jolly house—not too big, thoroughly comfortable. There'll be your cousins near for you to play with in the holidays. It's a very good idea, I think."

"I'm sure it is," said Vernon politely. "But I'd really like being here best, thank you."

"Ah! H'm," said Uncle Sydney. He blew his nose and looked questioningly at the lawyer, who assented to the look with a slight nod.

"It's not quite so simple as that, old chap," said Uncle Sydney. "I think you're quite old enough to understand if I explain things to you. Now that your father's dead—er—passed from us, Abbots Puissants belongs to you."

"I know," said Vernon.

"Eh? How do you know? Servants been talking?"

"Father told me before he went away."

"Oh!" said Uncle Sydney, rather taken aback. "Oh!—I see. Well, as I say, Abbots Puissants belongs to you, but a place like this takes a lot of money to run—paying wages and things like that—you understand? And then there are some things called Death Duties. When anyone dies you have to pay out a lot of money to the government.

"Now, your father wasn't a rich man. When his father died, and he came into this place, he had so little money that he thought he'd have to sell it."

"Sell it?" burst out Vernon incredulously.

"Yes, it's not entailed."

"What's entailed?"

Mr. Flemming explained carefully and clearly.

"But—but—you aren't going to sell it now?"

Vernon gazed at him with agonizing imploring eyes.

"Certainly not," said Mr. Flemming. "The estate is left to you, and nothing can be done until you are of age—that means twenty-one, you know."

Vernon breathed a sigh of relief.

"But you see," continued Uncle Sydney, "there isn't enough money to go on living here. As I say, your father would have had to sell it. But he met your mother and married her, and fortunately she had enough money to—to keep things going. But your father's death has made a lot of difference. For one thing, he has left certain—er—debts which your mother insists on paying."

There was a sniff from Myra. Uncle Sydney's tone was embarrassed and he hurried on.

"The common-sense thing to do is to let Abbots Puissants for a term of years—till you are twenty-one, in fact. By then, who knows? Things may—er—change for the better. Naturally your mother will be happier living near her own relations. You must think of your mother, you know, my boy."

"Yes," said Vernon. "Father told me to."

"So that's settled—eh?"

How cruel they were, thought Vernon. Asking him—when he could see that there was nothing to ask him about. They could do as they liked. They meant to. Why call him in here and *pretend!*

Strangers would come and live in Abbots Puissants.

Never mind! Some day he would be twenty-one.

"Darling," said Myra. "I'm doing it all for you. It would be so sad here without Daddy, wouldn't it?"

She held out her arms, but Vernon pretended not to notice. He walked out of the room, saying with difficulty:

"Thank you, Uncle Sydney, so much, for telling me."

4

He went out into the garden and wandered on till he came to the old Abbey. He sat down with his chin in his hands.

"Mother *could!*" he said to himself. "If she liked, she *could!* She wants to go and live in a horrid red brick house with pipes on it like Uncle Sydney's. She doesn't like Abbots Puissants—she never has. But she needn't pretend it's all for me. That's not true. She says things that aren't true. She always has. . . ."

He sat there smoldering with indignation.

"Vernon—Vernon—I've been looking for you everywhere. I couldn't think what had become of you. What's the matter?"

It was Joe. He told her. Here was someone who would understand and sympathize. But Joe startled him.

"Well, why not? Why shouldn't Aunt Myra go and live in Birmingham if she wants to? I think you're beastly. Why should she go on living here just so that you should be here in the holidays? It's *her* money. Why shouldn't she spend it on doing as *she* likes?"

"But Joe, Abbots Puissants—"

"Well, what's Abbots Puissants to Aunt Myra? In her heart of hearts she feels about it just like you feel about Uncle Sydney's house in Birmingham. Why should she pinch and scrape to live here if she doesn't want to? If your father had made her happier here, perhaps she would want to—but he didn't. Mother said so once. I don't like Aunt Myra terribly—I know she's good and all that, but I don't love her—but I *can* be fair. It's *her* money. You can't get away from that!"

Vernon looked at her. They were antagonists. Both had their point of view and neither could see the other's. They were both ablaze with indignation.

"I think women have a rotten time," said Joe. "And I'm on Aunt Myra's side."

"All right," said Vernon, "be on her side! I don't care."

Joe went away. He stayed there, sitting on the ruined wall of the old Abbey.

For the first time he questioned life. . . . Things weren't *sure*. How could you tell what was going to happen?

When he was twenty-one. . . .

Yes, but you couldn't be *sure!* You couldn't be *safe!*

Look at the time when he was a baby. Nurse, God, Mr. Green! How absolutely fixed they had seemed. And now they had all gone.

At least, God was still there, he supposed. But it wasn't the same God—not the same God at all.

What would have happened to everything by the time he was twenty-one? *What, strangest thought of all, would have happened to himself?*

He felt terribly alone. Father, Aunt Nina—both dead. Only Uncle

Sydney and Mummy—and they weren't—didn't—belong. He paused, confused. There was Joe! Joe understood. But Joe was queer about some things.

He clenched his hands. No everything would be all right.

When he was twenty-one....

BOOK II

NELL

Chapter One

The room was full of cigarette smoke. It eddied and drifted about, forming a thin blue haze. Through it came the sound of three voices occupied with the betterment of the human race and the encouragement of art—especially art that defied all known conventions.

Sebastian Levinne, leaning back against the ornate marble mantelpiece of his mother's town house, spoke didactically, gesticulating with the long yellow hand that held his cigarette. The tendency to lisp was still there, but very faint. His yellow Mongolian face, his surprised-looking ears, were much the same as they had been at eleven years old. At twenty-two he was the same Sebastian, sure of himself, perspective, with the same love of beauty and the same unemotional and unerring sense of values.

In front of him, reclining in two immense leather-covered armchairs, were Vernon and Joe. Very much alike these two, cast in the same sharply accentuated black-and-white mold. But, as of old, Joe's was the more aggressive personality, energetic, rebellious, vehement. Vernon, an immense length, lay back slothfully in his chair. His long legs rested on the back of another chair. He was blowing smoke rings and smiling thoughtfully to himself. He occasionally contributed grunts to the conversation, or a short easy sentence.

"That wouldn't pay," Sebastian had just said decisively.

As he had half expected, Joe was roused at once to the point of virulence.

"Who wants a thing to *pay?* It's so—so *rotten*—that point of view! Treating everything from a commercial standpoint. I hate it."

Sebastian said calmly: "That's because you've got such an incurably romantic view of life. You like poets to stave in garrets, and artists to toil unrecognized, and sculptors to be applauded after they are dead."

"Well—that's what happens. Always!"

"No, not *always.* Very often, perhaps. But it needn't be as often as it is. That's my point. The world never likes anything new—but I say it could be made to. Taken the right way, it could be made to. But you've got to know just what will go down and what won't."

"That's compromise," murmured Vernon indistinctly.

"It's common sense! Why should I lose money by backing my judgment?"

"Oh! Sebastian," cried Joe, "you—you—"

"Jew!" said Sebastian calmly. "That's what you mean. Well, we Jews have got taste—we know when a thing is fine and when it isn't. We don't go by the fashion—we back our own judgment, and we're *right!* People always see the money side of it, but the other's there too."

Vernon grunted. Sebastian went on:

"There are two sides to what we're talking about—there are the people who are thinking of new things, new ways of doing old things, new thoughts altogether, and who can't get their chance because people are afraid of anything new. And there are the other people—the people who know what the public has always wanted and who go on giving it to them, because it's safe and there's a sure profit. But there's a third way— to find things that are new and beautiful and take a chance on them. That's what I'm going to do. I'm going to run a picture gallery in Bond Street—I signed the deeds yesterday—and a couple of theaters—and later I want to run a weekly of some kind on entirely different lines from anything that has been done before. And what's more, I'm going to make the whole thing pay. There are all sorts of things that I admire, that a cultivated few would admire—but I'm not going out for those. Anything I run's going to be a popular success. Dash it all, Joe don't you see that half the fun of the thing is *making* it pay? It's justifying yourself by success."

Joe shook her head, unconvinced.

"Are you really going to have all those things?" said Vernon.

Both the cousins looked at Sebastian with a tinge of envy. Queer, and rather wonderful, to be in old Sebastian's position. His father had died some years before. Sebastian, at twenty-two, was master of so many millions that it took one's breath away to think about them.

The friendship with Sebastian, begun all those years ago at Abbots Puissants, had endured and strengthened. He and Vernon had been friends at Eton, they were at the same college at Cambridge. In the holidays the three had always managed to spend a good deal of time together.

"What about sculpture?" asked Joe suddenly. "Is that included?"

"Of course. Are you still keen about taking up modeling?"

"Rather. It's the only thing I really care about."

A derisive hoot of laughter came from Vernon.

"Yes, and what will it be this time next year? You'll be a frenzied poet or something."

"It takes one some time to find one's true vocation," said Joe with dignity. "But I'm really in earnest this time."

"You always are," said Vernon. "However, thank heaven you've given up that damned violin."

"Why do you hate music so, Vernon?"

"Dunno—I always have."

Joe turned back to Sebastian. Unconsciously her voice took on a different note. It sounded ever so faintly constrained.

"What do you think of Paul la Marre's work? Vernon and I went to his studio last Sunday."

"No guts," said Sebastian succinctly.

A slight flush rose in Joe's cheek.

"That's simply because you don't understand what he's aiming at. I think he's wonderful."

"Anemic," said Sebastian, unperturbed.

"Sebastian, I think you're perfectly hateful sometimes. Just because La Marre has the courage to break away from tradition—"

"That's not it at all," said Sebastian. "A man can break away from tradition by modeling a Stilton cheese and calling it his idea of a nymph bathing. But if he can't convince you and impress you by doing so, he's failed. Just doing things differently to anyone else isn't genius. Nine times out of ten it's aiming at getting cheap notoriety."

The door opened and Mrs. Levinne looked in.

"Tea'th ready, dearths," she said, and beamed on them.

Jet dangled and twinkled on her immense bust. A large black hat with feathers sat on top of her elaborately arranged coiffure. She looked the complete symbol of material prosperity. Her eyes dwelt adoration on Sebastian.

They got up, and prepared to follow her. Sebastian said in a low voice to Joe:

"Joe—you're not angry, are you?"

There was suddenly something young and pathetic about his voice—a pleading in it that exposed him as immature and vulnerable. A moment ago he had been the master spirit laying down the law in complete self-confidence.

"Why should I be angry?" said Joe coldly.

She moved toward the door without looking at him. Sebastian's eyes rested on her wistfully. She had that dark magnetic beauty that matures early. Her skin was dead white, and her eyelashes so thick and dark that they looked like jet against the even color of her cheeks. There was magic in her way of moving, something languorous and passionate that was wholly unconscious as yet of its own appeal. Although she was the youngest of the three, just past her twentieth birthday, she was at the same time the oldest. To her Vernon and Sebastian were boys, and she despised boys. That queer doglike devotion of Sebastian's irritated her. She liked men of experience, men who could say exciting, half-understood things. She lowered her white eyelids for a moment, remembering Paul la Marre.

2

Mrs. Levinne's drawing room was a curious mixture of sheer blatant opulence and an almost austere good taste. The opulence was due to her—she liked velvet hangings and rich cushions and marble and gilding—the taste was Sebastian's. It was he who had torn down a medley of pictures from the wall and substituted two of his own choosing. His mother was reconciled to their plainness, as she called it, by the immense price that had been paid for them. The old Spanish leather screen was one of her son's presents to her—so was the exquisite *cloisonné* vase.

Seated behind an unusually massive silver tea tray, Mrs. Levinne raised the teapot with two hands and made conversational inquiries, lisping slightly.

"And how'th your dear mother? She never comes to town nowadays. You tell her from me she'll be getting rusty."

She laughed, a good-natured fat wheezy chuckle.

"I've never regretted having this town hou'th as well as a country one. Deerfields is all very well, but one wantth a bit of life. And of course Sebastian will be home soon for good—and that full of schemes as he ith! Well, well, his father was much the same. Went into deals against everybody'th advice, and instead of losing his money he doubled and trebled it every time. A thmart fellow, my poor Yakob."

Sebastian thought to himself: "I wish she wouldn't. That's just the sort of remark Joe always hates. Joe's always against me nowadays. . . ."

Mrs. Levinne went on: "I've got a box for *Kings in Arcady* on Wednesday night. What about it, my dearth? Will you come?"

"I'm awfully sorry, Mrs. Levinne," said Vernon. "I wish we could. But we're going down to Birmingham tomorrow."

"Oh! you're going home."

"Yes."

Why hadn't he said "going home?" Why did it sound so fantastic in his ears? There was only one home, of course—Abbots Puissants. Home! A queer word, so many meanings to it. It reminded him of the ridiculous words of a song that one of Joe's young men used to bray out (What a damnable thing music was!) while he fingered his collar and looked at her sentimentally. "Home, love, is where the heart is, where'er the heart may be . . ."

But in that case his home ought to be in Birmingham where his mother was.

He experienced that faint feeling of disquietude that always came over him when he thought of his mother. He was very fond of her, naturally. Mothers, of course, were hopeless people to explain things to, they never understood. But he *was* very fond of her—it would be unnatural if he wasn't. As she so often said, he was all she had.

Suddenly a little imp seemed to jump in Vernon's brain. The imp said suddenly and unexpectedly: "What rot you are talking! She's got the house, and the servants to talk to and bully, and friends to gossip with, and her own people all round her. She'd miss all that far more than she'd miss you. She loves you, but she's relieved when you go back to Cambridge—and even then she's not as relieved as you are!"

"Vernon!" It was Joe's voice, sharp with annoyance. "What are you thinking of? Mrs. Levinne was asking about Abbots Puissants—if it's still let?"

How fortunate that when people said "What *are* you thinking about?" they didn't in the least mean that they wanted to know! Still, you could always say "Nothing much," just as when you were small you had said "Nothing."

He answered Mrs. Levinne's questions, promised to deliver her various messages to his mother.

Sebastian saw them to the door, they said a final good-bye and walked out into the London streets. Joe sniffed the air ecstatically.

"How I love London! You know, Vernon, my mind's made up. I'm coming up to London to study. I'm going to tackle Aunt Myra about it this time. And I won't live with Aunt Ethel, either. I'm going to be on my own."

"You can't do that, Joe. Girls don't."

"They *do*. I could share rooms with another girl or girls. But to live with Aunt Ethel, always asking me where I'm going, and who with—I just can't stand it. And anyway she hates me being a suffragette."

The Aunt Ethel they referred to was Aunt Carrie's sister, an aunt by courtesy only. They were staying with her at the present moment.

"Oh! and that reminds me," went on Joe. "You've got to do something for me, Vernon."

"What?"

"Tomorrow afternoon Mrs. Cartwright's taking me to that Titantic Concert as a special treat."

"Well?"

"Well, I don't want to go—that's all."

"You can make some excuse or other, I suppose."

"It's not so easy as that. You see, Aunt Ethel's got to think I've gone to the concert. I don't want her ferreting out where I am going."

Vernon gave a whistle.

"Oh! so that's it? What are you really up to, Joe? Who is it this time?"

"It's La Marre, if you really want to know."

"That bounder."

"He's not a bounder. He's wonderful—you don't know how wonderful he is."

Vernon grinned.

"No, indeed I don't. I don't like Frenchmen."

"You're so horribly insular. But it doesn't matter whether you like him or not. He's going to motor me down to the country to a friend's house where his *chef d'oeuvre* is. I do so want to go, and you know perfectly that Aunt Ethel would never let me."

"You oughtn't to go racketing about the country with a fellow like that."

"Don't be an ass, Vernon. Don't you know that I can look after myself?"

"Oh! I suppose so."

"I'm not one of those silly girls who know nothing about anything."

"I don't see, though, where *I* come in."

"Well, you see," Joe displayed a trace of anxiety, "you're to go to the concert."

"No, I won't do anything of the kind. You know I hate music."

"Oh! you must, Vernon. It's the only way. If I say I can't go she'll ring up Aunt Ethel and suggest one of the girls coming instead, and then the fat will be in the fire. But if you just turn up instead of me—I'm to meet her at the Albert Hall—and give some weak excuse, everything will be all right. She's very fond of you—she likes you heaps better than me."

"But I loathe music."

"I know, but you can just bear it for one afternoon. An hour and a half. That's all it will be."

"Oh! damn it all, Joe, I don't want to."

His hand shook with irritation. Joe stared at him.

"You are *funny* about music, Vernon! I've never known anyone who sort of—well, hates it like you. Most people just don't care for it. But I do think you might go—you know *I* always do things for *you*."

"All right," said Vernon abruptly.

It was no good. It had got to be. Joe and he always stood together. After all, as she had said, it would only be an hour and a half. Why should he feel that he had taken a momentous decision? His heart felt like lead—right down in his boots. He didn't want to go—oh! he didn't want to go!

Like a visit to the dentist—best not to think about it. He forced his mind away to other things. Joe looked up sharply as she heard him give vent to a chuckle.

"What is it?"

"I was thinking of you as a kid—so grand about saying you were never going to have anything to do with men. And now it's always men with you, one after the other. You fall in and out of love about once a month."

"Don't be so horrid, Vernon. Those were just silly girls' fancies. La Marre says if you have any temperament that always happens—but the real grand passion is quite different when it comes."

"Well, don't go and have a grand passion for La Marre."

Joe did not answer. Presently she said:

"I'm not like Mother. Mother was—was so *soft* about men. She gave in to them—would do anything for anyone she was fond of. I'm not like that."

"No," said Vernon, after thinking for a moment. "No, I don't think you are. You won't make a mess of your life in the same way she did. But you might make a mess of it in a different way."

"What sort of a way?"

"I don't quite know. Going and marrying someone you thought you had a grand passion for, just because everyone else disliked him, and then spending your life fighting him. Or deciding to go and live with someone just because you thought Free Love was a fine idea."

"So it is."

"Oh! I am not saying it isn't—though, as a matter of fact, I really think it is antisocial myself. But you're always the same. If anyone forbids you anything you always want to do it—quite irrespective of whether you really want to. I haven't put that well, but you know what I mean."

"What I really want is to *do* something! To be a great sculptor."

"That's because you've got a pash for La Marre."

"It isn't. Oh! Vernon, why will you be so trying? I've *always* wanted to do something—always—always! I used to say so at Abbots Puissants."

"It's odd," said Vernon thoughtfully. "Old Sebastian used to say then very much what he says now. Perhaps one doesn't change as much as one thinks."

"You were going to marry someone very beautiful and live at Abbots Puissant always," said Joe with slight scorn. "You don't still feel that to be your life's ambition, do you?"

"One might do worse," said Vernon.

"Lazy—downright lazy!"

Joe looked at him in unconcealed impatience. She and Vernon were so alike in some ways, and so different in others!

Vernon was thinking: "Abbots Puissants. In a year I shall be twenty-one."

They were passing a Salvation Army meeting. Joe stopped. A thin white-faced man was standing on a box. His voice, high and raucous, came echoing across to them:

"Why won't you be saved? Why won't you? Jesus wants you! Jesus wants *you!*" Tremendous emphasis on the you. "Yes, brothers and sisters, and I'll tell you something more. *You want Jesus.* You won't admit it to yourselves, you turn your back on him, you're afraid—that's what it is, you're afraid, because you want him so badly—you want him and you don't know!" His arms waved, his white face shone with ecstasy. "But you will know—you *will* know. There are things that you can't run away from forever." He spoke slowly, almost menacingly. "*I say unto you, this very night shall thy soul be required of thee.*"

Vernon turned away with a slight shiver. A woman on the outskirts of the crowd gave a hysterical sob.

"Disgusting," said Joe, her nose very much in the air. "Indecent and

hysterical! For my part, I can't see how any rational being can be anything but an atheist."

Vernon smiled to himself, though he said nothing. He was remembering the time, a year ago, when Joe had risen every day to attend early
service and had insisted on eating a boiled egg with some ostentation on
Fridays, and had sat spellbound listening to the somewhat uninteresting
but strictly dogmatical sermons of handsome Father Cuthbert at the
Church of St. Bartholemew which was reputed to be so "high" that
Rome itself could do no more.

"I wonder," he said aloud, "what it would feel like to be 'saved'?"

3

It was half-past six on the following afternoon when Joe returned from
her stolen day's pleasure. Her Aunt Ethel met her in the hall.

"Where's Vernon?" inquired Joe, in case she might be asked how she
had liked the concert.

"He came in about half an hour ago. He said there was nothing the
matter, but somehow I don't think he's very well."

"Oh!" Joe stared. "Where is he? In his room? I'll go up and see."

"I wish you would, dear. Really he didn't look well at all."

Joe ran quickly up the stairs, gave a perfunctory rap on Vernon's
door, and walked in. Vernon was sitting on his bed, and something in
his appearance gave Joe a shock. She had never seen Vernon look quite
like this.

"Vernon, what's the matter?"

He didn't answer. He had the dazed look of someone who has undergone a terrible shock. It was as though he were too far away to be
reached by mere words.

"Vernon." She shook him by the shoulder. "What *is* the matter with
you?"

He heard her this time.

"Nothing."

"There must be something. You're looking—you're looking—"

Words failed her to express how he was looking. She left it at that.

"Nothing," he repeated dully.

She sat down on the bed beside him.

"Tell me," she said gently but authoritatively.

A long shuddering sigh broke from Vernon.

"Joe, do you remember that man yesterday?"

"Which man?"

"That Salvation Army chap—those cant phrases he used. And that one—a fine one—from the Bible: *This night shall thy soul be required of thee.* I said afterward I wondered what it would be like to be saved. Just idly. Well, I *know!*"

Joe stared at him. *Vernon!* Oh! but such a thing was impossible.

"Do you mean—do you mean—" Difficult, somehow, to get the words. "Do you mean you've 'got religion'—suddenly—like people do?"

She felt it was ridiculous as she said it. She was relieved when he gave a sudden spurt of laughter.

"*Religion?* Good God, no! Or is it that for some people? I wonder . . . No, I mean—" he hesitated, brought the word out at last very softly, almost as though he dared not speak it: "*Music.*"

"Music?" She was still utterly at sea.

"Yes. Joe, do you remember Nurse Frances?"

"Nurse Frances? No, I don't think I do. Who was she?"

"Of course you wouldn't. It was before you came—the time I broke my leg. I've always remembered something she said to me. About not being in a hurry to run away from things before you've had a good look. Well, that's what happened to me today. I couldn't run away any longer—I just had to look. Joe, music's the most wonderful thing in the world."

"But—but—you've always said—"

"I know. That's why it's been such an awful shock. Not that I mean music is so wonderful *now*—but it *could* be—if you had it as it was meant to be! Little bits of it are ugly—it's like going up to a picture and seeing a nasty gray smear of paint—but go to a distance and it falls into its place as the most wonderful shadow. It's got to be a *whole.* I still think one violin's ugly, and a piano's beastly—but useful in a way, I suppose. But oh! Joe, music could be so wonderful—I know it could."

Joe was silent, bewildered. She understood now what Vernon meant by his opening words. His face had the queer dreamy exaltation that one associated with religious fervor. And yet she was a little frightened. His face had always expressed so little. Now, she thought, it expressed too much. It was a worse face or a better face, just as you chose to look on it.

He went on talking, hardly to her, more to himself.

"There were nine orchestras, you know. All massed. Sound can be glorious if you get enough of it. I don't mean just loudness—it shows more when it's soft. But there must be enough. I don't know what they played—nothing, I think, that was real. But it showed one—it showed one—"

He turned queer bright excited eyes upon her.

"There's so much to know—to learn. I don't want to play things—never that. But I want to know about every instrument there is. What it can do, what are its limitations, what are its possibilities. And the notes, too. There are notes they don't use—notes that they ought to use. I know there are. Do you know what music's like now, Joe? It's like the little sturdy Norman pillars in the crypt of Gloucester Cathedral. It's at its beginnings, that's all."

He sat silent, leaning forward dreamily.

"Well, I think you've gone quite mad," said Joe.

She tried on purpose to make her voice sound practical and matter of fact. But, in spite of herself, she was impressed. That white-hot conviction. And she had always thought Vernon rather a slow coach—reactionary, prejudiced, unimaginative.

"I've got to begin to learn. As soon as ever I can. Oh! it's awful—to have wasted twenty years!"

"Nonsense," said Joe. "You couldn't have studied music when you were an infant in a cot."

He smiled at that. He was coming out of his trance by degrees.

"You think I'm mad? I suppose it must sound like that. But I'm not. And oh! Joe, it's the most awful *relief*. As though you had been pretending for years, and now you needn't pretend anymore. I've been horribly afraid of music—always. Now—"

He sat up, squared his shoulders.

"I'm going to work—work like a nigger. I'm going to know the ins and outs of every instrument. By the way, there must be more instruments in the world—many more. There ought to be a kind of waily thing—I've heard it somewhere. You'd want ten—fifteen of those. And about fifty harps."

He sat there, planning composedly details that to Joe sounded sheer nonsense. Yet it was evident that to his inner vision some event was perfectly clear.

"It'll be suppertime in ten minutes," Joe reminded him timidly.

"Oh! will it? What a nuisance. I want to stay here and think and hear things in my head. Tell Aunt Ethel I've got a headache or that I've been frightfully sick. As a matter of fact, I think I *am* going to be sick."

And somehow that impressed Joe more than anything else. It was a homely familiar happening. When anything upset you very much, either pleasurably or otherwise, you always wanted to be sick! She had felt that herself, often.

She stood in the door hesitating. Vernon had relapsed into abstraction again. How queer he looked! Quite different. As though—as though— Joe sought for the words she wanted—as though he had suddenly come alive.

She was a little frightened.

Chapter Two

Carey Lodge was the name of Myra's house. It was about eight miles from Birmingham.

A subtle depression always weighed down Vernon's spirits as he got near Carey Lodge. He hated the house, hated its solid comfort, its thick bright-red carpets, its lounge hall, the carefully selected sporting prints that hung in the dining room, the superabundance of knick-knacks that filled the drawing room. And yet, was it so much those things he hated as the facts that stood behind them?

He questioned himself, trying for the first time to be honest with himself. Wasn't it the truth that he hated his mother being so at home there, so placidly content? He liked to think of her in terms of Abbots Puissants—liked to think of her as being, like himself, an exile.

And she wasn't! Abbots Puissants had been to her what a foreign kingdom might be to a queen consort. She had felt important there, and pleased with herself. It had been new and exciting. But it hadn't been home.

Myra greeted her son with extravagant affection as always. He wished she wouldn't. In some way it made it harder than ever for him to respond. When he was away from her he pictured himself being affectionate to his mother. When he was with her all that illusion faded away.

Myra Deyre had altered a good deal since leaving Abbots Puissants. She had grown much stouter. Her beautiful golden-red hair was flecked with gray. The expression of her face was different, it was at once more satisfied and more placid. There was now a strong resemblance between her and her brother Sydney.

"You've had a good time in London? I'm so glad. It's so exciting to have my fine big son back with me—I've been telling everybody how excited I am. Mothers are foolish creatures, aren't they?"

Vernon thought they were rather—then was ashamed of himself.

"Very jolly to see you, Mother," he mumbled.

Joe said: "You're looking splendidly fit, Aunt Myra."

"I've not really been very well, dear. I don't think Dr. Grey quite understands my case. I hear there's a new doctor—Dr. Littleworth—just bought Dr. Armstrong's practice. They say he is wonderfully clever. I'm sure it's my heart—and it's all nonsense Dr. Grey saying it's indigestion."

She was quite animated. Her health was always an absorbing topic to Myra.

"Mary's gone—the housemaid, you know. I was really very disappointed in that girl. After all I did for her."

It went on and on. Joe and Vernon listened perfunctorily. Their minds were full of conscious superiority. Thank heaven they belonged to a new and enlightened generation, far above this insistence on domestic details! For them, a new and splendid world opened out. They were deeply, poignantly sorry for the contented creature who sat there chattering to them.

Joe thought: "Poor—poor Aunt Myra! So terribly female! Of course Uncle Walter got bored with her. Not her fault! A rotten education, and brought up to believe that domesticity was all that mattered. And here she is, still young really—at least not too terribly old—and all she's got to do is to sit in the house and gossip, and think about servants, and fuss about her health. If she'd only been born twenty years later she could have been happy and free and independent all her life."

And out of her intense pity for her unconscious aunt she answered gently and pretended an interest that she certainly did not feel.

Vernon thought: "Was Mother always like this? Somehow she didn't seem so at Abbots Puissants. Or was I too much of a kid to notice? It's rotten of me to criticize her when she's been so good to me always. Only I wish she wouldn't treat me still as though I were about six years old. Oh, well, I suppose she can't help it. I don't think I shall ever marry."

And suddenly he jerked out abruptly, urged thereto by intense nervousness:

"I say, Mother. I'm thinking of taking music at Cambridge."

There, it was out! He had said it.

Myra, distracted from her account of the Armstrongs' cook, said vaguely:

"But darling, you always were so unmusical. You used to be quite unreasonable about it."

"I know," said Vernon gruffly. "But one changes one's mind about things sometimes."

"Well, I'm very glad, dear. I used to play quite brilliant pieces myself when I was a young girl. But one never keeps up anything when one marries."

"I know. It's a wicked shame," said Joe hotly. "I don't mean to marry—but if I did I'd never give up my own career. And that reminds me, Aunt Myra, I've just got to go to London to study if I'm ever going to be any good at modeling."

"I'm sure Mr. Bradford—"

"Oh, damn Mr. Bradford! I'm sorry, Aunt Myra, but you don't understand. I've got to study—*hard*. And I must be on my own. I could share diggings with another girl—"

"Joe, darling, don't be so absurd." Myra laughed. "I need my little Joe here. I always look on you as my daughter, you know, Joe dear."

Joe wriggled.

"I really am in earnest, Aunt Myra. It's my whole life."

This tragic utterance only made her aunt laugh more.

"Girls often think like that. Now don't let's spoil this happy evening by quarreling."

"But will you really seriously consider it?"

"We must see what Uncle Sydney says."

"It's nothing to do with him. He's not *my* uncle. Surely, if I like, I can take my own money."

"It isn't exactly your own money, Joe. Your father sends it to me as an allowance for you—though I'm sure I would be willing to have you without any allowance at all—and knows you are well and safely looked after with me."

"Then I suppose I'd better write to Father."

She said it valiantly, but her heart sank. She had seen her father twice in ten years, and the old antagonism held between them. The present plan doubtless commended itself to Major Waite. At the cost of a few hundreds a year, the problem of his daughter was lifted off his hands. But Joe had no money of her own. She doubted very much if her father would make her any allowance at all if she broke away from Aunt Myra and insisted on leading her own life.

Vernon murmured to her: "Don't be so damned impatient, Joe. Wait till I'm twenty-one."

That cheered her a little. One could always depend on Vernon.

Myra asked Vernon about the Levinnes. Was Mrs. Levinne's asthma any better? Was it true that they spent almost all of their time in London nowadays?

"No, I don't think so. Of course, they don't go down to Deerfields much in the winter, but they were there all the autumn. It'll be jolly to have them next door when we go back to Abbots Puissants, won't it?"

His mother started, and said in a flustered sort of voice: "Oh! yes—very nice."

She added almost immediately: "Your Uncle Sydney is coming round to tea. He's bringing Enid. By the way, I don't have late dinner anymore. I really think it suits me better to have a good sit-down meal at six."

"Oh!" said Vernon, rather taken aback.

He had an unreasoning prejudice against those meals. He disliked the juxtaposition of tea and scrambled eggs and rich plum cake. Why couldn't his mother have proper meals like other people? Of course, Uncle Sydney and Aunt Carrie always had high tea. Bother Uncle Sydney! All this was his fault.

His thought stopped—checked. All what? He couldn't answer—didn't quite know. But anyway, when he and his mother went back to Abbots Puissants everything would be different.

2

Uncle Sydney arrived very soon—very bluff and hearty, a little stouter than of old. With him came Enid, his third daughter. The two eldest were married, and the two youngest were in the schoolroom.

Uncle Sydney was full of jokes and fun. Myra looked at her brother admiringly. Really, there was nobody like Sydney? He made things go.

Vernon laughed politely at his uncle's jokes, which he privately thought both stupid and boring.

"I wonder where you buy your tobacco in Cambridge," said Uncle Sydney. "From a pretty girl, I'll be bound. Ha! Ha! Myra, the boy's blushing—actually blushing."

"Stupid old fool!" thought Vernon disdainfully.

"And where do *you* buy your tobacco, Uncle Sydney?" said Joe, valiantly entering the lists.

"Ha! Ha!" trumpeted Uncle Sydney. "That's a good one. You're a smart girl, Joe. We won't tell your Aunt Carrie the answer to that, eh?"

Enid said very little but giggled a good deal.

"You ought to write to your cousin," said Uncle Sydney. "He'd like a letter, wouldn't you, Vernon?"

"Rather," said Vernon.

"There you are," said Uncle Sydney. "What did I tell you, Miss? The child wanted to, but was shy. She's always thought a lot of you, Vernon. But I mustn't tell tales out of school, hey, Enid?"

Later, after the heavy composite meal was ended, he talked to Vernon at some length of the prosperity of Bent's.

"Booming, my boy, booming."

He went into long financial explanations: profits had doubled, he was extending the premises—and so on and so on.

Vernon much preferred this style of conversation. Not being the least interested, he could abstract his attention. An encouraging monosyllable from time to time was all that was needed.

Uncle Sydney talked on, developing the fascinating theme of the Power and Glory of Bent's, World without End, Amen.

Vernon thought about the book on musical instruments which he had bought that morning and read coming down in the train. There was a terrible lot to know. Oboes—he felt he was going to have ideas about oboes. And violas—yes, certainly, violas.

Uncle Sydney's talk made a pleasant accompaniment, like a remote double bass.

Presently Uncle Sydney said he must be getting along. There was more facetiousness—should or should not Vernon kiss Enid good-night?

How idiotic people were! Thank goodness he'd soon be able to get up to his own room!

Myra heaved a happy sigh as the door closed.

"Dear me!" she murmured. "I wish your father had been here. We've had such a happy evening. He would have enjoyed it."

"A jolly good thing he wasn't," said Vernon. "I don't remember that he and Uncle Sydney ever hit it off really well."

"You were only a little boy. They were the greatest of friends, and your father was always happy when I was. Oh, dear, how happy we were together!"

She raised a handkerchief to her eyes. Vernon stared at her. For a moment he thought: "This is the most magnificent loyalty." And then suddenly: "No, it isn't. She really believes it."

Myra went on in a soft reminiscent tone:

"You were never really fond of your father, Vernon. I think it must have grieved him sometimes. But then you were so devoted to me. It was quite ridiculous."

Vernon said suddenly and violently, and with a strange feeling that
he was defending his father by saying so:

"Father was a brute to you."

"Vernon, how dare you say such a thing? Your father was the best
man in the world."

She looked at him defiantly. He thought: "She's seeing herself being
heroic. 'How wonderful a woman's love can be—protecting her dead'—
that sort of thing. Oh! I hate it all. I hate it all."

He mumbled something, kissed her, and went up to bed.

3

Later in the evening Joe tapped at his door and was bidden to enter.
Vernon was sitting sprawled out in a chair. The book on musical instruments lay on the floor beside him.

"Hullo, Joe. God, what a beastly evening!"

"Did you mind it so much?"

"Didn't you? It's all wrong. What an ass Uncle Sydney is. Those
idiotic jokes! It's all so cheap."

"H'm," said Joe. She sat down thoughtfully on the bed and lit a
cigarette.

"Don't you agree?"

"Yes—at least I do in a way."

"Spit it out," said Vernon encouragingly.

"Well, what I mean is, *they're* happy enough."

"Who?"

"Aunt Myra. Uncle Sydney. Enid. They're a united happy lot, thoroughly content with one another. It's we who are wrong, Vernon. You
and I. We've lived here all these years—but we don't belong. That's
why—we've got to get out of it."

Vernon nodded thoughtfully.

"Yes, Joe, you're right. We've got to get out of it." He smiled happily, because the way was so clear. Twenty-one . . . Abbots Puissants . . .
Music.

Chapter Three

Do you mind just going over that once more, Mr. Flemming?"
"Willingly."

Precise, dry, even, word after word fell from the old lawyer's lips. His meaning was clear and unmistakable! Too much so! It didn't leave a loophole for doubt.

Vernon listened. His face was very white, his hands grasped the arms of the chair in which he was sitting.

It couldn't be true—it *couldn't!* And yet, after all, hadn't Mr. Flemming said very much the same, years ago? Yes, but then there had been the magic words "twenty-one" to look forward to. "Twenty-one" which by a blessed miracle was to make everything right. Instead of which:

"Mind you, the position is infinitely improved from what it was at the time of your father's death, but it is no good pretending we are out of the wood. The mortgage . . ."

Surely, surely, they had never mentioned a mortgage? Well, it wouldn't have been much use, he supposed, to a boy of nine. No good trying to get round it. The plain truth was that he couldn't afford to live at Abbots Puissants.

He waited till Mr. Flemming had finished and then said: "But if my mother . . ."

"Oh! of course. If Mrs. Deyre were prepared to . . ." He left the sentence unfinished, paused, and then added: "But, if I may say so, every time that I have had the pleasure of seeing Mrs. Deyre she has seemed to me to be very settled—very settled indeed. I suppose you know that she bought the freehold of Carey Lodge two years ago?"

Vernon hadn't known it. He saw plainly enough what it meant. Why hadn't his mother told him? Hadn't she had the courage? He had always taken it for granted that she would come back with him to Abbots Puissants, not so much because he longed for her presence there, as because it was—quite naturally—her home.

But it wasn't her home. It never could be in the sense that Carey Lodge was her home.

He could appeal to her, of course. Beg her, for his sake, because he wanted it so much.

No, a thousand times no! You couldn't beg favors from people you didn't really love. And he didn't really love his mother. He didn't believe he ever really had. Queer and sad and a little dreadful, but there it was.

If he never saw her again, would he mind? Not really. He would like to know that she was well and happy—cared for. But he wouldn't miss her, would never feel a longing for her presence. Because, in a queer way, he didn't really *like* her. He disliked the touch of her hands, always had to take a hold on himself before kissing her good-night. He'd never been able to tell her anything—she never understood or knew what he was feeling. She had been a good loving mother—and he didn't even like her! Rather horrible, he supposed, most people would say. . . .

He said quietly to Mr. Flemming: "You are quite right. I am sure my mother would not wish to leave Carey Lodge."

"Now, there are one or two alternatives open to you, Mr. Deyre. Major Salmon, who, as you know, has rented it furnished all these years, is anxious to buy—"

"No!" The word burst from Vernon like a pistol shot.

Mr. Flemming smiled.

"I was sure you would say that. And I must confess I am glad. There have been—er—Deyres at Abbots Puissants for, let me see, nearly five hundred years. Nevertheless, I should be failing in my duty if I didn't point out to you that the price offered is a good one, and that if, later, you should decide to sell, it may not be easy to find a suitable purchaser."

"It's out of the question."

"Very good. Then the best thing, I think, is to try and let once more. Major Salmon definitely wants to buy a place, so it will mean finding a new tenant. But I dare say we shall have no great difficulty. The point is, how long do you want to let for? To let the place for another long term of years is, I should say, not very desirable. Life is very uncertain. Who knows, in a few years the state of affairs may have—er—changed very considerably, and you may be in a position to take up residence there yourself."

"So I shall, but not the way you think, you old dunderhead," thought Vernon. "It'll be because I've made a name for myself in music—not because Mother is dead. I'm sure I hope she'll live to be ninety."

He exchanged a few more words with Mr. Flemming then rose to go.

"I'm afraid this has been rather a shock to you," said the old lawyer as he shook hands.

"Yes—just a bit. I've been building castles in the air, I suppose."

"You're going down to spend your twenty-first birthday with your mother, I suppose?"

"Yes."

"You might talk things over with your uncle, Mr. Bent. A very shrewd man of business. He has a daughter about your age, I think?"

"Yes, Enid. The two eldest are married, and the two youngest are at school. Enid's about a year younger than I am."

"Ah! very pleasant to have a cousin of one's own age. I dare say you will see a good deal of her."

"Oh! I don't suppose I shall," said Vernon vaguely.

Why should he be seeing a lot of Enid? She was a dull girl. But of course Mr. Flemming didn't know that.

Funny old chap. What on earth was there to put on such a sly knowing expression about?

2

"Well, Mother, I don't seem to be exactly the young heir!"

"Oh! well, dear, you mustn't worry. Things arrange themselves, you know. You must have a good talk with your Uncle Sydney."

Silly! What good could a talk with his Uncle Sydney do him?

Fortunately the matter was not referred to again. The extraordinary surprise was that Joe had been allowed to have her way. She was actually in London—somewhat dragoned and chaperoned, it is true—but still she had got her way.

His mother seemed always to be whispering mysteriously to friends. Vernon caught her at it one day.

"Yes . . . quite inseparable, they were . . . so I thought it wiser . . . it would be such a pity . . ." And what Vernon called the "other tabby" said something about "First cousins . . . most unwise . . ." and his mother, with a suddenly heightened color and raised voice, had said: "Oh! I don't think in *every* case."

"Who were first cousins?" asked Vernon later. "What was all the mystery about?"

"Mystery, darling? I don't know what you mean."

"Well, you shut up when I came in. I wondered what it was all about?"

"Oh! nothing interesting. Some people you don't know."

She looked rather red and confused.

Vernon wasn't curious. He asked no more.

He missed Joe most frightfully. Carey Lodge was pretty deadly without her. For one thing, he saw more of Enid than he ever had before. She was always coming in to see Myra, and Vernon would find himself let in for taking her to roller-skate at the new rink, or for some deadly party or other.

Myra told Vernon that it would be nice if he asked Enid up to Cambridge for May Week. She was so persistent about it that Vernon gave in. After all, it didn't matter. Sebastian would have Joe and he himself didn't much care. Dancing was rather rot. Everything was rot that interfered with music.

The evening before his departure Uncle Sydney came to Carey Lodge and Myra pushed Vernon into the study with him and said, "Your Uncle Sydney's come to have a little talk with you, Vernon."

Mr. Bent hemmed and hawed for a minute or two and then, rather surprisingly, came straight to the point. Vernon had never liked his uncle as much. His facetious manner had been entirely laid aside.

"I'm coming straight out with what I want to say, my boy—but I don't want you interrupting till I've finished. See?"

"Yes, Uncle Sydney."

"The long and short of it is just this. *I want you to come into Bent's.* Now remember what I said—no interruptions! I know you've never thought of such a thing, and I dare say the idea isn't very congenial to you now. I'm a plain man, and I can face facts as well as anyone. If you'd got a good income and could live at Abbots Puissants like a gentleman, there wouldn't be any question of the thing. Well, I accept that.

You're like your father's people. But for all that, you've got good Bent blood in your veins, my boy, and blood's bound to tell.

"I've got no son of my own. I'm willing—if you're willing—to look upon you as a son. The girls are provided for, and handsomely provided for at that. And mind you, it won't be a case of toiling for life. I'm not unreasonable—and I realize just as much as you do what that place of yours stands for. You're a young fellow. You go into the business when you come down from Cambridge—mind you, you go into it from the bottom. You'll start at a moderate salary and work up. If you want to retire before you're forty, well, you can do so. Please yourself. You'll be a rich man by then, and you'll be able to run Abbots Puissants as it should be run.

"You'll marry young, I hope. Excellent thing, young marriages. Your eldest boy succeeds to the place, the younger sons find a first-class business to step into where they can show what they're made of. I'm proud of Bent's—as proud of Bent's as you are of Abbots Puissants—that's why I understand your feeling about the old place. I don't want you to have to sell it. Let it go out of the family after all these years—that would be a shame. Well, there's the offer."

"It's most awfully good of you, Uncle Sydney—" began Vernon.

His uncle threw up a large square hand and stopped him.

"We'll leave it at that, if you please. I don't want an answer now. In fact, I won't have one. When you come down from Cambridge—that's time enough."

He rose.

"Kind of you to ask Enid up for May Week. Very excited about it, she is. If you knew what that girl thought of you, Vernon, you'd be quite conceited. Ah! well, girls will be girls."

Laughing boisterously, he slammed the front door.

Vernon remained in the hall frowning. It was really jolly decent of Uncle Sydney—*jolly* decent.

Not that he was going to accept. All the money in the world wouldn't tear him from music.

And, somehow, he would have Abbots Puissants as well.

3

May Week!

Joe and Enid were at Cambridge. Vernon had been let in for Ethel, too, as chaperon. The world seemed largely composed of Bents just at present.

Joe had burst out at once with: "Why on earth did you ask Enid?"

He had answered: "Oh! Mother went on about it—it doesn't really matter."

Nothing mattered to Vernon just then except one thing. Joe talked privately to Sebastian about that.

"Is Vernon really in earnest about this music business? Will he ever be any good? I suppose it's just a passing craze?"

But Sebastian was unexpectedly serious.

"It's extraordinarily interesting, you know," he said. "As far as I can make out, what Vernon is aiming at is something entirely revolutionary. He's mastering now what you might call the main facts, and mastering them at an extraordinary rate. Old Coddington admits that, though of course he snorts at Vernon's ideas—or would if Vernon ever let out about them. The person who's interested is old Jeffries—mathematics! He says Vernon's ideas of music are fourth dimensional.

"I don't know if Vernon will ever pull it off—or whether he'll be considered as a harmless lunatic. The borderline is very narrow, I imagine. Old Jeffries is very enthusiastic. But not in the least encouraging. He points out, quite rightly, that to attempt to discover something new and force it on the world is always a thankless task, and that in all probability the truths that Vernon is discovering won't be accepted for at least another two hundred years. He's a queer old codger. Sits about thinking of imaginary curves in space—that sort of thing.

"But I see his point. Vernon isn't creating something new. He's discovering something that's already there. Rather like a scientist. Jeffries says that Vernon's dislike of music as a child is perfectly understandable. To his ear music's incomplete—it's like a picture out of drawing. The whole perspective is wrong. It sounds to Vernon like—I suppose a primitive savage's music would sound to us—mostly unendurable discord.

"Jeffries is full of queer ideas. Start him off on squares and cubes and geometrical figures and the speed of light and he goes quite mad. He writes to a German fellow called Einstein. The queer thing is that he isn't a bit musical, and yet he can see—or says he can—exactly what Vernon is driving at."

Joe cogitated deeply.

"Well," she said at last, "I don't understand a word of all this. But it looks as though Vernon might make a success of it all."

Sebastian was discouraging.

"I wouldn't say that. Vernon may be a genius—and that's quite a different thing. Nobody welcomes genius. On the other hand, he may be just slightly mad. He sounds mad enough sometimes when he gets going—and yet, somehow, I've always got a kind of feeling that he's right—that in some odd way he knows what he's talking about."

"You've heard about Uncle Sydney's offer?"

"Yes. Vernon seems to be turning it down very lightheartedly, and yet, you know, it's a good thing."

"You wouldn't have him accept it?" flamed out Joe.

Sebastian remained provokingly cool.

"I don't know. It needs thinking about. Vernon may have wonderful theories about this music business—there's nothing to show that he's ever going to be able to put them into practice."

"You're maddening," said Joe, turning away.

Sebastian annoyed her nowadays. All his cool analytical faculties seemed to be uppermost. If he had enthusiasms, he hid them carefully.

And to Joe, just now, enthusiasm seemed the most necessary thing in the world. She had a passion for lost causes, for minorities. She was a passionate champion of the weak and oppressed.

Sebastian she felt, was only interested in successes. She accused him in her own mind of judging everyone and everything by a monetary standard. Most of the time they were together they fought and bickered incessantly.

Vernon, too, seemed separated from her. Music was the only thing he wanted to talk about, and even then on lines that were not familiar to her.

His preoccupation was entirely with instruments—their scope and power—and the violin which Joe herself played seemed the instrument in which he was least interested. Joe was quite unfitted to talk about clarionets, trombones, and bassoons. Vernon's ambition in life seemed to be to form friendships with players of these instruments so as to be able to acquire some practical as opposed to theoretical knowledge.

"Don't you know any bassoon players?"

Joe said she didn't.

Vernon said that she might as well make herself useful and try and pick up some musical friends. "Even a French horn would do," he said kindly.

He drew an experimental finger round the edge of his finger bowl. Joe shuddered and clapped both hands to her ears. The sound increased in volume. Vernon smiled dreamily and ecstatically.

"One ought to be able to catch that and harness it. I wonder how it could be done. It's a lovely round sound, isn't it? Like a circle."

Sebastian took the finger bowl forcibly away from him, and he wandered round the room and rang various goblets experimentally.

"Nice lot of glasses in this room," he said appreciatively.

"You're drowning sailors," said Joe.

"Can't you be satisfied with bells and a triangle?" asked Sebastian. "And a little gong to beat."

"No," said Vernon. "I want glass. . . . Let's have the Venetian and the Waterford together. . . . I'm glad you have these aesthetic tastes, Sebastian. Have you got a common glass that I can smash?—all the tinkling fragments. Wonderful stuff—glass!"

"Symphony of goblets," said Joe scathingly.

"Well, why not? I suppose somebody once pulled a bit of catgut tight and found it made a squawky noise, and somebody once blew through a reed and liked it. I wonder when they first thought of making things of brass and metal. I dare say some book tells you."

"Columbus and the egg. You and Sebastian's glass goblets. Why not a slate and a slate pencil?"

"If you've got one . . ."

"Isn't he too funny?" giggled Enid. And that stopped the conversation—for the time, at any rate.

Not that Vernon really minded her presence. He was far too wrapped up in his ideas to be sensitive about them. Enid and Ethel were welcome to laugh as much as they chose.

But he was slightly disturbed by the lack of harmony between Joe and Sebastian. The three of them had always been such a united trio.

"I don't think this 'living your own life' stunt agrees with Joe," said Vernon to his friend. "She's like an angry cat most of the time. I can't think why Mother agreed. She was dead against it about six months ago. I can't imagine what made her change her mind, can you?"

A smile creased Sebastian's long yellow face.

"I could make a guess," he said.

"What?"

"I shan't say. In the first place, I may be wrong, and in the second place I should hate to interfere with the (possibly) normal course of events."

"That's your tortuous Russian mind."

"I dare say."

Vernon didn't insist. He was much too lazy to probe for reasons that weren't given him.

Day succeeded day. They danced, breakfasted, drove at incredibly fast speeds through the countryside, sat and smoked and talked in Vernon's rooms, danced again. It was a point of honor not to sleep. At five in the morning they went on the river.

Vernon's right arm ached. Enid fell to his share and she was a heavy partner. Well, it didn't matter. Uncle Sydney had seemed pleased, and he was a decent old boy. Jolly good of him to make that offer. What a pity it was that he (Vernon) was not more of a Bent and less of a Deyre.

A vague memory stirred in his mind—somebody saying, "The Deyres, Vernon, are neither happy nor successful. They can't make good." Who was it who had said that? A woman's voice, it had been, in a garden—and there had been curling cigarette smoke. . . .

Sebastian's voice said: "He's going to sleep. Wake up, you blighter! Chuck a chocolate at him, Enid."

A chocolate whizzed past his head. Enid's voice said with a giggle:

"I can't throw straight for nuts."

She giggled again as though she thought it very funny. Tiresome girl—always giggling. Besides, her teeth stuck out.

He heaved himself over onto his side. Not usually very appreciative of the beauties of Nature, this morning he was struck by the beauty of the world. The pale gleaming river, here and there on the banks a flowering tree.

The boat drifted slowly down stream . . . a queer silent enchanted world. Because, he supposed, there were no human beings about. It was, when you came to think of it, an excess of human beings who spoiled the world. Always chattering and talking and giggling, and asking you what you were thinking of when all you wanted was to be let alone.

He always remembered feeling that as a kid. If they'd only let him alone! He smiled to himself as he remembered the ridiculous games he had been in the habit of inventing. Mr. Green! He remembered Mr. Green perfectly. And those three playmates—what were their names, now?

A funny child's world—a world of dragons and princesses and strangely concrete realities mixed up with them. There had been a story someone had told him—a ragged prince with a little green hat and a princess in a tower whose hair when she combed it was so golden that it could be seen in four kingdoms.

He raised his head a little, looked along the river bank. There was a punt tied up under some trees. Four people in it—but Vernon only saw one.

A girl in a pink evening frock with hair like spun gold standing under a tree laden with pink blossom.

He looked and he looked.

"Vernon." Joe kicked him correctively. "You're not asleep because your eyes are open. You've been spoken to four times."

"Sorry. I was looking at that lot over there. That's rather a pretty girl, don't you think so?"

He tried to make his tone light—casual. Inside him a riotous voice was saying: "Pretty? She's lovely. She's the most lovely girl in the world. I'm going to get to know her. I've got to know her. I'm going to marry her. . . ."

Joe heaved herself up on her elbows, looked, uttered an exclamation.

"Why!" she exclaimed. "I do believe—yes, I'm sure it is. It's Nell Vereker."

4

Impossible. It couldn't be. Nell Vereker? Pale scraggy Nell, with her pink nose and her inappropriate starched dresses. Surely it couldn't be. Was Time capable of that kind of practical joke? If so, one couldn't be sure of anything. That long-ago Nell, and this Nell—they were two different people.

The whole world felt dreamlike. Joe was saying:

"If that's Nell, I really must speak to her. Let's go across."

And then the greetings, exclamations, surprise.

"Why, of course. Joe Waite. And Vernon! It's years ago, isn't it?"

Very soft her voice was. Her eyes smiled into his—a trifle shyly. Lovely—lovely—lovelier even than he had thought. Tongue-tied fool, why couldn't he say anything? Something brilliant, witty, arresting. How blue her eyes were with their long soft golden-brown lashes. She was like the blossom above her head—untouched, springlike.

A great wave of despondency swept over him. She would never marry him. Was it likely? A great clumsy tongue-tied creature such as he was. She was talking to him. Heavens! he must try and listen to what she said—answer intelligently.

"We left very soon after you did. Father gave up his job."

An echo came into his head of past gossip:

Vereker got the sack. Hopelessly incompetent—it was bound to come.

Her voice went on—such a lovely voice. You wanted to listen to it instead of to the words.

"We live in London now. Father died five years ago."

He said, feeling idiotic, "Oh! I say, I'm sorry, awfully sorry."

"I'll give you our address. You must come and see us."

He blundered out hopes of meeting her that evening. What dance was she going to? She told him. No good there. The night after—thank goodness! they'd be at the same. He said hurriedly:

"Look here. You've got to save me a dance or two—you must—we've not seen each other for years."

"Oh! but can I?" Her voice was doubtful.

"I'll fix it somehow. Leave it to me."

It was over all too soon. Good-byes were said. They were going up-stream again.

Joe said in an incredibly matter-of-fact tone, "Well, isn't that strange? Who would ever have thought that Nell Vereker would have turned out so good-looking? I wonder if she's as much of an ass as ever."

Sacrilege! He felt oceans removed from Joe. Joe couldn't see anything at all.

Would Nell ever marry him? *Would* she? Probably she'd never look at him. All sorts of fellows must be in love with her.

He felt terribly despondent. Black misery swept over him.

5

He was dancing with her. Never had he imagined that he could be so happy. She was like a feather, a rose leaf in his arms. She was wearing a pink dress again—a different one. It floated out all round her.

If life could only go on like this forever . . . forever . . .

But of course, life never did. In what seemed to Vernon like one second, the music stopped. They were sitting together on two chairs.

He wanted to say a thousand things to her—but he didn't know how to begin. He heard himself saying foolish things about the floor and the music.

Fool—unutterable fool! In a few minutes another dance would begin. She would be swept away from him. He must make some plan—some arrangement to meet her again.

She was talking—desultory in-between-dance talk. London—the season. Horrible to think of—she was going to dances night after night—three dances a night sometimes. And here was he tied by the leg. She would marry someone—some rich clever amusing fellow would snap her up.

He mumbled something about being in town—she gave him their address. Mother would be so pleased to see him again. He wrote it down.

The music struck up. He said desperately: "Nell—I say, I do call you Nell, don't I?"

"Why, of course." She laughed. "Do you remember hauling me over the palings that day we thought the rhinoceros was after us?"

And he had thought her a nuisance, he remembered. Nell! A nuisance!

She went on: "I used to think you were wonderful then, Vernon."

She had, had she? But she couldn't think him wonderful now. His mood drooped to despondency once more.

"I—I was an awful little rotter, I expect," he mumbled.

Why couldn't he be intelligent and clever and say witty things?

"Oh! you were a dear. Sebastian hasn't changed much, has he?"

Sebastian. She called him Sebastian. Well, after all, he supposed she would—since she called him Vernon. What a lucky thing it was that Sebastian cared for nobody but him. Sebastian with his money and his brains. Did Nell like Sebastian? he wondered.

"One would know his ears anywhere," said Nell with a laugh.

Vernon felt comforted. He had forgotten Sebastian's ears. No girl who had noticed Sebastian's ears could go falling in love with him. Poor old Sebastian! Rather rough luck to be handicapped with those ears.

He saw Nell's partner arriving. He blurted out quickly and hurriedly:

"I say, it's wonderful to have seen you again, Nell. Don't forget me, will you? I shall be turning up in town. It's—it's been awfully jolly seeing you again. (Oh! damn, I said that before!) I mean—it's been simply ripping. You don't know. But you won't forget, will you?"

She was gone from him. He saw her whirling round in Barnard's arms. She couldn't like Barnard surely, could she? Barnard was such an absolute ass.

Her eyes met his over Barnard's shoulder. She smiled.

He was in Heaven again. She liked him—he knew she liked him. She had smiled. . . .

6

May Week was over. Vernon was sitting at a table writing.

Dear Uncle Sydney:

I've thought over your offer, and I'd like to come into Bent's if you still want me. I'm afraid I shall be rather useless but I will try all I know. I still think it's most awfully good of you.

He paused. Sebastian was walking up and down restlessly. His pacing disturbed Vernon.

"For goodness' sake, sit down," he said irritably. "What's the matter with you?"

"Nothing."

Sebastian sat down with unusual mildness. He filled and lighted a pipe. From behind a sheltering haze of smoke, he spoke:

"I say, Vernon. I asked Joe to marry me that last night. She turned me down."

"Oh! rough luck," said Vernon, trying to bring his mind back and be sympathetic. "Perhaps she'll change her mind," he said vaguely. "They say girls do."

"It's this damned money," said Sebastian angrily.

"What damned money?"

"Mine. Joe always said she would marry me when we were kids together. She likes me—I'm sure she does. And now—everything I say or do always seems to be wrong. If I were only persecuted, or looked down on, or socially undesirable, I believe she'd marry me like a shot. But she's always got to be on the losing side. It's a ripping quality in a way, but you can carry it to a pitch where it's damned illogical. Joe is illogical."

"Hm," said Vernon vaguely.

He was selfishly intent on his own affairs. It seemed to him curious that Sebastian should be so keen on marrying Joe. There were lots of other girls who would suit him just as well. He reread his letter and added another sentence:

I will work like a nigger.

Chapter Four

W e want another man," said Mrs. Vereker.
Her eyebrows, slightly enhanced by art, drew together in a straight line as she frowned.

"It's too annoying young Wetherill failing us," she added.

Nell nodded apathetically. She was sitting on the arm of a chair, not yet dressed. Her golden hair hung in a stream over the pale pink kimono she was wearing. She looked very lovely and very young and defenseless.

Mrs. Vereker, sitting at her inlaid desk, frowned still more and bit the end of her penholder thoughtfully. The hardness that had always been noticeable was now accentuated and, as it were, crystallized. This was a woman who had battled steadily and unceasingly through life and was now engaged in a supreme struggle. She lived in a house the rent of which she could not afford to pay and she dressed her daughter in clothes she could not afford to buy. She got things on credit—not, like some others, by cajolery, but by sheer driving power. She never appealed to her creditors, she browbeat them.

And the result was that Nell went everywhere and did everything that other girls did and was better dressed while doing so.

"Mademoiselle is lovely," said the dressmakers, and their eyes would meet Mrs. Vereker's in a glance of understanding.

A girl so beautiful, so well turned out, would marry probably in her first season, certainly in her second—and then a rich harvest would be reaped. They were used to taking risks of this kind—Mademoiselle was lovely, Madame her mother was a woman of the world and a woman, they could see, who was accustomed to success in her undertakings. She would assuredly see to it that her daughter made a good match and did not marry a nobody.

Nobody but Mrs. Vereker knew the difficulties, the setbacks, the galling defeats of the campaign she had undertaken.

"There is young Earnescliff," she said thoughtfully. "But he is really too much of an outsider—and not even money to recommend him."

Nell looked at her pink polished nails.

"What about Vernon Deyre?" she suggested. "He wrote he was coming up to town this weekend."

"He would do," said Mrs. Vereker. She looked sharply at her daughter. "Nell, you're not—you're not allowing yourself to become foolish about that young man, are you? We seem to have seen a great deal of him lately."

"He dances well," said Nell. "And he's frightfully useful."

"Yes," said Mrs. Vereker. "Yes. It's a pity."

"What's a pity?"

"That he hasn't got a few more of this world's goods. He'll have to marry money if he's ever going to be able to keep up Abbots Puissants. It's mortgaged, you know. I found that out. Of course, when his mother dies . . . But she's one of those large healthy women who go on living till they're eighty or ninety. And besides, she may marry again. No, Vernon Deyre is hopeless considered as a *parti*. He's very much in love with you, too, poor boy."

"Do you think so?" said Nell in a low voice.

"Anyone can see it. It sticks out all over him—it always does with boys of that age. Well, they've got to go through calf love, I suppose. But no foolishness on your part, Nell."

"Oh! Mother, he's only a boy—a very nice boy, but a boy."

"He's a good-looking boy," said her mother dryly. "I'm only warning you. Being in love is a painful process when you can't have the man you want. And worse—"

She stopped. Nell knew well enough how her thoughts ran on. Captain Vereker had once been a handsome blue-eyed impecunious young subaltern. Her mother had been guilty of the folly of marrying him for love. She had lived to rue the day bitterly. A weak man, a failure, a drunkard. Disillusionment enough there in all conscience.

"Someone devoted is always useful," said Mrs. Vereker, reverting to her utilitarian standpoint. "He mustn't, of course, spoil your chances with other men. But you're too wise to let him monopolize you to that extent. Yes, write and ask him to drive down to Ranelagh and dine with us there on Sunday next."

Nell nodded. She got up and went to her own room, flung off the trailing kimono and started dressing. With a stiff brush she brushed out the long golden hair before coiling it round her small lovely head.

The window was open. A sooty London sparrow chirped and sang with the arrogance of his kind.

Something caught at Nell's heart. Oh! why was everything so—so—

So what? She didn't know—couldn't put into words the feeling that surged over her. Why couldn't things be nice instead of nasty? It would be just as easy for God.

Nell never thought much about God, but she knew, of course, that he was there. Perhaps, somehow or other, God would make everything come right for her.

There was something childlike about Nell Vereker on that summer's morning in London.

2

Vernon was in the seventh heaven. He had had the luck to meet Nell in the park that morning, and now there was a whole glorious rapturous evening! So happy was he that he almost felt affectionate toward Mrs. Vereker.

Instead of saying to himself, "That woman is a gorgon!" as he usually did, he found himself thinking: "She may not be so bad after all. Anyway, she's very fond of Nell."

At dinner he studied the other members of the party. There was an inferior girl dressed in green, a being not to be mentioned in the same breath with Nell, and there was a tall dark man, a Major Somebody, whose evening dress was very faultless and who talked about India a lot. An insufferably conceited being—Vernon hated him. Boasting and swaggering and showing off! A cold hand closed round his heart. Nell would marry this blighter and go away to India. He knew it, he simply knew it. He refused a course that was handed to him and gave the girl in green a hard time, so monosyllabic were his responses to her efforts.

The other man was older—very old to Vernon. A rather wooden

figure, very upright. Gray hair, blue eyes, a square determined face. It turned out that he was an American, though no one would have known it, for he had no trace of accent.

He spoke stiffly and a little punctiliously. He sounded rich. A very suitable companion for Mrs. Vereker, Vernon thought him. She might even marry him, and then, perhaps, she would cease worrying Nell and making her lead this insane life. . . .

Mr. Chetwynd seemed to admire Nell a good deal, which was only natural, and he paid her one or two rather old-fashioned compliments. He sat between her and her mother.

"You must bring Miss Nell to Dinard this summer, Mrs. Vereker," he said. "You really must. Quite a party of us going. Wonderful place."

"It sounds delightful, Mr. Chetwynd, but I don't know whether we can manage it. We seem to have promised so many people for visits and one thing and another."

"I know you're always so much in request that it's hard to get hold of you. I hope your daughter's not listening when I congratulate you on being the mother of the beauty of the season."

"And I said to the syce . . ."

This from Major Dacre.

All the Deyres had been soldiers. Why wasn't he a soldier, thought Vernon, instead of being in business in Birmingham? Then he laughed to himself. Absurd to be so jealous. What could be worse than to be a penniless subaltern? There would be no hope of Nell then.

Americans were rather long-winded—he was getting tired of the sound of Chetwynd's voice. If only dinner could come to an end! If he and Nell could wander together under the trees.

Wandering with Nell wasn't easy. He was foiled by Mrs. Vereker. She asked him questions about his mother and Joe, kept him by her side. He was no match for her in tactics. He had to stay there, answer, pretend he liked it.

There was only one crumb of comfort. Nell was walking with the old boy—not with Dacre.

Suddenly they encountered friends. Everyone stood talking. It was his chance. He found his way to Nell's side.

"Come with me—do. Quickly—now."

He had done it! He had got her away from the others. He was hurrying so that she had almost to run to keep up with him, but she didn't
say anything—didn't protest or make a joke about it.

The voices sounded from farther and farther away. He could hear
other sounds now—the hurried unevenness of Nell's breathing. Was that
because they had walked so fast? He didn't somehow think it was.

He slowed up. They were alone now—alone in the world. They
couldn't have been more alone, he felt, on a desert island.

He must say something—something ordinary and commonplace. Otherwise she might think of going back to the others, and he couldn't bear
that. Lucky she didn't know how his heart was beating—in great throbs,
right up in his throat somewhere.

He said abruptly: "I've gone into my uncle's business, you know."

"Yes, I know. Do you like it?"

A cool sweet voice. No trace of agitation in it now.

"I don't like it much. I expect I shall get to, though."

"I suppose it will be more interesting when you understand it more."

"I don't see how it ever could be. It's making the shanks of buttons,
you know."

"Oh! I see—no, that doesn't sound very thrilling."

There was a pause, and then she said, very softly: "Do you hate it
very much, Vernon?"

"I'm afraid I do."

"I'm awfully sorry. I—I understand just how you feel."

If someone understood, it made the whole world different. Adorable
Nell! He said unsteadily:

"I say, that's—that's most awfully sweet of you."

Another pause—one of those pauses that are heavy with the weight
of latent emotion. Nell seemed to take fright. She said rather hurriedly:

"Weren't you—I mean I thought you were taking up music?"

"I was. I—I gave that up."

"But why? Isn't that the most awful pity?"

"It's the thing I wanted to do most in the world. But it's no good.
I've got to make some money somehow." Should he tell her? Was this
the moment? No, he daren't—he simply daren't. He blundered on
quickly: "You see, Abbots Puissants—you remember Abbots Puissants?"

"Of course. Why, Vernon, we were talking about it the other day."

"Sorry. I'm stupid tonight. Well, you see I want awfully to live there again some day."

"I think you're wonderful."

"Wonderful?"

"Yes. To give up everything you cared about and set to as you are doing. It's splendid!"

"It's ripping of you to say that. It makes—oh! you don't know what a difference it makes."

"Does it?" said Nell in a very low voice. "I'm glad."

She thought to herself: "I ought to go back. Oh! I ought to go back. Mother will be very angry about this. What am I doing? I ought to go back and listen to George Chetwynd, but he's so *dull*. Oh! God, don't let Mother be very cross."

And she walked on by Vernon's side. She felt out of breath. Strange—what was the matter with her? If only Vernon would say something. What was he thinking about?

She said in a would-be-detached voice: "How's Joe?"

"Very artistic at present. I thought perhaps you might have been seeing something of each other as you were both in town?"

"I've seen her once, I think. That's all." She paused and then added, rather diffidently: "I don't think Joe likes me."

"Nonsense! Of course she does."

"No, she thinks I'm frivolous, that I only care for social things—dances and parties."

"Nobody who really knew you could think that."

"I don't know. I feel awfully—well, stupid sometimes."

"You? Stupid?"

That warm incredulous voice. Darling Vernon! He did think her nice, then. Her mother had been right.

They came to a little bridge across some water. They walked onto it, stood there side by side, leaning over, looking down on the water below.

Vernon said in a choked kind of voice: "It's jolly here."

"Yes."

It was coming—it was coming. She couldn't have defined what she meant, but that was the feeling. The world standing still, gathering itself for a leap and a spring.

"Nell . . ."

Why did her knees feel so shaky? Why did her voice sound so far away?

"Yes."

Was that queer little "Yes" hers?

"Oh! Nell . . ."

He had got to tell her. He must.

"I love you so . . . I do love you so . . ."

"Do you?"

It couldn't be her speaking. What an idiotic thing to say!

"Do you?" Her voice sounded stiff and unnatural.

His hand found hers. His hand was hot—hers was cold. They both shook.

"Could you—do you—do you think you could ever manage to love me?"

She answered, hardly knowing what she was saying: "I don't know."

They continued to stand there like dazed children, hand in hand, lost in a kind of rapture that was almost fear.

Something must happen soon. They didn't know what.

Out of the darkness two figures appeared—a hoarse laugh, a girl's giggle.

"So here you are! What a romantic spot!"

The green girl and that ass Dacre. Nell said something, a saucy something—said it with the utmost self-possession. Women were wonderful. She moved out into the moonlight—calm, detached, at ease. They all walked together, talking, chaffing each other. They found George Chetwynd with Mrs. Vereker on the lawn. He looked very glum, Vernon thought.

Mrs. Vereker was distinctly nasty to him. Her manner when bidding him good-bye was quite offensive.

He didn't care. All he wanted was to get away and lose himself in an orgy of remembrance.

He'd told her—he'd told her. He'd asked her whether she loved him—yes, he had dared to do that—and instead of laughing at him she had said, *"I don't know."*

But that meant—that meant . . . Oh, it was incredible! Nell, fairy-like Nell, so wonderful, so inaccessible, loved him—or, at least, she was willing to love him.

He wanted to walk on and on through the night. Instead he had to catch the midnight train to Birmingham. Damn! If he could only have walked—walked—till morning.

With a little green hat and a magic flute like the prince in that tale!

Suddenly he saw the whole thing in music—the high tower and princess's cascade of golden hair, and the eerie haunting tune of the prince's pipe which called the princess out from her tower.

Insensibly, this music was more in accordance with recognized canons than Vernon's original conception had been. It was adapted to the limits of known dimensions, though at the same time the inner vision remained unaltered. He heard the music of the tower—the round globular music of the princess's jewels, and the gay wild lawless strain of the vagabond prince: "Come out, my love, come out . . ."

He walked through the bare drab streets of London as through an enchanted world. The black mass of Paddington Station loomed up before him.

In the train he didn't sleep. Instead, on the back of an envelope, he wrote microscopic notes: "Trumpets . . . French horns . . . Cor Anglais," and alongside them lines and curves that to his understanding represented what he heard.

He was happy.

3

"I'm ashamed of you. What can you be thinking of?"

Mrs. Vereker was very angry. Nell stood before her, dumb and lovely.

Her mother uttered a few more virulent and incisive words, then turned and left the room without saying good-night.

Ten minutes later, as Mrs. Vereker completed her preparations for the night, she suddenly laughed to herself—a grim chuckle.

"I needn't have been so angry with the child. As a matter of fact, it will do George Chetwynd good. Wake him up. He needed prodding."

She turned out her light and slept, satisfied.

Nell lay awake. Again and again she went over the evening, trying to recapture each feeling, each word that had been spoken.

What had Vernon said? What had she answered? Queer that she couldn't remember.

He had asked her whether she loved him. What had she said to that? She couldn't tell. But in the darkness the scene rose up before her eyes. She felt her hand in Vernon's, heard his voice, husky and ill-assured. . . . She shut her eyes, lost in a hazy delicious dream.

Life was so lovely—so lovely.

Chapter Five

"Then you can't love me!"

"Oh! but Vernon, I do. If you'd only try and understand."

They faced each other desperately, bewildered by this sudden rift between them—by the queer unexpected vagaries of life. One minute they had been so near that each thought even had seemed to be shared by the other. Now they were poles apart, angry and hurt by the other's lack of comprehension.

Nell turned away with a little gesture of despair and sank down on a chair.

Why was it all like this? Why couldn't things stay as they ought to be, as you had felt they were going to be forever? That evening at Ranelagh—and the night afterward when she had lain awake wrapped in a happy dream. Enough that night just to know that she was loved. Why, even her mother's scathing words had failed to upset her. They had come from so far away. They couldn't penetrate that shining web of misty dream.

She had wakened up happy the next morning. Her mother had been pleasant, had said nothing more. Wrapped in her secret thoughts, Nell had gone through the day doing all the usual things: chattering with friends, walking in the park, lunching, teaing, dancing. Nobody, she was sure, could have noticed anything different, and yet all the time she herself had been conscious of that one deep strand underneath everything else. Just for a minute, sometimes, she would lose the thread of what she was saying, she would remember. . . . "Oh! Nell, I do love you so . . ." The moonlight on the dark water. His hand in hers. . . . A little shiver and she would recall herself hastily, chatter, laugh. Oh! how happy one could be—how happy she had been.

Then she had wondered if, perhaps, he would write. She had watched for the post, her heart giving little throbs whenever the postman knocked. It had come the second day. She had hidden it beneath a pile of others, kept it till she went up to bed, then opened it with a beating heart.

Oh, Nell—oh, darling Nell! Did you really mean it? I've written three letters to you and torn them up. I'm so afraid of saying something that might make you angry. Because perhaps you didn't mean it after all. But you did, didn't you? You are so lovely, Nell, and I do love you so dreadfully. I'm always thinking about you, the whole time. I make awful mistakes at the office just because I'm thinking about you. But oh, Nell, I will work so hard! I want so dreadfully to see you. When can I come up to town? I must see you. Darling, darling, Nell, I want to say such lots and lots of things and I can't in a letter, and anyway perhaps I'm boring you. Write and tell me when I can see you. Very soon, please. I shall go mad if I can't see you very soon.

Yours ever,
Vernon

She had read it again and again, put it under her pillow when she slept, read it again the next morning. She had been so happy, so dreadfully happy. It was not till the day after that she had written to him. When the pen was in her hand she had felt stiff and awkward. She hadn't known what to say.

Dear Vernon.

Was that silly? Ought she to say Dearest Vernon? Oh! no, she couldn't—she couldn't.

Dear Vernon. Thank you for your letter.

A long pause. She bit the stem of her penholder and gazed in an agonized way at the wall in front of her.

A party of us are going to the Howards' dance on Friday. Will you dine here first and come with us? Eight o'clock.

A longer pause. She'd got to say something—she wanted to say something. She bent over and wrote hastily:

I want to see you too—very much. Yours, Nell.

He had written back:

Dear Nell, I'd love to come on Friday. Thanks ever so much.

Yours, Vernon

A little panic had swept over her when she read it. Had she offended him? Did he think she ought to have said more in her letter? Happiness fled. She lay awake, miserable, uncertain, hating herself in case it had been her fault.

Then had come Friday night. The moment she saw him she knew it was all right. Their eyes met across the room. The world changed back to radiant happiness again.

They did not sit near each other at dinner. It was not till the third dance at the Howards' that they were able really to speak to each other. They moved round the crowded room, gyrating in a deep-toned sentimental waltz. He whispered:

"I haven't asked for too many dances, have I?"

"No."

Queer how absolutely tongue-tied it made her feel being with Vernon. He held her just a minute longer when the music stopped. His fingers tightened over hers. She looked at him and smiled. They were both deliriously happy. In a few minutes he was dancing with another girl, talking airily in her ear. Nell was dancing with George Chetwynd. Once or twice her eyes met Vernon's and they both smiled very faintly. Their secret was so wonderful.

At his next dance with her his mood had changed.

"Nell, darling, isn't there anywhere I can talk to you? I've got such heaps of things I want to say. What a ridiculous house this is—nowhere to go."

They tried the stairs, mounting higher and higher as you do in London houses. Still, it seemed impossible to get away from people. Then they saw a tiny iron ladder that led to the roof.

"Nell, let's get up there? Could you? Would it ruin your dress?"

"I don't care about my dress."

Vernon went up first, unbolted the trap door, climbed out, and knelt down to help Nell. She climbed through safely.

They were alone, looking down on London. Insensibly they drew nearer to each other. Her hand found its way into his.

"Nell—darling . . ."

"Vernon . . ."

Her voice could only whisper.

"It *is* true? You do love me?"

"I do love you."

"It's too wonderful to be true. Oh! Nell, I do so want to kiss you."

She turned her face to his. They kissed—rather shakily and timidly.

"Your face is so soft and lovely," murmured Vernon.

Oblivious of dirt and smuts, they sat down on a little ledge. His arms went round her, held her. She turned her face to his kisses.

"I do love you so, Nell. I love you so much that I'm almost afraid to touch you."

She didn't understand that—it seemed queer. She drew a little closer to him. The magic of the night was made complete by their kisses. . . .

2

They woke from a happy dream. "Oh! Vernon, I believe we've been here *ages!*"

Conscience-stricken, they hurried to the trapdoor. On the landing below, Vernon surveyed Nell anxiously.

"I'm afraid you've been sitting on an awful lot of smuts, Nell."

"Oh! have I? How awful."

"It's my fault, darling. But oh! Nell, it was worth it, wasn't it?"

She smiled up at him, gently, happily.

"It was worth it," she said softly.

As they went down the stairs she said with a little laugh:

"What about all the things you wanted to say? Lots and lots of them."

They both laughed in perfect understanding. They reentered the dancing room rather sheepishly. They had missed six dances.

A lovely evening. Nell had gone to sleep and dreamed of more kisses.

And then, Saturday morning, Vernon had rung up.

"I want to talk to you. Can I come round?"

"Oh! Vernon dear, you can't. I'm going out now to meet people. I can't get out of it."

"Why not?"

"I mean I wouldn't know what to say to Mother."

"You haven't told her anything?"

"Oh, *no!*"

The vehemence of that "Oh, *no!*" had checked Vernon. He thought: "Poor little darling. Of course she hasn't." He said: "Hadn't I better do that? I'll come round now."

"Oh! no, Vernon, not until we've talked."

"Well, when can we talk?"

"I don't know. I'm lunching with people and going to a matinée and to the theater again tonight. If you'd only told me you were going to be up this weekend I'd have arranged something."

"What about tomorrow?"

"Well, there's church—"

"That'll do! Don't go to church. Say you've got a headache or something. I'll come round. We can talk then, and when your mother comes back from church I can have it out with her."

"Oh! Vernon, I don't think I can—"

"Yes, you can. I'm going to ring off now before you can make any more excuses. At eleven tomorrow."

He rang off. He hadn't even told Nell where he was staying. She admired him for this masculine decision even while it caused her anxiety. She was afraid he was going to spoil everything.

And now here they were, in the middle of a heated discussion. Nell had begged him to say nothing to her mother.

"It will spoil everything. We shan't be allowed to."

"Shan't be allowed to what?"

"See each other or anything."

"But Nell darling, I want to marry you. And you want to marry me, don't you? I want to marry you awfully soon."

She had her first feeling of exasperation then. Couldn't he see things as they were? He was talking like a mere boy.

"But, Vernon, we haven't any money."

"I know. But I'm going to work awfully hard. You won't mind being poor, will you, Nell?"

She said No since it was expected of her, but she was conscious that she did not say it wholeheartedly. It was dreadful being poor. Vernon didn't know how dreadful it was. She suddenly felt years and years older and more experienced than he. He was talking like a romantic boy—he didn't know what things were really like.

"Oh! Vernon, can't we just go on as we are? We're so happy now."

"Of course we're happy—but we could be happier still. I want to be really engaged to you—I want everyone to know that you belong to me."

"I don't see that that makes any difference."

"I suppose it doesn't. But I want to have a right to see you, instead of being miserable about you going round with chaps like that ass, Dacre."

"Oh! Vernon, you're not jealous?"

"I know I oughtn't to be. But you don't really know how lovely you are, Nell! Everyone must be in love with you. I believe even that solemn old American fellow is."

Nell changed colour slightly.

"Well, I think you'll spoil everything," she murmured.

"You think your mother will be horrid to you about it? I'm awfully sorry. I'll tell her it's all my fault. And after all, she's got to know. I expect she'll be disappointed because she probably wanted you to marry someone rich. That's quite natural. But it doesn't really make you happy, being rich, does it?"

Nell said suddenly in a hard desperate little voice:

"You talk like that, but what do you know about being poor?"

Vernon was astonished.

"But I am poor."

"No, you're not. You've been to schools and universities and in the holidays you've lived with your mother who's rich. You don't know anything at all about it. You don't know—"

She stopped in despair. She wasn't clever with words. How could she paint the picture she knew so well? The shifts, the struggles, the evasions, the desperate fight to keep up appearances, the ease with which friends dropped you if you "couldn't keep up with things," the slights, the snubs—worse, the galling patronage! In Captain Vereker's lifetime, and since his death, it had always been the same. You could, of course, live in a cottage in the country and never see anyone, never to go to dances like other girls, never have pretty clothes, live within your income and rot away slowly! Either way was pretty beastly. It was so unfair—one ought to have money. And always marriage lay ahead of you clearly designated as the way of escape. No more striving and snubs and subterfuges.

You didn't think of it as marrying for money. Nell, with the boundless optimism of youth, had always pictured herself falling in love with a nice rich man. And now she had fallen in love with Vernon Deyre. Her thoughts hadn't gone as far as marriage. She was just happy—wonderfully happy.

She almost hated Vernon for dragging her down from the clouds. And she resented his easy taking for granted of her readiness to face poverty for his sake. If he'd put it differently. If he'd said: "I oughtn't to ask you—but do you think you *could* for my sake?" Something like that.

So that she could feel that her sacrifice was being appreciated. For, after all, it *was* a sacrifice! She didn't want to be poor—she hated the idea of being poor. She was afraid of it. Vernon's contemptuous unwordly attitude infuriated her. It was so easy not to care about money when you'd never felt the lack of it. And Vernon hadn't. He wasn't aware of the fact, but there it was. He'd lived softly and comfortably and well.

He said now in an astonished kind of way: "Oh! Nell, surely you wouldn't mind being poor?"

"I've been poor, I tell you. I know what it's like."

She felt years and years older than Vernon. He was a child—a baby! What did he know of the difficulties of getting credit? Of the money that she and her mother already owed? She felt suddenly terribly lonely and miserable. What was the good of men? They said wonderful things to you, they loved you, but did they ever try to understand? Vernon wasn't trying now. He was just saying condemnatory things, showing her how she had fallen in his estimation.

"If you say that you can't love me."

She replied helplessly: "You don't understand."

They gazed at each other hopelessly. What had happened? Why were things like this between them?

"You don't love me," repeated Vernon angrily.

"Oh! Vernon, I do, I do. . . ."

Suddenly, like an enchantment, their love swept over them again. They clung together, kissing. They felt that age-long lovers' delusion that everything *must* come right because they loved. It was Vernon's victory. He still insisted on telling Mrs. Vereker. Nell opposed him no longer. His arms round her, his lips on hers . . . she couldn't go on arguing. Better to give oneself up to the joy of being loved, to say: "Yes—yes darling, if you like . . . anything you like."

Yet, almost unknown to herself, under her love was a faint resentment.

3

Mrs. Vereker was a clever woman. She was taken by surprise but she did not show it, and she adopted a different line from any that Vernon had pictured her taking. She was faintly derisively amused.

"So you children think you are in love with one another? Well, well!"

She listened to Vernon with such an expression of kindly irony that despite himself his tongue flustered and tripped.

She gave a faint sigh as he subsided into silence.

"What it is to be young! I feel quite envious. Now, my dear boy, just listen to me. I'm not going to forbid the banns or do anything melodramatic. If Nell really wants to marry you she shall. I don't say I won't be very disappointed if she does. She's my only child. I naturally hope that she will marry someone who can give her the best of everything, and surround her with every luxury and comfort. That, I think, is only natural."

Vernon was forced to agree. Mrs. Vereker's reasonableness was extremely disconcerting, being so unexpected.

"But, as I say, I'm not going to forbid the banns. What I do stipulate is that Nell should be thoroughly sure that she really knows her own mind. You agree to that, I'm sure?"

Vernon agreed to that with an uneasy feeling of being entangled in a mesh from which he was presently not going to be able to escape.

"Nell is very young. This is her first season. I want her to have every chance of being sure that she does like you better than any other man. If you agree between yourselves that you are engaged, that is one thing— a public announcement of your engagement is another. I could not agree to that. Any understanding between yourselves must be kept quite secret. I think you will see that that is only fair. Nell must be given every chance to change her mind if she wants to."

"She doesn't want to!"

"Then there is certainly no reason for objecting. As a gentleman you can hardly act otherwise. If you agree to these stipulations I will put no obstacle in the way of your seeing Nell."

"But, Mrs. Vereker, I want to marry Nell quite soon."

"And what exactly do you propose to marry on?"

Vernon told her the salary he was getting from his uncle and explained the position in regard to Abbots Puissants.

When he had finished she spoke. She gave a brief and succinct résumé of house rent, servants' wages, the cost of clothes, alluded delicately to possible perambulators, and then contrasted the picture with Nell's present position.

Vernon was like the Queen of Sheba—no spirit was left in him. He was beaten by the relentless logic of facts. A terrible woman, Nell's mother—implacable. But he saw her point. He and Nell would have to wait. He must, as Mrs. Vereker said, give her every chance of changing her mind. Not that she would, bless her lovely heart!

He essayed one last venture.

"My uncle might increase my salary. He has spoken to me several times on the advantages of early marriages. He seems very keen on the subject."

"Oh!" Mrs. Vereker was thoughtful for a minute or two. "Has he any daughters of his own?"

"Yes, five, and the two oldest are married already."

Mrs. Vereker smiled. A simple boy. He had quite misunderstood the point of her question. Still, she had found out what she wanted to know.

"We'll leave it like that, then," she said.

A clever woman!

4

Vernon left the house in a restless mood. He wanted badly to talk to someone sympathetic. He thought of Joe, then shook his head. He and Joe had almost quarreled about Nell. Joe despised Nell as what she called a "regular empty-headed society girl." She was unfair and prejudiced. As a passport to Joe's favor, you had to have short hair, wear art smocks, and live in Chelsea.

Sebastian, on the whole, was the best person. Sebastian was always willing to see your point of view, and he was occasionally unusually useful with his matter-of-fact common-sense point of view. A very sound fellow, Sebastian.

Rich, too. How queer things were! If only he had Sebastian's money he could probably marry Nell tomorrow. Yet, with all that money, Sebastian couldn't get hold of the girl he wanted. Rather a pity. He wished Joe would marry Sebastian instead of some rotter or other who called himself artistic.

Sebastian, alas, was not at home. Vernon was entertained by Mrs. Levinne. Strangely enough, he found a kind of comfort in her bulky presence. Funny fat old Mrs. Levinne with her jet and her diamonds and her greasy black hair managed to be more understanding than his own mother.

"You mustn't be unhappy, my dear," she said. "I can see you are. It's some girl, I suppose? Ah, well, well, Sebastian is just the same about Joe. I tell him he must be patient. Joe's just kicking up her heels at present. She'll settle down soon and begin to find out what it is she really does want."

"It would be awfully jolly if she married Sebastian. I wish she would. It would keep us all together."

"Yes—I'm very fond of Joe myself. Not that I think she's really the wife for Sebastian—they'd be too far away to understand each other. I'm old-fashioned, my dear. I'd like my boy to marry one of our own people. It always works out best. The same interests, and the same instincts, and Jewish women are good mothers. Well, well, it may come, if Joe is really in earnest about not marrying him. And the same thing with you, Vernon. There are worse things than marrying a cousin."

"Me? Marry Joe?"

Vernon stared at her in utter astonishment. Mrs. Levinne laughed, a fat good-natured chuckle that shook her various chins.

"Joe? No, indeed. It's your cousin Enid I'm talking about. That's the idea at Birmingham, isn't it?"

"Oh! no—at least—I'm sure it isn't."

Mrs. Levinne laughed again.

"I can see that you, at any rate, have never thought of it till this minute. But it would be a wise plan, you know—that is, if the other girl won't have you. Keeps the money in the family."

Vernon went away with his brain tingling. All sorts of things fell into line. Uncle Sydney's chaff and hints. The way Enid was always being thrust at him. That, of course, was what Mrs. Vereker had been hinting at. They wanted him to marry Enid! Enid!

Another memory came back to him. His mother and some old friend of hers whispering together. Something about first cousins. A sudden idea occurred to him. That was why Joe had been allowed to go to London. His mother had thought that he and Joe might . . .

He gave a sudden shout of laughter. He and Joe! It showed how little his mother had ever understood. He could never, under any circumstances, imagine himself falling in love with Joe. They were exactly like brother and sister and always would be. They had the same sympathies, the same sharp divergences and differences of opinion. They were cast in the same mold, devoid of any glamour and romance for each other.

Enid! So this was what Uncle Sydney was after. Poor old Uncle Sydney, doomed to disappointment—but he shouldn't have been such an ass.

Perhaps, though, he was jumping to conclusions. Perhaps it wasn't Uncle Sydney—only his mother. Women were always marrying you to someone in their minds. Anyway, Uncle Sydney would soon know the truth.

5

The interview between Vernon and his uncle wasn't very satisfactory. Uncle Sydney was both annoyed and upset, though he tried to conceal the fact from Vernon. He was uncertain at first which line to take and made one or two vague sallies in different directions.

"Nonsense, all nonsense, much too young to marry. Packet of nonsense."

Vernon reminded his uncle of his own words.

"Pooh!—I didn't mean this kind of marriage. Society girl—I know what they are."

Vernon broke out hotly.

"Sorry, my boy, I didn't mean to hurt your feelings. But that kind of girl wants to marry money. You'll be no use to her for many years to come."

"I thought perhaps—"

Vernon paused. He felt ashamed, uncomfortable.

"That I'd set you up with a large income, hey? Is that what the young lady suggested? Now, I put it to you, my boy, would that be business? No, I see that you know it isn't."

"I don't feel that I'm even worth what you give me, Uncle Sydney."

"Pooh, pooh, I wasn't saying that. You're doing very well for a start. I'm sorry about this affair—it will upset you. My advice to you is, give the whole thing up. Much the best thing to do."

"I can't do that, Uncle Sydney."

"Well, it's not my business. By the way, have you talked it over with your mother? No? Well, you have a good talk with her. See if she doesn't say the same as I do. I bet she will. And remember the old saying: a boy's best friend is his mother—hey?"

Why did Uncle Sydney say such idiotic things? He always had as far as Vernon could remember back. And yet he was a shrewd and clever business man.

Well, there was nothing for it. He must buckle to—and wait. The first misty enchantment of love was wearing off. It could be hell as well as heaven. He wanted Nell so badly—so badly.

He wrote to her:

Darling, there is nothing for it. We must be patient and wait. At any rate we'll see each other often. Your mother was really very decent about it—much more so than I thought she'd be. I do quite see the force of all she said. It's only fair that you should be free to see if you like anyone better than me. But you won't, will you, darling? I know you won't. We're going to love each other forever and ever. And it won't matter how poor we are . . . the tiniest place with you . . .

Nell was relieved by her mother's attitude. She had feared recriminations, reproaches. Insensibly she always shrank from harsh words or any kind of scene. Sometimes she thought to herself bitterly: "I'm a coward. I can't stand up to things."

She was definitely afraid of her mother. She had been dominated by her always, from the first moment she could remember. Mrs. Vereker had the hard imperious character which can rule most weaker natures with whom it comes in contact. And Nell was the more easily subdued because she understood well enough that her mother loved her and that it was because of that love that she was so determined that Nell should have the happiness out of life that she herself had failed to get.

So Nell was immeasurably relieved when her mother uttered no reproaches, merely observed:

"If you're determined to be foolish, well, there it is. Most girls have some little love affair or other which comes to nothing in the end. I haven't much patience with this sentimental nonsense myself. The boy can't possibly afford to marry for years to come and you'll only make yourself very unhappy. But you must please yourself."

In spite of herself, Nell was influenced by this contemptuous attitude. She hoped against hope that Vernon's uncle might perhaps do something. Vernon's letter dashed her hopes.

They must wait—and perhaps wait a very long time.

2

In the meantime Mrs. Vereker had her own methods. One day she asked Nell to go and see an old friend—a girl who had married some few years ago. Amelie King had been a brilliant dashing creature whom Nell, as a schoolgirl, had admired enviously. She might have made a very good marriage, but to everyone's surprise she had married a struggling young man and had dissappeared from her own particular gay world.

"It seems unkind to drop old friends," said Mrs. Vereker. "I'm sure Amelie would be pleased if you went to see her, and you're not doing anything this afternoon."

So Nell went off obediently to call on Mrs. Horton at 35 Glenster Gardens, Ealing.

It was a hot day. Nell took the District Railway and inquired her way from Ealing. Broadway Station when she got there.

Glenster Gardens proved to be about a mile from the station—a long depressing road of little houses, all exactly alike. The door of No. 35 was opened by a frowsy-looking maid with a dirty apron and Nell was shown into a small drawing room. There were one or two nice old pieces of furniture in it and the cretonnes and curtains were of an attractive pattern though very faded, but the place was very untidy and littered with children's toys and odd bits of mending. A child's fretful wail rose from somewhere in the house as the door opened and Amelie came in.

"Nell, why how nice of you! I haven't seen you for years."

Nell had quite a shock on seeing her. Could this be the well-turned-out attractive Amelie? Her figure had got sloppy, her blouse was shapeless and evidently homemade, and her face was tired and worried, with all the old dash and sparkle gone out of it.

She sat down and they talked. Presently Nell was taken to see the two children, a boy and a girl, the younger a baby in a cot.

"I ought to take them out now," said Amelie, "but really, I'm too tired this afternoon. You don't know how tired one can get pushing a perambulator all the way up from the shops as I did this morning."

The boy was an attractive child, the baby girl looked sickly and peevish.

"It's partly her teeth," said Amelie. "And then her digestion is weak, the doctor says. I do wish she wouldn't cry at night. It's annoying for Jack, who needs his sleep after working all day."

"You don't have a nurse?"

"Can't afford it, my dear. We have the half-wit—that's what we call the girl who opened the door to you. She's a complete idiot, but she comes cheap and she really will set to and do some work, which is more than most of them will do. A general servant hates coming anywhere where there are children."

She called out: "Mary, bring some tea," and led the way back to the drawing room.

"Oh! dear, Nell, do you know I almost wish you hadn't come to see me. You look so smart and cool—you remind me of all the fun one used to have in the old days. Tennis and dancing and golf and parties."

Nell said timidly: "But you're happy . . ."

"Oh! of course. I'm only enjoying a grumble. Jack's a dear, and then there are the children, only sometimes—well, one is really too tired to care for anyone or anything. I feel I'd sell my nearest and dearest for a tiled bathroom and bath salts and a maid to brush my hair and lovely silken garments to slip into. And then you hear some rich idiot holding forth on how money doesn't bring happiness. Fools!"

She laughed.

"Tell me some news, Nell. I'm so out of things nowadays. You can't keep up if you have no money. I never see any of the old crowd."

They gossiped a little. So and So was married, So and So had had a row with her husband, So and So had got a new baby, and about So and So there was the most terrible scandal.

Tea was brought, rather untidily, with smeary silver and thick bread and butter. As they were finishing, the front door was opened with a key and a man's voice sounded from the hall fretful and irritable.

"Amelie—I say, it is too bad. I only ask you to do one thing and you go and forget it. This parcel has never been taken down to Jones's. You said you would."

Amelie ran out to him in the hall. There was a quick exchange of whispers. She brought him into the drawing room where he greeted Nell. The child in the nursery began to wail again.

"I must go to her," said Amelie, and hurried away.

"What a life!" said Jack Horton. He was still very good-looking though his clothes were distinctly shabby and there were bad-tempered lines coming round his mouth. He laughed as though it were a great joke. "You've found us at sixes and sevens, Miss Vereker. We always are. Traveling to and fro in trains in this weather is very trying—and no peace in the home when you get there!"

He laughed again and Nell laughed too, politely. Amelie came back holding the child in her arms. Nell rose to go. They came with her to the door. Amelie sent messages to Mrs. Vereker and waved her hand.

At the gate Nell looked back and caught the expression on Amelie's face. A hungry envious look.

In spite of herself Nell's heart sank. Was this the inevitable end? Did poverty kill love?

She reached the main road and was walking along it in the direction of the station when an unexpected voice made her start.

"Miss Nell, by all that's wonderful!"

A big Rolls-Royce had drawn up to the curb. George Chetwynd sat behind the wheel smiling at her.

"If this isn't too good to be true! I thought I saw a girl who was mighty like you—from the back view anyhow—so I slowed down to have a look at her face, and it was your very self. Are you going back to town? Because if so, step in."

Nell stepped in obediently and settled herself contentedly beside the driver. The car glided forward smoothly, gathering power. A heavenly sensation, Nell thought—effortless, delightful.

"And what are you doing in Ealing?"

"I've been to see some friends."

Moved by some obscure prompting, she described her visit. Chetwynd listened sympathetically, nodding his head from side to side, all the while driving the car with the perfection of a master.

"If that isn't too bad," he said sympathetically. "You know, I hate to think of that poor girl. Women ought to be taken care of—to have their lives made easy for them. They ought to be surrounded with everything they want."

He looked at Nell and said kindly: "It's upset you, I can see. You must have a very soft heart, Miss Nell."

Nell looked at him with a sudden warming of her heart. She did like George Chetwynd. There was something so kind and reliable and strong about him. She liked his rather wooden face, and the way his graying hair grew back from his temples. She liked the square upright way he sat and the firm precision of his hands on the wheel. He looked the kind of man who could deal with any emergency, a man on whom you could *depend*. The brunt of things would always be on his shoulders, not on yours. Oh! yes, she liked George. He was a nice person to meet when you were tired at the end of a bothering day.

"Is my tie crooked?" he asked suddenly without looking round.

Nell laughed.

"Was I staring? I'm afraid I was."

"I felt the glance. What were you doing—sizing me up?"

"I believe I was."

"And I suppose I've been found utterly wanting."

"No, very much the other way about."

"Don't say these nice things—which I'm sure you don't mean. You excited me so much that I nearly collided with a tram then."

"I never say things I don't mean."

"Don't you? I wonder now." His voice altered. "There's something I've wanted to say to you for a long time. This is a funny place to say it, but I'm going to take the plunge here and now. Will you marry me, Nell? I want you very badly."

"Oh!" Nell was startled. "Oh! no, I couldn't."

He shot a quick glance at her before returning to his task of steering through the traffic. He slowed down a little.

"Do you mean that, I wonder? I know I'm too old for you—"

"No—you're not—I mean, it's not that."

A little smile twisted his mouth.

"I must be twenty years older than you, Nell, at least. It's a lot, you know. But I do honestly believe that I could make you happy. Queerly enough, I'm sure of it."

Nell didn't answer for a minute or two. Then she said rather weakly: "Oh! but really, I couldn't."

"Splendid! You said it much less decidedly that time."

"But indeed—"

"I'm not going to bother you anymore just now. We'll take it that you've said No this time. But you aren't always going to say No, Nell. I can afford to wait quite a long time for what I want to have. Someday you'll find yourself saying Yes."

"No, I shan't."

"Yes, you will, dear. There's no one else, is there? Ah! but I know there isn't.

Nell didn't answer. She told herself that she didn't know what to say. She had tacitly promised her mother that nothing should be said about her engagement.

And yet somewhere, deep down, she felt ashamed.

George Chetwynd began cheerfuly to talk of various outside topics.

Chapter Seven

August was a difficult month for Vernon. Nell and her mother were in Dinard. He wrote to her and she to him, but her letters told him little or nothing of what he wanted to know. She was having a gay time, he gathered, and enjoying herself though longing for Vernon to be there.

Vernon's work was of the purely routine order. It required little intelligence. You needed to be careful and methodical, that was all. His mind, free from other distractions, swung back to its secret love, music.

He had formed the idea of writing an opera and had taken for his theme the half-forgotten fairy story of his youth. It was now bound up in his mind with Nell—the whole strength of his love for her flowed into this new channel.

He worked feverishly. Nell's words about his living comfortably with his mother had rankled, and he had insisted on having rooms of his own. The ones he had found were very cheap, but they gave him an unexpected sense of freedom. At Carey Lodge he would never have been able to concentrate. His mother would have been, he knew, forever fussing after him, urging him to come to bed. Here, in Arthur Street, he could, and often did, sit up till five in the morning if he liked.

He got very thin and haggard-looking. Myra worried about his health and urged patent restoratives upon him. He assured her curtly that he was all right. He told her nothing of what he was doing. Sometimes he would be full of despair over his work, at others a sudden sense of power would rush over him as he knew that some small infinitesimal fragment was good.

Occasionally he went to town and spent a weekend with Sebastian, and on two occasions Sebastian came down to Birmingham. Sebastian was Vernon's most valued standby at this time. His sympathy was real and not assumed and it had a twofold character. He was interested as a friend and also from his own professional standpoint. Vernon had an enormous respect for Sebastian's judgment in all things artistic. He would play excerpts on the piano he had hired, explaining as he did so the proper orchestration. Sebastian listened, nodding very quietly, speaking little. At the end he would say:

"It's going to be good, Vernon. Get on with it."

He never uttered a word of destructive criticism, for in his belief such a word might be fatal. Vernon needed encouragement and nothing but encouragement.

He said one day: "Is this what you meant to do at Cambridge?"

Vernon considered for a minute.

"No," he said at last. "At least, it's not what I meant originally. After that concert, you know. It's gone again—the thing I saw then. Perhaps it'll come back again sometime. This is, I suppose, the usual sort of thing, conventional—and all that. But here and there I've got what I mean into it."

"I see."

To Joe, Sebastian said plainly what he thought.

"Vernon calls this the 'usual sort of thing,' but as a matter of fact it isn't. It's entirely unusual. The whole orchestration is conducted on an unusual plan. What it is, though, is immature. Brilliant but immature."

"Have you told him so?"

"Good Lord, no. One disparaging word and he'd shrivel up and consign the whole thing to the wastepaper basket. I know these people. I'm spoon-feeding him with praise at present. We'll have the pruning knife and the garden syringe later. I've mixed my metaphors, but you know what I mean."

In early September Sebastian gave a party to meet Herr Radmaager, the famous composer. Vernon and Joe were bidden to attend.

"Only about a dozen of us," said Sebastian. "Anita Quarll, whose dancing I'm interested in—she's a rotten little devil, though. Jane Harding—you'll like her. She's singing in this English Opera business. Wrong vocation—she's an actress, not a singer. You and Vernon—Radmaager—two or three others. Radmaager will be interested in Vernon—he's well disposed toward the younger generation."

Both Joe and Vernon were elated.

"Do you think I'll ever do anything, Joe? Really do anything, I mean." Vernon sounded dispirited.

"Why not?" said Joe valiantly.

"I don't know. Everything I've done just lately is rotten. I started all right. But now I'm stale as stale. I'm tired before I start."

"I suppose that's because you work all day."

"I suppose it is."

He was silent for a minute or two and then said: "It'll be wonderful meeting Radmaager. He's one of the few men who writes what I call music. I wish I could talk to him about what I really think—but it would be such awful cheek."

The party was of an informal character. Sebastian had a large studio, empty save for a dais, a grand piano, and a large quantity of cushions thrown down at random about the floor. At one end was a hastily put trestle table and on this were piled viands of all descriptions.

You collected what you wanted and then pitched your cushion. When Joe and Vernon arrived a girl was dancing—a small red-haired girl with a lithe sinewy body. Her dancing was ugly but alluring.

She finished to loud applause and leaped down from the dais.

"Bravo, Anita," said Sebastian. "Now then, Vernon and Joe, have you got what you want? That's right. You'd better sink down gracefully by Jane. This is Jane."

They sank down as bidden. Jane was a tall creature with a beautiful body and a mass of very dark brown hair coiled low on her neck. Her face was too broad for beauty and her chin too sharp. Her eyes were deep-set and green. She was about thirty, Vernon thought. He found her disconcerting, but attractive.

Joe began to talk to her eagerly. Her enthusiasm for sculpture had been waning of late. She had always had a high soprano voice and she was now coquetting with the idea of becoming an opera singer.

Jane Harding listened sympathetically enough, emitting a faintly amused monosyllable from time to time. Finally she said:

"If you like to come round to my flat, I'll try your voice, and I can tell you in two minutes just what your voice is good for."

"Would you really? That's awfully kind of you."

"Oh! not at all. You can trust me. You can't trust someone who makes their living by teaching to tell you the truth."

Sebastian came up and said: "What about it, Jane?"

She got up from the floor—rather a beautiful movement. Then, looking round, she said in the curt voice of command one would use to a dog:

"Mr. Hill."

A small man, rather like a white worm, bustled forward with an ingratiating twist of the body. He followed her up to the dias.

She sang a French song Vernon had never heard before.

"J'ai perdu mon amie—elle est morte,
Tout s'en va cette fois à jamais,
A jamais, pour toujours elle emporte
Le dernier des amours que j'aimais.

"Pauvre nous! Rien ne m'a crié l'heure
Où là-bas se nouait son linceul
On m'a dit, 'Elle est morte!' Et tout seul
Je répète, 'Elle est morte!' Et je pleure . . ."

Like most people who heard Jane Harding sing, Vernon was quite unable to criticize the voice. She created an emotional atmosphere—the voice was only an instrument. The sense of overwhelming loss, of dazed grief, the final relief of tears.

There was applause. Sebastian murmured: "Enormous emotional power—that's it."

She sang again. This time it was a Norwegian song about falling snow.

There was no emotion in her voice whatsoever—it was like the white flakes of the snow: monotonous, exquisitely clear, finally dying away to silence on the last line.

In response to applause she sang yet a third song. Vernon sat up, suddenly alert.

> *"I saw a Fairy lady there*
> *With long white hands and drowning hair*
> *And oh! her face was wild and sweet,*
> *Was sweet and wild and wild and strange and fair..."*

It was like a spell laid on the room—the sense of magic, of terrified enchantment. Jane's face was thrust forward. Her eyes looked out, past beyond—seeing—frightened yet fascinated.

There was a sigh as she finished. A stout burly man with white hair *en brosse* pushed his way to Sebastian.

"Ah! my good Sebastian, I have arrived. I will talk to that young lady—at once, immediately."

Sebastian went with him across the room to Jane. Herr Radmaager took her by both hands. He looked at her earnestly.

"Yes," he said at last. "Your physique is good. I should say that both the digestion and the circulation were excellent. You will give me your address and I will come and see you. Is it not so?"

Vernon thought: "These people are mad."

But he noticed that Jane Harding seemed to take it as a matter of course. She wrote her address, talked to Radmaager for a few minutes longer, then came and rejoined Joe and Vernon.

"Sebastian is a good friend," she remarked. "He knows that Herr Radmaager is looking for a Solveig for his new opera, *Peer Gynt*. That is why he asked me here tonight."

Joe got up and went to talk to Sebastian. Vernon and Jane Harding were left alone.

"Tell me," said Vernon stammering a little. "That song you sang—"

"Frosted snow?"

"No, the last one. I—I heard it years ago—when I was a kid."

"How curious. I thought it was a family secret."

"A hospital nurse sang it to me when I broke my leg. I always loved it, but never thought I should hear it again."

Jane Harding said thoughtfully: "I wonder now. Could that have been my Aunt Frances?"

"Yes, that was her name. Nurse Frances. Was she your aunt? What's happened to her?"

"She died a good many years ago. Diphtheria, caught from a patient."

"Oh! I'm sorry." He paused, hesitated, then blundered on. "I've always remembered her. She was—she was a wonderful friend to me as a kid."

He caught Jane's green eyes looking at him, a steady kindly glance, and he knew at once of whom she had reminded him the first moment he saw her. She was like Nurse Frances.

She said quietly: "You write music, don't you? Sebastian told me about you."

"Yes—at least, I try to."

He stopped, hesitated again. He thought: "She's terribly attractive. Do I like her? Why am I afraid of her?"

He felt suddenly excited and exalted. He could do things—he *knew* he could do things. . . .

"Vernon!"

Sebastian was calling him. He got up. Sebastian presented him to Radmaager. The great man was kindly and sympathetic.

"I am interested," he said, "in what I hear about your work from my young friend here." He laid his hand on Sebastian's shoulder. "He is very astute, my young friend. In spite of his youth, he is seldom wrong. We will arrange a meeting and you shall show me your work."

He moved on. Vernon was left quivering with excitement. Did he really mean it? He went back to Jane. She was smiling. Vernon sat down by her. A sudden wave of depression succeeded the exhilaration. What was the good of it all? He was tied, hand and foot, to Uncle Sydney and Birmingham. You couldn't write music unless you gave your whole time, your whole thoughts, your whole soul to it.

He felt injured—miserable—yearning for sympathy. If only Nell were here. Darling Nell who always understood.

He looked up and found Jane Harding watching him.

"What's the matter?" she said.

"I wish I were dead," said Vernon bitterly.

Jane raised her eyebrows slightly.

"Well," she said, "if you walk up to the top of this building and jump off, you can be."

It was hardly the answer that Vernon had expected. He looked up resentfully, but her cool kindly glance disarmed him.

"There's only one thing I care about in the whole world," he said passionately. "I want to write music. I *could* write music. And instead of that I'm stuck in a beastly business that I hate. Grinding away day after day! It's too sickening."

"Why do you do it if you don't like it?"

"Because I have to."

"I expect you want to really—otherwise you wouldn't," said Jane indifferently.

"Haven't I told you that I want to write music more than anything else in the world?"

"Then why don't you do it?"

"Because I can't, I tell you."

He felt exasperated with her. She didn't seem to understand at all. Her view on life seemed to be that if you wanted to do anything, you just went and did it.

He began pouring out things. Abbots Puissants, the concert, his uncle's offer, and then—Nell.

When he had finished she said: "You do expect life to be rather a fairy story, don't you?"

"What do you mean?"

"Just that. You want to be able to live in the house of your forefathers, and to marry the girl you love, and to grow immensely rich, and to be a great composer. I dare say you might manage to do one of those four things if you give your whole mind to it. But it's not likely that you'll have everything, you know. Life isn't like a penny novelette."

He hated her for the moment. And yet, even while he hated, he was attracted. He felt again the curious emotional atmosphere that she had created when singing. He thought to himself: "A magnetic field, that's what it is." And then again: "I don't like her. I'm afraid of her."

A longhaired young man came up and joined them. He was a Swede, but he spoke excellent English.

"Sebastian tells me that you will write the music of the future," he said to Vernon. "I have theories about the future. Time is only another dimension of space. You can move to and fro in time as you can move to and fro in space. Half your dreams are only confused memories of the future. And as you can be separated from your dear ones in space, so you can be separated from them in time, and that is the greatest tragedy there is or can be."

Since he was clearly mad, Vernon paid no attention. He was not interested in theories of space and time. But Jane Harding leaned forward.

"To be separated in time," she said. "I never thought of that."

Encouraged, the Swede went on. He talked of time, and of ultimate space, and of time one, and of time two. Whether Jane was interested or not, Vernon did not know. She looked straight in front of her and did not appear to be listening. The Swede went on to time three and Vernon escaped.

He joined Joe and Sebastian. Joe was being enthusiastic on the subject of Jane Harding.

"I think she's wonderful. Don't you, Vernon? She's asked me to go and see her. I wish I could sing like that."

"She's an actress, not a singer," said Sebastian. "A good sort, Jane. She's had rather a tragic life. For five years she lived with Boris Androv, the sculptor."

Joe glanced over in Jane's direction with enhanced interest. Vernon felt suddenly young and crude. He could still see those enigmatical slightly mocking green eyes. He heard that amused ironical voice. *You do expect life to be a fairy story, don't you?* Hang it all, that hurt!

And yet he had an immense desire to see her again.

Should he ask her if he might?

No, he couldn't.

Besides, he was so seldom in town.

He heard her voice behind him—a singer's voice, slightly husky.

"Good-night, Sebastian. Thank you."

She moved toward the door, looked over her shoulder at Vernon.

"Come and see me some time," she said carelessly. "Your cousin has got my address."

BOOK III

JANE

Chapter One

Jane Harding had a flat at the top of a block of mansions overlooking the river in Chelsea.

Here, on the evening following the party, came Sebastian Levinne.

"I've fixed it up, Jane," he said. "Radmaager is coming here to see you sometime tomorrow. He prefers to do that, it seems."

" 'Come, tell me how you live, he cried,' " quoted Jane. "Well, I'm living very nicely and respectably, entirely alone! Do you want something to eat, Sebastian?"

"If there is anything?"

"There are scrambled eggs and mushrooms, anchovy toast and black coffee if you'll sit here peaceably while I get them."

She put the cigarette box and the matches beside him and left the room. In a quarter of an hour the meal was ready.

"I like coming to see you, Jane," said Sebastian. "You never treat me as a bloated young Jew to whom only the flesh pots of the Savoy would make appeal."

Jane smiled without speaking.

Presently she said: "I like your girl, Sebastian."

"Joe?"

"Yes, Joe."

Sebastian said gruffly: "What—what do you really think of her?"

Again Jane paused before answering.

"So young," she said at last. "So terribly young."

Sebastian chuckled.

"She'd be very angry if she heard you."

"Probably." After a minute she said: "You care for her very much, don't you, Sebastian?"

"Yes. It's odd, isn't it, Jane, how little all the things you've got matter? I've got practically all the things I want, except Joe, and Joe is all that matters. I can see what a fool I am, but it doesn't make a bit of difference! What's the difference between Joe and a hundred other girls? Very little. And yet she's the only thing in the world that matters to me just now."

"Partly because you can't get her."

"Perhaps. But I don't think that's so entirely."

"Neither do I."

"What do you think of Vernon?" asked Sebastian after a pause.

Jane changed her position, shading her face from the fire.

"He's interesting," she said slowly, "partly, I think, because he is so completely unambitious."

"Unambitious, do you think?"

"Yes. He wants things made easy."

"If so, he'll never do anything in music. You want driving power for that."

"Yes, you want driving power. But music will be the power that drives *him!*"

Sebastian looked up, his face alight and appreciative.

"Do you know, Jane," he said, "I believe you're right!"

She smiled but made no answer.

"I wish I knew what to make of the girl he's engaged to," said Sebastian.

"What is she like?"

"Pretty. Some people might call it lovely—but I'd call it pretty. She does the things that other people do, and does them very sweetly. She's not a cat. I'm afraid—yes, I am afraid now that she definitely cares for Vernon."

"You needn't be afraid. Your pet genius won't be turned aside or held down. That doesn't happen. I'm more than ever sure, every day I live, that that doesn't happen."

"Nothing would turn *you* aside, Jane, but then you have got driving power."

"And yet, do you know, Sebastian, I believe I should be more easily 'turned aside,' as you call it, than your Vernon? I know what I want and go for it—he doesn't know what he wants, or rather doesn't want it, but *it* goes for *him*. . . . And that *It*, whatever It is, *will* be served—no matter at what cost."

"Cost to whom?"

"Ah! I wonder. . . ."

Sebastian rose.

"I must go. Thanks for feeding me, Jane."

"Thank you for what you've done for me with Radmaager. You're a very good friend, Sebastian. And I don't think success will ever spoil you."

"Oh! success . . ." He held out his hand.

She laid both hands on his shoulders and kissed him.

"My dear, I hope you will get your Joe. But if not I am quite sure you will get everything else!"

2

Herr Radmaager did not come to see Jane Harding for nearly a fortnight. He arrived without warning of any kind at half-past ten in the morning. He stumped into the flat without a word of apology and looked around the walls of the sitting room.

"It is you who have furnished and papered this? Yes?"

"Yes."

"You live here alone?"

"Yes."

"But you have not always lived alone?"

"No."

Radmaager said unexpectedly: "That is good." Then he said commandingly: "Come here."

He took her by both arms, and drew her toward the window. There he looked her over from head to foot. He pinched the flesh of her arm between finger and thumb, opened her mouth and looked down her throat, and finally put a large hand on each side of her waist.

"Breathe in—good! Now out—sharply."

He took a tape measure out of his pocket, made her repeat the two movements, passing the tape measure round her each time. Finally he pocketed it and put it away. Neither he nor Jane seemed to see anything curious in the proceedings.

"It is well," said Radmaager. "Your chest is excellent, your throat is strong. You are intelligent—since you have not interrupted me. I can find many singers with a better voice than yours—your voice is very true, very beautiful, but it is not clear, a silver thread. If you force it, it will go—and where will you be then, I ask you? The music you sing now is absurd—if you were not pigheaded as the devil you would not sing those roles, Yet I respect you because you are an artist."

He paused, then went on:

"Now listen to me. My music is beautiful and it will not hurt your voice. When Ibsen created Solveig he created the most wonderful woman character that has ever been created. My opera will stand and fall by its Solveig—and it is not sufficient to have a singer. There are Cavarossi, Mary Montner, Jeanne Dorta—all hope to sing Solveig. But I will not have it. What are they? Unintelligent animals with marvelous vocal chords. For my Solveig I must have a perfect instrument, an instrument with intelligence. You are a young singer—as yet unknown. You shall sing at Covent Garden next year in my *Peer Gynt* if you satisfy me. Now listen. . . ."

He sat down at Jane's piano and began to play—queer rhythmic monotonous notes.

"It is the snow, you comprehend—the Northern snow. That is what your voice must be like—the snow. It is white like damask—and the pattern runs through it. But the pattern is in the music, not in your voice."

He went on playing. Endless monotony, endless repetition, and yet suddenly the something that was woven through it caught your ear—what he had called the pattern.

He stopped.

"Well?"

"It will be very difficult to sing."

"Quite right. But you have an excellent ear. You wish to sing Solveig—yes?"

"Naturally. It's the chance of a lifetime. If I can satisfy you."

"I think you can." He got up again, laid his hands on her shoulders. "How old are you?"

"Thirty-three."

"And you have been very unhappy—that is so?"

"Yes."

"How many men have you lived with?"

"One."

"And he was not a good man?"

Jane answered evenly: "He was a very bad one."

"I see. Yes, it is that which is written in your face. Now listen to me. All that you have suffered, all that you have enjoyed, you will put it into my music—not with abandon, not with unrestraint, but with controlled and disciplined force. You have intelligence and you have courage. Without courage nothing can ever be accomplished. Those without courage turn their backs on life. You will never turn your back on life. Whatever comes you will stand there facing it with your chin up and your eyes very steady. . . . But I hope, my child, that you will not be too much hurt."

He turned away.

"I will send on the score," he said over his shoulder. "And you will study it."

He stumped out of the room and the flat door banged.

Jane sat down by the table. She stared at the wall in front of her with unseeing eyes. Her chance had come.

She murmured very softly to herself: "I'm afraid."

3

For a whole week Vernon debated the question of whether he should or should not take Jane at her word. He could get up to town at the weekend—but then perhaps Jane would be away. He felt miserably self-conscious and shy. Perhaps by now she had forgotten that she had asked him.

He let the weekend go by. He felt that certainly by now she would have forgotten him. Then he got a letter from Joe in which she mentioned having seen Jane twice. That decided Vernon. At six o'clock on the following Saturday he rang the bell of Jane's flat.

Jane herself opened it. Her eyes opened a little wider when she saw who it was. Otherwise she displayed no surprise.

"Come in," she said. "I'm finishing my practicing. But you won't mind."

He followed her into a long room whose windows overlooked the river. It was very empty. A grand piano, a divan, a couple of chairs and walls that were papered with a wild riot of bluebells and daffodils. One wall alone was papered in sober dark green and on it hung a single picture—a queer study of bare tree trunks. Something about it reminded Vernon of his early adventures in the Forest.

On the music stool was the little man like a white worm.

Jane pushed a cigarette box toward Vernon, said in her brutal commanding voice, "Now, Mr. Hill," and began to walk up and down the room.

Mr. Hill flung himself upon the piano. His hands twinkled up and down it with marvelous speed and dexterity. Jane sang. Most of the time *sotto voce*, almost under her breath. Occasionally she would take a phrase full pitch. Once or twice she stopped with an exclamation of what sounded like furious impatience, and Mr. Hill was made to repeat from several bars back.

She broke off quite suddenly by clapping her hands. She crossed to the fireplace, pushed the bell, and turning her head addressed Mr. Hill for the first time as a human being.

"You'll stay and have some tea, won't you, Mr. Hill?"

Mr. Hill was afraid he couldn't. He twisted his body apologetically several times and sidled out of the room. A maid brought in black coffee and hot buttered toast, which appeared to be Jane's conception of afternoon tea.

"What was that you were singing?"

"Electra—Richard Strauss."

"Oh! I liked it. It was like dogs fighting."

"Strauss would be flattered. All the same, I know what you mean. It is combative."

She pushed the toast toward him and added: "Your cousin's been here twice."

"I know. She wrote and told me."

He felt tongue-tied and uncomfortable. He had wanted so much to come, and now that he was here he didn't know what to say. Something about Jane made him uncomfortable. He blurted out at last:

"Tell me truthfully—would you advise me to chuck work altogether and stick to music?"

"How can I possibly tell? I don't know what you want to do."

"You spoke like that the other night. As though everyone can do just what they like."

"So they can. Not always, of course—but very nearly always. If you want to murder someone, there is really nothing to stop you. But you will be hanged afterwards—naturally."

"I don't want to murder anyone."

"No, you want your fairy story to end happily. Uncle dies and leaves you all his money. You marry your lady love and live at Abbots—whatever it's called—happily ever afterward."

Vernon said angrily: "I wish you wouldn't laugh at me."

Jane was silent a minute, then she said in a different voice: "I wasn't laughing at you. I was doing something I'd no business to do—trying to interfere."

"What do you mean, trying to interfere?"

"Trying to make you face reality, and forgetting that you are—what—about eight years younger than I am?—and that your time for that hasn't yet come."

He thought suddenly: "I could say anything to her—anything at all. She wouldn't always answer the way I wanted her to, though."

Aloud he said: "Please go on. I'm afraid it's very egotistical, my talking about myself like this, but I'm so worried and unhappy. I want to know what you meant when you said the other evening that of the four things I wanted, I could get any one of them but not all together."

Jane considered a minute.

"What did I mean exactly? Why, just this. To get what you want, you must usually pay a price or take a risk—sometimes both. For instance, I love music—a certain kind of music. My voice is suitable for a totally different kind of music. It's an unusually good concert voice—not an operatic one, except for very light opera. But I've sung in Wagner, in Strauss—in all the things I like. I haven't exactly paid a price—but I take an enormous risk. My voice may give out any minute. I know that. I've looked the fact in the face and I've decided that the game is worth the candle.

"Now, in your case, you mentioned four things. For the first, I suppose that if you remain in your uncle's business for a sufficient number of years you will grow rich without any further trouble. That's not very interesting. Secondly, you want to live at Abbots Puissants. You could do that tomorrow if you married a girl with money. Then the girl you're fond of, the girl you want to marry—"

"Can I get her tomorrow?" asked Vernon. He spoke with a kind of angry irony.

"I should say so—quite easily."

"How?"

"By selling Abbots Puissants. It is yours to sell, isn't it?"

"Yes, but I couldn't do that. I couldn't—I couldn't. . . ." Jane leaned back in her chair and smiled.

"You prefer to go on believing that life is a fairy story?"

"There must be some other way."

"Yes, of course there is another. Probably the simplest. There's nothing to stop you both going out to the nearest Registry Office. You've both got the use of your limbs."

"You don't understand. There are hundreds of difficulties in the way. I couldn't ask Nell to face a life of poverty. She doesn't want to be poor."

"Perhaps she can't."

"What do you mean by 'can't'?"

"Just that. Can't. Some people can't be poor, you know."

Vernon got up, walked twice up and down the room. Then he came back, dropped on the hearth rug beside Jane's chair, and looked up at her.

"What about the fourth thing? Music? Do you think I could ever do that?"

"That I can't say. Wanting mayn't be any use there. But if it does happen, I expect it will swallow up all the rest. They'll all go—Abbots Puissants, money, the girl. My dear, I don't feel life's going to be easy for you. Ugh! A goose is walking over my grave. Now tell me something about this opera Sebastian Levinne says you are writing."

When he had finished telling her, it was nine o'clock. They both exclaimed and went out to a little restaurant together. As he said good-bye afterward his first diffidence returned.

"I think you are one of the—the nicest people I ever met. You will let me come again and talk, won't you? If I haven't bored you too frightfully."

"Any time you like. Good-night."

4

Myra wrote to Joe:

Dearest Josephine:

I am so worried about Vernon and this woman he is always going up to town to see—some opera singer or other. Years older than he is. It's so dreadful the way women like that get hold of boys. I am terribly worried and don't know what to do about it. I have spoken to your Uncle Sydney, but he was not very helpful about it and just said that boys will be boys. But I don't want *my* boy to be like that. I was wondering, dear Joe, if it would be any good my seeing this woman and begging her to leave my boy alone. Even a *bad* woman would listen to a mother, I think. Vernon is too young to have his life ruined. I really don't know what to do. I seem to have no influence over Vernon nowadays.

With much love,
Your affectionate
Aunt Myra

Joe showed this letter to Sebastian.

"I suppose she means Jane," said Sebastian. "I'd rather like to see an interview between them. Frankly, I think Jane would be amused."

"It's too silly," said Joe hotly. "I wish to goodness Vernon *would* fall in love with Jane. It would be a hundred times better for him than being in love with that silly stick of a Nell."

"You don't like Nell, do you, Joe?"

"You don't like her either."

"Oh! yes, I do, in a way. She doesn't interest me very much, but I can quite see the attraction. In her own way, she's quite lovely."

"Yes, in a chocolate-box way."

"She doesn't attract me, because to my mind there's nothing there to attract as yet. The real Nell hasn't happened. Perhaps she never will. I suppose to some people that is very attractive because it opens out all sorts of possibilities."

"Well, I think Jane is worth ten of Nell! The sooner Vernon gets over his silly calf love for Nell and falls in love with Jane instead, the better it will be."

Sebastian lit a cigarette and said slowly: "I'm not sure that I agree with you."

"Why?"

"Well, it's not very easy to explain. But, you see, Jane is a real person—very much so. To be in love with Jane might be a whole-time job. We're agreed, aren't we, that Vernon is very possibly a genius? Well, I don't think a genius wants to be married to a real person. He wants to be married to someone rather negligible—someone whose personality won't interfere. Now it may sound cynical, but that's what will probably happen if Vernon marries Nell. At the moment she represents—I don't quite know what to call it—what's that line? 'The apple tree, the singing and the gold . . .' Something like that. Once he's married to her, that will go. She'll just be a nice pretty sweet-tempered girl whom, naturally, he loves very much. But she won't *interfere*. She'll never get between him and his work—she hasn't got sufficient personality. Now Jane might. She wouldn't mean to, but she might. It isn't Jane's beauty that attracts you—it's herself. She might be absolutely fatal to Vernon."

"Well," said Joe, "I don't agree with you. I think Nell's a silly little ass and I should hate to see Vernon married to her. I hope it will all come to nothing."

"Which is much the likeliest thing to happen," said Sebastian.

Chapter Two

Nell was back in London. Vernon came up to see her the day after her return. She noticed the change in him at once. He looked haggard, excited. He said abruptly:

"Nell, I'm going to chuck Birmingham."

"What?"

"Listen while I tell you. . . ."

He talked eagerly, excitedly. His music—he'd got to give himself up to it. He told her of the opera.

"Listen, Nell. This is you—in your tower—with your golden hair hanging down and shining—shining in the sun."

He went to the piano, began to play, explaining as he did so. "Violins—you see—and this is all for harps . . . and these are the round jewels. . . ."

He played what seemed to Nell to be a series of rather ugly discords. She privately thought it all hideous. Perhaps it would sound differently played by an orchestra.

But she loved him—and because she loved him, everything he did must be right. She smiled and said:

"It's lovely, Vernon."

"Do you really like it, Nell? Oh! sweetheart—you are so wonderful. You always understand. You're so sweet about everything."

He came across to her, knelt down and buried his face on her lap.

"I love you so . . . I love you so."

She stroked his dark head.

"Tell me the story of it."

"Shall I? Well, you see, there's a princess in a tower with golden hair, and kings and knights come from all over the world to try and get her to marry them. But she's too haughty to look at any of them—the real good old fairy-story touch. And at last one comes—a kind of gypsy fellow—very ragged, with a little green hat on his head and a kind of pipe he plays on. And he sings and says that he has the biggest kingdom of anyone because his kingdom is the whole world—and that there are no jewels like his jewels, which are dewdrops. And they say he's mad and throw him out. But that night when the princess is lying in bed she hears him playing his song in the castle garden and she listens.

"Then there's an old Jew pedlar man in the town and he offers the fellow gold and riches with which to win the princess, but the gypsy laughs and says, What could he give in exchange? And the old man says his green hat and the pipe he plays on, but the gypsy says he will never part with those.

"He plays in the palace garden every night. There's an old bard in the palace and he tells a tale of how a hundred years ago a prince of the royal house was bewitched by a gypsy maid and wandered forth and was never seen again. And the princess listens to it, and at last one night she gets up and comes to the window. And the gypsy tells her to leave all her robes and jewels behind and to come out in a simple white gown. But she thinks in her heart that it's as well to be on the safe side, so she puts a pearl in the hem of her skirt, and she comes out, and they go off in the moonlight while he sings. But the pearl in her dress weighs her down and she can't keep up. And he goes on, not realizing that she's left behind. . . .

"I've told this very badly, like a story, but that's the end of the first act—his going off in the moonlight and her left behind weeping. There are three scenes. The castle hall, the market place, and the palace garden outside her window."

"Won't that be very expensive—in the way of scenery, I mean?" suggested Nell.

"I don't know—I hadn't thought—oh! it can be managed, I expect." Vernon was irritated by these prosaic details.

"Now the second act is near the market place. There is a girl there mending dolls—with black hair hanging down round her face. The gypsy comes along, and asks her what she's doing, and she says she's mending the children's toys—she's got the most wonderful needle and thread in the world. He tells her all about the princess and how he's lost her again, and he says he's going to the old Jew pedlar to sell his hat and his pipe, and she warns him not to—but he says he must.

"I wish I could tell things better. I'm just giving you the story now—not the way I've divided it up, because I'm not exactly sure myself yet about that. I've got the music—that's the great thing: the heavy empty palace music—and the noisy clattering marketplace music—and the princess— like that line of poetry, 'a singing stream in a silent vale,' and the doll mender all trees and dark woods like the Forest used to sound at Abbots Puissants; you know, enchanted and mysterious and a little frightening . . . I think you'll have to have some instruments specially tuned for it. . . . Well, I won't go into that, it wouldn't interest you—it's too technical.

"Where was I? Oh! yes, he turns up at the palace—as a great king this time—all clanking swords and horse trappings and blazing jewels, and the princess is overjoyed and they're going to be married and every-thing's all right. But he begins to get pale and weary, worse every day, and when anyone asks him what is the matter, he says, 'Nothing.' "

"Like you when you were a little boy at Abbots Puissants," said Nell smiling.

"Did I say that? I don't remember. Well, then the night before the wedding he can't bear it anymore, and he steals away from the palace and down to the market and wakes up the old Jew and says he must have back his hat and his pipe. He'll give back everything he got in exchange. The old Jew laughs, and throws down the hat, torn across, and the pipe, broken, at the prince's feet.

"He's brokenhearted—the bottom knocked out of the world—and he wanders away with them in his hand, till he comes to where the doll mender is sitting with her feet tucked up under her, and he tells her what has happened and she tells him to lie down and sleep. And when he wakes in the morning there are his green hat and his pipe, mended so beautifully that no one could tell they had been mended.

"And then he laughs for joy, and she goes to a cupboard and pulls out a similar little green hat and a pipe, and they go out together through the forest, and just as the sun rises on the edge of the forest, he looks at her and remembers. He says, 'Why, a hundred years ago I left my palace and my throne for love of you.' And she says, 'Yes. But because you were afraid you hid a piece of gold in the lining of your doublet, and the gleam of it enchanted your eyes and we lost each other. But now the whole world is ours and we will wander through it together forever and ever.' "

Vernon stopped. He turned an enthusiastic face upon Nell. "It ought to be lovely, the end . . . so lovely. If I can get into the music what I see and hear: the two of them in their little green hats . . . playing their pipes . . . and the forest and the sun rising. . . ."

His face grew dreamy and ecstatic. He seemed to have forgotten Nell.

Nell herself felt indescribable sensations sweep over her. She was afraid of this queer rapt Vernon. He had talked of music before to her, but never with this strange exalted passion. She knew that Sebastian Levinne thought Vernon might do wonderful things someday, but she remembered lives she had read of musical geniuses, and suddenly she wished with all her heart that Vernon might not have this marvelous gift. She wanted him as he had been heretofore, her eager boyish lover, the two of them wrapped in their common dream.

The wives of musicians were always unhappy: she had read that somewhere. She didn't want Vernon to be a great musician. She wanted him to make some money quickly and live with her at Abbots Puissants. She wanted a sweet sane normal everyday life. Love—and Vernon.

This thing—this kind of possession—was *dangerous*. She was sure it was dangerous.

But she couldn't damp Vernon's ardor. She loved him far too much for that. She said, trying to make her voice sound sympathetic and interested:

"What an unusual fairy story! Do you mean to say you've remembered it from ever since you were a child?"

"More or less. I thought of it again that morning on the river at Cambridge—just before I saw you standing under that tree. Darling, you were so lovely—so lovely. . . . You always will be lovely, won't you? I couldn't bear it if you weren't. What idiotic things I am saying! And then, after that night at Ranelagh, that wonderful night when I told you that I loved you, all the music came pouring into my mind. Only I couldn't remember the story clearly—only really the bit about the tower.

"But I've had marvelous luck. I've met a girl who is actually the niece of the hospital nurse who told me the story. And she remembered it perfectly and helped me to get it quite clearly again. Isn't it extraordinary the way things happen?"

"Who is she, this woman?"

"She's really rather a wonderful person, I think. Awfully nice and frightfully clever. She's a singer—Jane Harding. She sings Electra and Brunhild and Isolde with the new English Opera Company, and she may sing at Covent Garden next year. I met her at a party of Sebastian's. I want you to meet her. I'm sure you'd like her awfully."

"How old is she? Young?"

"Youngish—about thirty, I should think. She has an awfully queer effect on one. In a way you almost dislike her, and yet she makes you feel you can do things. She's been very good to me."

"I dare say."

Why did she say that? Why should she feel an unreasoning prejudice against this woman—this Jane Harding?

Vernon was staring at her with rather a puzzled expression.

"What's the matter, darling? You said that so queerly."

"I don't know." She tried to laugh. "A goose walking over my grave, perhaps."

"Funny," said Vernon frowning. "Somebody else said that just lately."

"Lots of people say it," said Nell laughing. She paused and then said: "I'd—I'd like to meet this friend of yours very much, Vernon."

"I know. I want her to meet you. I've talked a lot about you to her."

"I wish you wouldn't. Talk about me, I mean. After all, we promised Mother no one should know."

"Nobody outside—but Sebastian knows and Joe."

"That's different. You've known them all your life."

"Yes, of course. I'm sorry. I didn't think. I didn't say we were engaged, or tell your name or anything. You're not cross, are you, Nell darling?"

"Of course not."

Even in her own ears her voice sounded hard. Why was life so horribly difficult? She was afraid of this music. Already it had made Vernon chuck up a good job. *Was* it the music? Or was it Jane Harding?

She thought to herself desperately: "I wish I'd never met Vernon. I wish I'd never loved him. I wish—oh! I wish I didn't love so much. I'm afraid. I'm afraid. . . ."

2

It was over! the plunge was taken! There was unpleasantness, of course. Uncle Sydney was furious; not, Vernon was forced to confess, without reason. There were scenes with his mother—tears—recriminations. A dozen times he was on the point of giving way, and yet, somehow or other, he didn't.

He had a curious sense of desolation all the time. He was alone in this thing. Nell, because she loved him, agreed to all he said, but he was uncomfortably conscious that his decision had grieved and disturbed her, and might even shake her faith in the future. Sebastian thought the move premature. For the time being, he would have advised making the best of two worlds. Not that he said so. Sebastian never gave advice to anybody. Even the staunch Joe was doubtful. She realized that for Vernon to sever his connection with the Bents was serious, and she had not the real faith in Vernon's musical future which would have made her heartily applaud the step.

So far in his life, Vernon had never had the courage to set himself definitely in opposition to everybody. When it was all over, and he was settled in the very cheap rooms which were all he could afford in London, he felt as one might who had overcome invincible odds. Then, and not till then, he went to see Jane Harding.

He had held boyish imaginary conversations with her in his mind.

"I have done what you told me."

"Splendid! I knew you had the courage really."

He was modest, she applauded. He was sustained and uplifted by her praise.

The reality, as always, fell out quite differently. His intercourse with Jane always did. He was always holding imaginary conversations with Jane in his mind, and the reality was always totally different.

In this case, when he announced, with due modesty, what he had done, she seemed to take it as a matter of course, with nothing particularly heroic about it. She said:

"Well, you must have wanted to do it or you wouldn't have done it."

He felt baffled, almost angry. A curious sense of constraint always came over him in Jane's presence. He could never be wholly natural with her. He had so much he wanted to say—but he found it difficult to say. He was tongue-tied—embarrassed. And then suddenly, for no reason, it seemed, the cloud would lift and he would be talking happily and easily, saying the things that came into his head.

He thought; "Why am I so embarrassed with her? *She's* natural enough."

It worried him. From the first moment he had met her, he had felt disturbed—afraid. He resented the effect she had on him and yet he was unwilling to admit how strong that effect was.

An attempt to bring about a friendship between her and Nell failed. Vernon could feel that behind the outward cordiality that politeness dictates there was very little real feeling.

When he asked Nell what she thought of Jane, she answered: "I like her very much. I think she's most interesting."

He was more awkward approaching Jane, but she helped him.

"You want to know what I think of your Nell? She is lovely—and very sweet."

He said: "And you really think you'll be friends?"

"No, of course not. Why should we?"

"Well, but—"

He stammered, taken aback.

"Friendship is not a kind of equilateral triangle. If A likes B and loves C, then C and B *et cetera, et cetera....* We've nothing in common, your Nell and I. She, too, expects life to be a fairy story, and is just beginning to be afraid, poor child, that it mayn't be, after all. She's a Sleeping Beauty waking in the forest. Love, to her, is something very wonderful and very beautiful."

"Isn't it that to you?"

He had to ask. He wanted to know so badly. So often, so often, he'd wondered about Boris Androv, about those five years.

She looked at him with a face from which all expression had died out.

"Some day—I'll tell you."

He wanted to say, "Tell me now," but he didn't. He said instead: "Tell me, Jane, what is life to you?"

She paused a minute and then said: "A difficult, dangerous, but endlessly interesting adventure."

3

At last he was able to work. He began to appreciate to the full the joys of freedom. There was nothing to fray his nerves, nothing to dissipate his energy. It could flow, all in one steady stream, into his work. There were few distractions. At the moment, he had only just enough money to keep body and soul together. Abbots Puissants was still unlet. . . .

The autumn passed and most of the winter. He saw Nell once or twice a week, stolen unsatisfactory meetings. They were both conscious of the loss of the first fine rapture. She questioned him closely about the progress of the opera. How was it going? When did he expect it would be finished? What chances were there of its being produced?

Vernon was vague as to all these practical aspects. He was concerned at the moment only with the creative side. The opera was getting itself born slowly, with innumerable pangs and difficulties, with a hundred setbacks owing to Vernon's own lack of experience and technique. His conversation was mostly of instrumental difficulties or possibilities. He went out with odd musicians who played in orchestras. Nell went to many concerts and was fond of music but it is doubtful if she could have told an oboe from a clarionet. She'd always imagined a horn and a French horn to be much the same thing. The technical knowledge needed in score writing appalled her, and Vernon's indifference to how and when the opera would be produced made her uneasy.

He hardly realized himself how much his uncertain answers depressed and alienated Nell. He was startled one day when she said to him— indeed, not so much said as wailed:

"Oh! Vernon, don't try me too hard. It's so difficult—so difficult. I must have some hope. You don't understand."

He looked at her astonished.

"But Nell, it's all right *really*. It's only a question of being patient."

"I know, Vernon. I shouldn't have said that, but you see—"

She paused.

"It makes it so much more difficult for me, darling," said Vernon, "if I feel that you're unhappy."

"Oh! I'm not—I won't be."

But underneath, choked down, that old feeling of resentment lifted its head again. Vernon didn't understand or care how difficult things were for her. He never had the faintest conception of her difficulties. He would, perhaps, have called them silly, or trivial. They were, in one sense, but in another they weren't—since the sum total of them went to make up her life. Vernon didn't see or realize that she was fighting a battle—fighting it all the time. She could never relax. If he could only realize that, give her a word of cheer, show her that he understood the difficult position in which she was placed. But he never would see.

A devastating sense of loneliness swept over Nell. Men were like that—they never understood or cared. Love—that seemed to solve everything. But really it didn't solve anything at all. She almost hated Vernon. Selfishly absorbed in his work, disliking her to be unhappy because it upset *him*. . . .

She thought: "Any *woman* would understand."

And, moved by some obscure impulse, she went of her own accord to see Jane Harding.

Jane was in, and if she was surprised to see Nell, she did not show it. They talked for some time of desultory things. Yet Nell had a feeling that Jane was waiting and watching, biding her time.

Why had she come? She didn't know. She feared and distrusted Jane—perhaps that was why! Jane was her enemy. Yes, but she had a fear that her enemy had a wisdom denied to her. Jane (she put it to herself) was clever. She was, very possibly, bad—yes, she was sure Jane was bad—but somehow or other one might learn from her.

She began rather blunderingly. Did Jane think that Vernon's music was likely to be successful—that is to say, successful *soon*? She tried in vain to keep a quaver out of her voice.

She felt Jane's cool green eyes upon her.

"Things getting difficult?"

"Yes, you see—"

It tumbled out, a great deal of it: the shifts, the difficulties, the un-spoken force of her mother's silent pressure, a dimly veiled reference to Someone, name not given, Someone who understood and was kind and was rich.

How easy to say these things to a woman—even a woman like Jane, who couldn't know anything about them. Women understood—they didn't pooh-pooh trifles and make everything out to be unimportant.

When she had finished, Jane said: "It's a little hard on you. When you first met Vernon you had no idea of this music business."

"I didn't think it would be like this," said Nell bitterly.

"Well, it's no good going back to what you didn't think, is it?"

"I suppose not." Nell felt vaguely annoyed at Jane's tone. "Oh!" she broke out. "You feel, of course, that everything ought to give way to his music—that he's a genius—that I ought to be glad to make any sacri-fice."

"No, I don't," said Jane. "I don't think any of those things. I don't know what good geniuses are, or works of art either. Some people are born with a feeling that they matter more than anything else, and some people aren't. It's impossible to say who's right. The best thing for you would be to persuade Vernon to give up music, sell Abbots Puissants and settle down with you on the proceeds. But I do know this, that you haven't an earthly chance of getting him to give up music. These things, genius, art, whatever you like to call them, are much stronger than you are. You might just as well be King Canute on the seashore. You can't turn back Vernon from music."

"What can I do?" said Nell hopelessly.

"Well, you can either marry this other man you were talking of and be reasonably happy, or you can marry Vernon and be actively unhappy with periods of bliss."

Nell looked at her.

"What would you do?" she whispered.

"Oh! I should marry Vernon and be unhappy, but then some of us like taking our pleasures sadly."

Nell got up. She stood in the doorway looking back at Jane who had not moved. She was lying back against the wall, smoking a cigarette, her eyes half closed. She looked a little like a cat, or a Chinese idol. A sudden wave of fury came over Nell.

"I hate you," she cried. "You're taking Vernon away from me. Yes— *you*. You're bad—evil. I know it, I can feel it. You're a bad woman."

"You're jealous," said Jane quietly.

"You admit then, there's something to be jealous of? Not that Vernon loves you. He doesn't. He never would. It's you who want to get hold of him."

There was silence—a pulsating silence. Then, without moving, Jane laughed. Nell hurried out of the flat, hardly knowing what she was doing.

4

Sebastian came very often to see Jane. He usually came after dinner, ringing up first to find out if she would be at home. They both found a curious pleasure in each other's company. To Sebastian Jane recounted her struggles with the role of Solveig, the difficulties of the music, the difficulty of pleasing Radmaager, the still greater difficulty of pleasing herself. To Jane Sebastian imparted his ambitious, his present plans, his future vague ideals.

One evening, after they had both been silent after a long spell of talking, he said:

"I can talk to you better than anyone I know, Jane. I don't quite know why, either."

"Well, in a way, we're both the same kind of person, aren't we?"

"Are we?"

"I think so. Not superficially, perhaps, but fundamentally. We both like truth. I think, as far as one can say that of oneself, we both see things as they are."

"And you think most people don't?"

"Of course they don't. Nell Vereker, for instance. She sees things as they've been shown her, as she hopes they are."

"A slave of convention, you mean?"

"Yes, but it works both ways. Joe, for instance, prides herself on being unconventional, but that makes just as much for narrowness and prejudice."

"Yes, if you're 'agin' everything irrespective of what it is. Joe is like that. She *must* be a rebel. She never really examines a thing on its merits. And that's what damns me so hopelessly in her eyes. I'm successful, and she admires failures. I'm rich, so she'd gain instead of lose if she married me. And being a Jew doesn't count against you much nowadays."

"It's even fashionable," said Jane laughing.

"And yet, do you know, Jane, I always have a queer feeling that Joe really likes me."

"Perhaps she does. She's the wrong age for you, Sebastian. That Swede at your party said something wonderfully true—about separation in time being worse than separation in space. If you're the wrong age for a person, nothing keeps you apart so hopelessly. You may be made for one another, but be born at the wrong time for each other. Does that sound nonsense? I believe when she's about thirty-five, Joe could love you—the real essential you—madly. It'll take a woman to love you, Sebastian, not a girl."

Sebastian was looking into the fire. It was a cold February day, and there were logs piled up on the coals. Jane hated gas fires.

"Have you ever wondered, Jane, why we don't fall in love with each other, you and I? Platonic friendship doesn't usually work. And you're very attractive. There's a lot of the siren about you—quite unconscious, but it's there."

"Perhaps we should under normal conditions."

"Aren't we under normal conditions? Oh! wait a minute—I know what you mean. You mean, the line's already engaged."

"Yes. If you didn't love Joe—"

"And if you—"

He stopped.

"Well?" said Jane. "You knew, didn't you?"

"Yes, I suppose so. You don't mind talking about it?"

"Not in the least. If a thing's there, what does it matter if you talk of it or not?"

"Are you one of the people, Jane, who believe that if you want a thing enough you can make it happen?"

Jane considered.

"No—I don't think I am. So many things happen to you naturally that it keeps you busy without—well, looking for things as well. When a thing's offered you, you've got to choose whether you'll accept it or refuse it. That's destiny. And when you've made your choice you must abide by it without looking back."

"That's the spirit of Greek tragedy. You've got Electra into your bones, Jane." He picked up a book from the table. *"Peer Gynt?* You're steeping yourself in Solveig, I see."

"Yes. It's more her opera than Peer's. You know, Sebastian, Solveig is a wonderfully fascinating character—so impassive, so calm, and yet so utterly certain that her love for Peer is the only thing in heaven or earth. She knows that he wants and needs her though he never tells her so, she is abandoned and deserted by him, and manages to turn that desertion into a crowning proof of his love. By the way, that Whitsuntide music of Radmaager's is perfectly glorious. You know: 'Blessed is he who has made my life blessed!' To show that the love of a man can turn into a kind of impassioned nun is difficult but rather wonderful."

"Is Radmaager pleased with you?"

"Sometimes he is. Yesterday, on the other hand, he consigned my soul to hell and shook me till my teeth rattled. He was perfectly right, too. I sang it all wrong—like a melodramatic stage-struck girl. It's got to be sheer force of will—restraint. Solveig must be so soft and gentle but really so terribly strong. It's like Radmaager said the first day. Snow—smooth snow—with a wonderful clear design running through it."

She went on to talk of Vernon's work.

"It's almost finished, you know. I want him to show it to Radmaager."

"Will he?"

"I think so. Have you seen it?"

"Parts of it only."

"What do you think of it?"

"I'll hear what you think of it first, Jane. Your judgment's as good as mine any day where music is concerned."

"It's crude. There's too much in it—too much good stuff. He hasn't

learned how to handle his material, but the material is there—masses
and masses of it. Do you agree?"

Sebastian nodded.

"Absolutely. I'm more sure than ever that Vernon is going to—well,
revolutionize things. But there's a nasty time coming. He'll have to face
the fact that what he's written isn't, when all's said and done, a commercial proposition."

"You mean, it couldn't be produced?"

"That's what I mean."

"*You* could produce it."

"You mean, out of friendship?"

"That's what I meant."

Sebastian got up and began to pace up and down.

"To my way of thinking, that's unethical," he said at last.

"And also you don't like losing money."

"Quite true."

"But you could afford to lose a certain amount without—well, noticing it?"

"I always notice losing money. It affects—well, my pride."

Jane nodded.

"I understand that. But I don't think, Sebastian, that you need lose
money."

"My dear Jane—"

"Don't argue with me till you know what I'm arguing about. You're
going to produce a certain amount of what the world calls 'highbrow'
stuff at the little Holborn theater, aren't you? Well, this summer—say
the beginning of July—produce *The Princess in the Tower* for—say—
two weeks. Don't produce it from the point of view of an opera (don't
tell Vernon this, by the way—but there, you wouldn't. You're not an
idiot) but from the point of view of a musical spectacular play. Unusual
scenery and weird lighting effects—you're keen on lighting, I know. The
Russian ballet—that's what you've got to aim at; that's the—the *tone* of
it. Have good singers, but attractive ones to look at as well. And now,
putting modesty in the background, I'll tell you this. I'll make a success
of it for you."

"You—as the princess?"

"No, my dear child, as the doll mender. It's a weird character—a character that will attract and arrest. The music of the doll mender is the best thing Vernon has done. Sebastian, you've always said I could act. They're going to let me sing at Covent Garden this season because I can act. I shall make a hit. I know I can act—and acting counts for a lot in opera. I can—I can *sway* people. I can make them *feel*. Vernon's opera will need licking into shape from the dramatic point of view. Leave that to me. From the musical side, you and Radmaager may be able to make suggestions—if he'll take them. Musicians are the devil to deal with, as we all know. The thing can be done, Sebastian."

She leaned forward, her face vivid and impressive. Sebastian's face grew more impassive, as it always did when he was thinking hard. He looked appraisingly at Jane, weighing her, not from the personal standpoint, but from the impersonal. He believed in Jane, in her dynamic force, inner magnetism, in her wonderful power of communicating emotion over the footlights.

"I'll think it over," he said quietly. "There's something in what you say."

Jane laughed suddenly.

"And you'll be able to get me very cheap, Sebastian," she said.

"I shall expect to," said Sebastian gravely. "My Jewish instincts must be appeased somehow. You're putting this thing over on me, Jane—don't imagine that I don't know it!"

Chapter Three

At last "The Princess in the Tower" was finished. Vernon suffered from a tremendous wave of reaction. The whole thing was rotten—hopeless. Best to chuck it into the fire.

Nell's sweetness and encouragement were like manna to him at this time. She had that wonderful instinct for always saying the words he longed to hear. But for her, as he constantly told her, he would have given way to despair long ago.

He had seen less of Jane during the winter. She had been on tour with the English Opera Company part of the time. When she sang in *Electra* in Birmingham, he went down for it. He was tremendously impressed—loved both the music and Jane's impersonation of Electra. That ruthless will, that determined: "Say naught but dance on!" She gave the impression of being more spirit than flesh. He was conscious that her voice was really too weak for the part, but somehow it didn't seem to matter. She *was* Electra—that fanatical fiery spirit of relentless doom.

He stayed a few days with his mother—days which he found trying and difficult. He went to see his Uncle Sydney and was received coldly. Enid was engaged to be married to a solicitor, and Uncle Sydney was not too pleased about it.

Nell and her mother were away for Easter. On their return Vernon rang up and said he must see her immediately. He arrived with a white face and burning eyes.

"Nell, do you know what I've heard? Everyone has been saying that you are going to marry George Chetwynd. *George Chetwynd!*"

"Who said so?"

"Lots of people. They say you go round with him everywhere."

Nell looked frightened and unhappy.

"I wish you wouldn't believe things. And Vernon, don't look so—so accusing. It's perfectly true that he has asked me to marry him—twice, as a matter of fact."

"That old man?"

"Oh! Vernon, don't be ridiculous. He's only about forty-one or-two."

"Nearly double your age. Why, I thought he wanted to marry your mother, perhaps."

Nell laughed in spite of herself.

"Oh! dear, I wish he would. Mother's really awfully handsome still."

"That's what I thought that night at Ranelagh. I never guessed—I never dreamed—that it was *you!* Or hadn't it begun then?"

"Oh! yes, it had begun—as you call it. That was why Mother was so angry that night—at my going off alone with you."

"And I never guessed! Nell, you might have told me!"

"Told you what? There wasn't anything to tell—then!"

"No, I suppose not. I'm being an idiot. But I do know he's awfully rich. I get frightened sometimes. Oh! darling Nell, it was beastly of me to doubt you—even for a minute. As though you'd ever care how rich anyone was."

Nell said irritably: "Rich, rich, rich! You harp on that. He's awfully kind and awfully nice, too."

"Oh, I dare say."

"He is, Vernon. Really he is."

"It's nice of you to stick up for him, darling, but he must be an insensitive sort of brute to hang round after you've refused him twice."

Nell did not answer. She looked at him in a way he did not understand—something piteous and appealing and yet defiant in that strange limpid gaze. It was as though she looked at him from a world so far removed from his that they might be on different spheres.

He said: "I feel ashamed of myself, Nell. But you're so lovely, everyone must want you."

She broke down suddenly—began to cry. He was startled. She cried on, sobbed on his shoulder.

"I don't know what to do—I don't know what to do. I'm so unhappy. If I could only talk to you."

"But you can talk to me, darling. I'm here listening."

"No, no, no . . . I can never talk to you. You don't understand. It's all no use."

She cried on. He kissed her, soothed her, poured out all his love. . . .

When he had gone her mother came into the room, an open letter in her hand.

She did not appear to notice Nell's tear-stained face.

"George Chetwynd sails for America on the thirtieth of May," she remarked as she went across to her desk.

"I don't care when he sails," said Nell rebelliously.

Mrs. Vereker did not answer.

That night Nell knelt longer than usual by her narrow white bed.

"Oh! God, please let me marry Vernon. I want to so much. I do love him so. Please let things come right and let us be married. Make something happen. . . . Please God. . . ."

2

At the end of April Abbots Puissants was let. Vernon came to Nell in some excitement.

"Nell, will you marry me now? We could just manage. It's a bad let— an awfully bad one—but I simply had to take it. You see, there's been the mortgage interest to pay and all the expenses of the upkeep while it's been unlet. I've had to borrow for all that and now of course it's got to be paid back. We'll be pretty short for a year or two, but then it won't be so bad. . . ."

He talked on, explaining the financial details.

"I've been into it all, Nell. I have really. Sensibly, I mean. We could afford a tiny flat and one maid and have a little left over to play with. Oh! Nell, you wouldn't mind being poor with me, would you? You said once I didn't know what it was to be poor, but you can't say that now. I've lived on frightfully little since I came to London, and I haven't minded a bit."

No, Nell knew he hadn't. The fact was in some way a vague reproach to her. And yet, though she couldn't quite express it to herself, she felt that the two cases were not on a par. It made much more difference to women. To be gay and pretty and admired and have a good time—none of those things affected men. They hadn't that everlasting problem of clothes—nobody minded if they were shabby.

But how explain these things to Vernon? One couldn't. He wasn't like George Chetwynd. George understood things like that.

"Nell."

She sat there, irresolute, his arm around her. She had got to decide. Visions floated before her eyes. Amelie . . . the hot little house, the wailing children . . . George Chetwynd and his car . . . a stuffy little flat, a dirty incompetent maid . . . dances . . . clothes . . . the money they owed dressmakers . . . the rent of the London house—unpaid . . . herself at Ascot, smiling, chattering in a lovely model gown . . . then, with a sudden revulsion, she was back at Ranelagh on the bridge over the water with Vernon. . . .

In almost the same voice as she had used that evening she said: "I don't know. Oh! Vernon, I don't know."

"Oh! Nell darling, do . . . do!"

She disengaged herself from him, got up.

"Please, Vernon—I must think . . . yes, think. I—I can't when I'm with you."

She wrote to him later that night:

Dearest Vernon:

Let us wait a little longer—say six months. I don't feel I want to be married now. Besides, something might have happened about your opera then. You think I'm afraid of being poor, but it's not quite that. I've seen people—people who loved each other—and they didn't anymore because of all the bothers and worries. I feel that if we wait and are patient everything will come right. Oh! Vernon, I know it will—and then everything will be so lovely. If only we wait and have patience . . .

Vernon was angry when he got this letter. He did not show the letter to Jane, but he broke out into sufficiently unguarded speech to let her see how the land lay. She said at once in her disconcerting fashion:

"You do think you're sufficient prize for any girl, don't you, Vernon?"

"What do you mean?"

"Well, do you think it will be awfully jolly for a girl who has danced and been to parties and had lots of fun and people admiring her to be stuck down in a poky hole with no more fun?"

"We'd have each other."

"You can't make love to her for twenty-four hours on end. While you're working, what is she to do?"

"Don't you think a woman can be poor and happy?"

"Certainly, given the necessary qualifications."

"Which are—what? Love and trust?"

"No, you idiotic child. A sense of humor, a tough hide, and the valuable quality of being sufficient unto oneself. You will insist on love in a cottage being a sentimental problem dependent on the amount of love concerned. It's far more a problem of mental outlook. You'd be all right stuck down anywhere—Buckingham Palace or the Sahara—because you've got your mental preoccupation—music. But Nell's dependent on extraneous circumstances. Marrying you will cut her off from all her friends."

"Why should it?"

"Because it's the hardest thing in the world for people with different incomes to continue friends. They're not all doing the same thing naturally."

"You always put me in the wrong," said Vernon savagely. "Or at any rate you try to."

"Well, it annoys me to see you put yourself on a pedestal and stand admiring yourself for nothing at all," said Jane calmly. "You expect Nell to sacrifice her friends and life to you, but you wouldn't make your sacrifice for her."

"What sacrifice? I'd do anything."

"Except sell Abbots Puissants!"

"You don't understand."

Jane looked at him gently.

"Perhaps I do. Oh! yes, my dear, I do very well. But don't be noble. It always annoys me to see people being noble! Let's talk about *The Princess in the Tower*. I want you to show it to Radmaager."

"Oh! it's so rotten. I couldn't. You know, I didn't realize myself, Jane, how rotten it was until I had finished it."

"No," said Jane. "Nobody ever does. Fortunately—or nothing ever would be finished. Show it to Radmaager. What he says will be interesting, at all events."

Vernon yielded rather grudgingly.

"He'll think it such awful cheek."

"No, he won't. He's a very high opinion of what Sebastian says, and Sebastian has always believed in you. Radmaager says that, for so young a man, Sebastian's judgment is amazing."

"Good old Sebastian! He's wonderful," said Vernon warmly. "Nearly everything he's done has been a success. Shekels are rolling in. God! how I envy him sometimes."

"You needn't. He's not such a very happy person, really."

"You mean Joe? Oh, that will all come right."

"I wonder. Vernon, do you see much of Joe?"

"A fair amount. Not as much as I used to. I can't stand that queer artistic set she's drifted into—their hair's all wrong and they look unwashed and they talk what seems to me the most arrant drivel. They're not a bit like your crowd—the people who really do things."

"We're what Sebastian would call the successful commercial propositions. All the same, I'm worried about Joe. I'm afraid she's going to do something foolish."

"That bounder La Marre, you mean?"

"Yes, I mean that bounder La Marre. He's clever with women, you know, Vernon. Some men are."

"You think she'd go off with him or something? Of course Joe is a damned fool in some ways." He looked curiously at Jane. "But I should have thought you—"

He stopped, suddenly crimson. Jane looked very faintly amused.

"You really needn't be embarrassed by my morals."

"I wasn't. I mean—I've always wondered—oh! I've wondered such an awful lot. . . ."

His voice died away. There was silence. Jane sat very upright. She did not look at Vernon. She looked straight ahead of her. Presently, in a quiet even voice, she began to speak. She spoke quite unemotionally and evenly, as though recounting something that had happened to someone else. It was a cold concise recital of horror, and to Vernon the most dreadful thing about it was her own detached calm. She spoke as a scientist might speak, impersonally.

He buried his face in his hands.

Jane brought her recital to an end. Her quiet voice ceased.

Vernon said in a low shuddering voice: "And you lived through *that?* I—I didn't know that such things were."

Jane said calmly: "He was a Russian and a degenerate. It's hard for an Anglo Saxon to understand that peculiar refined lust of cruelty. You understand brutality. You don't understand anything else."

Vernon said, feeling childish and awkward as he put the question: "You—you loved him very much?"

She shook her head slowly, began to speak and then stopped.

"Why dissect the past?" she said after a minute or two. "He did some fine work. There's a thing of his in the South Kensington. It's macabre, but it's good."

Then she began once more to talk of *The Princess in the Tower*.

Vernon went to the South Kensington two days later. He found the solitary representation of Boris Androv's work easily enough. A drowned woman—the face was horrible, puffed, bloated, decomposed, but the body was beautiful . . . a lovely body. Vernon knew instinctively that it was Jane's body.

He stood looking down on the bronze nude figure, with arms spread wide and long lank hair reaching out mournfully.

Such a beautiful body . . . Jane's body. Androv had modeled that nude body from her.

For the first time for years a queer remembrance of the Beast came over him. He felt afraid.

He turned quickly away from the beautiful bronze figure and left the building hurriedly, almost running.

3

It was the first night of Radmaager's new opera, *Peer Gynt*. Vernon was going to it and had been asked by Radmaager to attend a supper party afterward. He was dining with Nell at her mother's house. She was not coming to the opera.

Much to Nell's surprise, Vernon did not turn up to dinner. They waited some time, and then began without him. He arrived just as dessert was being put on the table.

"I'm most awfully sorry, Mrs. Vereker. I can't tell you how sorry I am. Something very—very unexpected occurred. I'll tell you later."

His face was so white and he was so obviously upset that Mrs. Vereker forgot her annoyance. She was always a tactful woman of the world and she treated the present situation with her usual discretion.

"Well," she said, rising, "now you are here, Vernon, you can talk to Nell. If you're going to the opera you won't have much time."

She left the room. Nell looked inquiringly at Vernon. He answered her look.

"Joe's gone off with La Marre."

"Oh, Vernon, she hasn't!"

"She has."

"Do you mean that she has eloped? That she's married him? That they've run away to get married?"

Vernon said grimly: "He can't marry her. He's got a wife already."

"Oh, Vernon, how awful! How could she?"

"Joe was always wrongheaded. She'll regret this—I know she will. I don't believe she really cares for him."

"What about Sebastian? Won't he feel this terribly?"

"Yes, poor devil. I've been with him now. He's absolutely broken up over it. I'd no idea how much he cared for Joe."

"I know he did."

"You see, there were the three of us—always. Joe and I and Sebastian. We belonged together."

A faint pang of jealousy shot through Nell. Vernon repeated:

"The three of us. It's—Oh! I don't know. I feel as though I'd been to blame in some way. I've let myself get out of touch with Joe. Dear old Joe, she was so staunch always—better than any sister could be. It hurts me to think of the things she used to say when she was a kid—how she'd never have anything to do with men. And now she's come a mucker like this."

Nell said in a shocked voice: "A married man. That's what makes it so awful. Had he any children?"

"How should I know anything about his beastly children?"

"Vernon—don't be so cross."

"Sorry, Nell. I'm upset, that's all."

"How could she do such a thing?" said Nell. She had always rather resented Joe's unspoken contempt of which she had been subconsciously aware. She would not have been human had she not felt a faint sense of superiority. "To run away with anyone married! It's dreadful!"

"Well, she had courage, anyway," said Vernon.

He felt a sudden passionate desire to defend Joe—Joe who belonged to Abbots Puissants and the old days.

"Courage?" said Nell.

"Yes, courage!" said Vernon. "At any rate she wasn't prudent. She didn't count the cost. She's chucked away everything in the world for love. That's more than some people will do."

"Vernon!"

She got up, breathing hard.

"Well, it's true." All his smoldering resentment came bursting out. "You won't even face a little discomfort for me, Nell. You're always saying 'Wait' and 'Let's be careful.' You aren't capable of chucking everything to the winds for love of anyone."

"Oh! Vernon, how cruel you are . . . how cruel!"

He saw the tears come into her eyes and was immediately all compunction.

"Oh! Nell, I didn't mean it—I didn't mean it, sweetheart."

His arms went round her, held her to him. Her sobs lessened. He glanced at his watch.

"Damn! I must go. Good-night, Nell darling. You do love me, don't you?"

"Yes, of course—of course I do."

He kissed her once more, hurried off. She sat down again by the disordered dinner table. Sat there, lost in thought. . . .

4

He got to Covent Garden late. *Peer Gynt* had begun. The scene was Ingrid's wedding, and Vernon arrived just at the moment of the first brief meeting of Peer and Solveig. He wondered if Jane were nervous. She managed to look marvelously young with her fair plaits and her innocent calm bearing. She looked nineteen. The act ended with the carrying off of Ingrid by Peer.

Vernon found himself interested less in the music than in Jane. Tonight was Jane's ordeal. She had to make good or go under. Vernon knew how anxious she was, above everything else to justify Radmaager's trust in her.

Presently he knew that all was well. Jane was the perfect Solveig. Her voice, clear and true—the crystal thread, as Radmaager had called it—

sang unfalteringly and her acting was wonderful. The calm steadfast personality of Solveig dominated the opera.

Vernon found himself for the first time interested in the story of the weak storm-torn Peer, the coward who ran from reality at every opportunity. The music of Peer's conflict with the great Boyg stirred him, reminding him of his childish terror of the Beast. It was the same formless bogy fear of childhood. Unseen, Solveig's clear voice delivered him from it. The scene in the forest where Solveig comes to Peer was infinitely beautiful, ending with Peer bidding Solveig remain while he went out to take up his burden. Her reply: "If it is so heavy it is best two should share it." And then Peer's departure, his final evasion: "Bring sorrow on her? No. Go roundabout, Peer, go roundabout."

The Whitsuntide music was the most beautiful, but in atmosphere very Radmaagian, Vernon thought. It led up to and prepared for the effect of the final scene: the weary Peer asleep with his head on Solveig's lap, and Solveig, her hair silvered, a Madonna blue cloak round her in the middle of the stage, her head silhouetted against the rising sun, singing valiantly against the buttons' moulder.

It was a wonderful duet—Chavaranov, the famous Russian bass, his voice deepening and deepening, and Jane, with her silver thread singing steadily upward and ever upward, higher and higher, till the last note was left to her—high and incredibly pure. . . . And the sun rose. . . .

Vernon, feeling boyishly important, went behind afterward. The opera had been a terrific success. The applause had been long and enthusiastic. He found Radmaager holding Jane by the hand and kissing her with artistic fervour and thoroughness.

"You are an angel—you are magnificent—yes, magnificent! You are an artist. Ah!" he burst into a torrent of words in his native language, then reverted to English. "I will reward you—yes, little one, I will reward you. I know very well how to do it. I will persuade the long Sebastian. Together we will—"

"Hush," said Jane.

Vernon came forward awkwardly, said shyly: "It was splendid!"

He squeezed Jane's hand, and she gave him a brief affectionate smile.

"Where's Sebastian? Wasn't he here just now?"

Sebastian was no longer to be seen. Vernon volunteered to go in search of him and bring him along to supper. He said vaguely that he thought he knew where he was. Jane knew nothing of the news about Joe and he didn't see how he could tell her at the moment.

He got a taxi and drove to Sebastian's house but did not find him. Vernon wondered if perhaps Sebastian might be at his own rooms where he had left him earlier in the evening. He drove there straight away.

He was feeling suddenly elated and triumphant. Even Joe did not seem to matter for the moment. He felt suddenly convinced that his own work was good—or rather that it would be some day. And somehow or other he also felt that things were coming right with Nell. She had clung to him differently tonight—more closely—more as though she could not bear to let him go. . . . Yes, he was sure of it. Everything was coming right.

He ran up the stairs to his room. It was in darkness. Sebastian was not here then. He switched on the light, looked round. A note lay on the table, sent by hand. He picked it up. It was addressed to him in Nell's handwriting. He tore it open. . . .

He stood there a long time. Then, carefully and methodically, he drew up a chair to the table, setting it very exactly straight, as though that were important, and sat down holding the note in his hand. He read it again for the tenth or eleventh time:

Dearest Vernon—forgive me—please forgive me. I am going to marry George Chetwynd. I don't love him as I love you but I shall be safe with him. Again—do forgive me—please.

Your always loving Nell

He said aloud: "*Safe with him.* What does she mean by that? She'd have been safe with me. *Safe with him?* That hurts. . . ."

He sat there. Minutes passed. . . . Hours passed. . . . He sat there, motionless, almost unable to think. . . . Once the thought rose dully in his brain: "Was this how Sebastian felt? I didn't understand. . . ."

When he heard a rustle in the doorway he didn't look up. His first sight of Jane was when she came round the table, dropped on her knees beside him.

"Vernon, my dear, what is it? I knew there was something when you didn't come to the supper. I came to see."

Dully, mechanically, he held out the note to her. She took it and read it. She laid it down again on the table.

He said in a dull bewildered voice: "She needn't have said that about not being safe with me. She would have been safe with me."

"Oh! Vernon—my dear . . ."

Her arms went round him. He clutched at her suddenly—a frightened clutch such as a child might give at its mother. A sob burst from his throat. He laid his face down on the gleaming white skin of her neck.

"Oh! Jane . . . Jane . . ."

She held him closer. She stroked his hair. He murmured:

"Stay with me. Stay with me. Don't leave me."

She answered: "I won't leave you. It's all right."

Her voice was tender—motherly. Something broke in him like the breaking of a dam. Ideas swirled and rushed through his head. His father kissing Winnie at Abbots Puissants . . . the statue in the South Kensington . . . Jane's body . . . her beautiful body.

He said hoarsely: "Stay with me."

Her arms round him, her lips on his forehead, she murmured back: "I'll stay with you, dear."

Like a mother to a child.

He wrenched himself suddenly free.

"Not like that. Not like that. Like this."

His lips fastened on hers—fiercely, hungrily—his hand clutched at the roundness of her breast. He'd always wanted her—always. He knew it now. It was her body he wanted, that beautiful gracious body that Boris Androv had known so well.

He said again: "Stay with me."

There was a long pause—it seemed to him as though minutes, hours, years passed before she answered.

She said: *"I'll stay. . . ."*

Chapter Four

On a day in July Sebastian Levinne walked along the Embankment in the direction of Jane's flat. It was a day more suggestive of early spring than of summer. A cold wind blew the dust in his face and made him blink.

There was a change visible in Sebastian. He had grown perceptibly older. There was very little of the boy about him now—there never had been much. He had always had that curious maturity of outlook which is the Semitic inheritance. As he walked along now, frowning to himself and pondering, he would easily have been taken for a man over thirty.

Jane herself opened the door of the flat to him. She spoke in a low unusually husky voice.

"Vernon's out. He couldn't wait for you. You said three, you know, and it's past four now."

"I was kept. Just as well, perhaps. I'm never quite sure of the best way of dealing with Vernon's nerves."

"Don't tell me any fresh crises have arisen? I couldn't bear it."

"Oh! you'll get used to them. I've had to. What's the matter with your voice, Jane?"

"A cold. A throat, rather. It's all right. I'm nursing it."

"My God! and *The Princess in the Tower* tomorrow night. Suppose you can't sing?"

"Oh! I shall sing. Don't be afraid. Only don't mind my whispering. I want to save it every bit I can."

"Of course. You've seen someone, I suppose?"

"My usual man in Harley Street."

"What did he say?"

"The usual things."

"He didn't forbid you to sing to-morrow?"

"Oh! no."

"You're an awfully good liar, aren't you, Jane?"

"I thought it would save trouble. But I might have known it would be no good with you. I'll be honest. He warned me that I'd been persistently overstraining my voice for years. He said it was madness to sing tomorrow night. But I don't care."

"My dear Jane, I'm not going to risk your losing your voice."

"Mind your own business, Sebastian. My voice is my affair. I don't interfere in your concerns, don't interfere in mine."

Sebastian grinned.

"The tiger cat at home," he remarked. "But you mustn't, Jane, all the same. Does Vernon know?"

"Of course not. What do you think? And you're not to tell him, Sebastian."

"I don't interfere really," said Sebastian. "I never have. But Jane dear, it will be ten thousand pities. The opera's not worth it. And Vernon's not worth it either. Be angry with me if you like for saying so."

"Why should I be angry with you? It's the truth and I know it. All the same, I'm going through with it. Call me any kind of a conceited egoist you like, but *The Princess in the Tower* won't be a success without me. I've been a success as Isolde and a furor as Solveig. It's my moment. And it's going to be Vernon's moment too. I can at least do that for him."

He heard the undercurrent of feeling, the unconscious betrayal of that "at least," but not by a muscle of his face did he show that he had realized its significance. He only said again very gently: "He's not worth it, Jane. Paddle your own canoe. It's the only way. You've arrived. Vernon hasn't and may never."

"I know. I know. No one's what you call 'worth it'—except perhaps one person."

"Who?"

"*You*, Sebastian. *You're* worth it—and yet it's not for you I'm doing it!"

Sebastian was surprised and touched. A sudden mist came over his eyes. He stretched out his hand and took Jane's. They sat for a minute or two in silence.

"That was nice of you, Jane," he said at last.

"Well, it's true. You're worth a dozen of Vernon. You've got brains, initiative, strength of character . . ."

Her husky voice died away. After another minute or two he said very gently:

"How are things? Much as usual?"

"Yes, I think so. You know Mrs. Deyre came to see me?"

"No, I didn't. What did she want?"

"She came to beg me to give up her boy. Pointed out how I was ruining his life. Only a really bad woman would do what I was doing. And so on. You can guess the kind of thing."

"And what did you say to her?" asked Sebastian curiously.

Jane shrugged her shoulders.

"What could I say? That to Vernon one harlot was as good as another?"

"Oh! my dear," said Sebastian gently. "Is it as bad as that?"

Jane got up, lighted a cigarette, and walked restlessly about the room. Sebastian noticed how haggard her face had become.

"Is he—more or less all right?" he ventured.

"He drinks too much," said Jane curtly.

"Can't you prevent it?"

"No, I can't."

"It's queer. I should have thought you would always have great influence over Vernon."

"Well, I haven't. Not now." She was silent for a moment and then said: "Nell's being married in the autumn, isn't she?"

"Yes. Do you think things will be—better then?"

"I haven't the least idea."

"I wish to God he'd pull up," said Sebastian. "If you can't keep him straight, Jane, nobody can. Of course, it's in the blood."

She came and sat down again.

"Tell me—tell me everything you know. About his people—his father, his mother."

Sebastian gave a succinct account of the Deyres. Jane listened.

"His mother you've seen," he concluded. "Queer, isn't it, that Vernon doesn't seem to have inherited one single thing from her? He's a Deyre through and through. They are all artistic, musical, weak-willed, self-indulgent, and attractive to women. Heredity's an odd thing."

"I don't quite agree with you," said Jane. "Vernon's not like his mother, but he *has* inherited something from her."

"What?"

"Vitality. She's an extraordinarily fine animal—have you ever thought of her that way? Well, Vernon's inherited some of that. Without it he'd never have been a composer. If he were a Deyre pure and simple he'd only have *dallied* with music. It's the Bent force that gives him the power to create. You say his grandfather built up their business single-handed. Well, there's the same thing in Vernon."

"I wonder if you're right."

"I'm sure I am."

Sebastian considered silently for some minutes.

"Is it only drink?" he said at last. "Or is it—well, I mean, are there—other people?"

"Oh! there are others."

"And you don't mind?"

"Mind? Mind? Of course I mind. What do you think I'm made of, Sebastian? I'm nearly killed with minding. . . . But what can I do? Make scenes? Rant and rave and drive Vernon away from me altogether?"

Her beautiful husky voice rose from its whisper. Sebastian made a quick gesture and she stopped.

"You're right. I must be careful."

"I can't understand it," grumbled Sebastian. "Even his music doesn't seem to mean anything to Vernon now. He's taken every suggestion from Radmaager and been like a lamb. It's unnatural!"

"We must wait. It will come back. It's reaction—reaction and Nell together. I can't help feeling that if *The Princess in the Tower* is a success, Vernon will pull himself together. He must feel a certain pride—a sense of achievement."

"I hope so," said Sebastian heavily. "But I'm a bit worried about the future."

"In what way? What are you afraid of?"

"War."

Jane looked at him in astonishment. She could hardly believe her ears. She thought she must have mistaken the word.

"*War?*"

"Yes. The outcome of this Sarajevo business." It still seemed to Jane a little absurd and ridiculous.

"War with whom?"

"Germany—principally."

"Oh! surely, Sebastian. Such a—a—far-away thing."

"What does the pretext matter?" said Sebastian impatiently. "It's the way money has been going. Money talks. I handle money—our relations in Russia handle money. We know. From the way money has been behaving for some time we can guess what is in the wind. War's coming, Jane."

Jane looked at him and changed her mind. Sebastian was in earnest, and Sebastian usually knew what he was talking about. If he said war was coming, then, fantastic as it seemed, war would come.

Sebastian sat still, lost in thought. Money, investments, various loans, financial responsibilities he had undertaken, the future of his theaters, the policy to be adopted by the weekly paper he owned. Then, of course, there would be fighting. He was the son of a naturalized Englishman. He didn't wish in the least to go and fight, but he supposed it would be necessary. Everyone below a certain age would do so as a matter of course. It was not the danger that worried him, it was the annoyance of leaving his pet schemes to be looked after by someone else. "They'll make a mess of it, sure to," thought Sebastian bitterly. He put the war down as being a long job—two years, perhaps more. In the end, he shouldn't wonder if America was dragged into it.

The government would issue loans—war loans would be a good investment. No highbrow stuff for the theatres. Soldiers on leave would want light comedy—pretty girls—legs—dancing. He thought it all out carefully. It was a good thing to get a chance to think uninterruptedly. Being with Jane was like being alone. She always knew when you didn't want to be spoken to.

He looked across at her. She, too, was thinking. He wondered what she was thinking about—you never quite knew with Jane. She and Ver-

non were alike there—didn't tell their thoughts. She was probably thinking about Vernon. If Vernon should go to the war and be killed! But
no—that mustn't be. Sebastian's artistic soul rebelled. Vernon mustn't
be killed.

2

The production of *The Princess in the Tower* has been forgotten by now.
It came at an unfortunate time, since war broke out only about three
weeks later.

At the time it was what is called "well received." Certain critics waxed
a little sarcastic over this "new school of young musicians" who thought
they could revolutionize all existing ideas. Others praised it with sincerity
as a work of great promise, though immature. But one and all spoke
enthusiastically of the perfect beauty and artistry of the whole performance. Everyone "went to Holborn, such miles out of the way, dear,
but really worth it," to see the attractive fantastic drama, and "that wonderful new singer, Jane Harding. Her *face,* dear, is simply wonderful—
quite medieval. It wouldn't be the same without her!" It was a triumph
for Jane, though a triumph that was short-lived. On the fifth day she
was forced to retire from the cast.

Sebastian was summoned by telephone at an hour when Vernon
would not be there. Jane met him with such a radiant smile that he
thought at first that his fears were not going to be realized.

"It's no good, Sebastian. Mary Lloyd must go on with it. She's not
too bad, considering. As a matter of fact, she's got a better voice than I
have and she's quite nice-looking."

"H'm, I was afraid Hershall would say that. I'd like to see him myself."

"Yes, he wants to see you. Not that there's anything to be done, I'm
afraid."

"What do you mean? Nothing to be done?"

"It's gone, my child. Gone for good. Hershall's too honest to hold
out any real hope. He says of course you never can be absolutely sure.
It might come back with rest, *et cetera, et cetera.* He said it very well,

and then looked at him and laughed—and then he had to look shamefaced and own up. He was relieved, I think, at the way I took it."

"But Jane, darling Jane . . ."

"Oh! don't mind so much, Sebastian. Please don't. It's so much easier
if you don't. It's been a gamble, you know, all along—my voice was
never really strong enough. I gambled with it. So far I won—now, I've
lost. Well, there it is! One must be a good gambler and not let the hands
twitch. Isn't that what they say at Monte Carlo?"

"Does Vernon know?"

"Yes. He's most awfully upset. He loved my voice. He's really quite
brokenhearted about it."

"But he doesn't know that—"

"That if I had waited two days, and not sung on the opening night
of his opera, it would have been all right? No, he doesn't know that.
And if you are loyal to me, Sebastian, he never will."

"I shan't make promises. I think he ought to know."

"No, because really it's unwarrantable what I've done! I've laid him
under an obligation to me without his knowledge. That's a thing one
shouldn't do. It isn't fair. If I had gone to Vernon and told him what
Hershall said, do you suppose he would ever have consented to let me
sing? He'd have prevented me by main force. It would be the meanest
and cruelest thing in the world to go to Vernon now and say: 'See what
I have done for you!' Sniveling and asking for sympathy and gratitude
ladled out in a soup plate."

Sebastian was silent.

"Come now, my dear, agree."

"Yes," said Sebastian at last. "You're right. What you did was unethical. You did it without Vernon's knowledge, and it's got to be kept
from him now. But oh! Jane darling, why did you? Is Vernon's music
worth it?"

"It will be—some day."

"Is that why you did it?"

Jane shook her head.

"I thought not."

There was a pause. Sebastian said: "What will you do now, Jane?"

"Possibly teach. Possibly go on the stage. I don't know. If the worst comes to the worst, I can always cook."

They both laughed, but Jane was very near tears.

She looked across the table at Sebastian and then suddenly rose and came and knelt down beside him. She laid her head down on his shoulder and he put his arm round her.

"Oh! Sebastian . . . Sebastian . . ."

"Poor old Jane!"

"I pretend I don't mind—but I do . . . I do. I loved singing. I loved it, loved it, loved it. . . . That lovely Whitsuntide music of Solveig. I shall never sing it again."

"I know. Why were you such a fool, Jane?"

"I don't know. Sheer idiocy."

"If you had the choice again—"

"I'd do the same thing again."

A silence. Then Jane lifted her head and said:

"Do you remember saying, Sebastian, that I had great 'driving power'? That nothing would turn me aside? And I said that I might be more easily turned aside than you thought. That between Vernon and me, I should go to the wall."

Sebastian said: "Things are queer."

Jane slipped down on the floor beside him, her hand still in his.

"You can be clever," said Sebastian, breaking the silence. "You can have the brains to foresee things, and the wits to plan things, and the force to succeed, but with all the cleverness in the world you can't avoid suffering some way or another. That's what's so odd. I know I've got brains, I know I'll get to the top of anything I undertake. I'm not like Vernon. Vernon will either be a heaven-sent genius, or else he'll be an idle dissipated young man. He's got a gift if he's got anything, I've got ability. And yet with all the ability in the world, I can't prevent myself getting hurt."

"No one can."

"One might, perhaps, if one gave up one's whole life to it. If you pursued safety and nothing but safety. You'd get your wings singed, perhaps, but that would be all. You'd build a nice smooth wall and hide yourself inside it."

"You're thinking of somebody in particular? Who?"

"Just a fancy. The future Mrs. George Chetwynd, if you want to be exact."

"Nell? Do you think Nell has the strength of character to shut herself out from life?"

"Oh! Nell has got an enormous power of developing protective colouring. Some species have." He paused, then went on: "Jane, have you ever heard from—Joe?"

"Yes, my dear, twice."

"What did she say?"

"Very little. Just what fun everything was, and how she was enjoying herself, and how splendid one felt when one had had the courage to defy convention." She paused and then added: "She's not happy, Sebastian."

"You think not?"

"I'm sure of it."

There was a long silence. Two unhappy faces looked into the empty fireplace. Outside taxis hooted as they sped rapidly down the Embankment. Life went on. . . .

3

It was the ninth of August. Nell Vereker turned out of Paddington Station and walked slowly down toward the park. Four-wheelers passed her with old ladies in them laden with many hams. Staring placards were flaunted at every street corner. In every shop was a queue of people anxious to buy commodities.

Nell had said to herself many times: "We're at war—actually at war," and had not been able to believe it. Today, for the first time, it seemed to come home to her. A train journey where the ticket office refused to change a five-pound note had proved the turning point. Ridiculous, but there it was.

A taxi passed and Nell hailed it. She got in, giving the address of Jane's flat in Chelsea. She glanced at her watch. It was just half-past ten. No fear that Jane would be out so early.

Nell went up in the lift and stood outside the door, having rung the bell. Her heart was beating nervously. In another minute the door would open. Her small face grew white and strained. Ah! now the door was opening. She and Jane were face to face.

She thought Jane started a little—that was all.

"Oh!" she said. "It's you."

"Yes," said Nell. "May I come in, please?"

It seemed to her that Jane hesitated a minute before drawing back to let her enter. She retreated into the hall, shut a door at the far end, and then drew open the sitting-room door for Nell to pass in. She followed her, closing the door behind her.

"Well?"

"Jane, I've come to ask you if you know where Vernon is."

"Vernon?"

"Yes. I went to his rooms—yesterday. He's left. The woman there didn't know where he'd gone. She said his letters were forwarded to you. I went home and wrote to you asking for his address. Then I was afraid you wouldn't tell me, wouldn't even answer, perhaps, and I thought I'd come instead."

"I see."

The tone was noncommittal, unhelpful. Nell hurried on.

"I was sure you'd know where he was. You do, don't you?"

"Yes, I know."

A slow answer, unnecessarily slow, Nell thought. Either Jane knew or she didn't.

Again a pause. Then Jane said: "Why do you want to see Vernon, Nell?"

Nell raised a white face.

"Because I've been such a beast—such a beast! I see it now—now that this awful war has come. I was such a miserable coward. I hate myself—simply hate myself. Just because George was kind and good and—yes, rich! Oh, Jane, how you must despise me! I know you do. You're quite right to despise me. Somehow this war has made everything clear—don't you find that?"

"Not particularly. There have been wars before and there will be wars again. They don't really alter anything underneath, you know."

Nell was not paying attention.

"It's wicked to do anything except marry the man you love. I do love Vernon. I always knew I loved him, but I just hadn't the courage. . . . Oh! Jane, do you think it's too late? Perhaps it is. Perhaps he won't want me now. But I *must* see him. Even if he doesn't want me. I must tell him."

She stood there looking piteously up at Jane. Would Jane help her? If not, she must try Sebastian—but she was afraid of Sebastian. He might refuse flatly to do anything.

"I could get hold of him for you," said Jane slowly, after a minute or two.

"Oh! thank you, Jane. And Jane—tell me—the war?"

"He's applied to join up, if that's what you mean."

"Yes. Oh! it's dreadful—if he should be killed. But it can't last long. It'll be over by Christmas—everybody says so."

"Sebastian says it will last two years."

"Oh! but Sebastian can't know. He's not really English. He's Russian."

Jane shook her head. Then she said: "I'll go and—" she paused— "telephone. Wait here."

She went out, closing the door behind her. She went to the end of the passage and into the bedroom. Vernon raised a dark rumpled head from the pillow.

"Get up," said Jane curtly. "Wash yourself and shave yourself and try and make yourself reasonably decent. Nell's here and wants to see you."

"Nell! But—"

"She thinks I'm telephoning to you. When you're ready, you can go outside the front door and ring the bell—and may God have mercy on both our souls."

"But Jane. Nell . . . what does she want?"

"If you want to marry her, Vernon, now is your chance."

"But I'll have to tell her—"

"What? That you've been leading a 'gay life,' that you've been 'wild'? All the usual euphemisms! That's all she'll expect—and she'll be grateful to you for laying as little stress on that as possible. But tell her about you and me and you bring it from the general to the particular—and take the child through hell. Muzzle that noble concience of yours and think of her."

Vernon rose slowly from the bed.

"I don't understand you, Jane."

"No, probably you never will."

He said: "Has Nell thrown over George Chetwynd?"

"I haven't asked for details. I'm going back to her now. Hurry up."

She left the room. Vernon thought: "I've never understood Jane. I never shall. She's so damned disconcerting. Well, I suppose I've been a sort of passing amusement to her. No, that's ungrateful. She's been damned decent to me. Nobody could have been more decent than Jane has been. But I couldn't make Nell understand that. She'd think Jane was dreadful. . . ."

As he shaved and washed rapidly he said to himself: "All the same, it's out of the question. Nell and I could never come together again. Oh! I don't suppose there's any question of that. She's probably only come to ask me to forgive her, to make her feel comfortable in case I get killed in this bloody war. The sort of thing a girl would do. Anyway, I don't believe I care anymore."

Another voice, deep down, said ironically: "Oh! no, not at all. Then why is your heart beating and your hand shaking? You bloody ass, of course you care!"

He was ready. He went outside—rang the bell. A mean subterfuge— unworthy—he felt ashamed. Jane opened the door. She said, rather like a parlor maid, "In here," and waved him toward the sitting room. He went in, closing the door behind him.

Nell had risen at his entrance. She stood with her hands clasped in front of her.

Her voice came faint and weak, like a guilty child.

"Oh! Vernon . . ."

Time swept backward. He was in the boat at Cambridge . . . on the bridge at Ranelagh. He forgot Jane, he forgot everything. He and Nell were the only people in the world.

"Nell!"

They were clinging together, breathless as though they had been running. Words tumbled from Nell's lips.

"Vernon—if you want—I do love you—Oh! I do. . . . I'll marry you anytime—at once—today. I don't mind about being poor or *anything!*"

He lifted her off her feet, kissed her eyes, her hair, her lips.

"Darling—oh! darling. Don't let's waste a minute—not a minute. I don't know how you get married. I've never thought about it. But let's go out and see. We'll go to the Archbishop of Canterbury—isn't that what you do? and get a special licence. How the devil *do* you get married?"

"We might ask a clergyman?"

"Or there's a Registry Office. That's the thing."

"I don't think I want to be married at a Registry Office. I'd feel rather like a cook or a house parlormaid being engaged."

"I don't think it's that kind, darling. But if you'd rather be married in a church, let's be married in a church. There are thousands of churches in London, all with nothing to do. I'm sure one of them will love to marry us."

They went out together, laughing happily. Vernon had forgotten everything—remorse, conscience, Jane. . . .

At half-past two that afternoon Vernon Deyre and Eleanor Vereker were married in the church of St. Ethelred's, Chelsea.

BOOK IV

WAR

Chapter One

It was six months later that Sebastian Levinne had a note from Joe.

St. George's Hotel, Soho

Dear Sebastian: I'm over in England for a few days. I should love to see you. Yours, Joe.

Sebastian read and reread the brief note. He was at his mother's house on a few days' leave, so it had reached him with no delay. Across the breakfast table he was conscious of his mother's eyes watching him, and he marveled as he had often done before, at the quickness of her maternal apprehension. She read his face, which most people found so inscrutable, as easily as he read the note in his hand.

When she spoke it was in ordinary commonplace tones.

"Thome more marmalade, dear?" she said.

"No, thanks, Mother." He answered the spoken question first, then went on to the unspoken one of which he was so keenly conscious. "It's from Joe."

"Joe," said Mrs. Levinne. Her voice expressed nothing.

"She's in London."

There was a pause.

"I see," said Mrs. Levinne.

Still her voice expressed nothing. But Sebastian was aware of a whole tumult of feeling. It was the same to him as though his mother had burst out: "My son, my son! And you were just beginning to forget her! Why does she come back like this? Why can't she leave you alone? This girl who has nothing to do with us or our race? This girl who was never the right wife for you and never will be."

Sebastian rose.

"I think I must go round and see her."

His mother answered in the same voice: "I suppose so."

They said no more. They understood each other. Each respected the other's point of view.

As he swung along the street it suddenly occurred to Sebastian that Joe had given him no clues as to what name she was staying under at the hotel. Did she call herself Miss Waite or Madame de la Marre? Unimportant, of course, but one of those silly conventional absurdities that made one feel awkward. He must ask for her under one or the other. How like Joe it was to have completely overlooked the point!

But as it happened there was no awkwardness, for the first person he saw as he passed through the swing doors was Joe herself. She greeted him with a glad cry of surprise.

"Sebastian! I'd no idea you could possibly have got my letter so soon!"

She led the way to a retired corner of the lounge and he followed her.

His first feeling was that she had changed—she had gone so far away that she was almost a stranger. It was partly, he thought, her clothes. They were ultra-French clothes. Very quiet and dark and discreet, but utterly un-English. Her face, too, was very much made up. Its creamy pallor was enhanced by art, her lips were impossibly red, and she had done something to the corners of her eyes.

He thought: "She's a stranger—and yet she's Joe! She's the same Joe but she's gone a long way away—so far away that one can only just get in touch with her."

But they talked together easily enough, each, as it were, putting out little feelers, as though sounding the distance that separated them. And suddenly the distance itself lessened and the elegant Parisian stranger melted into Joe.

They talked of Vernon. Where was he? He never wrote or told one anything.

"He's on Salisbury Plain, near Wiltsbury. He may be going out to France any minute."

"And Nell married him after all! Sebastian, I feel I was rather a beast about Nell. I didn't think she had it in her. I don't think she *would* have had it in her if it hadn't been for the war. Sebastian, isn't the war wonderful? What it's doing for people, I mean."

Sebastian said dryly that he supposed it was very much like any other war. Joe flew out at him vehemently.

"It isn't! It isn't! That's just where you're wrong. There's going to be a new world after it. People are beginning to see things—things they never saw before. All the cruelty and the wickedness and the waste of war. And they'll stand together so that such a thing shall never happen again."

Her face was flushed and exalted. Sebastian perceived that the war had, as he phrased it, "got" Joe. The war did get people. He had discussed it and deplored it with Jane. It made him sick to read the things that were printed and said about the war: "A world fit for heroes." "The war to end war." "The fight for democracy." And really, all the time it was the same old bloody business it always had been. Why couldn't people speak the truth about it?

Jane had disagreed with him. She maintained that the claptrap (for she agreed it *was* claptrap) which was written about war was inevitable, a kind of accompanying phenomenon inseparable from it. It was Nature's way of providing a way of escape—you had to have that wall of illusion and lies to help you to endure the solid facts. It was, to her, pitiable and almost beautiful—these things that we wanted to believe and told ourselves so speciously.

Sebastian had said: "I dare say, but it's going to play hell with the nation afterward."

He was saddened and a little depressed by Joe's fiery enthusiasm. And yet, after all, it was typical of Joe. Her enthusiasm always was red-hot. It was a toss-up which camp he found her in, that was all. She might just as easily have been a white-hot pacifist, embracing martyrdom with fervor.

She said now accusingly to Sebastian: "You don't agree! You think everything's going to be just the same."

"There have always been wars, and they have never made any great difference."

"Yes, but this is a different kind of war altogether."

He smiled. He could not help it.

"My dear Joe, the things that happen to us personally are always different."

"Oh! I've no patience with you. It's people like you—"

She stopped.

"Yes," said Sebastian encouragingly. "People like me—"

"You usen't to be like that. You used to have ideas. Now—"

"Now," said Sebastian gravely, "I am sunk in money. I'm a capitalist. Everyone knows what a hoggish creature the capitalist is."

"Don't be absurd. But I do think that money is rather—well, stifling."

"Yes," said Sebastian. "That's true enough. But that's a question of effect on an individual. I will quite agree with you that poverty is a blessed state. Talking in terms of art, it's probably as valuable as manure in a garden. But it's nonsense to say that because I've got money I'm unfit to make prognostications as to the future, and especially as to the state obtaining after the war. Just because I've got money I'm all the more likely to be a good judge. Money has got a lot to do with war."

"Yes, but because you think of everything in terms of money, you say that there always will be wars."

"I didn't say anything of the kind. I think war will eventually be abolished. I'd give it roughly another two hundred years."

"Ah! you do admit that by then we may have purer ideals."

"I don't think it's got anything to do with ideals. It's probably a question of transport. Once you get flying going on a commercial scale, you fuse countries together. Air charabancs to the Sahara Wednesdays and Saturdays—that kind of thing. Countries getting mixed up and matey. Trade revolutionized. For all practical purposes, you make the world smaller. You reduce it in time to the level of a nation with countries in it. I don't think what's always alluded to as the Brotherhood of Man will ever develop from fine ideas—it will be a simple matter of common sense."

"Oh, Sebastian!"

"I'm annoying you. I'm sorry, Joe dear."

"You don't believe in anything."

"Well, it's you who are the atheist, you know. Though, as a matter of fact, that word has gone out of fashion. We say nowadays that we believe in *Something!* Personally, I'm quite satisfied with Jehovah. But I know what you meant when you said that, and you're wrong. I believe in beauty, in creation, in things like Vernon's music. I can't see any real defense for them economically, and yet I'm perfectly sure that they matter more than anything else in the world. I'm even prepared (sometimes) to drop money over them. That's a lot for a Jew!"

Joe laughed in spite of herself. Then she asked: "What was *The Princess in the Tower* really like? Honestly, Sebastian."

"Oh! rather like a giant toddling—an unconvincing performance, and yet a performance on a different scale from anything else."

"You think that someday—"

"I'm sure of it. There's nothing I'm so sure of as that. If only he isn't killed in this bloody war."

Joe shivered.

"It's so awful," she murmured. "I've been working in the hospitals in Paris. Some of the things one sees!"

"I know. If he's only maimed it doesn't matter—not like a violinist who is finished if he loses his right hand. No, they can mess up his body any way they like, so long as his brain is left untouched. That sounds brutal, but you know what I mean."

"I know. But sometimes—even then—" She broke off and then went on, speaking in a new tone of voice: "Sebastian, I'm married."

If something in him winced he didn't show it.

"Are you, my dear? Did La Marre get a divorce?"

"No. I left him. He was a beast—a beast, Sebastian."

"I can imagine he might be."

"Not that I regret anything. One has to live one's life—to gain experience. Anything is better than shrinking from life. That's just what people like Aunt Myra can't understand. I'm not going near them at Birmingham. I'm not ashamed or repentant of anything I've done."

She gazed at him defiantly and his mind went back to Joe in the woods at Abbots Puissants. He thought: "She's just the same. Wrong-headed, rebellious, adorable. One might have known then that she'd do this sort of thing."

He said gently: "I'm only sorry that you've been unhappy. Because you've been unhappy, haven't you?"

"Horribly. But I've found my real life now. There was a boy in hospital—terribly badly wounded. They gave him morphia. He's been discharged now—cured, though of course he isn't fit for service. But the morphia—it's got hold of him. That's why we were married. A fortnight ago. We're going to fight it together."

Sebastian did not trust himself to speak. Joe all over. But why, in the name of fortune, couldn't she have been content with physical disabilities? Morphia. A ghastly business.

And suddenly a pang shot through him. It was as though he resigned his last hope of her. Their ways led in opposite directions—Joe amongst her lost causes and her lame dogs, and he on an upward route. He might, of course, be killed in the war, but somehow he didn't think he would be. He was almost certain that he wouldn't even be picturesquely wounded. He felt a kind of certitude that he would come through safely, probably with moderate distinction; that he would come back to his enterprises, reorganizing and revitalizing them; that he would be successful, notably successful, in a world that did not tolerate failures. And the higher he climbed the farther he would be separated from Joe.

He thought bitterly: "There's always some woman to pull you out of a pit, but nobody will come and keep you company on a mountain peak, and yet you may be damned lonely there."

He didn't quite know what to say to Joe. No good depressing her, poor child. He said rather weakly:

"What's your name now?"

"Valnière. You must meet François some time, I've just come over to settle up some legal bothers. Father died about a month ago, you know."

Sebastian nodded. He remembered hearing of Major Waite's death. Joe went on.

"I want to see Jane. And I want to see Vernon and Nell."

It was settled that he should motor her down to Wiltsbury on the following day.

2

Nell and Vernon had rooms in a small prim house about a mile out of Wiltsbury. Vernon, looking well and brown, fell upon Joe and hugged her with enthusiasm.

They all went into a room full of antimacassars and lunched off boiled mutton and caper sauce.

"Vernon, you look splendid—and almost good-looking, doesn't he, Nell?"

"That's the uniform," said Nell demurely.

She had changed, Sebastian thought, looking at her. He had not seen her since her marriage. To him she had always fallen into a class—a certain type of charming young girl. Now he saw her as an individual— the real Nell bursting out of her chrysalis.

There was a subdued radiance about her. She was quieter than she used to be, and yet she was more alive. They were happy together—no one who looked at them could doubt it. They seldom looked at each other, but when they did you felt it. Something passed between them— delicate, evanescent, but unmistakable.

It was a happy meal. They talked of old days—of Abbots Puissants.

"And here we are, all four of us together again," said Joe.

A warm feeling fastened round Nell's heart. Joe had included her. All *four* of us, she had said. Nell remembered how once Vernon had said, "We three," and the words had hurt her. But that was over now. She was one of them. That was her reward—one of her rewards. Life seemed full of rewards at the moment.

She was happy—so terribly happy. And she might so easily not have been happy. She might have been actually married to George when the war broke out. How could she ever have been so incredibly foolish as to think that anything mattered except marrying Vernon? How extraordinarily happy they were and how right he had been to say poverty didn't matter.

It wasn't as though she were the only one. Lots of girls were doing it—flinging up everything, marrying the man they cared for no matter how poor he was. After the war something would turn up. That was the attitude. And behind it lay that awful secret fear that you never took out and looked at properly. The nearest you ever got to it was saying defiantly: "And no matter *what* happens, we'll have had *something*."

She thought: "The world's changing. Everything's different now. It always will be. We'll never go back. . . ."

She looked across the table at Joe. Joe looked different somehow—very *queer*. What you would have called before the war—well, *"not quite."* What had Joe been doing with herself? That nasty man, La Marre . . . Oh! well, better not think about it. Nothing mattered nowadays.

Joe was very nice to her—so different from what she used to be in the old days when Nell had always felt uncomfortable that Joe despised her. Perhaps she had cause. She *had* been a little coward.

The war was awful, of course, but it had simplified things. Her mother, for instance, had come round almost at once. She was disappointed, naturally, about George Chetwynd (poor George, he really *was* a dear and she'd been a beast to him), but Mrs. Vereker proceeded to make the best of things with admirable common sense.

"These war marriages!" she used that phrase with a tiny shrug of the shoulders. "Poor children—you can't blame them. Not wise, perhaps—but what is wisdom at a time like this?" Mrs. Vereker needed all her skill and all her wit to deal with her creditors and she had come off pretty well. Some of them even felt sympathy for her.

If she and Vernon didn't really like each other, they concealed the fact quite creditably, and as a matter of fact had met only once since the marriage. It had all been very easy.

Perhaps, if you had courage, things were always easy. Perhaps that was the great secret of life.

Nell pondered, then waking from her reverie plunged once more into the conversation.

Sebastian was speaking.

"We're going to look Jane up when we get back to town. I've not so much as heard of her for ages. Have you, Vernon?"

Vernon shook his head.

"No," he said, "I haven't."

He tried to speak naturally but didn't quite succeed.

"She's very nice," said Nell. "But—well, rather difficult, isn't she? I mean, you never quite know what she's thinking about."

"She might be occasionally disconcerting," Sebastian allowed.

"She's an angel," said Joe with vehemence.

Nell was watching Vernon. She thought: "I wish he'd say something . . . anything. I'm afraid of Jane. I always have been. She's a devil. . . ."

"Probably," said Sebastian, "she's gone to Russia or Timbuctoo or Mozambique. One would never be surprised with Jane."

"How long is it since you've seen her?" asked Joe.

"Exactly? Oh, about three weeks."

"Is that all? I thought you meant really ages."

"It seems like it," said Sebastian.

They began to talk of Joe's hospital in Paris. Then they talked of Myra and Uncle Sydney. Myra was very well and making an incredible quantity of swabs and also did duty twice a week at a canteen. Uncle Sydney was well on the way to making a second fortune, having started the manufacture of explosives.

"He's got off the mark early," said Sebastian appreciatively. "This war's not going to be over for three years at least."

They argued the point. The days of an "optimistic six months" were over, but three years were regarded as too gloomy a view. Sebastian talked about explosives, the state of Russia, the food question, and submarines. He was a little dictatorial, since he was perfectly sure that he was right.

At five o'clock Sebastian and Joe got into the car and drove back to London. Vernon and Nell stood in the road waving.

"Well," said Nell, "that's that." She slipped her arm through Vernon's. "I'm glad you were able to get off today. Joe would have been awfully disappointed not to see you."

"Do you think she's changed?"

"A little. Don't you?"

They were strolling along the road and they turned off where a track led over the downs.

"Yes," said Vernon, with a sigh. "I suppose it was inevitable."

"I'm glad she's married. I think it's very fine of her. Don't you?"

"Oh, yes. Joe was always warmhearted, bless her!"

He spoke abstractedly. Nell glanced up at him. She realized now that he had been rather silent all day. The others had done most of the talking.

"I'm glad they came," she said again.

Vernon didn't answer. She pressed her arm against his and felt him press it against his side. But his silence persisted.

It was getting dark and the air came sharp and cold, but they did not turn back, walked on and on without speaking. So they had often walked before—silent and happy. But this silence was different. There was weight in it and menace.

Suddenly Nell knew.

"Vernon! It's come! You've got to go. . . ."

He pressed her hand closer still but did not speak.

"Vernon . . . when?"

"Next Thursday."

"Oh!" she stood still. Agony shot through her. It had come. She had known it was bound to come, but she hadn't known—quite—what it was going to feel like.

"Nell, Nell. . . . Don't mind so much. Please don't mind so much." The words came tumbling out now. "It'll be all right. I *know* it'll be all right. I'm not going to get killed. I couldn't now that you love me—now that we're so happy. Some fellows feel their number's up when they go out—but I don't. I've a kind of certainty that I'm going to come through. I want you to feel that too."

She stood there frozen. This was what war was really. It took the heart out of your body, the blood of out your veins. She clung to him with a sob. He held her to him.

"It's all right, Nell. We knew it was coming soon. And I'm really frightfully keen to go—at least I would be if it wasn't for leaving you. You wouldn't like me to have spent the whole war guarding a bridge in England, would you? And there will be the leaves to look forward to— we'll have the most frightfully jolly leaves. There will be lots of money, and we'll simply blow it. Oh! Nell darling, I just know that nothing can happen to me now that you care for me."

She agreed with him.

"It can't—it can't. God couldn't be so cruel."

But the thought came to her that God was letting a lot of cruel things happen.

She said valiantly, forcing back her tears: "It'll be all right, darling. I know it too."

"And even—even if it isn't, you must remember—how perfect this has been. . . . Darling, you have been happy, haven't you?"

She lifted her lips to his. They clung together, dumb, agonizing, the shadow of their first parting hanging over them.

How long they stood there they hardly knew.

3

When they went back to the antimacassars they talked cheerfully of ordinary things. Vernon touched only once on the future.

"Nell, when I'm gone will you go to your mother, or what?"

"No. I'd rather stay down here. There are lots of things to do in Wiltsbury—hospital, canteen."

"Yes, but I don't want you to do anything. I think you'd be better distracted in London. There will still be theaters and things like that."

"No, Vernon, I must do something—work, I mean."

"Well, if you want to work you can knit me socks. I hate all this nursing business. I suppose it's necessary, but I don't like it. You wouldn't care to go to Birmingham?"

Nell said very decidedly that she would *not* like to go to Birmingham.

The actual parting when it came was less strenuous. Vernon kissed her almost offhandedly.

"Well, so long. Cheer up. Everything's going to be all right. I'll write as much as I can, though I expect we're not allowed to say much that's interesting. Take care of yourself, Nell darling."

One almost involuntary tightening of his arms round her, and then he almost pushed her from him.

He was gone.

She thought: "I shall never sleep tonight . . . never . . ."

But she did. A deep heavy sleep. She went down into it as into an abyss. A haunted sleep—full of terror and apprehension that gradually faded into the unconsciousness of exhaustion.

She woke with a keen sword of pain piercing her heart.

She thought: "Vernon's gone to the war. I must get something to do."

Chapter Two

Nell went to see Mrs. Curtis, the Red Cross commandant. Mrs. Curtis was benign and affable. She was enjoying her importance and was convinced that she was a born organizer. Actually, she was a very bad one. But everyone said she had a wonderful manner. She condescended graciously to Nell.

"Let me see, Mrs.—ah! Deyre. You've got your V.A.D. and nursing certificates?"

"Yes."

"But you don't belong to any of the local detachments?"

Nell's exact standing was discussed at some length.

"Well, we must see what we can do for you," said Mrs. Curtis. "The hospital is fully staffed at present, but of course they are always falling out. Two days after the first convoy came in, we had seventeen resignations. All women of a certain age. They didn't like the way the Sisters spoke to them. I myself think the Sisters were perhaps a little unnecessarily brutal, but of course there's a great deal of jealousy of the Red Cross. And these were well-to-do women who didn't like being 'spoken to.' You are not sensitive in that way, Mrs. Deyre?"

Nell said that she didn't mind anything.

"That is the spirit," said Mrs. Curtis approvingly. "I myself," she continued, "consider it in the light of good discipline. And where should we all be without discipline?"

It shot through Nell's mind that Mrs. Curtis had not had to endure any discipline, which robbed her pronouncement of some of its impressiveness. But she continued to stand there looking attentive and impressed.

"I have a list of girls on the reserve," continued Mrs. Curtis. "I will add your name. Two days a week you will attend at the Out Patient Ward at the Town Hospital, and thereby gain a little experience. They are short-handed there and are willing to accept our help. Then you and Miss—" she consulted a list—"I think Miss Cardner—yes, Miss Cardner—will go with the district nurse on her rounds on Tuesdays and Fridays. You've got your uniform, of course? Then that is all right."

Mary Cardner was a pleasant plump girl whose father was a retired butcher. She was very friendly to Nell, explained that the days were Wednesday and Saturday and not Tuesday and Friday, "but old Curtis always gets something wrong," that the district nurse was a dear and never jumped on you, and that Sister Margaret at the hospital was a holy terror.

On the following Wednesday Nell did her first round with the district nurse, a little bustling woman very much overworked. At the end of the day she patted Nell kindly on the shoulder.

"I'm glad to see you have a head on your shoulders, my dear. Really some of the girls who come seem to be half-witted—they do indeed. And such fine ladies, you wouldn't believe—Not by birth—I don't mean that. But half-educated girls who think nursing is all smoothing a pillow and feeding the patient with grapes. You'll know your way about in no time."

Heartened by this, Nell presented herself at the Out Patient Department at the given time without too much trepidation. She was received by a tall gaunt Sister with a malevolent eye.

"Another raw beginner," she grumbled. "Mrs. Curtis sent you, I suppose? I'm sick of that woman. Takes me more time and trouble teaching silly girls who think they know everything than it would to do everything myself."

"I'm sorry," said Nell meekly.

"Get a couple of certificates, attend a dozen lectures, and think you know everything," said Sister Margaret bitterly. "Here they come. Don't get in my way more than you can help."

A typical batch of patients was assembled: a young boy with legs riddled with ulcers, a child with scalded legs from an overturned kettle, a girl with a needle in her finger, various sufferers with "bad ears," "bad legs," "bad arms."

Sister Margaret said sharply to Nell: "Know how to syringe an ear? I thought not. Watch me."

Nell watched.

"You can do it next time," said Sister Margaret. "Get the bandage off that boy's finger, and let him soak it in hot boracic water till I'm ready for him."

Nell felt nervous and clumsy. Sister Margaret was paralyzing her. Almost immediately, it seemed, Sister was by her side.

"We haven't got all day here to do things in," she remarked. "Here, leave it to me. You seem to be all thumbs. Soak the bandages off that kid's legs. Tepid water."

Nell got a basin of tepid water and knelt down before the child, a mere mite of three. She was badly burnt and the bandages had stuck to the tiny legs. Nell sponged and soaked very gently, but the baby screamed. It was a loud long-drawn yell of terror and agony, and it defeated Nell utterly.

She felt suddenly sick and faint. She couldn't do this work—she simply couldn't do it. She drew back, and as she did so she glanced up to find Sister Margaret watching her, a gleam of malicious pleasure showing in her eye.

"I thought you couldn't stick it," that eye said.

It rallied Nell as nothing else would have done. She bent her head, and setting her teeth, went on with her job, trying to avert her mind from the child's shrieks. It was done at last, and Nell stood up, white and trembling and feeling deathly sick.

Sister Margaret came along. She seemed disappointed.

"Oh! you've done it," she said. She spoke to the child's mother. "I'd be a bit more careful how you let the child get at the kettle in future, Mrs. Somers," she said.

Mrs. Somers complained that you couldn't be everywhere at once.

Nell was ordered off to foment a poisoned finger. Next, she assisted Sister to syringe the ulcerated leg, and after that stood by while a young doctor extracted the needle from the girl's finger. As he probed and cut, the girl winced and shrank and he spoke to her sharply.

"Keep quiet, can't you?"

Nell thought: "One never sees this side of things. One is only used to a doctor with a bedside manner. *I'm afraid this will hurt a little. Be as still as you can.*"

The young doctor proceeded to extract a couple of teeth, flinging them carelessly on the floor, then he treated a smashed hand that had just come in from an accident.

It was not, Nell reflected, that he was unskillful. It was the absence of manner that was so disturbing to one's preconceived ideas. Whatever he did, Sister Margaret accompanied him, tittering in a sycophantic manner at any joke he was pleased to make. Of Nell he took no notice.

At last the hour was over. Nell was thankful. She said good-bye timidly to Sister Margaret.

"Like it?" asked Sister with a demoniac grin.

"I'm afraid I'm very stupid," said Nell.

"How can you be anything else?" said Sister Margaret.

"A lot of amateurs like you Red Cross people. And thinking you know everything on earth. Well, perhaps, you'll be a little less clumsy next time!"

Such was Nell's encouraging debut at the hospital.

It grew less terrible as time went on, however. Sister Margaret softened and relaxed her attitude of fierce defensiveness. She even permitted herself to answer questions.

"You're not so stuck-up as most," she allowed graciously.

Nell, in her turn, was impressed by the enormous amount of competent work Sister Margaret managed to put in in a very short time. And she understood a little her soreness on the subject of amateurs.

What struck Nell most was the enormous number of "bad legs" and their prototypes, most of them evidently old friends. She asked Sister Margaret timidly about them.

"Nothing much to be done about it," Sister Margaret replied. "Hereditary, most of them. Bad blood. You can't cure it."

Another thing that impressed Nell was the uncomplaining heroism of the poor. They came and were treated, suffered great pain, and went off to walk several miles home without a thought.

She saw it too in their homes. She and Mary Cardner had taken over a certain amount of the district nurse's round. They washed bedridden old women, tended "bad legs," occasionally washed and tended babies whose mothers were too ill to do anything. The cottages were small, the windows usually hermetically sealed, and the places littered with treasures dear to the hearts of the owners. The stuffiness was often unbearable.

The worst shock was about two weeks after beginning work, when they found a bedridden old man dead in his bed and had to lay him out. But for Mary Cardner's matter-of-fact cheerfulness Nell felt she could not have done it.

The district nurse praised them.

"You're good girls. And you're being a real help."

They went home glowing with satisfaction. Never in her life had Nell so appreciated a hot bath and a lavish allowance of bath salts.

She had had two postcards from Vernon. Mere scrawls saying he was all right and everything was splendid. She wrote to him every day, describing her adventures, trying to make them sound as amusing as possible. He wrote back:

Somewhere in France—

Darling Nell:

I'm all right. Feeling splendidly fit. It's all a great adventure, but I do long to see you. I do wish you wouldn't go into these beastly cottages and places and mess about with diseased people. I'm sure you'll catch something. Why you want to, I can't think. I'm sure it isn't necessary. Do give up.

We think mostly about our food out here, and the Tommies think of nothing but their tea. They'll risk being blown to bits any time for a cup of 'ot tea. I have to censor their letters. One man always ends "Yours till hell freezes," so I'll say the same.

Yours, Vernon

One morning Nell received a telephone call from Mrs. Curtis.

"There is a vacancy for a ward maid, Mrs. Deyre. Afternoon duty. Be at the hospital at two-thirty."

The Town Hall of Wiltsbury had been turned into a hospital. It was a big new building standing in the cathedral square and overshadowed by the tall spire of the cathedral. A handsome being in uniform with a game leg and medals received her kindly at the front entrance.

"You've come to the wrong door, missie. Staff through the quarter-master's stores. Here, the scout will show you the way."

A dimunitive scout conducted her down steps, through a kind of gloomy crypt where an elderly lady in Red Cross uniform sat surrounded with bales of hospital shirts—wearing several shawls and shivering a good deal—then along stone-flagged passages, and finally into a gloomy underground chamber where she was received by Miss Curtain, the chief of the ward maids, a tall thin lady with a face like a dreaming duchess and charming gentle manners.

Nell was instructed in her duties, which were simple enough to understand. They entailed hard work, but no difficulty. A certain area of stone passages and steps to scrub. Then the nurses' tea to lay, wait on, and finally clear away. Then the ward maids had their own tea. Then the same routine for supper.

Nell soon got the hang of things. The salient points of the new life were: one, war with the kitchen; two, the difficulty of providing the Sisters with the right kind of tea.

There was a long table where the V.A.D. nurses sat, pouring down in a stream, frantically hungry, and always the food seemed to fail before the last three were seated. You then applied to the kitchen through a tube and got a biting rejoinder. The right amount of bread and butter had been sent up, three pieces for each. Somebody must have eaten more than her share. Loud disclaimers from the V.A.D.'s. They chatted to each other amiably and freely, addressing each other by their surnames.

"I didn't eat your slice of bread, Jones. I wouldn't do such a mean thing!" "They always send it up wrong." "Look here, Catford's got to have something to eat. She's got an op. in half an hour." "Hurry up, Bulgy [an affectionate nickname, this]. We've got all those mackintoshes to scrub."

Very different the behavior at the Sisters' table at the other side of the room. Conversation there went on genteelly in frosty whispers. Before each Sister was a small brown pot of tea. It was Nell's business to know exactly how strong each Sister liked it. It was never a question of how weak! To bring "washy" tea to a Sister was to fall from grace forever.

The whispers went on incessantly.

"I said to her: 'Naturally the surgical cases receive the first attention.'" "I only passed the remark, so to speak." "Pushing herself forward. Always the same thing." "Would you believe it, she forgot to hold the towel for the doctor's hands." "I said to doctor this morning . . ." "I passed the remark to Nurse . . ."

Again and again that one phrase recurred: "I passed the remark." Nell grew to listen for it. When she approached the table the whispers became lower and the Sisters looked at her suspiciously. Their conversation was secretive and shrouded in dignity. With enormous formality, they offered each other tea.

"Some of mine, Sister Westhaven? There's plenty in the pot." "Would you oblige me with the sugar, Sister Carr?" "Pardon me."

Nell had just begun to realize the hospital atmosphere, the feuds, the jealousies, the cabals, and the hundred-and-one undercurrents, when she was promoted to the ward, one of the nurses having gone sick.

She had a row of twelve beds to attend to, mostly surgical cases. Her companion was Gladys Potts, a small giggling creature, intelligent but lazy. The ward was under the charge of Sister Westhaven, a tall thin acid woman with a look of permanent disapproval. Nell's heart sank when she saw her, but later she congratulated herself. Sister Westhaven was far the pleasantest nurse in the hospital to work under.

There were five Sisters in all. Sister Carr, round and good-tempered looking. The men liked her and she giggled and joked with them a good deal, and was then late over her dressings and hurried over them. She called the V.A.D.'s "dear," and patted them affectionately, but her temper was uncertain. She herself was so unpunctual that everything went wrong and the "dear" was blamed for it. She was maddening to work under.

Sister Barnes was impossible. Everyone said so. She ranted and scolded from morning to night. She hated V.A.D.'s and let them know it. "I'll teach them to come here thinking they know everything," was her constant declaration. Apart from her biting sarcasm, she was a good nurse, and some of the girls liked working under her in spite of her lashing tongue.

Sister Dunlop was a dug-out. She was kindly and placid, but thoroughly lazy. She drank a great deal of tea and did as little work as possible.

Sister Norris was Theater Sister. She was competent at her job, rouged her lips, and was cattish to her underlings.

Sister Westhaven was by far the best nurse in the hospital. She was enthusiastic over work and was a good judge of those under her. If they showed promise she was reasonably amiable to them. If she judged them fools they led a miserable life.

On the fourth day she said to Nell: "I thought you weren't worth much at first, Nurse. But you've got a good lot of work in you."

So much imbued by now was Nell by the hospital spirit that she went home in the seventh heaven.

Little by little she sank into the hospital rut. At first she had suffered a heart-rending pang at the sight of the wounded. The first dressing of wounds at which she assisted was almost more than she could bear. Those who "longed to nurse" usually brought a certain amount of emotionalism to the task. But they were soon purged of it. Blood, wounds, suffering were everyday matters.

Nell was popular with the men. In the slack hour after tea she wrote letters for them, fetched books she thought they would like from the shelves at the end of the ward, heard stories of their families and sweethearts. She became, in common with the other nurses, zealous to defend them from the cruelties and stupidities of the would-be kind.

On visitors' days streams of elderly ladies arrived. They sat down by beds and did their best to "cheer our brave soldier." Certain things were conventions. "You're longing to get back, I suppose?" And "Yes, ma'am," was always the answer given. Descriptions were sought of the Angels at Mons.

There were also concerts. Some were well organized and were thoroughly enjoyed. Others—! They were summed up by the nurse on the next row to Nell, Phillis Deacon:

"Anybody who thinks they can sing, but has never been allowed to by their families, has got their chance now!"

There were also clergymen. Never, Nell thought, had she seen so many clergymen. One or two were appreciated. They were fine men, with sympathy and understanding, and they knew the right things to say and did not stress the religious side of their duties unduly. But there were many others.

"Nurse."

Nell paused in a hurried progress along the ward, having just been told sharply by Sister: "Nurse, your beds are crooked. No. 7's sticking out."

"Yes."

"Couldn't you wash me now, Nurse?"

Nell stared at the unusual request.

"It's not nearly half-past seven."

"It's the parson. He's at me to be confirmed. He's coming in now."

Nell took pity on him. The Reverend Canon Edgerton found his prospective convert barred from him by screens and basins of water.

"Thank yer, Nurse," said the patient hoarsely. "It seems a bit hard to go on nagging at a feller when he can't get away from yer, doesn't it?"

Washing—interminable washing. The patients were washed, the ward was washed, and at every hour of the day there were mackintoshes to scrub.

And eternal tidiness.

"Nurse—your beds. The bedclothes are hanging down on No. 9. No. 2 has pushed his bed sideways. What will Doctor think?"

Doctor—Doctor—Doctor. Morning, noon, and night, Doctor! Doctor was a god. For a mere V.A.D. to speak to Doctor was *lesé majestè* and brought down the vials of wrath on your head from Sister. Some of the V.A.D.'s offended innocently. They were Wiltsbury girls and they knew the doctors—knew them as ordinary human beings. They said good-morning blithely. Soon they knew better—knew they had been guilty of that awful sin, "pushing yourself forward." Mary Cardner "pushed herself forward." Doctor asked for some scissors and, unthinkingly, she handed him the pair she wore. Sister explained her crime to her at length. She ended thus:

"I don't say you mightn't have done this. Seeing you had the exact thing that was wanted, you might have said to me—in a whisper, that is—'Is this what is needed, Sister?' And I would have taken them from you and handed them to Doctor. No one could have objected to that."

You got tired of the word "Doctor." Every remark Sister made was punctuated with it, even when speaking to him.

"Yes, Doctor . . . 102 this morning, Doctor. . . . I don't think so, Doctor. . . . Pardon, Doctor? I didn't quite catch. . . . Nurse, hold the towel for Doctor's hands."

And you held the towel meekly, standing like a glorified towel horse. And Doctor, having wiped his sacred hands, flung the towel on the floor where you meekly picked it up. You poured water for Doctor, you handed soap to Doctor, and finally you received the command:

"Nurse, open the door for Doctor."

"And what I'm afraid is, we shan't be able to grow out of it afterward," said Phillis Deacon wrathfully. "I shall never feel the same about doctors again. Even the scrubbiest little doctors I shall be subservient to, and when they come to dine I shall find myself rushing to open the door for them. I know I shall."

There was a great freemasonry in the hospital. Class distinctions were a thing of the past. The dean's daughter, the butcher's daughter, Mrs. Manfred who was the wife of a draper's assistant, Phillis Deacon who was the daughter of a baronet—they all called each other by their surname and shared the common interest of "what would there be for supper, and would it go round?" Undoubtedly there was cheating. Gladys Potts, the giggler, was discovered to go down early and surreptitiously to filch an extra piece of bread and butter or an unfair helping of rice.

"You know," said Phillis Deacon, "I do sympathize with servants now. One always thinks they mind so much about their food—and here are we getting just the same. It's having nothing else to look forward to. I could have cried when the scrambled eggs didn't go round last night."

"They oughtn't to have scrambled eggs," said Mary Cardner angrily.

"The eggs ought to be separate, poached or boiled. Scrambled gives too much opportunity to unscrupulous people."

And she looked with significance at Gladys Potts, who giggled nervously and moved away.

"That girl's a slacker," said Phillis Deacon. "She's always got something else to do when it's screens. And she sucks up to Sister. It doesn't matter with Westhaven. Westhaven's fair. But she flattered little Carr till she got all the soft jobs."

Little Potts was unpopular. Strenuous efforts were made to force her to do the more disagreeable work sometimes, but Potts was wily. Only the resourceful Deacon was a match for her.

There were also the jealousies amongst the doctors themselves. Naturally they all wanted the more interesting surgical cases. The allotting of cases to different wards gave rise to feeling.

Nell soon knew all the doctors and their various attributes. There was Dr. Lang, tall, untidy, slouching, with long nervous fingers. He was the cleverest surgeon of the lot. He had a sarcastic tongue, and was ruthless in his treatments but he was clever. All the Sisters adored him.

Then there was Dr. Wilbraham, who had the fashionable practice of Wiltsbury. A big florid man, genial in temper when things went well, and the manners of a spoiled child when he was put out. If he was tired and cross he was unnecessarily rough and Nell hated him.

There was Dr. Meadows, a quiet efficient G. P. He was content not to do operations and he gave every case unfailing attention. He always spoke politely to the V.A.D.'s and omitted to throw towels on the floor.

Then there was Dr. Bury, who was not supposed to be much good and who was himself convinced that he knew everything. He was always wishing to try extraordinary new methods and he never continued one treatment for more than a couple of days. If one of his patients died, it was the fashion to say: "Do you wonder, with Dr. Bury?"

Then there was young Dr. Keen, who had been invalided home from the front. He was little more than a medical student but he was full of importance. He even demeaned himself to chat with the V.A.D.'s, explaining the importance of an operation that had just taken place. Nell said to Sister Westhaven: "I didn't know Dr. Keen was operating. I thought it was Dr. Lang." Sister replied grimly: "Dr. Keen held the leg. That's all."

Operations had been a nightmare to Nell at first. At the first one she attended, the floor rose at her and a nurse led her out. She hardly dared to face Sister, but Sister was unexpectedly kind.

"It's partly the lack of air and the smell of the ether, Nurse," she said kindly. "Go into a short one next. You'll get used to it."

Next time Nell felt faint but did not have to go out, the time after she felt sick only, and the time after that she didn't feel sick at all.

Once or twice she was lent to help the theater nurse clear up the operating theater after an unusually big op. The place was like a shambles, blood everywhere. The theater nurse was only eighteen, a determined slip of a thing. She owned to Nell that she had hated it at first.

"The very first op. was a leg," she said. "Amputation. And Sister went off afterward and left me to clear up, and I had to take the leg down to the furnace myself. It was awful."

On her days out Nell went to tea with friends. Some of them were kindly old ladies and sentimentalized over her and told her she was splendid.

"You don't work on Sundays, do you, dear? Really? Oh! but that isn't right. Sunday should be a day of rest."

Nell pointed out gently that the soldiers had to be washed and fed on Sundays just as any other day, and the old ladies admitted this but seemed to think that the matter should have been better organized. They were also very distressed at Nell's having to walk home alone at midnight.

Others were even more difficult.

"I hear those hospital nurses give themselves great airs, ordering everyone about. I shouldn't stand that kind of thing myself. I am willing to do anything I can to help in this dreadful war, but impertinence I will not stand. I told Mrs. Curtis so, and she agreed it would be better for me not to do hospital work."

To these ladies Nell made no reply at all.

The rumor of "the Russians" was sweeping through England at this time. Everyone had seen them—or if not actually seen them, their cook's second cousin had, which was practically the same thing. The rumor died hard—it was so pleasing and so exciting.

A very old lady who came to the hospital took Nell aside.

"My dear," she said, "don't believe that story. It's true, but not in the way we think."

Nell looked inquiringly at her.

"Eggs!" said the old lady in a poignant whisper. "Russian eggs! Several millions of them—to keep us from starving."

Nell wrote all these things to Vernon. She felt terribly cut off from him. His letters were naturally terse and constrained and he seemed to dislike the idea of her working in hospital. He urged her again and again to go to London—enjoy herself.

How queer men were, Nell thought. They didn't seem to understand. She would hate to be one of the "keeping themselves bright for the boys" brigade. How soon you drifted apart when you were doing different things! She couldn't share Vernon's life and he couldn't share hers.

The first agony of parting, when she had felt sure he would be killed, was over. She had fallen into the routine of wives. Four months had passed and he hadn't been even wounded. He wouldn't be. Everything was all right.

Five months after he had gone out he wired that he had got leave. Nell's heart almost stopped beating. She was so excited! She went off to Matron and was granted leave of absence.

She traveled to London feeling strange and unusual in ordinary clothes. Their first leave!

2

It was true—really true! The leave train came in and disgorged its multitudes. She saw him. He was actually there. They met. Neither could speak. He squeezed her hand frantically. She knew then how afraid she had been. . . .

That five days went by in a flash. It was like some queer delirious dream. She adored Vernon and he adored her, but they were in some ways like strangers to each other. He was offhand when she spoke about

France. It was all right—everything was all right. One made jokes about it and refused to treat it seriously. "For goodness' sake, Nell, don't sentimentalize. It's awful to come home and find everyone with long faces. And don't talk slush about our brave soldiers laying down their lives, *etc.* That sort of stuff makes me sick. Let's get tickets for another show."

Something in his absolute callousness perturbed her—it seemed somehow rather dreadful to treat everything so lightly. When he asked her what she had been doing she could only give him hospital news, and that he didn't like. He begged her again to give it up.

"It's a filthy job, nursing. I hate to think of your doing it."

She felt chilled, rebuffed, then rebuked herself. They were together again. What did anything else matter?

They had a wild delightful time. They went to a show and danced every night. In the daytime they went shopping. Vernon bought her everything that took his fancy. They went to a Paris firm of dressmakers and sat there whilst airy young duchesses floated past in wisps of chiffon and Vernon chose the most expensive model. They felt horribly wicked but dreadfully happy when Nell wore it that night.

Then Nell told him he ought to go and see his mother. Vernon rebelled.

"Oh! darling, I don't want to! Our little short precious time. I can't miss a minute of it."

Nell pleaded. Myra would be terribly hurt and disappointed.

"Well, then, you've got to come with me."

"No, that wouldn't do at all."

In the end, he went down to Birmingham for a flying visit. His mother made a tremendous fuss over him—greeted him with floods of what she called "glad proud tears," and trotted him round to see the Bents. Vernon came back seething with conscious virtue.

"You are a hard-hearted devil, Nell. We've missed a whole day! God, how I've been slobbered over."

He felt ashamed as soon as he had said it. Why couldn't he love his mother better? Why did she always manage to rub him up the wrong way, no matter how good his resolutions were? He gave Nell a hug.

"I didn't mean it. I'm glad you made me go. You're so sweet, Nell.

You never think of yourself. It's so wonderful being with you again. You don't know . . ."

And she put on the French model gown and they went out to dine with a ridiculous feeling of having been model children and deserving a reward.

They had nearly finished dinner when Nell saw Vernon's face change. It stiffened and grew anxious.

"What is it?"

"Nothing," he said hastily.

But she turned and looked behind her. At a small table against the wall was Jane.

Something cold seemed for a moment to rest on Nell's heart. Then she said easily:

"Why, it's Jane! Let's go and speak to her."

"No, I'd rather not." She was a little surprised by the vehemence of his tone. He saw that and went on: "I'm stupid, darling. I want to have you and nothing but you—not other people butting in. Have you finished? Let's go. I don't want to miss the beginning of the play."

They paid the bill and went. Jane nodded to them carelessly and Nell waved her hand to her. They arrived at the theater ten minutes early.

Later, as Nell was slipping the gown from her white shoulders, Vernon said suddenly: "Nell, do you think I shall ever write music again?"

"Of course. Why not?"

"Oh! I don't know. I don't think I want to."

She looked at him in surprise. He was sitting on a chair, frowning into space.

"I thought it was the only thing you cared about."

"Cared about—cared about—that doesn't express it in the least. It isn't the things you care about that matter. It's the things you can't get rid of—the things that won't let you go—that haunt you—like a face that you can't help seeing even when you don't want to. . . ."

"Darling Vernon—don't."

She came and knelt down beside him. He clutched her to him convulsively.

"Nell—darling Nell—nothing matters but you. Kiss me. . . ."

But he reverted presently to the topic. He said irrelevantly: "Guns make a pattern, you know. A musical pattern, I mean. Not the sound one hears. I mean the pattern the sound makes in space. I suppose that's nonsense—but I know what I mean."

And again a minute or two later: "If one could only get hold of it properly."

Ever so slightly, she moved her body away from him. It was as though she challenged her rival. She never admitted it openly, but secretly she feared Vernon's music. If only he didn't care so much.

And tonight, at any rate, she was triumphant. He drew her back, holding her close, showering kisses on her.

But long after Nell was asleep, Vernon lay staring into the darkness, seeing against his will Jane's face and the outline of her body in its dull green satin sheath as he had seen it against the crimson curtain at the restaurant.

He said to himself very softly under his breath: "Damn Jane!"

But he knew that you couldn't get rid of Jane as easily as that.

He wished he hadn't seen her.

There was something so damnably disturbing about Jane.

He forgot her the next day. It was their last, and it went terribly quickly.

All too soon, it was over.

3

It had been like a dream. Now the dream was over. Nell was back at the hospital. It seemed to her she had never been away. She waited desperately for the post—for Vernon's first letter. It came—more ardent and unrestrained than usual, as though even censorship had been forgotten. Nell wore it against her heart and the indelible pencil came off on her skin. She wrote and told him so.

Life went on as usual. Dr. Lang went out to the front and was replaced by an elderly doctor with a beard who said, "Thank ye, thank ye, Sister," every time he was offered a towel or was helped on with his white linen coat. They had a slack time with most of the beds empty and Nell found the enforced idleness trying.

One day, to her surprise and delight, Sebastian walked in. He was home on leave and had come down to look her up. Vernon had asked him to.

"You've seen him then?"

Sebastian said Yes, his lot had taken over from Vernon.

"And he's all right?"

"Oh! yes, he's all *right!*"

Something in the way he said it caused her alarm. She pressed him. Sebastian frowned in perplexity.

"It's difficult to explain, Nell. You see, Vernon's an odd beggar—always has been. He doesn't like looking things in the face."

He quelled the fierce retort that he saw rising to her lips.

"I don't mean in the least what you think I mean. He isn't *afraid.* Lucky devil, I don't think he knows what fear is. I wish I didn't. No, it's different from that. It's the whole life—it's pretty ghastly, you know. Dirt and blood and filth, and noise—above all, noise! Recurrent noise at fixed times. It gets on my nerves, so what must it do to Vernon's?"

"Yes, but what did you mean by not facing things."

"Simply that he won't admit that there's anything to face. He's afraid of minding, so he says there's nothing *to* mind. If he'd only admit that it's a bloody filthy business like I do he'd be all right. But it's like that old piano business—he won't look at the thing fair and square. And it's no good saying 'there ain't no such thing' when there *is*. But that's always been Vernon's way. He's in good spirits—enjoying everything—and it isn't natural. I'm afraid of his— Oh! I don't know what I'm afraid of. But I know that telling yourself fairy stories is about the worst thing you can do. Vernon's a musician, and he's got the nerves of a musician. The worst of him is that he doesn't know anything about himself. He never has."

Nell looked troubled.

"Sebastian, what do you think will happen?"

"Oh! nothing, probably. What I should like to happen would be for Vernon to stop one, in as conveniently painless a place as possible, and come back to be nursed for a bit."

"How I wish that would happen!"

"Poor old Nell! It's rotten for all you people. I'm glad I haven't got a wife."

"If you had—" Nell paused, then went on. "Would you want her to work in a hospital or would you rather she did nothing?"

"Everybody will be working sooner or later. It's as well to get down to it as soon as possible, I should say."

"Vernon doesn't like my doing this."

"That's his ostrich act again, plus the reactionary spirit that he's inherited and will never quite outgrow. Sooner or later he'll face the fact that women are working—but he won't admit it till the last minute."

Nell sighed.

"How worrying everything is."

"I know. And I've made things worse for you. But I'm awfully fond of Vernon. He's the one friend I care about. And I hoped if I told you what I thought you'd encourage him to—well, give way a little—at any rate to you. But perhaps to you he does let himself go?"

Nell shook her head.

"He won't do anything but joke about the war."

Sebastian whistled.

"Well, next time—get it out of him. Stick to it."

Nell said suddenly and sharply: "Do you think he'd talk better—to Jane?"

"To Jane?" Sebastian looked rather embarrassed. "I don't know. Perhaps. It all depends."

"You do think so! Why? Tell me why? Is she more sympathetic, or what?"

"Oh! Lord, no. Jane's not exactly sympathetic. Provocative is more the word. You get annoyed with her—and out pops the truth. She makes you aware of yourself in ways you don't want to be. There's nobody like Jane for pulling you off your high horse."

"You think she's a lot of influence over Vernon?"

"Oh! I wouldn't say that. And anyway, it wouldn't matter if she had. She's doing relief work in Serbia. Sailed a fortnight ago."

"Oh!" said Nell. She drew a deep breath and smiled.

Somehow, she felt happier.

4

Darling Nell:

Do you know I dream of you every night? Usually you're nice
to me, but sometimes you're a little beast. Cold and hard and far
away. You couldn't be that really, could you? Not now. Darling,
will the indelible pencil ever come off?

Nell sweetest, I never believe I'm going to be killed, but if I
were, what would it matter? We've had so much. You'd think
of me always as happy and loving you, wouldn't you, sweetheart? I know I'd go on loving you after I was dead. That's the
only bit of me that couldn't die. I love you—love love you—love
you. . . .

He had never written to her quite like that before. She put the letter
in its usual place.

That day she was absentminded at the hospital. She forgot things.
The men noticed it.

"Nurse is daydreaming," they teased her, making little jokes. And she
laughed back.

It was so wonderful, so very wonderful, to be loved. Sister Westhaven
was in a temper. Nurse Potts slacked more than usual. But it didn't
matter. Nothing mattered.

Even the monumental Sister Jenkins, who came on night duty and
was always full of pessimism, failed to impress her with any kind of
gloom.

"Ah!" Sister Jenkins would say, settling her cuffs and moving three
double chins round inside her collar in an effort to alleviate their mass.
"No. 3 still alive? You surprise me. I didn't think he'd last through the
day. Well, he'll be gone tomorrow, poor young chap. [Sister Jenkins was
always prophesying that patients would be gone tomorrow, and the failure of her prognostications to come true never seemed to induce in her
a more hopeful attitude.] I don't like the look of No. 18—that last
operation was worse than useless. No. 8 is going to take a turn for the

worse, unless I'm much mistaken. I said so to Doctor, but he didn't listen to me. Now then, Nurse [with sudden acerbity], no good for you to hang about. Off duty is off duty."

Nell accepted this gracious permission to depart, well aware that if she had not lingered Sister Jenkins would have asked her "what she meant by hurrying away like that?—not even willing to wait a minute overtime."

It took twenty minutes to walk home. The night was a clear starry one and Nell enjoyed the walk. If only Vernon could have been walking beside her!

She let herself into the house very quietly with her latchkey. Her landlady always went to bed early. On the tray in the hall was an orange-colored envelope.

She knew then.

Telling herself that it wasn't—that it couldn't be—that he was only wounded—surely he was only wounded . . . yet she knew.

A sentence from the letter she had received that morning leaped out at her: *Nell sweetest, I never believe I am going to be killed, but if I were, what would it matter? We've had so much. . . .*

He had never written like that before. He must have felt—have known. Sensitive people did know sometimes beforehand.

She stood there, holding the telegram. Vernon—her lover, her husband . . . She stood there a long time.

Then at last she opened the telegram, which informed her with deep regret that Lieutenant Vernon Deyre had been Killed in Action.

Chapter Three

A memorial service was held for Vernon in the little old church at Abbotsford under the shadow of Abbots Puissants, as it had been held for his father. The two last of the Deyres were not to lie in the family vault. One in South Africa, one in France.

In Nell's memory afterward the proceedings seemed shadowed by the monumental bulk of Mrs. Levinne—a vast matriarchal figure dwarfing everything else. She herself had to bite her lips not to laugh hysterically. The whole thing was so funny somehow—so unlike Vernon.

Her mother was there, elegant and aloof. Uncle Sydney was there, in black broadcloth, restraining himself from jingling his money with great difficulty, and with a suitable "mourner's" face. Myra Deyre was there in heavy crape, weeping copiously and unrestrainedly. But it was Mrs. Levinne who dominated the proceedings. She came back with them afterward to the sitting room at the inn, identifying herself with the family.

"Poor dear boy—poor dear gallant boy! I've always thought of him like another thon."

She was genuinely distressed. Tears splashed down on her black bodice. She patted Myra on the shoulder.

"Now, now, my dear, you mustn't take on so, You mustn't indeed. It's our duty, all of us, to bear up. You gave him to his country. You couldn't do more. Here's Nell—as brave as can be."

"Everything I had in the world," sobbed Myra. "First husband, then son. Nothing left."

She stared ahead of her through blood-suffused eyes in a kind of ecstasy of bereavement.

"The very best son—we were everything to each other." She caught Mrs. Levinne's hand. "You'll know what it feels like if Sebastian . . ."

A spasm of fear passed across Mrs. Levinne's face. She clenched her hands.

"I see they've sent up some sandwiches and some port," said Uncle Sydney, creating a diversion. "Very thoughtful. Very thoughtful. A little drop of port, Myra dear. You've been through a great strain, you know."

Myra waved away port with a horror-stricken hand. Uncle Sydney was made to feel that he had displayed callousness.

"We've all got to keep up," he said. "It's our duty."

His hand stole to his pocket and he began to jingle.

"Syd!"

"Sorry, Myra."

Again Nell felt that wild desire to giggle. She didn't want to cry. She wanted to laugh and laugh and laugh. . . . Awful—to feel like that.

"I thought everything went off very nicely," said Uncle Sydney. "Very nicely indeed. A most impressive lot of the villagers attended. You wouldn't like to stroll round Abbots Puissants? That was a very nice letter putting it at our disposal today."

"I hate the place," said Myra vehemently. "I always have."

"I suppose, Nell, you've seen the lawyers? I understand Vernon made a perfectly simple will before going out to France, leaving everything to you. In that case, Abbots Puissants is now yours. It was not entailed, and in any case there are no Deyres now in existence."

Nell said: "Thank you, Uncle Sydney, I've seen the lawyer. He was very kind and explained everything to me."

"That's more than any lawyer can do as a rule," said Uncle Sydney. "They make the simplest thing sound difficult. It's not my business to advise you, but I know there's no man in your family who can do so. Much the best thing you can do is to sell it. There's no money to keep it up, you know. You understand that?"

Nell did understand. She saw that Uncle Sydney was making it clear to her that no Bent money was coming her way. Myra would leave her money back to her own family. That, of course, was only natural. Nell would never have dreamed of anything else.

As a matter of fact, Uncle Sydney had at once tackled Myra as to whether there was a child coming. Myra said she didn't think so. Uncle Sydney said she had better make sure. "I don't know exactly how the law stands, but as it is, if you were to pop off tomorrow, having left your money to Vernon, it might go to her. No good taking any chances."

Myra said tearfully that it was very unkind of him to suggest that she was going to die.

"Nothing of the sort. You women are all alike. Carrie sulked for a week when I insisted on her making a proper will. We don't want good money to go out of the family."

Above all, he did not want good money to go to Nell. He disliked Nell, whom he regarded as Enid's supplanter. And he loathed Mrs. Vereker, who always managed to make him feel hot and clumsy and uncertain about his hands.

"Nell, of course, will take legal advice," said Mrs. Vereker sweetly.

"Don't think I want to butt in," said Uncle Sydney.

Nell felt a passionate pang of regret. If only she were going to have a child! Vernon had been so afraid for her. "It would be so dreadful for you, darling, if I were to be killed and you were left with all the trouble and worry of a child and very little money—Besides—you never know—you might die. I couldn't bear to risk it."

And really, it *had* seemed better and more prudent to wait.

But now she was sorry. Her mother's consolations had seemed coldly brutal to her.

"You're not going to have a baby, are you, Nell? Well, I must say I'm thankful. Naturally, you'll marry again, and it's so much better when there are no encumbrances."

In answer to a passionate protest, Mrs. Vereker had smiled. "I oughtn't to have said that just now. But you are only a girl still. Vernon himself would have wanted you to be happy."

Nell thought: "Never! She doesn't understand!"

"Well, well, it's a sad world," said Mr. Bent, surreptitiously helping himself to a sandwich. "The flower of our manhood being mown down. But all the same, I'm proud of England. I'm proud of being an Englishman. I like to feel that I'm doing my bit in England just as much as these boys are doing it out here. We're doubling our output of explosives next month. Night and day shifts. I'm proud of Bent's, I can tell you."

"It must be wonderfully profitable," said Mrs. Vereker.

"That's not the way I like to look at it," said Mr. Bent. "I like to look at it that I'm serving my country."

"Well, I hope we all try to do our bit," said Mrs. Levinne. "I have been a working party twice a week, and I'm interethting myself in all these poor girls who are having war babieths."

"There's too much loose thinking going about," said Mr. Bent. "We mustn't get lax. England has never been lax."

"Well, we've got to look after the children at any rate," said Mrs. Levinne. She added: "How is Joe? I thought I might see her here to-day."

Both Uncle Sydney and Myra looked embarrassed. It was clear that Joe was what is known as a "delicate subject." They skated lightly over the topic. War work in Paris—very busy—unable to get leave.

Mr. Bent looked at his watch.

"Myra, we've not too much time before the train. Must get back tonight. Carrie, my wife you know, is very far from well. That's why she wasn't able to be here today." He sighed. "It's odd how often things turn out for the best. It was a great disappointment to us not having a son. And yet, in a way, we've been spared a good deal. Think of the anxiety we might be in today. The ways of Providence are wonderful."

Mrs. Vereker said to Nell when they had taken leave of Mrs. Levinne, who motored them back to London: "One thing I do hope, Nell, is that you won't think it your duty to see a lot of your in-laws. I dislike the way that woman wallowed in her grief more than I can tell you. She was thoroughly enjoying herself, though I dare say she'd have preferred a proper coffin."

"Oh! Mother—she was really unhappy. She was awfully fond of Vernon. As she said, he was all she had in the world."

"That's a phrase women like her are very fond of using. It means nothing at all. And you're not going to pretend to me that Vernon adored his mother. He merely tolerated her. They had nothing in common. He was a Deyre through and through."

Nell couldn't deny that.

She stayed at her mother's flat in town for three weeks. Mrs. Vereker was very kind within her own limits. She was not a sympathetic woman at any time, but she respected Nell's grief and did not intrude upon it. Upon practical matters her judgment was, as it had always been, excellent. There were various interviews with lawyers and Mrs. Vereker was present at all of them.

Abbots Puissants was still let. The tenancy would be up the following year, and the lawyer strongly advised its sale rather than reletting it. Mrs. Vereker, to Nell's surprise, did not seem to concur with this view. She suggested a further let of not too long duration.

"So much may happen in a few years," she said.

Mr. Flemming looked hard at her and seemed to catch her meaning. His glance rested for just a moment on Nell, fair and childish-looking in her mourning.

"As you say," he remarked, "much may happen. At any rate, nothing need be decided for a year."

Business matters settled, Nell returned to the hospital at Wiltsbury. She felt that there, and there only, could life be at all possible. Mrs.

Vereker did not oppose her. She was a sensible woman and she had her own plans.

A month after Vernon's death Nell was once more back in the ward. Nobody ever referred to her loss and she was grateful. To carry on as usual was the motto of the moment.

Nell carried on.

2

"There's someone asking for you, Nurse Deyre."

"For me?" Nell was surprised.

It must be Sebastian. Only he was likely to come down here and look her up. Did she want to see him or not? She hardly knew.

But to her great surprise, her visitor was George Chetwynd. He explained that he was passing through Wiltsbury, and had stopped to find out if he could see her. He asked whether she couldn't come out to lunch with him.

"I thought you were on afternoon duty," he explained.

"I was changed to the morning shift yesterday. I'll ask Matron. We're not very busy."

Permission was accorded her, and half an hour later she was sitting opposite George Chetwynd at the County Hotel with a plate of roast beef in front of her and a waiter hovering over her with a vast dish of cabbage.

"The only vegetable the County Hotel knows," observed Chetwynd.

He talked interestingly and made no reference to her loss. All he said was that her continuing to work here was the pluckiest thing he had ever heard of.

"I can't tell you how I admire all you women. Carrying on, tackling one job after another. No fuss—no heroics—just sticking to it as though it were the most natural thing in the world. I think Englishwomen are fine."

"One must do something."

"I know. I can understand that feeling. Anything's better than sitting with your hands in your lap, eh?"

"That's it."

She was grateful. George always understood. He told her that he was off to Serbia in a day or two, organizing relief work there.

"Frankly," he said, "I'm ashamed of my country for not coming in. But it will. I'm convinced of that. It's only a matter of time. In the meantime we do what we can to alleviate the horrors of war."

"You look very well."

He looked younger than she remembered him—well set up, bronzed, the gray in his hair a mere distinction rather than a sign of age.

"I'm feeling well. Nothing like having plenty to do. Relief work's pretty strenuous."

"When are you off?"

"Day after tomorrow." He paused, then said in a different voice: "Look here—you didn't mind my looking you up like this? You don't feel I'd no business to butt in?"

"No—no. It was very kind of you. Especially after I—I—"

"You know I've never borne any rancor over that. I admire you for following your heart. You loved him, and you didn't love me. But there's no reason we shouldn't be friends, is there?"

He looked so friendly, so very unsentimental, that Nell answered happily that there wasn't.

He said: "That's fine. And you'll let me do anything for you that a friend can? Advise you in any bothers that arise, I mean?"

Nell said she'd be only too grateful.

They left it like that. He departed in his car shortly after lunch, wringing her hand and saying he hoped they'd meet again in about six months' time, and begging her again to consult him if she were in a difficulty any time.

Nell promised that she would.

3

The winter was a bad one for Nell. She caught a cold, neglected to take proper care of herself, and was ill for a week or so. She was quite unfit to resume hospital work at the end of it, and Mrs. Vereker carried her off to London to her flat. There she regained strength slowly.

Endless bothers seemed to arise. Abbots Puissants appeared to need an entire new roof. New water pipes had to be installed. The fencing was in a bad state.

Nell appreciated for the first time the awful drain property can be. The rent was eaten up many times over with the necessary repairs, and Mrs. Vereker had to come to the rescue to tide Nell over a difficult corner and not let her get too much in debt. They were living as penuriously as possible. Vanished were the days of outward show and credit. Mrs. Vereker managed to make both ends meet by a very narrow margin, and would hardly have done that but for what she won at the bridge table. She was a first-class player and added materially to her income by play. She was out most of the day at a bridge club that still survived.

It was a dull unhappy life for Nell. Worried over money, not strong enough to undertake fresh work, nothing to do but sit and brood. Poverty combined with love in a cottage was one thing. Poverty without love to soften it was another. Sometimes Nell wondered how she was ever going to get through a life that stretched drear and bleak ahead of her. She couldn't bear things. She simply couldn't.

Then Mr. Flemming urged her to make a decision concerning Abbots Puissants. The tenancy would be up in a month or two. Something must be done. He could not hold out any hopes of letting it for a higher rent. Nobody wanted to rent big places without central heating or modern conveniences. He strongly advised her to sell.

He knew the feeling her husband had had about the place. But since she herself was never likely to be able to afford to live in it . . .

Nell admitted the wisdom of what he said, but still pleaded for time to decide. She was reluctant to sell it but she could not help feeling that, the worry of Abbots Puissants once off her mind she would be relieved from her heaviest burden. Then one day Mr. Flemming rang up to say that he had had a very good offer for Abbots Puissants. He mentioned a sum far in excess of her—or indeed his—expectations. He very strongly advised her to close with it without delay.

Nell hesitated a minute, then said, "Yes."

4

It was extraordinary how much happier she felt at once. Free of that terrible incubus! It wasn't as though Vernon had lived. Houses and estates were simply white elephants when you hadn't the necessary money to keep them up properly.

She was undisturbed even by a letter from Joe in Paris.

> How *can* you sell Abbots Puissants when you know what Vernon felt about it? I should have thought it would be the last thing you could have done.

She thought: "Joe doesn't understand."
She wrote back:

> What was I to do? I don't know where to turn for money. There's been the roof and the drains and the water—it's endless. I can't go on running into debt. Everything's so tiring I wish I were dead. . . .

Three days later she got a letter from George Chetwynd asking if he might come and see her. He had, he said, something to confess.

Mrs. Vereker was out. She received him alone. He broke it rather apprehensively to her. It was he who had purchased Abbots Puissants.

Just at first she recoiled from the idea. Not George! Not George at Abbots Puissants! Then with admirable common sense he argued the point.

Surely it was better that it should pass into his hands instead of those of a stranger? He hoped that sometimes she and her mother would come and stay there.

"I'd like you to feel that your husband's home is open to you at any time. I want to change things there as little as possible. You shall advise me. Surely you prefer my having it to its passing into the hands of some vulgarians who will fill it with gilt and spurious Old Masters?"

In the end she wondered why she had felt any objection. Better

George than anyone. And he was so kind and understanding about everything. She was tired and worried. She broke down suddenly, cried on his shoulder whilst he put an arm round her and told her that everything was all right, that it was only because she'd been ill.

Nobody could have been kinder or more brotherly.

When she told her mother Mrs. Vereker said: "I knew George was looking out for a place. It's lucky he's chosen Abbots Puissants. He's probably haggled less about the price simply because he was once in love with you."

The remote way she said "once in love with you" made Nell feel comfortable. She had imagined that her mother might have "ideas" still about George Chetwynd.

5

That summer they went down and stayed at Abbots Puissants. They were the only guests. Nell had not been there since she was a child. A deep regret came upon her that she could not have lived there with Vernon. The house was truly beautiful and so were the stately gardens and the ruined Abbey.

George was in the middle of doing up the house and he consulted her taste at every turn. Nell began to feel quite a proprietary interest. She was almost happy again, enjoying the ease and luxury and the freedom from anxiety.

True, once she received the money from Abbots Puissants and had invested it she would have a nice little income, but she dreaded the onus of deciding where to live and what to do. She was not really happy with her mother, and all her own friends seemed to have drifted out of touch. She hardly knew where to go or what to do with her life.

Abbots Puissants gave her just the peace and rest she needed. She felt sheltered there and safe. She dreaded the return to town.

It was the last evening. George had pressed them to remain longer but Mrs. Vereker had declared that they really couldn't trespass further on his hospitality.

Nell and George walked together on the long flagged walk. It was a still balmy evening.

"It has been lovely here," said Nell, with a little sigh. "I hate going back."

"I hate your going back, too." He paused, and then said very quietly: "I suppose there's no chance for me, is there, Nell?"

"I don't know what you mean."

But she did know—she knew at once.

"I bought this house because I hoped someday you'd live here. I wanted you to have the home that was rightfully yours. Are you going to spend your whole life nursing a memory, Nell? Do you think he—Vernon—would wish it? I never think of the dead like that—as grudging happiness to the living. I think he would want you to be looked after and taken care of, now that he isn't here to do it."

She said in a low voice: "I can't . . . I can't."

"You mean you can't forget him? I know that. But I'd be very good to you, Nell. You'd be wrapped round with love and care. I think I could make you happy—happier, at any rate, than you'll be facing life by yourself. I do honestly and truly believe that Vernon would wish it."

Would he? She wondered. She thought George was right. People might call it disloyalty, but it wasn't. That life of hers with Vernon was something by itself—nothing could touch it ever.

But oh! to be looked after, cared for, petted, and understood. She always *had* been fond of George.

She answered very softly: "Yes."

6

The person who was angry about it was Myra. She wrote long abusive letters to Nell.

> You can forget so soon. Vernon has only one home—in my heart. You never loved him.

Uncle Sydney twirled his thumbs and said: "That young woman knows which side her bread is buttered on," and wrote her a stereotyped letter of congratulations.

An unexpected ally was Joe, who was paying a flying visit to London and came round to see Nell at her mother's flat.

"I'm very glad," she said, kissing her. "And I'm sure Vernon would be. You're not the kind that can face life on your own. You never were. Don't you mind what Aunt Myra says. *I'll* talk to her. Life's a rotten business for women. I think you'll be happy with George. Vernon would want you to be happy, I know."

Joe's support heartened Nell more than anything. Joe had always been the nearest person to Vernon. On the night before her wedding she knelt by her bed and looked up to where Vernon's sword hung over the head of it.

She pressed her hands over her closed eyes.

"You do understand, beloved? You do? You do? It's you I love and always shall. . . . Oh! Vernon, if only I could know that you understood."

She tried to send her very soul out questing in search of him. He must—he *must*—know and understand.

Chapter Four

In the town of A—— in Holland, not far from the German frontier, is an inconspicuous inn. Here on a certain evening in 1917 a dark young man with a haggard face pushed open the door and in very halting Dutch asked for a lodging for the night. He breathed hard and his eyes were restless. Anna Schlieder, the fat proprietress of the inn, looked at him attentively up and down in her usual deliberate way before she replied. Then she told him that he could have a room. Her daughter Freda took him up to it. When she came back her mother said laconically: "English—escaped prisoner."

Freda nodded but said nothing. Her china-blue eyes were soft and sentimental. She had reasons of her own for taking an interest in the English. Presently she again mounted the stairs and knocked on the door. She went in on top of the knock, which as a matter of fact the young man had not heard. He was so sunk in a stupor of exhaustion that external sounds and happenings had hardly any meaning for him. For days and weeks he had been on the *qui vive*, escaping dangers by a hair's-breadth, never daring to be caught napping either physically or mentally. Now he was suffering the reaction. He lay where he had fallen, half sprawling across the bed. Freda stood and watched him. At last she said:

"I bring you hot water."

"Oh!" He started up. "I'm sorry. I didn't hear you."

She said slowly and carefully in his own language: "You are English—yes?"

"Yes. Yes, that is—"

He stopped suddenly in doubt. One must be careful. The danger was over—he was out of Germany. He felt slightly lightheaded. A diet of raw potatoes, dug up from the fields, was not stimulating to the brain. But he still felt he *must* be careful. It was so difficult. He felt queer—felt that he wanted to talk and talk, pour out everything now that at last that fearful long strain was over.

The Dutch girl was nodding her head at him gravely, wisely.

"I know," she said. "You come from over there." Her hand pointed in the direction of the frontier.

He looked at her, still irresolute.

"You have escaped—yes. We had before one like you."

A wave of reassurance passed over him. She was all right, this girl. His legs suddenly felt weak under him. He dropped down on the bed again.

"You are hungry? Yes. I see. I go and bring you something."

Was he hungry? He supposed he was. How long was it since he had eaten? One day, two days? He couldn't remember. The end had been like a nightmare—just keeping blindly on. He had had a map and a compass. He had known the place where he wanted to cross the frontier, the spot that seemed to him to offer the best chance. A thousand-to-one chance against his being able to pass the frontier—but he had passed it. They had shot at him and missed. Or was that all a dream? He had swum down the river—that was it. No, that was all wrong, too. Well, he wouldn't think about it. He had escaped, that was the great thing.

He leaned forward, supporting his aching head in his hands.

Very soon Freda returned carrying a tray with food on it and a great tankard of beer. He ate and drank whilst she stood watching him. The effect was magical. His head cleared. He *had* been lightheaded, he realized that now. He smiled up at Freda.

"That's splendid," he said. "Thanks awfully."

Encouraged by his smile, she sat down on a chair.

"You know London?"

"Yes, I know it." He smiled a little. She had asked that so quaintly. Freda did not smile. She was in deadly earnest.

"You know a soldier there? A what is it?—Corporal Green?"

He shook his head, a little touched.

"I'm afraid not," he said gently. "Do you know his regiment?"

"It was a London regiment—the London Fusiliers." She had no further information than that.

He said kindly: "When I get back to London I'll try to find out, if you like to give me a letter."

She looked at him doubtfully, yet with a certain air of trusting appeal. In the end the doubt was vanquished.

"I will write—yes," she said.

She rose to leave the room and said abruptly: "We have an English paper here—two English papers here. My cousin brought them from the hotel. You would like to see them, yes?"

He thanked her and she returned, bringing a tattered *Eve* and a *Sketch* which she handed to him with some pride.

When she left the room again he laid down the papers by his side and lighted a cigarette—his last cigarette! What would he have done without those cigarettes—stolen at that! Perhaps Freda would bring him some—he had money to pay for them. A kind girl, Freda, in spite of her thick ankles and an unprepossessing exterior.

He took out a small notebook from his pocket. The pages were blank and he wrote in it: *Corporal Green, London Fusiliers.* He would do what he could for the girl. He wondered idly what story lay behind it. What had Corporal Green been doing in Holland in A——? Poor Freda! It was the usual thing, he supposed.

Green—it reminded him of his childhood. *Mr. Green*. The omnipotent delightful Mr. Green—his playfellow and protector. Funny, the things one thought of when one was a kid!

He'd never told Nell about Mr. Green. Perhaps she'd had a Mr. Green of her own. Perhaps all children did.

He thought: "Nell—oh! Nell . . ." and his heart missed a beat. Then he turned his thoughts resolutely away. Very soon now. Poor darling, what she must have suffered knowing him to be a prisoner in Germany! But that was all over now. Very soon now they'd be together. Very soon. Oh! he mustn't think of it. The task in hand—no looking forward.

He picked up the *Sketch* and idly turned over the pages. A lot of new shows seemed to be on. What fun to go to a show again. Pictures of generals all looking very fierce and warlike. Pictures of people getting married. Not a bad-looking crowd. That one— Why—

It wasn't true—it couldn't be true. Another dream—a nightmare.

> Mrs. Vernon Deyre, who is to marry Mr. George Chetwynd.
> Mrs. Deyre's first husband was killed in action over a year
> ago. Mr. George Chetwynd is an American who has done
> very valuable relief work in Serbia.

Killed in action—yes, he supposed, that might be. In spite of all conceivable precautions, mistakes like that *did* arise. A man Vernon knew had been reported killed. A thousandth chance, but it happened.

Naturally, Nell would have believed—and naturally, quite naturally, she would marry again.

What nonsense he was talking! Nell—marry again! So soon. Marry George—*George* with his gray hair.

A sudden sharp pang shot through him. He had visualized George too clearly. Damn George. Blast and curse George!

But it wasn't true. No, it wasn't true!

He stood up, studying himself as he swayed on his feet. To anyone who had seen him, he would have appeared a little drunk.

He was perfectly calm—yes, he was perfectly calm. The thing was not to believe—not to think. Put it away—right away. It wasn't true—

it couldn't be true. If you once admitted that it might be true, you were done.

He went out of his room, down the stairs. He passed the girl Freda, who stared at him. He said very quietly and calmly (marvelous that he should be so calm):

"I'm going out for a walk."

He went out, oblivious of old Anna Schlieder's eyes that raked his back as he passed her. The girl Freda said to her:

"He passed me on the stairs like—like—what has happened to him?"

Anna tapped her forehead significantly. Nothing ever surprised her.

Out on the road Vernon was walking—walking very fast. He must get away—get away from the thing that was following him. If he looked round—if he thought about it—but he wouldn't think about it.

Everything was all right—*everything*.

Only he mustn't think. This queer dark thing that was following him—following him . . . If he didn't think, he was all right.

Nell—Nell with her golden hair and her sweet smile. His Nell. Nell and George . . . No, no, no! It wasn't so. He was in time.

And suddenly, lucidly, there ran through his mind the thought: "That paper was six months old at least. They've been married five months."

He reeled. He thought: "I can't bear it. No, this I can't bear. Something must happen."

He held on blindly to that: *Something must happen.*

Somebody would help him. Mr. Green. What was this awful thing that was dogging him? Of course, the Beast. The Beast.

He could hear it coming. He gave one panic-stricken glance over his shoulder. He was out of the town now, walking on a straight road between dykes. The Beast was coming lumbering along at a great pace, rattling and bumping.

The Beast . . . Oh! if only he could go back—to the Beast and Mr. Green, the old terrors, the old comforts. They didn't hurt you like the new things—like Nell and George Chetwynd. George . . . Nell belonging to George . . .

No! no, it wasn't true—it mustn't be true. He couldn't face anymore. Not that—not that.

There was only one way to get out of it all, to be at peace—only one way. Vernon Deyre had made a mess of life. Better to get out of it.

One last flaming agony shot through his brain. Nell—George—no! He thrust them out with a last effort. Mr. Green—kind Mr. Green.

He stepped out into the roadway right in the path of the lurching lorry that tried to avoid him too late—and struck him down and backward.

A horrible searing shock. Thank God, this was death.

BOOK V

GEORGE GREEN

Chapter One

In the yard of the county hotel in Wiltsbury two chauffeurs were busy with cars. George Green finished his work on the interior of the big Daimler, wiped his hands on a bit of oily rag, and stood upright with a sigh of satisfaction. He was a cheerful young fellow and was smiling now because he was pleased with himself for locating the trouble and dealing with it. He strolled along to where his fellow chauffeur was completing the toilet of a Minerva.

The latter looked up.

"Hullo, George. You through? Your boss is a Yank, isn't he? What's he like?"

"He's all right. Fussy, though. Won't go more than forty."

"Well, thank your stars you don't drive for a woman," said the other. His name was Evans. "Always changing their minds. And no idea of the proper times for meals. Picnic lunches as often as not—and you know what that means, a hard-boiled egg and a leaf of lettuce."

Green sat down on an adjacent barrel.

"Why don't you chuck it?"

"Not so easy to get another job these days," said Evans.

"No, that's true," said Green. He looked thoughtful.

"And I've got a missus and two kids," went on the other. "What's the rot that was talked about a country fit for heroes? No, if you've got a job—any kind of a job—it's better to freeze on to it in 1920."

He was silent for a minute, and then went on.

"Funny business—the war. I was hit twice—shrapnel. Makes you go a bit queer afterward. My missus says I frighten her—go quite batty sometimes. Wake up in the middle of the night hollering and not knowing where I am."

"I know," said Green. "I'm the same. When my guvnor picked me up—in Holland that was—I couldn't remember a thing about myself except my name."

"When was that? After the war?"

"Six months after the armistice. I was working in a garage there. Some chaps who were drunk ran me down one night in a lorry. Fairly scared 'em sober. They picked me up and took me along with them. I'd got a whacking great bash on the head. They looked after me and got me a job. Good chaps they were. I'd been working there two years when Mr. Bleibner came along. He hired a car from our place once or twice and I drove him. He talked to me a good bit and finally he offered to take me on as chauffeur."

"Mean to say you never thought of getting back home before that?"

"No—I didn't want to, somehow. I'd no folks there as far as I could remember, and I've an idea I'd had a bit of trouble there of some kind."

"I shouldn't associate trouble with you, mate," said Evans with a laugh.

George Green laughed, too. He was indeed a most cheerful-looking young man, tall and dark with broad shoulders and an ever-ready smile.

"Nothing much ever worries me," he boasted. "I was born the happy-go-lucky kind, I guess."

He moved away, smiling happily. A few minutes later he was reporting to his employer that the Daimler was ready for the road.

Mr. Bleibner was a tall thin dyspeptic-looking American with pure speech.

"Very good. Now, Green, I am going to Lord Datchet's for luncheon. Abingworth Friars. It's about six miles from here."

"Yes, sir."

"After luncheon I am going to a place called Abbots Puissants. Abbotsford is the village. Do you know it?"

"I've heard of it, I think, sir. But I don't know exactly where it is. I'll look it up on the map."

"Yes, please do so. It cannot, I think, be more than twenty miles—in the direction of Ringwood, I fancy."

"Very good, sir."

Green touched his cap and withdrew.

2

Nell Chetwynd stepped through the French window of the drawing room and came out upon the terrace at Abbots Puissants.

It was one of those still early autumn days when there seems no stirring of life anywhere, as though Nature herself feigned unconsciousness. The sky was pale, not a deep blue and there was a very faint haze in the atmosphere.

Nell leaned against a big stone urn and gazed out over the silent prospect. Everything was very beautiful and very English. The formal gardens were exquisitely kept. The house itself had been very judiciously and carefully repaired.

Not habitually given to emotion, as Nell looked up at the rose-red brick of the walls she felt a sudden swelling of the heart. It was all so perfect. She wished that Vernon could know—could see.

Four years of marriage had dealt kindly with Nell, but they had changed her. There was no suggestion of the nymph about her now. She was a beautiful woman instead of a lovely girl. She was poised, assured. Her beauty was a very definite kind of beauty—it never varied or altered. Her movements were more deliberate than of old, she had filled out a little—there was no suggestion of immaturity. She was the perfect full-blown rose.

A voice called her from the house.

"Nell!"

"I'm here, George, on the terrace."

"Right. I'll be out in a minute."

What a dear George was! A little smile creased her lips. The perfect husband! Perhaps that was because he was an American. You always heard that Americans made perfect husbands. Certainly, George had been one to her. The marriage had been a complete success. It was true that she had never felt for George what she had felt for Vernon, but almost reluctantly she had admitted that perhaps that was a good thing. These tempestuous emotions that tore and rent one—they couldn't last. Every day you had evidence that they *didn't* last.

All her old revolt was quelled now. She no longer questioned passionately the reason why Vernon should have been taken from her. God knew best. One rebelled at the time, but one came at last to realize that whatever happened was really for the best.

They had known supreme happiness, she and Vernon, and nothing could ever mar or take away from it. It was there forever—a precious secret possession, a hidden jewel. She could think of him now without regret or longing. They had loved each other and had risked everything to be together. Then had come that awful pain of separation—and then peace.

Yes, that was the predominant factor in her life now—peace. George had given her that. He had wrapped her round with comfort, with luxury, with tenderness. She hoped that she was a good wife to him, even if she didn't care as she had cared for Vernon. But she *was* fond of him—of course she was! The quiet affectionate feeling she had for him was by far the safest emotion to go through life with.

Yes, that expressed exactly what she felt—safe and happy. She wished that Vernon knew. He would be glad, she was sure.

George Chetwynd came out and joined her. He wore English country clothes and looked very much the country squire. He had not aged at all—indeed, he looked younger. In his hand he held some letters.

"I've agreed to share that shooting with Drummond. I think we'll enjoy it."

"I'm so glad."

"We must decide who we want to ask."

"Yes, we'll talk about it tonight. I'm rather glad the Hays couldn't come and dine. It will be nice to have an evening to ourselves."

"I was afraid you were overdoing it in town, Nell."

"We *did* rush about, rather. But I think it's good for one really. And anyway, it's been splendidly peaceful down here."

"It's wonderful." George threw an appreciative glance over the land-scape. "I'd rather have Abbots Puissants than any place in England. It's got an atmosphere."

Nell nodded.

"I know what you mean."

"I should hate to think of it in the hands of—well, people like the Levinnes, for instance."

"I know. One would resent it. And yet Sebastian is a dear—and his taste, at any rate, is perfect."

"He knows the taste of the public all right," said George dryly. "One success after another—with occasionally a *succès d'estine*, just to show he's not a mere moneymaker. He's beginning to look the part though—getting not exactly fat, but sleek. Adopting all sorts of mannerisms. There's a caricature of him in *Punch* this week. Very clever."

"Sebastian would lend himself to caricaturing," said Nell smiling. "Those enormous ears, and those funny high cheekbones. He was an extraordinary-looking boy."

"It's odd to think of you all playing together as children. By the way, I've got a surprise for you. A friend you haven't seen for some time is coming to lunch today."

"Not Josephine."

"No. Jane Harding."

"Jane Harding! But how on earth—?"

"I ran into her at Wiltsbury yesterday. She's on tour, acting in some company or other."

"Jane! Why, George, I didn't even realize you knew her?"

"I came across her when we were both doing relief work in Serbia. I saw a lot of her. I wrote to you about it."

"Did you? I don't remember."

Something in her tone seemed to strike him and he said anxiously: "It's all right, isn't it, dear? I thought it would be a pleasant surprise for you. I always thought she was a great friend of yours. I can put her off in a minute if—"

"No, no. Of course, I'll be delighted to see her. I was only surprised."

George was reassured.

"That's all right then. By the way, she told me that a man called

Bleibner, a man I knew very well in New York, is also in Wiltsbury. I'd like him to see the Abbey ruins—that sort of thing is a specialty of his. Do you mind if I ask him to lunch, too?"

"No, of course not. Do ask him."

"I'll see if I can get him on the phone now. I meant to do it last night, but it slipped my memory."

He went indoors again. Nell was left on the terrace frowning slightly.

George in this had been right. For some reason or other, she was not pleased at the thought of Jane's coming to lunch. She felt very definitely that she didn't want to see Jane. Already, the mere mention of Jane seemed to have disturbed the serenity of the morning. She thought: "I was so peaceful and now—"

Annoying—yes, it was annoying. She was, had always been, afraid of Jane. Jane was the kind of person you could never be sure about. She—how could one put it?—she upset things. She was disturbing, and Nell didn't want to be disturbed.

She thought unreasonably: "Why on earth did George have to meet her in Serbia? How trying things are."

But it was absurd to be afraid of Jane. Jane couldn't hurt her—now. Poor Jane, she must have made rather a mess of things, to have come down to acting in a touring company.

One must be loyal to one's old friends. Jane was an old friend. She should see how loyal Nell could be. And with a glow of self-approval she went upstairs and changed into a dress of dove-colored georgette with which she wore one very beautifully matched string of pearls that George had given her on the last anniversary of their marriage. She took particular pains over her toilet, satisfying thereby some obscure female instinct.

"At any rate," she thought, "the Bleibner man will be there and that will make things easier."

Though why she expected things to be difficult she could not have explained.

George came up to fetch her just as she was applying a final dusting of powder.

"Jane's arrived," he said. "She's in the drawing room."

"And Mr. Bleibner?"

"He's engaged for lunch, unfortunately. But he's coming along this afternoon."

"Oh!"

She went downstairs slowly. Absurd to feel so apprehensive. Poor Jane—one simply must be nice to her. It was such terribly bad luck to have lost her voice and come down to this.

Jane, however, did not seem aware of bad luck. She was sprawling back on the sofa in an attitude of easy unconcern, looking round the room with keen appreciation.

"Hullo, Nell," she said. "Well, you seem to have dug yourself in pretty comfortably."

It was an outrageous remark. Nell stiffened. She couldn't think for a moment of what to say. She met Jane's eyes, which were full of mocking maliciousness. They shook hands and Nell said at the same time: "I don't know what you mean."

Jane subsided on the sofa again.

"I meant all this. Palatial dwelling, well-proportioned footmen, highly paid cook, soft-footed servants, possibly a French maid, baths prepared for one with the latest unguents and bath salts, five or six gardeners, luxurious limousines, expensive clothes, and, I perceive, genuine pearls! Are you enjoying it all frightfully? I am sure you are."

"Tell me about yourself," said Nell, seating herself beside Jane on the sofa.

Jane's eyes narrowed.

"That's a very clever answer. And I fully deserved it. Sorry, Nell. I was a beast. But you were being so queenly and so gracious. I never can stand people being gracious."

She got up and began to stroll round the room.

"So this is Vernon's home," she said softly. "I've never seen it before—only heard him talk about it."

She was silent for a minute, then asked abruptly: "How much have you changed?"

Nell explained that everything had been left as it was, as far as possible. Curtains, covers, carpets, and so forth, had all been renewed. The old ones were too shabby. And one or two priceless pieces of furniture had been added. Whenever George came across anything that was in keeping with the place he bought it.

Jane's eyes were fixed on her while she made this explanation, and Nell felt uneasy because she couldn't read the expression in them.

George came in before she had finished talking and they went in to lunch.

The talk was at first of Serbia, of a few mutual friends out there. Then they passed on to Jane's affairs. George referred delicately to Jane's voice—the sorrow he had felt, that everyone must feel. Jane passed it off carelessly enough.

"My own fault," she said. "I would sing a certain kind of music and my voice wasn't made for it."

Sebastian Levinne, she went on to say, had been a wonderful friend. He was willing now to star her in London, but she had wished to learn her trade first.

"Singing in opera is, of course, acting too. But there are all sorts of things to learn—to manage one's speaking voice, for instance. And then one's effects are all different—they must be more subtle, less broad."

Next autumn, she explained, she was to appear in London in a dramatized version of *Tosca*.

Then, dismissing her own affairs, she began to talk of Abbots Puissants. She led George on to discuss his plans, his ideas about the estate. He was made to display himself the complete country squire.

There was, apparently, no mockery in Jane's eyes or her voice, but nevertheless Nell felt acutely uncomfortable. She wished George would stop talking. It was a little ridiculous, the way he spoke as though he and his forefathers before him had lived for centuries at Abbots Puissants.

After coffee they went out on the terrace again, and here George was summoned to the telephone and left them with a word of excuse. Nell suggested a tour through the gardens and Jane acquiesced.

"I'd like to see everything," she said.

Nell thought: "It's Vernon's home she wants to see. That's why she's come. But Vernon never meant to her what he meant to me!"

She had a passionate desire to vindicate herself, to make Jane see—

See what? She didn't quite know herself, but she felt that Jane was judging her—condemning her, even.

She stopped suddenly as they were walking down a long herbaceous border, gay with Michaelmas daisies against the old rose-colored brick wall behind it.

"Jane. I want to tell you—to explain—"

She paused, gathering herself together. Jane merely looked at her inquiringly.

"You must think it—very dreadful of me—marrying again so soon."

"Not at all," said Jane. "It was very sensible."

Nell didn't want that. That wasn't the point of view at all.

"I adored Vernon—*adored* him. When he was killed it nearly broke my heart. I mean it. But I knew so well that he himself wouldn't wish me to grieve. The dead don't want us to grieve—"

"Don't they?"

Nell stared at her.

"Oh! I know you're voicing the popular idea," said Jane. "The dead want us to be brave and bear up and carry on as usual. They hate us being unhappy about them. That's what everybody goes about saying—but I never have seen that they've any foundation for that cheering belief. I think they've invented it themselves to make things easier for them. The living don't all want exactly the same thing, so I don't see why the dead should either. There must be heaps of selfish dead. If they exist at all, they must be very much the same as they were in life. They can't be full of beautiful and unselfish feelings all at once. It always makes me laugh when I see a bereaved widower tucking into his breakfast the day after the funeral and saying solemnly: 'Mary wouldn't wish me to grieve!' How does he know? Mary may be simply weeping and gnashing her teeth (astral teeth, of course) at seeing him going on as usual, just as though she had never existed. Heaps of women like a fuss made over them. Why should they change their characters when they're dead?"

Nell was silent. She couldn't for the moment collect her thoughts.

"Not that I mean Vernon was like that," went on Jane. "He may really have wished you not to grieve. You'd know best about that, because you knew him better than anyone else."

"Yes," said Nell eagerly. "That's just it. I know he would want me to be happy. And he wanted me to have Abbots Puissants. I know he'd love to think of my being here."

"He wanted to live here with you. That's not quite the same thing."

"No, but it isn't as though I were living here with George as—as it would have been with him. Oh! Jane, I want to make you understand. George is a dear, but he isn't—he can never be—what—what Vernon was to me."

There was a long pause and then Jane said: "You're lucky, Nell."

"If you think I really love all this luxury! Why, for Vernon I'd give it up in a minute!"

"I wonder."

"Jane! You—"

"You think you would, but—I wonder."

"I did before."

"No—you only gave up the prospect of it. That's different. It hadn't eaten into you as it has now."

"Jane!"

Nell's eyes filled with tears. She turned away.

"My dear, I'm being a beast. There's no harm in what you've done. I dare say you're right—about Vernon wishing it. You need kindness and protection—but all the same, soft living does eat into one. You'll know what I mean someday. By the way, I didn't mean what you thought when I said just now that you were lucky. By lucky, I meant that you'd had the best of both worlds. If you'd married your George when you originally intended, you'd have gone through life with a secret regret, a longing for Vernon, a feeling that you'd been cheated out of life through your own cowardice. And if Vernon had lived you might have grown away from each other, quarreled, come to hate each other. But as it is, you've had Vernon, made your sacrifice. You've got him where nothing can ever touch him. Love will be a thing of beauty to you forever. And you've got all the other things as well. This!"

She swept her arm around in a sudden embracing gesture.

Nell had hardly paid any attention to the end part of the speech. Her eyes had grown soft and melting.

"I know. Everything turns out for the best. They tell you so when you're a child and later you find it out for yourself. God does know best."

"What do you know about God, Nell Chetwynd?"

There was a savagery in the question that brought Nell's eyes to Jane in astonishment. She looked menacing—fiercely accusing. The gentleness of a minute ago was gone.

"The will of God! Would you be able to say that, if God's will didn't happen to coincide with Nell Chetwynd's comfort, I wonder? You don't know anything about God or you couldn't have spoken like that, gently patting God on the back for making life comfortable and easy for you. Do you know a text that used to frighten me in the Bible? *This night shall thy soul be required of thee.* When God requires *your* soul of you, be sure you've got a soul to give him!"

She paused and then said quietly: "I'll go now. I shouldn't have come. But I wanted to see Vernon's home. I apologize for what what I've said. But you're so damned smug, Nell. You don't know it, but you are. Smug—that's the word. Life to you means yourself, and yourself only. What about Vernon? Was it best for him? Do you think *he* wanted to die—right at the beginning of everything he cared for?"

Nell flung her head back defiantly.

"I made him happy."

"I wasn't thinking of his happiness. I was thinking of his music. You and Abbots Puissants—what do you matter? Vernon had genius. That's the wrong way of putting it—he *belonged* to his genius. And genius is the hardest master there is—everything has got to be sacrificed to it. Your trumpery happiness, even, would have had to go if it stood in the way. Genius has got to be served. Music wanted Vernon—and he's dead. That's the crying shame, the thing that matters, the thing you never even consider. I know why—because you were afraid of it, Nell. It doesn't make for peace and happiness and security. But I tell you, *it's got to be served.*"

Suddenly her face relaxed, the old mocking light that Nell hated came back to her eyes. She said:

"Don't worry, Nell. You're much the strongest of us all. Protective coloring! I told Sebastian so long ago, and I was right. You'll endure when we've all perished. Good-bye. I'm sorry I've been a devil, but I'm made that way."

Nell stood staring after her retreating figure. She clenched her hands and said under her breath:

"I hate you. I've always hated you."

3

The day had begun so peacefully—and now it was spoiled. Tears came into Nell's eyes. Why couldn't people let her alone? Jane and her horrid sneering. Jane was a beast—an uncanny beast. She knew where things hurt you most.

Why, even Joe had said that she, Nell, was quite right to marry George! Joe had understood perfectly. Nell felt aggrieved and hurt. Why should Jane be so horrid? And saying things like that about the dead—irreligious things—when everyone knew that the dead liked one to be brave and cheerful.

The impertinence of Jane to hurl a text at her head! A woman like Jane, who had lived with people and done all kinds of immoral things. Nell felt a glow of superior virtue. In spite of everything that was said nowadays, there were two kinds of women. She belonged to one kind and Jane to the other. Jane was attractive—that kind of woman always was attractive. That was why in the past she had felt afraid of Jane. Jane had some queer power over men—she was bad through and through.

Thinking these thoughts, Nell paced restlessly up and down. She felt disinclined to go back to the house. In any case, there was nothing particular to do this afternoon. There were some letters that must be written sometime, but she really couldn't settle to them at present.

She had forgotten about her husband's American friend, and was quite surprised when George joined her with Mr. Bleibner in tow. The American was a tall thin man, very precise. He paid her grave compliments on the house. They were now, he explained, going to view the ruins of the Abbey. George suggested she should come with them.

"You go on," said Nell. "I'll follow you presently. I must get a hat. The sun is so hot."

"Shall I get it for you, dear?"

"No, thanks. You and Mr. Bleibner go on. You'll be ages pottering about there, I know."

"Why, I should say that is very certain to be the case, Mrs. Chetwynd. I understand your husband has some idea of restoring the Abbey. That is very interesting."

"It's one of our many projects, Mr. Bleibner."

"You are fortunate to own this place. By the way, I hope you've no objection. I told my chauffeur (with your husband's assent, naturally) that he might stroll round the grounds. He is a most intelligent young man of quite a superior class."

"That's quite all right. And if he'd like to see the house the butler can take him over to it later."

"Now I call that very kind of you, Mrs. Chetwynd. What I feel is that we want beauty appreciated by all classes. The idea that's going to weld together the League of Nations—"

Nell felt suddenly that she couldn't bear to hear Mr. Bleibner's views on the League of Nations. They were sure to be ponderous and lengthy. She excused herself on the plea of the hot sun.

Some Americans could be very boring. What a mercy George was not like that! Dear George—really, he was very nearly perfect. She experienced again that warm happy feeling that had surged over her earlier in the day.

What an idiot she was to have let herself be upset by Jane! *Jane* of all people! What did it matter what Jane said or thought? It didn't, of course, but there was something about Jane—she had the power of— well—upsetting one.

But that was all over now. The old tide of reassurance and safety welled up again. Abbots Puissants, George, the tender memory of Vernon. Everything was all right.

She ran down the stairs happily, hat in hand. She paused a minute to adjust it in front of the mirror. She would go now and join them at the Abbey. She would make herself absolutely charming to Mr. Bleibner.

She went down the steps of the terrace and along the garden walk. It was later than she thought. The sun was not far from setting—a beautiful sunset with a crimson sky.

By the goldfish pond a young man in chauffeur's livery was standing with his back to her. He turned at her approach and civilly raised a finger to his cap.

She stopped stock-still, and slowly an unconscious hand crept up to her heart as she stood there staring.

4

George Green stared.

Then he ejaculated to himself: "Well, that's a rum go!"

On arrival at their destination his master had said to him: "This is one of the oldest and most interesting places in England, Green. I shall be here at least an hour—perhaps longer. I will ask Mr. Chetwynd if you may stroll about the grounds."

A kind old buffer, Green thought indulgently, but terribly keen on what was called "uplift." Couldn't let one alone. And he had that extraordinary American reverence for anything that was hallowed by antiquity.

Certainly, this was a nice old place, though. He looked up at it appreciatively. He'd seen pictures of it somewhere, he was sure. He wouldn't mind having a stroll round as he'd been told to do so.

It was well kept up, he noticed that. Who owned it? Some American chap? These Americans, they had all the money. He wondered who had owned it originally. Whoever it was must have been sick at having to let it go.

He thought wistfully: "I wish I'd been born a toff. I'd like to own a place like this."

He wandered some way through the gardens. In the distance he noticed a heap of ruins and amongst them two figures, one of which he recognized as being that of his employer. Funny old josser—always poking about ruins.

The sun was setting, there was a wonderful lurid sky, and against it Abbots Puissants stood out in all its beauty.

Funny, the way you thought of things as having happened before! Just for a minute Green could have sworn that he had once stood just where he was standing now and seen the house outlined against a red sky. Could swear, too, that he had felt just that same keen pang as of something that hurt. But it wanted something else—a woman with red hair like the sunset.

There was a step behind him and he started and turned. For a minute he felt a vague pang of disappointment. For standing there was a young slender woman, and her hair, escaping each side from under her hat, was golden, not red.

He touched his cap respectfully.

A queer sort of lady, he thought. She stared at him with every bit of color draining slowly from her face. She looked absolutely terrified.

Then, with a sudden gasp, she turned and almost ran down the path. It was then that he ejaculated: "Well, that's a rum go!"

She must, he decided, be a bit queer in the head.

He resumed his aimless strolling.

Chapter Two

Sebastian Levinne was in his office going into the details of a ticklish contract when a telegram was brought to him. He opened it carelessly, for he received forty or fifty telegrams a day. After he had read it he held it in his hand, looking at it.

Then he crumpled it up, slipped it into his pocket, and spoke to Lewis, his right-hand man.

"Get on with this thing as best you can," he said curtly. "I'm called out of town."

He took no heed of the protestations that arose, but left the room. He paused to tell his secretary to see to the canceling of various appointments and then went home, packed a bag, and took a taxi to Waterloo. There he unfolded the telegram again and read it:

> Please come at once if you can very urgent Jane Wilts Hotel Wiltsbury.

It was a proof of his confidence and respect for Jane that he never hesitated. He trusted Jane as he trusted no one else in the world. If Jane said a thing was urgent, it was urgent. He obeyed the summons without wasting a thought of regret on the necessary complications it would cause. For no one else in the world, be it said, would he have done that.

On arriving at Wiltsbury he drove straight to the hotel and asked for her. She had engaged a private room, and there she met him with outstretched hands.

"Sebastian, my dear, you've been marvelously quick."

"I came at once." He slipped off his coat and threw it over the back of a chair. "What is it, Jane?"

"It's Vernon."

Sebastian looked puzzled.

"What about him?"

"He's not dead. I've seen him."

Sebastian stared at her for a minute, then drew a chair to the table and sat down.

"It's not like you, Jane, but I think, for once in your life, you must have been mistaken."

"I wasn't mistaken. It's possible, I suppose, for the War Office to have made an error?"

"Errors have been made more than once—but they've usually been contradicted fairly soon. It stands to reason that they must be. If Vernon's alive, what's he been doing all this time?"

She shook her head.

"That I can't say. But I'm as sure about its being Vernon as I am that it's you here now."

She spoke curtly but very confidently.

He stared at her very hard, then nodded.

"Tell me," he said.

Jane spoke quietly and composedly.

"There's an American here, a Mr. Bleibner. I met him out in Serbia. We recognized each other in the street. He told me he was staying at the County Hotel and asked me to lunch today. I went. Afterward it was raining. He wouldn't hear of my walking back. His car was there and would take me. His car did take me. Sebastian, the chauffeur was Vernon—*and he didn't know me.*"

Sebastian considered the matter.

"You're sure you weren't deceived by some strong resemblance?"

"Perfectly sure."

"Then why didn't Vernon recognize you? He was pretending, I suppose."

"No, I don't think so—in fact, I'm sure he wasn't. He would be bound to give some sign—a start—something. He couldn't have been *expecting* to see me. He couldn't have controlled his first surprise. Besides, he looked—different."

"How different?"

Jane considered.

"It's hard to explain. Rather happy and jolly and—just faintly—like his mother."

"Extraordinary," said Sebastian. "I'm glad you sent for me. If it *is* Vernon—well, it's going to be the devil of a business. Nell having married again and everything. We don't want reporters coming down like wolves on the fold. I suppose there'll have to be *some* publicity." He got up, walked up and down. "The first thing is to get hold of Bleibner."

"I telephoned to him, asking him to be here at six-thirty. I didn't dare leave, though I was afraid you wouldn't be able to get here so soon. Bleibner will be here any minute."

"Good for you, Jane. We must hear what he's got to say."

There was a knock at the door and Mr. Bleibner was announced. Jane rose to meet him.

"It's very good of you to come, Mr. Bleibner," she began.

"Not at all," said the American. "Always delighted to oblige a lady. And you said that the matter you wanted to see me about was urgent."

"It is. This is Mr. Sebastian Levinne."

"*The* Mr. Sebastian Levinne? I'm very pleased to meet you, sir."

The two men shook hands.

"And now, Mr. Bleibner," said Jane. "I'll come straight to what I want to talk to you about. How long have you had your chauffeur, and what can you tell us about him?"

Mr. Bleibner was plainly surprised and showed it.

"Green? You want to know about Green?"

"Yes."

"Well—" The American reflected. "I've no objections to telling you what I know. I guess you wouldn't ask without a good reason. I know you well enough for that, Miss Harding. I picked up Green in Holland not long after the Armistice. He was working in a local garage. I discovered he was an Englishman and began to take an interest in him. I asked him his history and he was pretty vague about it. I thought at first he had something to conceal, but I soon convinced myself that he was genuine enough. The man was in a kind of mental fog. He knew his name and where he came from, but very little else."

"Lost memory," said Sebastian softly. "I see."

"His father was killed in the South African war, he told me. He remembered his father singing in the village choir, and he remembered a brother whom he used to call Squirrel."

"And he was quite sure about his own name?"

"Oh! yes. As a matter of fact, he'd got it written down in a small pocketbook. There was an accident, you know, He was knocked down by a lorry. That's how they knew who he was. They asked him if his name was Green and he said Yes—George. He was very popular at the garage, he was so sunny and lighthearted. I don't believe I've ever seen Green out of temper.

"Well, I took a fancy to the young chap. I've seen a few shell-shocked cases and his state wasn't any mystery to me. He showed me the entry in his pocketbook and I made a few inquiries. I soon found the reason—there always is a reason, you know—for his loss of memory. Corporal George Green, London Fusiliers, was a deserter.

"There, you have it. He'd funked things—and being a decent young fellow really, he couldn't face the fact. I explained it all to him. He said, rather wonderingly: 'I shouldn't have thought I could ever desert—not *desert*.' I explained to him that that point of view was just the reason he couldn't remember. He couldn't remember because he didn't want to remember.

"He listened but I don't think he was very convinced. I felt, and still feel, extremely sorry for him. I didn't think there was any obligation on my part to report his existence to the military authorities. I took him into my service and offered him a chance to make good. I've never had cause to regret it. He's an excellent chauffeur—punctual, intelligent, a good mechanic, and always sunny-tempered and obliging."

Mr. Bleibner paused and looked inquiringly at Jane and Sebastian. Their pale serious faces impressed him.

"It's frightening," said Jane in her low voice. "It's one of the most frightening things that could happen."

Sebastian took her hand and squeezed it.

"It's all right, Jane."

Jane roused herself with a slight shiver and spoke to the American.

"I think it's our turn to explain. You see, Mr. Bleibner, in your chauffeur I recognized an old friend—and he didn't recognize me."

"In—deed!"

"But his name wasn't Green," said Sebastian.

"No? You mean he enlisted under another name?"

"No. There's something there that seems incomprehensible. I suppose we shall get at it someday. In the meantime, I will ask you, Mr. Bleibner, not to repeat this conversation to *anyone*. There's a wife in the matter, and—oh! many other considerations."

"My dear sir," said Mr. Bleibner, "you can trust me to be absolutely silent. But what next? Do you want to see Green?"

Sebastian looked at Jane and she bowed her head.

"Yes," said Sebastian slowly. "I think perhaps that would be the best plan."

The American rose.

"He's below now. He brought me here. I'll send him up right away."

2

George Green mounted the stairs with his usual buoyant step. As he did so he wondered what had happened to upset the old josser—by that term meaning his employer. Very queer the old buffer had looked.

"The door at the top of the stairs," Mr. Bleibner had said.

George Green rapped on it sharply with his knuckles and waited. A voice called "Come in" and he obeyed.

There were two people in the room—the lady he had driven home today (whom he thought of in his own mind as a tip-topper) and a big, rather fat man with a very yellow face and projecting ears. His face seemed vaguely familiar to the chauffeur. For a moment he stood there while they both stared at him. He thought: "What's the matter with everybody this evening?"

He said, "Yes, sir?" in a respectful voice to the yellow gentleman. He went on: "Mr. Bleibner told me to come up."

The yellow gentleman seemed to recover himself.

"Yes, yes," he said. "That's right. Sit down—er—Green. That's your name, isn't it?"

"Yes, sir. George Green."

He sat down respectfully in the chair indicated. The yellow gentleman handed him a cigarette case and said, "Help yourself." And all the time, his eyes, small piercing eyes, never left Green's face. That intent burning gaze made the chauffeur uneasy. What *was* up with everyone tonight?

"I wanted to ask you a few questions. To begin with, have you ever seen me before?"

Green shook his head.

"No, sir."

"Sure?" persisted the other.

A faint trace of uncertainty crept into Green's voice.

"I—I don't think so," he said doubtfully.

"My name is Sebastian Levinne."

The chauffeur's face cleared.

"Of course, sir, I've seen your picture in the papers. I thought it seemed familiar somehow."

There was a pause, and then Sebastian Levinne asked casually: "Have you ever heard the name of Vernon Deyre?"

"Vernon Deyre," Green repeated the name thoughtfully. He frowned perplexedly. "The name seems somehow familiar to me, sir, but I can't quite place it." He paused, the frown deepening. "I think I've heard it." And then added, "The gentleman's dead, isn't he?"

"So that's your impression, is it? That the gentleman is dead."

"Yes, sir, and a good—"

He stopped suddenly, crimsoning.

"Go on," said Levinne. "What were you going to say?" He added shrewdly, perceiving where the trouble lay. "You need not mince your words. Mr. Deyre was no relation of mine."

The chauffeur accepted the implication.

"I was going to say a good job, too—but I don't know that I ought to say it, since I can't remember anything about him. But I've got a kind of impression that—well, that he was best out of the way, so to speak. Made rather a mess of things, hadn't he?"

"You knew him?"

The frown deepened in an agony of attempted recollection.

"I'm sorry, sir," the chauffeur apologized. "Since the war things seemed to have got a bit mixed up. I can't always recollect things clearly. I don't know where I came across Mr. Deyre, and why I disliked him, but I do know that I'm thankful to hear that he's dead. He was no good—you can take my word for that."

There was a silence, only broken by something like a smothered sob from the other occupant of the room. Levinne turned to her.

"Telephone to the theater, Jane," he said. "You can't appear tonight."

She nodded and left the room. Levinne looked after her and then said abruptly:

"You've seen Miss Harding before?"

"Yes, sir. I drove her home today."

Levinne sighed. Green looked at him inquiringly.

"Is—is that all, sir? I'm sorry to have been so little use. I know I've been a bit—well, queer since the war. My own fault. Perhaps Mr. Bleibner told you—I—didn't do my duty as I should have done."

His face flushed but he brought out the words resolutely. Had the old josser told them or not? Better to say that anyway. At the same time, a pang of shame pierced him keenly. He was a deserter, a man who had run away! A rotten business.

Jane Harding came back into the room and resumed her place behind the table. She looked paler than when she had gone out, Green thought. Curious eyes she had—so deep and tragic. He wondered what she was thinking about. Perhaps she had been engaged to this Mr. Deyre. No, Mr. Levinne wouldn't have urged him to speak out if that had been the case. It was probably all to do with money. A will, or something like that.

Mr. Levinne began questioning him again. He made no reference to the last sentence.

"Your father was killed in the Boer War, I believe?"

"Yes, sir."

"You remember him?"

"Oh! yes, sir."

"What did he look like?"

Green smiled. The memory was pleasant to him.

"A burly sort of chap. Muttonchop whiskers. Very bright blue eyes. I remember him as well as anything singing in the choir. Baritone voice he had."

He smiled happily.

"And he was killed in the Boer War?"

A sudden look of doubt crept into Green's face. He seemed worried—distressed. His eyes looked pathetically across the table like a dog at fault.

"It's queer," he said. "I never thought of that. He'd be too old. He—and yet I'd swear—I'm sure—"

The look of distress in his eyes was so acute that the other said, "Never mind," and went on: "Are you married, Green?"

"No, sir."

The answer came with prompt assurance.

"You seem very certain about that," said Mr. Levinne, smiling.

"I am, sir. It leads to nothing but trouble—mixing yourself up with women." He stopped abruptly and said to Jane: "I beg your pardon."

She smiled faintly and said: "It doesn't matter."

There was a pause. Levinne turned to her and said something so quickly that Green could not catch it. It sounded like:

"Extraordinary likeness to Sydney Bent. Never imagined it was there."

Then they both stared at him again.

And suddenly he was afraid—definitely childishly afraid—in the same way that he remembered being afraid of the dark when he was a baby.

There was something up—that was how he put it to himself—and these two knew it. Something about him.

He leaned forward, acutely apprehensive.

"What's the matter?" he said sharply. "There's something . . ."

They didn't deny it—just continued to look at him.

And his terror grew. Why couldn't they tell a chap? They knew something that he didn't. Something dreadful. He said again, and this time his voice was high and shrill:

"What's the matter?"

The lady got up—he noticed in the background of his mind as it were how splendidly she moved. She was like a statue he'd seen somewhere. She came round the table and laid a hand on his shoulder. She said comfortingly and reassuringly: "It's all right. You mustn't be frightened."

But Green's eyes continued to question Levinne. This man knew—this man was going to tell him. What was this horrible thing that they knew and he didn't?

"Very odd things have happened in this war," began Levinne. "People have sometimes forgotten their own names."

He paused significantly, but the significance was lost on Green. He said with a momentary return to cheerfulness:

"I'm not as bad as that. I've never forgotten my name."

"But you *have*." He stopped, then went on: "Your real name is Vernon Deyre."

The announcement ought to have been dramatic, but it wasn't. The words seemed to Green simply silly. He looked amused.

"I'm Mr. Vernon Deyre? You mean I'm his double or something?"

"I mean you *are* him."

Green laughed frankly.

"I can't monkey about with that stuff, sir. Not even if it means a title or a fortune! Whatever the resemblance, I'd be bound to be found out."

Sebastian Levinne leaned forward over the table and rapped out each word separately, with emphasis.

"You—are—Vernon—Deyre."

Green stared. The emphasis impressed him.

"You're kidding me?"

Levinne slowly shook his head. Green turned suddenly to the woman who stood beside him. Her eyes, very grave and absolutely assured, met his. She said very quietly:

"You are Vernon Deyre. We both know it."

There was dead silence in the room. To Green, it seemed as though the whole world were spinning round. It was like a fairy story, fantastic and impossible. And yet something about these two compelled credence. He said uncertainly:

"But—but things don't happen like that. You couldn't forget your own name!"

"Evidently—since you have done so."

"But—but, look here, sir, I *know* I'm George Green. I—well, I just know it!"

He looked at them triumphantly, but slowly and remorselessly Sebastian Levinne shook his head.

"I don't know how that's come about," he said. "A doctor would probably be able to tell you. But I do know this—that you are my friend Vernon Deyre. There is no possible doubt of that."

"But—but, if that's true, I ought to know it."

He felt bewildered, horribly uncertain. A strange sickening world where you couldn't be sure of anything. These were kindly sane people; he trusted them. What they said must be so—and yet something in him refused to be convinced. They were sorry for him—he felt that. And that frightened him. There was something more yet—something that he hadn't been told.

"Who is he?" he said sharply. "This Vernon Deyre, I mean."

"You come from this part of the world. You were born and spent most of your childhood at a place called Abbots Puissants—"

Green interrupted him in astonishment.

"Abbots Puissants? Why, I drove Mr. Bleibner there yesterday. And you say it's my old home, and I never recognized it!"

He felt suddenly buoyed up and scornful. The whole thing was a pack of lies! Of course it was! He had known it all the time. These people were honest, but they were mistaken. He felt relieved—happier.

"After that you went to live near Birmingham," continued Levinne. "You went to school at Eton and from there you went on to Cambridge.

After that you went to London and studied music. You composed an opera."

Green laughed outright.

"There you're quite wrong, sir. Why, I don't know one note of music from another."

"The war broke out. You obtained a commission in the yeomanry. You were married—" he paused, but Green gave no sign—"and went out to France. In the spring of the following year you were reported Killed in Action."

Green stared at him incredulously. What sort of a rigmarole was this? He couldn't remember a thing about any of it.

"There must be some mistake," he said confidently. "Mr. Deyre must have been what they call my 'double.'"

"There is no mistake, Vernon," said Jane Harding.

Green looked from her to Sebastian. The confident intimacy of her tone had done more to convince him than anything else. He thought: "This is awful. A nightmare. Such things can't happen." He began to shake all over, unable to stop.

Levinne got up, mixed him a stiff drink from materials that stood on a tray in the corner and brought it back to him.

"Swallow this," he said. "And you'll feel better. It's been a shock."

Green gulped down the draught. It steadied him. The trembling ceased.

"Before God, sir," he said, "is this true?"

"Before God, it is," said Sebastian.

He brought a chair forward, sat down close by his friend.

"Vernon, dear old chap—don't you remember me at all?"

Green stared at him—an anguished stare. Something seemed to stir ever so faintly. How it hurt, this trying to remember! There was *something*—what was it. He said doubtfully:

"You—you've grown up." He stretched out a hand and touched Sebastian's ear. "I seem to remember—"

"He remembers your ears, Sebastian," cried Jane, and going over to the mantelpiece she laid her head down upon it and began to laugh.

"Stop it, Jane." Sebastian rose, poured out another drink and took it to her. "Some medicine for you."

She drank it, handed the glass back to him, smiled faintly, and said: "I'm sorry. I won't do it again."

Green was going on with his discoveries.

"You're—you're not a brother, are you? No, you lived next door. That's it—you lived next door."

"That's right, old chap." Sebastian patted him on the shoulder. "Don't worry to think—it'll come back soon. Take it easy."

Green looked at Jane. He said timidly and politely: "Were you—are you—my sister? I seem to remember something about a sister."

Jane shook her head, unable to speak. Green flushed.

"I'm sorry. I shouldn't have—"

Sebastian interrupted.

"You didn't have a sister. There was a cousin who lived with you. Her name was Josephine. We called her Joe."

Green pondered.

"Josephine—Joe. Yes, I seem to remember something about that." He paused and then reiterated pathetically: "Are you *sure* my name isn't Green?"

"Quite sure. Do you still feel it is?"

"Yes. . . . And you say I made up music—music of my own? Highbrow stuff—not ragtime?"

"Yes."

"It all seems—well, mad. Just that—mad!"

"You mustn't worry," said Jane gently. "I dare say we have been wrong to tell you all this the way we have."

Green looked from one to the other of them. He felt dazed.

"What am I to do?" he asked helplessly.

Sebastian gave an answer with decision.

"You must stay here with us. You've had a great shock, you know. I'll go and square things with old Bleibner. He's a very decent chap and he'll understand."

"I shouldn't like to put him out in any way. He's been a thundering good boss to me."

"He'll understand. I've already told him something."

"What about the car? I don't like to think of another chap driving that car. She's running now as sweetly—"

He was once again the chauffeur, intent on his charge.

"I know. I know." Sebastian was impatient. "But the great thing, my dear fellow, is to get you right as soon as possible. We want to get a first-class doctor on to you."

"What's a doctor got to do with it?" Green was slightly hostile. "I'm perfectly fit."

"Perhaps a doctor ought to see you all the same. Not here—in London. We don't want any talk down here."

Something in the tone of the speaker's voice attracted Green's attention. The flush came over his face.

"You mean the deserting business."

"No, no. To tell the truth, I can't get the hang of that. I mean something quite different."

Green looked at him inquiringly.

Sebastian thought: "Well, I suppose he's got to know sometime." Aloud he said:

"You see, thinking you were dead, you wife has—well—married again."

He was a little afraid of the effect of those words. But Green seemed to see the matter in a humorous light.

"That *is* a bit awkward," he said with a grin.

"It doesn't upset you in any way?"

"You can't be upset by a thing you don't remember." He paused, as though really considering the matter for the first time. "Was Mr. Deyre—I mean, was I—fond of her?"

"Well—yes."

But again the grin came over Green's face.

"And I to be so positive I wasn't married. All the same"—his face changed—"it's rather frightening—all this!"

He looked suddenly at Jane, as though seeking assurance.

"Dear Vernon," she said, "it will be all right."

She paused, and then said in a quiet casual tone: "You drove Mr. Bleibner over to Abbots Puissants, you say. Did you—did you see anyone there? Any of the people of the house?"

"I saw Mr. Chetwynd—and I saw a lady in the sunk gardens. I took her to be Mrs. Chetwynd, fair-haired and good-looking."

"Did—did she see you?"

"Yes. Seemed—well, scared. Went dead-white and bolted like a rab-bit."

"Oh, God!" said Jane, and bit off the exclamation almost before it was uttered.

Green was cogitating quietly over the matter.

"Perhaps she thought she knew me," he said. "She must have been one of them who knew him—me—in the old days, and it gave her a turn. Yes, that must have been it."

He was quite happy with his solution.

Suddenly he asked: "Had my mother got red hair?"

Jane nodded.

"Then that was it." He looked up apologetically. "Sorry. I was just thinking of something."

"I'll go and see Bleibner now," said Sebastian. "Jane will look after you."

He left the room. Green leaned forward in his chair, his head held between his hands. He felt acutely uncomfortable and miserable—es-pecially with Jane. Clearly he ought to know her—and he didn't. She had said "Dear Vernon" just now. It was terribly awkward when people knew you and you felt they were strangers. If he spoke to her he sup-posed he ought to call her Jane—but he couldn't. She was a stranger. Still, he supposed he'd have to get used to it. They'd have to be Sebastian and George and Jane together—no, not George—Vernon. Silly sort of name, Vernon. Probably he'd been a silly sort of chap.

"I mean," he thought, trying desperately to force the realization upon himself, "*I* must have been a silly sort of chap."

He felt horribly lonely—cut off from reality. He looked up to find Jane watching him, and the pity and understanding in her eyes made him feel a shade less forlorn.

"It's rather terrible just at first, isn't it?" she said.

He said politely: "It is rather difficult. You don't—you don't know where you are with things."

"I understand."

She said no more, just sat there quietly beside him. His head jerked forward. He began to doze. In reality he only slept for a few minutes, but it seemed to him hours. Jane had turned all the lamps out but one. He woke with a start. She said quickly:

"It's all right."

He stared at her, his breath coming in gasps. He was still in the nightmare then, he hadn't wakened. And there was something worse to come—something he didn't know yet. He was sure of it. That was why they all looked at him so pityingly.

Jane got up suddenly. Wildly, he cried out:

"Stay with me. Oh! please stay with me."

He couldn't understand why her face should suddenly twist with pain. What was there in what he had said to make her look like that? He said again: "Don't leave me. Stay with me."

She sat down again beside him and took his hand in hers. She said very gently:

"I won't go away."

He felt soothed, reassured. After a minute or two he dozed again. He woke quietly this time. The room was as before and his hand was still in Jane's. He spoke diffidently:

"You—you aren't my sister? You were—you are, I mean—a friend of mine?"

"Yes."

"A great friend?"

"A great friend."

He paused. Yet the conviction in his mind was growing stronger and stronger. He blurted out suddenly:

"You're—you're my wife, aren't you?"

He was sure of it.

She drew her hand away. He wouldn't understand the look in her face. It frightened him. She got up.

"No," she said. "I'm not your wife."

"Oh! I'm sorry. I thought—"

"It's all right."

And at that minute Sebastian came back. His eyes went to Jane. She said, with a little twisted smile:

"I'm glad you've come. . . . I'm—glad you've come."

3

Jane and Sebastian talked long into the night. What was to be done? Who was to be told?

There was Nell and Nell's position to consider. Presumably Nell should be told first of all. She was the one most vitally concerned.

Jane agreed. "If she doesn't know already."

"You think she knows?"

"Well, evidently she met Vernon yesterday face to face."

"Yes, but she must have thought it just a very strong resemblance." Jane was silent.

"Don't you think so?"

"I don't know."

"But hang it all, Jane, if she said she'd recognized him, she'd have done something—got hold of him or Bleibner. It's nearly two days ago now."

"I know."

"She can't have recognized him. She just saw Bleibner's chauffeur, and his likeness to Vernon gave her such a shock that she couldn't stand it and rushed away."

"I suppose so."

"What's in your mind, Jane?"

"*We* recognized him, Sebastian."

"You mean you did. I'd been told by you."

"But you would have known him anywhere, wouldn't you?"

"Yes, I would. . . . But then, I know him so well."

Jane said in a hard voice: "So does Nell."

Sebastian looked sharply at her and said: "What are you getting at, Jane?"

"I don't know."

"Yes, you do. What do you really think happened?"

Jane paused before speaking.

"I think Nell came upon him suddenly in the garden and thought it was Vernon. Afterward she persuaded herself that it had only been a chance resemblance that had upset her so."

"Well, that's very much what I said."

He was a little surprised when she said meekly: "Yes, it is."

"What's the difference?"

"Practically none, only—"

"Yes?"

"You and I would have wanted to believe it was Vernon even if it wasn't."

"Wouldn't Nell? Surely she hasn't come to care for George Chetwynd to such an extent—"

"Nell is very fond of George, but Vernon is the only person she's ever been in love with."

"Then that's all right. Or is it worse that way? It's the deuce of a tangle. What about his people?—Mrs. Deyre and the Bents."

Jane said decidedly: "Nell must be told before they are. Mrs. Deyre will broadcast it over England as soon as she knows, and that will be very unfair to both Vernon and Nell."

"Yes, I think you're right. Now my plan is this: to take Vernon up to town tomorrow and go and see a specialist—then be guided by what he advises."

Jane said Yes, she thought that would be the best plan. She got up to go to bed. On the stairs she paused and said to Sebastian:

"I wonder if we're right. Bringing him back, I mean. He looked so happy. Oh! Sebastian, he looked so happy. . . ."

"As George Green, you mean?"

"Yes. Are you sure we're right?"

"Yes, I'm pretty sure. It can't be right for anyone to be in that unnatural sort of state."

"I suppose it *is* unnatural. The queer thing is he looked so normal and commonplace. And happy—that's what I can't get over, Sebastian—*happy*. . . . We're none of us very happy, are we?"

He couldn't answer that.

Chapter Three

Two days later Sebastian came to Abbots Puissants. The butler was not sure that Mrs. Chetwynd could see him. She was lying down.

Sebastian gave his name and said he was sure Mrs. Chetwynd would see him. He was shown into the drawing room to wait. The room seemed empty and silent but unusually luxurious—very different from what it had looked in his childish days. He thought to himself, "It was a *real* house then," and wondered what exactly he meant by that. He got it presently. Now it suggested, very faintly, a museum. Everything was beautifully arranged, and harmonized perfectly. Every piece that was not perfect had been replaced by one that was. All the carpets and covers and hangings were new.

"And they must have cost a pretty penny," thought Sebastian appreciatively, and priced them with a fair degree of accuracy. He always knew the cost of things.

He was interrupted in this salutary exercise by the door opening. Nell came in, a pink color in her cheeks and her hand outstretched.

"Sebastian! What a surprise! I thought you were too busy ever to leave London except at a weekend—and not often then!"

"I've lost just twenty thousand pounds in the last two days," said Sebastian gruffly as he took her hand. "Simply from gadding about and letting things go anyhow. How are you, Nell?"

"Oh! I'm feeling splendid."

She didn't look very splendid, though, he thought, now that the flush of surprise had died away. Besides, hadn't the butler said she was lying down, not feeling well? He fancied that her face looked a little strained and haggard.

She went on: "Sit down, Sebastian. You look as though you were on the point of going off to catch a train. George is away—in Spain. He had to go on business. He'll be away a week at least."

"Will he?"

That was a good thing anyway. A damned awkward business. Nell had simply no idea . . .

"You're very glum, Sebastian. Is anything the matter?"

She asked the question quite lightly, but he seized upon it eagerly. It was the opening he needed.

"Yes, Nell," he said gravely. "As a matter of fact, there is."

He heard her draw in her breath with a sudden catch. Her eyes looked watchful.

"What is it?" she said.

Her voice sounded different—hard and suspicious.

"I'm afraid what I'm going to say will be a great shock to you. It's about Vernon."

"What about Vernon?"

Sebastian waited a minute. Then he said: "Vernon—is alive, Nell."

"Alive?" she whispered. Her hand crept up to her heart.

"Yes."

She didn't do any of the things he expected her to do—didn't faint, or cry out, or ask eager questions. She just stared straight ahead of her. And a sudden quick suspicion came into his shrewd Jewish mind.

"You knew it?"

"No, no."

"I thought perhaps you saw him, the other day, when he came here?"

"Then it *was* Vernon!"

It broke from her like a cry. Sebastian nodded his head. It was as he thought and said to Jane. She had not trusted her eyes.

"What did you think—that it was a very close resemblance?"

"Yes—yes, that's what I thought. How could I think it was Vernon? He looked at me and didn't know me."

"He's lost his memory, Nell."

"Lost his memory?"

"Yes."

He told her the story, giving the details as carefully as possible. She listened but paid less attention than he expected. When he had finished she said: "Yes, but what's to be done about it all? Will he get it back? What are we to do?"

He explained that Vernon was having treatment from a specialist.

Already, under hypnosis, part of the lost memory had returned. The whole process would not be long delayed. He did not enter into the technical details, judging rightly that these would have no interest for her.

"And then he'll know—everything?"

"Yes."

She shrank back in her chair. He felt a sudden rush of pity.

"He can't bame you, Nell. You didn't know—nobody could know. The report of his death was absolutely definite. It's an almost unique case. I've heard of one other. In most cases, of course, a report of death was contradicted almost immediately. Vernon loves you enough to understand and forgive."

She said nothing but she put up both hands to cover her face.

"We think—if you agree—that everything had better be kept quiet for the present. You'll tell Chetwynd, of course. And you and he and Vernon can—well, thrash it out together."

"Don't! Don't! Don't go into details. Just let's leave it for the present—till I've seen Vernon."

"Do you want to see him at once? Will you come up to town with me?"

"No—I can't do that. Let him come here—to see me. Nobody will recognize him. The servants are all new."

Sebastian said slowly: "Very well . . . I'll tell him."

Nell got up.

"I—I—you must go away now, Sebastian. I can't bear any more. I can't indeed. It's all so dreadful. And only two days ago I was so happy and peaceful . . ."

"But Nell, surely to have Vernon back again—"

"Oh! yes, I didn't mean *that*. You don't understand. That's wonderful, of course. Oh! do go, Sebastian. It's awful of me turning you out like this, but I can't bear any more. You must go."

Sebastian went. On the way back to town he wondered a good deal.

2

Left alone, Nell went back to her bedroom and lay down on her bed, pulling the silk eiderdown tightly over her.

So it was true after all. It *had* been Vernon. She had told herself that it couldn't be—that she had made a ridiculous mistake. But she'd been uneasy ever since.

What was going to happen? What would George say about it all? Poor George! He'd been so good to her.

Of course there were women who'd married again, and then had found their first husbands were alive. Rather an awful position. She had never really been George's wife at all.

Oh! it couldn't be true. Such things didn't happen. God wouldn't let—

But perhaps she had better not think of God. It reminded her of those very unpleasant things that Jane had said the other day. That very same day.

She thought with a rush of self-pity: "I was so happy!"

Was Vernon going to understand? Would he—perhaps—blame her? He'd want her, of course, to come back. Or wouldn't he, now that she and George . . . What *did* men think?

There could be a divorce, of course, and then she could marry George. But that would make a lot of talk. How difficult everything was.

She thought with a sudden shock: "But I *love* Vernon. How can I contemplate a divorce and marrying George when I love Vernon? He's been given back to me—from the dead."

She turned over restlessly on the bed. It was a beautiful Empire bed. George had bought it out of on old château in France. It was perfect and quite unique. She looked round the room: a charming room, everything in harmony—perfect taste, perfect unostentatious luxury.

She remembered suddenly the horsehair sofa and the antimacassars in the furnished rooms at Wiltsbury. . . . Dreadful! But they had been happy there.

But now? She looked round the room with new eyes. Of course, Abbots Puissants belonged to George. Or didn't it, now that Vernon had come back? Anyway, Vernon would be just as poor as ever. They couldn't afford to live here. There were all the things that George had done to it.... Thought after thought raced confusedly through her brain.

She must write to George—beg him to come home. Just say it was urgent—nothing more. He was so clever. He might see a way.

Or perhaps she wouldn't write to him—not till she had seen Vernon. Would Vernon be very angry? How terrible it all was.

The tears came to her eyes. She sobbed: "It's unfair—it's unfair. I've never done anything. Why should this happen to me? Vernon will blame me, and I couldn't know. How could I know?"

And again the thought flitted across her mind: "I *was* so happy!"

3

Vernon was listening, trying to understand what the doctor was saying to him. He looked across the table at him. A tall thin man, with eyes that seemed to see right into the center of you and to read there things that you didn't even know about yourself.

And he made you see all the things you didn't want to see. Made you bring things up out of the depths. He was saying:

"Now that you have remembered, tell me again exactly how you saw the announcement of your wife's marriage."

Vernon cried out: "Must we go over it again and again? It was all so horrible. I don't want to think of it anymore."

And then the doctor explained, gravely and kindly, but very impressively. It was because of that desire not to "think of it anymore" that all this had come about. It must be faced now—thrashed out. Otherwise the loss of memory might return.

They went all over it again.

And then, when Vernon felt he could bear no more, he was told to lie down on a couch. The doctor touched his forehead and his limbs, told him that he was resting—was rested—that he would become strong and happy again....

A feeling of peace came over Vernon.

He closed his eyes....

4

Vernon came down to Abbots Puissants three days later. He came in Sebastian Levinne's car. To the butler he gave his name as Mr. Green. Nell was waiting for him in the little white-paneled room where his mother had sat in the mornings. She came forward to meet him, forcing a conventional smile to her lips. The butler shut the door behind him just in time for her to stop short before offering him her hand.

They looked at each other. Then Vernon said:

"Nell. . . ."

She was in his arms. He kissed her—kissed her—kissed her. . . .

He let her go at last. They sat down. He was quiet, rather tragic, very restrained, but for that one wild greeting. He'd gone through so much—so much in these last few days.

Sometimes he wished they'd left him alone—as George Green. It had been jolly being George Green.

He said stammeringly: "It's all right, Nell. You mustn't think I blame you. I understand. Only it hurts. It hurts like hell! Naturally."

She said: "I didn't mean—"

He interrupted her.

"I *know*, I tell you—I *know!* Don't talk about it. I don't want to hear about it. I don't want to think about it even." He added in a different tone: "They say that's my trouble. That's how it happened."

She said, rather eagerly: "Tell me about it—about everything."

'There isn't much to tell." He spoke without interest, abstractedly. "I was taken prisoner. How I got to be reported killed, I don't know. At least, I have a sort of vague idea. There was a fellow very like me—one of the Huns. I don't mean a double, or anything of that sort, but just a general superficial resemblance. My German's pretty rotten but I heard them commenting on it. They took my kit and my identification disc. I think the idea was for him to penetrate into our lines as me—we were being relieved by Colonial troops, and they knew it. The fellow would pass muster for a day or so and would gain the information he wanted. That's only an idea, but it explains why I wasn't returned in the list of prisoners and I was sent to a camp that was practically all French and Belgians. But none of that matters, does it? I suppose the Hun was killed getting through our lines and was buried as me. I had a pretty bad time in Germany—nearly died with some kind of fever on top of being wounded. Finally I escaped— Oh! it's a long story. I'm not going into all that now. I had the hell of a time—without food and water sometimes for days at a stretch. It was a sort of miracle that I came through—but I did. I got into Holland. I was exhausted and at the same time all strung up. And I could only think of one thing—getting back to you."

"Yes?"

"And then I saw it—in a beastly illustrated paper. Your marriage. It—it finished me. But I wouldn't face it. I kept on saying that it couldn't be true. I went out—I don't know where I went. Things got all mixed up in my mind.

"There was a whacking great lorry coming down the road. I saw my chance—end it all, get out of it. I stepped out in front of it."

"Oh, Vernon!" she shuddered.

"And that *was* the end. Of me as Vernon Deyre, I mean. When I came to there was just one name in my head—George. That lucky chap, George. George Green."

"Why Green?"

"A sort of fancy of mine when I was a child. And then the Dutch girl at the inn had asked me to look up a pal of hers whose name was Green and I'd written it down in a little book."

"And you didn't remember anything?"

"No."

"Weren't you very frightened?"

"No, not at all. I didn't seem to be worrying about anything." He added with lingering regret: "I was awfully happy and jolly."

Then he looked across at her.

"But that doesn't matter now. Nothing matters—but you."

She smiled at him, but her smile was flickering and uncertain. He barely noticed it at the moment, but went on.

"It's been rather hell—getting back, remembering things. All such beastly things. All the things that—really—I didn't want to face. I seem to have been a most awful coward all my life. Always turning away from things I didn't want to look at. Refusing to admit them."

He got up suddenly and came across to her, dropping his head upon her knees.

"Darling Nell, it's all right. I know I come first. I do, don't I?"

She said: "Of course."

Why did her voice sound so mechanical in her own ears? He did come first. Just now, with his lips on hers, she had been swept back again to those wonderful days at the beginning of the war. She had never felt about George like that . . . drowned, carried away.

"You say that so strangely—as though you didn't mean it."

"Of course I mean it."

"I'm sorry for Chetwynd—rotten luck for him. How has he taken it? Very hard?"

"I haven't told him."

"What?"

She was moved to vindicate herself.

"He's away—in Spain. I haven't got his address."

"Oh! I see. . . ."

He paused.

"It'll be rather rotten for you, Nell. But it can't be helped. We'll have each other."

"Yes."

Vernon looked around.

"Chetwynd will have this place, anyway. I'm such an ungenerous beggar that I even grudge him that. But, damn it all, it *is* my home. It's been in the family five hundred years. Oh! what does it all matter? Jane told me once that I couldn't get everything. I've got you—that's all that matters. We'll find some place. Even if it's only a couple of rooms, it will do."

His arms stole up, closing round her. Why did she feel that cold dismay at those words, "A couple of rooms"?

"Damn these things! They get in my way!"

Impetuously, half laughing, he held up the string of pearls she wore. He switched them off—flung them on the floor. Her lovely pearls! She thought: "Anyway, I suppose I'll have to give them back." Another cold feeling. All those lovely jewels that George had given her.

What a brute she was to go on thinking of things like that.

He had seen something at last. He was kneeling upright, looking at her.

"Nell, is—is anything the matter?"

"No—of course not."

She couldn't meet his eyes. She felt too ashamed.

"There is something. Tell me."

She shook her head.

"It's nothing."

She couldn't be poor again. She couldn't—she couldn't.

"Nell, you must tell me."

He mustn't know—he must never know what she was really like. She was so ashamed.

"Nell, you do love me, don't you?"

"Oh, yes!" The words came eagerly. *That* at any rate was true.

"Then what is it? I know there's something. . . . Ah!"

He got up. His face had gone white. She looked up at him inquiringly.

"Is it that?" he asked in a low voice. "It must be. You're going to have a child."

She sat as though carved in stone. She had never thought of that. If it were true, it solved everything. Vernon would never know.

"It *is* that?"

Again it seemed as though hours passed. Thoughts went whirling round in her brain. It was not herself, but something outside herself that at last made her bow her head ever so slightly.

He moved a little away. He spoke in a hard dry voice.

"That alters everything. . . . My poor Nell! You can't—*we* can't . . . Look here, nobody knows—about me, I mean—except the doctor and Sebastian and Jane. They won't split. I was reported dead. I *am* dead."

She made a movement, but he held up a hand to stop her and backed away toward the door.

"Don't say anything—for God's sake, don't say anything. Words will make it worse, I'm going. I daren't touch you or kiss you. I—good-bye."

She heard the door open, made a movement as if to call out—but no sound came from her throat. The door shut again.

There was still time. The car hadn't started.

But still she didn't move.

She had one moment of searing bitterness when she looked into herself and thought: "So that's what I'm really like."

But she made no sound or movement.

Four years of soft living fettered her will, stifled her voice, and paralyzed her body.

Chapter Four

"Miss Harding to see you, madam."

Nell started. Twenty-four hours had elapsed since her interview with Vernon. She had thought it was finished. And now Jane!

She was afraid of Jane.

She might refuse to see her.

She said: "Show her up here."

It was more private up here in her own sitting room.

What a long time it was waiting. Had Jane gone away again? No, here she was.

She looked very tall. Nell cowered down on the sofa. Jane had a wicked face—she had always thought so. There was a look on her face now as of an avenging Fury.

The butler left the room. Jane stood towering over Nell. Then she flung back her head and laughed.

"Don't forget to ask me to the christening," she said.

Nell flinched. She said haughtily:

"I don't know what you mean?"

"It's a family secret at present, is it? Nell, you damned little liar, you're not going to have a child. I don't believe you ever will have a child—too much risk and pain. What made you think of telling Vernon such a peculiarly damnable lie?"

Nell said sullenly: "I never told him. He—he guessed."

"That's even more damnable."

"I don't know what you mean, coming here and—and saying things like this."

Her protest sounded weak—spiritless. For the life of her she couldn't put the necessary indignation into it. With anyone else—not with Jane. Jane had always been disagreeably clear-eyed. It was awful! If only Jane would go away.

She rose to her feet, trying to sound decisive.

"I don't know why you have come here. If it is only to make a scene . . ."

"Listen, Nell. You're going to hear the truth. You chucked Vernon once before. He came to me. Yes—to me. He lived with me for three months. He was living with me when you came to my flat that day. Ah! that hurts you. You've still got a bit of raw womanhood left in you, I'm glad to see.

"You took him from me then. He went to you and never gave me a thought. He's yours now if you want him. But I tell you this, Nell, if you let him down a second time, he'll come to me again. Oh! yes, he will. You've thought things about me in your mind—turned up your nose at me as 'a certain kind of woman.' Well, because of that, perhaps, I've got power. I know more about men than you will ever learn. I can get Vernon if I want him. And I do want him. I always have."

Nell shuddered. She turned her face away, digging her nails into the palms of her hands.

"Why do you tell me all this? You're a devil."

"I tell it to you to hurt you! To hurt you like hell before it's too late. No, you shan't turn your head away. You shan't shrink away from what I'm telling you. You've got to look at me and see—yes, see—with your eyes and your heart and your brain. . . . You love Vernon with the last remaining corner of your miserable little soul. Think of him in my arms—think of his lips on mine, of his kisses burning my body. . . . Yes, you shall think of it.

"Soon you won't mind even that. But you mind now. . . . Aren't you enough of a woman to jib at handing over the man you love to another woman? To a woman you hate? 'A present for Jane with love from Nell.' "

"Go away," said Nell faintly. "Go away."

"I'm going. It's not too late. You can undo the lie you told."

"Go away. . . . Go away."

"Do it soon—or you'll never do it." Jane paused at the door, looking back over her shoulder. "I came for Vernon's sake—not mine. I want him back. And I shall have him . . ." she paused, "unless . . ."

She went out.

Nell sat with her hands clenched.

She murmured fiercely: "She shan't have him. She shan't."

She wanted Vernon. She wanted him. He had loved Jane once. He would love her again. What had she said? ". . . his lips on mine . . . his kisses burning my . . ." Oh! God, she couldn't bear it. She started up—moved toward the telephone.

The door opened. She turned slowly. George came in. He looked very normal and cheerful.

"Hullo, sweetheart." He crossed the room and kissed her. "Here I am—back again. A nasty crossing, I'd rather have the Atlantic than the Channel any day."

She had completely forgotten that George was coming home today! She couldn't tell him this minute—it would be too cruel. And besides, it was so difficult—to burst in with tragic news in the middle of a flow of banalities. This evening—later. In the meantime she would play her part.

She returned his embrace mechanically, sat down and listened while he talked.

"I've got a present for you, honey. Something that reminded me of you."

He took a velvet case from his pocket.

Inside, on a bed of white velvet, lay a big rose-colored diamond—exquisite, flawless—depending from a long chain. Nell gave a little gasp of pleasure.

He lifted the jewel from the case and slipped the chain over her head. She looked down. The exquisite rose-colored stone blinked up at her from its resting place between her breasts. Something about it hypnotized her.

He led her to the glass. She saw a golden-haired beautiful woman, very calm and elegant. She saw the waved and shingled hair, the manicured hands, the foamy negligee of soft lace, the cobweb-silk stockings and little embroidered mules. She saw the hard cold beauty of the rose-colored diamond.

And behind them she saw George Chetwynd—kindly, generous, deliciously safe.

Dear George, she couldn't hurt him. . . .

Kisses. . . . What, after all, were kisses? You needn't think about them. Better not to think of them.

Vernon . . . Jane . . .

She wouldn't think of them. For good or evil, she'd made her choice. There would be bad moments sometimes, but on the whole it would be for the best. Better for Vernon, too. If she weren't happy she couldn't make him happy.

She said gently: "You are a dear to bring me such a lovely present. Ring for tea. We'll have it up here."

"That will be fine. But weren't you going to telephone to someone? I interrupted you."

She shook her head.

"No," she said. "I've changed my mind."

2

LETTERS FROM VERNON DEYRE TO SEBASTIAN LEVINNE

Moscow

Dear Sebastian:

Do you know that there was once a legend in Russia that concerned a "nameless beast" that was coming?

I mention this not because of any political significance (by the way, the Antichrist hysteria is curious, isn't it?) but because it reminded me of my own terror of "the Beast." I've thought about the Beast a great deal since coming to Russia—trying to get at its true significance.

Because there's more in it than just being afraid of a piano. That doctor in London opened my eyes to a great many things. I've begun to see that all through my life I've been a coward. I think you've known that, Sebastian. You wouldn't put it in that offensive way, but you hinted as much to me once. I've run away from things. . . . Always I've run away from things.

And thinking it all over now, I see the Beast as something symbolical—not a mere piece of furniture composed of wood and wires. Don't mathematicians say that the future exists at the same time as the past?—that we travel through time as we travel through space?—from a thing that is to another thing that is? Don't some even hold that remembering is a mere habit of the mind—that we could remember forward as well as back if we had only learned the trick of it? It sounds nonsense when I say it, but I believe there is some theory of that kind.

I believe that there is some part of us that *does* know the future, that is always intimately aware of it.

That explains, doesn't it, why we should shrink sometimes? The burden of our destiny is going to be heavy and we recoil from its shadow. I tried to escape from music—but it got me. It got me at that concert, in the same way that religion got those people at the Salvation Army meeting.

It's a devilish thing—or is it godlike? If so it's an Old Testament jealous God—all the things I've tried to cling to have been swept away. Abbots Puissants . . . Nell . . .

And, damn it all, what's left? Nothing. Not even the cursed thing itself. I've no wish to write music. I hear nothing—feel nothing. Will it ever come back. Jane says it will. She seems very sure. She sends her love to you, by the way.

Yours,
Vernon

3

Moscow

You're an understanding devil, Sebastian. You don't complain that I ought to have written you a description of samovars, the political situation, and life in Russia generally. The country, of

course, is in a bloody muddle. What else could it be in? But it's
jolly interesting. . . . Love from Jane.

Vernon

4

Moscow

Dear Sebastian:

Jane was right to bring me here. Point No. 1, no one is likely
to come across me here and joyously proclaim my resurrection
from the dead. Point No. 2, this is about the most interesting place
in the world to be from my point of view. A kind of free-and-easy
laboratory where everyone is trying experiments of the most dangerous kind. The whole world seems concerned with Russia from
a purely political point of view. Economic, starvation, morals, lack
of liberty, diseased and decadent children . . . *etc.*

But amazing things are sometimes born out of vice and filth and
anarchy. The whole trend of Russian thought in art is extraordinary—part of it the most utter childish drivel you ever heard, and
yet wonderful gleams peeping through, like shining flesh through
a beggar's rags.

The Nameless Beast—Collective Man. Did you ever see that
plan for a monument to the Communist Revolution? The Colossus
of Iron? I tell you, it stirs the imagination.

Machinery—an Age of Machinery. . . . How the Bolsheviks worship anything to do with machinery—and how little they know
about it! That's why it's so wonderful to them, I suppose. Imagine
a real mechanic of Chicago composing a dynamic poem describing
his city as ". . . built upon a screw! Electro dynamo mechanical
city! Spiral-shaped on a steel disc. At every stroke of the hour
Turning round itself—Five thousand skyscrapers . . ." Anything
more alien from the spirit of America!

And yet, do you ever see a thing when you're too close to it?
It's the people who don't know machinery who see its soul and its
meaning. The Nameless Beast. . . . My Beast? . . . I wonder.

Collective Man—forming himself in turn into a vast machine. The same herd instinct that saved the race of old coming out again in a different form.

Life's becoming too difficult—too dangerous—for the individual. What was it Dostoevsky says in one of his books?

"The flock will collect again and submit once more, and then it will be forever, forever. We will give them a quiet modest happiness."

Herd instinct. . . . I wonder.

Yours,
Vernon

5

Moscow

I have found the other passage in Dostoevsky. I think it is the one you mean:

"And we alone, we who guard the mystery, we alone shall be unhappy. There will be thousands of millions of happy children and only a hundred thousand martyrs who have taken on themselves the curse of good and evil."

You mean, and Dostoevsky meant, that there must always be individualists. It is the individualists who carry on the torch. Men welded into a vast machine must ultimately perish. For the machine is soulless and will end as scrap iron.

Men worshipped stone and built Stonehenge—and to-day the men who built it have perished and are unknown and Stonehenge stands. And yet, by a paradox, the men are alive in you and me, their descendants, and Stonehenge and what it stood for is dead. The things that die endure, and the things that endure perish.

It is Man that goes on forever. (Does he? Isn't that unwarrantable arrogance? Yet we believe it!) And so, there must be individualists behind the Machine. So Dostoevsky says and so you say. But then, you're both Russians. As an Englishman I'm more pessimistic.

Do you know what that passage from Dostoevsky reminds me of? My childhood. Mr. Green's hundred children—*and* Poodle, Squirrel, and Tree. Representatives of the hundred thousand.

Yours,
Vernon

6

Moscow

Dear Sebastian:

I suppose you're right. I never have thought much before. It seemed to me an unprofitable exercise. In fact, I'm not sure I don't still regard it as such.

The trouble is, you see, that I can't "say it in music." Damn it all, why *can't* I say it in music? Music's my job. I'm more sure of that than ever. And yet—nothing doing.

It's hell.

Vernon

7

Dear Sebastian:

Haven't I mentioned Jane? What is there to say about her? She's splendid. We both know that. Why don't you write to her yourself?

Yours ever,
Vernon

8

Dear old Sebastian:

Jane says you may be coming out here. I wish to God you would. I'm sorry I haven't written for six months—I never was one of the world's ready letter writers.

Have you seen anything of Joe? I'm glad Jane and I looked her up passing through Paris. Joe's staunch, she'll never split on us, and I'm glad she at any rate knows. We never write to each other, she and I, we never have. But I wondered if you'd heard anything. I didn't think she looked awfully fit. Poor old Joe! She's made a mess of things.

Have you heard anything of Tatlin's scheme for a monument to the Third Internationale? To consist of a union of three great glass chambers connected by a system of vertical axes and spirals. By means of special machinery they would be kept in perpetual motion but at different rates of speed.

And inside, I suppose, they'd sing hymns to a Holy Acetylene Blowpipe!

Do you remember, one night, we were motoring back to town, and we took the wrong turning somewhere amongst the tramlines of Lewisham, and instead of making for the haunts of civilization we turned up somewhere among the Surrey docks and through an opening in the frowsy houses we saw a queer kind of cubist picture of cranes and cloudy steam and iron girders? And immediately your artistic soul bagged it for a drop scene—or whatever the technical term is.

My God, Sebastian! What a magnificent spectacle of machinery you could build up—sheer effects and lighting, and masses of humans with inhuman faces—mass, not individuals. You've something of the kind in mind, haven't you?

The architect, Tatlin, said something that I think good and yet a lot of nonsense:

"Only the rhythm of the metropolis, of factories and machines together with the organization of the masses, can give the impulse to the new art—"

And he goes on to speak of the "monument of the machine" the only adequate expression of the pression.

You know, of course, all about the modern Russian theater. That's your job. I suppose Mayerhold is as marvelous as they say he is. But can one mix up drama and propaganda?

All the same, it's exciting to arrive at a theater and be compelled at once to join a marching crowd—up and down, in strict step, till the performance begins—and the scenery, composed of rocking chairs and cannons and revolving bays and God knows what! It's babyish—absurd—and yet one feels that baby has got hold of a dangerous and rather interesting toy that in other hands . . .

Your hands, Sebastian—you're a Russian. But thank heaven and geography, no propagandist—just a showman pure and simple.

The Rhythm of the metropolis—made pictorial.

My God!—if I could give you the music. It's the music that's needed.

Lord—their "noise orchestras"—their symphonies of factory sirens! There was a show at Baku in 1922—batteries of artillery, machine guns, choirs, naval fog horns. Ridiculous! Yes, but if they had a composer . . .

No woman ever longed for a child as I long to produce music.

And I'm barren—sterile.

Vernon

9

Dear Sebastian:

It seems like a dream, your having come and gone. Will you really do *The Tale of the Rogue Who Outwitted Three Other Rogues?* I wonder.

I'm only just beginning to recognize what a howling success you've made of things. I've at last grasped that you're simply IT nowadays. Yes, found your National Opera House—God knows it's time we had one. But what do you want with opera? It's archaic—dead—ridiculous individual love affairs.

Music up to now seems to me like a child's drawing of a house—four walls, a door, two windows, and a chimney pot. There you are—and what more do you want?

At any rate Feinberg and Prokofiev do more than that.

Do you remember how we used to jeer at the cubists and futurists? At least, I did. Now that I come to think of it, I don't believe you agreed.

And then one day—at a cinema—I saw a view of a big city from the air. Spires turning over, buildings bending—everything behaving as one simply knew concrete and steel and iron couldn't behave! And for the first time I got a glimmering of what old Einstein meant when he talked about relativity.

We don't know anything about the shape of music. We don't know anything about the shape of anything, for that matter—because there's always one side open to space.

Some day you'll know what I mean—what music can mean—what I've always known it meant.

What a mess that opera of mine was. All opera is a mess. Music was never intended to be representational. To take a story and write descriptive music to it is as wrong as to write a passage of music—in the abstract so to speak—and then find an instrument capable of playing it! When Stravinsky wrote a clarionet passage, you can't even conceive of it as being played by anything else!

Music should be like mathematics—a pure science, untouched by drama, or romanticism, or any emotion other than the pure emotion which is the result of *sound* divorced from ideas.

I've always known that in my heart. Music must be Absolute.

Not, of course, that I shall realize my ideal. To create pure sound untouched by ideas is a counsel of perfection.

My music will be the music of machinery. I leave the dressing of it to you. It's an age of choreography, and choreography will reach heights we don't as yet dream of. I can trust you with the visual side of my masterpiece as yet unwritten—and which in all probability never will be written.

Music must be four dimensional—timbre, pitch, relative speed, and periodicity.

I don't think even now we appreciate Schönberg enough. That clean remorseless logic that is the spirit of today. He and he alone had the courage to disregard tradition—to get down to bedrock, and discover Truth.

He's the one man to my mind who matters. Even his scheme of score writing will have to be adopted universally. It's absolutely necessary if scores are going to be intelligible.

The thing I have against him is scorn of his instruments. He's afraid of being a slave to them. He makes them serve him whether they will or no.

I'm going to glorify my instruments. I'm going to give them what they want—what they've always wanted.

Damn it all, Sebastian, *what is this strange thing, music?* I know less and less.

Yours,
Vernon

10

I know I haven't written. I've been busy. Making experiments. Means of expression for the Nameless Beast. In other words, instrument making. Metals are jolly interesting. I'm working with alloys just at present.

What a fascinating thing sound is.

Jane sends her love.

In answer to your question—No, I don't suppose I shall ever leave Russia—not even to attend at your newly planned opera house, disguised in my beard!

It's even more barbarous and beautiful now than when you saw it! Full and flowing, the perfect temperamental Slav Beaver!

But in spite of the forest camouflage, here I am and here I stay, till I am exterminated by one of the bands of wild children.

Yours ever,
Vernon

TELEGRAM FROM VERNON DEYRE TO SEBASTIAN LEVINNE

Just heard Joe dangerously ill feared dying stranded in New York Jane and I sailing *Resplendent* hope see you London.

Chapter Five

"Sebastian!"

Joe started up in bed, then fell back weakly. She stared unbelievingly. Sebastian, big, fur-coated, calm, and omniscient, smiled placidly down at her.

There was no sign in his face of the sudden pang her appearance had given him. Joe—poor little Joe!

Her hair had grown—it was arranged in two short plaits, one over each shoulder. Her face was horribly thin, with a high hectic flush on each cheekbone. The bones of her shoulders showed through her thin nightdress.

She looked like a feverish child. There was something childlike in her surprise, in her pleasure, in her eager questioning. The nurse had left them.

Sebastian sat down by the bed and took Joe's thin hand in his.

"Vernon wired me. I didn't wait for him. I caught the first boat."

"To come to me?"

"Of course."

"Dear Sebastian!"

Tears came into her eyes. Sebastian was alarmed and went on hastily:

"Not that I shan't do a bit of business while I am over. I often come over on business, and as a matter of fact I can do one or two good deals just now."

"Don't spoil it."

"But it's true," said Sebastian, surprised.

Joe began to laugh, but coughed instead. Sebastian watched anxiously, ready to call the nurse. He had been warned. But the fit passed.

Joe lay there contentedly, her hand creeping into Sebastian's again.

"Mother died this way," she whispered. "Poor Mother! I thought I was going to be so much wiser than she was, and I've made such a mess of things. Oh! such a mess of things."

"Poor old Joe!"

"You don't know what a mess I've made of things, Sebastian."

"I can imagine it," said Sebastian. "I always thought you would."

Joe was silent a minute, then she said: "You don't know what a comfort it is to see you, Sebastian. I have seen and known so many rotters. I didn't like your being strong and successful and cocksure—it annoyed me. But now—oh, it's wonderful!"

He squeezed her hand.

"There's no one else in the world who would have come—as you've come—miles—at once. Vernon, of course, but then he's a relation—a kind of brother. But you—"

"I'm just as much a brother—more than a brother. Ever since Abbots Puissants I've been—well, ready to stand by if you wanted me."

"Oh! Sebastian." Her eyes opened wide—happily. "I never dreamt that you'd feel like that still."

He started ever so slightly. He hadn't meant that exactly. He had meant something that he couldn't explain—not at any rate to Joe. It was a feeling peculiarly and exclusively Jewish. The undying gratitude of the Jew who never forgets a benefit conferred. As a child he had been an outcast and Joe had stood by him—she had been willing to defy her world. The child Sebastian had never forgotten—would never forget. He would, as he had said, have gone to the ends of the earth if she had wanted him.

She went on.

"They moved me into this place—from that horrible ward. Was that you?"

He nodded.

"I cabled."

Joe sighed.

"You're so terribly efficient, Sebastian."

"I'm afraid so."

"But there's nobody like you—nobody. I've thought of you so often lately."

"Have you?"

He thought of the lonely years—the aching longing—the baffled desire. Why did things always come to you at the wrong time?

She went on.

"I never dreamt you'd still think about me. I always fancied that some day you and Jane—"

A queer pang shot through him. *Jane* . . .

He and Jane . . .

He said gruffly: "Jane, to my mind, is one of the finest things God ever made. But she belongs body and soul to Vernon and always will."

"I suppose so. But it's a pity. You and she are the strong ones. You belong together."

They did, in a curious way. He knew what she meant.

Joe said with a flickering smile: "This reminds me of the books one reads as a child. Edifying death-bed scenes. Friends and relations gathering round. Wan smiles of heroine."

Sebastian had made up his mind. Why had he felt this wasn't love? It was. This passion of pure disinterested pity and tenderness—this deep affection lasting through the years. A thousand times better worthwhile than those stormy or tepid affairs that occurred with monotonous regularity—that punctuated his life without ever touching any real depths.

His heart went out to the childlike figure. Somehow, he'd bring it off.

He said gently: "There aren't going to be any death-bed scenes, Joe. You're going to get well and marry me."

"Darling Sebastian! Tie you to a consumptive wife? Of course not."

"Nonsense! You'll do one of two things—either get well or die. If you die you die, and there's an end of it. If you get cured you marry me. And no expense will be spared to cure you."

"I'm pretty bad, Sebastian dear."

"Possibly. But nothing is more uncertain than tubercle—any doctor will tell you so. You've been just letting yourself go. I think myself you'll get well. A long weary business, but it can be done."

She looked at him. He saw the color rising and falling in her thin cheeks. He knew then that she loved him, and a queer little stir of warmth woke round his heart. His mother had died two years ago. Since then no one had really cared.

Joe said in a low voice: "Sebastian, do you really need me? I—I've made such a mess of things."

He said with sincerity: "Need you? I'm the loneliest man on earth."

And suddenly he broke down. It was a thing he had never done in his life—never thought he would do. He knelt by Joe's bed, his face buried, his shoulders heaving.

Her hand stroked his head. He knew she was happy—her proud spirit appeased. Dear Joe—so impulsive, so warmhearted, so wrongheaded. She was dearer to him than anyone on earth. They could help one another.

The nurse came in—the visitor had been there long enough. She withdrew again for Sebastian to say good-bye.

"By the way," he said. "That French fellow—what's his name?"

"François? He's dead."

"That's all right. You could have got a divorce, of course. But being a widow makes it easier."

"You *do* think I shall get well?"

Pathetic, the way she said that!

"Of course."

The nurse reappeared and he took his departure. He called on the doctor—had a long talk. The doctor was not hopeful. But he agreed that there was a chance. They decided on Florida.

Sebastian left the home. He walked along the street deep in thought. He saw a placard with "Terrible Disaster to *Resplendent*" on it, but it conveyed nothing to his mind.

He was too busy with his own thoughts. What was really best for Joe? To live or to die? He wondered.

She'd had such a rotten life. He wanted the best for her.

He went to bed and slept heavily.

2

He awoke to a vague uneasiness. There was something—something. For the life of him he couldn't put a name to it.

It wasn't Joe. Joe was in the foreground of his mind. This was something in the background—shoved away—something that he hadn't been able to give consideration to at the time.

He thought: "I shall remember presently." But he didn't.

As he dressed he thought out the problem of Joe. He was all for moving her to Florida as soon as possible. Later, perhaps, Switzerland. She was very weak, but not too weak to be moved. As soon as she had seen Vernon and Jane . . .

They were arriving—when? The *Resplendent*, wasn't it? The *Resplendent* . . .

The razor he was holding dropped from his hand. He'd got it now! Before his eyes rose the vision of a newspaper placard.

The *Resplendent*—Terrible Disaster.

Vernon and Jane were on the *Resplendent*.

He rang furiously. A few minutes later he was scanning the morning newspaper. There were now full details to hand. His eyes scanned them rapidly. The *Resplendent* had struck an iceberg—the death roll—survivors.

A list of names . . . survivors. He found the name there of Groen; Vernon was alive anyway. Then he searched the other list and found at last what he was looking for, fearing—the name of Jane Harding.

3

He stood quite still, staring at the news sheet in his hand. Presently he folded it up neatly, laid it on a side table and rang the bell. In a few minutes a curt order given to the bellhop sent his secretary hurrying to him.

"I've got an appointment at ten o'clock I can't break. There are some things you've got to find out for me. Have the information ready for me when I return."

He detailed the points succinctly. The fullest particulars as to the *Resplendent* were to be collected, and certain radios were to be sent off.

Sebastian telephoned himself to the hospital and warned them that no mention of the *Resplendent* disaster was to be made to the patient. He had a few words with Joe herself which he managed to make normal and commonplace.

He stopped at a florist's to send her some flowers and then went off to embark on a long day of meetings and business appointments. It is to be doubted if anyone noticed that the great Sebastian Levinne was unlike himself in the smallest detail. He had never been more shrewd in driving a bargain and his power of getting his own way was never more in evidence.

It was six o'clock when he returned to the Biltmore.

His secretary met him with all the information available. The survivors had been picked up by a Norwegian ship. They would be due in New York in three days' time.

Sebastian nodded, his face unchanged. He gave further instructions.

On the evening of the third day following that he returned to his hotel, to be met by the information that Mr. Groen had arrived and was installed in the suite adjoining his own.

Sebastian strode there.

Vernon was standing by the window. He turned round. Sebastian felt something like a shock. In some strange way he no longer recognized his friend. Something had happened to him.

They stood staring at each other. Sebastian spoke first. He said the thing that all day had been present in his mind.

"Jane's dead," he said.

Vernon nodded—gravely—understandingly.

"Yes," he said quietly. "Jane's dead—and I killed her."

The old unemotional Sebastian revived and protested.

"For God's sake, Vernon, don't take it like that. She came with you—naturally. Don't be morbid about it."

"You don't understand," said Vernon. "You don't know what happened."

He paused and then went on, speaking very quietly and collectedly.

"I can't describe the thing. It happened quite suddenly, you know—in the middle of the night. There was very little time. The boat heeled over, you know, at an appalling angle. The two of them came together—slipping—sliding down the deck. They couldn't save themselves."

"What two?"

"Nell and Jane, of course."

"What's Nell got to do with it?"

"She was on board."

"What?"

"Yes. I didn't know. Jane and I were second class, of course, and I don't think we ever glanced at a passenger list. Yes, Nell and George Chetwynd were on board. That's what I'm telling you, if you wouldn't interrupt. It happened—a sort of nightmare, no time for lifeboats or anything. I was hanging onto a stanchion—or whatever you call it—to save myself from falling into the sea.

"And they came drifting along the deck, those two, right by me— slipping, sliding—faster and faster—and the sea waiting for them below.

"I'd no idea Nell was on board till I saw her drifting down to destruction, and crying out, '*Vernon!*'

"There isn't time to think on these occasions, I tell you. One can just make an instinctive gesture. I could grab on to one or other of them— Nell or Jane. I grabbed Nell and held her, held her like grim death."

"And Jane?"

Vernon said quietly: "I can see her face still, looking at me as she went—down into that green swirl."

"My God!" said Sebastian hoarsely.

Then suddenly his impassivity forsook him. His voice rang out bellowing like a bull.

"You saved Nell? You bloody fool! To save Nell—and let Jane drown. Why, Nell isn't worth the tip of Jane's little finger. Damn you!"

"I know that."

"You know it? Then—"

"I tell you, it isn't what you *know*—it's some blind instinct that takes hold of you."

"Damn you! Damn you!"

"I'm damned all right. You needn't worry. I let Jane drown—and I love her."

"Love her?"

"Yes, I've always loved her. I see that now. Always, from the beginning, I was afraid of her—because I loved her. I was a coward there, like everywhere else—trying to escape from reality. I fought against her. I was ashamed of the power she had over me. I've taken her through hell.

"And now I want her—I want her. Oh! you'll say that's like me, to want a thing as soon as it's out of my reach. Perhaps it's true—perhaps I am like that.

"I only know that I love Jane—that I love her—and that she's gone from me forever."

He sat down on a chair and said in his normal tone: "I want to work. Get out of here, Sebastian, there's a good fellow."

"My God, Vernon, I didn't think I could ever hate you—"

Vernon repeated: "I want to work."

Sebastian turned on his heel and left the room.

4

Vernon sat very still.

Jane . . .

Horrible to suffer like this—to want anyone so much.

Jane . . . Jane . . .

Yes, he'd always loved her. After that very first meeting he'd been unable to keep away. He'd been drawn toward her by something stronger than himself.

Fool and coward to be afraid—always afraid. Afraid of any deep reality—of any violent emotion.

And she had known—she had always known, and been unable to help him. What had she said: "Divided in time"? That first evening at Sebastian's party when she had sung:

> "I saw a Fairy lady there
> With long white hands and drowning hair. . . ."

Drowning hair . . . no, no, not that. Queer she should have sung that song. And the statue of the drowned woman . . . that was queer, too.

What was the other thing she had sung that night?

> "J'ai perdu mon amie—elle est morte.
> Tout s'en va cette fois, à jamais,
> A jamais, pour toujours elle emporte
> Le dernier des amours que j'aimais. . . ."

He had lost Abbots Puissants, he had lost Nell.

But with Jane, he had indeed lost *"le dernier des amours que j'aimais."*

For the rest of his life he would be able to see only one woman—Jane.

He loved Jane . . . he loved her. . . .

And he'd tortured her, slighted her, finally abandoned her to that green evil sea.

The statute in the South Kensington Museum . . .

God!—he mustn't think of that.

Yes, he'd think of everything. This time he wouldn't turn away.

Jane . . . Jane . . . Jane . . .

He wanted her. Jane . . .

He'd never see her again.

He'd lost everything now . . . everything.

Those days, months, years in Russia. Wasted years.

Fool—to live beside her, to hold her body in his arms, and all the time to be afraid . . . afraid of his passion for her.

That old terror of the Beast . . .

And suddenly, as he thought of the Beast, he knew . . .

Knew that at last he had come into his heritage.

5

It was like the day he had come back from the Titanic Concert. It was the vision he had had then. He called it vision for it seemed more that than sound. Seeing and hearing were one—curves and spirals of sound, ascending, descending, returning.

And now he *knew*—he had the technical knowledge.

He snatched at paper, jotted down brief scrawled hieroglyphics, a kind of frantic shorthand. There were years of work in front of him, but he knew that he should never again recapture this first freshness and clearness of vision.

It must be so—and so: a whole weight of metal—brass—all the brass in the world.

And those new glass sounds . . . ringing, clear.

He was happy.

An hour passed . . . two hours.

For a moment he came out of his frenzy—remembered . . . Jane!

He felt sick—ashamed. Couldn't he mourn her for even one evening? There was something base—cruel—in the way he was using his sorrow, his desire—transmuting it into terms of sound.

That was what it meant to be a creator—ruthlessness, using everything.

And people like Jane were the victims.

Jane . . .

He felt torn in two—agony and wild exultation.

He thought: "Perhaps women feel like this when they have a child."

Presently he bent again over his sheets of paper, writing frenziedly, flinging them on the floor as he finished them.

When the door opened he did not hear it. He was deaf to the rustle of a woman's dress. Only when a small frightened voice said, "Vernon," did he look up.

With an effort he forced the abstracted look from his face.

"Hullo," he said. "Nell."

She stood there, twisting her hands together—her face white and ravaged. She spoke in breathless gasps.

"Vernon . . . I found out. They told me . . . where you were . . . and I came."

He nodded.

"Yes," he said. "You came?"

Oboes—no, cut out oboes. Too soft a note. It must be strident—brazen. But harps—yes, he wanted the liquidness of harps—like water. You wanted water as a source of power.

Bother! Nell was speaking. He'd have to listen.

"Vernon, after that awful escape from death—I knew. . . . There's only one thing that matters—love. I've always loved you. I've come back to you—for always."

"Oh!" he said stupidly.

She had come nearer, was holding out her hands to him.

He looked at her as if from a great distance. Really, Nell was extraordinarily pretty. He could well see why he had fallen in love with her. Queer, that he wasn't the least bit in love with her now. How awkward it all was. He did wish she would go away and let him get on with what he was doing. What about trombones? One could improve on a trombone . . .

"Vernon!" Her voice was sharp—frightened. "Don't you love me anymore?"

It was really best to be truthful. He said with an odd formal politeness:

"I'm awfully sorry. I—I'm afraid I don't. You see, I love Jane."

"You're angry with me—because of that lie about the—the child."

"What lie? About what child?"

"Don't you even remember? I said I was going to have a child and it wasn't true. . . . Oh! Vernon, forgive me . . . forgive me."

"That's quite all right, Nell. Don't you worry. I'm sure everything's for the best. George is an awfully good chap and you're really happiest with him. And now, for God's sake, do go away. I don't want to be rude, but I'm most awfully busy. The whole thing will go if I don't pin it down."

She stared at him.

Then slowly she moved toward the door. She stopped, turned, flung out her hands toward him.

"Vernon . . ."

It was a last cry of despairing appeal.

He did not even look up, only shook his head impatiently.

She went out, shutting the door behind her.

Vernon gave a sigh of relief.

There was nothing now to come between him and his work.

He bent over the table.

· THE ROSE AND THE YEW TREE ·

The moment of the rose and the moment of the yew tree
Are of equal duration

—T. S. ELIOT

Prelude

I was in Paris when Parfitt, my man, came to me and said that a lady had called to see me. She said, he added, that it was very important.

I had formed by then the habit of never seeing people without an appointment. People who call to see you about urgent business are nearly invariably people who wish for financial assistance. The people who are in real need of financial assistance, on the other hand, hardly ever come and ask for it.

I asked Parfitt what my visitor's name was, and he proffered a card. The card said: Catherine Yougoubian—a name I had never heard of and which, frankly, I did not much fancy. I revised my idea that she needed financial assistance and deduced instead that she had something to sell— probably one of those spurious antiques which command a better price when they are brought by hand and forced on the unwilling buyer with the aid of voluble patter.

I said I was sorry that I could not see Madame Yougoubian, but she could write and state her business.

Parfitt inclined his head and withdrew. He is very reliable—an invalid such as I am needs a reliable attendant—and I had not the slightest doubt that the matter was now disposed of. Much to my astonishment, however, Parfitt reappeared. The lady, he said, was very insistent. It was a matter of life and death and concerned an old friend of mine.

Whereupon my curiosity was suddenly aroused. Not by the message— that was a fairly obvious gambit; life and death and the old friend are the usual counters in the game. No, what stimulated my curiosity was the behavior of Parfitt. It was not like Parfitt to come back with a message of that kind.

I jumped, quite wrongly, to the conclusion that Catherine Yougoubian was incredibly beautiful, or at any rate unusually attractive. Nothing else, I thought, would explain Parfitt's behavior.

And since a man is always a man, even if he be fifty and a cripple, I fell into the snare. I wanted to see this radiant creature who could overcome the defenses of the impeccable Parfitt.

So I told him to bring the lady up—and when Catherine Yougoubian entered the room, revulsion of feeling nearly took my breath away!

True, I understand Parfitt's behavior well enough now. His judgment of human nature is quite unerring. He recognized in Catherine that persistence of temperament against which, in the end, all defenses fall. Wisely, he capitulated straight away and saved himself a long and wearying battle. For Catherine Yougoubian has the persistence of a sledge hammer and the monotony of an oxyacetylene blowpipe: combined with the wearing effect of water dropping on a stone! Time is infinite for her if she wishes to achieve her object. She would have sat determinedly in my entrance hall all day. She is one of those women who have room in their heads for one idea only—which gives them an enormous advantage over less single-minded individuals.

As I say, the shock I got when she entered the room was tremendous. I was all keyed up to behold beauty. Instead, the woman who entered was monumentally, almost awe-inspiringly, plain. Not ugly, mark you; ugliness has its own rhythm, its own mode of attack, but Catherine had a large flat face like a pancake—a kind of desert of a face. Her mouth was wide and had a slight—a very slight—moustache on its upper lip. Her eyes were small and dark and made one think of inferior currants in an inferior bun. Her hair was abundant, ill-confined, and preeminently greasy. Her figure was so nondescript that it was practically not a figure at all. Her clothes covered her adequately and fitted her nowhere. She appeared neither destitute nor opulent. She had a determined jaw and, as I heard when she opened her mouth, a harsh and unlovely voice.

I threw a glance of deep reproach at Parfitt who met it imperturbably. He was clearly of the opinion that, as usual, he knew best.

"Madame Yougoubian, sir," he said, and retired, shutting the door and leaving me at the mercy of this determined-looking female.

Catherine advanced upon me purposefully. I had never felt so helpless, so conscious of my crippled state. This was a woman from whom it would be advisable to run away, and I could not run.

She spoke in a loud firm voice.

"Please—if you will be so good—you must come with me, please?"

It was less of a request than a command.

"I beg your pardon?" I said, startled.

"I do not speak the English too good, I am afraid. But there is not time to lose—no, no time at all. It is to Mr. Gabriel I ask you to come. He is very ill. Soon, very soon, he dies, and he has asked for you. So to see him you must come at once."

I stared at her. Frankly, I thought she was crazy. The name Gabriel made no impression upon me at all, partly, I daresay, because of her pronunciation. It did not sound in the least like Gabriel. But even if it had sounded like it, I do not think that it would have stirred a chord. It was all so long ago. It must have been ten years since I had even thought of John Gabriel.

"You say someone is dying? Someone—er—that I know?"

She cast at me a look of infinite reproach.

"But yes, you know him—you know him well—and he asks for you."

She was so positive that I began to rack my brains. What name had she said? Gable? Galbraith? I had known a Galbraith, a mining engineer. Only casually, it is true; it seemed in the highest degree unlikely that he should ask to see me on his deathbed. Yet it is a tribute to Catherine's force of character that I did not doubt for a moment the truth of her statement.

"What name did you say?" I asked. "Galbraith?"

"No—no. Gabriel. *Gabriel!*"

I stared. This time I got the word right, but it only conjured up a mental vision of the Angel Gabriel with a large pair of wings. The vision fitted in well enough with Catherine Yougoubian. She had a resemblance to the type of earnest woman usually to be found kneeling in the extreme lefthand corner of an early Italian Primitive. She had that peculiar simplicity of feature combined with the look of ardent devotion.

She added, persistently, doggedly, "*John* Gabriel—" and I got it!

It all came back to me. I felt giddy and slightly sick. St. Loo, and the old ladies, and Milly Burt, and John Gabriel with his ugly dynamic little face, rocking gently back on his heels. And Rupert, tall and handsome like a young god. And, of course, Isabella. . . .

I remembered the last time I had seen John Gabriel in Zagrade and what had happened there, and I felt rising in me a surging red tide of anger and loathing. . . .

"So he's dying, is he?" I asked savagely. "I'm delighted to hear it!"

"Pardon?"

There are things that you cannot very well repeat when someone says "Pardon?" politely to you. Catherine Yougoubian looked utterly uncomprehending. I merely said:

"You say he is dying?"

"Yes. He is in pain—in terrible pain."

Well, I was delighted to hear that, too. No pain that John Gabriel could suffer would atone for what he had done. But I felt unable to say so to one who was evidently John Gabriel's devoted worshipper.

What was there about the fellow, I wondered irritably, that always made women fall for him? He was ugly as sin. He was pretentious, vulgar, boastful. He had brains of a kind, and he was, in certain circumstances (low circumstances!) good company. He had humor. But none of these are really characteristics that appeal to women very much.

Catherine broke in upon my thoughts.

"You will come, please? You will come quickly? There is no time to lose."

I pulled myself together.

"I'm sorry, my dear lady," I said, "but I'm afraid I cannot accompany you."

"But he asks for you," she persisted.

"I'm not coming," I said.

"You do not understand," said Catherine. "He is ill. He is dying; and he asks for you."

I braced myself for the fight. I had already begun to realize (what Parfitt had realized at the first glance) that Catherine Yougoubian did not give up easily.

"You are making a mistake," I said. "John Gabriel is not a friend of mine."

She nodded her head vigorously.

"But yes—but yes. He read your name in the paper—it say you are here as member of the Commission—and he say I am to find out where you live and to get you to come. And please you must come quick—very quick— for the doctor say very soon now. So will you come at once, please?"

It seemed to me that I had got to be frank. I said:

"He may rot in Hell for all I care!"

"Pardon?"

She looked at me anxiously, wrinkling her long nose, amiable, trying to understand. . . .

"John Gabriel," I said slowly and clearly, "is *not* a friend of mine. He is a man I hate—*hate*! Now do you understand?"

She blinked. It seemed to me that at last she was beginning to get there.

"You say—" she said it slowly, like a child repeating a difficult lesson, "you say that—you—hate—John Gabriel? Is that what you say, please?"

"That's right," I said.

She smiled—a maddening smile.

"No, no," she said indulgently, "that is not possible. . . . No one could hate John Gabriel. He is very great—very good—man. All of us who know him, we die for him gladly."

"Good God," I cried, exasperated. "What's the man ever done that people should feel like that about him?"

Well, I had asked for it! She forgot the urgency of her mission. She sat down, she pushed back a loop of greasy hair from her forehead, her eyes shone with enthusiasm, she opened her mouth, and words poured from her. . . .

She spoke, I think, for about a quarter of an hour. Sometimes she was incomprehensible, stumbling with the difficulties of the spoken word. Sometimes her words flowed in a clear stream. But the whole performance had the effect of a great epic.

She spoke with reverence, with awe, with humility, with worship. She spoke of John Gabriel as one speaks of a Messiah—and that clearly was what he was to her. She said things of him that to me seemed wildly fantastic and wholly impossible. She spoke of a man tender, brave, and strong. A leader and a succorer. She spoke of one who risked death that others might live; of one who hated cruelty and injustice with a white and burning flame. He was to her a Prophet, a King, a Saviour—one who could give to people courage that they did not know they had, and strength that they did not know they possessed. He had been tortured more than once; crippled, half-killed; but somehow his maimed body had overcome its disabilities by sheer willpower, and he had continued to perform the impossible.

"You do not know, you say, what he has done?" she ended. "But everyone knows Father Clement—*everyone!*"

I stared—for what she said was true. Everyone has heard of Father Clement. His is a name to conjure with, even if some people hold that it is only a name—a myth—and that the real man has never existed.

How shall I describe the legend of Father Clement? Imagine a mixture of Richard Coeur de Lion and Father Damien and Lawrence of Arabia. A man at once a fighter and a Saint and with the adventurous recklessness of a boy. In the years that had succeeded the war of 1939–1945, Europe and the East had undergone a black period. Fear had been in the ascendant, and Fear had bred its new crop of cruelties and savageries. Civilization had begun to crack. In India and Persia abominable things had happened: wholesale massacres, famines, tortures, anarchy. . . .

And through the black mist a figure, an almost legendary figure had appeared—the man calling himself "Father Clement"—saving children, rescuing people from torture, leading his flock by impassable ways over mountains, bringing them to safe zones, settling them in communities. Worshipped, loved, adored—a legend, not a man.

And according to Catherine Yougoubian, Father Clement was John Gabriel, former M.P. for St. Loo, womanizer, drunkard; the man who first, last, and all the time, played for his own hand. An adventurer, an opportunist, a man with no virtues save the virtue of physical courage.

Suddenly, uneasily, my incredulity wavered. Impossible as I believed

Catherine's tale to be, there was one point of plausibility. Both Father Clement and John Gabriel were men of unusual physical courage. Some of those exploits of the legendary figure, the audacity of the rescues, the sheer bluff, the—yes, the impudence of his methods, were John Gabriel's methods all right.

But John Gabriel had always been a self-advertiser. Everything he did, he did with an eye on the gallery. If John Gabriel was Father Clement, the whole world would surely have been advised of the fact.

No, I didn't—I couldn't—believe. . . .

But when Catherine stopped breathless, when the fire in her eyes died down, when she said in her old persistent monotonous manner, "You will come now, yes, please?" I shouted for Parfitt.

He helped me up and gave me my crutches and assisted me down the stairs and into a taxi, and Catherine got in beside me.

I had to know, you see. Curiosity, perhaps? Or the persistence of Catherine Yougoubian? (I should certainly have had to give way to her in the end!) Anyway, I wanted to see John Gabriel. I wanted to see if I could reconcile the Father Clement story with what I knew of the John Gabriel of St. Loo. I wanted, perhaps, to see if I could see what Isabella had seen—what she must have seen to have done as she had done. . . .

I don't know what I expected as I followed Catherine Yougoubian up the narrow stairs and into the little back bedroom. There was a French doctor there, with a beard and a pontifical manner. He was bending over his patient, but he drew back and motioned me forward courteously.

I noticed his eyes appraising me curiously. I was the person that a great man, dying, had expressed a wish to see. . . .

I had a shock when I saw Gabriel. It was so long since that day in Zagrade. I would not have recognized the figure that lay so quietly on the bed. He was dying, I saw that. The end was very near now. And it seemed to me that I recognized nothing I knew in the face of the man lying there. For I had to acknowledge that, as far as appearances went, Catherine had been right. That emaciated face was the face of a Saint. It had the marks of suffering, of agony. . . . It had the asceticism. And it had, finally, the spiritual peace. . . .

And none of these qualities had anything to do with the man whom I had known as John Gabriel.

Then he opened his eyes and saw me—and he grinned. It was the same grin, the same eyes—beautiful eyes in a small ugly clown's face.

His voice was very weak. He said, "So she got you! Armenians are wonderful!"

Yes, it was John Gabriel. He motioned to the doctor. He demanded in his weak suffering imperious voice, a promised stimulant. The doctor demurred—Gabriel overbore him. It would hasten the end, or so I guessed, but Gabriel made it clear that a last spurt of energy was important and indeed necessary to him.

The doctor shrugged his shoulders and gave in. He administered the injection and then he and Catherine left me alone with the patient.

Gabriel began at once.

"I want you to know about Isabella's death."

I told him that I knew all about that.

"No," he said, "I don't think you do . . ."

It was then that he described to me that final scene in the café in Zagrade.

I shall tell it in its proper place.

After that, he only said one thing more. It is because of that one thing more that I am writing this story.

Father Clement belongs to history. His incredible life of heroism, endurance, compassion, and courage belongs to those people who like writing the lives of heroes. The communities he started are the foundation of our new tentative experiments in living, and there will be many biographies of the man who imagined and created them.

This is not the story of Father Clement. It is the story of John Merryweather Gabriel, a V.C. in the war, and opportunist, a man of sensual passions and of great personal charm. He and I, in our different way, loved the same woman.

We all start out as the central figure of our own story. Later we wonder, doubt, get confused. So it has been with me. First it was *my* story. Then I thought it was Jennifer and I together—Romeo and Juliet, Tristan and Iseult. And then, in my darkness and disillusionment, Isabella sailed across my vision like the moon on a dark night. She became the central theme of the embroidery, and I—I was the cross-stitch background—no more. No more, but also no less, for without the drab background, the pattern will not stand out.

Now, again, the pattern has shifted. This is not my story, not Isabella's story. It is the story of John Gabriel.

The story ends here, where I am beginning it. It ends with John Gabriel. But it also begins here.

Chapter One

Where to begin? At St. Loo? At the meeting in the Memorial Hall when the prospective Conservative candidate, Major John Gabriel, V.C., was introduced by an old (a very old) General, and stood there and made his speech, disappointing us all a little by his flat common voice and his ugly face, so that we had to fortify ourselves by the recollection of his gallantry and by reminding ourselves that it was necessary to get into touch with the People—the privileged classes were now so pitifully small!

Or shall I begin at Polnorth House, in the long low room that faced the sea, with the terrace outside where my invalid couch could be drawn out on fine days and I could look out to the Atlantic with its thundering breakers, and the dark gray rocky point which broke the line of the horizon and on which rose the battlements and the turrets of St. Loo Castle—looking, as I always felt, like a watercolor sketch done by a romantic young lady in the year 1860 or thereabouts.

For St. Loo Castle has that bogus, that phony air of theatricality, of spurious romance which can only be given by something that is in fact genuine. It was built, you see, when human nature was unself-conscious enough to enjoy romanticism without feeling ashamed of it. It suggests sieges, and dragons, and captive princesses and knights in armor, and all the pageantry of a rather bad historical film. And of course when you come to think of it, a bad film is exactly what history really is.

When you looked at St. Loo Castle, you expected something like Lady

St. Loo, and Lady Tressilian, and Mrs. Bigham Charteris, and Isabella. The shock was that you got them!

Shall I begin there, with the visit paid by those three old ladies with their erect bearing, their dowdy clothing, their diamonds in old-fashioned settings? With my saying to Teresa in a fascinated voice, "But they can't—they simply can't—be *real?*"

Or shall I start a little earlier; at the moment, for instance, when I got into the car and started for Northolt Aerodrome to meet Jennifer . . . ?

But behind that again is *my* life—which had started thirty-eight years before and which came to an end that day. . . .

This is not *my* story. I have said that before. But it began as my story. It began with me, Hugh Norreys. Looking back over my life, I see that it has been a life much like any other man's life. Neither more interesting, nor less so. It has had the inevitable disillusionments and disappointments, the secret childish agonies; it has had also the excitements, the harmonies, the intense satisfactions arising from oddly inadequate causes. I can choose from which angle I will view my life—from the angle of frustration, or as a triumphant chronicle. Both are true. It is, in the end, always a question of selection. There is Hugh Norreys as he sees himself, and Hugh Norreys as he appears to others. There must actually be, too, Huge Norreys as he appears to God. There must be the essential Hugh. But his story is the story that only the recording angel can write. It comes back to this: How much do I know, now, of the young man who got into the train at Penzance in the early days of 1945 on his way to London? Life had, I should have said if asked, on the whole treated me well. I liked my peacetime job of schoolmastering. I had enjoyed my war experiences—I had my job waiting to return to—and the prospect of a partnership and a headmastership in the future. I had had love affairs that had hurt me, but none that went deep. I had family ties that were adequate, but not too close. I was thirty-seven and on that particular day I was conscious of something of which I had been half-conscious for some time. I was waiting for something . . . for an experience, for a supreme event. . . .

Everything up to then in my life, I suddenly felt, had been superficial—I was waiting now for something *real*. Probably everyone experiences such a feeling once at least in their lives. Sometimes it comes early, sometimes late. It is a moment that corresponds to the moment in a cricket match when you go in to bat. . . .

I got on the train at Penzance and I took a ticket for third lunch (because I had just finished a rather large breakfast) and when the attendant came along the train shouting out nasally, "Third lunch, please, tickets ooonlee . . ." I got up and went along to the dining car and the attendant took my ticket and gestured me into a single seat, back to the engine, opposite the place where Jennifer was sitting.

That, you see, is how things happen. You cannot take thought for them, you cannot plan. I sat down opposite Jennifer—and Jennifer was crying.

I didn't see it at first. She was struggling hard for control. There was no sound, no outward indication. We did not look at each other, we behaved with due regard to the conventions governing the meeting of strangers on a restaurant car. I advanced the menu towards her—a polite but meaningless action since it only bore the legend: Soup, Fish or Meat, Sweet or Cheese. 4/6.

She accepted my gesture with the answering gesture, a polite ritualistic smile and an inclination of the head. The attendant asked us what we would have to drink. We both had light ale.

Then there was a pause. I looked at the magazine I had brought in with me. The attendant dashed along the car with plates of soup and set them in front of us. Still the little gentleman, I advanced the salt and pepper an inch in Jennifer's direction. Up to now I had not looked at her—not really looked, that is to say—though of course I knew certain basic facts. That she was young, but not very young, a few years younger than myself, that she was of medium height and dark, that she was of my own social standing and that while attractive enough to be pleasant, she was not so overwhelmingly attractive as to be in any sense disturbing.

Presently I intended to look rather more closely, and if it seemed indicated I should probably advance a few tentative remarks. It would depend.

But the thing that suddenly upset all my calculations was the fact that my eyes, straying over the soup plate opposite me, noticed that something unexpected was splashing into the soup. Without noise, or sound, or any indication of distress, tears were forcing themselves from her eyes and dropping into the soup.

I was startled. I cast swift surreptitious glances at her. The tears soon stopped, she succeeded in forcing them back, she drank her soup. I said, quite unpardonably, but irresistibly:

"You're dreadfully unhappy, aren't you?"

And she replied fiercely, "I'm a perfect fool!"

Neither of us spoke. The waiter took the soup plates away. He laid minute portions of meat pie in front of us and helped us from a monstrous dish of cabbage. To this he added two roast potatoes with the air of one doing us a special favor.

I looked out of the window and made a remark about the scenery. I proceeded to a few remarks about Cornwall. I said I didn't know it well. Did she? She said, Yes, she did, she lived there. We compared Cornwall with Devonshire, and with Wales, and with the East coast. None of our conversation meant anything. It served the purpose of glossing over the fact that she had been guilty of shedding tears in a public place and that I had been guilty of noticing the fact.

It was not until we had coffee in front of us and I had offered her a cigarette and she had accepted it, that we got back to where we had started.

I said I was sorry I had been so stupid, but that I couldn't help it. She said I must have thought her a perfect idiot.

"No," I said. "I thought that you'd come to the end of your tether. That was it, wasn't it?"

She said, Yes, that was it.

"It's humiliating," she said fiercely, "to get to such a pitch of self-pity that you don't care what you do or who sees you!"

"But you *did* care. You were struggling hard."

"I didn't actually howl," she said, "if that's what you mean."

I asked her how bad it was?

She said it was pretty bad. She had got to the end of everything, and she didn't know what to do.

I think I had already sensed that. There was an air of taut desperation about her. I wasn't going to let her get away from me while she was in that mood. I said, "Come on, tell me about it. I'm a stranger—you can say things to a stranger. It won't matter."

She said, "There's nothing to tell except that I've made the most bloody mess of everything—*everything*."

I told her it wasn't probably as bad as all that. She needed, I could see, reassurance. She needed new life, new courage—she needed lifting up from a pitiful slough of endurance and suffering and setting on her feet again. I had not the slightest doubt that I was the person best qualified to do that. . . . Yes, it happened as soon as that.

She looked at me doubtfully, like an uncertain child. Then she poured it all out.

In the midst of it, of course, the attendant came with the bill. I was glad then that we were having the third lunch. They wouldn't hustle us out of the dining car. I added ten shillings to my bill, and the attendant bowed discreetly and melted away.

I went on listening to Jennifer.

She'd had a raw deal. She'd stood up to things with an incredible amount of pluck, but there had been too many things, one after the other, and she wasn't physically, strong. Things had gone wrong for her all along—as a child, as a girl, in her marriage. Her sweetness, her impulsiveness, had landed her every time in a hole. There had been loopholes for escape and she hadn't taken them—she'd preferred to try and make the best of a bad job. And when that had failed, and a loophole had presented itself, it had been a bad loophole, and she'd landed herself in a worse mess than ever.

For everything that had happened, she blamed herself. My heart warmed to that lovable trait in her—there was no judgment, no resentment. "It must," she ended up wistfully every time, "have been my fault somehow . . ."

I wanted to roar out, "Of course it wasn't your fault! Don't you see that you're a victim—that you'll always be a victim—so long as you adopt that fatal attitude of being willing to take all the blame for everything?"

She was adorable sitting there, worried and miserable and defeated. I think I knew then, looking at her across the narrow table, what it was

I had been waiting for. It was Jennifer . . . not Jennifer as a possession, but to give Jennifer back her mastery of life, to see Jennifer happy, to see her *whole* once more.

Yes, I knew then . . . though it wasn't until many weeks afterwards that I admitted to myself that I was in love with her.

You see, there was so much more to it than that.

We made no plans for meeting again. I think she believed truly that we would not meet again. I knew otherwise. She had told me her name. She said, very sweetly, when we at last left the dining car, "This is good-bye. But please believe I shall never forget you and what you've done for me. I was desperate—quite desperate."

I took her hand and I said good-bye—but I knew it wasn't good-bye. I was so sure of it that I would have been willing to agree not even to try and find her again. But as it chanced there were friends of hers who were friends of mine. I did not tell her, but to find her again would be easy. What was odd was that we had not happened to meet before this.

I met her again a week later, at Caro Strangeways's cocktail party. And after that, there was no more doubt about it. We both knew what had happened to us. . . .

We met and parted and met again. We met at parties, in other people's houses, we met at small quiet restaurants, we took trains into the country and walked together in a world that was all a shining haze of unreal bliss. We went to a concert and heard Elizabeth Schumann sing "And in that pathway where our feet shall wander, we'll meet, forget the earth and lost in dreaming, bid heaven unite a love that earth no more shall sunder . . ."

And as we went out into the noise and bustle of Wigmore Street I repeated the last words of Strauss's song "—in love and bliss ne'er ending . . ." and met her eyes.

She said, "Oh no, not for us, Hugh . . ."

And I said, "Yes, for us . . ."

Because, as I pointed out to her, we had got to go through the rest of our lives together. . . .

She couldn't, she said, throw everything over like that. Her husband, she knew, wouldn't consent to let her divorce him.

"But he'd divorce you?"

"Yes, I suppose so . . . Oh Hugh, can't we go on as we are?"

No, I said, we couldn't. I'd been waiting, watching her fight her way back to health and sanity. I hadn't wanted to let her vex herself with decisions until she was once more the happy joyful creature Nature had created her to be. Well, I'd done it. She was strong again—strong mentally and physically. And we'd got to come to a decision.

It wasn't plain sailing. She had all sorts of queer, quite unpredictable objections. Chiefly, it was because of me and my career that she demurred. It would mean a complete breakup for me. Yes, I said, I knew that. I'd thought it out, and it didn't matter. I was young—there were other things that I could do besides schoolmastering.

She cried then and said that she'd never forgive herself if, because of her, I were to ruin my life. I told her that nothing could ruin it, unless she herself were to leave me. Without her, I said, life would be finished for me.

We had a lot of ups and downs. She would seem to accept my view, then suddenly, when I was no longer with her, she would retract. She had, you see, no confidence in herself.

Yet, little by little, she came to share my outlook. It was not only passion between us—there was more than that. That harmony of mind and thought—that delight in mind answering mind. The things that she would say—which had just been on my own lips—the sharing of a thousand small minor pleasures.

She admitted at last that I was right, that we belonged together. Her last defenses went down.

"It *is* true! Oh Hugh, how it can be, I don't know. How can I really mean to you what you say I do? And yet I don't really doubt."

The thing was tested—proved. We made plans, the necessary mundane plans.

It was a cold sunny morning when I woke up and realized that on that day our new life was starting. From now on Jennifer and I would be together. Not until this moment had I allowed myself to believe fully. I had always feared that her strange morbid distrust of her own capabilities would make her draw back.

Even on this, the last morning of the old life, I had to make quite sure. I rang her up.

"Jennifer . . ."

"Hugh . . ."

Her voice, soft with a tiny tremor in it . . . It was true, I said:

"Forgive me, darling. I had to hear your voice. Is it all true?"

"It's all true. . . ."

We were to meet at Northolt Aerodrome. I hummed as I dressed, I shaved carefully. In the mirror I saw a face almost unrecognizable with sheer idiotic happiness. This was *my* day! The day I had waited for for thirty-eight years. I breakfasted, checked over tickets, passport. I went down to the car. Harriman was driving. I told him I would drive—he could sit behind.

I turned out of the Mews into the main road. The car wound in and out of the traffic. I had plenty of time. It was a glorious morning—a lovely morning created specially for Hugh and Jennifer. I could have sung and shouted.

The lorry came at forty miles an hour out of the side road—there was no seeing or avoiding it—no failure in driving—no faulty reaction. The driver of the lorry was drunk, they told me afterwards—how little it matters *why* a thing happens!

It struck the Buick broadside on, wrecking it—pinning me under the wreckage. Harriman was killed.

Jennifer waited at the Aerodrome. The plane left . . . I did not come. . . .

Chapter Two

There isn't much point in describing what came next. There wasn't, to begin with, any continuity. There was confusion, darkness, pain. . . . I wandered endlessly, it seemed to me, in long underground corridors. At intervals I realized dimly that I was in a hospital ward. I was aware of doctors, white-capped nurses, the smell of antiseptics—the flashing of steel instruments, glittering little glass trolleys being wheeled briskly about. . . .

Realization came to me slowly—there was less confusion, less pain . . .

but no thoughts as yet of people or of places. The animal in pain knows only pain or the surcease of pain, it can concentrate on nothing else. Drugs, mercifully dulling physical suffering, confuse the mind; heightening the impression of chaos.

But lucid intervals began to come—there was the moment when they told me definitely that I had had an accident.

Knowledge came at last—knowledge of my helplessness—of my wrecked broken body. . . . There was no more life for me as a man amongst men.

People came to see me—my brother, awkward, tongue-tied, with no idea of what to say. We had never been very close. I could not speak to him of Jennifer.

But it was of Jennifer I was thinking. As I improved, they brought me my letters. Letters from Jennifer . . .

Only my immediate family had been admitted to see me. Jennifer had had no claim, no right. She had been technically only a friend.

They won't let me come, Hugh darling, she wrote. *I shall come as soon as they do. All my love. Concentrate on getting better, Jennifer.*

And another:

Don't worry, Hugh. Nothing matters so long as you are not dead. That's all that matters. We shall be together soon—for always. Yours Jennifer.

I wrote to her, a feeble pencil scrawl, that she mustn't come. What had I to offer Jennifer now?

It was not until I was out of the hospital and in my brother's house that I saw Jennifer again. Her letters had all sounded the same note. We loved each other! Even if I never recovered we must be together. She would look after me. There would still be happiness—not the happiness of which we had once dreamed, but still happiness.

And though my first reaction had been to cut the knot ruthlessly, to say to Jennifer, "Go away, and never come near me," I wavered. Because I believed, as she did, that the tie between us was not of the flesh only. All the delights of mental companionship would still be ours. Certainly it would be best for her to go and forget me—but if she would not go?

It was a long time before I gave in and let her come. We wrote to each other frequently and those letters of ours were true love letters. They were inspiring—heroic in tone—

And so, at last, I let her come. . . .

Well, she came.

She wasn't allowed to stay very long. We knew then, I suppose—but we wouldn't admit it. She came again. She came a third time. After that, I simply couldn't stand it any longer. Her third visit lasted ten minutes, and it seemed like an hour and a half! I could hardly believe it when I looked at my watch afterwards. It had seemed, I have no doubt, just as long to her. . . .

For you see we had nothing to say to each other. . . .

Yes, just that. . . .

There wasn't, after all, anything there.

Is there any bitterness like the bitterness of a fool's paradise? All that communion of mind with mind, our thoughts that leapt to complete each other, our friendship, our companionship: illusion—nothing but illusion. The illusion that mutual attraction between man and woman breeds. Nature's lure, Nature's last and most cunning piece of deceit. Between me and Jennifer there had been the attraction of the flesh only—from that had sprung the whole monstrous fabric of self-deception. It had been passion and passion only, and the discovery shamed me, turned me sour, brought me almost to the point of hating her as well as myself. We stared at each other desolately—wondering each in our own way what had happened to the miracle in which we had been so confident.

She was a good-looking young woman, I saw that. But when she talked she bored me. And I bored her. We couldn't talk about anything or discuss anything with any pleasure.

She kept reproaching herself for the whole thing, and I wished she wouldn't. It seemed unnecessary and just a trifle hysterical. I thought to myself, Why on earth has she got to fuss so?

As she left the third time she said, in her persevering bright way, "I'll come again very soon, Hugh darling."

"No," I said. "Don't come."

"But of course I shall." Her voice was hollow, insincere.

I said savagely, "For God's sake don't pretend, Jennifer. It's finished—it's all finished."

She said it wasn't finished, that she didn't know what I meant. She was going to spend her life looking after me, she said, and we would be very happy. She was determined on self-immolation, and it made me see red. I felt apprehensive, too, that she would do as she said. Perhaps she would always be there, chattering, trying to be kind, uttering foolish bright remarks . . . I got in a panic—a panic born of weakness and illness.

I yelled at her to go away—go *away*. She went, looking frightened. But I saw relief in her eyes.

When my sister-in-law came in later to draw the curtains, I spoke. I said, "It's over, Teresa. She's gone, she's gone . . . She won't come back, will she?"

Teresa said in her quiet voice, No, she wouldn't come back.

"Do you think, Teresa," I asked, "that it's my illness that makes me see things—wrong?"

Teresa knew what I meant. She said that, in her opinion, an illness like mine tended to make you see things as they really were.

"You mean that I'm seeing Jennifer now as she really is?"

Teresa said she didn't mean quite that. I wasn't probably any better able to know what Jennifer was really like now than before. But I knew now exactly what effect Jennifer produced on *me*, apart from my being in love with her.

I asked her what she herself thought of Jennifer.

She said that she had always thought Jennifer was attractive, nice, and not at all interesting.

"Do you think she's very unhappy, Teresa?" I asked morbidly.

"Yes, Hugh, I do."

"Because of me?"

"No, because of herself."

I said, "She goes on blaming herself for my accident. She keeps saying that if I hadn't been coming to meet *her*, it would never have happened—it's all so *stupid*!"

"It is, rather."

"I don't want her to work herself up about it. I don't want her to be unhappy, Teresa."

"Really, Hugh," said Teresa. "Do leave the girl something!"

"What do you mean?"

"She *likes* being unhappy. Haven't you realized that?"

There is a cold clarity about my sister-in-law's thought processes that I find very disconcerting.

I told her that that was a beastly thing to say.

Teresa said thoughtfully that perhaps it was, but that she hadn't really thought it mattered saying so now.

"You haven't got to tell yourself fairy stories any longer. Jennifer has always loved sitting down and thinking how everything has gone wrong. She broods over it and works herself up—but if she likes living that way, why shouldn't she?" Teresa added, "You know, Hugh, you can't feel pity for a person unless there's self-pity there. A person has to be sorry for themselves before you can be sorry for them. Pity has always been your weakness. Because of it you don't see things clearly."

I found momentary satisfaction in telling Teresa that she was an odious woman. She said she thought she probably was.

"You are never sorry for anyone."

"Yes, I am. I'm sorry for Jennifer in a way."

"And me?"

"I don't know, Hugh."

I said sarcastically:

"The fact that I'm a maimed broken wreck with nothing to live for doesn't affect you at all?"

"I don't know if I'm sorry for you or not. This means that you're going to start your life all over again, living it from an entirely different angle. That might be very interesting."

I told Teresa that she was inhuman, and she went away smiling.

She had done me a lot of good.

Chapter Three

It was soon afterwards that we moved to St. Loo in Cornwall.

Teresa had just inherited a house there from a great-aunt. The doctor wanted me to be out of London. My brother Robert is a painter with what most people think is a perverted vision of landscapes. His war service, like most artists', had been agricultural. So it all fitted in very well.

Teresa went down and got the house ready and, having filled up a lot of forms successfully, I was borne down by special ambulance.

"What goes on here?" I asked Teresa on the morning after my arrival.

Teresa was well-informed. There were, she said, three separate worlds. There was the old fishing village, grouped round its harbor, with the tall slate-roofed houses rising up all round it, and the notices written in Flemish and French as well as English. Beyond that, sprawling out along the coast, was the modern tourist and residential excrescence. The large luxury hotels, thousands of small bungalows, masses of little boarding houses—all very busy and active in summer, quiet in winter. Thirdly, there was St. Loo Castle, ruled over by the old dowager, Lady St. Loo, a nucleus of yet another way of life with ramifications stretching up through winding lanes to houses tucked inconspicuously away in valleys beside old world churches. County, in fact, said Teresa.

"And what are we?" I asked.

Teresa said we were "county" too, because Polnorth House had belonged to her great-aunt Miss Amy Tregellis, and it was hers, Teresa's, by inheritance and not by purchase, so that we belonged.

"Even Robert?" I asked. "In spite of his being a painter?"

That, Teresa admitted, would take a little swallowing. There were too many painters at St. Loo in the summer months.

"But he's my husband," said Teresa superbly, "and besides, his mother was a Bolduro from Bodmin way."

It was then that I invited Teresa to tell us what we were going to do in the new home—or rather what she was going to do. My role was clear. I was the looker-on.

Teresa said she was going to participate in all the local goings-on.

"Which are?"

Teresa said she thought mainly politics and gardening, with a dash of Women's Institutes and good causes such as Welcoming the Soldiers Home.

"But principally politics," she said. "After all, a General Election will be on us any minute."

"Have you ever taken any interest in politics, Teresa?"

"No, Hugh, I haven't. It has always seemed to me unnecessary. I have confined myself to voting for the candidate who seems to me likely to do least harm."

"An admirable policy," I murmured.

But now, Teresa said, she would do her best to take politics seriously. She would have, of course, to be a Conservative. Nobody who owned Polnorth House could be anything else, and the late Miss Amy Tregellis would turn in her grave if the niece to whom she had bequeathed her treasures was to vote Labour.

"But if you believe Labour to be the better party?"

"I don't," said Teresa. "I don't think there's anything to choose between them."

"Nothing could be fairer than that," I said.

When we had been settled in at Polnorth House a fortnight, Lady St. Loo came to call upon us.

She brought with her her sister, Lady Tressilian, her sister-in-law, Mrs. Bigham Charteris, and her granddaughter, Isabella.

After they had left, I said in a fascinated voice to Teresa that they couldn't be real.

They were, you see, so exactly right to have come out of St. Loo Castle. They were pure fairy story. The Three Witches and the Enchanted Maiden.

Adelaide St. Loo was the widow of the seventh Baron. Her husband had been killed in the Boer War. Her two sons had been killed in the war of 1914–1918. They left behind them no sons, but the younger left a daughter, Isabella, whose mother had died at her birth. The title passed to a cousin, then resident in New Zealand. The ninth Lord St. Loo was only too pleased to rent the Castle to the old dowager. Isabella was brought up there, watched over by her guardians, her grandmother and her two great-aunts. Lady St. Loo's widowed sister, Lady Tressilian, and her widowed sister-in-law, Mrs. Bigham Charteris, came to join her. They shared expenses and so made it possible for Isabella to be brought up in what the old ladies considered her rightful home. They were all over seventy, and had somewhat the appearance of three black crows. Lady St. Loo had a vast bony face, with an eagle nose and a high forehead. Lady Tressilian was plump and had a large round face with little twinkling eyes. Mrs. Bigham Charteris was lean and leathery. They achieved in their appearance a kind of Edwardian effect—as though time had stood still for them. They wore jewelry, rather dirty, indubitably real, pinned on them in unlikely places—not too much of it. It was usually in the form of crescents or horseshoes or stars.

Such were the three old ladies of St. Loo Castle. With them came Isabella—a very fair representative of an enchanted maiden. She was tall and thin, and her face was long and thin with a high forehead, and straight-falling ash-blond hair. She was almost incredibly like a figure out of an early stained-glass window. She could not have been called actually pretty, nor attractive, but there was about her something that you might almost call beauty—only it was the beauty of a time long past—it was most definitely not at all the modern idea of beauty. There was no animation in her, no charm of coloring, no irregularity of feature. Her beauty was the severe beauty of good structure—good bone formation. She looked medieval, severe and austere. But her face was not characterless; it had what I can only describe as nobility.

After I had said to Teresa that the old ladies weren't real, I added that the girl wasn't real either.

"The Princess imprisoned in the ruined castle?" Teresa suggested.

"Exactly. She ought to have come here on a milk white steed and not in a very old Daimler." I added with curiosity, "I wonder what she thinks about."

For Isabella had said very little during the official visit. She had sat very upright, with a sweet rather faraway smile. She had responded politely to any conversational overtures made to her, but there had not been much need for her to sustain the conversation since her grandmother and aunts had monopolized most of the talk. I wondered if she had been bored to come, or interested in something new turning up in St. Loo. Her life, I thought, must be rather dull.

I asked curiously, "Didn't she get called up at all during the war? Did she stay at home through it all?"

"She's only nineteen. She's been driving for the Red Cross here since she left school."

"School?" I was astonished. "Do you mean she's been to school? Boarding school?"

"Yes. St. Ninian's."

I was even more surprised. For St. Ninian's is an expensive and up-to-date school—not co-educational, or in any sense a crank school—but an establishment priding itself on its modern outlook. Not in any sense a fashionable finishing school.

"Do you find that astonishing?" Teresa asked.

"Yes, do you know, I do," I said slowly. "That girl gives you the impression that she's never been away from home, that she's been brought up in some bygone medieval environment that is completely out of touch with the twentieth century."

Teresa nodded her head thoughtfully. "Yes," she said. "I know what you mean."

My brother Robert chimed in here. It just showed, he said, how the only environment that counted was home environment—that and hereditary disposition.

"I still wonder," I said curiously, "what she thinks about . . ."

"Perhaps," said Teresa, "she doesn't think."

I laughed at Teresa's suggestion. But I wondered still in my own mind about this curious stick of a girl.

At that particular time I was suffering from an almost morbid self-consciousness about my own condition. I had always been a healthy and athletic person—I had disliked such things as illness or deformity, or ever having my attention called to them. I had been capable of pity, yes, but with pity had always gone a faint repulsion.

And now I was an object to inspire pity and repulsion. An invalid, a cripple, a man lying on a couch with twisted limbs—a rug pulled up over him.

And sensitively I waited, shrinking, for everyone's reaction to my state. Whatever it was, it invariably made me flinch. The kindly commiserating glance was horrible to me. No less horrible was the obvious tact that managed to pretend that I was an entirely natural object, that the visitor hadn't noticed anything unusual. But for Teresa's iron will, I would have shut myself up and seen nobody at all. But Teresa, when she is determined on anything, is not easy to withstand. She was determined that I should not become a recluse. She managed, without the aid of the spoken word, to suggest that to shut myself up and make a mystery of myself would be a form of self-advertisement. I knew what she was doing and why she was doing it, but nevertheless I responded. Grimly I set out to show her I could take it—no matter what it was! Sympathy, tact, the extra kindliness in a voice, the conscientious avoidance of any reference to accidents or illness, the pretense that I was as other men—I endured them all with a poker face.

I had not found the old ladies' reaction to my state too embarrassing. Lady St. Loo had adopted the line of tactful avoidance. Lady Tressilian, a maternal type, had not been able to help exuding maternal compassion. She had stressed, rather obviously, the latest books. She wondered if, perhaps, I did any reviewing? Mrs. Bigham Charteris, a blunter type, had shown her awareness only by rather obviously checking herself when speaking of the more active blood sports. (Poor devil, mustn't mention hunting or the beagles.)

Only the girl, Isabella, had surprised me by being natural. She had looked at me without any suggestion of having to look away quickly. She had looked at me as though her mind registered me along with the other occupants of the room and with the furniture. *One man, age over thirty, broken.* . . . An item in a catalogue—a catalogue of things that had nothing to do with her.

When she had finished with me, her eyes went on to the grand piano, and then to Robert and Teresa's Tang Horse which stood on a table by itself. The Tang Horse seemed to awaken a certain amount of interest in her. She asked me what it was. I told her.

"Do you like it?" I asked her.

She considered quite carefully before replying. Then she said—and gave the monosyllable a lot of weight, as though it was important— "Yes."

I wondered if she was a moron.

I asked her if she was fond of horses.

She said this was the first one she'd seen.

"No," I said, "I meant real horses."

"Oh, I see. Yes, I am. But I can't afford to hunt."

"Would you like to hunt?"

"Not particularly. There's not very much good country round here."

I asked her if she sailed and she said she did. Then Lady Tressilian began talking to me about books, and Isabella relapsed into silence. She had, I noticed then, one art highly developed: the art of repose. She could sit still. She didn't smoke, she didn't cross her legs, or swing them, or fiddle with her hands, or pat her hair. She sat quite still and upright in the tall grandfather chair, with her hands on her lap—long narrow hands. She was as immobile as the Tang Horse—it on its table, she in her chair. They had something, I thought, of the same quality—highly decorative—static—belonging to a bygone age. . . .

I laughed when Teresa suggested that she didn't think, but later it occurred to me that it might be true. Animals don't think—their minds are relaxed, passive, until an emergency arises with which they have to deal. Thinking (in the speculative sense of the word) is really a highly artificial process which we have taught ourselves with some trouble. We worry over what we did yesterday, and debate what we are going to do today and what will happen tomorrow. But yesterday, today and tomorrow exist quite independently of our speculation. They have happened and will happen to us no matter what we do about it.

Teresa's prognostications of our life at St. Loo were singularly accurate. Almost at once we became plunged up to the neck in politics. Polnorth House was large and rambling, and Miss Amy Tregellis, her income diminished by taxation, had shut off a wing of it, providing this with a separate kitchen. It had been done originally for evacuees from the bombed areas. But the evacuees, arriving from London in midwinter, had been unable to stomach the horrors of Polnorth House. In St. Loo itself, with its shops and its bungalows, they might have been able to support life, but a mile from the town, along "that narsty winding lane—the mud, yer wouldn't believe it—and no lights—and anybody might jump out on yer from be'ind the hedge. And vegetables all mud out of the garden, too much green stuff, and milk—coming right from a cow—quite hot sometimes—disgusting—and never a tin of condensed handy!" It was too much for Mrs. Price and Mrs. Hardy and their offspring. They departed secretly at early dawn taking their broods back to the dangers of London. They were nice women. They left the place clean and scrubbed and a note on the table.

"Thanking you, Miss, for your kindness, and we know you've done all you can, but it's just too awful in the country, and the children having to walk in the mud to school. But thanking you all the same. I hope as everything has been left all right."

The billeting officer did not try anymore. He was learning wisdom. In due course Miss Tregellis let the detached wing to Captain Carslake, the Conservative agent, who also led a busy life as an Air Raid Warden and an officer in the Home Guard.

Robert and Teresa were perfectly willing for the Carslakes to continue as tenants. Indeed, it was doubtful if they could have turned them out. But it meant that a great deal of preelection activity centerd in and around Polnorth House as well as the Conservative offices in St. Loo High Street.

Teresa, as she had foreseen, was swept into the vortex. She drove cars, and distributed leaflets, and did a little tentative canvassing. St. Loo's recent political history was unsettled. As a fashionable seaside watering place, superimposed on a fishing port, and with agricultural surroundings, it had naturally always returned a Conservative. The outlying agricultural districts were Conservative to a man. But the character of St. Loo had changed in the last fifteen years. It had become a tourist resort in summer with small boardinghouses. It had a large colony of artists' bungalows, like a rash, spread along the cliffs. The people who made up the present population were serious, artistic, cultured and, in politics, definitely pink if not red.

There had been a by-election in 1943 on the retirement of Sir George Borrodaile at the age of sixty-nine after his second stroke. And to the horror of the old inhabitants, for the first time in history, a Labour M.P. was returned.

"Mind you," said Captain Carslake, swaying to and fro on his heels as he imparted past history to Teresa and myself, "I'm not saying we didn't ask for it."

Carslake was a lean little dark man, horsy-looking, with sharp almost furtive eyes. He had become a captain in 1918 when he had entered the Army Service Corps. He was competent politically and knew his job.

You must understand that I myself am a tyro in politics—I never really understand the jargon. My account of the St. Loo election is probably wildly inaccurate. It bears the same relation to reality as Robert's pictures of trees do the particular trees he happens to be painting at the moment. The actual trees are trees, entities with barks and branches and leaves and acorns or chestnuts. Robert's trees are blodges and splodges of thick oil paint applied in a certain pattern and wildly surprising colors to a certain area of canvas. The two things are not at all alike. In my own opinion, Robert's trees are not even recognizable as trees—they might just as easily be plates of spinach or a gas works. But they are Robert's *idea* of trees. And my account of politics in St. Loo is my impression of a political election. It is probably not recognizable as such to a politician. I daresay I shall get the terms and the procedure wrong. But to me the election was only the unimportant and confusing background for a life-size figure—John Gabriel.

Chapter Four

The first mention of John Gabriel came on the evening when Carslake was explaining to Teresa that as regards the result of the by-election they had asked for it.

Sir James Bradwell of Torington Park had been the Conservative candidate. He was a resident of the district, he had some money, and was a good dyed-in-the-wool Tory with sound principles. He was a man of upright character. He was also sixty-two, devoid of intellectual fire, or quick reactions—had no gift of public speaking and was quite helpless if heckled.

"Pitiful on a platform," said Carslake. "Quite pitiful. Er and ah and erhem—just couldn't get on with it. We wrote his speeches, of course, and we had a good speaker down always for the important meetings. It would have been all right ten years ago. Good honest chap, local, straight as a die, and a gentleman. But nowadays—they want more than that!"

"They want brains?" I suggested.

Carslake didn't seem to think much of brains.

"They want a downy sort of chap—slick—knows the answers, can get a quick laugh. And, of course, they want someone who'll promise the earth. An old-fashioned chap like Bradwell is too conscientious to do that sort of thing. He won't say that everyone will have houses, and the war will end tomorrow, and every woman's going to have central heating and a washing machine.

"And of course," he went on, "the swing of the pendulum had begun. We've been in too long. Anything for a change. The other chap, Wilbraham, was a competent fellow, earnest, been a schoolmaster, invalided out of the Army, big talk about what was going to be done for the returning ex-serviceman—and the usual hot air about Nationalization and the Health Schemes. What I mean is, he put over his stuff well. Got in with a majority of over two thousand. First time such a thing's ever happened in St. Loo. Shook us all up, I can tell you. We've got to do better this time. We've got to get Wilbraham out."

"Is he popular?"

"So so. Doesn't spend much money in the place, but he's conscientious and got a nice manner with him. It won't be too easy getting him out. We've got to pull our socks up all over the country."

"You don't think Labour will get in?"

We were incredulous about such a possibility before the election of 1945.

Carslake said of course Labour wouldn't get in—the county was solidly behind Churchill.

"But we shan't have the same majority in the country. Depends, of course, how the Liberal vote goes. Between you and me, Mrs. Norreys, I shan't be surprised if we see a big increase in the Liberal vote."

I glanced sideways at Teresa. She was trying to assume the face of one politically intent.

"I'm sure you'll be a great help to us," said Carslake heartily to her.

Teresa murmured, "I'm afraid I'm not a very keen politician."

Carslake said breezily, "We must all work hard."

He looked at me in a calculating manner. I at once offered to address envelopes.

"I still have the use of my arms," I said.

He looked embarrassed at once and began to rock on his heels again.

"Splendid," he said. "Splendid. Where did you get yours? North Africa?"

I said I had got it in the Harrow Road. That finished him. His embarrassment was so acute as to be catching.

Clutching at a straw, he turned to Teresa.

"Your husband," he said, "he'll help us too?"

Teresa shook her head.

"I'm afraid," she said, "he's a Communist."

If she had said Robert had been a black mamba she couldn't have upset Carslake more. He positively shuddered.

"You see," explained Teresa, "he's an artist."

Carslake brightened a little at that. Artists, writers, that sort of thing . . .

"I see," he said broad-mindedly. "Yes, I see."

"And that gets Robert out of it," Teresa said to me afterwards.

I told her that she was an unscrupulous woman.

When Robert came in, Teresa informed him of his political faith.

"But I've never been a member of the Communist party," he protested. "I mean, I do like their ideas. I think the whole ideology is right."

"Exactly," said Teresa. "That's what I told Carslake. And from time to time we'll leave Karl Marx open across the arm of your chair—and then you'll be quite safe from being asked to do anything."

"That's all very well, Teresa," said Robert doubtfully. "Suppose the other side get at me?"

Teresa reassured him.

"They won't. As far as I can see, the Labour party is far more frightened of the Communists than the Tories are."

"I wonder," I said, "what our candidate's like?"

For Carslake had been just a little evasive on the subject.

Teresa had asked him if Sir James was going to contest the seat again and Carslake had shaken his head.

"No, not this time. We've got to make a big fight. I don't know how it will go, I'm sure." He looked very harassed. "He's not a local man."

"Who is he?"

"A Major Gabriel. He's a V.C."

"This war? Or the last?"

"Oh, this war. He's quite a youngish chap. Thirty-four. Splendid war record. Got his V.C. for 'Unusual coolness, heroism and devotion to duty.' He was in command of a machine-gun position under constant enemy fire in the attack at Salerno. All but one of his crew were killed and although wounded himself he held the position alone until all the ammunition was exhausted. He then retired to the main position, killed several of the enemy with hand-grenades and dragged the remaining seriously wounded member of his crew to safety. Good show, what? Unfortunately, he's not much to look at—small insignificant chap."

"How will he stand the test of the public platform?" I asked.

Carslake's face brightened.

"Oh, he's all right there. Positively slick, if you know what I mean. Quick as lightning. Good at getting a laugh, too. Some of it, mind you, is rather cheap stuff—" For a moment Carslake's face showed a sensitive distaste. He was a real Conservative, I perceived, he preferred acute boredom to the meretriciously amusing. "But it goes down—oh yes, it goes down.

"Of course," he added, "he had no background . . ."

"You mean he isn't a Cornishman?" I said. "Where does he come from?"

"To tell you the truth,. I've no idea. . . . He doesn't come from any- where exactly—if you know what I mean. We shall keep dark on all that. Play up the war angle—gallant service—all that. He can stand, you know, for the plain man—the ordinary Englishman. He's not our usual type, of course. . . ." He looked unhappy about it. "I'm afraid Lady St. Loo doesn't really approve."

Teresa asked delicately if it mattered whether Lady St. Loo approved. It transpired that it did. Lady St. Loo was the head of the Conservative Women's Association, and the Conservative Women were a power in St. Loo. They ran things, and managed things, and got up things, and they had, so Carslake said, a great influence on the women's vote. The women's vote, he said, was always tricky.

Then he brightened up a little.

"That's one reason why I'm optimistic about Gabriel," he said. "He gets on with women."

"But not with Lady St. Loo?"

Lady St. Loo, Carslake said, was being very good about it. . . . She acknowledged quite frankly that she was old-fashioned. But she was wholeheartedly behind whatever the Party thought necessary.

"After all," said Carslake sadly, "times have changed. We used to have gentlemen in politics. Precious few of them now. I wish this chap was a gentleman, but he isn't, and there it is. If you can't have a gentleman, I suppose a hero is the next best thing."

Which, I remarked to Teresa after he had left, was practically an epigram.

Teresa smiled. Then she said she was rather sorry for Major Gabriel.

"What do you think he's like?" she said. "Pretty dreadful?"

"No, I should think he was rather a nice chap."

"Because of his V.C.?"

"Lord, no. You can get a V.C. for being merely reckless—or even for being just stupid. You know, it's always said that old Freddy Elton got his V.C. for being too stupid to know when to retire from an advanced position. They called it holding on in face of almost insurmountable odds. Really he had no idea that everyone else had gone."

"Don't be ridiculous, Hugh. Why do you think this Gabriel person must be nice?"

"Simply, I think, because Carslake doesn't like him. The only man Carslake would like would be some awful stuffed shirt."

"What you mean is, that you don't like poor Captain Carslake!"

"No poor about it. Carslake fits into his job like a bug in a rug. And what a job!"

"Is it worse than any other job? It's hard work."

"Yes, that's true. But if your whole life is spent on the calculation of what effect *this* has on *that*—you'll end up by not knowing what this and that really are."

"Divorced from reality?"

"Yes, isn't that what politics really boil down to in the end? What people will believe, what they will stand, what they can be induced to think? Never plain fact."

"Ah!" said Teresa. "How right I am not to take politics seriously."

"You are always right, Teresa," I said and kissed my hand to her.

• • •

I myself didn't actually see the Conservative Candidate until the big meeting in the Drill Hall.

Teresa had procured for me an up-to-date type of wheeled invalid couch. I could be wheeled out on the terrace on it and lie there in a sheltered sunny place. Then, as the movement of the chair caused me less pain, I went further afield. I was occasionally pushed into St. Loo. The Drill Hall meeting was an afternoon one, and Teresa arranged that I should be present at it. It would, she assured me, amuse me. I replied that Teresa had curious ideas of amusement.

"You'll see," said Teresa, adding, "it will entertain you enormously to see everyone taking themselves so seriously."

"Besides," she went on, "I shall be wearing my Hat."

Teresa, who never wears a hat unless she goes to a wedding, had made an expedition to London and had returned with the kind of hat which was, according to her, suitable for a Conservative Woman.

"And what," I enquired, "is a hat suitable to a Conservative Woman?"

Teresa replied in detail.

It must, she said, be a hat of good material, not dowdy, but not too fashionable. It must set well on the head and it must not be frivolous.

She then produced the hat, and it was indeed all that Teresa had set forth that it should be.

She put it on and Robert and I applauded.

"It's damned good, Teresa," said Robert. "It makes you look earnest and as though you had a purpose in life."

You will understand, therefore, that to see Teresa sitting on the platform wearing the Hat lured me irresistibly to the Drill Hall on a remarkably fine summer's afternoon.

The Drill Hall was well filled by prosperous-looking elderly people. Anybody under forty was (wisely, in my opinion) enjoying the pleasures of the seaside. As my invalid couch was carefully wheeled by a boy scout to a position of vantage near the wall by the front seats, I speculated as to the usefulness of such meetings. Everyone in this hall was sure to vote our way. Our opponents were holding an opposition meeting in the Girls' School. Presumably they, too, would have a full meeting of staunch supporters. How, then, was public opinion influenced? The loudspeaker truck? Open-air meetings?

My speculations were interrupted by the shuffling of a small party of people coming onto the platform which hitherto had held nothing but chairs, a table, and a glass of water.

They whispered, gesticulated, and finally got settled in the required positions. Teresa, in the hat, was relegated to the second row amongst the minor personalities.

The Chairman, several tottery old gentlemen, the speaker from Headquarters, Lady St. Loo, two other women and the Candidate arranged themselves in the front row.

The Chairman began to speak in a quavery, rather sweet voice. His mumbled platitudes were practically inaudible. He was a very old general who had served with distinction in the Boer War. (Or was it, I queried to myself, the Crimean?) Whatever it was, it must have been a long time ago. The world he was mumbling about did not, I thought, now exist. . . . The thin apple-sweet old voice stopped, there was spontaneous and enthusiastic applause—the applause given always, in England, to a friend who has stood the test of time. . . . Everyone in St. Loo knew old General S——. He was a fine old boy, they said, one of the old school.

With his concluding words, General S—— had introduced to the meeting a member of the new school, the Conservative Candidate, Major Gabriel, V.C.

It was then, with a deep and gusty sigh, that Lady Tressilian, whom I suddenly discovered to be in the end seat of a row close to me (I suspected that her maternal instinct had placed her there), breathed poignantly:

"It's such a pity that he's got such common legs."

I knew immediately what she meant. Yet asked to define what is or is not common in a leg, I could not for the life of me tell you. Gabriel was not a tall man. He had, I should say, the normal legs for his height— they were neither unduly long nor unduly short. His suit was quite a well-cut one. Nevertheless, indubitably, those trousered legs were *not* the legs of a gentleman. Is it, perhaps, in the structure and poise of the nether limbs that the essence of gentility resides? A question for the Brains Trust.

Gabriel's face did not give him away, it was an ugly, but quite interesting face, with remarkably fine eyes. His legs gave him away every time.

He rose to his feet, smiled (an engaging smile), opened his mouth and spoke in a flat slightly cockney voice.

He spoke for twenty minutes—and he spoke well. Don't ask me what he said. Offhand I should say that he said the usual things—and said them more or less in the usual manner. But he got across. There was something dynamic about the man. You forgot what he looked like, you forgot that he had an ugly voice and accent. You had instead a great impression of earnestness—of single-minded purpose. You felt: this chap jolly well means to do his best. Sincerity—that was it, sincerity.

You felt—yes—that he *cared*. He *cared* about housing, about young couples who couldn't set up housekeeping—he *cared* about soldiers who had been overseas for many years and were due home, he *cared* about building up industrial security—about staving off unemployment. He cared, desperately, about seeing his country prosperous, because that prosperity would mean the happiness and well-doing of every small component part of that country. Every now and then, quite suddenly, he let off a squib, a flash of cheap, easily understood humor. They were quite obvious jokes—jokes that had been made many times before. They came out comfortingly because they were so familiar. But it wasn't the humor, it was his earnestness that really counted. When the war was finally over, when Japan was out of it, then would come the peace, and it would be vital then to get down to things. He, if they returned him, meant to get down to things. . . .

That was all. It was, I realized, entirely a personal performance. I don't mean that he ignored the party slogans, he didn't. He said all the correct things, spoke of the leader with due admiration and enthusiasm, mentioned the Empire. He was entirely correct. But you were being asked to support, not so much the Conservative Party Candidate as Major John Gabriel who was going to get things done, and who cared, passionately, that they should get done.

The audience liked him. They had, of course, come prepared to like him. They were Tories to a man (or woman), but I got the impression that they liked him rather more than they had thought they would. They seemed, I thought, even to wake up a little. And I said to myself, rather pleased with my idea, "Of course, the man's a dynamo!"

After the applause which was really enthusiastic, the Speaker from Headquarters was introduced. He was excellent. He said all the right things, made all the right pauses, got all the right laughs in the right places. I will confess that my attention wandered.

The meeting ended with the usual formalities.

As everyone got up and started streaming out, Lady Tressilian came and stood by me. I had been right—she was being a guardian angel. She said in her breathless, rather asthmatic voice:

"What do *you* think? Do tell me what you think?"

"He's good," I said. "Definitely he's good."

"I'm *so* glad you think so." She sighed gustily.

I wondered why my opinion should matter to her. She partially enlightened me when she said:

"I'm not as clever as Addie, you know, or Maud. I've never really studied politics—and I'm old-fashioned. I don't like the idea of M.P.s being paid. I've never got used to it. It should be a matter of serving your country—not recompensed."

"You can't always afford to serve your country, Lady Tressilian," I pointed out.

"No, I know that. Not nowadays. But it seems to me a pity. Our legislators should be drawn from the class that doesn't need to work for its living, the class that can really be indifferent to gain."

I wondered whether to say, "My dear lady, you come out of the Ark!"

But it was interesting to find a pocket of England where the old ideas still survived. The ruling class. The governing class. The upper class. All such hateful phrases. And yet—be honest—something in them?

Lady Tressilian went on:

"My father stood for Parliament, you know. He was M.P. for Garavissey for thirty years. He found it a great tax upon his time and very wearisome—but he thought it his *duty*."

My eyes strayed to the platform. Major Gabriel was talking to Lady

St. Loo. His legs were definitely ill-at-ease. Did Major Gabriel think it his duty to stand for Parliament? I very much doubted it.

"I thought," said Lady Tressilian, following the direction of my eyes, "that he seemed very *sincere*. Didn't you?"

"That was how it struck me."

"And he spoke so beautifully about dear Mr. Churchill . . . I think there is no doubt at all that the country is solidly behind Mr. Churchill. Don't you agree?"

I did agree. Or rather, I thought that the Conservatives would certainly be returned to power with a small majority.

Teresa joined me and my boy scout appeared, prepared to push.

"Enjoy yourself?" I asked Teresa.

"Yes, I did."

"What do you think of our candidate?"

She did not answer until we were outside the Hall. Then she said, "I don't know."

Chapter Five

I met the candidate a couple of days later when he came over to confer with Carslake. Carslake brought him in to us for a drink.

Some question arose about clerical work done by Teresa, and she went out of the room with Carslake to clear the matter up.

I apologized to Gabriel for not being able to get up, and directed him where the drinks were, and told him to get himself one. He poured himself a pretty stiff one, I noticed.

He brought me mine, saying as he did so:

"War casualty?"

"No," I said, "Harrow Road." It was, by now, my stock answer, and I had come to derive a certain amount of amusement from the various reactions to it. Gabriel was much amused.

"Pity to say so," he remarked. "You're passing up an asset there."

"Do you expect me to invent a heroic tale?"

He said there was no need to invent anything.

"Just say, 'I was in North Africa'—or in Burma—or wherever you actually were—you have been overseas?"

I nodded. "Alamein and on."

"There you are then. Mention Alamein. That's enough—no one will ask details—they'll think they know."

"Is it worth it?"

"Well," he considered, "it's worth it with women. They love a wounded hero."

"I know that," I said with some bitterness.

He nodded with immediate comprehension.

"Yes. It must get you down sometimes. Lot of women round here. Motherly, some of them." He picked up his empty glass. "Do you mind if I have another?"

I urged him to do so.

"I'm going to dinner at the Castle," he explained. "That old bitch fairly puts the wind up me!"

We might have been Lady St. Loo's dearest friends, but I suppose he knew quite well that we weren't. John Gabriel seldom made mistakes.

"Lady St. Loo?" I asked. "Or all of them?"

"I don't mind the fat one. She's the kind you can soon get where you want them, and Mrs. Bigham Charteris is practically a horse. You've only got to neigh at her. But that St. Loo woman is the kind that can see through you and out the other side. You can't put on any fancy frills with her!

"Not that I'd try," he added.

"You know," he went on thoughtfully, "when you come up against a real aristocrat you're licked—there isn't anything you can do about it."

"I'm not sure," I said, "that I understand you."

He smiled.

"Well, in a way, you see, I'm in the wrong camp."

"You mean that you're not really a Tory in politics?"

"No, no. I mean I'm not their kind. They like, they can't help liking, the old school tie. Of course, they can't be too choosy nowadays, they've got to have blokes like me." He added meditatively, "My old man was a plumber—not a very good plumber either."

He looked at me and twinkled. I grinned back at him. In that moment I fell under his charm.

"Yes," he said, "Labour's really my ticket."

"But you don't believe in their program?" I suggested.

He said easily, "Oh, I've no beliefs. With me it's purely a matter of expediency. I've got to have a job. The war's as good as over, and the plums will soon be snapped up. I've always thought I could make a name for myself in politics. You see if I don't."

"So that's why you're a Tory? You prefer to be in the party that will be in power?"

"Good Lord," he said. "You don't think the Tories are going to get in, do you?"

I said I certainly did think so. With a reduced majority.

"Nonsense," he said. "Labour's going to sweep the country. Their majority's going to be terrific."

"But then—if you think so—"

I stopped.

"Why don't I want to be on the winning side?" He grinned. "My dear chap. That's why I'm not Labour. I don't want to be swamped in a crowd. The Opposition's the place for me. What is the Tory party anyway? Taken by and large it's the most muddle-headed crowd of gentlemanly inefficients combined with unbusinesslike business men. They're hopeless. They haven't got a policy, and they're all at sixes and sevens. Anyone with any ability at all will stick out a mile. You watch. I shall shoot up like a rocket!"

"If you get in," I said.

"Oh, I shall get in all right."

I looked at him curiously.

"You really think so?"

He grinned again.

"If I don't make a fool of myself. I've got my weak spots." He tossed off the remainder of his drink. "Mainly women. I must keep off women. Won't be difficult down here. Although there's a nice little number at the St. Loo Arms. Have you come across her? No," his eyes fell on my immobile state. "Sorry, of course you haven't." He was moved to add, with what seemed genuine feeling, "Hard lines."

It was the first bit of sympathy that I had not resented. It came out so naturally.

"Tell me," I said, "do you talk to Carslake like this?"

"That ass? Good Lord, no."

I have since wondered why Gabriel chose to be so frank with me that first evening. The conclusion that I have come to is that he was lonely. He was putting up a very good performance, but there was not much chance of relaxing between the acts. He knew, too, he must have known, that a crippled and immobile man always falls in the end into the role of the listener. I wanted entertainment. John Gabriel was quite willing to provide entertainment by taking me behind the scenes of his life. Besides, he was by nature a frank man.

I asked, with some curiosity, how Lady St. Loo behaved to him.

"Beautifully," he said. "Quite beautifully—damn her eyes! That's one of the ways she gets under my skin. There's nothing you can take hold of anywhere—there wouldn't be—she knows her stuff. These old hags— if they want to be rude they're so rude it takes your breath away—and if they don't want to be rude you can't make 'em."

I wondered a little at his vehemence. I didn't see that it could really matter to him whether an old lady like Lady St. Loo was rude to him or not. She surely didn't matter in the least. She belonged to a past era.

I said as much and he shot me a queer sideways glance.

"You wouldn't understand," he said.

"No, I don't think I do."

He said very quietly, "She thinks I'm dirt."

"My dear fellow!"

"They *look* at you—that kind. Look *through* you. You don't count. You're not there. You don't exist for them. You're just the boy with the papers, or the boy who brings the fish."

I knew then that it was Gabriel's past that was active. Some slight, some casual rudeness long ago to the plumber's son.

He took the words out of my mouth.

"Oh yes," he said. "I've got it. I'm class-conscious. I hate these arrogant upper-class women. They make me feel that nothing I do will ever get me there—that to them I'll always be dirt. They know all right, you see, what I really am."

I was startled. That glimpse of depths of resentment was so unexpected. There was hate there—real implacable hate. I wondered exactly what incident in the past still fermented and rankled in John Gabriel's subconscious mind.

"I know they don't count," he said. "I know their day is over. They're living, all over the country, in houses that are tumbling down, on incomes that have shrunk to practically nothing. Lots of 'em don't get enough to eat. They live off vegetables from the garden. They do their own housework as often as not. But they've got something that I can't get hold of—and never shall get hold of—some damned feeling of superiority. I'm as good as they are—in many ways I'm better, but when I'm with them I don't *feel* it."

Then he broke off with a sudden laugh.

"Don't mind me. I'm just blowing off steam." He looked out of the window. "A sham gingerbread castle—three old croaking ravens—and a girl like a stick, so stuck up she can't find a word to say to you. That's the kind of girl who felt a pea through all the mattresses, I expect."

I smiled.

"I always have thought," I said, "that the Princess and the Pea was a rather far-fetched fairy tale."

He fastened on one word.

"Princess! That's how she behaves—that's how they treat her. Like something royal out of a storybook. She's not a Princess, she's an ordinary flesh-and-blood girl—she ought to be, anyway, with that mouth."

Teresa and Carslake came back at that moment. Presently Carslake and Gabriel departed.

"I wish he hadn't had to go," said Teresa. "I'd like to have talked to him."

"I expect," I said, "we shall see him fairly often."

She looked at me.

"You're interested," she said. "Aren't you?"

I considered.

"It's the first time," said Teresa, "the very first time that I've seen you interested in anything since we came here."

"I must be more politically minded than I thought."

"Oh," she said, "it isn't politics. It's that man."

"He's certainly a dynamic personality," I admitted. "It's a pity he's so ugly."

"I suppose he is ugly." She added thoughtfully, "He's very attractive, though."

I was quite astonished.

Teresa said: "Don't look at me like that. He *is* attractive. Any woman would tell you so."

"Well," I said, "you surprise me. I shouldn't have thought he was at all the sort of man women would have found attractive."

"You thought wrong," said Teresa.

Chapter Six

On the following day, Isabella Charteris came over with a note from Lady St. Loo to Captain Carslake. I was out on the terrace in the sun. When she had delivered the note she came back along the terrace and presently sat down near me on a carved stone seat.

If she had been Lady Tressilian I should have suspected kindness to the lame dog, but Isabella was quite clearly not concerned with me at all. I have never seen anyone less so. She sat for some time quite silently. Then she said that she liked the sun.

"So do I," I said. "You're not very brown, though."

"I don't go brown."

Her skin was lovely in the clear light—it had a kind of magnolia whiteness. I noticed how proudly her head was set on her shoulders. I could see why Gabriel had called her a Princess.

Thinking of him made me say, "Major Gabriel dined with you last night, didn't he?"

"Yes."

"Did you go to his meeting at the Drill Hall?"

"Yes."

"I didn't see you there."

"I was sitting in the second row."

"Did you enjoy it?"

She considered a moment before replying.

"No."

"Why did you go then?" I asked.

Again she thought a moment before saying, "It's one of the things we do."

I was curious.

"Do you like living down here? Are you happy?"

"Yes."

It struck me suddenly how rare it was to receive monosyllabic replies. Most people elaborate. The normal reply would be, "I love being by the sea" or "It's my home" . . . "I like the country" . . . "I love it down here." This girl contented herself with saying "Yes." But that "Yes" was curiously forceful. It really meant yes. It was a firm and definite assent. Her eyes had gone towards the Castle, and a very faint smile showed on her lips.

I knew then what she reminded me of. She was like those Acropolis Maidens of the 5th century B.C. She had that same inhuman exquisite smile. . . .

So Isabella Charteris was happy living at St. Loo Castle with three old women. Sitting here now in the sun, looking towards the Castle, she was happy. I could almost feel the quiet confident happiness that possessed her. And suddenly I was afraid—afraid for her.

I said, "Have you always been happy, Isabella?"

But I knew the answer before it came, although she considered a little before she said, "Yes."

"At school?"

"Yes."

I could not, somehow, imagine Isabella at school. She was totally unlike the ordinary product of an English boarding school. Still, presumably it takes all sorts to make a school.

Across the terrace came running a brown squirrel. It sat up, looking at us. It chattered a while, then darted off to run up a tree.

I felt suddenly as though a kaleidoscopic universe had shifted, setting into a different pattern. What I saw now was the pattern of a sentient world where existence was everything, thought and speculation nothing. Here was morning and evening, day and night, food and drink, cold and heat—here movement, purpose, consciousness that did not yet know it *was* consciousness. This was the squirrel's world, the world of green grass pushing steadily upward, of trees, living and breathing. Here in this world, Isabella had her place. And strangely enough I, the broken wreck of a man, could find my place also. . . .

For the first time since my accident I ceased to rebel . . . the bitterness, the frustration, the morbid self-consciousness left me. I was no longer Hugh Norreys, twisted away from his path of active and purposeful manhood. I was Hugh Norreys, the cripple, conscious of sunshine, of a stirring breathing world, of my own rhythmic breathing, of the fact that this was a day in eternity going on its way towards sleep. . . .

The feeling did not last. But for a moment or two I had known a world in which I belonged. I suspected that it was the world in which Isabella always lived.

Chapter Seven

It must, I think, have been a day or two after that that a child fell into St. Loo harbor. Some children had been playing in a group on the edge of the quay, and one of them, screaming and running away in the course of the game, tripped and fell headlong over the edge down twenty feet into the water below. It was half tide and there was about twelve feet of water in the harbor.

Major Gabriel who happened to be walking along the quay at the time, did not hesitate. He plunged straight in after the child. About twenty-five people crowded to the edge. By the steps on the far side a fisherman pushed off a boat and began rowing towards them. But before he could get to them, another man had dived in to the rescue having grasped the fact that Major Gabriel could not swim.

The incident ended happily. Gabriel and the child were rescued—the child unconscious but quickly brought round by artificial respiration. The child's mother, in acute hysteria, more or less fell upon Gabriel's neck, sobbing out thanks and blessings. Gabriel pooh-poohed it all, patted her on the shoulder and hurried off to the St. Loo Arms for dry clothes and alcoholic refreshment.

Later in the day, Carslake brought him along to tea.

"Pluckiest thing I ever saw in my life," he said to Teresa. "Not a moment's hesitation. Might easily have been drowned—remarkable that he *wasn't* drowned."

But Gabriel himself was properly modest and depreciatory.

"Just a damn silly thing to do," he said. "Much more to the point if I'd dashed for help or got a boat out. Trouble is, one doesn't stop to think."

Teresa said, "One of these days you'll do just one dashing thing too many."

She said it rather drily. Gabriel shot her a quick look.

After she had gone out with the tea things and Carslake had excused himself on the plea of work, Gabriel said meditatively:

"She's sharp, isn't she?"

"Who is?"

"Mrs. Norreys. She knows what's what. You can't really put much over on her." He added that he'd have to be careful.

Then he inquired, "Did I sound all right?"

I asked him what on earth he meant.

"My attitude. It was the right one, wasn't it? I mean—pooh-pooh the whole thing. Make out that I'd just been rather an ass?"

He smiled engagingly, and added:

"You don't mind my asking you, do you? It's awfully hard for me to know if I'm getting my effects right."

"Do you have to calculate effects? Can't you just be natural?"

He said meditatively that that would hardly do.

"I can't very well come in here and rub my hands with satisfaction and say, 'What a godsend!' can I?"

"Is that what you really think it was? A godsend?"

"My dear fellow, I've been going around all keyed up looking for something in that line to turn up. You know, runaway horses, burning buildings, snatching a child from under the wheels of a car. Children are the best for sob-stuff purposes. You'd think with all the fuss in the papers about death on the roads, that an opportunity would come soon enough. But it hasn't—either bad luck, or else the children of St. Loo are just damnably cautious little brutes."

"You didn't give that child a shilling to throw itself into the harbor, did you?" I inquired.

He took my remark quite seriously and replied that the whole thing had happened quite naturally.

"Anyway, I wouldn't risk doing a thing like that. The kid would probably tell its mother, and then where should I be?"

I burst out laughing.

"But look here," I said. "Is it really true that you can't swim?"

"I can keep myself afloat for about three strokes."

"But then weren't you taking a frightful risk? You might easily have been drowned."

"I might have been, I suppose . . . but look here, Norreys, you can't have it both ways. You can't go in for heroism unless you're prepared to be more or less heroic. Anyway, there were lots of people about. None of them wanted to get wet, of course, but somebody would be bound to do something about it. They'd do it for the kid if they wouldn't do it for me. And there were boats. The fellow who jumped in after me held up the kid and the man with the boat arrived before I finally went under. In any case artificial respiration usually brings you back even if you have more or less drowned."

His own particular engaging grin spread across his face.

"It's all so damned silly, isn't it?" he said. "People, I mean, are such damned fools. I shall get far more kudos for going in after that kid when I couldn't swim, than if I had dived in and saved her in the approved life-saving scientific way. Lots of people are going about now saying how damned plucky it was. If they'd any sense they'd say it was just plain damned stupid—which it was. The fellow who really did the trick—the fellow who went in after me and saved us both—he won't get half as much kudos. He's a first-class swimmer. He's ruined a good suit, poor devil, and my being floundering there as well as the child just made things more difficult for him. But nobody will look at it that way—unless, perhaps, it's people like your sister-in-law, but there aren't many of them.

"Just as well that there aren't," he added. "The last thing you want in an election is a lot of people who think things out and really use their heads."

"Didn't you feel a qualm or two before you jumped? An uneasy feeling in the pit of the stomach?"

"I hadn't time for that. I was just so blissfully exultant that the thing was being handed to me on a platter."

"I'm not sure that I see why you think this—this sort of spectacular business is necessary."

His face changed. It became grim and determined.

"Don't you realize that I've only got the one asset? I've no looks to speak of. I'm not a first-class speaker. I've no background—no influence. I've no money. I was born with one talent—" he laid a hand on my knee—"physical courage. Do you think, if I hadn't been a V.C. that I'd ever have been put up as Conservative candidate here?"

"But, my dear fellow, isn't a V.C. enough for you?"

"You don't understand psychology, Norreys. One silly stunt like this morning, has far more effect than a V.C. gained in Southern Italy. Italy's a long way off. They didn't see me win that V.C.—and unfortunately I can't tell them about it. I could make them see it all right if I did tell them. . . . I'd take them along with me and by the time I'd finished, they'd have won that V.C. too! But the conventions of this country don't allow me to do that. No, I've got to look modest and mutter that it was nothing—any chap could have done it. Which is nonsense—very few chaps could have done what I did. Half a dozen in the regiment could have—not more. You want judgment, you know, and calculation and the coolness not to be flurried, and you've got in a way to enjoy what you're doing."

He was silent for a moment or two. Then he said, "I meant to get a V.C when I joined up."

"My dear Gabriel!"

He turned his ugly intent little face towards me, with the shining eyes.

"You're right—you can't say definitely you'll get a thing like that. You've got to have luck. But I meant to try for it. I saw then that it was my big chance. Bravery's about the last thing you need in everyday life— it's hardly ever called for, and it's long odds against its getting you any- where if it does. But war's different—war's where bravery comes into its own. I'm not putting on any frills about it—it's all a matter of nerves or glands or something. It just boils down to the fact that you just don't happen to be afraid of dying. You can see what an enormous advantage that gives you over the other man in a war.

"Of course I couldn't be certain that my chance would ever come. . . . You can go on being quietly brave all through a war and come out of it without a single medal. Or you can be reckless at the wrong moment and get blown to bits with nobody thanking you for it."

"Most V.C.s are posthumous," I murmured.

"Oh I know. I wonder I'm not one of them. When I think how those bullets went singing round my head, I simply can't imagine why I'm here today. Four of them got me—and not one in a vulnerable spot. Odd, wasn't it? I shall never forget the pain of dragging myself along with my broken leg. That, and the loss of blood from my shoulder . . . and then old Spider James to haul along—he never stopped cursing—and the weight of him—"

Gabriel meditated for a minute, then he sighed and said:

"Oh well, happy days," and went and got himself a drink.

"I owe you a debt of gratitude," I said, "for debunking the popular belief that all brave men are modest."

"It's a damned shame," said Gabriel. "If you're a city magnate and bring off a smart deal, you can boast about it and everyone thinks more of you. And you can admit you've painted a pretty good picture. As for golf, if you do a round under bogey, everyone hears the good news. But this war hero stuff—" he shook his head. "You've got to get another fellow to blow the trumpet for you. Carslake's not really any good at that kind of thing. He's been bitten by the Tory bug of understatement. All they do is attack the other fellow instead of blowing their own trum- pet." He meditated again. "I've asked my Brigadier to come down here and speak next week. He might put it about in a quiet kind of way what a really remarkable fellow I am—but of course I can't ask him to. Awk-ward!"

"What with that and today's little incident, you ought not to do too badly," I said.

"Don't underestimate today's incident," said Gabriel. "You'll see. It will set everyone talking about my V.C. again. Bless that kid. I'll go round and give her a doll or something tomorrow. That will be good publicity too."

"Just tell me," I said, "a matter of curiosity. If there had been nobody there to see what happened—nobody at all, would you still have gone in after her?"

"What would have been the use if there had been nobody to see? We'd both have been drowned and nobody would have known about it until the tide washed us up somewhere."

"Then you would have walked home and let her drown?"

"No, of course not. What do you take me for? I'm a humane man. I'd have sprinted like mad round to the steps, got a boat and rowed like fury to where she'd gone in. With any luck I'd have fished her out and she'd have come round all right. I'd have done what I thought gave *her* the best chance. I like kids." He added, "Do you think the Board of Trade will give me some extra coupons for those clothes I ruined? Don't think I can ever wear that suit again. It's shrunk to nothing. These Gov-ernment departments are so mean."

On this practical note he departed.

I speculated a good deal about John Gabriel. I could not decide whether I liked the man or not. His blatant opportunism rather disgusted me—his frankness was attractive. As to the accuracy of his judgment, I soon had ample confirmation of the correct way he had gauged public opin-ion.

Lady Tressilian was the first person to give me her views. She had brought me some books.

"You know," she said breathlessly, "I always did feel there was something really nice about Major Gabriel. This proves it, don't you think so?"

I said, "In what way?"

"Not counting the cost. Just jumping straight into the water although he couldn't swim."

"It wasn't much good, was it? I mean, he could never have rescued the child without help."

"No, but he didn't stop to think about that. What I admire is the brave impulse, the absence of all calculation."

I could have told her that there was plenty of calculation.

She went on, her round pudding face flushing like a girl's:

"I do so admire a *really* brave man . . ."

One up to John Gabriel, I thought.

Mrs. Carslake, a feline and gushing woman whom I did not like, was positively maudlin.

"The pluckiest thing I've ever heard of. I'd been told, you know, that Major Gabriel's gallantry during the war was simply *incredible*. He absolutely didn't know what fear was. All his men *worshipped* him. For sheer heroism his record is just *too* wonderful. His C.O. is coming down here on Thursday. I shall pump him shamelessly. Of course Major Gabriel would be angry if he knew what I meant to do—he's so modest, isn't he?"

"That is the impression he manages to give, certainly," I said.

She did not notice any ambiguity in my wording.

"But I do think that these wonderful wonderful boys of ours ought not to hide their light under a bushel. It ought to be *known* all the splendid things they've done. Men are so *inarticulate*. I think it's the duty of women to spread these things abroad. Our present Member, Wilbraham, you know, he's never been out of an office all through the war."

Well, I supposed John Gabriel would say that she had the right ideas, but I did not like Mrs. Carslake. She gushed, and even as she gushed, her small dark eyes were mean and calculating.

"It's a pity, isn't it," she said, "that Mr. Norreys is a Communist."

"Every family," I said, "has its black sheep."

"They have such dreadful ideas—attack property."

"They attack other things," I said. "The Resistance movement in France is largely Communist."

That was rather a poser for Mrs. Carslake—and she retired.

Mrs. Bigham Charteris, calling in for some circulars to distribute had also her views on the harbor incident.

"Must be good blood in him somewhere," she said.

"You think so?"

"Sure to be."

"His father was a plumber," I said.

Mrs. Bigham Charteris took that in her stride.

"I imagined something of the kind. But there's good blood some-where—far back perhaps."

She went on.

"We must have him over at the Castle a bit more. I'll talk to Adelaide. She has an unfortunate manner sometimes—it makes people ill at ease. I never felt we saw Major Gabriel at his best there. Personally, I get on with him very well."

"He seems popular in the place generally."

"Yes, he's doing very well. A good choice. The Party needs new blood—needs it badly."

She paused and said, "He might be, you know, another Disraeli."

"You think he'll go far."

"I think he might get to the top. He's got the vitality."

Lady St. Loo's comment on the affair was brought to me by Teresa who had been over to the Castle.

"Hm!" she had said. "Did it with an eye on the gallery, of course—"

I could understand why Gabriel usually referred to Lady St. Loo as an old bitch.

Chapter Eight

The weather remained fine. I spent much of my time pushed out onto the sunny terrace. There were rose beds along it and a very old yew tree at one end of it. From there I could look across to the sea and the battlements of St. Loo Castle, and I could see Isabella walking across the fields from the Castle to Polnorth House.

She had formed the habit of walking over most days. Sometimes she had the dogs with her, sometimes she was alone. When she arrived she would smile, say good morning to me, and sit on the big carved stone seat near my invalid chair.

It was an odd friendship, but friendship was what it was. It was not kindness to an invalid, not pity, not sympathy that brought Isabella to me. It was something that was, from my point of view, much better. It was liking. Because she liked me Isabella came and sat in the garden beside me. She did it as naturally and as deliberately as an animal might have done.

When we talked, we talked mostly about the things we could see: the shape of a cloud, the light on the sea, the behavior of a bird . . .

It was a bird that showed me another facet of Isabella's nature. The bird was a dead bird; it had dashed its head against the glass of the drawing-room window and lay there under the window on the terrace, its legs sticking pathetically, stiffly up in the air, its soft bright eyes closed.

Isabella saw it first and the shock and horror in her voice gave me quite a start.

"Look," she said. "It's a bird—dead."

It was the note of panic in her voice that made me look so searchingly at her. She was looking like a frightened horse, her lips drawn back and quivering.

"Pick it up," I said.

She shook her head vehemently.

"I can't touch it."

"Do you dislike touching birds?" I asked. Some people did, I knew.

"I can't touch anything *dead*."

I stared at her.

She said, "I'm afraid of death—horribly afraid. I can't bear *anything* to be dead. I suppose it reminds me that I—that I shall be dead myself one day."

"We shall all be dead someday," I said.

(I was thinking of what lay at that moment conveniently close to my hand.)

"And don't you mind? Don't you mind terribly? To think it's there ahead of you—coming nearer all the time. And one day," her long beautiful hands, so seldom dramatic, struck her breast, "*it will come*. The end of living."

"What an odd girl you are, Isabella," I said. "I never knew you felt like this."

She said bitterly, "It's lucky, isn't it, that I'm a girl and not a boy. In the war I should have had to be a soldier—and I'd have disgraced us—run away or something. Yes," she spoke quietly again, almost meditatively, "it's terrible to be a coward. . . ."

I laughed a little uncertainly.

"I don't suppose you would have been a coward when the time came. Most people are—well—really it's afraid of being afraid."

"Were you afraid?"

"Good Lord, yes!"

"But when it came it was—all right?"

I cast my mind back to a particular moment—the strain of waiting in darkness—waiting for the order to move forward . . . the sick feeling in the pit of the stomach. . . .

I was truthful.

"No," I said. "I wouldn't describe it as all right. But I found that I could more or less take it. That is to say, I could take it as well as anybody else. You see, after a bit, you get into the way of feeling that it's never you who are going to stop the bullet—it may be the other fellow, but not you."

"Do you think Major Gabriel felt like that, too?"

I paid Gabriel his tribute.

"I rather fancy," I said, "that Gabriel is one of the rare and lucky people who simply don't know what fear is."

"Yes," she said. "I thought that, too."

There was a queer expression on her face.

I asked her if she had always been afraid of death. If she had had some shock that had given her a special terror.

She shook her head.

"I don't think so. Of course, my father was killed before I was born. I don't know if that—"

"Yes," I said, "I think that's very likely. I think that would account for it."

Isabella was frowning. Her mind was on the past.

"My canary died when I was about five. It was quite well the night before—and in the morning it was lying in the cage—with its feet sticking up stiff—like that bird just now. I took it in my hand," she shivered. "It was *cold* . . ." She struggled with words. "It—it wasn't *real* anymore . . . it was just a *thing* . . . it didn't see . . . or hear . . . or feel . . . it—it wasn't *there*!"

And suddenly, almost pathetically, she asked of me:

"Don't you think it's awful that we have to die?"

I don't know what I ought to have said. Instead of a considered reply I blurted out the truth—my own particular truth.

"Sometimes—it's the only thing a man has got to look forward to."

She looked at me with blank uncomprehending eyes.

"I don't know what you mean . . ."

"Don't you?" I said bitterly. "Use your eyes, Isabella. What do you think life is like, washed, dressed, got up in the morning like a baby, hauled about like a sack of coals—an inanimate useless broken hulk, lying here in the sun with nothing to do and nothing to look forward to, and nothing to hope for. . . . If I was a broken chair or table they'd throw me on the junk heap—but because I'm a man they put civilized garments on me, and throw a rug over the worst of the wreckage and lay me out here in the sun!"

Her eyes grew wide, wide with puzzlement, with questioning. For the first time, or so it seemed to me, they looked not beyond me but at me. They focused on me. And even then they saw and understood nothing—nothing but bare physical facts.

She said, "But at any rate you *are* in the sun . . . You *are* alive. You might easily have been killed . . ."

"Very easily. Don't you understand that I wish to God I had been killed?"

No, she didn't understand. To her, it was a foreign language I was speaking. She said, almost timidly:

"Are you—in a lot of pain always? Is it *that*?"

"I have a good deal of pain from time to time, but no, Isabella, it's not that. Can't you understand that I've nothing to live *for*?"

"But—I know I'm stupid—does one have to have anything to live for? I mean why? Can't one just live?"

I caught my breath before the simplicity of that.

And then, as I turned, or tried to turn on my couch, an awkward gesture on my part jerked the little bottle labeled Aspirin out of the place I kept it onto the grass and in falling the cap fell off and the little tablets inside scattered far and wide all over the grass.

I almost screamed. I heard my voice, hysterical, unnatural, calling out:

"Don't let them be lost . . . oh, pick them up . . . find them . . . don't let them go!"

Isabella bent, deftly picking up the tablets. Turning my head, I saw Teresa coming through the window. It was with almost a sob in my voice that I cried out under my breath:

"Teresa's coming . . ."

And then, to my astonishment, Isabella did something of which I would never have suspected her capable.

With a single rapid but unflurried gesture she loosened the colored scarf she was wearing round the neck of her summer frock, and let it float down on the grass covering the sprawled tablets. . . . And at the same time she said in a quiet conversational voice:

"—you see, everything may be quite different when Rupert comes home—"

You would have sworn that we were in the middle of a conversation. Teresa came to us and asked:

"What about a drink, you two?"

I suggested something rather elaborate. As Teresa was turning back to the house, she half bent as though to pick up the scarf. Isabella said in her unhurried voice:

"Do leave it, Mrs. Norreys—the colors look nice against the grass."

Teresa smiled and went back through the window.

I was left staring at Isabella.

"My dear girl," I said, "why did you do that?"

She looked at me shyly.

"I thought," she said, "that you didn't want her to see them. . . ."

"You thought right," I said grimly.

In the early days of my convalescence I had formed a plan. I foresaw only too plainly my helpless state, my complete dependence on others. I wanted a means of exit ready to my hand.

So long as they injected morphia, I could do nothing. But there came a time when morphia was replaced by sleeping draughts or tablets. That was my opportunity. At first I cursed, for I was given chloral in draught form. But later, when I was with Robert and Teresa, and medical attendance was less frequent, the doctor prescribed sleeping tablets—seconal, I think, or it may have been amytal. In any case there was an arrangement by which I was to try and do without the tablets, but a couple were left handy to take if sleep did not come. Little by little I accumulated my store. I continued to complain of sleeplessness, and fresh tablets were prescribed. I endured long nights of pain wide-eyed, fortified by the knowledge that my gate of departure was opening wider. For some time now I had had enough and more than enough to do the trick.

And with the accomplishment of my project, the urgent need for it retreated. I was content to wait a little while longer. But I did not mean to wait forever.

For an agonized few minutes, I had seen my plan jeopardized, retarded, perhaps ruined altogether. From that disaster Isabella's quick wits had saved me. She was picking up the tablets now and replacing them in the bottle. Presently she gave it to me.

I put the bottle back in its place and breathed a deep sigh.

"Thank you, Isabella," I said with feeling.

She showed no curiosity, no anxiety. She had been astute enough to realize my agitation and to come to my rescue. I apologized mentally for having once thought her a moron. She was no fool.

What did she think? She must have realized that those tablets were something other than aspirin.

I looked at her. There was no clue at all to what she thought. I found her very difficult to understand . . .

And then a sudden curiosity stirred in me.

She had mentioned a name . . .

"Who is Rupert?" I said.

"Rupert is my cousin."

"You mean Lord St. Loo?"

"Yes. He may be coming here soon. He's been in Burma during most of the war." She paused and said, "He may come here to live . . . the Castle is his, you know. We only rent it."

"I just wondered," I said, "why—well, why you suddenly mentioned him."

"I just wanted to say something quickly to make it seem as though we were talking." Then she meditated a minute. "I suppose—I spoke of Rupert—because I am always thinking of him. . . ."

Chapter Nine

Up to now Lord St. Loo had been a name, an abstraction—the absent owner of St. Loo Castle. Now he came into the round—a living entity. I began to wonder about him.

Lady Tressilian came over in the afternoon to bring me what she described as "a book I thought might interest you." It was not, I saw at a glance, the kind of book that would interest me. It was the kind of smartly written pep talk that wants you to believe that you can make the world brighter and better by lying on your back and thinking beautiful thoughts. Lady Tressilian, her thwarted maternal instincts asserting themselves, was always bringing me something. Her favorite idea was that I should become an author. She had brought me the literature of at least three correspondence courses on "How to make a living by writing in twenty-four lessons" or something of that kind. She was one of those nice kind women who cannot, by any possible chance, leave anyone who is suffering to suffer alone.

I could not dislike her, but I could, and did, try to dodge her ministrations. Sometimes Teresa helped, but sometimes she didn't. Sometimes she looked at me, smiled, and deliberately left me to my fate. When I swore at her afterward she said that a counterirritant was a good thing occasionally.

On this particular afternoon Teresa was out on political canvassing, so I had no chance of escape.

When Lady Tressilian had sighed and asked me how I was and told me how much better I was looking and I had thanked her for the book and said it looked very interesting, we dropped into local chat. At the moment all our local chat was political. She told me how the meetings had gone and how well Gabriel had tackled some hecklers. She went on to talk of what the country really wanted and how terrible it would be if everything was nationalized, and how unscrupulous the other side were, and exactly what the farmers felt about the Milk Marketing Board. The conversation was practically identical with one we had had three days ago.

It was then, after a slight pause, that Lady Tressilian sighed and said how wonderful it would be if Rupert came soon.

"Is there a chance of it?" I asked.

"Yes. He was wounded—out in Burma, you know. It is so wicked the newspapers hardly mention the Fourteenth Army. He has been in hospital for some time, and he is due for a long spell of leave. There are a lot of things for him to settle here. We have all done the best we can, but conditions are changing the whole time."

I gathered that with taxation and other difficulties, Lord St. Loo would probably soon have to sell some of his land.

"The part by the sea is good building land, but one hates to have more of those dreadful little houses springing up."

I agreed that the builders who had developed the East Cliff had not been overburdened with artistic sensibility.

She said, "My brother-in-law, the seventh Lord St. Loo, gave that land to the town. He wanted it to be saved for the people, but he did not think of attaching specific safeguards, and consequently the Council sold it all, bit by bit, for building. It was very dishonest, for it was *not* what my brother-in-law meant."

I asked if Lord St. Loo was thinking of coming here to live.

"I don't know. He has not said anything definite." She sighed. "I hope so—I do very much hope so."

She added, "We have not seen him since he was sixteen—he used to come here for his holidays when he was at Eton. His mother was a New

Zealander—a very charming girl—when she was left a widow she went back to her own people and took the child with her. One cannot blame her, and yet I always regret that the boy was not brought up on what was to be his own estate from the beginning. He is bound, I feel, when he comes here, to be out of touch. But then, of course, everything is changing . . ."

Her nice round face looked distressed.

"We have done our best. Death duties were heavy. Isabella's father was killed in the last war. The place had got to be let. By clubbing together Addie and I and Maud could manage to rent it—and it seemed so much better than letting it to strangers. It has always been Isabella's home."

Her face softened as she bent towards me confidentially.

"I daresay I am a very sentimental old woman, but I have so hoped that Isabella and Rupert—it would be, I mean, the *ideal* solution . . ."

I did not speak and she went on:

"Such a handsome boy—so charming and affectionate to us all—and he always seemed to have a special fondness for Isabella. She was only eleven then. She used to follow him about everywhere. She was quite devoted to him. Addie and I used to look at them and say to each other, 'If only—' Maud, of course, kept saying that they were first cousins and it wouldn't do. But then Maud is always thinking of things from the pedigree point of view. Lots of first cousins do marry and it turns out quite all right. It's not as though we were an R.C. family and had to get a dispensation."

Again she paused. This time her face had that absorbed, intensely feminine expression that women put on when they are matchmaking.

"He has always remembered her birthday every year. He writes to Asprey's. I think, don't you, that that is rather touching? Isabella is such a dear girl—and she loves St. Loo so much." She looked out towards the battlements of the castle. "If they could settle down there to-gether . . ." I saw tears gathering in her eyes. . . .

("This place becomes more like a fairy story than ever," I said to Teresa that evening. "A fairy Prince may arrive any minute to marry the Princess. Where *are* we living? In a story from Grimms?")

"Tell me about your cousin Rupert," I said to Isabella when she was sitting on the stone seat the next day.

"I don't think there is anything to tell."

"You think about him all the time, you said. Is that really true?"

She considered for a moment or two.

"No, I don't think about him. I meant—he is there in my mind. I think—that one day I shall marry Rupert."

She turned towards me as though my silence disquieted her.

"Does that seem to you an absurd thing to say? I haven't seen Rupert since I was eleven and he was sixteen. He said then he would come back and marry me someday. I've always believed it . . . I still believe it."

"And Lord and Lady St. Loo were married and lived happy ever afterwards in St. Loo Castle by the sea," I said.

"You think it won't happen?" Isabella asked.

She looked at me as though my opinion on the point might be final. I drew a deep breath.

"I'm inclined to think it will happen. It's that kind of fairy story."

We were recalled bluntly from fairy stories to reality by Mrs. Bigham Charteris who made an abrupt appearance on the terrace.

She had a bulging parcel with her which she flapped down beside her, requesting me brusquely to give it to Captain Carslake.

"I think he's in his office," I began, but she interrupted:

"I know—but I don't want to go in there. I'm not in the mood for that woman."

Personally I was never in the mood for Mrs. Carslake, but I saw that there was something more than that behind Mrs. Bigham Charteris's almost violently brusque manner.

Isabella saw it too. She asked:

"Is anything the matter, Aunt Maud?"

Mrs. Bigham Charteris, her face rigid, jerked out:

"Lucinda's been run over."

Lucinda was Mrs. Bigham Charteris's brown spaniel whom she adored passionately.

She went on, speaking still more jerkily, and fixing me with a glacial eye to prevent me expressing sympathy:

"Down by the quay—some of those bloody tourists—driving much too fast—didn't even stop—Come on, Isabella—we must get home—"

I didn't offer tea or sympathy.

Isabella asked, "Where is Lucy?"

"Took her into Burt's. Major Gabriel helped me. He was very kind, very kind indeed."

Gabriel had come upon the scene when Lucinda was lying whimpering in the road and Mrs. Bigham Charteris was kneeling by her. He had knelt down also and had felt the dog's body all over with skillful sensitive fingers.

He said:

"There's a loss of power in the hind legs—it might be internal injury. We ought to get her to a vet."

"I always have Johnson from Polwithen—he's wonderful with dogs. But that's too far."

He nodded. "Who's the best vet in St. Loo?"

"James Burt. He's clever, but he's a brute. I'd never trust him with dogs—not to send them to his place. He drinks, you know. But he's quite near here. We'd better take Lucy there. Mind—she may bite."

Gabriel said with confidence:

"She won't bite me." He spoke to her soothingly. "All right, old girl, all right." He slid his arms under her gently. The crowd of small boys, fishermen and young women with shopping bags made sympathetic noises and offered advice.

Mrs. Bigham Charteris said jerkily, "Good girl, Lucy, good girl."

To Gabriel she said, "It's very kind of you. Burt's house is just round the corner in Western Place."

It was a prim Victorian house, slate-roofed, with a worn brass plate on the gate.

The door was opened by a rather pretty woman of about twenty-eight who turned out to be Mrs. Burt.

She recognized Mrs. Bigham Charteris at once.

"Oh, Mrs. Bigham Charteris, I'm ever so sorry. My husband's out. And the assistant too."

"When will he be back?"

"I think Mr. Burt will be back any minute now. Of course, his surgery hours are nine to ten or two to three—but I'm sure he'll do all he can. What's the matter with the dog? Run over?"

"Yes, just now—by a car."

"It's wicked, isn't it?" said Milly Burt. "They go far too fast. Bring her into the surgery, will you?"

She talked on in her soft, slightly over-refined voice. Mrs. Bigham Charteris stood by Lucinda, stroking her. Her weatherbeaten face was twisted with pain. She could pay no attention to Milly Burt, who talked on, kindly, inadequately, rather at a loss.

She said presently that she would telephone to Lower Grange Farm and see if Mr. Burt was there. The telephone was in the hall. Gabriel went with her, leaving Mrs. Bigham Charteris alone with her dog and her own agony. He was a perceptive man.

Mrs. Burt dialed the number, and recognized the voice at the other end.

"Yes, Mrs. Whidden—it's Mrs. Burt speaking. Is Mr. Burt there—well, yes, I would if you don't mind—yes—" There was a pause, and then Gabriel, watching her, saw her flush and wince. Her voice changed—it became apologetic—timid.

"I'm sorry, Jim. No, of course—" Gabriel could hear the sound of Burt's voice at the other end, though not what he said—a domineering, ugly voice. Milly Burt's voice became more apologetic.

"It's Mrs. Bigham Charteris—from the Castle—her dog—it's been run over. Yes, she's here now."

She flushed again and replaced the receiver, but not before Gabriel had heard the voice at the other end say angrily:

"Why couldn't you say so at once, you fool?"

There was a moment's awkwardness. Gabriel felt sorry for Mrs. Burt—a pretty gentle little thing, scared of that husband of hers. He said in his sincere friendly way:

"It's awfully good of you to take so much trouble and to be so sympathetic, Mrs. Burt." And he smiled at her.

"Oh, that's quite all right, Major Gabriel. It *is* Major Gabriel, isn't it?" She was just a little excited by his appearance in her house. "I came to your meeting in the Institute the other night."

"That was very nice of you, Mrs. Burt."

"And I hope you get in—but I'm sure you will. Everybody's dreadfully tired of Mr. Wilbraham, I'm sure. He doesn't really belong here, you know. He's not a Cornishman."

"No more am I for that matter."

"Oh, *you*—"

She looked at him with eyes that were rather like Lucinda's brown eyes, capable of hero worship. Her hair was brown, too, pretty chestnut hair. Her lips parted, she was looking at John Gabriel, seeing him against a background of no particular place—just as a figure against a war landscape. Desert, heat, shots, blood, staggering over open country. . . . A film landscape like the picture she'd seen last week.

And he was no natural—so kind—so *ordinary*!

Gabriel exerted himself to talk to her. He particularly didn't want her to go back into the surgery and worry that poor old bean who wanted to be alone with her dog. Especially as he was fairly sure the dog was for it. Pity, a lovely bitch and not more than three or four years old. This was a nice little woman, but she would want to show her sympathy by talking. She'd go on and on, exclaiming about motors and the number of dogs killed each year, and what a lovely dog Lucinda was, and wouldn't Mrs. Charteris like a cup of tea?

So John Gabriel talked to Milly Burt, and made her laugh, so that she showed her pretty teeth and a nice dimple that she had at one corner of her mouth. She was looking quite lively and animated when the door suddenly opened and a thickset man in riding breeches stumped in.

Gabriel was startled by the way Burt's wife flinched and shrank.

"Oh, Jim—here you are," she exclaimed nervously. "This is Major Gabriel."

James Burt nodded curtly and his wife went on:

"Mrs. Charteris is in the surgery with the dog—"

Burt interrupted: "Why didn't you take the dog in there and keep her out? You never have the least sense."

"Shall I ask her—"

"I'll see to it."

He shouldered his way past her and went down the stairs into the surgery.

Milly Burt blinked hasty tears out of her eyes.

She asked Major Gabriel if he would like a cup of tea.

Because he was sorry for Mrs. Burt and because he thought her husband was an unmannerly brute, he said he would.

And that was the beginning of that.

Chapter Ten

It was, I think, the following day—or possibly the day after—that Teresa brought Mrs. Burt into my sitting room.

She said, "This is my brother-in-law, Hugh. Hugh, this is Mrs. Burt who has kindly offered to help us."

"Us" was not personal but denoted the Conservative Party.

I looked at Teresa. She did not bat an eyelash. Mrs. Burt was already yearning over me with soft brown eyes full of womanly sympathy. If I had occasionally indulged in the luxury of pitying myself, moments such as these were wholesome correctives. Against the eager sympathy in Mrs. Burt's eyes I had no defense. Teresa basely left the room.

Mrs. Burt sat down beside me and prepared to be chatty. When I had recovered from my self-consciousness and raw misery, I was forced to admit that she was a nice woman.

"I do feel," she was saying, "that we must all do what we can for the election. I'm afraid I can't do much. I'm not clever. I couldn't go and talk to people, but as I said to Mrs. Norreys if there is any clerical work to be done, or leaflets to be delivered, I could do that. I thought Major Gabriel spoke so splendidly at the Institute about the part women can play. It made me feel I'd been terribly slack up to now. He's such a wonderful speaker, don't you think? Oh, I forgot—I suppose you—"

Her distress was rather touching. She looked at me in a dismayed fashion. I came to her rescue quickly.

"I heard his opening speech at the Drill Hall. He certainly gets his effects."

She suspected no irony. She said with a rush of feeling:

"I think he's splendid."

"That's exactly what we—er—want everyone to think."

"So they ought," said Milly Burt. "I mean—it will make all the difference to have a man like that standing for St. Loo. A real man. A man who's really been in the Army and fought. Mr. Wilbraham is all right, of course, but I always think these socialists are so cranky—and after all, he's only a schoolmaster or something of that sort—and very weedy looking and such an affected voice. One doesn't feel he's really *done* things."

I listened to the voice of the electorate with some interest, and observed that John Gabriel had certainly done things.

She flushed with enthusiasm.

"I've heard he's one of the bravest men in the whole Army. They say he could have won the V.C. over and over again."

Gabriel had evidently succeeded in getting the right kind of publicity across. That is, unless it was just personal enthusiasm on the part of Mrs. Burt. She was looking very pretty with her cheeks slightly flushed and her brown eyes alight with hero worship.

"He came in with Mrs. Bigham Charteris," she explained. "The day her dog was run over. It was nice of him, wasn't it? He was ever so concerned about it."

"Possibly he's fond of dogs," I said.

That was a little too ordinary for Milly Burt.

"No," she said. "I think it's because he is so kind—so wonderfully kind. And he talked so naturally and so pleasantly."

She paused and went on, "I felt quite ashamed. I mean, ashamed that I hadn't been doing more to help the cause. Of course, I always vote Conservative, but just voting isn't nearly enough, is it?"

"That," I said, "is a matter of opinion."

"So I really felt I must do *something*—and I came along to ask Captain Carslake what I can do. I've really got a lot of time on my hands, you see. Mr. Burt is so busy—out all day except just for surgery—and I haven't any children."

A different expression showed in her brown eyes for a moment—I felt sorry for her. She was the kind of woman who ought to have had children. She would have made a very good mother.

The thwarted maternity was still in her face as she abandoned her memories of John Gabriel and concentrated on me instead.

"You were wounded at Alamein, weren't you?" she said.

"No," I said furiously, "in the Harrow Road."

"Oh." She was taken aback. "But Major Gabriel told me—"

"Gabriel would," I said. "You mustn't believe a word he says."

She smiled doubtfully. She admitted a joke that she couldn't quite see.

"You look wonderfully fit," she said encouragingly.

"My dear Mrs. Burt, I neither look fit nor feel it."

She said, very nicely, "I'm really dreadfully sorry, Captain Norreys."

Before I could attempt murder, the door opened and Carslake and Gabriel came in.

Gabriel did his stuff very well. His face lighted up and he came across to her.

"Hullo, Mrs. Burt. This *is* nice of you! It really is nice."

She looked happy and shy.

"Oh, really, Major Gabriel—I don't suppose I shall be any use. But I do want to do *something* to help."

"You are going to help. We're going to make you *work*." He had her hand still in his and was smiling all over his ugly face. I could feel the charm and the magnetism of the man—and if I felt it, the woman felt it far more. She laughed and flushed.

"I'll do my best. It's important, isn't it, that we should show that the country is loyal to Mr. Churchill?"

It was far more important, I could have told her, that we should be loyal to John Gabriel and return him with a good majority.

"That's the spirit," said Gabriel heartily. "It's the women who have the real power in elections nowadays. If only they'll use it."

"Oh, I know." She was grave. "We don't *care* enough."

"Oh well," said Gabriel. "After all, one candidate isn't much better than another perhaps."

"Oh, Major Gabriel," she was shocked. "Of course, there is all the difference in the world."

"Yes, indeed, Mrs. Burt," said Carslake. "I can tell you Major Gabriel is going to make them sit up at Westminster."

I wanted to say "Oh yeah?" but restrained myself. Carslake took her off to give her some leaflets or some typing or something and Gabriel said as the door closed behind them:

"Nice little woman, that."

"You certainly have her eating out of your hand."

He frowned at me.

"Come off it, Norreys. I like Mrs. Burt. And I'm sorry for her. If you ask me, she hasn't got too easy a life."

"Possibly not. She doesn't look very happy."

"Burt's a callous devil. Drinks a lot. I should fancy he could be brutal. I noticed yesterday that she had a couple of nasty bruises on her arm. I bet he knocks her about. Things like that make me see red."

I was a little surprised. Gabriel noticed my surprise, and gave a vigorous nod of the head.

"I'm not putting it on. Cruelty always does rile me. . . . Have you ever thought about the kind of lives women may have to lead? And hold their tongues about?"

"There's legal redress, I suppose," I said.

"No, there isn't, Norreys—not until the last resort. Systematic bullying, steady sneering unkindness, a bit of rough stuff if he's had a drop too much—what's a woman able to do about that? What can she do but sit down under it—and suffer quietly? Women like Milly Burt have got no money of their own—where could they go if they walked out on their husbands? Relations don't like fomenting marital troubles. Women like Milly Burt are quite alone. No one will lift a finger to help them."

"Yes," I said, "that's true . . ."

I looked at him curiously.

"You're very heated?"

"Don't you think I'm capable of a little decent sympathy? I like that girl. I'm sorry for her. I wish there were anything I could do about it—but I suppose there isn't."

I stirred uneasily. Or rather, to be accurate, I tried to stir—and was rewarded by a twinge of sharp pain from my maimed body. But with the physical pain went another, more subtle pain, the pain of memory. I was sitting again in a train going from Cornwall to London and watching tears drop into a plate of soup. . . .

That was the way things started—not the way you imagined they'd start. It was one's helplessness in face of pity that laid you open to the assaults of life, that led you—where? In my case to an invalid chair with no future before me and a past that mocked me. . . .

I said abruptly to Gabriel (and there was a connection in my mind, though to him the transition must have seemed abrupt indeed):

"How's the nice little number at the St. Loo Arms?"

He grinned.

"That's all right, my boy. I'm being very discreet. Strictly business whilst I'm in St. Loo." He sighed. "It's a pity. She's just my type. . . . But there—you can't have everything! Mustn't let down the Tory Party."

I asked if the Tory Party was so particular, and he replied that there was a very strong Puritan element in St. Loo. Fishermen, he added, tended to be religious.

"In spite of having a wife in every port?"

"That's the Navy, old boy. Don't get things mixed up."

"Well, don't *you* get mixed up—with the St. Loo Arms or with Mrs. Burt."

He flared up unexpectedly at that.

"Look here, what are you driving at? Mrs. Burt's straight—dead straight. She's a nice kid."

I looked at him curiously.

"She's all right, I tell you," he insisted. "She wouldn't stand for any funny business."

"No," I agreed. "I don't think she would. But she admires you very much, you know."

"Oh, that's the V.C. and the harbor business and various rumors that get around."

"I was going to ask you about that. Who's circulating these rumors?"

He winked.

"I'll tell you this—they're useful—very useful. Wilbraham's C.3, poor devil."

"Who starts them off—Carslake?"

Gabriel shook his head.

"Not Carslake. Too heavy-handed. I couldn't trust him. I've had to get to work myself."

I burst out laughing.

"Do you seriously mean to tell me you've got the nerve to tell people that you could have won the V.C. three times over?"

"It's not quite like that. I use women—the less-brainy type. They drag details out of me—details that I'm reluctant to give them—then, when I get horribly embarrassed and beg them not to mention it to a soul, they hurry off and tell all their best friends."

"You really are shameless, Gabriel."

"I'm fighting an election. I've got my career to think of. These things count a great deal more than whether I'm sound on the subject of tariffs, or reparations, or equal pay for equally bad work. Women always go for the personal element."

"That reminds me; what the devil do you mean by telling Mrs. Burt that I was wounded at Alamein?"

Gabriel sighed.

"I suppose you disillusioned her. You shouldn't do it, old boy. Cash in on what you can while the going's good. Heroes have got a high points value just at present. They'll slump later. Cash in while you can."

"Under false pretenses?"

"Quite unnecessary to tell women the truth. I never do. They don't like it, you'll find."

"That's a little different from telling a deliberate lie."

"No need to lie. I'd done the lying for you. You'd only got to mutter, 'Nonsense . . . all a mistake . . . Gabriel should have held his tongue . . .' And then start talking about the weather—or the pilchard catch—or what's cooking in darkest Russia. And the girl goes away all big-eyed with enthusiasm. Damn it, don't you want *any* fun?"

"What fun can I have nowadays?"

"Well, I realize you can't actually go to bed with anyone—" Gabriel seldom minced his words. "But a bit of sob stuff's better than nothing. Don't you want women to make a fuss of you?"

"No."

"Funny—I should."

"I wonder."

Gabriel's face changed. He frowned. He said slowly:

"You may be right . . . I suppose when you come down to it none of us really know ourselves . . . *I* think I'm pretty well acquainted with John Gabriel. You're suggesting that I mayn't know him so well as I think I do. Meet Major John Gabriel—I don't think you know each other. . . ."

He paced swiftly up and down the room. I sensed that my words had plumbed some deep disquiet. He looked—yes, I realized it suddenly— he looked like a frightened little boy.

"You're wrong," he said. "You're dead wrong. I *do* know myself. It's the one thing I do know. Sometimes I wish I didn't . . . I know exactly what I am, and what I'm capable of. I'm careful, mind you, not to let other people catch on. I know where I've come from and I know where I'm going. I know what I want—and I mean to make sure of getting it. I've worked it all out fairly carefully—and I don't think I'm likely to slip up." He considered for a moment or two. "No, I think I'm well set. I'm going to get where I want to be!"

The ring in his voice interested me. Just for a moment I believed that John Gabriel was more than a charlatan—I saw him as a power.

"So *that's* what you want," I said. "Well—perhaps you'll get it."

"Get what?"

"Power. That's what you meant, wasn't it?"

He stared at me, then broke out laughing.

"Good Lord, no. Who do you think I am—Hitler? I don't want power—I've no ambition to lord it over my fellow creatures or the world generally. Good God, man, what do you think I'm in this racket for? Power's poppycock! What I want is a soft job. That's all."

I stared at him. I was disappointed. Just for a moment John Gabriel had attained titanic proportions. Now he had shrunk back again to life size. He flung himself down in a chair and thrust out his legs. I saw him suddenly as he was apart from his charm—a gross, mean little man—a greedy little man.

"And you can thank your stars," he said, "that that's all I *do* want! Men who are greedy and self-seeking don't hurt the world—the world's got room for them. And they're the right kind of men to have governing you. Heaven help any country that has men in power with ideas! A man with an idea will grind down the common people, and starve children, and break women, without even noticing what's happening to them. He won't even *care*. But a selfish grasping bloke won't do much harm—he only wants his own little corner made comfortable, and once he's got that, he's quite agreeable to having the average man happy and contented. In fact, he prefers him happy and contented—it's less trouble. I know pretty well what most people want—it isn't much. Just to feel important and to have a chance of doing a bit better than the other man and not to be too much pushed around. You mark my words, Norreys, that's where the Labour Party will make their big mistake when they get in—"

"If they get in," I interrupted.

"They'll get in all right," said Gabriel confidently. "And I'm telling you where they'll make their mistake. They'll start pushing people round. All with the best intentions. The ones who aren't really dyed-in-the-wool Tories are cranks. And God save us from cranks! It's really remarkable the amount of suffering a really high-minded idealistic crank can inflict on a decent law-abiding country."

I argued, "It still boils down to the fact that you think you know what is best for the country?"

"Not at all. I know what's best for John Gabriel. The country's safe from my experiments because I shall be occupied thinking about myself and how to dig myself in comfortably. I don't care in the least about being Prime Minister."

"You surprise me!"

"Now don't make any mistake, Norreys, I probably *could* become Prime Minister if I wanted to. It's amazing what you can do, if you just study what people want to hear said and then say it to them! But to be Prime Minister means a lot of worry and hard work. I mean to make a name for myself, that's all—"

"And where's the money coming from? Six hundred a year doesn't go far."

"They'll have to put it up if Labour gets in. Probably make it a clear thousand. But don't make any mistake, there are plenty of ways of making money in a political career—some on the side, some straightforward. And there's marriage—"

"You've planned your marriage, too? A title?"

For some reason he flushed.

"No," he spoke with vehemence. "I'm not marrying out of my class. Oh yes, I know what my class is. I'm not a gentleman."

"Does that word mean anything nowadays?" I asked skeptically.

"The word doesn't. But the thing the word means is still there."

He stared in front of him. When he spoke his voice was reflective and far away.

"I remember going round to a big house with my father. He was doing a job on the kitchen boiler. I stayed around outside the house. A kid came and spoke to me. Nice kid, a year or two older than I was. She took me along with her into the garden—rather a super garden— fountains, you know, and terraces, and big cedar trees and green grass like velvet. Her brother was there, too. He was younger. We played games. Hide and Seek—I Spy—It was fine—we got on together like a house on fire. And then a nannie came out of the house—all starched and got up in uniform. Pam, that was the kid's name, went dancing up to her and said I must come to tea in the nursery, she wanted me to come to tea.

"I can see that stuck-up nurse's face now—the primness of it, I can hear the mincing voice!

" 'You can't do that, dear. He's just a common little boy.' "

Gabriel stopped. I was shocked—shocked at what cruelty, uncon- scious unthinking cruelty, can do. He'd been hearing that voice, seeing that face, ever since. . . . He'd been hurt—hurt to the core.

"But look here," I said, "it wasn't the children's mother. It was— well—a very second-class thing to say—apart from the cruelty—"

He turned a white somber face on me.

"You don't get the point, Norreys. I agree a gentlewoman wouldn't have said a thing like that—she'd have been more considerate—but the fact remains that it was true. I *was* a common little boy. I'm *still* a common little boy. I'll die a common little boy."

"Don't be absurd! What do these things matter?"

"They don't matter. They've left off mattering. In actual fact, it's an advantage not to be a gentleman nowadays. People sneer at those rather pathetic straight-backed old ladies and gentlemen who are well con- nected and haven't enough to live on. All we're snobbish about nowadays is education. Education's our fetish. But the trouble is, Norreys, that I didn't want to be a common little boy. I went home and said to my father, 'Dad, when I grow up I want to be a Lord. I want to be Lord John Gabriel.' 'And that's what you'll never be,' he said. 'You've got to be born that kind of a Lord. They can make you a Peer if you get rich enough but it's not the same thing.' And it isn't the same thing. There's something—something I can never have—oh, I don't mean the title. I mean being born sure of yourself—knowing what you're going to do or say—being rude only when you mean to be rude—and not being rude just because you feel hot and uncomfortable and want to show you're as good as anyone else. Not having to go about hot under the collar and wondering all the time what people are thinking of you, but just concerned with what *you* think of *them*. Knowing that if you're queer or shabby or eccentric it doesn't matter a damn because you are what you are . . ."

"Because, in fact, you're Lady St. Loo?" I suggested.

"Blast and damn the old bitch!" said John Gabriel.

I looked at him with considerable interest.

"You know," I said, "you're really very interesting."

"It isn't real to you, is it? You don't know what I mean. You think you do—but you don't really get near it."

"I knew," I said slowly, "that there had been something . . . that you'd had, once, some shock. . . . You were wounded as a child, hurt. In a sense you've never got over it—"

"Cut out the psychology," said Gabriel curtly. "But you see, don't you, why, when I get with a nice girl like Milly Burt, I'm happy. And that's the kind of girl I'm going to marry. She'll have to have money, of course—but money or no money she'll be of my own class. You can imagine, can't you, the Hell it would be if I married some stuck-up girl with a face like a horse and spent my life trying to live up to her?"

He paused and said abruptly:

"You were in Italy. Did you ever get to Pisa?"

"I have been in Pisa—some years ago."

"I think it's Pisa I mean. . . . There's a thing there painted on the wall—Heaven and Hell and Purgatory and all the rest of it. Hell's rather jolly, little devils pushing you down with pitchforks. Heaven's up above—a row of the blessed sitting under trees with a smug expression on their faces. My God, those women! They don't know about Hell, they don't know about the damned—they don't know *anything*! They just sit there, smiling smugly—" His passion rose. "Smug, smug, self-satisfied—God, I'd like to tear them down from their trees and their state of beatitude and pitch them down into the flames! Hold them there writhing; make them feel, make them suffer! What right have they not to know what suffering is? There they sit, smiling, and nothing can ever touch them. . . . Their heads among the stars. . . . Yes, that's it, among the stars. . . ."

He got up, his voice fell, his eyes looked past me, vague searching eyes . . .

"Among the stars," he repeated.

Then he laughed.

"Sorry to have inflicted all this on you. But after all, why not? The Harrow Road may have made a pretty fair wreck of you, but you're still good for *something*—you can listen to me when I feel like talking . . . You'll find, I expect, that people will talk to you a good deal."

"I do find that."

"Do you know why? It isn't because you're such a wonderfully sympathetic listener or anything like that. It's because you're no good for anything else."

He stood, his head a little on one side, his eyes, angry eyes still, watching me. He wanted his words to hurt me, I think. But they did not hurt me. I experienced instead considerable relief in hearing put into spoken words the things that I had been thinking inside my head. . . .

"Why the Hell you don't get out of it all I can't think," he said, "or haven't you got the means?"

"I've got the means all right," I said, and my hand closed round my bottle of tablets.

"I see," he said. "You've got more guts than I thought. . . ."

Chapter Eleven

Mrs. Carslake spent some time talking to me next morning. I did not like Mrs. Carslake. She was a thin dark woman with an acid tongue. I don't think that all the time I was at Polnorth House I ever heard her say a nice thing about anyone. Sometimes, for sheer amusement, I used to mention name after name and wait for the first sweetness of her comments to go sour.

She was talking now of Milly Burt.

"She's a nice little thing," she said. "And so anxious to help. She's rather stupid, of course, and not very well educated politically. Women of that class are very apathetic politically."

It was my own impression that Milly Burt's class was also Mrs. Carslake's class. To annoy her, I said:

"Just like Teresa, in fact."

Mrs. Carslake looked shocked.

"Oh, but Mrs. Norreys is very clever—" then came the usual touch of venom—"far too clever for *me* sometimes. I get the impression often that she quite despises us all. Intellectual women are often very wrapped up in themselves, don't you think so? Of course, I wouldn't exactly call Mrs. Norreys selfish—"

Then she reverted to Milly Burt.

"It's a good thing for Mrs. Burt to have something to do," she said. "I'm afraid, you know, she has a very unhappy home life."

"I'm sorry to hear it."

"That man Burt is going right down the hill. He comes reeling out of the St. Loo Arms at closing time. Really, I wonder they serve him. And I believe he's quite violent sometimes—or so the neighbors say. She's frightened to death of him, you know."

Her nose quivered at the tip—it was, I decided, a quiver indicating pleasurable sensations.

"Why doesn't she leave him?" I asked.

Mrs. Carslake looked shocked.

"Oh really, Captain Norreys, she couldn't do a thing like *that*! Where could she go? She's no relations. I've sometimes thought that if a sympathetic young man came along—I don't feel, you know, that she has very strong principles. And she's quite good looking in a rather obvious sort of way."

"You don't like her very much, do you?" I said.

"Oh yes—I do—but of course I hardly know her. A vet—well, I mean it isn't like a doctor."

Having made this social distinction quite clear, Mrs. Carslake asked solicitously if there wasn't anything she could do for me.

"It's very kind of you. I don't think there's anything."

I was looking out of the window. She followed my eyes and saw what I was looking at.

"Oh," she said. "It's Isabella Charteris."

Together we watched Isabella coming nearer, passing through the field gate, coming up the steps to the terrace.

"She's quite a handsome girl," said Mrs. Carslake. "Very quiet, though. I often think these quiet girls are inclined to be sly."

The word sly made me feel indignant. I couldn't say anything because Mrs. Carslake had made her statement an exit line.

Sly—it was a horrible word! Especially as applied to Isabella. The quality most in evidence in Isabella was honesty—a fearless and almost painstaking honesty.

At least—I remembered suddenly the way she had let her scarf fall over those wretched tablets. The ease with which she had pretended to be in the middle of a conversation. And all without excitement or fuss—simply, naturally—as though she had been doing that sort of thing all her life.

Was that, perhaps, what Mrs. Carslake had meant by the word "sly"?

I thought to myself that I would ask Teresa what she thought about it. Teresa was not given to volunteering opinions, but if you asked for them you could have them.

When Isabella arrived, I saw that she was excited. I don't know that it would have been apparent to anybody else, but I spotted it at once. Up to a point, I was beginning to know Isabella fairly well.

She began abruptly without wasting time in greetings.

"Rupert is coming—really coming," she said. "He may arrive any day now. He's flying home, of course."

She sat down and smiled. Her long narrow hands were folded in her lap. Behind her head the yew tree outside made a pattern against the sky. She sat there looking beatific. Her attitude, the picture she made, reminded me of something. Something that I had seen or heard just lately. . . .

"Does his coming mean a lot to you?" I asked.

"Yes, it does. Oh yes." She added, "You see, I have been waiting a long time."

Was there possibly a touch of Mariana in the moated Grange about Isabella? Did she belong, just a little, to the Tennyson period?

"Waiting for Rupert?"

"Yes."

"Are you—so fond of him?"

"I think I am fonder of Rupert than anyone in the world." Then she added, managing somehow to give a different intonation to the repetition of the same words, "I—think I am."

"Aren't you sure?"

She looked at me with a sudden grave distress.

"Can one ever be sure of anything?"

It was not a statement of her feelings. It was definitely a question.

She asked me because she thought I might know the answer she did not know. She could not guess how that particular question hurt me.

"No," I said, and my voice was harsh in my own ears. "One can never be sure."

She accepted the answer, looking down at the quietness of her folded hands.

"I see," she said. "I see."

"How long is it since you have seen him?"

"Eight years."

"You are a romantic creature, Isabella," I said.

She looked at me questioningly.

"Because I believe that Rupert will come home and that we shall be married? But it isn't really romantic. It's more that it's a pattern—" Her long still hands quivered into life, tracing something on the surface of her frock. "My pattern and his pattern. They will come together and join. I don't think I could ever leave St. Loo. I was born here and I've always lived here. I want to go on living here. I expect I shall—die here."

She shivered a little as she said the last words, and at the same time a cloud came over the sun.

I wondered again in my own mind at her queer horror of death.

"I don't think you'll die for a long time, Isabella," I said consolingly. "You're very strong and healthy."

She assented eagerly.

"Yes, I'm very strong. I'm never ill. I think I might live to be ninety, don't you? Or even a hundred. After all, people do."

I tried to picture to myself an Isabella of ninety. I just couldn't see it. And yet I could easily imagine Lady St. Loo living to be a hundred. But then Lady St. Loo had a vigorous and forceful personality, she impinged on life, she was conscious of herself as a director and creator of events. She battled for life—Isabella accepted it.

Gabriel opened the door and came in, saying:

"Look here, Norreys—" and then stopped when he saw Isabella.

He said, "Oh—good morning, Miss Charteris."

His manner was slightly awkward and self-conscious. Was it, I wondered amusedly, the shadow of Lady St. Loo?

"We are discussing life and death," I said cheerfully. "I've just been prophesying that Miss Charteris will live to be ninety."

"I shouldn't think she'd want to," said Gabriel. "Who would?"

"I would," said Isabella.

"Why?"

She said, "I don't want to die."

"Oh," said Gabriel cheerfully, "nobody wants to die. At least they don't mind death, but they're afraid of dying. A painful messy business."

"It's death that I mind," said Isabella. "Not pain. I can stand a lot of pain."

"That's what you think," said Gabriel.

Something in his amused scornful tone angered Isabella.

She flushed.

"I can stand pain."

They looked at each other. His glance was still scornful, hers was challenging.

And then Gabriel did something that I could hardly credit.

I had laid my cigarette down. With a quick gesture he leaned across me, picked it up and brought its glowing tip close to Isabella's arm.

She did not flinch or move her arm away.

I think I cried out in protest, but neither of them paid any attention to me. He pressed the glowing end down onto the skin.

The whole ignominy and bitterness of the cripple was mine at that moment. To be helpless, bound, unable to act. I could do nothing. Revolted by Gabriel's savagery, I could do nothing to prevent it.

I saw Isabella's face slowly whiten with pain. Her lips closed tight. She did not move. Her eyes looked steadily into Gabriel's.

"Are you mad, Gabriel?" I cried. "What the hell do you think you're doing?"

He paid absolutely no attention to me. I might not have been in the room.

Suddenly, with a quick movement, he tossed the cigarette into the fireplace.

"I apologize," he said to Isabella. "You can take it all right."

And thereupon, without a further word, he went out of the room.

I was almost inarticulate, trying to get words out.

"The brute—the savage—what the hell did he think he was doing? He ought to be shot . . ."

Isabella, her eyes on the door, was slowly winding a handkerchief round her burned arm. She was doing it, if I can use the term, almost absentmindedly. As though her thoughts were elsewhere.

Then, from a long way away, as it were, she looked at me.

She seemed a little surprised.

"What's the matter?" she asked.

I tried, incoherently, to tell her just what I felt about Gabriel's action.

"I don't see," she said, "why you should be so upset. Major Gabriel was only seeing if I could stand pain. Now he knows I can."

Chapter Twelve

We had a tea party that afternoon. A niece of Mrs. Carslake's was staying in St. Loo. She had been at school with Isabella, so Mrs. Carslake told us. I had never been able to picture Isabella at school, so I agreed readily when Teresa suggested asking the niece, now a Mrs. Mordaunt, and Mrs. Carslake to tea. Teresa also asked Isabella.

"Anne Mordaunt is coming. I believe she was at school with you."

"There were several Annes," said Isabella vaguely. "Anne Trenchard and Anne Langley and Anne Thompson."

"I forget what her name was before she married. Mrs. Carslake did tell me."

Anne Mordaunt turned out to have been Anne Thompson. She was a lively young woman with a rather unpleasantly assertive manner. (Or, at any rate, that was my view.) She was in one of the Ministries in London, and her husband was in another Ministry, and she had a child who was conveniently parked somewhere where it wouldn't interfere with Anne Mordaunt's valuable contribution to the war effort.

"Though my mother seems to think that we might have Tony back now that the bombs are over. But really I do think a child in London is too difficult at present. The flat's so small, and one just can't get proper nannies, and there are meals, and of course I am out all day."

"I really think," I said, "that it was very public spirited of you to have a child at all when you have so much important work to do."

I saw Teresa, sitting behind the large silver tea tray, smile a little. She also, very gently, shook her head at me.

But my remark went down quite well with young Mrs. Mordaunt. In fact, it seemed to please her.

"One does feel," she said, "that one doesn't want to shirk any of one's responsibilities. Children are badly needed—especially in our class." She added, as a kind of afterthought, "Besides, I am absolutely devoted to Tony."

She then turned to Isabella and plunged into reminiscences of the old days at St. Ninian's. It seemed to me a conversation in which one of the two participants did not really know her part. Anne Mordaunt had to help her out more than once.

Mrs. Carslake murmured apologetically to Teresa:

"I'm so sorry Dick is late. I cannot think what is keeping him. He expected to be home by half-past four."

Isabella said, "I think Major Gabriel is with him. He passed along the terrace about a quarter of an hour ago."

I was surprised. I had not heard anyone pass. Isabella was sitting with her back to the window and could not possibly have seen anyone go by. I had had my eyes on her and she certainly had not turned her head or shown any awareness of anybody. Of course, her hearing was unusually quick, I knew that. But I wondered how she had known it was Gabriel.

Teresa said, "Isabella, I wonder if you would mind—no, please don't move, Mrs. Carslake—would you go along next door and ask them both if they wouldn't like to come and have some tea."

We watched Isabella's tall figure disappear through the doorway and Mrs. Mordaunt said:

"Isabella really hasn't changed at all. She's just the same. She always was the oddest girl. Walked about as though she were in a dream. We always put it down to her being so brainy."

"Brainy?" I said sharply.

She turned to me.

"Yes, didn't you know? Isabella's frightfully clever. Miss Curtis—the Head—was simply heartbroken because she wouldn't go on to Somerville. She matriculated when she was only fifteen and had several distinctions."

I was still inclined to think of Isabella as a creature charming to look at but not overgifted with brains. I still stared at Anne Mordaunt unbelievingly.

"What were her special subjects?" I asked.

"Oh, astronomy and mathematics—she was frightfully good at maths—and Latin and French. She could learn anything she put her mind to. And yet, you know, she just didn't care a bit. It quite broke

Miss Curtis's heart. All Isabella seemed to want to do was to come back and settle down in this stuffy old Castle place."

Isabella came back with Captain Carslake and Gabriel.

The tea party went with a swing.

"What is so bewildering to me, Teresa," I said later that evening, "is the impossibility of ever knowing what any particular human being is really like. Take Isabella Charteris. That Mordaunt woman described her as brainy. I myself used to think she was practically a moron. Then again, I should have said that one of her special characteristics was honesty. Mrs. Carslake, however, says that she's sly. Sly! An odious word. John Gabriel says she's smug and stuck up. You—well, actually I don't know what you think—because you hardly ever say anything personal about people. But—well—what is the real truth of a human creature who can appear so differently to different people?"

Robert, who seldom joined in our conversations, moved restlessly and said rather unexpectedly:

"But isn't that just the point? People do appear differently to different people. So do things. Trees, for instance, or the sea. Two painters would give you an entirely different idea of St. Loo harbor."

"You mean one painter would paint it naturalistically and another symbolically?"

Robert shook his head rather wearily. He hated talking about painting. He never could find the words to express what he meant.

"No," he said. "They'd actually *see* it differently. Probably—I don't know—you pick out of everything the things in it which are significant to *you*."

"And one does the same to people, you think? But you can't have two diametrically opposite qualities. Take Isabella, she can't be brainy *and* a moron!"

"I think you're wrong there, Hugh," said Teresa.

"My dear Teresa!"

Teresa smiled. She spoke slowly and thoughtfully.

"You can have a quality and not use it. Not, that is, if you have a simpler method that gives the same results, or that—yes, that's more probable—costs you less trouble. The point is, Hugh, that we have, all of us, progressed such a long way from simplicity that we don't now know what it is when we meet it. To *feel* a thing is always much easier—much less trouble—than to *think* it. Only, in the complexities of civilized life, feeling isn't accurate enough.

"As an instance of what I mean, you know, roughly, if asked, what time of day it is. Morning, midday—late afternoon—evening—you don't have to *think*—and you don't need, for that, accurate knowledge or any apparatus—sundials, water clocks, chronometers, watches or clocks. But if you have to keep appointments and catch trains and be at specific places at specific times, you do have to take thought and devise complicated mechanisms to provide accuracy. I think an attitude to life might be much the same. You feel happy, you are roused to anger, you like someone or something, you dislike someone or something, you feel sad. People like you and me, Hugh (but not Robert so much), *speculate* on what they feel, they *analyze* it, they *think* about it. They examine the whole thing and give themselves the *reason*. 'I am happy because of so and so—I like so and so because of so and so—I am sad today because of so and so.' Only, very often, they give themselves the wrong reasons, they willfully deceive themselves. But Isabella, I think, does not speculate—does not ask herself, ever, *why*. Because, quite frankly, she isn't interested. If you asked her to think—to tell you *why* she feels about something as she does feel, she could, I think, reason it out with perfect accuracy, and give you the correct answer. But she is like a person who has a good and expensive clock on the mantelpiece, but never winds it up because, in the kind of life she leads, it isn't important to know exactly what time it is.

"But at St. Ninian's she was asked to use her intellect, and she has got an intellect—but not, I should say, a particularly speculative intellect. Her bent is for mathematics, languages, astronomy. Nothing that requires imagination. We, all of us, use imagination and speculation as a means of escape—a way of getting outwards, away from ourselves. Isabella doesn't need to get away from herself. She can live with herself—she's in harmony with herself. She has no need for a more complex way of life.

"Possibly human beings were all like that in medieval times—even in Elizabethan days. I read in some book that a 'great man' in those days bore one meaning only—a person who had a big establishment, who was, quite simply, significance that we attach to it. The term had nothing to do with character."

"You mean," I said, "that people were direct and concrete in their attitude to life—they did not speculate much."

"Yes, Hamlet, with his musings, his 'to be or not to be,' was an entirely alien figure to his age. So much so that then and for long afterwards critics wrote condemning Hamlet as a play because of the fatal weakness of plot. 'There is no reason,' one of them said, 'why Hamlet should not kill the King in the first act. The only reason he does not do so is that if he had done, there would be no play!' It is quite unbelievable to them that there could be a play about character.

"But nowadays we are practically *all* Hamlets and Macbeths. We are all asking ourselves the whole time—" (her voice held suddenly a great weariness) " '*to be or not to be?*' Whether it is better to be alive or dead. Analyzing the successful as Hamlet analyzes (and envies!) Fortinbras.

"It is Fortinbras nowadays who would be the little understood figure. Moving ahead, confident, asking no questions of himself. How many of his sort are there in these days? Not many, I think."

"You think Isabella is a kind of female Fortinbras?" I asked smiling.

Teresa smiled too.

"Not so warlike. But direct of purpose and entirely single-minded. She would never ask herself, 'Why am I like I am? What do I really feel?' She knows what she feels and she is what she is." Teresa added softly, "And she will do—what she has to do."

"You mean she is fatalistic?"

"No. But for her I do not think there are ever alternatives. She will never see two possible courses of action—only one. And she will never think of retracing her steps, she will always go on. There's no backward way for the Isabellas...."

"I wonder if there is any backward way for any of us!"

I spoke with bitterness.

Teresa said calmly, "Perhaps not. But there is usually, I think, a loophole."

"What do you mean exactly, Teresa?"

"I think one usually gets one chance of escape.... You don't usually realize it until afterwards . . . when you are looking back . . . but it's there . . ."

I was silent for a moment or two, smoking and thinking . . .

When Teresa had said that I had had a sudden vivid memory. I had just arrived at Caro Strangeways's cocktail party. I was standing in the doorway, hesitating a moment as my eyes accustomed themselves to the dim lamps and the haze of smoke. And there, at the far end of the room, I saw Jennifer. She didn't see me, she was talking to someone else her usual vivid animated way.

I was conscious of two sharply conflicting feelings. First a leap of triumph. I had known that we should meet again—and here was my instinctive knowledge proved true. That meeting in the train was not an isolated incident. I had always known it was not, and here was my belief being proved true. And yet—in spite of my excitement, my triumph—I had a sudden wish to turn round and leave the party . . . I had a wish to keep my meeting with Jennifer in the train as a single isolated happening—a happening that I should never forget. It was as though someone had said to me, "*That* was the best you could ever have of each other—a short space of perfection. Leave it like that."

If Teresa was right, that had been *my* "chance of escape . . ."

Well, I hadn't taken it. I had gone on. And Jennifer had gone on. And everything else had happened in sequence. Our belief in our mutual love, the lorry in the Harrow Road, my invalid chair, and Polnorth House. . . .

And brought back again, thus, to my original point of departure, my mind reverted to Isabella again, and I made a final protest to Teresa.

"But not sly, Teresa? Such an odious word. Not sly."

"I wonder," said Teresa.

"Sly? Isabella?"

"Isn't slyness the first—the easiest line of defense? Isn't cunning one of the most primitive characteristics—the hare that crouches in her form—the grouse that flutters across the heather to distract you from her nest? Surely, Hugh, cunning is elemental. It's the only weapon you can use when you're helpless with your back to the wall."

She got up and moved towards the door. Robert had slipped off to bed already. With her fingers on the handle, Teresa turned her head.

"I believe," she said, "that you can really throw those tablets of yours away. You won't want them now."

"Teresa," I cried. "So you knew about them?"

"Of course I knew."

"But then—" I stopped. "Why do you say I shan't want them now?"

"Well, do you want them?"

"No," I said slowly. "You're right . . . I don't. I shall throw them away tomorrow."

"I'm so glad," said Teresa. "I've often been afraid . . ."

I looked at her curiously.

"Why didn't you try to take them away from me?"

She did not speak for a moment. Then she said:

"They've been a comfort to you, haven't they? They've made you feel secure—knowing that you always had a way out?"

"Yes," I said. "It's made a lot of difference."

"Then why are you so stupid as to ask why I didn't take them away from you?"

I laughed.

"Well, tomorrow, Teresa—they'll go down the drainpipe. That's a promise."

"So at last you've begun to live again—to want to live."

"Yes," I said wonderingly. "I suppose I have. I really can't think why. But it's true. I'm actually interested in waking up tomorrow morning."

"You're interested, yes. I wonder who's responsible for that. Is it life in St. Loo? Or Isabella Charteris? Or John Gabriel?"

"It certainly isn't John Gabriel," I said.

"I'm not so sure. There's something about that man—"

"There certainly seems to be plenty of sex appeal!" I said. "But he's the type I dislike—I can't stand a blatant opportunist. Why, that man would sell his grandmother if he saw a chance of making a profit out of her."

"I shouldn't be surprised."

"I wouldn't trust him an inch."

"No, he's not very trustworthy."

I went on, "He boasts. He's a flagrant publicity hound. He exploits himself and everybody else. Do you seriously think that that man is capable of one single disinterested action?"

Teresa said thoughtfully, "I think just possibly he might be—but if so, it would probably finish him for good."

I was to remember that remark of Teresa's within the next few days.

Chapter Thirteen

Our next local excitement was the whist drive. It was being got up by the Women's Institute.

It was being held where such affairs had always been held, in the Long Barn of Polnorth House. The Long Barn, I gather, was something rather special. Enthusiastic antiquarians came to gloat over it, measure it, photograph it, and write about it. It was considered in St. Loo as a kind of public possession. The inhabitants were proud of it.

There was a great hum of activity during the next two days. Organizing members of the Women's Institute drifted in and out.

I remained mercifully segregated from the mainstream, but Teresa occasionally introduced what I can only describe as particularly choice specimens for my amusement and entertainment.

Since Teresa knew that I liked Milly Burt, Milly was admitted fairly frequently to my sitting room and we engaged together in various miscellaneous tasks such as writing out tickets, sticking or gumming decorations.

It was while we were engaged on these operations that I heard Milly's life story. As Gabriel had so brutally told me, I could only justify my existence by becoming a kind of ever-ready receiving set. I might be good for nothing else, but I was still good for that.

Milly Burt talked to me without self-consciousness—a kind of burbling self-revelation, like a gentle little stream.

She talked a great deal about Major Gabriel. Her hero worship where he was concerned had increased rather than diminished.

"What I think so wonderful about him, Captain Norreys, is that he's so *kind*. I mean when he's so busy and so rushed and has so many important things to do, yet he always remembers things and has such a nice teasing way of talking. I've never met anyone quite like him."

"You're probably right there," I said.

"With his wonderful war record and everything, he isn't a bit proud or stuck up—he's just as nice to me as to somebody important. He's nice to everybody—and he remembers about people and if their sons have been killed or if they're out in Burma or somewhere dreadful, and he always knows the right thing to say and how to make people laugh and cheer up. I don't know how he manages it all."

"He must have been reading Kipling's *If*," I said coldly.

"Yes. I'm sure he fills the unforgiving minute with sixty seconds' worth of distance run if anybody does."

"Probably a hundred and twenty seconds' worth," I suggested. "Sixty seconds wouldn't be enough for Gabriel."

"I wish I knew more about politics," said Milly wistfully. "I have read up all the pamphlets, but I'm not really good at canvassing or persuading people to vote. You see, I don't know the answers to the things they say."

"Oh well," I said consolingly, "all that sort of thing is just a knack. Anyway, to my mind canvassing is quite unethical."

She looked at me uncomprehendingly.

I explained:

"You shouldn't ever try to make people vote against their convictions," I said.

"Oh, I see—yes, I see what you mean. But we do think that the Conservatives are the only people who can finish off the war and make the peace the right way, don't we?"

"Mrs. Burt," I said, "what a really splendid little Tory you are. Is that what you say when you go canvassing?"

She blushed.

"No, I don't really know enough to talk about the political side. But I *can* say what a splendid man Major Gabriel is, and how sincere, and how it's people like him who are really going to matter."

Well, I thought to myself, that would be right down Gabriel's street . . .

I looked into her flushed serious face. Her brown eyes were shining. I had an uncomfortable moment wondering whether perhaps a little more than hero worship was involved.

As though responding to my unexpressed thought, Milly's face clouded over.

"Jim thinks I'm an awful fool," she said deprecatingly.

"Does he? Why?"

"He says I'm such a fool I can't understand anything about politics—and anyway, the whole thing's a racket. And he says what the—I mean he says I can't possibly be any use, and if I go round talking to people it's as good as a vote for the other side from everyone I talk to. Captain Norreys, do you think that's true?"

"No," I said firmly.

She brightened up.

"I know I'm stupid in some ways. But it's only when I'm rattled, and Jim always can rattle me. He likes upsetting me. He likes—" She stopped. Her lips were quivering.

Then suddenly she scattered the white slips of paper she was working on and began to cry—deep heartrending sobs.

"My dear Mrs. Burt—" I said helplessly.

What the hell can a man do who lies helpless in an invalid chair? I couldn't pat her shoulder. She wasn't near enough. I couldn't push a handkerchief into her hand. I couldn't mutter an excuse and sidle out of the room. I couldn't even say, "I'll get you a cup of tea."

No, I had to fulfill my function, the function which, as Gabriel had been kind (or cruel) enough to tell me, was the only one left to me. So I said, helplessly, "My dear Mrs. Burt—" and waited.

"I'm so unhappy—so terribly unhappy—I see now—I should never have married Jim."

I said feebly, "Oh, come now, it's not so bad as that, I'm sure."

"He was so gay and so dashing—and he made such nice jokes. He used to come round to see the horses if anything went wrong. Dad kept a riding school, you know. Jim looks wonderful on a horse."

"Yes—yes."

"And he didn't drink so much then—at least perhaps he did, but I didn't realize it. Though I suppose I ought to have realized it, because people came and talked about it to me. Said he lifted his elbow too much. But you see, Captain Norreys, I didn't believe it. One doesn't, does one?"

"No," I said.

"I thought he would give all that up when we were married. I'm sure he didn't drink at all while we were engaged. I'm *sure* he didn't."

"Probably not," I said. "A man is capable of anything when he's courting."

"And they said he was cruel, too. But that I didn't believe. Because he was so sweet to me. Although I did see him once with a horse—he'd lost his temper with it—he was punishing it—" She gave a little quick shiver and half closed her eyes. "I felt—I felt quite differently—just for a moment or two. 'I'm not going to marry you if that's the sort of man you are,' I said to myself. It was funny, you know—I felt suddenly as though he was a stranger—not my Jim at all. It would have been funny if I had broken it off, wouldn't it?"

Funny was not what she really meant, but we agreed that it would have been funny—and also very fortunate.

Milly continued, "But it all passed over—Jim explained, and I realized that every man does lose his temper now and then. It didn't seem important. You see, I thought that I'd make him so happy that he'd never want to drink or lose his temper. That's really why I wanted to marry him so much—to make him happy."

"To make anyone happy is not the real purpose of marriage," I said. She stared at me.

"But surely, if you love anyone, the first thing you think about is to make them happy?"

"It is one of the more insidious forms of self-indulgence," I said. "And fairly widespread. It has probably caused more unhappiness than anything else in matrimonial statistics."

She still stared. I quoted to her those lines of Emily Brontë's sad wisdom:

> *"I've known a hundred ways of love*
> *And each one made the loved one rue."*

She protested, "I think that's *horrid*!"

"To love anyone," I said, "is always to lay upon that person an almost intolerable burden."

"You do say funny things, Captain Norreys."

Milly seemed almost disposed to giggle.

"Pay no attention to me," I said. "My views are not orthodox, only the result of sad experience."

"Oh, have you been unhappy too? Do you—"

I shied from the awakening sympathy in her eyes. I steered the conversation back to Jim Burt. It was unfortunate for Milly, I thought, that she had been the gentle easily browbeaten type—the worst type for marriage with a man like Burt. From what I heard of him, I guessed that he was the type of man who likes spirit in both horseflesh and women. An Irish termagant might have held him and aroused his unwilling respect. What was fatal for him was to have power over an animal or a human being. His sadistic disposition was fed by his wife's flinching fear of him, and her tears and sighs. The pity of it was that Milly Burt (or so at least I thought) would have made a happy and successful wife to most men. She would have listened to them, flattered them, and made a fuss over them. She would have increased their self-esteem and good humor.

She would, I thought suddenly, have made John Gabriel a good wife. She might not have advanced his ambitions (but was he really ambitious? I doubted it) but she would have assuaged in him that bitterness and self-distrust that now and then showed through the almost insufferable cocksureness of his manner.

James Burt, it seemed, combined jealousy with neglect, as is by no means uncommon. Railing at his wife for her poor spiritedness and stupidity, he yet resented violently any signs of friendship shown her by another man.

"You wouldn't believe it, Captain Norreys, but he even said horrible things about Major Gabriel. Just because Major Gabriel asked me to have morning coffee at the Ginger Cat last week. He was so nice—Major Gabriel, I mean, not Jim—and we sat on there a long time, although I'm sure he couldn't really spare the time—and talking so nicely, asking me about Dad and the horses and about how things used to be at St. Loo then. He couldn't have been nicer! And then—and then—to have Jim say the things he did—and get in one of his rages—he twisted my arm—I got away and locked myself in my room. I'm terrified of Jim sometimes . . . Oh, Captain Norreys—I'm so dreadfully unhappy. I do wish I was dead."

"No, you don't, Mrs. Burt, not really."

"Oh, but I *do*. What's going to happen to me? There's nothing to look forward to. It'll just go on getting worse and worse . . . Jim's losing a lot of his practice because of drinking. And that makes him madder than ever. And I'm frightened of him. I really am frightened . . ."

I soothed her as best I could. I did not think things were quite as bad as she made out. But she was certainly a very unhappy woman.

I told Teresa that Mrs. Burt led a very miserable life, but Teresa did not seem much interested.

"Don't you want to hear about it?" I asked reproachfully.

Teresa said, "Not particularly. Unhappy wives so resemble each other that their stories get rather monotonous."

"Really, Teresa!" I said. "You are quite inhuman."

"I admit," said Teresa, "that sympathy has never been my strong point."

"I have an uneasy feeling," I said, "that the wretched little thing is in love with Gabriel."

"Almost certainly, I should say," said Teresa drily.

"And you're still not sorry for her?"

"Well—not for that reason. I should think that to fall in love with Gabriel would be a most enjoyable experience."

"Really, Teresa! You're not in love with him yourself, are you?"

No, Teresa said, she wasn't. Fortunately, she added.

I pounced on that and told her she was illogical. She had just said that to fall in love with John Gabriel would be enjoyable.

"Not to me," said Teresa. "Because I resent—and have always resented—feeling emotion."

"Yes," I said thoughtfully. "I believe that's true. But why? I can't understand that."

"And I can't explain."

"Try," I urged.

"Dear Hugh, how you like to probe! I suppose because I have no instinct for living. To feel that my will and my brain can be entirely swamped and overridden by emotion is insufferable to me. I can control my actions and to a large extent my thoughts—not to be able to control my emotions is galling to my pride—it humiliates me."

"You don't think there is really any danger of anything between John Gabriel and Mrs. Burt, do you?" I asked.

"There has been some talk. Carslake is worried about it. Mrs. Carslake says there is a lot of gossip going about."

"That woman! She would."

"She would, as you say. But she represents public opinion. The opinion of the malicious gossipy strata of St. Loo. And I understand Burt's tongue has wagged rather freely when he's had a couple—which is very often. Of course he's known to be a jealous husband and a lot of what he says is discounted, but it all causes talk."

"Gabriel will have to be careful," I said.

"Being careful isn't quite his line of country, is it?" said Teresa.

"You don't think he really cares for the woman?"

Teresa considered before she replied, "I think he's very sorry for her. He's a man easily moved to pity."

"You don't think he'd get her to leave her husband? That would be a disaster."

"Would it?"

"My dear Teresa, it would bust up the whole show."

"I know."

"Well, that would be fatal, wouldn't it?"

Teresa said in an odd voice, "For John Gabriel? Or for the Conservative Party?"

"I was really thinking of Gabriel," I said. "But for the Party too, of course."

"Of course, I'm not really politically minded," said Teresa. "I don't care in the least if one more Labour Member gets elected to Westminster—though it would be too awful if the Carslakes heard me say so. What I am wondering is, if it would be a disaster for John Gabriel or not? Suppose it resulted in his being a happier man?"

"But he's frightfully keen on winning the election," I exclaimed.

Teresa said that success and happiness were two entirely different things.

"I don't really believe," she said, "that they ever go together."

Chapter Fourteen

On the morning of the whist drive, Captain Carslake came and unburdened himself of a great deal of alarm and despondency.

"There's nothing *in* it," he said. "Of course there's nothing *in* it! I've known little Mrs. Burt all my life. She's *quite* all right—very strictly brought up and all that—a thoroughly nice little woman. But you know what people's minds are."

I knew what his wife's mind was. It was probably his criterion for judging other people's.

He continued walking up and down and rubbing his nose in an exasperated fashion.

"Gabriel's a good-natured chap. He's been nice to her. But he's been careless—you can't afford to be careless during an election."

"What you really mean is you can't afford to be kind."

"Exactly—exactly. Gabriel's been too kind—kind in public. Having morning coffee with her at the Ginger Cat café. It doesn't look well. Why should he have coffee with her there?"

"Why shouldn't he?"

Carslake ignored that.

"All the old cats are there having their elevenses at that time. Then I believe he walked quite a long way with her in the town the other morning—he actually carried her shopping bag for her."

"A Conservative gentleman could do no less," I murmured.

Carslake still paid no attention to my remarks.

"And he gave her a lift in his car one day—out by Sprague's farm it was. Quite a long way out. Made it look as though they'd been off together for an outing."

"After all, this is nineteen forty-five not eighteen forty-five," I said.

"Things haven't altered much down here," said Carslake. "I don't mean the new bungalows and the arty crowd—they're up-to-date, no morals to speak of—but they'll vote Labour anyway. It's the solid respectable old-fashioned part of the town that we've got to worry about. Gabriel will really have to be more careful."

Half an hour later I had Gabriel burst in upon me in a white heat of indignation. Carslake had made tactful representations to him and the result had been the usual result of tactful words spoken in season.

"Carslake," he said, "is a foul-minded old woman! Do you know what he's had the cheek to say to me?"

"Yes," I said. "I know all about it. And by the way, this is the time of day when I rest. I don't have visitors."

"Nonsense," said Gabriel. "You don't need to rest. You're perpetually resting. You've got to listen to what I have to say about this. Damn it, I've got to let off steam to someone, and as I told you the other day, it's about all you're good for, and you might as well make up your mind to listen gracefully to people when they want to hear the sound of their own voices!"

"I remember the particularly charming way you put it," I said.

"I really said it because I wanted to get under your skin."

"I knew that."

"I suppose it was rather a brutal thing to say, but after all, it's no good your being thin-skinned."

"Actually," I said, "your saying it rather bucked me up. I've been so wrapped in consideration and tactfulness that to hear a little plain speaking was quite a relief."

"You're coming on," said Gabriel, and went on unburdening himself about his own affairs.

"Can't I offer an unhappy girl a cup of coffee in a public café without being suspected of immorality?" he demanded. "Why should I pay any attention to what people think who have minds like a public sewer?"

"Well, you want to be an M.P., don't you?" I said.

"I'm going to be an M.P."

"Carslake's point is that you won't be one, if you parade your friendship with Mrs. Burt."

"What damned swine people are!"

"Oh yes, yes!"

"As if politics isn't the dirtiest racket there is!"

"Again, yes, yes."

"Don't grin, Norreys. I find you damned annoying this morning. And if you think there's anything there shouldn't be between me and Mrs. Burt, you're wrong. I'm sorry for her, that's all. I've never said a word to her that her husband or the whole Watch Committee of St. Loo couldn't overhear if they wanted to. My God, when you think of the way I've held myself in where women are concerned! And I *like* women!"

He was deeply injured. The matter had its humorous side.

He said earnestly, "That woman's terribly unhappy. You don't know—you can't guess what she's had to put up with. How brave she's been. And how loyal. And she doesn't complain. Says she feels it must be partly her fault somehow. I'd like to get my hands on Burt—he's an unutterable brute. His own mother wouldn't recognize him when I'd done with him!"

"For Heaven's sake," I cried, really alarmed. "Haven't you got any prudence, Gabriel? A public row with Burt and your chances of the election would be dished."

He laughed and said, "Who knows? It might be worth it. I'll tell you—" He stopped.

I looked to see what had stopped the flow. It was Isabella. She had just come in through the window. She said good morning to us both, and said Teresa had asked her to come over and help arrange the Barn for tonight.

"You are going to honor us with your presence, I hope, Miss Charteris?" said Gabriel.

His speech held a mixture of oiliness and sprightliness that did not at all become him. Isabella always seemed to have a bad effect on him.

She said, "Yes." She added, "We always come to these things."

Then she went off in search of Teresa and Gabriel exploded.

"Very kind of the Princess," he said. "Very condescending. Nice of her to mix with the common herd! So gracious! I tell you, Norreys, Milly Burt is worth a dozen stuck-up girls like Isabella Charteris. Isabella Charteris! Who is she, after all?"

It seemed obvious who Isabella was. But Gabriel enjoyed himself developing the theme.

"Poor as a church mouse. Living in a ruined tumbledown old castle and pretending to be grander than anybody else. Hanging about there twiddling her fingers and doing nothing and hoping that the precious heir will come home and marry her. She's never seen him and she can't care a button for him, but she's willing to marry him. Oh yes. Faugh! These girls make me sick. Sick, Norreys. Pampered Pekinese dogs, that's what they are. Lady St. Loo, that's what she means to be. What the hell is the good of being Lady St. Loo nowadays? All that kind of thing is over and done with. Comic, that's all it is nowadays—a music-hall joke—"

"Really, Gabriel," I said. "You are undoubtedly in the wrong camp. You'd make a magnificent speech on Wilbraham's platform. Why don't you change places?"

"To a girl like that," said Gabriel, still breathing hard, "Milly Burt is just the vet's wife! Someone to be condescended to at political bean-feasts—but not to be asked to tea at the Castle—oh, no, not good enough for *that*! I tell you Milly Burt's worth six of Isabella Stuck-Up Charteris."

I closed my eyes with determination.

"Could you go away, Gabriel?" I said. "No matter what you say, I am still a very sick man, and I insist on having my rest. I find you extremely tiring."

Chapter Fifteen

Everybody had a word to say on the subject of John Gabriel and Milly Burt, and everybody said it, sooner or later, to me. My room, in the throes of preparation for the whist drive, became a kind of Green Room. People repaired there for cups of tea or glasses of sherry. Teresa could, of course, have barred them out, but she did nothing of the kind, and I was glad that she didn't for I found myself deeply interested in this rapidly woven pattern of hearsay and malice and obscure jealousy.

Between Milly Burt and John Gabriel there existed, of that I was sure, nothing that could be taken exception to. Friendliness and pity on his side, adoring hero worship on hers.

Yet I realized, reluctantly, that implicit in the present position were the further developments that malicious hearsay had anticipated. Technically innocent, Milly Burt was already more than half in love with Gabriel whether she knew it herself or not. Gabriel was essentially a man of sensual appetites. At any moment protective chivalry might be transformed into passion.

I thought that but for the exigencies of the election, their friendship might already have turned into a love affair. Gabriel, I suspected, was a man who needed to be loved and at the same time admired. The black subterranean venom in him could be appeased so long as he could cherish and protect. Milly Burt was the kind of woman who needed to be cherished and protected.

I thought cynically to myself that it would be one of the better kinds of adulteries—based less on lust than on love, pity, kindness, and gratitude. Still, it would, undoubtedly, be adultery and a large proportion of the voting electorate of St. Loo would see it as adultery without extenuating circumstances, and would forthwith record votes for the desiccated Mr. Wilbraham of blameless private life, or else sit at home and refrain from voting at all. Rightly or wrongly, Gabriel was fighting this election on personal appeal—the votes recorded would be given for John Gabriel not for Winston Churchill. And John Gabriel was skating on thin ice.

"I know I oughtn't to mention such a thing perhaps," Lady Tressilian said breathlessly. She had been walking fast. She undid her gray flannel coat and sipped gratefully at tea served in one of the late Miss Amy Tregellis's Rockingham cups. She dropped her voice in a conspiratorial manner. "But I wonder if anyone has said anything to you about—about Mrs. Burt and—and our candidate."

She looked at me like a spaniel in distress.

"I'm afraid," I said, "that people have been talking a little."

Her nice face looked very worried.

"Oh dear," she said. "I wish they wouldn't. She's very nice, you know, very nice indeed. Not at all the type that—I mean, it's so unfair. Of course, if there were anything in it, anything to be careful about—why, then they would be careful and no one would know anything about it. It's just because it's quite all right and there's nothing to conceal that they haven't, well—thought—"

Mrs. Bigham Charteris stumped in energetically at this point. She was full of indignation about some horse or other.

"Disgraceful carelessness," she said. "That man Burt is absolutely un-reliable. He's drinking more and more—and now it's beginning to show in his work. Of course, I've always known he was hopeless with dogs, but he did pull himself together over horses and cows—the farmers all swear by him—but now I hear that Polneathy's cow died calving—just due to negligence. And now Bentley's mare. Burt will do for himself if he's not careful."

"I was just talking to Captain Norreys about Mrs. Burt," said Lady Tressilian. "Asking if he'd heard anything—"

"All a pack of nonsense," said Mrs. Bigham Charteris robustly, "but these things stick. Now people are saying that *that's* the reason Burt's drinking so much. More stuff and nonsense. He drank too much and knocked his wife about long before Major Gabriel ever came to this place.

"Still," she added, "something's got to be done about it. Somebody's got to speak to Major Gabriel."

"Carslake has mentioned the matter to him, I believe," I said.

"That man's got no tact," said Mrs. Bigham Charteris. "I suppose Gabriel flew right off the handle?"

"Yes," I said. "He did."

"Gabriel's a damned fool," said Mrs. Bigham Charteris. "Soft-hearted—that's his trouble. H'm—somebody had better speak to *her*. Give her a hint to keep out of the way until after the election. I don't suppose she's the least idea what people are saying." She turned on her sister-in-law. "You'd better do it, Agnes."

Lady Tressilian turned purple and bleated miserably:

"Oh really, Maud—I shouldn't know what to say. I'm sure I'm *quite* the wrong person."

"Well, we mustn't risk letting Mrs. Carslake do it. That woman's just poison."

"Hear, hear," I said, with feeling.

"And I've a shrewd suspicion that she's at the bottom of a lot of the talk herself."

"Oh, surely not, Maud. She wouldn't do anything to prejudice our own candidate's chances."

"You'd be surprised, Agnes," said Mrs. Bigham Charteris darkly, "at what I've seen go on in a regiment. If a woman wants to be spiteful it seems to override everything else—her husband's chances of promotion—*everything*. If you ask me," she went on, "she'd have liked a mild flirtation with John Gabriel herself!"

"Maud!"

"Ask Captain Norreys what he thinks. He's been on the spot, and lookers-on see most of the game, they say."

Both ladies looked at me expectantly.

"I certainly don't think—" I began—and then changed my mind. "I think you're perfectly right," I said to Mrs. Bigham Charteris.

The significance of some of Mrs. Carslake's half-finished remarks and glances had suddenly dawned on me. I thought it possible that, unlikely as it seemed, Mrs. Carslake had not only taken no steps to scotch any flying rumors, but might actually have secretly encouraged them.

It was, I reflected, an unpleasant world.

"If anyone's going to tackle Milly Burt, I think Captain Norreys is the person," said Mrs. Bigham Charteris unexpectedly.

"No," I cried.

"She likes you and an invalid is always in rather a privileged position."

"Oh, I do so agree," said Lady Tressilian delighted at a suggestion which released her from an unpleasant task.

"No!" I said.

"She's decorating the Barn now," said Mrs. Bigham Charteris rising energetically. "I'll send her along—tell her there's a cup of tea waiting for her."

"I shan't do anything of the kind," I cried.

"Oh yes, you will," said Mrs. Bigham Charteris, who had not been a colonel's wife for nothing. "We've all got to do *something* to prevent those dreadful Socialists from getting in."

"It's to help dear Mr. Churchill," said Lady Tressilian. "After all he's done for the country."

"Now that he's won the war for us," I said, "he ought to sit back and write his history of the war (he's one of the best writers of our times) and have a nice rest while Labour mismanages the peace."

Mrs. Bigham Charteris had gone energetically through the window. I continued to address Lady Tressilian.

"Churchill deserves a rest," I said.

"Think of the terrible mess Labour would make of things," said Lady Tressilian.

"Think of the terrible mess anyone will make of it," I said. "Nobody can help making a mess of things after a war. Don't you think, really, that it had better not be our side? Anyway," I added frantically as I heard footsteps and voices outside, "*you're* obviously the person to hint things to Milly Burt. These things come better from another woman."

But Lady Tressilian was shaking her head.

"No," she said. "They don't—they don't really. Maud is quite right. You're the right person. I'm sure she'll understand."

The last pronoun referred, I presumed, to Milly Burt. I myself had very grave doubts whether she would understand.

Mrs. Bigham Charteris brought Milly Burt into the room like a naval destroyer convoying a merchant ship.

"Here you are," she said breezily. "There's the tea. Pour out a cup and sit down and amuse Captain Norreys. Agnes, I want you. What did you do with the prizes?"

The two women swept out of the room. Milly Burt poured out her cup of tea and came to sit down by me. She looked a little bewildered.

"There isn't anything wrong, is there?" she asked.

Perhaps if she had not used that opening phrase I should have shirked the task imposed upon me. As it was, the opening made it slightly easier for me to say what I had been told to say.

"You're a very nice person, Milly," I said. "Do you ever realize that a lot of people aren't particularly nice?"

"What do you mean, Captain Norreys?"

"Look here," I said. "Do you know that there's a lot of ill-natured talk going on about you and Major Gabriel?"

"About me and Major Gabriel?" She stared at me. A slow burning blush suffused her face up to the roots of the hair. It embarrassed me and I averted my eyes. "You mean that it's not only Jim—that outside people say so too—that they really think—?"

"When an election is on," I said, hating myself, "the prospective candidate has to be particularly careful. He has, in St. Paul's words, to avoid even the appearance of evil. . . . You see? Silly little things like having coffee with him at the Ginger Cat or his meeting you in the street and carrying your parcels, are quite enough to set people off."

She looked at me with wide frightened brown eyes.

"But you do believe, don't you, that there's never been *anything*, that he's never said a word? That's he's been just very very kind? That's all! *Really*, that's all."

"Of course, I know that. But a prospective candidate can't even afford to be kind. Such," I added bitterly, "is the purity of our political ideals."

"I wouldn't do him any harm," said Milly. "Not for the world."

"I'm sure you wouldn't."

She looked at me appealingly.

"What can I do to—to put things right?"

"I should simply suggest that you—well, keep out of his way until the election's over. Try not to be seen together in public if you can help it."

She nodded quickly.

"Yes, of course. I'm ever so grateful to you for telling me, Captain Norreys. I should never have thought of it. I—he's been so wonderful to me—"

She got up and everything would have ended very satisfactorily if John Gabriel had not chosen that moment to come in.

"Hullo," he said. "What's going on here? I've just come from a meeting, been talking till my throat's hoarse. Got any sherry? I'm visiting some mothers next—and whiskey isn't too good on the breath."

"I must be off now," said Milly. "Good-bye, Captain Norreys. Good-bye, Major Gabriel."

Gabriel said, "Wait a moment. I'll walk home with you."

"No. No, please. I—I must hurry."

He said, "All right. I'll sacrifice the sherry then."

"Please!" She was flushed, embarrassed. "I don't want you to come. I—I want to go alone."

She almost ran from the room. Gabriel wheeled round on me.

"Who's been saying things to her? You?"

"I have," I said.

"What do you mean by butting into my affairs?"

"I don't care a damn about your affairs. This is the affair of the Conervative Party."

"And do you care a damn about the Conservative Party?"

"When I actually come to think of it, no," I admitted.

"Then why do the Nosey Parker?"

"If you want to know, it's because I like little Mrs. Burt, and if she were to feel later that you had lost the election from any reason connected with your friendship for her, she would be very unhappy."

"I shan't lose the election through my friendship with her."

"It's quite possible that you might, Gabriel. You underestimate the force of prurient imagination."

He nodded.

"Who put you up to talking to her?"

"Mrs. Bigham Charteris and Lady Tressilian."

"Those old hags! And Lady St. Loo?"

"No," I said. "Lady St. Loo had nothing to do with it."

"If I thought *she* was issuing orders," said Gabriel, "I'd take Milly Burt away for the weekend and to hell with the lot of them!"

"That would finish things very nicely!" I said. "I thought you wanted to win this election?"

He grinned suddenly, his good temper restored.

"I'll win it all right," he said.

Chapter Sixteen

That evening was one of the loveliest evenings of the whole summer. People flocked along to the Long Barn. There was fancy dress and dancing as well as the whist drive proper.

Teresa wheeled me along to have a look at the scene. Everyone seemed very animated. Gabriel was in good form, telling stories, mixing with the crowd, quick with back chat and repartee. He looked particularly cheerful and confident. He seemed to be paying special attention to the ladies present, rather exaggerating his manner to them. I thought that was astute of him. His infectious good spirits made themselves felt—and everything was going with a swing.

Lady St. Loo, gaunt and impressive, was there to set things in motion. Her presence was taken as a compliment. I had discovered that she was both liked and feared. She was a woman who did not hesitate to speak her mind on occasions—on the other hand, her kindness, though unspectacular, was very real, and she took a keen interest in the town of St. Loo and its vicissitudes.

"The Castle" was much respected. When the billeting officer had been tearing his hair over the difficulties of placing evacuees early in the war, an uncompromising message had arrived from Lady St. Loo. Why had she not been allocated any evacuees?

To Mr. Pengelley's halting explanations that he had been unwilling that she should be troubled—some of the children were very undisciplined—she had replied:

"Naturally we shall do our share. We can easily take five children of school age, or two mothers with families, whichever you prefer."

The mothers and families had not been a success. The two London women had been terrified of the long echoing stone passages of the Castle, they had shivered and murmured about ghosts. When the gales blew from the sea the inadequate heating set them huddling together with their teeth chattering. The place was a nightmare to them after the cheery warmth and humanity of a London tenement. They soon departed and were replaced with children of school age to whom the Castle was one of the most exciting things that had ever happened. They climbed about its ruins, hunted insatiably for a rumored underground passage, and enjoyed the echoing corridors inside. They submitted to being mothered by Lady Tressilian, were awed and fascinated by Lady St. Loo, were taught not to fear horses and dogs by Mrs. Bigham Charteris, and got on excellent terms with the old Cornish cook who made them saffron buns.

Later Lady St. Loo twice made representations to the billeting officer. Certain children had been placed on lonely farms—the farmers in question were not, according to her, either kindly or trustworthy. She insisted on inquiries being made. It was found that in one case the children were being badly underfed. In the other they were adequately fed but dirty and neglected.

It all heightened the respect in which the old lady was held. The Castle wouldn't stand for things being done wrong, people said.

Lady St. Loo did not grace the whist drive with her presence too long. She and her sister and sister-in-law departed together. Isabella remained on to help Teresa, Mrs. Carslake and other ladies.

I myself stayed watching it all for about twenty minutes. Then Robert pushed my chair back to the house. I stopped him on the terrace. It was a warm night and the moonlight was magnificent.

"I'll stay out here," I said.

"Right. Do you want a rug or anything?"

"No, it's quite warm."

Robert nodded. He turned on his heel and strode back to the Barn where he had undertaken certain tasks.

I lay there smoking peacefully. The Castle was silhouetted against the moonlit sea and looked more than ever like a stage property. A hum of music and voices came from the direction of the Barn. Behind me the house was dark and shuttered save for one open window. A freak of the moonlight made it look as though a causeway of light stretched from the Castle to Polnorth House.

Along it, I pleased myself by imagining, rode a figure in shining armor—young Lord St. Loo returned to his home . . . A pity that battle-dress was so much less romantic than chain mail.

At variance with the far-off human noises from the Barn came the thousand and one noises of the summer night, small creakings and rustlings—tiny animals creeping about their lawful occasions, leaves stirring, the faint far off hoot of an owl. . . .

Vague contentment stole over me. It was true what I had told Teresa—I was beginning to live again. The past and Jennifer were like a brilliant unsubstantial dream—between it and me was the morass of pain and darkness and lethargy from which I was only now emerging. I could not take up my old life—the break was clean. The life that I was beginning was a new life. What was this new life of mine going to be? How was I going to shape it? Who and what was the new Hugh Norreys? I felt interest beginning to stir. What did I know? What could I hope? What was I going to do?

I saw a tall white-clad figure come out from the Long Barn. It hesitated a moment then walked in my direction. I had known at once it was Isabella. She came and sat down on the stone bench. The harmony of the night was complete.

We were quite a long time without saying anything. I was very happy. I didn't want to spoil it by talking. I didn't even want to think.

It was not till a sudden breeze sprang up off the sea and ruffled Isabella's hair so that she raised her arm to her head that the spell was broken. I turned my head to look at her. She was staring, as I had stared earlier, at the moonlit causeway leading to the Castle.

"Rupert ought to come tonight," I said.

"Yes." There was a tiny catch in her voice. "He ought."

"I've been picturing his arrival," I said, "in chain mail on a horse. But really, I suppose, he'll come in battle-dress and a beret."

"He must come soon," Isabella said. "Oh, he must come soon . . ."

There was urgency, almost distress, in her voice.

I didn't know what was in her mind, but I felt vaguely alarmed for her.

"Don't set your heart too much on his coming," I warned her. "Things have a knack of turning out all wrong."

"I suppose they do, sometimes."

"You expect something," I said, "and it isn't there. . . ."

Isabella said, "Rupert must come *soon*."

There was distress, real urgency in her voice.

I would have asked her what she meant, but at that moment John Gabriel came out of the Long Barn and joined us.

"Mrs. Norreys sent me along to see if there was anything you wanted," he said to me. "Like a drink?"

"No, thank you."

"Sure?"

"Quite sure."

He more or less ignored Isabella.

"Fetch yourself one," I said.

"No, thanks. I don't want one." He paused and then said, "Lovely night. On such a night did young Lorenzo etcetera etcetera."

We were all three silent. Music came faintly from the Long Barn. Gabriel turned to Isabella.

"Would you care to come and dance, Miss Charteris?"

Isabella rose and murmured in her polite voice, "Thank you. I would like to very much."

They walked away together rather stiffly without saying anything to each other.

I began to think about Jennifer. I wondered where she was and what she was doing. Was she happy or unhappy? Had she found, as the phrase goes, "someone else?" I hoped so. I hoped so very much.

There was no real pain in thinking about Jennifer, because the Jennifer that I had once known had not really existed. I had invented her to please myself. I had never bothered about the real Jennifer. Between her and me there had stood the figure of Hugh Norreys caring for Jennifer.

I remembered vaguely as a child going carefully and unsteadily down a big flight of stairs. I could hear the faint echo of my own voice saying importantly, "Here's Hugh going downstairs . . ." Later, a child learns to say *"I."* But somewhere, deep inside himself, that "I" doesn't penetrate. He goes on being not "I" but a spectator. He sees himself in a series of pictures. I had seen Hugh comforting Jennifer, Hugh being all the world to Jennifer, Hugh going to make Jennifer happy, going to make up to Jennifer for all that had happened to her.

Yes, I thought to myself suddenly, just like Milly Burt. Milly Burt deciding to marry her Jim, seeing herself making him happy, curing him of drinking, not caring, really, to acknowledge the real Jim.

I tried this process on John Gabriel. Here's John Gabriel, sorry for the little woman, cheering her up, being kind to her, helping her along.

I switched to Teresa. Here's Teresa marrying Robert, here's Teresa— No, that wouldn't work. Teresa, I thought to myself, was adult—she had learned to say *"I."*

Two figures came out from the Barn. They did not come towards me. Instead they turned the other way down the steps to the lower terrace and the water garden. . . .

I pursued my mental researches. Lady Tressilian, seeing herself persuade me back to health, to interest in life. Mrs. Bigham Charteris seeing herself as the person who always knew the right way to tackle things, still in her own eyes the efficient wife of the Colonel of the regiment. Well, why the hell not? Life is hard, and we must have our dreams.

Had Jennifer had dreams? What was Jennifer really like? Had I ever bothered to find out? Hadn't I seen always what I wanted to see, my loyal unhappy wonderful Jennifer?

What was she really? Not so very wonderful, not so very loyal (when one came to think of it!), certainly unhappy . . . determinedly unhappy. I remembered her remorse, her self-accusations when I had lain there, a broken and shattered wreck. Everything was *her* fault, her doing. What did that mean after all but Jennifer seeing herself in a tragic role?

Everything that has happened must have been caused by Jennifer. This is Jennifer, the tragic, the unhappy figure, for whom everything goes wrong, and who takes the blame for everything that goes wrong with everyone else. Milly Burt, probably, would do much the same. Milly— my thoughts switched abruptly from theories of personality to present everyday problems. Milly hadn't come tonight. Perhaps that was wise of her. Or would her absence cause equal comment?

I shivered suddenly and gave a start. I must have been nearly asleep. It was getting much colder . . .

I heard steps coming up from the lower terrace. It was John Gabriel. He walked towards me and I noticed that he walked unsteadily. I wondered if he had been drinking.

He came up to me. I was startled at his appearance. His voice when he spoke was thick, the words were slurred. He presented every appearance of a man who had been drinking, but it was not alcohol that had got him into this state.

He laughed, a drunken sort of laugh.

"That girl!" he said. "That girl! I told you that girl was just like any other girl. Her head may be in the stars, but her feet are set in clay all right."

"What are you talking about, Gabriel?" I said sharply. "Have you been drinking?"

He let out another laugh.

"That's a good one! No, I haven't been drinking. There are better things to do than drink. A proud stuck-up bit of goods! Too much of a fine lady to associate with the common herd! I've shown her where she belongs. I've pulled her down from the stars—I've shown her what she's made of, common earth. I told you long ago she wasn't a saint—not with a mouth like that. . . . She's human all right. She's just like all the rest of us. Make love to any woman you like, they're all the same . . . all the same!"

"Look here, Gabriel," I said furiously, "what have you been up to?"

He let out a cackle of laughter.

"I've been enjoying myself, old boy," he said. "That's what I've been doing, enjoying myself. Enjoying myself in my own way—and a damned good way too."

"If you've insulted that girl in any way—"

"Girl? She's a full-grown woman. She knows what she's doing, or she ought to know. She's a woman all right. Take my word for it."

Again he laughed. The echo of that laugh haunted me for many years. It was a gross materialistic chuckle, horribly unpleasant. I hated him then and I went on hating him.

I was horribly conscious of my own helplessness, my immobility. He made me conscious of it by his swift contemptuous glance. I can imagine no one more odious than John Gabriel was that night . . .

He laughed again and went unsteadily towards the Barn.

I looked after him full of angry rage. Then, while I was still revolving the bitter pill of my invalid status I heard someone coming up the terrace steps. Lighter, quieter footfalls this time.

Isabella come up onto the terrace and across towards me and sat down on the stone bench by my side.

Her movements, as always, were assured and quiet. She sat there in silence as she had sat earlier in the evening. Yet I was conscious, distinctly conscious, of a difference. It was as though, without outward sign, she sought reassurance. Something within her was startled and awake. She was, I felt certain, in deep trouble of spirit. But I did not know, I could not even guess, what exactly was passing through her mind. Perhaps she did not know herself.

I said, rather incoherently, "Isabella, my dear—is it all right?"

I did not quite know what I meant.

She said presently, "I don't know . . ."

A few minutes later she slipped her hand into mine. It was a lovely trustful gesture, a gesture I have never forgotten. We did not say anything. We sat there for nearly an hour. Then the people began to come out of the Long Barn and various women came and chatted and congratulated each other on the way everything had gone, and one of them took Isabella home in her car.

It was all dreamlike and unreal.

Chapter Seventeen

I expected that Gabriel would keep away from me the next day, but Gabriel was always unaccountable. He came into my room just before eleven o'clock.

"Hoped I'd find you alone," he said. "I suppose I made the most thundering fool of myself last night."

"You can call it that. I should call it something stronger. You're an unutterable swine, Gabriel."

"What did she say?"

"She didn't say anything."

"Was she upset? Was she angry? Damn it all, she must have said *something*. She was with you almost an hour."

"She didn't say anything at all," I repeated.

"I wish to God I'd never—" He stopped. "Look here, you don't think I seduced her, do you? Nothing of that kind. Good Lord, no. I only— well—I only made love to her a bit, that's all. Moonlight, a pretty girl— well, I mean it might have happened to anybody."

I didn't answer. Gabriel answered my silence as if it had been spoken words.

"You're right," he said. "I'm not particularly proud of myself. But she drove me mad. She's driven me mad ever since I met her. Looking as though she was too holy to be touched. That's why I made love to her last night—yes, and it wasn't pretty lovemaking either—it was pretty beastly. But she responded, Norreys . . . She's human all right—as human as any little piece you pick up on a Saturday night. I daresay she hates me now. I've not slept a wink—"

He walked violently up and down. Then he asked again:

"Are you sure she didn't say anything? Anything at all?"

"I've told you twice," I said coldly.

He clutched his head. It might have been a funny gesture, but it was actually purely tragic.

"I never know what she thinks," he said. "I don't know anything about her. She's somewhere where I can't get at her. It's like that damned frieze at Pisa. The blessed, sitting there in Heaven under the trees, smiling. I *had* to drag her down—I had to! I couldn't stand it any more. I tell you I just couldn't stand it. I wanted to humble her, to drag her down to earth, to see her look ashamed. I wanted her down in Hell with me—"

"For God's sake, Gabriel, shut up," I said angrily. "Haven't you any decency?"

"No, I haven't. You wouldn't have if you'd been through what I've been through. All these weeks. I wish I'd never seen her. I wish I could forget her. I wish I didn't know she existed."

"I'd no idea—"

He interrupted me.

"*You* wouldn't have any idea. You never do see an inch in front of your nose! You're the most selfish individual I've ever met, entirely wrapped up in your own feelings. Can't you see that I'm licked? A little more of this and I shan't care whether I get into Parliament or not."

"The country," I said, "may be the gainer."

"The truth is," said Gabriel gloomily, "that I've made the most unholy hash of everything."

I did not reply. I had stood so much from Gabriel in his boastful moods, that I was able to take a certain amount of satisfaction in seeing him thoroughly cast down.

My silence annoyed him. I was glad. I had meant it to annoy him.

"I wonder, Norreys, if you have any idea how smug and puritanical you look? What do you think I ought to do—apologize to the girl—say I lost my head—something like that?"

"It's nothing to do with me. You've had so much experience with women that you ought to know."

"I've never had anything to do with a girl like that before. Do you think she's shocked—disgusted? Does she think I'm a complete swine?"

Again I found pleasure in telling him what was the simple truth— that I did not know what Isabella thought or felt.

"But I think," I said, looking through the window, "that she's coming here now."

Gabriel went very red in the face and his eyes took on a hunted look.

He took up his position in front of the fireplace, an ugly position, his legs straddled, his chin thrust forward. He had a hangdog sheepish look that sat very ill upon him. It gave me pleasure to observe that he looked common and furtive and mean.

"If she looks at me as though I were something the cat had brought in—" he said, but did not finish the sentence.

Isabella, however, did not look at him as though he were something the cat had brought in. She said good morning, first to me and then to him. Her manner made no difference between us. It was, as usual, grave and perfectly courteous. She had the serene and untouched look that she always had. She had brought a message for Teresa and when she learned Teresa was next door with the Carslakes she went in search of her, giving us both a small gracious smile as she left the room.

When she had shut the door behind her Gabriel began to swear. He cursed her steadily and vitriolically. I tried to stem the torrent of his malice but without avail. He shouted at me:

"Hold your tongue, Norreys. This has nothing to do with you. I tell you I'll get even with that proud stuck-up bitch if it's the last thing I ever do."

And with that he charged out of the room, banging the door behind him so that Polnorth House shook with the impact.

I did not want to miss Isabella on her way back from the Carslakes so I rang my bell and had my chair pushed out onto the terrace.

I had not long to wait. Isabella came out of the far French window and along the terrace towards me. With her usual naturalness she came straight to the stone seat and sat down. She did not say anything. Her long hands were, as usual, loosely folded on her lap.

Usually I was content enough, but today my speculative mind was active. I wanted to know what went on in that rather nobly shaped head. I had seen the state that Gabriel was in. I had no idea what impression, if any, had been left on Isabella by the happenings of the preceding evening. The difficulty of dealing with Isabella was that you had to put things into plain words—to proffer any accepted euphemisms merely resulted in her giving you a stare of blank bewilderment.

Yet custom being what it is, my first remark was completely ambiguous.

"Is it all right, Isabella?" I asked.

She turned her level inquiring gaze on me.

"Gabriel," I said, "is upset this morning. I think he wants to apologize to you for what happened last night."

She said, "Why should he apologize?"

"Well—" I said, hesitating, "he thinks he behaved rather badly."

She looked thoughtful and said, "Oh, I see."

There was no trace of embarrassment in her manner. My curiosity drove me on to ask further questions, notwithstanding the fact that the whole subject was no business of mine.

"Don't *you* think he behaved badly?" I asked.

She said, "I don't know . . . I simply don't know . . ." She added, in a faintly apologetic manner, "You see, it's something I simply haven't had time to think about."

"You weren't shocked, or frightened, or upset?"

I was curious, really curious.

She seemed to turn over my words in her mind. Then she said, still with that air of viewing something with detachment that was a long way off:

"No, I don't think so. Ought I to have been?"

And there, of course, she turned the tables on me. Because I didn't know that answer. What ought a normal girl to feel when she first meets—not love—certainly not tenderness—but the easily awakened passion of a man of somewhat gross disposition?

I had always felt (or had I only wanted to feel?) that there was something extraordinarily virginal about Isabella. But was that really so? Gabriel, I remembered, had twice mentioned her mouth. I looked at that mouth now. The underlip was full—it was almost a Hapsburg mouth—it was unpainted—a fresh natural red—yes, it was a sensuous—a passionate mouth.

Gabriel had wakened response in her. But what was that response? Purely sensual? Instinctive? Was it a response to which her judgment assented?

Then Isabella asked me a question. She asked me quite simply if I liked Major Gabriel.

There were times when I would have found it hard to answer that question. But not today. Today I was quite definite in my feelings about Gabriel.

I said, uncompromisingly, "No."

She said thoughtfully, "Mrs. Carslake doesn't like him either."

I disliked a good deal being bracketed with Mrs. Carslake.

I, in my turn, asked a question.

"Do you like him, Isabella?"

She was silent for a very long time. And when words did struggle to the surface, I realized that they had arisen from a deep morass of bewilderment.

"I don't know him . . . I don't know anything about him. It's terrible when you can't even talk to anyone."

It was difficult for me to understand what she meant because always, where I had been attracted towards women, understanding had been, as it were, the lure. The belief (sometimes an erroneous belief) in a special sympathy between us. The discovery of things we both liked, things we disliked, discussions of plays, of books, of ethical points, of mutual sympathies or mutual aversions.

The sensation of warm comradeship had always been the start of what was quite frequently not comradeship at all, but merely camouflaged sex.

Gabriel, according to Teresa, was a man attractive to women. Presumably Isabella had found him attractive—but if so his male attractiveness was a bald fact to her—it was not disguised by a veneer of spurious understanding. It was as a stranger, an alien, that he came. But did she really find him attractive? Was it possibly his lovemaking that she found attractive and not the man himself?

These, I perceived, were all speculations. And Isabella did not speculate. Whatever her feelings toward Gabriel, she would not analyze them. She would accept them—accept them as a woven part of Life's tapestry, and go on to the next portion of the design.

And it was that, I suddenly realized, that had aroused Gabriel's almost maniacal rage. For a split second I felt a stirring of sympathy for him.

Then Isabella spoke.

She asked me in her serious voice why I thought it was that red roses never lasted in water.

We discussed the question. I asked her what her favorite flowers were.

She said red roses and very dark brown wallflowers and what she called thick-looking pale mauve stocks.

It seemed to me rather an odd selection. I asked her why she liked those particular flowers. She said she didn't know.

"You've got a lazy mind, Isabella," I said. "You know perfectly well if only you'd take the trouble to think."

"Would I? Very well, then, I will think."

She sat there, upright and serious, thinking. . . .

(And that, when I remember Isabella, is how I see her—and always shall see her to the end of time. Sitting in the sunlight on the upright carved stone seat, her head proud and erect, her long narrow hands folded peacefully on her lap and her face serious, thinking of flowers.)

She said at last, "I think it is because they all look as though they would be lovely to touch—rich—like velvet. . . . And because they have a lovely smell. Roses don't look right growing—they grow in an ugly way. A rose wants to be by itself, in a glass—then it's beautiful—but only for a very short time—then it droops and dies. Aspirin and burning the stems and all those things don't do any good—not to red roses— they're all right for the others. But nothing keeps big dark red roses long—I wish they didn't die."

It was quite the longest speech Isabella had ever made to me. She was more interested in talking about roses than she had been in talking about Gabriel.

It was, as I have said, a moment I shall always remember. It was the climax, you see, of our friendship. . . .

From where my chair was placed, I faced the footpath across the fields from St. Loo Castle. And along that footpath a figure was approaching—a figure in battle-dress and a beret. With a sudden pang that astonished me, I knew that Lord St. Loo had come home.

Chapter Eighteen

Sometimes one has the illusion of a certain series of events having happened a wearisome number of times before. I had that impression as I watched young Lord St. Loo coming towards us. It seemed to me that again and again and again I had lain here, helpless, immobile, watching Rupert St. Loo coming across the fields . . . It had happened often before, it would happen again . . . it would happen throughout Eternity.

Isabella, my heart said, *this is good-bye*. This is Fate coming for you.

It was the fairy story atmosphere again; it was illusion, unreality. I was going to assist at the familiar end of a familiar story.

I gave a little sigh as I looked at Isabella. She was quite unaware of

Fate approaching. She was looking down at her long narrow white hands. She was still thinking of roses—or possibly of very dark brown wallflowers . . .

"Isabella," I said gently. "Someone is coming . . ."

She looked up, without haste, mildly interested. She turned her head. Her body went rigid, then a little tremor went through it.

"Rupert," she said . . . "Rupert. . . ."

It mightn't, of course, have been Rupert at all. Nobody could have told at that distance. But it was Rupert.

He came, a little hesitantly, through the gate and up the steps to the terrace, a faintly apologetic air about him. Because Polnorth House belonged to strangers whom he hadn't yet met. . . . But they had told him, at the Castle, that he would find his cousin there.

Isabella rose to her feet as he came up onto the terrace and she took two steps towards him. He quickened his own steps towards her.

She said, "Rupert . . ." very softly as they met.

He said, "Isabella!"

They stood there together, their hands clapsed, his head bent just a little protectively.

It was perfect—quite perfect. If it had been a film scene there would have been no necessity for a retake . . . On the stage, it would have brought a lump to the throat of any romantic playgoing woman over middle age. It was idyllic—unreal—a fairy story's happy ending. It was Romance with a capital R.

It was the meeting of a boy and girl who had been thinking of each other for years, each building up an image that was partly illusory, and finding when they at last came together, that miraculously the illusion was at one with reality. . . .

It was the sort of thing which doesn't happen, one says, in real life. But it was happening, here before my eyes.

They settled things, really, in that first moment. Rupert had always held tenaciously, in the back of his mind, to the determination to come back to St. Loo and marry Isabella. Isabella had always had the calm certainty that Rupert would come home and marry her, and that they would live together at St. Loo . . . happy ever after.

And now, for both of them, their faith was justified and the vision was fulfilled.

Their moment didn't last long. Isabella turned to me. Her face was shining with happiness.

"This is Captain Norreys," she said. "My cousin Rupert."

St. Loo came forward and shook hands with me and I took a good look at him.

I still think that I have never seen anyone handsomer. I don't mean that he was of the "Greek God" type. His was an entirely virile and masculine beauty. A lean weather-beaten brown face, a rather large moustache, deep blue eyes, a head perfectly set on broad shoulders, narrow flanks, and well-shaped legs. His voice was attractive, deep and pleasant. He had no Colonial accent. There was humor in his face, intelligence, tenacity, and a certain calm stability.

He apologized for coming across informally like this, but he had just arrived by air, and had come straight across country from the aerodrome by car. On arrival, he had been told by Lady Tressilian that Isabella had gone over to Polnorth House and that he would probably find her there.

He looked at Isabella as he finished speaking and a twinkle came into his eye.

"You've improved a lot from a schoolgirl, Isabella," he said. "I remember you with immensely long spindly legs, two flapping plaits, and an earnest air."

"I must have looked terrible," said Isabella thoughtfully.

Lord St. Loo said he hoped he would meet my sister-in-law and my brother whose paintings he admired very much.

Isabella said that Teresa was with the Carslakes and she would go and tell her. Did Rupert want the Carslakes too?

Rupert said he didn't want the Carslakes, and he couldn't remember them anyway, even if they had been here when he was last at St. Loo as a schoolboy.

"I expect, Rupert," said Isabella, "that you will have to have them. They will be very excited about your coming. Everyone will be excited."

Young Lord St. Loo looked apprehensive. He had only got a month's leave, he said.

"And then you have to go back to the East?" asked Isabella.

"Yes."

"And after the Japanese war is over—will you come back here then, to live?"

She asked him the question with gravity. His face too became grave.

"It depends," he said, "on several things. . . ."

There was a little unexplained pause . . . it was as though both of them were thinking of the same things. There was already full harmony and understanding between them.

Then Isabella went away in search of Teresa, and Rupert St. Loo sat down and began to talk to me. We talked shop and I enjoyed it. Since I had come to Polnorth House I had lived perforce in a feminine atmosphere. St. Loo was one of those pockets in a country which remain consistently out of the war. Their connection with it is only by hearsay, gossip and rumors. Such soldiers as there are about are soldiers on leave who want to leave their war mentality behind them.

I had been plunged, instead, into a purely political world—and the political world, at any rate in places like St. Loo, is essentially female. It is a world of calculation of effects, of persuasion, of a thousand small subtleties, coupled with that large amount of sheer uninteresting drudgery that is, again, the female quota to existence. It is a world in miniature—the outside universe of bloodshed and violence has its place only as a stage backcloth might have its place. Against the background of a world war not yet terminated we were engaged in a parochial and intensely personal struggle. The same thing was going on all over England camouflaged by noble clichés. Democracy, Freedom, Security, Empire, Nationalization, Loyalty, Brave New World—those were the words, the banners.

But the actual elections, as I began to suspect was always the case, were swayed by those personal insistencies which are so much greater, so much more urgent, than the Words and Names—the Banners—under which the fight is enrolled.

Which side will give me a house to live in? Which side will bring my boy Johnnie, my husband David back from overseas? Which side will give my babies the best chance in the future? Which side will keep further wars from taking and killing my man, and perhaps my sons?

Fine words butter no parsnips. Who will help me to reopen my shop?

Who will build me a house? Who will give us all more food, more clothing coupons, more towels, more soap?

Churchill's all right. He won the war for us. He saved us from having the Germans here. I'll stick by Churchill.

Wilbraham's a schoolmaster. Education's the thing to get children on in the world. Labour will give us more houses. They say so. Churchill won't bring the boys home as quickly. Nationalize the mines—then we'll all have coal.

I like Major Gabriel. He's a real man. He cares about things. He's been wounded, he's fought all over Europe, he hasn't stayed at home in a safe job. He knows what we feel about the boys out there. He's the kind we want—not a blasted schoolmaster. Schoolteachers! Those evacuated teachers wouldn't even help Mrs. Polwidden to wash up the breakfast things. Stuck up, that's what they are.

What are politics after all but adjacent booths at the world's fair, each offering their own cheap-jack specific to cure all ills? . . . And the gullible public swallows the chatter.

That was the world I had lived in since I returned to life and began living it once more. It was a world I had never known before, a world entirely new to me.

At first I had despised it indulgently. I had characterized it to myself as just another racket. But now I was beginning to realize on what it was based, what passionate realities, what endless struggling hopes for survival. The woman's world—not the man's. Man was still the hunter— carefree, ragged, often hungry, pushing ahead, a woman and a child at his tail. No need for politics in *that* world, only the quick eyes, the ready hand, the stalking of the prey.

But the civilized world is based on earth, earth that grows and produces. That is a world that erects buildings, and fills them with possessions—a maternal, fecund world where survival is infinitely more complicated and may succeed and fail in a hundred different ways. Women do not see the stars, they see the four walls of a shelter from the wind, the cooking pot on the hearth, the faces of well-fed children asleep.

I wanted—badly—to escape from that female world. Robert was no help to me—he was a painter. An artist, maternally concerned with the bringing forth of new life. Gabriel was masculine enough—his presence had cut welcomely across the infinitesimal web of intrigue—but essentially he and I were out of sympathy.

With Rupert St. Loo, I was back in my own world. The world of Alamein and Sicily, of Cairo and Rome. We talked the old language, in the old idiom, discovering mutual acquaintances. I was back again, a whole man, in the wartime careless world of imminent death, good cheer, and physical enjoyment.

I liked Rupert St. Loo enormously. He was, I felt sure, a first-class officer, and he had an extremely attractive personality. He had brains, good humor, and a sensitive intelligence. He was the kind of man, I thought, who was needed to build up the new world. A man with traditions and yet with a modern and forward-looking mind.

Presently Teresa came and joined us, with Robert, and she explained how we were engaged in a fury of electioneering, and Rupert St. Loo confessed that he wasn't much of a politician: and then the Carslakes came in with Gabriel, and Mrs. Carslake gushed, and Carslake put on his hearty manner, and was delighted to see Lord St. Loo, and this was our candidate Major Gabriel.

Rupert St. Loo and Gabriel greeted each other pleasantly and Rupert wished him luck and talked a little about the campaign and how things were going. They stood together outlined against the sunlight, and I noted the contrast, the really cruel contrast, between them. It wasn't only that Rupert was handsome and Gabriel was an ugly little man—it went deeper than that. Rupert St. Loo was poised, assured. He had a naturally courteous and kindly manner. You felt, too, that he was dead straight. A Chinese merchant, if I may put it that way, would have trusted him to take away any amount of goods without paying for them—and the Chinese merchant would have been right. Gabriel showed up badly against the other—he was nervous, too assertive, he straddled his legs and moved about uneasily. He looked, poor devil, rather a nasty common little man—worse, he looked the kind of man who would be honest as long as it paid him. He was like a dog of doubtful ancestry that has got along all right until it is brought into the show ring side by side with a thoroughbred.

Robert was standing by my couch, and I drew his attention to the two men with a mumbled word.

He caught my meaning and looked thoughtfully at them both. Gabriel was still weaving uneasily from foot to foot. He had to look up at Rupert as they talked, and I don't think he liked having to do that.

Someone else was watching the two men—Isabella. Her eyes seemed at first to look at them both and then, unmistakably, they focused on Rupert. Her lips parted, she threw back her head proudly, a little color crept up in her cheeks. That proud glad look of hers was a lovely thing to see.

Robert noticed her attitude by a quick glance. Then his eyes returned thoughtfully to Rupert St. Loo's face.

When the others went in for drinks, Robert stayed on the terrace—I asked him what he thought of Rupert St. Loo. His answer was a curious one.

"I should say," he said, "that there wasn't a single bad fairy at his christening."

Chapter Nineteen

Well, Rupert and Isabella didn't take long to settle things. My own opinion is that it had been settled that very first moment when they met on the terrace by my chair.

There was, I think, an agonized relief on the part of both of them that the dream each had cherished secretly for so long had not let them down when it came to the testing.

For as Rupert told me, somedays later, he had cherished a dream.

We had become fairly intimate, he and I. He, too, was glad of male society. The atmosphere of the Castle was overloaded with feminine adoration. The three old ladies doted openly on Rupert, even Lady St. Loo herself dropped some of her own particular astringent quality.

So Rupert liked coming across and talking to me.

"I used to think," he said abruptly one day, "that I was a damned fool about Isabella. It's curious, say what you like, to make up your mind you're going to marry someone—when that someone is a child—and a scraggy child at that—and then find you don't change your mind."

I told him that I had known of similar cases.

He said thoughtfully, "The truth of it is, I suppose, that Isabella and I belong . . . I've felt always that she's a part of me, a part that I couldn't get hold of yet, but that I'd have to get hold of someday to make things complete. Funny business. She's an odd girl."

He smoked a minute or two in silence and then said:

"I think what I like best about her is that she's got no sense of humor."

"You don't think she has?"

"None whatever. It's wonderfully restful . . . I've always suspected that a sense of humor is a kind of parlor trick we civilized folk have taught ourselves as an insurance against disillusionment. We make a conscious effort to see things as funny, simply because we suspect they are unsatisfactory."

Well, there was something in that. . . . I thought about it with a slightly wry smile. . . . Yes, Rupert St. Loo had got something there.

He was staring out at the Castle. He said jerkily:

"I love that place. I've always loved it. Yet I'm glad I was brought up in New Zealand until the time I came over to Eton. It's given me detachment. I can see the place from outside, as well as identifying myself with it without reflection. To come here from Eton for holidays, to know it was really mine, that someday I should live here—to recognize it, as it were, as something I had always wanted to have . . . to have the feeling—the first time I saw it—a queer eerie feeling—of coming home.

"And Isabella was part of it. I was sure then and have been ever since that we would marry and live here for the rest of our mortal lives." His jaw set grimly. "And we *will* live here! In spite of taxation, and expenses and repairs—and the threat of land nationalization. That is our home, Isabella's and mine."

They were officially engaged on the fifth day after Rupert's return.

It was Lady Tressilian who told us the news. It would be in the *Times* tomorrow, or the day after, she said, but she wanted us to hear of it first. And she was so very *very* happy about it all!

Her nice round face was quivering with sentimental pleasure. Both

Teresa and I felt touched by her happiness. It showed so clearly the lack of certain things in her own life. In the joy of the moment, she became far less maternal in her attitude to me which made me enjoy her company a great deal better. For the first time she brought me no booklets and hardly tried at all to be bright and encouraging. It was clear that Rupert and Isabella occupied all her thoughts.

The attitudes of the other two old ladies varied slightly. Mrs. Bigham Charteris redoubled her energy and briskness. She took Rupert on immense walks around the estate, introduced him to his tenants and lectured him on roofs and repairs and what had positively got to be done, and what could and indeed must, be left undone.

"Amos Polflexen always grouses. He had entirely new pointing to the walls two years ago. Something must be done about Ellen Heath's chimney. She's been very patient. The Heaths have been tenants of the estate for three hundred years."

But it was Lady St. Loo's attitude that I found the most interesting. For some time I could not understand it. Then one day I got the clue. It was triumph. A curious sort of triumph—a kind of gloating as over a battle won against an invisible and non-existent antagonist.

"It will be all right now," she said to me.

And then she gave a sigh—a long tired sigh. It was as though she said, *"Lord, now lettest thou thy servant depart in peace . . ."* She gave me the impression of one who has been afraid—but has not dared to show fear—and who knows the occasion for fear is now over.

Well, I suppose that the odds against young Lord St. Loo returning and marrying a cousin he had not seen for eight years were pretty heavy. Far the most likely thing was for Rupert to have married a stranger in the war years. Marriages take place quickly in wartime. Yes, it must have been long odds against Rupert marrying Isabella.

And yet there was a rightness about it—a fitness.

I asked Teresa if she did not agree and she nodded her head thoughtfully.

"They're a wonderful pair," she said.

"Made for each other. That's what old family servants say at weddings, but this time it really is true."

"It *is* true. It's incredible . . . Don't you feel sometimes, Hugh, as though you'll wake up?"

I considered a moment or two because I knew what she meant.

"Nothing to do with St. Loo Castle is real," I said.

I was bound to hear John Gabriel's opinion. He kept up his habit of frankness with me. As far as I could make out, Gabriel disliked Lord St. Loo. That was natural enough, because Rupert St. Loo necessarily stole a good deal of Gabriel's thunder.

The whole of St. Loo was thrilled by the arrival of the Castle's rightful owner. The original inhabitants were proud of the antiquity of his title and remembered his father. The new inhabitants were more snobbishly thrilled.

"Disgusting lot of sheep," said Gabriel. "It's amazing to me how, say what they will, the Englishman always loves a title."

"Don't call a Cornishman an Englishman," I said. "Haven't you learned that yet?"

"It slipped out. But it's true, isn't it? Either they come fawning round—or else they go to the other extreme and say what a farce the whole thing is and get violent, and that's just inverted snobbery."

"What about your feelings?" I said.

Gabriel immediately grinned. He was always appreciative of a point that told against him.

"I'm an inverted snob all right," he said. "The thing I'd really like better than anything in the world would be to have been born Rupert St. Loo."

"You astonish me," I said.

"There are some things you've got to be born with—I'd give anything to have his legs," said Gabriel thoughtfully.

I remembered what Lady Tressilian had said at Gabriel's first meeting, and it interested me to see what a perceptive person Gabriel was.

I asked whether Gabriel felt that Rupert St. Loo was stealing his thunder?

Gabriel considered the question seriously on its merits without showing any signs of annoyance.

No, he said, he thought it was quite all right because Lord St. Loo wasn't his political opponent. It was all additional propaganda for the Conservative Party.

"Though I daresay if he *did* stand—I mean if he *could* stand (which of course he can't, being a peer) he'd be quite likely to stand for Labour."

"Surely not," I objected. "Not as a landowner."

"He wouldn't like land nationalization, of course—but things are very twisted round nowadays, Norreys. Farmers and solid working-class men are the staunch Conservatives—and young men with intellects and degrees and lots of money are Labour, mainly, I suppose, because they don't know the first thing about really working with their hands and haven't an idea what a working man really wants."

"And what does the working man want?" I asked, because I knew Gabriel was always giving one different answers to this question.

"He wants the country to be prosperous—so that he can be prosperous. He thinks the Conservatives are more likely to make the country prosperous because they know more about money, which of course is really very sound. I should say Lord St. Loo is really an old-fashioned Liberal—and of course nobody's got any use for a Liberal. No, they haven't, Norreys, it's no use your opening your mouth to say what you're going to say. You wait for the result of the elections. The Liberals will have diminished so much that you'll have to look for them with a magnifying glass. Nobody ever does like Liberal ideas, really, by which I mean that nobody ever likes the middle course. It's too damned tame."

"And you consider Rupert St. Loo is an advocate of the middle way?"

"Yes. He's a reasonable man—keeps in with the old and welcomes the new—in fact, neither fish, flesh, nor good red herring. Gingerbread—that's what he is!"

"What?" I demanded.

"You heard what I said. Gingerbread! Gingerbread castle! Gingerbread owner of castle." He snorted. "Gingerbread wedding!"

"And a gingerbread bride?" I asked.

"No. She's all right . . . she's just strayed in—like Hansel and Gretel into the gingerbread house. It's attractive, gingerbread, you can break off a bit of it and eat it. It's edible all right."

"You don't like Rupert St. Loo much, do you?"

"Why should I? Come to that, he doesn't like me."

I considered for a moment or two. No, I did not think Rupert St. Loo did like John Gabriel.

"Still, he'll have to have me," said Gabriel. "Here I shall be—member of Parliament for his part of the world. They'll have to ask me to dinner from time to time and he'll sit on platforms with me."

"You're very sure of yourself, Gabriel. You're not in yet."

"I tell you the thing's a certainty. It's *got* to be. I shouldn't get another chance, you know. I'm by way of being an experiment. If the experiment fails, my name's mud and I'm done for. I can't go back to soldiering, either. You see, I'm not an administrative soldier—I'm only useful when there's a real scrap on. When the Japanese war ends, I'm finished. Othello's occupation's gone."

"I have never," I said, "found Othello a credible character."

"Why not? Jealousy never is credible."

"Well, shall we say—not a sympathetic character. One isn't sorry for him. One feels he is merely a damned fool."

"No," said Gabriel reflectively. "No—one isn't sorry for him. Not sorry for him in the way one is sorry for Iago."

"Sorry for Iago? Really, Gabriel, you seem to have the oddest sympathies."

He flashed me a queer look.

"No," he said. "*You* wouldn't understand."

He got up and walked about, moving jerkily. He pushed some of the things on the writing table about unseeingly. I saw with some curiosity that he was laboring under some deeply felt inarticulate emotion.

"I understand Iago," he said. "I understand even why the poor devil never says anything in the end except

"Demand me nothing, what you know, you know.
From this time forth, I never will speak word."

He turned on me. "Fellows like you, Norreys, fellows who've lived on good terms with yourself all your life, who've been able to grow up with yourself without flinching (if I can put it like that) well, what the hell can you know about the Iagos—the doomed men, the little mean men? My God, if I ever produced Shakespeare, I'd go to town on Iago—I'd get an actor who was an actor—an actor who could move you to the bowels! Imagine to yourself what it's like to be born a coward—to lie and cheat and get away with it—to love money so much that you wake up and eat and sleep and kiss your wife with money foremost in your brain. And all the time to *know* what you are. . . .

"That's the hell of life—to have one good fairy at the christening in amongst all the bad ones. And when the rest of the crew have turned you into a dirty skunk, to have Fairy Daydream wave her wand and flute out, 'I give him the gift of seeing and knowing . . .'

" 'We needs must love the highest when we see it.' What damned fool said that? Wordsworth, probably—a man who couldn't even see a primrose and be satisfied with the lovely thing . . .

"I tell you, Norreys, you hate the highest when you see it—hate it because it's not for you—because you can never be what you'd sell your soul to be. The man who really values courage is often the man who runs away when danger comes. I've seen that, more than once. Do you think a man is what he wants to be? A man is what he is born. Do you think the poor devil who worships money wants to worship money? Do you think the man with a sensual imagination wants to have a sensual imagination? Do you think the man who runs away wants to run away?

"The man you envy (really envy) isn't the man who's done better than you. The man you envy is the man who is better than you.

"If you're down in the mud, you hate the human being who's up amongst the stars. You want to pull her down . . . down . . . down . . . to where you're wallowing in your pigsty . . . pity Iago, I say. He'd have been all right if he hadn't met Othello. He'd have got along very well doing the confidence trick. Nowadays he'd have been selling non-existent goldmining shares to chumps in the Ritz Bar.

"A plausible fellow, Iago, so honest, always able to take in the simple soldier. Nothing easier than to take in a soldier—the greater the soldier, the more of a fool he is in business matters. It's always soldiers who buy dud shares, and believe in schemes for getting up Spanish treasure from sunk galleons, and buy chicken farms that are on their last legs. Soldiers are the believing kind. Othello was the kind of mug who would have fallen for any plausible tale put across by an artist—and Iago was an artist. You've only got to read between the lines in that play and it's as clear as day that Iago's been embezzling the regimental funds. Othello doesn't believe that—oh no, not honest stupid Iago—it's just muddle-headedness on the dear old fellow's part—but he gets in Cassio and puts him in over Iago's head. Cassio was a countercaster and that's an accountant or I'll eat my hat. A good honest fellow, Iago (so Othello thought), but not bright enough for promotion.

"Remember all that swashbuckling stuff Iago spouts about his prowess in battles? All hooey, Norreys—it never happened. It's what you can hear any day in a pub from the man who was never near the front line. Falstaff stuff, only this time it's not comedy but tragedy. Iago, poor devil, wanted to be an Othello. He wanted to be a brave soldier and an upright man, and he couldn't be, any more than a hunchback can stand upright. He wanted to cut a dash with women, and women hadn't any use for him. That good-natured trollop of a wife of his despised him as a man. She was only too ready to hop into bed with other men. You bet all the women wanted to go to bed with Othello! I tell you, Norreys, I've seen some odd things happen with men who are sexually shamed. It turns them pathological. Shakespeare knew. Iago can't open his mouth without a stream of black, thwarted, sexual venom pouring out of it. What nobody ever seems to see is, that that man suffered! He could see beauty—he knew what it was—he knew a noble nature. My God, Norreys, material envy, envy of success, of possessions, of riches—is nothing—nothing at all to spiritual envy! That's vitriol all right—eating in, destroying you. You see the highest, and against your will you love it, and so you hate it, and you don't rest till you have destroyed it—till you've torn it down and stamped it out . . . Yes, Iago suffered, poor devil . . .

"And if you ask me, Shakespeare knew that and was sorry for the poor wretch. In the end, I mean. I daresay he started out dipping his quill pen in the ink, or whatever they used in those days, and setting out to draw a thorough black-hearted villain. But to do it, he had to go all the way with Iago, he had to go along with him and go down into the depths with him, he had to feel what Iago felt. And that's why when retribution comes, when Iago is for it, Shakespeare saves his pride for him. He lets him keep the only thing he's got left—his reticence. Shakespeare's been down among the dead men himself. He knows that when you've been in Hell, you don't talk about it . . ."

Gabriel wheeled round. His queer ugly face was contorted, his eyes shone with an odd kind of sincerity.

"You know, Norreys, I've never been able to believe in God. God the father, who made the pretty beasts and flowers, God who loves us and takes care of us, God who created the world. No, I don't believe in that God. But sometimes—I can't help it—I do believe in Christ . . . because Christ descended into Hell . . . His love went as deep as that. . . .

"He promised the repentant thief paradise. But what about the other one? The one who cursed and reviled him. Christ went with him down into Hell. Perhaps after that—"

Suddenly Gabriel shivered. He shook himself. His eyes became once more just rather beautiful eyes in an ugly face.

"I've been talking too much," he said. "Good-bye."

He departed abruptly.

I wondered whether he had been talking about Shakespeare or about himself. I thought, just a little, about himself. . . .

Chapter Twenty

Gabriel had been confident about the result of the election. He had said that he did not see what could go wrong.

The unforeseen in this case was a girl called Poppy Narracott. She was the barmaid at the Smugglers Arms at Greatwithiel. She was a girl whom John Gabriel had never seen and did not know existed. Yet it was Poppy Narracott who set the events in motion which placed Gabriel's chances of election in real jeopardy.

For James Burt and Poppy Narracott were on very close terms. But James Burt, when he had taken too much drink, was rough—sadistically rough. The girl Poppy turned against him. She refused, categorically, to have anything more to do with him, and she stuck to her decision.

Which was why James Burt came home one night rolling drunk and in a raging temper and was further infuriated by the terrified demeanor of his wife Milly. He let himself go. All the fury and balked desire that he felt for Poppy he vented on his wretched wife. He behaved like a complete madman and Milly Burt, small blame to her, lost her head completely.

She thought Jim Burt would kill her.

Twisting herself out of his grasp, she rushed out of the front door into the street. She had no idea of where she was going or to whom to go. To go to the police station would never have occurred to her. There were no near neighbors, only shops closely shuttered at night.

She had nothing but instinct to guide her fleeing footsteps. Instinct took her to the man she loved—the man who had been kind to her. There was no conscious thought in her head, no realization that scandal might result, she was terrified and she ran to John Gabriel. She was a desperate hunted animal looking for sanctuary.

She ran, disheveled and breathless, into the Kings Arms, and to the Kings Arms James Burt pursued her, roaring out threats of vengeance.

Gabriel, as it happened, was in the hall.

Personally, I don't see that John Gabriel could have behaved in any other way than he did. She was a woman he liked, he was sorry for her, and her husband was both drunk and dangerous. When James Burt came roaring in and swore at him and told him to give up his wife, accusing him point blank of being on terms of intimacy with her, Gabriel told him to go to hell, that he wasn't fit to have a wife, and that he, John Gabriel, was going to see that she was kept safe from him.

James Burt went for Gabriel like a charging bull and Gabriel knocked him down. After that he engaged a room for Mrs. Burt and told her to stay in it and lock her door. She couldn't possibly go back home now, he told her, and everything would come right in the morning.

By the next morning the news was all round St. Loo. Jim Burt had "found out" about his wife and Major Gabriel. And Gabriel and Mrs. Burt were staying together at the Kings Arms.

You can imagine, perhaps, the effect of this on the eve of the poll. Polling day was in two days' time.

"He's done for himself now," Carslake murmured distractedly. He walked up and down my sitting room. "We're finished—licked—Wilbraham's bound to get in. It's a disaster—a tragedy. I never liked the fellow. Hairy at the heel. I knew he'd end by letting us down."

Mrs. Carslake, in refined accents, lamented, "That's what comes of having a candidate who isn't a gentleman."

My brother seldom took part in our political discussions. If he was present at all he smoked a pipe in silence. But on this occasion he took his pipe out of his mouth and spoke.

"Trouble is," he said, "he *has* behaved like a gentleman."

It seemed to me then that it was an ironical thought that Gabriel's more blatant lapses from accepted gentlemanly standards had only increased his standing, but that his isolated piece of quixotic chivalry should be the circumstance to lay him low.

Presently Gabriel himself came in. He was dogged and unrepentant.

"No good making a song and dance about it, Carslake," he said. "Just tell me what the hell else I could do."

Carslake asked where Mrs. Burt was now.

Gabriel said she was still at the Kings Arms. He didn't see, he said, where else she was to go. And anyway, he added, it was too late. He whirled on Teresa whom he seemed to consider the realist of the assembly. "Isn't it?" he demanded.

Teresa said certainly it was too late.

"A night's a night," said Gabriel. "And it's nights people are interested in, not days."

"Really, Major Gabriel . . ." Carslake spluttered. He was shocked to the core.

"God, what a filthy mind you've got," said Gabriel. "I didn't spend the night with her, if that's what you're getting at. What I'm saying is that to the entire population of St. Loo it's the same thing. We were both at the Kings Arms."

That, he said, was all that people would mind about. That and the scene Burt had made and the things he went about saying about his wife and Gabriel.

"If she were to go away," said Carslake, "anywhere—just bundle her out of the place. Perhaps then—" He looked hopeful for a moment, then shook his head. "It would only look fishy," he said, "very fishy . . ."

"There's another thing to consider," said Gabriel. "What about her?" Carslake stared at him uncomprehendingly.

"What do you mean?"

"You haven't thought of her side of it, have you?"

Carslake said loftily, "We really can't consider these minor points now. What we've got to try and find is some possibility of getting you out of this mess."

"Exactly," said Gabriel. "Mrs. Burt doesn't really count, does she? Who's Mrs. Burt? Nobody in particular. Only a wretched decent girl who's been bullied and ill-treated and frightened half out of her wits and who's got nowhere to go and no money."

His voice rose.

"Well—I'll tell you this, Carslake. I don't like your attitude. And I'll tell you who Mrs. Burt is—she's a human being. To your blasted machine nobody and nothing matters but the election. That's what's always been rotten in politics. What did Mr. Baldwin say in the dark ages, 'If I had told the truth I should have lost the election. Well, I'm not Mr. Baldwin—I'm nobody in particular. But what you're saying to me is, 'You've behaved like an ordinary human being so you'll lose the election!' All right then, to hell with the election! You can keep your damned creaking stinking election. I'm a human being first and a politician second. I've never said a word I shouldn't to that poor kid. I've never made love to her. I've been damned sorry for her, that's all. She came to me last night because she hadn't got anybody else to turn to. All right, she can stay with me. I'll look after her. And to hell with St. Loo and Westminster and the whole blasted business."

"Major Gabriel." It was Mrs. Carslake's fluting agonized voice. "You *can't* do a thing like that! Supposing Burt divorces her?"

"If he divorces her, I'll marry her."

Carslake said angrily, "You can't let us down like that, Gabriel. You can't flaunt this thing as an open scandal."

"Can't I, Carslake? You watch me." Gabriel's eyes were the angriest things I had ever seen. I had never liked him so well.

"You can't bully me. If a lot of tinpot electors vote for the principle that a man can knock his wife about and terrify her out of her senses and bring foul unfounded charges against her—well then, let 'em! If they want to vote for bare Christian decency they can vote for me."

"They won't though," said Teresa and she sighed.

Gabriel looked at her and his face softened.

"No," he said, "they won't."

Robert took his pipe out of his mouth again.

"More fools they," he said unexpectedly.

"Of course, Mr. Norreys, we know you're a Communist," said Mrs. Carslake acidly.

What she meant I have no idea.

Then into the midst of this seething bitterness stepped Isabella Charteris. She came through the window from the terrace. She was cool and grave and composed.

She paid no attention to what was going on. She had come to say something and she said it. She came right up to Gabriel as though he were alone in the room and spoke to him in a confidential voice.

"I think," she said, "it will be quite all right."

Gabriel stared at her. We all stared at her.

"About Mrs. Burt, I mean," said Isabella.

She displayed no embarrassment. She had instead the pleased air of a simple-minded person who thinks they have done the right thing.

"She's at the Castle," she went on.

"At the *Castle?*" said Carslake unbelievingly.

Isabella turned to him.

"Yes," she said. "As soon as we heard what had happened, I thought that would be much the best thing. I spoke to Aunt Adelaide and she agreed. We went straight in the car to the Kings Arms."

It had been, I discovered later, positively a Royal Progress. Isabella's quick brain had hit on the only possible countermove.

Old Lady St. Loo, as I have said, had tremendous ascendency in St. Loo. From her emanated, so to speak, correct Greenwich moral time. People might sneer and call her old-fashioned and reactionary, but they respected her, and where she approved no one was likely to disapprove.

She had driven up in the aged Daimler in state, Isabella with her. An indomitable figure, Lady St. Loo had marched into the Kings Arms and had asked for Mrs. Burt.

A red-eyed, tearful, shrinking Milly had in due course descended the stairs and had been received with a kind of Royal Accolade. Lady St. Loo had not minced her words or lowered her voice.

"My dear," she boomed, "I am more sorry than I can say to hear of what you have been through. Major Gabriel should have brought you to us last night—but he is so considerate that he did not like to disturb us so late, I suppose."

"I—I—you are very kind."

"Get your things together, my dear. I will take you back with me now."

Milly Burt flushed and murmured that she hadn't—really—any things . . .

"Stupid of me," said Lady St. Loo. "We will stop at your house and get them."

"But—" Milly shrank . . .

"Get into the car. We will stop at your house and get them."

Milly bowed her head to superior authority. The three women got into the Daimler. It stopped a few yards further down Fore Street.

Lady St. Loo got out with Milly and accompanied her into the house. From the surgery James Burt, his eyes bloodshot, lurched out, prepared to break into a furious tirade.

He met old Lady St. Loo's eye and checked himself.

"Pack a few things, dear," said Lady St. Loo.

Milly fled upstairs quickly. Lady St. Loo addressed James Burt.

"You have behaved disgracefully to your wife," she said. "Quite disgracefully. The trouble with you is, Burt, that you drink too much. In any case you're not a nice man. I shall advise your wife to have nothing more to do with you. The things you have been saying about her are lies—and you know very well they are lies. Isn't that right?"

Her fierce eye hypnotized the twitching man.

"Oh well—I suppose—if you say so . . ."

"You know they are lies."

"All right—all right—I wasn't myself last night."

"Mind you let it be known they *were* lies. Otherwise I shall advise Major Gabriel to take proceedings. Ah, there you are, Mrs. Burt."

Milly Burt was descending the stairs with a small suitcase.

Lady St. Loo took her by the arm and turned to the door.

"Here—where's Milly going?" asked Milly's husband.

"She is coming with me to the Castle." She added militantly, "Have you anything to say to that?"

Burt shook his head vaguely. Lady St. Loo said sharply:

"My advice to you, James Burt, is to pull yourself together before it is too late. Stop drinking. Attend to your profession. You've got a good deal of skill. If you go on as you are going you will come to a very sticky end. Pull up, man. You can if you try. And curb that tongue of yours."

Then she and Milly got into the car. Milly sat beside Lady St. Loo. Isabella opposite them. They drove down the main street and along by the harbor and up by the market and so to the Castle. It was a Royal Progress and nearly everybody in St. Loo saw it.

That evening people were saying:

"It *must* be all right or Lady St. Loo wouldn't have her at the Castle."

Some people said that there was no smoke without fire and why should Milly Burt rush out of the house at night to Major Gabriel, and of course Lady St. Loo backed him up because of politics.

But the latter were in the minority. Character tells. Lady St. Loo had character. She had a reputation of absolute integrity. If Milly Burt was received at the Castle, if Lady St. Loo took her side, then Milly Burt was all right. Lady St. Loo wouldn't stand for anything else. Not old Lady St. Loo. Why, she was ever so particular!

The bare outline of these happenings was told to us by Isabella. She had come over from the Castle as soon as Milly was installed there.

As Carslake grasped the significance of what she was saying, his gloomy face brightened. He slapped his leg.

"My God," he said. "I believe it will do the trick. The old lady's smart. Yes, she's smart. Clever idea."

But the cleverness and the idea had been Isabella's. It amazed me how quick she had been to grasp the situation and to act.

"I'll get busy right away," said Carslake. "We must follow this up. Outline what our story's to be exactly. Come on, Janet. Major Gabriel—"

"I'll come in a minute," said Gabriel.

The Carslakes went out. Gabriel went closer to Isabella.

"You did this," he said. "Why?"

She stared at him—puzzled.

"But—because of the election."

"You mean you—you care very much that the Conservatives shall get in?"

She looked at him with surprise.

"No. I mean *you*."

"Me?"

"Yes. You want to win the election very much, don't you?"

A queer bewildered look came over Gabriel's face. He turned away. He said—more to himself than to her or to any of us:

"Do I? I wonder. . . ."

Chapter Twenty-one

As I have said before, this is not on accurate account of a political campaign. I was out of the main stream, in a backwater where I only caught echoes of what went on. I was aware of an increasing sense of urgency, which seemed to be striking everyone but myself.

There were two last frenzied days of electioneering. Gabriel came in twice during the time for a drink. When he relaxed, he looked fagged out, his voice was hoarse with addressing open-air meetings but though tired his vitality was unimpaired. He said very little to me, probably because he was saving both his voice and his energy.

He tossed off his drink and murmured, "What a hell of a life this is! The damn fool things you have to say to people. Serves 'em right that they're governed the way they are."

Teresa spent most of her time driving cars. The morning of Polling Day came with a gale driving in from the Atlantic. The wind howled and rain beat against the house.

Isabella dropped in early after breakfast. She wore a black mackintosh, her hair was wet, her eyes bright. An immense blue rosette was pinned to the mackintosh.

"I'm driving people to the polls all day," she said. "So's Rupert. I've suggested to Mrs. Burt that she should come over and see you. Do you mind? You'll be all alone won't you?"

I didn't mind, though I had actually been quite contented at the prospect of a peaceful day with my books. I had had almost too much company lately.

For Isabella to show herself concerned about my solitary state seemed singularly unlike Isabella. It was as though she had suddenly shown signs of adopting her Aunt Agnes's attitude towards me.

"Love seems to be having a softening effect upon you, Isabella," I said disapprovingly. "Or did Lady Tressilian think of it?"

Isabella smiled.

"Aunt Agnes wanted to come and sit with you herself," she said. "She thought it might be lonely for you and—what was it she said—that you might feel out of things."

She looked at me inquiringly. It was an idea, I saw, that would not have entered her own head.

"You don't agree?" I asked.

Isabella replied with her usual candor, "Well, you are out of things."

"Admirably true."

"I'm sorry if you mind about it, but I don't see that Aunt Agnes coming and breathing over you would make it any better. It would only mean that she would be out of things, too."

"And I'm sure she would like to be in things."

"I suggested Mrs. Burt coming because she's got to keep out of the way anyway. And I thought you might talk to her, perhaps."

"Talk to her?"

"Yes." A slight frown appeared on Isabella's white forehead. "You see, I'm no good at—at talking to people. Or letting them talk to me. She goes on and on."

"Mrs. Burt goes on and on?"

"Yes, and it seems so senseless—but I can't put things properly. I thought perhaps you could."

"What does she go on and on about?"

Isabella sat down on the arm of a chair. She spoke slowly, frowning a little, and giving a very good imitation of a traveler describing the more puzzling rites of some savage tribe.

"About what happened. About rushing to Major Gabriel. About its being all her fault. That if he loses the election she will be to blame. That if only she'd been more careful to begin with—that she ought to have seen what it might lead to. That if she'd been nicer to James Burt and understood him better, he might never have drunk so much. That she blames herself dreadfully and that she lies awake at night worrying about it and wishing she'd acted differently. That if she's injured Major Gabriel's career she'll never forgive herself as long as she lives. That nobody is to blame but her. That everything, always, has been her fault."

Isabella stopped. She looked at me. She was presenting me, as it were, on a platter, something that was to her quite incomprehensible.

A faint echo from the past came to me. Jennifer, knitting her adorable brows and shouldering manfully the blame for what other people had done.

I had thought it one of Jennifer's more lovable traits. Now, when Milly Burt was indulging in the same attitude, I saw that such a point of view might be distinctly irritating. Which, I reflected cynically, was the difference between thinking someone was a nice little woman, and being in love!

"Well," I said thoughtfully, "I suppose she might very well feel that way. Don't you?"

Isabella replied with one of her definite monosyllables.

"No," she said.

"But why not? Explain yourself."

"You know," said Isabella reproachfully, "that I can't say things." She paused, frowned and then began to speak—rather doubtfully. She said, "Things either have happened, or they haven't happened. I can see that you might worry beforehand—"

Even that, I could see, was not a really acceptable position to Isabella.

"But to go on worrying now—oh, it's as if you went for a walk in the fields and stepped in a cow pat. I mean, it wouldn't be any use spending the whole of the walk talking about it, wishing you hadn't stepped in the cow pat, that you'd gone another way, saying that it was all because you hadn't been looking where you were stepping, and that you always did do silly things like that. After all, the cow pat's there on your shoe— you can't get away from it—but you needn't have it in your *mind* as well! There's everything else—the fields and the sky and the hedges and the person you're walking with—they're all there too. The only time you've got to think about the cow pat again is when you actually get home when you have to deal with your shoe. Then you do have to think about it—"

Extravagance in self-blame was an interesting field on which to speculate. I could see that it was something in which Milly Burt might indulge rather freely. But I didn't really know why some people were more prone to it than others. Teresa had once implied that people like myself, who insisted on cheering people up, and putting things right, were not really being as helpful as they thought themselves. But that still didn't touch the question of why human beings enjoyed exaggerating their responsibility for events.

Isabella said hopefully, "I thought you could talk to her?"

"Supposing she likes—well, blaming herself," I said. "Why shouldn't she?"

"Because I think it makes it rather dreadful for *him*—for Major Gabriel. It must be very tiring having to go on and on assuring someone that it's quite all right."

It would undoubtedly, I thought to myself, be very tiring . . . It had been tiring, I remembered. . . . Jennifer had always been excessively tiring. But Jennifer had also had a lovely sweep of blue black hair, big sad gray eyes and the most adorable and ridiculous nose. . . .

Possibly John Gabriel enjoyed Milly's chestnut hair and soft brown eyes and didn't mind assuring her that it was quite all right.

"Has Mrs. Burt any plans?" I asked.

"Oh yes. Grandmother has found her a post in Sussex, as a companion housekeeper to someone she knows. It will be quite well paid and very little work. And there is a good train service to London, so that she can go up and meet her friends."

By friends, did Isabella, I wondered, mean Major John Gabriel? Milly was in love with Gabriel. I wondered if Gabriel was a little in love with her. I rather thought he might be.

"She could divorce Mr. Burt, I think," said Isabella. "Only divorce is expensive."

She got up, "I must go now. You will talk to her, won't you?" She paused by the door. "Rupert and I are being married a week from to-day," she said softly. "Do you think you could come to the church? The scouts could push you there if it's a fine day."

"Would you like me to come?"

"Yes, I would—very much."

"Then I will."

"Thank you. We shall have a week together before he goes back to Burma. But I don't think the war will last very much longer, do you?"

"Are you happy, Isabella?" I asked gently.

She nodded.

"It seems almost frightening—when a thing you've thought about for a long time really comes true . . . Rupert was there in my mind but getting so faint . . ."

She looked at me.

"Even though it is all real—it doesn't *seem* real yet. I still feel I might—wake up. It's like a dream. . . ."

She added very softly, "To have everything . . . Rupert . . . St. Loo . . . all one's wishes come true . . ."

Then, with a start, she cried, "I oughtn't to have stayed so long. They gave me twenty minutes off for a cup of tea."

I gathered that I had been Isabella's cup of tea.

Milly Burt came over to see me in the afternoon. When she had struggled out of her mackintosh and pixie hood and galoshes, she smoothed her brown hair back and powdered her nose a little self-consciously and came to sit beside me. She was really, I thought, very pretty and also very nice. You couldn't dislike Milly Burt even if you wanted to, and I, for one, didn't want to.

"I hope you don't feel dreadfully neglected?" she said. "Have you had lunch and everything all right?"

I assured her that my creature comforts had been attended to.

"Later," I said, "we'll have a cup of tea."

"That will be very nice." She moved restlessly. "Oh, Captain Norreys, you do think he'll get in, don't you?"

"Too early to say."

"Oh, but I mean what do you think?"

"I'm sure he stands a very good chance," I said soothingly.

"It would have been a certainty but for me! How I could be so stupid—so *wicked*. Oh, Captain Norreys, I just think about it all the time. I blame myself *dreadfully*."

Here we go, I thought.

"I should stop thinking about it," I advised.

"But how can I?" Her large pathetic brown eyes opened wide.

"By the exercise of self-control and will power," I said.

Milly looked highly skeptical and slightly disapproving.

"I don't feel I *ought* to take it lightly. Not when it's been all my fault."

"My dear girl, your brooding over it won't help Gabriel to get into Parliament."

"No-o, of course not. . . . But I shall never forgive myself if I've injured his career."

We argued on familiar lines. I had been through a lot of this with Jennifer. There was the difference that I was now arguing in cold blood, unaffected by the personal equation of romantic susceptibility. It was a big difference. I liked Milly Burt—but I found her quite infuriating.

"For God's sake," I exclaimed, "don't make such a song and dance about it! For Gabriel's sake if nobody else's."

"But it's for *his* sake I mind."

"Don't you think the poor fellow has enough on his back without your adding a load of tears and remorse?"

"But if he loses the election—"

"If he loses the election (which he hasn't lost yet) and if you've contributed to that result (which there is no means of knowing and which mayn't be so at all) won't it be disappointing enough for him to have lost the fight without having a remorseful woman piling her remorse on to make things worse?"

She looked bewildered and obstinate.

"But I want to make up for what I've done."

"Probably you can't. If you can, it will only be by managing to convince Gabriel that losing the election is a marvelous break for him, and that it has set him free for a much more interesting attack upon life."

Milly Burt looked scared.

"Oh," she said. "I don't think I could possibly do *that*."

I didn't think she could, either. A resourceful and unscrupulous woman could have done it. Teresa, if she had happened to care for John Gabriel, could have done it quite well.

Teresa's method with life is, I think, ceaseless attack.

Milly Burt's was, undoubtedly, ceaseless picturesque defeat. But then possibly John Gabriel liked picking up pieces and putting them together again. I had once liked that kind of thing myself.

"You're very fond of him, aren't you?" I asked.

Tears came into her brown eyes.

"Oh, I am . . . I am indeed. He's—I've never met anyone quite like him . . ."

I hadn't met anyone like John Gabriel myself, not that it affected me as it did Milly Burt.

"I'd do anything for him, Captain Norreys—I would indeed."

"If you care very much for him, that is something in itself. Just leave it at that."

Who had said "Love 'em and leave 'em alone"? Some psychologist writing advice to mothers? But there was a lot of wisdom in it applied to others beside children. But can we, really, leave anybody alone? Our enemies, perhaps, by an effort. But those we love?

I desisted from what has been termed unprofitable speculation and rang the bell and ordered tea.

Over tea I talked determinedly of films I remembered from last year. Milly liked going to the pictures. She brought me up-to-date with descriptions of the latest masterpieces. It was all quite pleasant and I enjoyed it, and I was quite sorry when Milly left me.

The far-flung battle line returned at varying hours. They were weary and in differing moods of optimism and despair. Robert alone returned in normal and cheerful mood. He had found a fallen beech tree in a disused quarry and it had been exactly what his soul had been longing for. He had also had an unusually good lunch at a small pub. Subjects to paint and food are Robert's main topics of conversation. And not at all bad topics, either.

Chapter Twenty-two

It was late the following evening when Teresa came abruptly into the room, pushed back her dark hair from her tired face and said, "Well, *he's in!*"

"What majority?" I asked.

"Two hundred and fourteen."

I gave a whistle.

"A near thing, then."

"Yes, Carslake thinks that if it hadn't been for the Milly Burt business, he'd have had at least a thousand."

"Carslake doesn't know what he's talking about more than anybody else."

"It's a terrific sweep to the Left all over the country. Labour's in everywhere. Ours will be one of the few Conservative gains."

"Gabriel was right," I said. "He prophesied that, you remember."

"I know. His judgment's uncanny."

"Well," I said, "little Milly Burt will go to bed happy tonight. She hasn't gummed up the works after all. What a relief that will be to her."

"Will it?"

"What a cat you are, Teresa," I said. "The little thing's devoted to Gabriel."

"I know she is." She added thoughtfully, "They suit each other, too. I think he might be reasonably happy with her—that is, if he wants to be happy. Some people don't."

"I've never noticed anything unduly ascetic about John Gabriel," I said. "I should say he thought of very little beyond doing himself well and grabbing as much as he can out of life. Anyway, he's going to marry money. He told me so. I expect he will, too. He's clearly marked for success—the grosser forms of success. As for Milly, she seems obviously cast for the role of victim. Now, I suppose, you'll tell me she enjoys it, Teresa."

"No, of course not. But it takes a really strong character, Hugh, to say 'I've made a complete ass of myself,' and laugh about it, and go on to the next thing. The weak have to have something to take hold of. They have to see their mistakes, not simply as a failure to cope, but as a definite fault, a tragic sin."

She added abruptly, "I don't believe in evil. All the harm in the world is caused by the weak—usually meaning well—and managing to appear in a wonderfully romantic light. I'm afraid of them. They're dangerous. They are like derelict ships that drift in the darkness and wreck the sound seaworthy craft."

I did not see Gabriel till the following day. He looked deflated and almost devoid of vitality. I hardly recognized him for the man I knew.

"Election hangover?" I suggested.

He groaned.

"You've said it. What a nauseating thing success is. Where's the best sherry?"

I told him and he helped himself.

"I don't suppose Wilbraham feels particularly elated by failure," I remarked.

Gabriel gave a pale grin.

"No, poor devil. Besides, he takes himself and politics quite seriously, I believe. Not too seriously, but seriously enough. Pity he's so wet."

"I suppose you said all the proper things to each other about a fair fight and good sportsmanship and all that?"

Gabriel grinned again.

"Oh, we went through the right drill. Carslake saw to that. What an ass that man is! Knows his job by heart—word perfect—and absolutely no intelligence behind it."

I raised my glass of sherry.

"Well," I said, "here's success to your future career. You're started now."

"Yes," said Gabriel without enthusiasm, "I'm started."

"You don't seem very cheerful about it?"

"Oh, it's just what you called it—election hangover. Life's always dull when you've licked the other fellow. But there will be plenty more battles to fight. You watch out for the way I'm going to force myself into the public eye."

"Labour's got a pretty hefty majority."

"I know. It's splendid."

"Really, Gabriel. Strange words for our new Tory M.P."

"Tory M.P. be hanged! I've got my chance now. Who have we got to put the Tory Party on its feet again? Winston's a grand old fighter of wars, especially when you're up against it. But he's too old to tackle a peace. Peace is tricky. Eden's a nice mealy-mouthed English gentleman—"

He proceeded, working through various well-known names of the Conservative Party.

"Not a constructive idea among them. They'll bleat against Nationalization, and fall with glee upon the Socialists' mistakes. (And boy, will they make mistakes! They're a fat-headed crowd. Old diehards of Trades Unionists—and irresponsible theorists from Oxford.) Our side will do all the old Parliamentary tricks—like pathetic old dogs at a Fair. Yap yap yap first, then stand on their hind legs and revolve in a slow waltz."

"And where does John Gabriel come in, in this attractive picture of the Opposition?"

"You can't have D Day until you've got it thoroughly worked out to the last detail. Then—let it rip. I shall get hold of the young fellows— the people with new ideas who are normally 'agin the Government.' Sell 'em an idea, and go all out *for* that idea."

"What idea?"

Gabriel threw me an exasperated glance.

"You always get things the wrong way round. It doesn't matter a tuppenny ha'penny damn *what* idea! I could think up half a dozen any time I like. There are only two things that ever stir people politically. One is put something in their pockets. The other is the sort of idea that sounds as though it would make everything come right and which is extremely easy to grasp, noble but woolly—and which gives you a nice inner glow. Man likes to feel a noble animal as well as being a well-paid one. You don't want too practical an idea, you know—just something humane and that isn't directed toward anyone you'll have to meet personally. Have you noticed how subscriptions will pour in for earthquake victims in Turkey or Armenia or somewhere? But nobody really wanted to take an evacuated child into their house, did they? That's human nature."

"I shall follow your career with great interest," I assured him.

"In twenty years' time you'll find me growing fat and living soft and probably regarded as a public benefactor," Gabriel told me.

"And then?"

"What do you mean by 'And then'?"

"I just wondered if you might be bored."

"Oh, I shall always find some racket or other—just for the fun of it."

I was always fascinated by the complete assurance with which Gabriel sketched out his life. I had come to have faith in the fulfillment of his prognostications. He had a knack, I thought, of being right. He had foreseen that the country would vote Labour. He had been sure of his own victory. His life would follow the course he now predicted, not deviating by a hair's breadth.

I said rather tritely, "So all's for the best in the best of possible worlds."

He frowned quickly and irritably, and said:

"What a way you've got of putting your finger on a sore spot, Norreys."

"Why, what's wrong?"

"Nothing's wrong . . . nothing, really." He was silent a moment, then went on. "Ever gone about with a thorn in your finger? Know how maddening it can be—nothing really bad—but always reminding you— pricking you—hampering you . . ."

"What's the thorn?" I asked. "Milly Burt?"

He stared at me in astonishment. I saw it wasn't Milly Burt.

"She's all right," he said. "No harm done there luckily. I like her. I hope I'll see something of her in London. None of this beastly local gossip in London."

Then, a flush coming over his face, he tugged a package out of his pocket.

"I wonder if you'd have a look at this. Is it all right, do you think? Wedding present. For Isabella Charteris. Suppose I have to give her something. When is it? Next Thursday? Or do you think it's a damn fool kind of present."

I unrolled the package with great interest. What I found gave me a complete surprise. It was the last thing I would have expected John Gabriel to produce as a wedding present.

It was a book of hours—exquisitely and delicately illuminated. It was a thing that should have been in a museum.

"Don't know exactly what it is," said Gabriel. "Some Catholic business. Couple of hundred years old. But I felt—I don't know—I thought it seemed to go with her. Of course, if you think it's just silly—"

I hastened to reassure him.

"It's beautiful," I said. "A thing anyone would be glad to possess. It's a museum piece."

"Don't suppose it's the sort of thing she'll care for particularly but it rather fits with her, if you know what I mean—" I nodded. I did know. "And after all, I've got to give her something. Not that I like the girl. I've no use for her at all. Stuck-up haughty bit of goods. She's managed to snaffle his Lordship all right. I wish her joy of that stuffed shirt."

"He's a good deal more than a stuffed shirt."

"Yes—as a matter of fact he is. At any rate, I've got to remain on good terms with them. As the local M.P. I shall dine at the Castle and go to the annual garden party and all that. I suppose old Lady St. Loo will have to move over to the Dower House now—that moldy ruin near the church. I should say that anyone who lives there will soon die of rheumatism."

He took back the illuminated missal and wrapped it up again.

"You really think that it's all right? That it will do?"

"A magnificent and most unusual present," I assured him.

Teresa came in. Gabriel said he was just going.

"What's the matter with him?" she asked me, when he had gone.

"Reaction, I suppose."

Teresa said, "It's more than that."

"I can't help feeling," I said, "that it's a pity he won the election. Failure might have had a sobering effect on him. As it is, he'll be blatant in a couple of years' time. By and large, he's a nasty bit of goods. But I rather fancy that he'll get to the top of the tree all right."

I suppose it was the word tree that roused Robert to speech. He had come in with Teresa but in his own inconspicuous way, so that, as usual, we were quite startled when he spoke.

"Oh no, he won't," he said.

We looked at him inquiringly.

"He won't get to the top of the tree," said Robert "Not a chance of it, I should say—"

He wandered disconsolately round the room and asked why someone always had to hide his palette knife.

Chapter Twenty-three

The wedding of Lord St. Loo to Isabella Charteris was fixed for Thursday. It was very early, about one in the morning, I suppose, when I heard footsteps outside the window on the terrace.

I had not been able to sleep. It was one of my bad nights with a good deal of pain.

I thought to myself that fancy plays queer tricks, for I could have sworn that they were Isabella's footsteps on the terrace outside.

Then I heard her voice.

"Can I come in, Hugh?"

The French windows were ajar as they always were unless there was a gale blowing. Isabella came in and I switched on the lamp by my couch. I still had a feeling that I was dreaming.

Isabella looked very tall. She had on a long dark tweed coat and a dark red scarf over her hair. Her face was grave, calm and rather sad.

I could not imagine what she could be doing here at this time of the night—or rather morning. But I felt vaguely alarmed.

I no longer had the impression that I was dreaming. In point of fact I felt exactly the opposite. I felt as though everything that had happened since Rupert St. Loo had come home was a dream, and this was the wakening.

I remembered Isabella saying, "I still feel I might wake up."

And I suddenly realized that that was what had happened to her. The girl who was standing by me was no longer in her dream—she had woken up.

And I remembered another thing—Robert saying that there had been no bad fairies at Rupert St. Loo's christening. I had asked him afterwards what he meant and he had replied, "Well, if there's not one bad fairy—where's your story?" That, perhaps, was what made Rupert St. Loo not quite real, in spite of his good looks, his intelligence, his "rightness."

All these things passed through my mind confusedly in the second or two that elapsed before Isabella said:

"I came to say good-bye to you, Hugh."

I stared at her stupidly.

"Good-bye?"

"Yes. You see, I'm going away . . ."

"Going away? With Rupert, you mean?"

"No. With John Gabriel. . . ."

I was conscious then of the strange duality of the human mind. Half of my brain was thunderstruck, unbelieving. What Isabella was saying seemed quite incredible—a thing so fantastic that it simply couldn't happen.

But somewhere, another part of me was not surprised. It was like an inner voice saying mockingly, "But surely, you've known this all along . . ." I remembered how, without turning her head, Isabella had known John Gabriel's step on the terrace. I remembered the look on her face when she had come up from the lower garden on the night of the whist drive, and the way she had acted so swiftly in the crisis of Milly Burt. I remembered her saying, "Rupert must come soon . . ." with a strange urgency in her voice.

She had been afraid then, afraid of what was happening to her.

I understood, very imperfectly, the dark urge that was driving her to Gabriel. For some reason or other the man had a strange quality of attraction for women. Teresa had told me so long ago . . .

Did Isabella love him? I doubted it. And I could see no happiness for her with a man like Gabriel—a man who desired her but did not love her.

On his part it was sheer madness. It would mean abandoning his political career. It would be the ruin of all his ambitions. I couldn't see why he was taking this crazy step.

Did he love her? I didn't think so. I thought that in a way he hated her. She was part of the things (the Castle, old Lady St. Loo) that had humiliated him ever since he came here. Was that the obscure reason for this act of insanity? Was he avenging that humiliation? Was he willing to smash up his own life if he could smash up the thing that had humiliated him? Was this the "common little boy" taking his revenge?

I loved Isabella. I knew that now. I loved her so much that I had been happy in her happiness—and she *had* been happy with Rupert in her dream come true—of life at St. Loo. . . . She had only feared that it might not be real—

What, then, was real? John Gabriel? No, what she was doing was madness. She must be stopped—pleaded with, persuaded.

The words rushed to my lips . . . but they remained unspoken. To this day I don't know why. . . .

The only reason I can think of is that Isabella—was Isabella.

I said nothing.

She stooped and kissed me. It was not a child's kiss. Her mouth was a woman's mouth. Her lips were cool and fresh, they pressed mine with a sweetness and intensity I shall never forget. It was like being kissed by a flower.

She said good-bye and she went away, out of the window—out of my life, to where John Gabriel was waiting for her.

And I did not try to stop her. . . .

Chapter Twenty-four

With the departure of John Gabriel and Isabella from St. Loo the first part of my story ends. I realize how much it is their story and not mine, because once they had gone I can remember little or nothing that happened. It is all vague and confused.

I had never been interested in the political side of our life in St. Loo. For me, it was only a backcloth against which the protagonists in the drama moved. But the political repercussions must have been—indeed, I know they were—quite far-reaching.

If John Gabriel had had any political conscience he would not, of course, have done what he did do. He would have been appalled at the prospect of letting his side down. For it did let it down. The local feeling aroused was so tremendous that pressure would have been brought to bear on him on make him resign his newly won seat if he had not resigned it without being asked. The affair brought great discredit on the Conservative Party. A man with traditions and a more delicate sense of honor would have been acutely sensitive to that. I don't think John Gabriel cared in the slightest. What he had been out for was his own career—by his crazy conduct he had wrecked this career. That was how he looked at it. He had spoken truly enough when he had prophesied that only a woman would be able to spoil his life. He had not in the least foreseen who that woman would be.

He was not fitted by temperament or upbringing to understand the shock and horror felt by people like Lady Tressilian and Mrs. Bigham Charteris. Lady Tressilian had been brought up to believe that to stand for election to Parliament was a duty owed by a man to his country. That was how her father had envisaged it.

Gabriel could not even have begun to appreciate such an attitude. The way he looked at it was that the Conservative Party had picked a dud when they picked him. It was a gamble—and they had lost. If things had taken a normal course they would have done very well for themselves. But there was always the hundredth chance—and the hundredth chance had happened.

Curiously enough the person who took exactly the same point of view as Gabriel was the dowager Lady St. Loo.

She spoke of it once and once only, in the drawing room at Polnorth House when she was alone with Teresa and myself.

"We cannot," she said, "avoid our share of blame. We knew what the man was like. We nominated a man who was an outsider, who had no real beliefs, no traditions, no true integrity. We knew perfectly well that the man was an adventurer, nothing else. Because he had qualities that appeal to the masses, a good war record, a specious appeal, we accepted him. We were prepared to let him use us, because *we* were prepared to use him. We excused ourselves by saying that we were going with the times. But if there is any reality, any meaning, in the Conservative tradition, it must live up to its tradition. We must be represented by men who, if not brilliant, are sincere, who have a stake in the country, who are prepared to take responsibility for those under them, who are not ashamed or uneasy at calling themselves the upper classes, because they accept not only the privileges but the duties of an upper class."

It was the voice of a dying *régime* speaking. I did not agree with it, but I respected it. New ideas; a new way of life was being born, the old was being swept away, but as an example of the best of the old, Lady St. Loo stood firm. She had her place and would hold that place until her death.

Of Isabella she did not speak. There the wound had gone deep into the heart. For Isabella, in the old lady's uncompromising view, had betrayed her own class. For John Gabriel the old martinet could find excuses—he was of the lesser breed without the law—but Isabella had betrayed the citadel from within.

Though Lady St. Loo said nothing of Isabella, Lady Tressilian did. She talked to me, I think, because she could talk to no one else—and also because she felt that owing to my invalid state I did not count. She had an incorrigibly motherly feeling towards my helplessness, and I think she felt almost justified in talking to me as though I were indeed her son.

Adelaide, she said, was unapproachable. Maude snapped her head off and immediately went out with the dogs. That vast sentimental heart of Lady Tressilian's had to unburden itself.

She would have felt disloyal discussing the family with Teresa. She did not feel disloyal in discussing it with me, possibly because she knew I loved Isabella. She loved Isabella, loved her dearly, and she could not stop thinking about her, and being puzzled and bewildered by what she had done.

"It was so unlike her—so very unlike her, Hugh. I do feel that man must have bewitched her. A very dangerous man, I always thought. . . . And she seemed so happy—so perfectly happy—she and Rupert seemed made for each other. I can't understand it. They were happy—they really were. Didn't you think so, too?"

I said, feeling my way, that yes, I thought they had been happy. I wanted to add, but I did not think that Lady Tressilian would understand, that sometimes happiness is not enough. . . .

"I can't help feeling that that horrible man must have *enticed* her away—that somehow or other he hypnotized her. But Addie says no. She says that Isabella would never do anything unless she fully meant to do it. I don't know, I'm sure."

Lady St. Loo was, I thought, right there.

Lady Tressilian asked, "Do you think they are married? Where do you think they are?"

I asked if they had had no word from her.

"No. Nothing. Nothing but the letter Isabella left. It was written to Addie. She said that she didn't expect Addie would ever forgive her and that probably Addie was right. And she said, 'It is no good saying I am sorry for all the pain I shall cause. If I were really sorry I wouldn't do it. I think Rupert may understand, but perhaps not. I shall always love you all, even if I never see you again.' "

Lady Tressilian looked at me, her eyes full of tears.

"That poor boy—that poor poor boy. Dear Rupert—and we had all got so fond of him."

"I suppose he took it very hard?"

I had not seen Rupert St. Loo since Isabella's flight. He had left St. Loo on the following day. I don't know where he went or what he did. A week later, he had rejoined his unit in Burma.

Lady Tressilian shook her head tearfully.

"He was so kind, so gentle to us all. But he didn't want to talk about it. Nobody wants to talk about it." She sighed. "But I can't help wondering where they are and what they are doing. Will they get married? Where will they live?"

Lady Tressilian's mind was essentially feminine. It was direct, practical, occupied with the events of daily life. I could see that already, nebulously, she was building up a picture of Isabella's domestic life—

marriage, a house, children. She had forgiven easily. She loved Isabella. What Isabella had done was shocking. It was disgraceful. It had let the family down. But it was also romantic. And Lady Tressilian was nothing if not romantic.

As I say my memories of the next two years at St. Loo are vague. There was a by-election in which Mr. Wilbraham was returned by a large majority. I don't even remember who was the Conservative candidate—some country gentleman of blameless life and no mass appeal, I fancy. Politics, without John Gabriel, no longer held my attention. My own health began to occupy most of my thoughts. I went to a hospital and started a series of operations which left me no worse, if little better. Teresa and Robert remained on in Polnorth House. The three old ladies of St. Loo Castle left the Castle and moved into a small Victorian house with an attractive garden. The Castle was let for a year to some people from the North of England. Eighteen months later, Rupert St. Loo came back to England and married an American girl with money. They had, Teresa wrote me, great plans for the complete restoration of the Castle as soon as building regulations permitted. Illogically I hated to think of St. Loo Castle restored.

Where Gabriel and Isabella actually were and what Gabriel was doing—nobody knew.

In 1947 Robert had a successful show in London of his Cornish pictures.

At that time, great advances were being made in surgery. On the Continent various foreign surgeons had been doing remarkable things in cases like mine. One of the few advantages that war brings in its train is a leap forward in the alleviation of human suffering. My own surgeon in London was enthusiastic about the work done by a Jewish doctor in Slovakia. Working in the Underground movements during the war, he had made daring experiments and had achieved really spectacular results. In a case like mine, it was possible, so my own man thought, that he could attempt something which no English surgeon would undertake.

That was why in the Autumn of 1947 I traveled out to Zagrade to consult Dr. Crassvitch.

There is no need to go into details of my own history. Suffice to say that Dr. Crassvitch, whom I found a sensitive and clever surgeon, pronounced his belief that by an operation my condition could be immensely improved. It would be possible, he hoped, that I should be able to move about freely on crutches—instead of lying prone, a helpless shattered wreck. It was arranged that I should go into his clinic forthwith.

My hopes and his were realized. At the end of six months I emerged able, as he had promised, to walk with the aid of crutches. I cannot hope to describe how exciting it made life for me. I remained on in Zagrade—since I had to have manipulative treatment several times a week. On a summer evening I swung myself slowly and painfully along the Zagrade main street and came to anchor in a small open air café where I ordered beer.

It was then, looking across the occupied tables, that I saw John Gabriel.

It was a shock. I had not thought of him for some time. I had no idea that he was in this part of the world. But what was a worse shock was the appearance of the man.

He had gone down in the world. His face had always been slightly coarse but it was coarsened now almost out of recognition. It was bloated and unhealthy, the eyes bloodshot. At this very moment I realized that he was slightly drunk.

He looked across, saw me, and rising, came unsteadily over to my table.

"Well," he said, "look who's here! Last man in the world I'd have expected to see."

It would have given me enormous pleasure to have driven my fist into John Gabriel's face—but apart from the fact that I was not in fighting condition, I wanted to learn news of Isabella. I invited him to sit down and have a drink.

"Thanks, Norreys, I will. How's St. Loo and the gingerbread Castle and all the old tabby cats?"

I told him that it was some time since I had been in St. Loo, that the Castle was let and that the three old ladies had moved out.

He said hopefully that that must have been a nasty pill for the Dowager to swallow. I said I thought that she had been glad to go. I told him that Rupert St. Loo was engaged to be married.

"In fact," said Gabriel, "everything's turned out very nicely for everybody."

I managed not to reply. I saw the old grin curving his mouth upwards.

"Come on, Norreys," he said. "Don't sit there looking as though you've swallowed a poker. Ask about her. That's what you want to know, isn't it?"

The trouble with Gabriel was that he always carried the war into the enemy's camp. I acknowledged defeat.

"How is Isabella?" I said.

"She's all right. I haven't done the characteristic seducer's act and abandoned her in a garret."

It became still more difficult for me to refrain from hitting Gabriel. He had always had the power of being offensive. He was far more offensive now that he had begun to go downhill.

"She's here in Zagrade?" I asked.

"Yes, you'd better come and call. Nice for her to see an old friend and hear the St. Loo news."

Would it be nice for her? I wondered. Was there some taint, some far-off echo of sadism in Gabriel's voice?

I said, my voice slightly embarrassed, "Are you—married?"

His grin was positively fiendish.

"No, Norreys, we're not married. You can go back and tell that to the old bitch at St. Loo."

(Curious the way Lady St. Loo still rankled.)

"I'm not likely to mention the subject to her," I said coldly.

"It's like that, is it? Isabella's disgraced the family." He tilted his chair backwards. "Lord, I'd like to have seen their faces that morning—the morning when they found we'd gone off together."

"My God, you're a swine, Gabriel," I said, my self-control slipping.

He was not at all annoyed.

"Depends how you look at it," he said. "Your outlook on life is so very narrow, Norreys."

"At any rate I've got a few decent instincts," I said sharply.

"You're so English. I must introduce you to the wide cosmopolitan set in which Isabella and I move."

"You don't look frightfully well, if I may say so," I said.

"That's because I drink too much," said Gabriel promptly. "I'm a bit high now. But cheer up," he went on, "Isabella doesn't drink. I can't think why not—but she doesn't. She's still got that schoolgirl complexion. You'll enjoy seeing her again."

"I would like to see her," I said slowly, but I wasn't sure as I said it, if it was true.

Would I like to see her? Wouldn't it, really, be sheer pain? Did she want to see me? Probably not. If I could know how she felt. . . .

"No illegitimate brats, you'll be glad to hear," said Gabriel cheerfully.

I looked at him. He said softly:

"You do hate me, don't you, Norreys?"

"I think I've good reason to."

"I don't see it that way. You got a lot of entertainment out of me at St. Loo. Oh yes, you did. Interest in my doings probably kept you from committing suicide. I should certainly have committed suicide in your place. It's no good hating me just because you are crazy about Isabella. Oh yes, you are. You were then and you are now. That's why you're sitting here pretending to be amicable and really loathing my guts."

"Isabella and I were friends," I said. "A thing I don't suppose you're capable of understanding."

"I didn't mean you made passes at her, old boy. I know that isn't your line of country. Soul affinity, and spiritual uplift. Well, it will be nice for her to see an old friend."

"I wonder," I said slowly. "Do you really think that she would like to see me?"

His demeanor changed. He scowled furiously.

"Why the devil not? Why shouldn't she want to see you?"

"I'm asking you," I said.

He said, "I'd like her to see you."

That grated on me. I said, "In this case, we'll go by what *she* prefers."

He suddenly beamed into a smile again.

"Of course she'll want to see you, old boy. I was just ragging you. I'll give you the address. Look her up any time you like. She's usually in."

"What are you doing nowadays?" I asked.

He winked, closing one eye and tilting his head sideways.

"Undercover work, old boy. Very hush hush. Poorly paid, though.

£1,000 a year I'd be getting now as an M.P. (I told you if Labour got in it would go up.) I often remind Isabella how much I've given up for her sake."

How I loathed that coarse jeering devil. I wanted to—well, I wanted to do many things that were physically impossible to me. Instead, I contained myself and accepted the bit of dirty paper with the address scrawled on it that he shoved across to me.

It was a long time before I could get to sleep that night. I was beset by fears for Isabella. I wondered if it was possible to get her to leave Gabriel. Obviously the whole thing had turned out badly.

How badly I only realized on the following day. I found the address that Gabriel had given me. It was a disreputable-looking house in a mean backstreet. That quarter of the town was a bad one. The furtive men and the brazen painted women I passed told me that. I found the house and asked, in German, of a vast blowsy woman who was standing in the doorway, for the English lady.

She understood German fortunately, and directed me to the top floor. I climbed with difficulty, my crutches slipping. The house was filthy. It smelt. My heart dropped down into my boots. My beautiful proud Isabella. To have come down to this. But at the same time my own resolve strengthened.

I would get her out of all this. Take her back to England. . . .

I arrived, panting, on the top floor, and knocked on the door.

A voice called out something in Czech from inside. I knew that voice—it was Isabella's. I opened the door and went in.

I don't think I can ever explain the extraordinary effect that room had on me.

To begin with, it was definitely squalid. Broken-down furniture, tawdry hangings, an unpleasant-looking and somehow lewd brass bedstead. The place was at once clean and dirty; that is, the walls were streaked with dirt, the ceiling black, and there was the faint unpleasant odor of bugs. There was no surface dirt. The bed was made, the ashtrays empty, there was no litter and no dust.

But it was nevertheless a sordid room. In the middle of it, sitting with her feet tucked up under her, and embroidering a piece of silk, was Isabella.

She looked exactly as she had looked when she left St. Loo. Her dress, actually, was shabby. But it had cut and style, and though old, she wore it with ease and distinction. Her hair was still in its long shimmering page-boy bob. Her face was beautiful, calm, and grave. She and the room had, I felt, nothing to do with each other. She was here, in the midst of it, exactly as she might have been in the midst of a desert, or on the deck of a ship. It was not her home. It was a place where she happened, just at the moment, to be.

She stared for a second, then, jumping up, came towards me with a glad surprised face, her hands outstretched. I saw then, that Gabriel had not told her of my being in Zagrade. I wondered why.

Her hands came affectionately into mine. She raised her face and kissed me.

"Hugh, how lovely."

She did not ask how I happened to be in Zagrade. She did not comment on the fact that I could now walk whereas when she had last seen me I was prone on a couch. All that concerned her was that her friend had come, and that she was glad to see him. She was, in fact, my Isabella.

She found a chair for me and drew it up to her own.

"Well, Isabella," I said, "what are you doing with yourself?"

Her reply was typical. She immediately showed me her embroidery.

"I began it three weeks ago. Do you like it?"

Her voice was anxious.

I took the piece of work into my hand. It was a square of old silk—a delicate dove gray in color, slightly faded, very soft to handle. On it Isabella was embroidering a design of dark red roses, wallflowers and pale mauve stocks. It was beautiful work, very fine, exquisitely executed.

"It's lovely, Isabella," I said, "quite lovely."

I felt as always the strange fairy story quality that always surrounded Isabella. Here was the captive maiden doing fine embroidery in the ogre's tower.

"It's beautiful," I said, handing it back to her. "But this place is awful."

She looked round with a casual, almost surprised, glance.

"Yes," she said. "I suppose it is."

Just that, no more. It baffled me—as Isabella had always baffled me.

I saw vaguely that it mattered very little to Isabella what her surroundings were. She was not thinking of them. They mattered to her no more than the upholstery or decorations in a railway train matters to someone who is engaged upon an important journey. This room was the place she happened to be living in at the moment. Her attention drawn to it, she agreed that it was not a nice place but the fact did not really interest her.

Her embroidery interested her far more.

I said, "I saw John Gabriel last night."

"Did you? Where? He didn't tell me."

I said, "That's how I got your address. He invited me to come and look you up."

"I'm so glad you did. Oh, I *am* glad!"

How warming it was—her eager pleasure in my presence.

"Isabella—dear Isabella," I said. "Are you all right? Are you happy?"

She stared at me, as though doubtful of my meaning.

"All this," I said. "It's so different from what you've been used to. Wouldn't you like to leave it all—to come back with me. To London if not to St. Loo."

She shook her head.

"John's doing something here. I don't know what exactly—"

"What I'm trying to ask you is if you're happy with him? I don't think you can be . . . If you once made a dreadful mistake, Isabella, don't be too proud to own it now. Leave him."

She looked down at her work—strangely, a little smile hovered on her lips.

"Oh no, I couldn't do that."

"Do you love him so much, Isabella? Are you—are you really happy with him? I ask because I care for you so much."

She said gravely, "You mean happy—happy in the way I was happy at St. Loo?"

"Yes."

"No, of course I'm not . . ."

"Then chuck it all up, come back with me and start afresh."

Again she gave that funny little smile.

"Oh no, I couldn't do that."

"After all," I said, rather embarrassed, "you're not married to him."

"No, I'm not married. . . ."

"Don't you think—" I felt awkward—embarrassed—all the things that so palpably Isabella was not. Still, I had to find out exactly how matters stood between these two strange people. "Why aren't you married?" I said brazenly.

She was not offended. I had, instead, the impression that it was the first time the question had presented itself to her. Why was it that she and John Gabriel were not married? She sat quite still, thoughtful, asking herself why?

Then she said, doubtfully, in a rather puzzled way:

"I don't think John—wants to marry me."

I managed not to explode into anger.

"Surely," I said, "there is no reason why you should *not* marry?"

"No," her tone was doubtful.

"He owes it to you. It is the least he can do."

She shook her head slowly.

"No," she said. "It was not like that at all."

"What was not like that?"

She brought the words out slowly, following up events in her mind.

"When I came away from St. Loo . . . it was not to marry John instead of marrying Rupert. He wanted me to come away with him, and I came. He didn't speak of marriage. I don't think he thought of it. All this—" she moved her hands slightly—by "this" I took it she meant not so much the actual rooms, the squalid surroundings, as the transitory character of their life together—"this isn't marriage. Marriage is something quite different."

"You and Rupert—" I began.

She interrupted me, relieved apparently that I had grasped her point.

"Yes," she said, "that would have been marriage."

Then what, I wondered, did she consider her life with John Gabriel to be? I didn't like to ask outright.

"Tell me, Isabella," I said. "What do you actually understand by marriage—what does marriage mean to you—apart from its pure legal significance?"

She was very thoughtful about that.

"I think it would mean becoming part of someone's life ... fitting
in ... taking your place ... and its being your rightful place—where you
belong."

Marriage to Isabella had, I saw, a structural significance.

"You mean," I said, "that you can't share Gabriel's life?"

"No. I don't know how. I wish I could. You see—" she stretched
out her long narrow hands in front of her—"I don't know anything
about him."

I stared at her, fascinated. I thought that she was instinctively right.
She did not know the first thing about John Gabriel. She never would
know the first thing about him, however long she stayed with him. But
I could see, also, that that might not affect her emotional feeling for him.

And he, I thought suddenly, was in the same boat. He was like a man
who had bought (or rather had looted) an expensive and delicate piece
of craftsmanship and who had no conception of the scientific principles
underlying its elaborate mechanism.

"So long," I said slowly, "as you are not unhappy."

She looked back at me with blind unseeing eyes. Either she deliberately concealed the answer to my question, or she did not know the
answer herself. I think the latter. She was living through a deep and
poignant experience, and she could not define it for my benefit in exact
terms.

I said gently, "Shall I give them your love at St. Loo?"

She sat very still. Tears came up in her eyes and spilled.

They were tears not of sorrow but of remembrance.

"If you could put the clock back, Isabella," I said. "If you were free
to choose—would you make the same choice again?"

It was cruel of me, perhaps, but I had to know, to be sure.

But she looked at me without comprehension.

"Does one ever really have any choice? About anything?"

Well, that is a matter of opinion. Life is easier, perhaps, for uncompromising realists like Isabella Charteris who cannot perceive any alter-
native way. Yet, as I now believe, there was to come a moment when
Isabella had a definite choice and took one way in preference to the
other with full knowledge that it was a choice. But that was not yet.

Then as I stood looking at Isabella I heard footsteps stumbling up the stairs. John Gabriel flung the door open with a flourish and lurched into the room. He was not a particularly pretty sight.

"Hullo," he said, "found your way here all right?"

"Yes," I said shortly.

For the life of me I couldn't say any more. I went toward the door.

"Sorry," I mumbled, "I've got to be going. . . ."

He stood aside a little to let me pass.

"Well," he said, and there was something in his expression that I didn't understand, "don't ever say I didn't give you your chance . . ."

I didn't know quite what he meant.

He went on, "Dine with us at the Café Gris tomorrow night. I'm throwing a party. Isabella would like you to come, wouldn't you, Isabella?"

I looked back. She was smiling at me gravely.

"Yes, do come," she said.

Her face was calm and unperturbed. She was smoothing and sorting her silks.

I caught a fleeting glimpse of something in Gabriel's face that I didn't understand. It might have been desperation.

I went down that horrid staircase quickly—as quickly as a cripple could go. I wanted to get out into the sunlight—away from the strange conjunction of Gabriel and Isabella. Gabriel had changed—for the worse. Isabella had not changed at all.

In my puzzled mind I felt that there must be some significance in that if only I could find it.

Chapter Twenty-five

There are some horrible memories you can never manage to forget. One of those was that nightmare evening in the Café Gris. I am convinced that that party was arranged entirely to satisfy Gabriel's malice towards me. It was, in my view, an infamous party. John Gabriel's friends and associates in Zagrade were introduced to me there—and in the midst of them sat Isabella. They were men and women she should never have been allowed to meet. There were drunkards and perverts, coarse-painted trollops, diseased dope addicts. Everything that was mean, base, and depraved.

And they were not redeemed, as might so easily have been the case, by artistic talent. Here were no writers, musicians, poets or painters; not even witty talkers. They were the dregs of the cosmopolitan world. They were Gabriel's choice. It was as though he had deliberately wished to show how low he could go.

I was wild with resentment for Isabella's sake. How dared he bring her into such a company?

And then I looked at her and resentment dropped from me. She showed no avoidance, no disgust, still less did she display any anxiety to gloss over a difficult situation. She sat there smiling quietly, the same remote Acropolis Maiden smile. She was gravely polite and quite untouched by her company. They did not, I saw, affect her—any more than the squalid lodgings in which she lived affected her. I remembered from long ago her answer to my question as to whether she was interested in politics. She had said then, looking a little vague, "It is one of the things we do." Tonight, I divined, came into the same category. If I had asked her what she felt about this party she would have said in the same tone, "It's the kind of party we have." She accepted it without resentment, and without any particular interest, as one of the things John Gabriel chose to do.

I looked across the table at her and she smiled back at me. My agony and distress on her behalf were simply not needed. A flower can bloom as well on a dung heap as anywhere else. Perhaps better—for you notice that it is a flower. . . .

We left the Café in a body. Nearly everybody was drunk.

As we stepped into the street to cross it, a large car came noiselessly out of the darkness. It nearly hit Isabella, but she saw her danger in time and made a sudden leap for the pavement—I saw the whiteness of her face and the sharp terror in her eyes as the car went hooting down the street.

Here, then, she was still vulnerable. Life, in all its vicissitudes, was powerless to affect her. She could stand up to life—but not to death—

or the threat of death. Even now, with the danger over, she was white and shaken.

Gabriel cried out:

"My God, that was a near shave. Are you all right, Isabella?"

She said, "Oh, yes! I'm all right."

But the fear was still in her voice. She looked at me and said, "You see, I'm still a coward."

There isn't very much more to tell. That evening at the Café Gris was the last time I was to see Isabella.

Tragedy came, as it usually comes, unheralded, without forewarning.

I was just wondering whether to go and see Isabella again, whether to write, whether to leave Zagrade without seeing her when Gabriel was shown in to see me.

I can't say that I noticed anything unusual in his appearance. A certain nervous excitement, perhaps, a tightness. I don't know. . . .

He said quite calmly, "Isabella's dead."

I stared at him. I didn't take it in at first. I simply didn't feel that it could be true.

He saw my disbelief.

"Oh yes," he said. "It's true. She was shot."

I found my tongue, as a cold sense of catastrophe—of utter loss—spread through me.

"Shot?" I said. "*Shot?* How could she be shot? How did it happen?"

He told me. They had been sitting together in the café where I had first met him.

He asked me, "Have you ever seen pictures of Stolanov? Do you see any likeness to me in him?"

Stolanov was at that time virtual dictator of Slovakia. I looked at Gabriel carefully and I realized that there was quite a strong facial resemblance. When Gabriel's hair fell forward untidily over his face, as it frequently did, that slight resemblance was heightened.

"What happened?" I asked.

"A damn fool of a student. He thought he recognized me as Stolanov. He had a revolver with him. He ran shooting across the café, yelling out 'Stolanov—Stolanov—I've got you at last.' There wasn't any time to do anything at all. He fired. He didn't hit me. He hit Isabella . . ."

He paused. Then added, "She was killed instantaneously. The bullet went through her heart."

"My God," I said, "and you couldn't do anything?"

It seemed to me incredible that Gabriel hadn't been able to do anything.

He flushed.

"No," he said. "I couldn't do anything . . . I was behind the table against the wall. There wasn't *time* to do anything . . ."

I was silent. I was still stunned—numb.

Gabriel sat watching me. He still showed no sign of emotion.

"So that's what you've brought her to," I said at last.

He shrugged his shoulders.

"Yes—if you like to put it that way."

"It's your doing that she was here—in that foul house, in this foul town. But for you she might have been—"

I stopped. He finished the sentence for me.

"She might have been Lady St. Loo, living in a castle by the sea—living in a gingerbread castle with a gingerbread husband and a gingerbread child on her knee, perhaps."

The sneer in his voice maddened me.

"My God, Gabriel," I said. "I don't think I shall ever forgive you!"

"I can't say it interests me very much, Norreys, if you forgive me or not."

"What are you doing here, anyway?" I asked angrily. "Why come to me? What do you want?"

He said quietly, "I want you to take her back to St. Loo . . . You can manage it, I expect. She ought to be buried there, not here where she doesn't belong."

"No," I said. "She doesn't belong here." I looked at him. In the midst of the pain I was beginning to feel I was aware of a rising curiosity.

"Why did you ever bring her away? What was the idea behind it all? Did you want her so much? Enough to chuck up your career? All the things you set so much store by?"

Again he shrugged his shoulders.

I cried angrily, "I don't understand!"

"Understand? Of course you don't understand." His voice startled me. It was hoarse and rasping. "*You'll* never understand anything. What do *you* know about suffering?"

"A good deal," I said, stung.

"No, you don't. You don't know what suffering, real suffering, is. Don't you understand that I've never known—once—what she's been thinking . . . ? I've never been able to talk to her. I tell you, Norreys, I've done everything to break her spirit—*everything*. I've taken her through the mud—through the dregs—and I don't think she even knows what I've been doing! 'She can't soil and she can't scare.' That's what Isabella is like. It's frightening, I tell you, frightening. Rows, tears, defiance— that's what I'd always imagined. And myself winning! But I didn't win. You can't win when you're fighting someone who doesn't know there is a fight. And I couldn't talk to her—I could never talk to her. I've drunk myself paralytic, I've tried drugs, I've gone with other women. . . . It hasn't touched her. She's sat there with her feet tucked up, embroidering her silk flowers, and sometimes singing to herself. . . . She might be still in her castle by the sea—she's still in her blasted fairy story—she brought it with her—"

He had slid insensibly into the present tense. But he stopped suddenly. He dropped into a chair.

"You don't understand," he said. "How can you? Well, I'm licked. I've had her body. I've never had anything else. Now her body's escaped me. . . ." He got up. "Take her back to St. Loo."

"I will," I said. "And God forgive you, Gabriel, for what you've done to her!"

He swerved round on me.

"For what I've done to her? What about what she's done to me? Hasn't it ever penetrated your smug mind, Norreys, that from the first moment I saw that girl, I suffered tortures? I can't explain to you what the mere sight of her did to me—I don't understand it now. It was like chilies and cayenne pepper rubbed into a raw wound. All the things I'd wanted and minded about all my life seemed to crystallize in her. I knew I was coarse, filthy, sensual—but I didn't mind about it till I saw her.

"She hurt me, Norreys. Don't you understand? She hurt me as nothing had ever hurt me before. I had to destroy her—to pull her down to my level. Don't you see—no, you don't! You don't understand anything.

You're incapable of it. You curl yourself up in the window seat as though life were a book you were reading! I was in Hell, I tell you, in *Hell*.

"Once, just once, I thought I'd got a break—a loophole of escape. When that nice silly woman came bolting into the St. Loo Arms and jammed up the works. It meant that the election was dished, and I was dished. I'd have Milly Burt on my hands. That brute of a husband of hers would have divorced her, and I'd have done the decent thing and married her. Then I'd have been safe. Safe from this awful torturing obsession . . .

"And then she, Isabella herself, took a hand. She didn't know what she was doing to me. I'd got to go on! There was no escape. I hoped, all along, that I'd just pull through. I even bought her a wedding present.

"Well, it was no use. I couldn't stick it. I had to have her . . ."

"And now," I said, "she's dead. . . ."

This time he let me have the last word.

He repeated, very softly, "And now—she's dead . . ."

He turned on his heel and went out of the room.

Chapter Twenty-six

That was the last time I saw John Gabriel. We parted in anger in Zagrade and did not meet again.

With some difficulty I made the arrangements which permitted Isabella's body to be brought home to England.

She was buried in the small churchyard by the sea at St. Loo where the other members of her family are buried. After the funeral, I went back with the three old ladies to the little Victorian house and was thanked by them for bringing Isabella home. . . .

They had aged terribly in the last two years. Lady St. Loo was more like an eagle than ever, her flesh stretched tightly over her bones. She looked so frail that I thought she might die any moment. Actually, though, she lived for many years after that. Lady Tressilian was stouter and very asthmatic. She told me in a whisper that they all liked Rupert's wife very much.

"Such a practical girl and so bright. I'm sure they'll be happy. Of course it isn't what we once dreamed of . . ."

The tears came into her eyes. She murmured, "Oh why—*why* did this have to happen?"

It was an echo of what had never ceased to reiterate in my own brain.

"That wicked—wicked man . . ." she went on.

We were united, three old ladies and myself in our sorrow for a dead girl and our hatred of John Gabriel.

Mrs. Bigham Charteris was more leathery than ever. She said as I finally bid them good-bye, "Do you remember little Mrs. Burt?"

"Yes, of course. What's happened to her?"

Mrs. Bigham Charteris shook her head.

"I'm sadly afraid she's going to make a fool of herself. You know what happened to Burt?"

"No, I don't."

"Upset into a ditch one night when he'd had one over the eight. Struck his head on a stone. Killed him."

"So she's a widow?"

"Yes. And I hear from my friends in Sussex that she's taken up with one of the farmers near there. Going to marry him. Man has a bad reputation. Drinks. Bit of a bully too."

So Milly Burt, I thought, was repeating her pattern . . .

Did anyone ever profit by having a second chance . . . ?

I wondered more than ever when I was on my way to London the following day. I had boarded the train at Penzance and taken a ticket for first lunch. As I sat there waiting for the soup to be served, I thought about Jennifer.

I had had news of her from time to time from Caro Strangeways. Jennifer, Caro had told me, was very unhappy. She had complicated her life in an incredible fashion, but she was being very plucky over it. One couldn't, Caro said, help admiring her.

I smiled a little to myself, thinking of Jennifer. Jennifer was rather a darling. But I felt no urge to see her—no real interest.

One doesn't care for hearing the same record too often. . . .

So I came at last to Teresa's house in London and Teresa let me talk . . .

She heard my bitter diatribes against John Gabriel. I described the happenings in Zagrade to her and ended with the account of Isabella's grave in St. Loo.

Then I was silent for a moment, hearing the noise of the Atlantic breakers against the rocks and seeing the outline of St. Loo Castle against the sky. . . .

"I suppose I ought to feel that I've left her there in peace—but I don't, Teresa. I'm full of rebellion. She died before her time. She said to me once that she hoped she would live to be a very old woman. She could have lived to be old. She was very strong. I think that's what I find so unendurable—that her life was cut short . . ."

Teresa stirred a little against the background of a large painted screen. She said:

"You're going by Time. But Times doesn't mean anything at all. Five minutes and a thousand years are equally significant." She quoted softly, "The moment of the Rose and the moment of the Yew Tree are of equal duration . . ."

(A dark red rose embroidered on faded gray silk. . . .)

Teresa went on, "You will insist on making your own design for life, Hugh, and trying to fit other people into it. But they've got their own design. Everyone has got their own design—that's what makes life so confusing. Because the designs are interlaced—superimposed.

"Just a few people are born clear-eyed enough to know their own design. I think Isabella was one of them. . . . She was difficult to understand—for us to understand—not because she was complex but because she was simple—almost terrifyingly simple. She recognized nothing but essentials.

"You persist in seeing Isabella's life as a thing cut short, twisted out of shape, broken off. . . . But I have a strong suspicion that it was a thing complete in itself . . ."

"The moment of the rose?"

"If you like to call it that." She added softly, "You're very lucky, Hugh."

"Lucky?" I stared at her.

"Yes, because you loved her."

"I suppose I did love her. And yet I never was able to do anything for her . . . I didn't even try to stop her going away with Gabriel . . ."

"No," said Teresa, "because you really loved her. You loved her enough to leave her alone."

Almost unwillingly I accepted Teresa's definition of love. Pity has always, perhaps, been my undoing. It has been my cherished indulgence. By pity, the facile easy going of pity, I have lived and warmed my heart.

But Isabella, at least, I had kept free of pity. I had never tried to serve her, to make her path easy for her, to carry her burdens. In her short life she was completely and perfectly herself. Pity is an emotion she neither needed, nor would have understood. As Teresa said, I had loved her enough to leave her alone . . .

"Dear Hugh," said Teresa gently, "of course you loved her. And you've been very happy loving her."

"Yes," I said, a little surprised. "Yes, I've been very happy."

Then anger swept over me.

"But," I said, "I still hope that John Gabriel will suffer the tortures of the damned in this world and the next!"

"I don't know about the next," said Teresa, "but in this world I should say that you had got your wish. John Gabriel is the most unhappy man I have ever known . . ."

"I suppose you're sorry for him, but I can tell you—"

Teresa interrupted. She said she wasn't exactly sorry for him. She said it went deeper than that.

"I don't know what you mean. If you'd seen him in Zagrade—he did nothing but talk about himself—he wasn't even broken up by Isabella's death."

"You don't know. I don't suppose you even looked at him properly. You never do look at people."

It struck me when she said that, that I had never really looked properly at Teresa. I have not even described her in this story.

I looked at her and it seemed to me that I was, perhaps, seeing her for the first time . . . seeing the high cheekbones and the upward sweep of black hair that seemed to need a mantilla and a big Spanish comb.

Seeing that her head was set on her neck very proudly like her Castilian great-grandmother's.

Looking at her, it seemed to me just for a moment that I saw exactly what Teresa must have been like as a young girl. Eager, passionate, stepping adventurously forward into life.

I did not know in the least what she had found there . . .

"Why are you staring at me, Hugh?"

I said slowly, "I was thinking that I had never looked at you properly."

"No, I don't think you have." She smiled faintly. "Well, what do you see?"

There was irony in her smile and laughter in her voice and something in her eyes that I could not fathom.

"You have been very good to me always, Teresa," I said slowly. "But I don't really know anything about you . . ."

"No, Hugh. You know nothing at all."

She got up brusquely and pulled the curtain that was letting in too much sun.

"As to John Gabriel—" I began.

Teresa said in her deep voice, "Leave him to God, Hugh."

"That's an odd thing to say, Teresa."

"No, I think it's the right thing to say. I've always thought so."

She added, "One day—perhaps you'll know what I mean."

Epilogue

Well, that is the story.

The story of the man I first knew at St. Loo in Cornwall and whom I had last seen in a hotel room at Zagrade.

The man who was now dying in a back bedroom in Paris.

"Listen, Norreys," his voice was weak but clear. "You've got to know what really happened in Zagrade. I didn't tell you at the time. I think I hadn't really taken in what it meant . . ."

He paused, gathering breath.

"You know that she—Isabella—was afraid of dying? More afraid of it than anything else in the world?"

I nodded. Yes, I knew. I remembered the blind panic in her eyes when she had looked down at a dead bird on the terrace at St. Loo, and I remembered how she had leaped to avoid the car in Zagrade and the whiteness of her face.

"Then listen. *Listen*, Norreys: the student came for me with the revolver. He was only a few feet away. He couldn't miss. And I was pinned behind the table. I couldn't move.

"Isabella saw what was going to happen. *She flung herself in front of me as he pressed the trigger . . .*"

Gabriel's voice rose.

"Do you understand, Norreys? She knew what she was doing. She knew that it meant death—for her. She chose death—to save me."

Warmth came into his voice.

"I hadn't understood—not until then. I didn't realize even then, what it meant, until I came to think about it. I'd never understood, you see, that she *loved* me. . . . I thought—I was convinced—that I held her by her senses. . . .

"But Isabella loved me—she loved me so much that she gave her life for me—in spite of her fear of death. . . ."

My mind moved backward. I was in the café in Zagrade. I saw the fanatical hysterical young student, saw Isabella's sharp alarm, her realization, her momentary panic fear—and then her swift choice. I saw her fling herself forward shielding John Gabriel with her body. . . .

"So that was the end . . ." I said.

But Gabriel pulled himself up on his pillows. His eyes, those eyes that had always been beautiful, opened very wide. His voice rang out loud and clear—a triumphant voice.

"Oh no," he said, "that's where you are wrong! It wasn't the end. *It was the beginning. . . .*"